THOSE BOYS ARE TROUBLE

VALETTI CRIME FAMILY

WILLOW WINTERS

COPYRIGHT

DIRTY DOM

SYNOPSIS

From *USA Today* bestselling author Willow Winters comes a HOT mafia, standalone romance.

I'm not always proud of the man I am, but when you grow up in a crime family, there aren't a lot of options.
    I do what I have to do, and more than often, I f*cking love it.

The power, the women, the money. All of it comes easy to me.
    Until Becca walked into my office.

Everything about her was tempting. Her beautiful eyes that pierced into me, her body that was made for sin.
    She came to pay off a debt, but I wanted more.
    So I did what I've always done, I took what I wanted.

She's a good girl who never should have walked through that door.
    I never should have touched her, but now that I have, I can't stop.

I'll push her boundaries, she'll cave to temptation.

We'll both forget about the danger.
And that's a mistake I can't afford...

PROLOGUE

Dom

Becca

Dom

   I crack my knuckles and stretch my arms above my head while looking out over the football stadium from my suite. I fucking love that this is my office. But then again, when you do what I do, your "office" can be anywhere. I snatch my scotch from the bar and tell Johnny to grab our lunch. Taking a seat on the sectional, I pull out my phone to look at my schedule. My first drop-off should be here soon.

Becca

   I'm so fucking nervous. I click my phone on and see I have fifteen minutes to find the bookie's suite. I clutch my purse tighter, holding the Coach Hobo closer to my side. I've got twelve thousand in cash under a scarf, and the idea I'm going to be mugged and then killed by the bookie is making my blood rush with adrenaline and anxiety. I can't believe Rick would put me in this position. Shit. I'm such a bitch. I swallow the lump in my throat and square my shoulders to keep the tears pricking the back of my eyes from surfacing. Now is not the time to think about Rick. And it's not like he asked me to do this. His problems keep coming after me, and I want to cover my bases.

The knock at the door seems hesitant, and that makes a deep, rough chuckle rumble in my hard chest. Whoever's behind the door is scared, and I live for that fear. They're right to be scared. I didn't get where I am today by being kind and understanding. Fuck that. I'm a ruthless prick, and I know it. Doubt fills my chest for a fraction of a second, but I shut that shit down ASAP. I'm a tough fucker, and I'm not going to let some pussy emotions make me weak. Some days I wish I didn't have to be such a cruel asshole. I don't like fucking guys up, breaking their legs and hands or whatever body part they pick – if I let them choose. But they know what they're signing up for when they do business with me. Damn shame they don't have a doctorate degree in Statistics from Stanford, like me. A devilish grin pulls at my lips. If you're gonna be making bets with me, you better be ready to pay up.

I wipe the cold sweat from my hands and onto my dress, ball up my small fist even tighter and knock on the door a little harder. I wonder if the people walking by know why I'm here. I swallow thickly, feeling like a dirty criminal. My eyes dart to an older woman with kind eyes and grey-speckled hair pushing a caterer's cart past me. I'm sure she knows. I'm sure everyone who looks at me knows I'm up to no good.

My eyes glance from left to right as I wait impatiently. Sarah's waiting outside, and I have to pick up my son from soccer practice soon. I lick my lower lip as the nerves start to creep up again. I'll just pretend this isn't real. Just hand them the money and walk away. Back to real life. Back to my assistant, and move on with my normal, nonthreatening, everyday life.

I take my time getting to the door. No matter how much money they owe me, or how much they've won, they need to know I do everything when-ever the fuck I please. If they have to wait, they have to wait. But I sure as shit don't wait for them. I open the door and my cold, hard heart pumps with hot blood and desire.

A petite woman in fuck-me pink heels and a grey dress that clings to her curves and ends just above her knees is staring back at me with wide, frightened hazel eyes. Her breasts rise and fall, peeking out of the modest neckline. Her black cardigan is covering up too much of her chest, and I narrowly resist the urge to push it off her shoulders. My eyes travel along her body in obvious appreciation before stopping at her purse. She's clinging to it like it's her lifeline. A tic in my jaw starts to twitch. What's a woman like her doing making bets with a guy like me? Johnny handles most of that shit now. We aren't supposed to take bets from women. I don't like it. I'm definitely going to have to ask him about her.

The door opens, and I nervously peek up through my thick, dark lashes at the gorgeous man looking down at me. The lines around his eyes mean he's every bit the man he looks, but his devilish white-toothed grin gives him a boyish charm meant to fool women like me. He's fucking hot in a black three-piece suit that's obviously been tailored to fit his large chiseled frame perfectly. With that crisp white button-down shirt and simple black tie you'd think he was a young CEO, but his muscular body, piercing blue eyes and messy dark hair that's long enough to grab, make him a sex god. Lust and power radiate from his broad chest as his eyes travel down my body. He looks like a man who knows how to destroy you.

A wave of desire shoots through me when my eyes meet his heated stare. My breathing hitches, and I swallow down the distress I'm feeling at my treacherous body. I'll just give him the money Rick owed him and get the fuck out of here. At the reminder of why I'm standing in his doorway, I push my purse toward him.

I grin at her obvious nervousness and cock a brow as I say, "Purses aren't my style, doll." Pulling the door open wider, I step aside just enough for her to get through. Her soft body gently brushes against mine as she walks through the small opening I gave her. The subtle touch sends a throbbing need to my dick and I feel it harden, pushing against my zipper. She hustles a little quicker when I lean closer to her. Her hips sway, and I stifle a groan when I see that dress clinging to her lush ass. Fuck, I want that ass. I never mix business with pleasure, but there's an exception to every rule.

Something about her just pulls me in. Something about the way she's carrying herself. It's like she needs me, or maybe I need her. My dick jumps as she turns around to fully face me. Fuck, at least one part of me desperately wants her attention.

His body touching mine makes every nerve ending in my core ignite; I nervously squeeze the strap of my purse. I just want to get the hell out of here, but my stupid heart is longing for comfort. My trembling body is aching with need. What the hell is wrong with me? It's only been three days; I should have more respect for Rick than this. I will the tears to go away. I just want to be held. But I know better. This man staring back at me isn't a man who will hold me and console me. I take in a gasp of air and turn around to face the man my husband owed money to while digging in my purse to gather the bundles of cash.

"Is it all there?" I have no fucking clue who she is, or what she's supposed to be giving me. Johnny has the list, but he's not back yet with our lunch. It's a rarity that I even have to speak during drops. I just like to watch. And when it comes to people not paying up, it's best if I'm here for that.

"I'm sorry it's late." His rough fingers brush mine as I hold out the thick stacks of hundreds. His touch sends a shot of lust to my heated core and I close my eyes, denying the desperate need burning inside me. It would feel so good to let him take me the way a man should. I haven't been touched in months. I haven't felt desire in nearly a year, and I know for a fact I've never felt such a strong pull to a man before, never wanted to give myself to someone like I do him.

"What about the interest?" Her eyes widen with fear, and her breath stalls as her plump lips part. If it's late, then she should know to pay that extra five percent per day. Compounded. Johnny should've told her all that shit. But judging by her silence and that scared look on her face, she doesn't have a clue. A grin pulls at my lips, but I stifle it. I want her to think I'm mad. I want her to feel like she owes me. I don't want her money though. She can pay me in a way I've never been paid before. I don't accept ass as payment, but for her, fuck yeah I'll take it.

The man on the phone said not to worry about being late. He said he was sorry for my loss, and that he understood. I feel my breath coming up short as a lump grows in my throat. Fuck! What the hell am I going to do? Fucking Rick, leaving me with this shit to deal with. I wish I could just fucking hide as these damn tears start pricking my eyes. My hands start to shake as I realize I'm trapped in the bookie's suite and I owe him more money that I don't have.

"Aw, doll. Don't cry. We can work something out." Her bottom lip's trembling, and her gorgeous hazel eyes are brimming with tears. I feel like a fucking asshole for taking advantage of the situation. But then again, what the fuck did she expect? First, she made a bet with a bookie – not fucking smart on her part. Then she's late with handing over the dough. She had to know there'd be consequences. She parts her lips to respond, but she's too shaken up. My heart clenches looking at her small frame quaking with worry.

I'll make it good for her. She looks like a girl I could keep. My brow furrows as I reach out to brush her cheek with my hand. I'm not sure where that thought came from, but the more I think about it, the more I like it. She closes her eyes and leans into my touch as I wipe away the tears trailing down her sun-kissed skin. As I reach her lips, I part them with my thumb.

I hate the bastard tears that've escaped. I feel too raw and vulnerable. I can't help but love the warmth of his skin. How long has it been since someone's touched me with kindness and looked at me with desire? I *need* this. I need to be held, if only for a little while. His thumb brushes my bottom lip, and I instantly part them for him. He can hold me for a moment. I can pretend it's more. I can pretend he really wants me. I can pretend he loves me.

Fuck, she's so damn perfect. She's leaning into me like she really wants me. Like she needs me. She radiates sweet innocence, but there's something more about her, something I can't quite put my finger on. A sting of loneliness pulses through me. I was playing with the thought of having her on her knees in exchange for payment. But I want more. I want her to fucking love what I do to her. I'll make her want me when it's over. A coldness sweeps through me. Women always act like they want me after, but it's the money they want, not me. A sad smirk plays at my lips as she licks my thumb and massages the underside with her hot tongue. Fuck, I'll take it. If she only wants me for my money, I'll take it. I feel a burning need to keep her.

My brows creases with anger at my thoughts. My fucking heart is turning me into a little bitch. "Strip. Now." My words come out hard, making her take a hesitant step back as I pull my thumb from her lips. I instantly regret being the fucking asshole I am. But I can't take it back. I turn my back to her, to lock the door. I slip the gun out from under my belt and easily hide it from her sight to set it down on the table by the door. God knows what she'd think if she got a look at it.

My body flinches as the hard sound of the door locking echoes through the room. He moves with power and confidence, his gaze like one of a predator. I swallow my pride and slip off my cardigan. I don't need pride and self-respect right now; I need a man to desire me. The thought and his hungry eyes on me have me peeling off my dress without hesitation. I don't care if this is a payment or if he's just using the interest as an excuse to fuck me; I want this. Or at least I want him.

As I reach behind my back to unhook my bra, he reaches for me, wrapping his strong arms around my body and molding his hard chest to mine. His lips crush against mine, and I part them for his hot tongue to taste me. He kisses me with passion and need. His hard dick pushes into my stomach. The feeling makes my pussy heat and clench. Yes. The tears stop, but my chest is still in agony. *Make it go away, please. Take my pain away.*

She fucking needs me; I can feel it. And I sure as fuck need her. I don't even hesitate to unleash my rigid cock from my pants. I rip her skimpy lace panties from her body, easily shredding them and tossing them to the floor. I squeeze her lush ass in my hands, pulling her body to mine. I slam her against the wall, keeping my lips to hers the entire time. My chest pounds as hot blood pumps through me. I need to be inside her now. I line my dick up with her hot entrance, rubbing my head between her slick pussy lips.

Fuck, she wants me just as much I want her. I slam inside of her, all the way to the hilt. She breaks our kiss to lean her head back, banging it against the wall and screaming out with pleasure as I fuck her tight pussy recklessly. My right hand roams her body while my left keeps her pinned to the wall. Her arousal leaks from her hot pussy and down to my thighs.

My legs wrap tightly around him as he ruts into me with a primitive need. My body knows I need his touch, but my heart needs his lips and it clenches as he gives them to me. He frantically kisses me as he pounds into me with desperation. The position he has me in ensures he pushes against my throbbing clit with each thrust. I feel my body building toward my release, every nerve ending on high alert.

His lips trail down my neck to my shoulder and collarbone, leaving small bites and open-mouth kisses in his wake. He licks the dip in my throat before trailing his hot tongue back up my neck. I moan my pleasure into the cold air above us. My heart stills, and my body trembles as a numbness and heat attack my body at once. "Yes!" I scream out as my pussy pulses around his thick cock. My body convulses against his as pleasure races through my heavy limbs. I feel waves of hot cum soak my aching pussy. My eyes widen as the after-shocks settle. What the fuck did I just do? I need to get out of here.

She's pushing against me like she can't wait to leave, and that makes my damn heart drop in my chest. Fine. It's fine. It's not like this was anything more than a payment. I say that over and over while I turn my back on her to grab my pants. I walk across the suite to grab a tissue from the desk for her to clean up with, but when I face her, she's already dressed. My blood runs cold with her dismissal of me and what we just shared. It wasn't just some random fuck. There was something there. I've never felt like that before. I never felt THAT before. Whatever it is, I fucking want it. And I'm a man who gets what he wants. My conviction settles as I stride back to her. I'll have her again. I'll make sure it happens.

What the fuck have I done? I need to go. I have to go to my son. I want nothing more than for this man to hold me, but I know that's not going to happen. I'm so fucking stupid. I don't even know his name. These feelings in my fucked up chest aren't the same for him. This was just a payment. The thought makes my heart stop and my chest pain, but I brush it aside. I refuse to be any weaker in front of him. I need to be strong for just a moment longer. I try to fix my hair as best as I can without a mirror. I straighten my back and grab my purse as he walks back over to me.

Women like it when I'm an asshole. Don't know why and I don't care, but it always has them coming back to me. I definitely want to see this girl again; I fucking need to be inside her as often as I can. So after I walk her sweet ass to the door, I give her a cocky smirk and kiss her cheek.

He leans in and whispers against my ear, letting his hot breath tickle my neck, "Thanks for the payment, doll." With that he turns his back and shuts the door without giving me a second glance. That's the moment the lust-filled hope dies, and my heart cracks and crumbles in my hollow chest.

I count the money and start pacing. I need her info from Johnny. I need to know who this woman is. Whoever she is, she's going to end up being mine. Not five minutes after she's gone, Johnny comes back. "The first drop just left. She came with everything but the interest." I pocket her panties so he won't see them. "Twelve grand, right?"

"We didn't charge her interest; she didn't know about her husband's debt until yesterday."

"Since when is that how we do business?" I don't even try to keep my voice down. Blood starts pounding in my ears. "Why the fuck is she paying her husband's debt, anyway? He doesn't have the balls to come here himself? He sends his woman?!" The words jump from my lips before I have a moment to think.

I'm usually more controlled, more thoughtful. If this job has taught me anything, it's that silence is deadly, and being a hothead will get you killed. But I'm shaking with rage. Anger seeps out of my pores. Anger that she's married to a fucking coward and a bastard. But more than that, I'm fucking pissed that she's taken.

Johnny shakes his head in confusion and slows his movements as he takes in my temper. "No, it's not like that. He died last week, heart attack or something."

The moment Sarah sees me, the last bit of my hardened exterior cracks. I feel my lips tremble, and bite down to prevent the tears. "What did you do, Becca?" Sarah's pleading eyes makes me feel even shittier. She knows; she can tell. I'm sure I look like I just got fucked. My neck is pulsing from where he was biting me.

Her eyes want me to tell her she's wrong, and they're begging me to tell her she's mistaken, but I can't lie. I can feel his cum leaking out of me and running down my thigh. Evidence of my weakness, and my betrayal. The tears well up in my eyes and I can't stop a few from leaving angry, hot trails down my cheeks. All I can manage to reply is the barest of truths, "I slept with him."

"Don't cry, Becca. It's alright."

"Rick just died, and I slept with a stranger." I can't keep my own disgust out of my voice.

"It's not like you two were even together in the end anyway. You'd been separated for nearly two months." My breath comes in spasms as I rest my head on the door of my car. I loved my husband, but I can't remember the last time he held me, the last time we made love. A criminal who probably would've hurt me had I shown up empty-handed gave me more compassion and showed more desire for me than Rick had in years.

My breath catches in my throat. I took advantage of her in a moment of weakness, but I didn't fucking know how vulnerable she was. I slam my fist against the window. I didn't fucking know! A sick, twisted churning in the pit of my stomach makes me want to heave. Fuck, I treated her like some random slut. She probably thinks I'm a fucking animal for doing that to her. Fuck! I knew she needed me. I fucking knew it.

I just needed to be held and feel like I was loved. This shattering feeling in my chest, jagged pieces of glass digging into my heart, tells me it wasn't worth it. It hurts too much. The worst part is that a very large part of me wants--no, *needs* to crawl back to him and beg him to hold me again. Just one more time.

I wish I hadn't let her go.

I wish I'd never had to meet with him.

I clench my teeth and close my eyes, wondering if I'll ever see her again.

I breathe deep and steady myself as I drive away, knowing I'll never see him again.

I hate myself.
I hate myself.

I'm such a dirty bastard.

DOM

"Give me her number." After I've had a moment to calm down, I finally take a seat and decide to work out a plan to see her again. I can't fucking let her go, especially not after the way I treated her.

"It's her husband's number." The tic in my jaw twitches again, and I grind my teeth at his words.

"The fucker's dead, right?" My eyes bore into Johnny's as my words come out with enough bite to let him know I'm still on edge. He starts to answer verbally, but then decides just to nod his head. I keep staring at him, letting him get a good fucking idea of how pissed I am when he refers to that prick as her husband. "So he's not her fucking husband."

"Alright, boss. You got it. I just-" he stops himself and looks at the floor before continuing, "I just have his number. Not hers."

"What's her name?" I'm a fucking fool for not even getting her name.

He shuffles his feet, but keeps his eyes on me. He knows better than to back down, even if I am pissed off. I don't have pussies working for me. I don't fucking like weakness. "I don't know." My rage is getting the best of me. Of course he doesn't fucking know. He probably doesn't even know her dead husband's real name.

"What's his number? Give it to me." Johnny immediately takes out his cell and pushes a few buttons. My phone, still on the sectional, beeps with a text.

It's my doll's dead husband's number. Perfect. I call it right away. Why? I don't fucking know why. I immediately hang the fuck up on the first ring. What the hell is wrong with me? What am I going to say? *Hey, sorry I fucked you like you were some slut. Didn't mean to take advantage.* Fucking hell, I'm losing my touch. "I'm gonna send this over to Tony." Tony will tell me everything he can about this number. From who it belonged to, to what that fucker ate for breakfast the day he died. More importantly, I'll find out who his widow is.

"Johnny, how many of these fucking drops do I have to sit through today?"

"We've got three more lined up, boss," he answers.

"Fan-fucking-tastic." I can't shake my irritation. I need to calm down before shit gets out of hand. I roll my shoulders, throw my scotch back and pour myself another.

"Your ma having dinner tonight?" Johnny asks me like he has no clue. Must be his fucking nerves getting the best of him.

"Relax, I'm just a bit wound up."

"What'd she say to you that's got you on edge?" he asks.

"She didn't say a goddamn thing, Johnny. I'm just curious." He raises a brow in question.

"Her pussy that good?" he asks with a smirk.

"You really wanna push me right now?" That wipes the smile off his face and puts one on mine. I laugh at him and pour him a drink. I walk over to him, a glass in each hand. He takes his drink from my hand and gives a small nod in thanks. "*Salute,*" I say, clinking my glass with his

"*Salute.*" He takes a small sip and winces as the burn stings his throat. I chuckle and gulp back the rest. I shake out my arms and already feel a bit more relaxed. I throw my feet on the table and get ready to text Tony.

"What's the cheers for, boss?"

I grin and press send on the text. I adjust in my seat and lean my head back on the sleek, black leather sectional. "Just found my new girl."

His brow furrows in confusion and then disbelief, but he's quick to straighten out his face. He takes another sip and walks to the window to look out over the field. It's Sunday, but there's nothing going on today. Team's on break, I take it. "Been a while for you, hasn't it?"

"Yeah, it's been a bit. I wanna take her on though."

"She into that?" he asks with very real curiosity in his voice.

"Nah, I doubt it; that's not how I like 'em. I enjoy breaking 'em in." I groan and adjust my dick, which is already getting hard again just from thinking about taking a belt to her lush ass. Fuck, I didn't even get a chance to truly enjoy her body. I smirk to myself, thinking of how I'm gonna punish her the second I get her alone for leaving like she did.

Johnny says, "I've been thinking about trying a thing or two, in the bedroom." He looks out the window like he's thinking real fucking hard about it. I snort at him, but before he can respond there's a hard knock at the door. I run a hand down my face and then through my hair. I can't wait to get this shit over with so I can go to Ma's and finally eat something. As Johnny opens the door, my phone goes off on the coffee table. Perfect fucking timing. I don't want to deal with whatever prick owes me money. I lean down to pick it up, and as I do all hell breaks loose. A fucking bullet whizzes by my head, right where I just was.

Johnny's scuffling with the fucker who's screaming for his life at the door. Johnny pushes him down, laying all his weight on top of him, with one hand over his mouth and the other on the silencer attached to the gun. I'm real fucking aware of exactly how the gun is pointed, so I stay out of the line of fire as I jump over the sofa and make my way to the two of them. Johnny's a pretty big dude. He's all muscle, broad-chested, and this puny fucker doesn't stand a chance. He's putting up one hell of a fight though.

My hand reaches into the waistline of my pants, but my gun isn't there. Fuck! I don't have my gun. I always fucking have my gun, but I belatedly remember removing it so I wouldn't scare off my doll earlier. I look over to the door and it's on the other side of the room. The worst fucking place possible. I keep low to the ground with my eyes on Johnny and this dumb shit. You gonna take a shot at me, you better fucking make sure it takes me out. Johnny carries reverse. I know right where his piece is. I come up from behind him and let him know it's me.

"Grabbing your piece, Johnny." In one swift move I've got his gun pointed at this fucker's head. He looks up with his eyes wide and finally stills, ending the struggle. "Keep your hand on his mouth and grab the gun."

The guy's eyes dart from me to Johnny. I can tell he's figuring out that he's going to die right about now. He loosens his grip on the gun and starts shaking his head and screaming something through Johnny's hand. It's not "help," like I expected it to be. Even if he could scream out for help, no one's

17

coming for him. I've had this suite for years. This wouldn't be the first time some chump thought he'd just kill me instead of paying his debt.

His muffled voice utters a sound that gets my attention. "Johnny, let the fucker talk."

Johnny looks up at me with sweat covering his brow from the struggle. His face is red, and he's still breathing like he's run a mile. I jerk my head to the table by the door and say, "Get mine; I wanna switch."

Johnny rises slowly, grabbing the bastard's gun and walks to the door calmly, straightening out his jacket and tucking his shirt back in. I track him in my peripheral vision, but my focus is on this skinny fuck looking straight into the barrel of the gun I've got pointed right between his eyes.

"Last words?" I ask, closer to pulling the trigger more than I really should. I shouldn't kill him here. Not with Johnny's gun. This fucker brought one with a silencer though. So it's his funeral. And I'll have to fix the flooring. But I bought extra wood the last time I remodeled for this very fucking reason.

"De Luca sent me." He spits the words out with terrified eyes. I smirk at him. Yeah, that's what I thought he said. I don't want to kill him with this gun anyway. So he can talk a bit more. Maybe I'll learn something new.

"Oh yeah? Why's that?" I ask him, switching guns with Johnny and motioning for him to give me this fucker's gun. How damn sweet is that? He comes to kill me; I unload his gun in his head. Seems fair enough to me. The only thing that's unfair is that I'll have to rip out some of the hardwood flooring and replace it.

The scrawny prick is crying his eyes out. The smell of urine hits me, and I look back at him with disgust. Did De Luca really think he'd get rid of me with this little piece of shit? I squat down to see him better and to put the gun closer to his head. I take a good look at his face and then settle for just reaching into his pants for his wallet. I toss it at Johnny without taking my eyes off this chump. This punk is young and scared for his life, but I don't underestimate anyone. Not now, not ever. You never know when someone might surprise you. And I don't fucking like surprises.

Not like that nice piece of ass today. *She* was a welcome surprise. My dick starts getting all fucking excited thinking about being in that hot pussy again. Fuck. Now is not the time to let my mind go there. Although it does make me wanna end this shit sooner, rather than later.

"De Luca's pissed about the territory, he wants all yous dead."

"All *yous?*" I echo, and arch an eyebrow.

"You need to learn to speak properly, Mr...?" I ask him, but not really. I know Johnny's gonna answer, and he does.

"Marco, Marco Bryant. Twenty-three, and an organ donor." Johnny's confident voice rings out from behind me and ends with a snort. Yeah, these organs are getting donated. I see him pocketing Marco's wallet as I nod my head. *Bryant.* Just like I thought, he's not full blood. No way De Luca gives a fuck about him.

"So, Marco. You need to get your shit together. You think De Luca was really giving you a chance?" Marco starts trembling beneath me, and widens his eyes. He doesn't know how to answer. Fuck, I wanna roll my eyes at this prick. But I don't take chances.

"Don't answer; I don't really give a fuck." I push the barrel of the gun between his eyes and ask, "You got anything else for me?"

"I'll give you everything!" His eyes are darting between me and Johnny, and his face is sweating like he's stranded in a desert in July. Or like he's about to lose his life. I can practically hear his heart pounding in his chest.

"Everything?" I ask with a smirk. He's got nothing that I want. I've got more money than I know what to do with. Unless he's got that chick's number, there's nothing I want from him.

"I've got a house on the southside and forty grand that's-" I pull the trigger before he can finish. I miss the bang of the bullet, but it's better this way. Nice and quiet. I get up quick so I don't get any blood on my suit.

"Grab the list and see if he was one of the drop-offs. If not, this is gonna be one long fucking day." I head over to the bar and finally get my gun positioned right where I like it. That's better.

"Got it, boss. Yeah, he's one of 'em." My chest rumbles with a laugh. "Wonder if he has a history of making bets and he got that forty grand by winning?" Johnny laughs as he picks Marco's head up and starts wrapping it with plastic wrap. Really distorts the fucker's head, but it works well for keeping all the blood from getting everywhere.

"Drop him off at the vet before Ma's." Everyone in my family *knows* someone. My vet was a wonderful addition to my contacts. If you can cremate a hundred and fifty pound dog, you can cremate a hundred and fifty pound corpse.

"You really wanna push it? You know your Ma hates it when you're late."

Johnny talks while he wipes up the blood. I flip the scrawny bastard over and pull him by his feet away from the mess.

I don't answer Johnny. I'm always fucking late. She'd be surprised if I showed up on time. I stare at the rag in Johnny's hand that's soaking up the blood. Damn, it's a lot of blood. Never gets old. I stand up from the dead bastard and head back to the bar for a drink. Our glasses are somewhere else, but there's plenty of new ones to fill. And plenty of liquor to fill them with.

This is why I'm the bookie in the family. I didn't really want to be a part of this shit. But with a name like Valetti, this shit tracks you down. "Yours is up here when you're ready, Johnny." As soon as I set my glass down, there's a knock at the door. Fucking perfect.

I walk over to Johnny and pick up Marco's legs while he gets his upper body. This fucker looks small, but his dead, limp body is fucking heavy. We'll dump him in the corner for now. I take a look at Johnny and straighten his jacket.

"You look good, just wipe your face," I tell him and return to my glass.

"Uh, Dom?" Johnny asks while another knock echoes through the suite.

"What?" I tilt my chin to the door. After that shit, I'm not opening it. I smirk at the thought.

Johnny motions to his hips while looking at mine. I take a glance down. "Fuck!" Motherfucker; fucking Marco ruined my Brioni suit. It cost more than that dumb fuck had in the bank. I look over to his carcass slumped in the corner of the room behind the pool table as Johnny opens the door. With one hand positioned firmly on the butt of my gun, and the other on my drink, I'm listening but I keep my eyes on the dead body in the room.

I'm vaguely aware of the transaction as the pit in my stomach sinks and blood rushes in my ears as their voices turn to white noise. I fucking hate that I was born a Valetti. But it's sure as shit better than being born Marco.

BECCA

*T*he car door shuts as Sarah gets out of the car. It closes lightly. I'm surprised the fucking light isn't flashing to tell me it's not closed all the way. Too gentle. Sarah is too gentle, too nice. We spent most of the car ride in silence. She kept opening her mouth like she was going to say something, but never did. What is she really going to say?

I swallow the lump in my throat and dig through the console for some tissues. I swear to God if his cum has leaked onto this dress I'm going to be mortified. I don't have a change of clothes, and it's not like I can just hide in the car. It's Jax's first game of the season. He may only be three and never remember this, but I will.

I close my eyes and wipe myself, feeling like a dirty slut. I've only ever been with one man. Rick the prick, as I'd recently started calling him. Until he died, anyway. I shake my head and shove the used tissue into the leftover paper bag from Dunkin' Donuts this morning. I crumple up the bag and toss it onto the passenger's seat. Taking a few deep breaths, I open my door and slide out of my seat. No one knows. I keep repeating that to myself as I turn my head to take a look at the back of my dress. Thank fuck there's no mark. Honestly, they'd probably believe I sneezed and pissed myself a bit over me actually having had sex with… him. Tears well up again, and my throat closes. I don't even know his fucking name.

I start walking along the tree line, looking over at the soccer fields. A loud whistle blows through the air and practically scratches my eardrums like nails on a chalkboard. I wince and rub my temples. Jax is at the very last field. Fuck these heels. I feel like a damn moron walking in heels on grass. I nearly topple over pulling one off, but the second is easier. I shake out my fears and anxiety; no one knows.

My heart clenches in pain once again. I can't say I didn't enjoy it. I can't say I never fantasized about being taken like that. Ruthlessly. Being devoured by a man consumed with lust. My cheeks heat with a violent blush. I need to get my shit together. I can't let these bitches smell any blood in the water.

"You're late, Becca," Cynthia says in a singsong voice, but there's a ring of disdain on the end. I hope she's fucking burning up in that strawberry tweed Chanel skirt suit. Her blonde hair is in a perfect bun, showing off her too fucking large diamond earrings. She's a picture-perfect housewife. The kind of twig who doesn't even finish all of her salad and knows exactly how everything is *supposed* to be done and doesn't mind chiming in to correct others constantly. Yeah, she's what Rick thought he was getting when he married me. Fuck her.

My eyes drop to her heels. All the moms are wearing heels even though they're digging slightly into the dirt. I don't know how they don't fall down on their asses. I tossed my pumps into my bag, and now I'm walking barefoot. As I come up next to them, their lips turn down in frowns. Zero fucks given.

"I had an errand to run. How are our boys doing?" I give her the same fake smile she's giving me before turning to face the field.

"They *really* need to step up their defense. How is Marshal ever going to score when the defense is this poor?"

They're three years old, for fuck's sake. I don't even try to hide my eye roll, not that she would see anyway since now she's texting away on her phone.

I spot Jax running after a boy who's kicking the ball. I pray to God he doesn't just push the kid over and pick up the ball with his hands. Rick and I decided it would be good to get him into sports early. One sport, one language, one instrument. But for fuck's sake, he's only three. I am glad I got him into sports to work off some of that excess energy, but these people drive me up the damn wall. I didn't come from daddy's money like these other women. I worked hard to get my restaurant up and running. I put everything I had in me into this industry. It took ten years to get to this point, and at thirty-one I'm the proud owner of an award-winning Italian bistro.

Jax kicks the ball, thankfully misses the kid, and runs down the field. "Go Jax!" I can't help screaming excitedly and hopping up and down on the balls of my feet. My voice gets the attention of the other moms. I see them smirk and look at each other from the corner of my eye, but I learned to ignore them early on. Mommy playgroups are cutthroat in this social group. I know they talk shit about me. That they defended Rick cheating on me because I work too much, and didn't make enough one-on-one time for the two of us. But they'd be fucking stupid to say that shit to my face.

The thought of Rick hits me hard. My chest hurts, and my heart twists in agony. He may have been an asshole of a husband who was going to try to get every cent from me that he could in our divorce, and try to take my baby away from me, but he was also the father of my baby boy. I smile weakly watching Jax in his little black and blue striped jersey. Number three, because that was Daddy's number. Tears well up in my eyes, and my throat closes as a bastard lump forms. I shake my head and try to think about happy times.

My eyes pop open wide, and my thighs clench. Thoughts of the bookie rutting into me like he fucking owned me make my heart race, and my blood heat. My senses are flooded with the image of his corded muscles pinning me to the wall, the masculine smell in the hot air, and the sounds of him fucking me. I shift my weight and try to cool down, feeling much hotter than I did a moment ago. I'm extremely aware of the fact that I'm no longer wearing any panties. I was in such a fucking rush to get out of there, I left them wherever they fell. My forehead pinches as I try to recollect what happened to them.

A shudder runs through my body as I remember. *He ripped them off of me.* That was the hottest fucking thing I've ever done. But with *him*? With a stranger? A criminal? I don't even fucking know his name. Shame washes over me, and that damn lump in my throat returns. I never lusted after a man before. Never. School and work were all that mattered. I married a nice man when I finally had life all worked out. Had a baby at twenty-seven. I did everything the exact way my parents would have wanted. My blood turns to ice and I look down at my feet, wondering if they'd be ashamed of me now. Now that my marriage failed, and I've fallen to a new level of filth I'd never thought I'd reach.

For fuck's sake, I let him cum in me. I cringe, but my treacherous pussy clenches. I have to repress a moan, remembering how good it felt. My lips purse as I pull out my phone and text Sarah. She's out getting dinner for Jax and me so I can be here to watch his game.

Plan B ASAP please.

I never thought I'd be texting my PA to pick up the morning-after pill. But hell, in the last few months we've grown close. I imagine we're as close as sisters would be, but I wouldn't know. I'm an only child, and I haven't had any family since my parents passed a few years ago. Just after I found out I was pregnant. Tears well up in my eyes as I remember. I was picking out a cute little mug for my mom to tell her. It was going to have the ultrasound on it. I wipe at my burning eyes and try to return my focus to my little man on the field, but all I can see in my head is a picture of that damn mug. *Grandmom in April.* She would've been so happy. I told everyone we were trying. The moment we got married, I wanted to be pregnant. In hindsight, I shouldn't have done that. 'Cause then everyone asks you constantly, "Are you pregnant yet?" It took a little longer than I'd hoped, but stress will do that to you. And when you work the hours I used to work, well, it's fucking stressful. That's why I got Sarah. That's why I cut back and hired more help. It was the best thing for me, and then for my little man, too.

It was supposed to be the best thing for my marriage. But I don't think anything would've helped us survive. Once a cheater, always a cheater. I'm too fucking forgiving. I never should've believed him. Never should've married that sweet-talking liar. But I wanted a baby. I wanted the whole package, the perfect life.

I didn't want a cheating ass husband who blew his business in a shit deal, wanted control of my business, and then gambled away nearly everything I had. Thank fuck I grabbed a hold of my self-respect and started putting my foot down. It was even better when I started feeling he was messing around on me that I confronted it head on. There are givers and takers in this world. I'm a giver, always have been. I know the givers have to set the limits, because the takers have none. Unfortunately, I've learned from experience. From my shit husband. I loosen my clenched fists as the reality of his death hits me again.

I feel like such a bitch for being angry at him. He's dead. He put me through hell and back, but he's not here for me to be mad at anymore. I'm so confused by my emotions. Six months ago, he let his business be torn to shreds and sold off, then he blew that money on a shit deal. Two months ago, I caught him in bed with another woman. Literally. She had her legs wrapped around his hips and her heels digging into his ass as he was fucking her. On our bed. Since then he'd been trying to get every penny of mine and hired the best lawyers he could to try to get full custody, with my fucking money. But a week ago he dropped dead of a heart attack, out of nowhere. Left me with a shit ton of debt, and a giant mess to clean up. I feel like a bitch for hating him in the end, for being relieved this divorce and custody battle are no longer an issue, but most of all I hate myself for not being more upset with him dying. I literally wished he would die. I was hoping that fucker would drop dead. And then he did. How fucking horrible am I that I'm not more upset? That I don't have more regrets?

Some days I absolutely despise myself.

And then I miss him. I see something, like a commercial for a restaurant we used to go to, and it hits me hard. The tears come on before I can hold them back, and I miss the old Rick. And then I hate myself for missing him. Maybe I've just turned into a hateful person.

Everything in the last year has gone to shit, but not Jax; he's perfect. I keep going just for him. He's my everything. As I watch him stumble on the grass and fall, I swear I see a movement to my left. A dark figure behind the trees. A cold shiver runs through my body as I jolt and stare into the trees. But I don't see anything. My body tingles with anxiety as my heart tries to beat its way out of my chest. I swallow thickly and turn back to the field.

There's no one there. I close my eyes and open them when I hear the women to my right clapping and cheering. One of the boys somehow managed to actually score a goal. I clap and yell and smile at my son, who's furiously waving at me. But somewhere deep inside me, fear settles.

I'm certain I saw something. Or someone.

I force another wide smile for my son and keep my feet planted where they are, but I can't wait to get out of here. I need to shake this feeling.

DOM

"**Y**ou're late, Dom!" My mom's high-pitched voice hits me with a touch of humor as she flicks a kitchen hand towel at me. "You're lucky I'm running behind." Ma's always running behind. Maybe it's in our genes. The kitchen smells like her signature Sunday dinner dish of sauce and meatballs.

"Sorry, Ma," I say and give her a kiss on the cheek as I pull the flowers in my hand around to the front. "Got you a gift though."

She pats my cheek with her hand and smiles as she says, "Aw, you spoil me!"

"Dante! Why do you never get me any flowers! You should take notes from your son!" she screams past me to the dining hall, and I all-out grin. I love it when she does this shit. Calling my dad out in front of everyone. I chuckle as I walk to the dining room and see the family gathered around the table.

My dad made sure to build this house with a large enough dining hall for everyone. There's at least twenty people in here. And it feels comfortable, it feels like home. I may not like everything about being a Valetti, but I fucking love Sunday night dinner.

"Pops," I greet as I slap my hand on father's shoulder, "looking good tonight." Pops is getting old, but he still looks good. He's got dark eyes, with dark hair that's grey at the temples. I have his high cheekbones and sharp jawline. He looks exactly like a mafia boss. And that's good, 'cause that's exactly who he is. I take a seat on his right, across from my brother.

"What up, Dom?" Vince is two years younger, making him twenty-seven. My chest pains realizing the dead fuck in my office was four years younger than my brother. Marco whatever-the-fuck his last name was. My jaw clenches tight, knowing I gotta tell them what happened. Not here though, not at dinner. Ma doesn't approve of that shit.

"What the hell did I do to you?" Vince looks back at me like I slapped him.

I shake my head and reply, "Not you. I got to talk to you guys later." The room goes quiet as I reach for some butter for the roll that's on my plate. I don't wait till dinner's served. Never have. Everyone else waits, but Ma doesn't mind if I get started without her. I don't know why Ma bothers with the rolls though. I'm the only one who eats them. Everyone else always waits for the garlic bread.

"What's going on, Dom, everything alright?" Jack asks. Jack is like a second father to me. He's just under my father in the business, or family, whatever you want to call it.

"Not at the table." My mom bends down with a hot bowl of meatballs, and places it in the center of the table.

I throw her an asymmetric grin as I say, "Aw, Ma, you know I wouldn't." I take a bite of my roll and lean back in my chair, trying to lighten the mood for my mother. "I love the smell of your sauce, Ma."

She smiles at me and seems to forget the cloud of tension still lingering in the room.

Jack is sitting with his wife next to my brother, but his eyes are on my father. The two have their eyes locked on one another like they're having a silent conversation. I try to stay out of family business. Pops told me I'd take the lead one day, but I passed it on to Vince. He's got the brains and the stomach to handle this shit. I'm more of a numbers guy. I help out with the books, but I like my side business I have going on. It's fun. ...well, most of the time.

Jack's wife, Jessica, gives me a tight smile from across the table. She's new. Jack divorced his wife, and then she disappeared. He wasn't right for a while. We all knew what happened. She got pissed one day, and he didn't keep his dick in his pants like he fucking should have. And she went blabbing about the wrong shit to the wrong people. The thought makes me want to put my roll down, but I don't. After all these years, I've toughened up some. Jessica's only been a part of the life for a little under a year. The women stay out of the business at all times. That's our rule. It prevents the shit that happened with Jack's ex from going down. Yet another reason Jack blames himself. She should've known, though. What did she really think was going to happen?

Sitting around the table are more people in the family. Tommy and Anthony are good friends of mine, but they're also my cousins. They're a year older and a year younger than me, respectively. Although they're brothers, they look nothing alike. Tommy's a wall of muscle. His fucking muscles have muscles. I'd be shocked if he didn't take steroids. I hope he doesn't, 'cause that shit will shrink up your dick. He's a fucking hothead like my Uncle Enzo, so it's hard to say if it's from 'roids or just genetic. The younger one, Anthony, looks scrawny next to his brother, but he's lean and works out to keep himself in shape. His eyes are darker, almost black. Anthony is a sick fuck. Tommy might be the muscle, but when we need to get information from someone, we turn to Anthony. Put him in a room with anyone, I don't care who it is, he'll get what he wants.

Two seats down from them is Uncle Enzo; he owns the bistro and the club. If someone's trying to meet my father, they have to go through my uncle first. He's leaning over telling Jack something I'd wager is a dirty joke, if his tone and hand gestures are anything to go by. A second later, that half of the table is laughing up a storm and my father's yelling out with a grin. There are some others around the table: Paulie, Joe and a few other guys I know. I don't hang out with them really. I do the books like Pop says, and I keep my nose clean.

Pops wasn't fond of me being a bookie at first. He said it's not good to do shit that could bring heat around the family. But when I started making valuable contacts, like my vet friend, he changed his mind. I know he's still proud of me even if I'm not looking to take over his empire. I'm not who he thought I'd be, but I'm still family and still worthy of being part of this particular *family*. Ma takes a seat at the other end and smacks Uncle Enzo over the head. "Hey!" he yells out and rubs the back of his head as everyone gets a good laugh in. Tony's on my right, the nerd of the group and also a lifelong friend. He gets the intel that we need. And that reminds me of my girl. My hands itch wanting to feel her lush ass again, and my dick jumps in my pants. I slip off my jacket and drape it over the back of the chair as Johnny walks in.

He takes a seat next to my sister, Clara. I've been noticing that lately. Not sure I like it. They've been friends for a while, but they seem *different* lately. The only people missing are my cousin Jimmy and his little boy, Gino. Gino's a hoot. His mom's a bitch and is lucky she's alive, to be honest. Not that I'd ever do anything to the kid's mother, but still, she's lucky.

The bowls are going around the table. I close my eyes and breathe in deep. It smells like home. With the laughter and loud voices of my uncle and father talking over one another, it sounds like home.

And then Ma opens her mouth and ruins it by asking, "Dom, when are you going to bring home a nice girl for dinner?" The room goes silent except for a few chuckles from my uncle and Jack.

"Come on Ma, why don't you pick on Vince for a while?"

"'Cause he's my baby," she says and shoots him a smile and he snorts a laugh in return, but I can tell he's embarrassed, too. Good. If she's gonna go after me, she should be digging at him as well.

"Ma, as soon as I find a keeper I'll bring her home, alright?" As soon as the words come out of my mouth, my beautiful doll pops into mind. She's got something about her I think Ma would like. I think it's her innocent yet confident nature, but I can't tell exactly what it is just yet.

Ma starts to respond with one brow cocked, but I'm saved by little Gino. "Mammie!" The little tyke squeals as he runs in with his little knit hat and thick jacket that billows around him. How can he even move in that thing?

"Gino, bambino!" Ma loves that little man.

I grin at Jimmy and nod my head as he walks around the table to take a seat. He's a tall, good-looking guy, with broad shoulders, and a pretty boy face. "Dom, who am I betting on this week?" I chuckle at him and shake my head.

"You read that book I gave you?" I ask, knowing full well he didn't.

He snorts and looks at me like I'm crazy. "Fuck no."

"Then my guess is that you'll be betting like all the rest of 'em."

The room laughs, and I just sit back in my seat until the meatballs come my way. Ma fries them before she covers them with her sauce. They're so good, but so fucking bad for you.

"C'mon Dom, give me something."

"Don't ever bet against me," I answer as I pile up the meatballs. "There's something for you, Jimmy. You wanna win bets, you stay on my side."

"Dude, just tell me this, New York or Dallas over under forty-five point five?" I shake my head at this fool.

"Giants, over." I lick my lips and slice my meatball as I ask, "How's construction going?"

"It's alright. Same old, same old. Wish I had a fun job, like you." It's important that we have someone in the construction business. Now that we have the vet, it's not quite as important, but it's still good for bookkeeping and all.

"It wasn't fun today." Johnny shakes his head and grabs another piece of garlic bread.

I don't respond; we don't talk about shit at the table. I stare at my food and shovel down another bite. I never wanna get dinner over with, but I've got two conversations that need to happen. One about De Luca, and one about my doll. I'll get De Luca dealt with first. But now is not the time.

"What happened today?" Clara asks, and the room goes silent. She knows better. I stare down at her, but all I see is the back of her head as she looks to Johnny for an answer.

"No game today; they're on break." Johnny answers with a smile and a twinkle in his eye. He's real fucking good at playing it off. Still, she should know not to ask questions. He should know not to bring that shit up. And they should both know not to be eye-fucking each other like that. I look to Pops, who looks exactly how I feel.

"I wanna play game!" Gino shouts from his seat next to Ma. Jimmy pulled a chair up from the corner so he could sit as close to Ma as possible. Just the way both of them like it. The little tyke gets the good mood going and all's well for now, but if some shit is going on between Johnny and Clara, they better square that up fast. I take a peek at my Pops and see he seems to have gotten over it.

But I know he didn't forget.

BECCA

"Four," I hold up my fingers for Jax to see, "little ladybugs sitting on a tree." He giggles and holds up four fingers. I love his toothy grin. We're on his rocket ship bed with his Mickey space-themed bedding, reading a story to settle him down for bed. "Along came a frog, and then there were..." I try to turn the page, but he shuts the book on my fingers.

"Little man-" I stop my scolding as he yawns. He's so tuckered out. He almost fell asleep in the bath, and that never happens. He freaking loves splashing in the tub. Especially if he can soak me. It's his favorite pastime. He yawns again and rubs his eyes with his little fists. A soft smile plays at my lips, and I put the book on the little nightstand next to his bed. His cup of water is there, but I really should take it; I don't want him to have an accident. I lean down and give him a kiss on the forehead. "I love you, baby boy. Have sweet dreams."

"Love you, Mommy." Hearing those words melts my heart, and they get me every time. I rise slowly and walk to the door. I double-check the nightlight before I hit the light switch and close the door. I wait a minute, listening by the door. Some days he's a little deviant and gets up to play, but tonight he's pretty beat. After a few minutes of silence, I walk to my own bedroom.

It fucking sucks being in here. Everything reminds me of Rick. I don't know why I haven't gotten rid of anything. The picture frames on the wall are full of our pictures. A couple are from my pregnancy and Jax's birth. But then there are wedding pictures on the dresser. *His* dresser. I rub the back of my neck and sigh. I should take care of this. I really should. I can't live like this. I fall back against the wall and look around the room. The comforter is a stormy blue; it's what he picked. The rug is the modern shag one he wanted. The furniture was all his. There's hardly anything in here that's *mine*. Everything has him written all over it. At least I picked my own clothes out. Thank God he didn't have a preference for that.

And heels. I refused to budge on that shit. Heels are my one indulgence. I don't care if I spend a little extra on them occasionally.

I turn around and walk out of the bedroom; I'll sleep in the guest room tonight. It seems like every other night this happens. I come to the realization that our bedroom was really his bedroom and instead of dealing with it, I just leave. I cringe as the thought hits me. I'm a stronger woman than that, but I'm so fucking tired. I'm way too tired to deal with this shit. I grin and think about messaging Sarah. That's why I have a PA, to take care of this shit for me. I can't message her this late though. That would make me a shit boss.

I grin as I turn on the light to the guest bedroom. This room is mine. All mine. From the antique furniture and cream paisley bedspread, to the pale aqua paint and plush chenille woven rug, it's all me. I curl my toes in the rug and sigh. I can sleep in here. I should just burn the old bedroom. After I relocate the pictures of Jax... and my heels.

I rub my sore eyes and climb into bed. I need to be up at four to make sure everything's good with the restaurant and that the orders came in. And hopefully Jax will sleep in until seven, fingers crossed for eight, so I can get all the morning shit done before the lunch rush starts. I settle down deep into the covers and rest my eyes. Tomorrow will be a better day. I will make it a better day. I no longer have to deal with any of this shit with Rick. The familiar pain in my chest forms yet again. I'm not sure if it's from Rick dying, or leaving me or cheating on me... or trying to take Jax away from me. That fucking bastard. I shake my head and push down the emotions. It doesn't matter. None of it matters now. It's all over. Paying his debt was the last thing I had to do.

My teeth grind against one another. It's a good fucking thing they gave me his phone and I had the balls to look at it. What if I'd never seen it? "Fucking Rick," I mutter with every bit of disdain I have left in me and roll over under the sheets.

I pull them up close to my chest and snuggle deep into the pillow top mattress. Happy thoughts. Positive thoughts. *Do good things, think good things, and good things will happen.* I repeat my mantra a few times and then open my eyes. I bite my bottom lip, feeling like a bitter bitch, but really – where the fuck did thinking like that get me?

I throw the covers back and head to the shower. I don't care that it's going to fuck my hair up in the morning by sleeping with it wet. I need a real shower. I need to wash all this shit off of me.

I clear my mind of everything and put a few drops of eucalyptus oil into the back of the shower as the room fills with steam. Deep breaths. Deep breaths. The cream marble tiles on the floor of the stall heat instantly under my feet. I step into the water, letting the warm spray wash away the day. I turn around and soak my hair, breathing in deep. Everything will be alright. Everything happens for a reason.

Just as I start to feel the heavy pull of relaxation, I remember today. I remember *him*.

A soft moan leaves my lips as I think of my dirty criminal. Although I can't, I pretend like I can still smell him on me. I wish I could. The eucalyptus suddenly feels like a bad idea. I try to remember that masculine scent he had, all woodsy and raw. Raw is a good word to describe him. A heat rushes up my chest and into my cheeks as I remember that's how he took me, raw. My fingers brush against my hips, trailing down to my thighs. My lips part as I remember him pushing me against the wall and slamming into me. It was almost surreal. Like a dark fantasy I've dreamed about. I pull my fingers back and open my eyes, realizing where my thoughts have gone. I can't do this shit. It's one thing to fantasize; it's another to indulge. *Indulge?* I shake my head. No, that's not what that was. That was him taking advantage. Even if I enjoyed it. I bite my lip and start washing my body. It's so fucking wrong I enjoyed that. No wonder I'm alone. I start to feel dizzy, and I have to lean against the stall. Fuck. I turn the temperature down and steady myself. I'm just too fucked up for this right now. My emotions are out of control. I don't know what's normal, what's rational, and what is just truly fucked.

Other than me. I was, in fact, truly fucked today. I turn off the water and step out. The bathroom is chillier than I like it to be, but it was a quick shower. I grab a towel and quickly dry off. I need to get to bed. I take out my face moisturizer and the serum for my hair and apply both. As I shut the cabinet, I catch sight of the spot where my birth control should be. I haven't had any for months.

Thank God I took the morning-after pill. And just like that, every bit of desire and heat leaves me. I don't have time for fantasies. I don't have time to indulge in something that would destroy the small piece of me that survived Rick.

I huff and throw on a nightshirt to quickly get into bed. Today was a one-off. Whatever I did today – I shake my head with my eyes closed – it doesn't count. Sarah will never mention it again. I wish she hadn't been there. I wish she hadn't seen me after that. After him. Fuck, the thought of him lights every nerve ending in my core aflame. FUCK!

I bury my head into the pillow and try to forget the shameful desire burning deep down in my core. It only takes the thought of him closing the door on me without a second look to shut down my longing. What a fucking prick. He may be hot and powerful and he may have fucked me like he owns me, but he's still an asshole. All men are fucking assholes.

It's wrong to want a man like him. But I can't lie to myself; I really fucking want him.

DOM

"*S*o tell me what you know about her." I question Tony as soon as I get him alone. De Luca's fucked. He's been fucked. We gotta keep our heads low. Yada yada. Same shit as last week. Motherfucker came for me; I took care of it. Pops is proud, and he's sending a message. Beyond that, I don't want a damn thing to do with this shit.

Back to making bets and hunting down my doll. Just thinking about her owing me makes my dick grow rigid. I shift my weight to cover it up, waiting for Tony to get all the info on the iPad. He takes that thing everywhere. I don't really like the idea, even if it is password protected and encrypted. I told Pops, I told everyone. Apparently this technology is fine, and it doesn't have *everything* on it. Still, I don't like having a device with any information on it pertaining to the business.

I have to admit though, when he hands it over to me and my doll's picture looks back at me, suddenly I don't really give a fuck about the iPad. I read the description and go through the photos.

Rebecca Lynn Harrison. Maiden name: Bartley.

Thirty-one years old. Birthday: January 2nd 1985.

Widow to Richard Francis Harrison. Married: December 14th 2011.

Died of heart attack at thirty-four years old. Birthday: May 12th 1982.

Mother to Jax Liam Harrison.
Three years old. Birthday: April 5th 2013.

MY JAW TICS as I read that part about a son. Kids complicate shit. I can't just keep her to myself whenever I want and expect her to submit without any question.

OWNER OF MARCELLO'S Italian Bistro.
127 Pattinsons Plaza. Value: Two million.
Owner of two-story family home in Harmony Place.
42 Hills Lane. Value: 600,000.

RECENT LEGAL ACTION
Divorce and distribution of assets – dismissed
Questions regarding custody – also dismissed

"WHAT THE FUCK IS THIS ABOUT?" Anger rises in my chest. Is she not a good mother? I won't fuck with someone who doesn't take care of their own. That's not the kind of woman I want.

"Her husband was a piece of shit. I've got his info on there, too." He motions to the iPad, and I suck in a deep breath.

I scroll past a few pictures of my doll in front of her restaurant. *Marcello's Italian Bistro*. I'll have to see about that. I doubt her meatballs are as good as Ma's. I smirk, taking in the façade of the restaurant. I've never been there; never even heard of it. We have our own upscale bistro. But the people who come to us are looking for an experience, not necessarily our food. It's not like Pops isn't known as the head of the mafia. The cops have been on him throughout the years, but they've never been able to get anything to stick. The papers crucify him any time there's bloodshed in the streets. Most of the time it's got nothing to do with us though. Sometimes it's deserved, but it's a rare day the papers get their information right.

So when people come into our bistro, they're hoping to see some shit from the Sopranos or something. The thought makes me chuckle. I stare at the picture of her restaurant. Of Rebecca's restaurant. I like that name. Rebecca. It feels good on my tongue. It looks like a nice place. I bet it's decent inside. But Italian? Real Italian? Nah, I doubt it. I smirk and keep scrolling. I'll have to go in and find out for myself.

I stop on a picture of her holding a little boy in her arms. He must be her son. I look past the kitchen doorway to the den and take a peek at Gino.

"What's Gino now? Is he three?" I ask him as I lean against the granite countertops.

He shrugs as he says, "No clue, Dom."

"Ma!" I yell through the kitchen to the dining room where her and Jessica are having a cup of tea. I know I'm interrupting them, but Ma won't mind.

She walks to the doorway with her hands on her hips and her lips pursed. "Why do you have to yell, Dom? Huh? You can't just walk into the room like a normal person?"

"Sorry Ma, just wanted to know how old Gino is."

"He'll be three in June." She narrows her eyes at me and says, "Why are you asking?"

I shrug as I reply, "No reason." I don't lie to my Ma, not ever. But of course the one time I do, she sees right through me. I guess I don't lie 'cause I'm a shitty liar. Her eyes focus on the iPad in my hands. "Not now, Ma," I warn her. Her lips part and she takes a step back, giving me a look of disappointment.

"I wanna see, Dominic." She puts one hand on her hip, and the other is palm up, extended in front of her. Fuck me.

"Ma. It's just a girl; she doesn't even know me." Well, she kind of knows me, in the biblical sense, but Ma doesn't need to hear that.

"There's a lot of broads out there, Dom," Pops says as he comes up from behind me and takes the iPad out of my hand. He's the only one in here I'd let get away with that shit. He chuckles. "You always go for the challenge, don't you? You can't be happy with a nice single twenty-something. You wanna go for a chick with baggage."

"Dante! A child is not baggage!" Ma looks pissed. I raise my eyebrows and stare past my ma to the dining room. My parents don't fight. Never. Can't tell you one time they ever got into an argument. But Ma sure as shit likes to beat up on Pops. She doesn't let him get away with a damn thing.

"Oh hush, I'm only saying having a kid creates extra work." He hands the iPad back to me and adds, "If he's not looking for anything but a good time, there's no reason to go after a broad who has to worry about a little one." I nod my head, hearing what my pops is saying, but I don't fucking like it.

"What you need to do is knock it off with all the girls and find a good woman to settle down with."

"All the girls?" I scrunch my face up in distaste. "What girls?" It's not like I bounce from girl to girl. I'm not some fucking manwhore. Not that I really see a problem either way. By that I mean I'm not into slut-shaming. You do what you want, how you want. Vince has a fleet of women coming and going. They know what they're signing up for, and I don't give him a hard time over it. I just prefer something different. I like to build some trust. A one-night stand is nothing that can give me the high I need. It's a quick release, and that's just not my thing. I like gaining trust and pushing limits. I enjoy finding out a woman's deepest, darkest fantasies. Hard to make that come true if they don't trust you enough to tell you.

I hear Vince laugh from the den. Great, the whole fucking family is in on it now. He walks into the kitchen, moving to lean against the fridge with a huge fucking grin on his face. I cut him off as his mouth opens. "Shut it." I point my thumb in Ma's direction. "She gets a pass." Then at Pops. "He gets a pass." Then I point at him with my brows raised. "Not you. Fuck off."

"Dom!" Ma scolds me.

"I know, I know." I roll my eyes and pass the iPad back to Tony. "Language." I look at Tony and say, "Email it to me."

Ma looks at me expectantly. "Ma, really." I don't fucking want her involved. This is just pussy. I can't get this broad out of my head. Partly because I want to apologize, but mostly because I want her cunt wrapped around my dick again. And that ass. Just thinking of it makes my dick come to attention. And that's my cue to fucking leave. I did my part; I came to Sunday dinner. I told them about that little shit Marco, and De Luca's bullshit.

I give Ma a hug as she asks, "You're leaving already?" She sounds hurt, and it would make me feel guilty if she didn't say it like that every time.

"Gotta go, Ma; I love you." She gets a kiss on the cheek. Pops gets a quick hug, and the rest get a wave as I walk my ass out the door to my Benz.

Time to go home and really look into this woman. I already know I want her; I've just got to figure out how I'm gonna get her to owe me again. The smirk on my face vanishes as I remember I'm gonna have to address how I behaved the first time. My hands twist the leather steering wheel. I'm not so good with apologies, but I'm sure I'll figure out a way to make it up to her. I groan, thinking up all the ways I'll make it up to my doll.

I can't fucking wait to get inside her tight pussy again. I haven't got anything planned for tomorrow. Well, now I do.

BECCA

*J*cringe as I take off my heels the second I get inside the house and drop my purse on the front hall table. Fuck, today was a long day. I wince and suck in air through my teeth as my feet finally have some relief. I drop the heels at the front door and start walking to the sofa, but I stop and sigh. Damn it, I can't fucking leave them there. I hate not being organized. I lean down and pick them up so I can put them back in the closet. Back on their spot on the shelf. It'll make me feel better. If I leave one little mess, then it'll just grow. I can't be lazy, it's not like anyone else is going to clean up after me. Besides, it's easier to maintain a tidy home than it is to let it go to shit and then have to clean it all up.

As I slide my Jimmy Choos back on the shelf, I hear the doorbell ring. I look down at my watch with my brow furrowed. It's only five. I have an hour before Jax will be home. I need this time to prep dinner, which today means ordering out, and to go through my emails and payroll. I really do need to hire someone. I pick up my pace to open the door as it rings again. I can't keep up this pace. I can't keep doing *everything* by myself, especially with how shitty I've been feeling. I swing open the door with a sigh and without bothering to look through the peephole.

My lips part, and my heart stills when I see the man on the other side. He fucking haunted my dreams last night in the best possible way. If I wasn't terrified at the moment, my pussy would be clenching in need. He's in dark dress slacks and a crisp, light blue button-down shirt with a dark blue tie. His exposed neck makes me want to lick it and feel the rough stubble on my tongue. As if he knows exactly what I'm thinking he gives me a cocky smirk, which only makes him look even hotter.

I swallow thickly and try to speak. Why is he here? Fuck. Fuck. Fuck. I gave him everything. Maybe he wants more? Maybe Rick's debt isn't completely paid. My eyes widen at the thought. I shouldn't be so turned on by that. I should be scared shitless, and part of me is. But another part of me wants him to fuck me against this wall and have him leave with the warning that he'll be back to collect again tomorrow. I must be fucking sick in the head.

"May I come in, Rebecca?" His smooth baritone voice drips with sex appeal. My core heats instantly. I can't speak, I don't trust my voice, so I just nod and open the door wider. As his tall, broad frame passes me I seem to snap out of my lust-filled haze. What the fuck did I just do? I should've said no!

I start shaking my head as though this isn't real. He turns around in my living room to face me. I paid a designer to make this room look like it belonged on a page of Good Housekeeping. All plush, cream-colored cushions and dark antique finishes. He doesn't belong here. He stands out amongst all the clean white lines. He may be in expensive, custom-tailored clothing, but he doesn't fool me. He's bad. His hair is messy and rugged. His hands are callused and scarred. His smirk is cocky and sexy as fuck. It's like he was placed in this room by accident.

Looking around the room to avoid his piercing gaze, I spot a family picture on the wall and I'm reminded of how tainted it is by my husband – ex-husband – deceased husband. Fuck. Tears well up in my eyes. I can't fucking handle this. I rub my temples. I just want to get whatever this is over with. I shut the door and follow him into the entryway of the living room. I should offer him tea or a drink. My parents raised me right. But fuck that. He's a criminal. I run my hands through my hair as anxiety consumes me.

"Can I help you?" I'm barely able to get the words out.

A deep chuckle rumbles from his chest. He grins, showing off his perfect white teeth. "I think you can, Rebecca." His smile falters a bit before he asks, "Are you going by Bartley now, or Harrison?"

I need to shut this shit down. I don't need someone barging into my life and walking all over me. I'll give him whatever he wants to just get the fuck out. I should've known he'd be back for the interest. For actual money.

A blush travels from my chest to my cheeks. I shouldn't have been so stupid to think that he'd be satisfied humiliating me like he did. My heart clenches. Was it really humiliating? I shake the thought away. I'm sure he intended it to be. Why else would he be here smirking at me like he owns me? Fucking asshole. I clench my fists and push out the words, "How much is it that I owe you?" I have a few grand in the safe in the bedroom. I fucking hope it's enough. I thought all this was behind me. I told Sarah to never speak of it again, and I fucking moved on. It was only awkward for the first few minutes. Thank fuck for Sarah; I need to give her a raise.

He smiles with that boyish charm I'm sure he's used on more than a handful of women and says, "Doll, you don't owe me. *You* never did."

A lump forms in my throat, making it hard to answer, "Why are you here?" I barely breathe the question. The way his eyes narrow and he licks his lips, he's looking at me like I'm his prey. Every bit of fear I had is replaced with pure desire. My core heats, and my shoulders shudder under his lust-filled gaze. "I want you to go." The words come out weak. But I need to say them.

He looks hurt for a split second, and I almost think I imagined it, but I didn't. I saw it. He gives me a tight smile. "I came to," he clears his throat and looks out of the large bay window for a moment. "I just wanted to apologize for the way I treated you." He shoves his hands in his pockets as his forehead pinches, as though he's truly considering something. "I didn't mean-"

"It's fine." My voice hitches on the end. I shake my head, turning my back on him to open the door for him. If he just came to apologize, then he can get the fuck out.

A small gasp escapes me as his hand covers mine and pushes the front door closed with a loud bang. The lock engages with a menacing click. My body jumps from the noise and then from his hard chest pushing against my back. His large frame boxes me in, and my breasts push against the front door. My heart races, and I struggle to breathe as his hot breath tickles my neck. His lips graze my ear as he whispers, "You didn't hear me, doll. I wanna make it up to you."

A wave of heat rips through my body as I close my eyes. The tips of my fingers tingle, and my pussy clenches as his other hand gently grabs my waist

42

and he pulls my ass into his hips. A strangled moan leaves my lips as I feel his hard dick push into my ass. I can feel the wetness between my thighs, preparing me for him. His hand reaches up my blouse and splays across my stomach. "I owe you, doll. Let me make it up to you." His hand gently travels down my side. A shiver runs through my body as he kisses the crook of my neck.

My breath hitches, and the word is on my lips. *Stop.* But I don't say it. I lean my back into his hard, hot body and rock against him. What the fuck is wrong with me? He wraps his hand around my throat. I love the possession. He could break me. He could crush me. He could take me like he did yesterday. And I want it. Fuck, I want it so bad.

This is so wrong. I shouldn't want this. I shouldn't feel like I need him. I shouldn't feel so empty and hollow, needing to be filled. I bite my bottom lip, warring with myself. It was so good. Fuck, it was so fucking good before. I can only imagine how good it would be now.

My head falls back against his chest, and my lips part as a breathy moan fills the hot air. A dark, masculine chuckle leaves his lips and tickles my neck. It sends an urgent need to my throbbing clit. He nips at my earlobe and then pulls it with his teeth.

"You want me, doll?" His question lingers in the hot air. I can't. I can't want this. But I can't say no. I close my eyes and shake my head. Tears leak from the corners of my eyes. I shove my back against his hard chest. He doesn't move. He's too strong.

"Yes you do, I know you do." His voice is hard and unmoving, like his muscular body caging me in.

I do. I want it so fucking bad. But I push against him again and turn around in his grasp. I yelp as his hand grabs both of my wrists and pins them above my head. His erection digs into my stomach as his hips keep me pinned to the door. He leans into my neck and hisses, "I hate liars."

My eyes close tight, and I struggle to swallow the lump in my throat. I can't explain it. I can't do this, no matter how much my body begs me for it. My lips find his neck, but instead of kissing him, I bite down. HARD. I sink my teeth deep into his flesh to *hurt* him. I don't know why. I don't want to fight him. But a sick part of me does.

"Fuck!" he yells out and pulls his upper body away while his hips stay pinned to mine, and his hand tightens on my wrists. His dick jumps from my attack. My eyes stare at his neck. That's gonna leave a bruise. There's no blood though. Good. I don't want to really hurt him, just...

His hand that isn't holding my wrists touches his neck in disbelief. My breathing comes in sharp pants as his eyes widen. I expect him to hit me. To slap me across the face. My cheek would sting with a violent red mark. I want him to pin me down on the ground, my knees burning as they scrape against the carpet while I struggle beneath him. I want him to rip my pants down and tear my panties off. I want him to fuck me. To punish me and treat me like he owns my body. I scissor my thighs, searching for relief from the heated need of my fantasy.

But I won't admit I want it, because it's wrong.

I swallow thickly as his eyes darken and narrow. They travel along my body with dark desire as he contemplates what to do with me. I'm paralyzed with a deadly mixture of lust and fear. His hand tightens on my wrists while the other wraps around my throat. He squeezes just before the point of too much. It's not a struggle to breathe, but I'm pinned to the door. I'm completely at his mercy. He holds my body still while he leans in. "You wanna fight me, doll?"

I press my lips into a hard line and struggle in his grasp. My body twists and writhes, but it's no use. He huffs a humorless laugh. "All you had to do was tell me," he says and leans in closer and bites down hard on my neck, making me scream out. The painful pinch of his bite intensifies the throbbing need burning in my core. He whispers in my ear, "Say red."

I still with confusion. *Red?*

"Say red, and it all stops. Do you understand?" My eyes widen as I realize what he's saying.

"Yes." The word comes out easy in absolute submission. Hope and lust stir in my blood.

"Say it." His words are hard and short.

"Red." It whips from my mouth.

His hand loosens on my throat and he says, "Good girl, now fight me like you want to." In a flash, he turns my body and pushes me hard against the door. His left hand keeps my wrists pinned while his other rips my pants down my thighs; the fabric burns across my skin as he forces them down. I think to scream, but I don't.

I don't want to scream. I don't want anyone to know.

His thick fingers tear away the lace scrap covering my pussy, and his fingers dip into my heat as I whimper. "You're such a fucking slut. So wet for me. Wet for a dirty, hard fuck." I hear his zipper, and that's when it hits me. Fuck! He's not going to put on a condom. I start to open my mouth, but I don't. I can't ruin this. I buck my body against his, and his grasp on my wrists slips. I hear him stumble back, and I run for the living room.

My pants fall even farther down my legs and hinder my movements. I trip and scream out, but his corded arms wrap around my body and cushion my blow. He pins me down as I thrash under him. My fingers dig into the carpet. I try to move away, but I can't. I can't get out from under him. I can't turn around.

His blunt fingernails dig into the flesh of my hips, tilting me up. And before I can move, before I can think of a way to fight him, he thrusts himself into me to the hilt.

"Fuck!" he yells out as I moan into the carpet.

I feel the sting of his massive size stretching my walls. I try to get up, but his strong hand splays across my back and pushes me down while his other keeps a firm grip on my hip as he pounds into me. Again and again. My body heats as pleasure grows in my core. He ruts into me like a beast claiming his prey.

"Yes!" I scream into the floor.

He leans down, keeping up his relentless pace. "That's right, doll; you fucking love this. You love me fucking your tight little cunt." His dirty words send me over the edge. My body convulses under him as intense pleasure wracks through my body. My back tries to arch, but he keeps me pinned and pounds into me without mercy. My walls pulse around him, and he pushes deeper into me. I scream into the floor as waves and waves of hot cum fill me. I lie limp on the ground, loving the feeling of being used. Loving how he took everything he wanted from me.

My bliss is shattered as I hear a beep alert that I got a text message. Reality slaps me in the fucking face. I scramble underneath of him to get up. The word is there, ready to pounce, but he lets me up. I kick my pants off and dig in my purse in the front hall for my iPhone.

Running 5 mins late – sorry!

It's a text from Sarah. I check the time. Shit! It's almost six. My hand covers my mouth. Fuck! Fuck! Fuck! I didn't get shit done. I drop the phone and grab my pants, searching frantically for my torn underwear. Holy fuck. Sarah's coming with Jax and his play date. I don't even remember which kid it is that's coming over. Holy hell, I'm a fucking mess.

"Are you okay?" I look up at the sex god standing in the middle of my living room. He just fucked me for a second time, and I don't even know his name. Tears form in my eyes as I shake my head. *Slut.* His word rings in my head as my throat closes, and my chest hollows.

He wraps his arms around me as he says, "It's alright, doll. It's okay."

He doesn't understand. I push away from him. "You need to leave. I'm sorry. I shouldn't-" I can't finish. I don't know what to say to him.

He looks at me like I've slapped him. And I guess I may as well have. But what did he honestly expect? He came here to fuck me, and he did. He won. It's over. I open the front door and stay behind it so no one will see. I lower my gaze to the floor as I say, "I can't."

"What the fuck?" My eyes reach his as he stands in front of me zipping up his pants, and shaking his head. He walks with confidence toward me, and I can tell he's not going to leave.

"My son." It's all I say. It's all I have to say. He stops a foot away from me and looks me up and down. I want to ask him his name. I want to do much more than I can. More than I should. I have to take a deep breath and try to calm myself.

"I'll go, but I want to see you again." *I do, too.* His words shock me. My lips part, and I stand there speechless.

He picks up my phone off the table and says, "I'm putting my number in here. Dom." He looks at me with a smirk. I feel my cheeks heat, and I cringe. That's so fucking embarrassing. I don't even respond.

He puts the phone down, but then laughs and shakes his head. He picks it back up and smiles broadly at me. "Dirty Dom, since that's the way you like it, doll." He puts the phone back down and then walks to me. His hand cups my face and tilts it so I'm forced to look at him.

He's so relaxed, so at ease. I want to melt into him. I bite my lip to keep myself from caving to him.

He turns his cheek toward me and taps it with his finger.

I look at him like he's fucking crazy. He wants me to kiss his cheek? "You don't have all day, Rebecca; your son will be here soon." My eyes widen. I don't want that. I have to stand on my tiptoes to plant a kiss on his cheek, but I do. I love the feel of his rough stubble under my soft lips.

"Good girl." An asymmetric grin pulls his lips up.

"Becca." I don't know why, but I correct him. No one calls me Rebecca. Only my mother, when she was mad at me. When I disappointed her. I don't want him calling me that. Shit, I'd rather he call me his dirty slut again than Rebecca.

"Becca," he repeats to me. "I like that even better," he mutters under his breath, and then leaves. I watch as he gets into a silver car without looking back at me. I quickly close the door and lean my back against it. My mind replays everything that happened as my fingertips touch my lips.

What the fuck did I just do?

DOM

hat the fuck just happened? I went there to smooth shit over and apologize. I start the ignition and run my hand through my hair. I lean back against the seat and take a look back at her house.

A two-story, single family home. Where the fuck is her picket fence?

Her door's closed. She didn't even wait to watch me leave. Probably has to clean up all the evidence that she was with me. For some reason, that really fucking hurts. But then I remember she's got a little boy. And fuck that, I don't want to be here and have to do all that shit. I just wanted to get laid. And I did. I pull out and snort at a few of the houses that actually do have white picket fences.

But why does it feel so... wrong? It was hot as fuck. I've never had a woman who wanted to do that, to fight me like that. I groan, leaning my head back against the seat as I pull up to a red light. That was fucking hot. My fingers graze the skin of my neck. She fucking bit me. My Becca is one kinky bitch.

The cocky grin on my lips slips as I remember how she looked after. Not after I got done fucking her. She was gorgeous when she came on my dick. Her teeth sank into her bottom lip as she tried to fight her need to scream in pleasure. The memory makes me want to fuck her again. Right now. This broad keeps me wanting to go back for more. I shake my head, not quite knowing how I feel about it all.

I FEEL A LITTLE USED, to be honest. I fucking enjoyed it, but damn, did she have to kick me out right fucking then? The aftershocks were probably still racing through her body when she shut the damn door.

She should've at least taken me to dinner if she was gonna fuck me like that. I bark a laugh out at my little joke.

Okay, okay. Now I know what I'm working with. If we're gonna keep fucking, I know exactly where I stand with her. I'd be her dirty, little secret. Usually women brag about fucking me. There's no way Becca will.

As I pull up to the house, my phone goes off. I look at the monitor on the dashboard and see it's Vince. I park the car in the driveway, but leave it running.

"Yeah?" I ask him. I don't really feel like fucking around. I want to get inside and look at my schedule. I gotta figure out when I'm hooking up with my doll again.

"We got a problem." I don't like his tone. My blood runs ice cold.

"What is it?" I ask.

"Detective Marshall took Jack in." Hearing that name pisses me off. Jack's ex threatened to go to him. You don't threaten a mobster, even if he's your husband. And you sure as fuck don't use names either. 'Cause that means you've already talked to law enforcement.

"What's he got on him?" I ask.

"Nothing. But we all need to lay low for now."

"Why'd he get picked up?" Marshall is always trying to hunt us down and pin anything he can on us. Every stupid thing used to get us taken in. Now they're careful, since Pops threatened a lawsuit and the judge in his pocket is on our side.

"Expired license." He's gotta be shitting me.

"Are you fucking serious?" I practically yell.

"Yeah, just lay low, Dom," he answers with a pissed off tone. Jack should fucking know better.

"Not a problem." My hands twist the steering wheel. I always lay low. I'm not out there like the rest of them.

"Yeah, it is a problem." My brow furrows. The fuck it is? "Don't you remember what happened yesterday?"

I close my eyes and pinch the bridge of my nose. De Luca. Damn is he a pain in my ass. "That hasn't been dealt with yet?" We have to be careful about how we talk. No names, nothing that could be used as evidence. Just in case.

"Not yet. We have some issues standing in the way, and now this." My fist slams on the wheel. It's not hard to whack a guy. Really, it's not. And the quicker, the better. Which is why it was supposed to happen last night.

"Why didn't the call happen last night?" It's hard to keep the anger out of my voice. Usually I stay calm and indifferent on the outside. That's how I am. That's how I like it to be. Other than with this broad. She's gotten under my skin.

"We got tied up." What the fuck could be more important than taking care of someone who's trying to *take care* of us? I wanna ask him, but my temper is starting to get the best of me. I can't let that get out of hand. I can't slip up on a phone call.

"What do you need me to do, Vince?" I fucking hate this. I hate knowing someone is out there gunning for us, and we're just sitting ducks. My mind flashes with an image of Becca, her lying on the ground, blood pooling around her pale, lifeless body. Even worse, her son. Fuck that. That can't happen. I won't let that happen.

No. No, they didn't see her. Right? There was plenty of time that passed between when she left and that young prick coming into my office. But who the fuck knows how long they were waiting out there?

Johnny looked at the footage, had to cross every "T" and dot every "I." He said there wasn't anyone with Marco. His car was left in the lot. Johnny dumped it, of course. But still, an uneasiness creeps up on me.

My body stills and freezes. I'm not risking it. I put the car in reverse. "I gotta go, Vince."

"Just hang tight and lay low."

"Got it." I hit end and immediately dial Johnny.

"Yo, boss," he answers casually. Too fucking casual for my liking.

"Did you watch my girl leave when you saw the footage?" I feel fucking stupid for not doing it myself. I grit my teeth as I come up to a red light and resist the urge to gun it. *Stay low.* Besides, I just left her. She's fine.

Fuck! What if they had a tail on me? I haven't been paying attention since this fucker is supposed to be dead. He was supposed to be taken care of. Fucking Jack! My fist slams against the wheel as I stare at the longest fucking red light I've ever sat at.

"Nah, boss. I di-"

I cut him off and say sharply, "Do it. Make sure no one followed her. Do it now, and get back to me when you're done. I'm heading to her house now." It's gonna take another forty minutes to get back to her place. At least it gets dark pretty early in the fall. I'll just scout it out, make sure she's good until Johnny gets back to me.

There's a short hesitation and I know he's confused and wants to ask what's going on, but he knows better than to ask. And realistically, I have no clue what's going on between us. But if they are hoping to get to us, those spineless rats will use any means necessary. Including our women. It wouldn't be the first time a competitor targeted us that way. But I'm sure as fuck not going to let it happen to her.

I pull up a few houses away, park and turn off my lights. I'm glad she lives in a nice neighborhood; my car doesn't really stand out much here. There's a car parked along the curb of her house, but I know she was expecting some-one, so I don't freak out. I stay calm. She'll be fine. I'm just gonna make sure she's alright. That's all. I put my hand on the butt of my gun, just to make sure it's where I like it, and get out with my phone in my hand. I flick it to vibrate and I shut the door quietly. Right before I pocket my phone, it goes off.

"Yeah?" I ask Johnny.

"She's good. There's nothing on there." His answer is quick and to the point. I like it.

"Thanks." I end the call and debate just getting back in my car and leaving. But I drove all the way back out here. I check the time on the phone. It's nearly eight. I'll go check to make sure she's alright.

I chuckle deep and low. That's a fucking lie. I wanna see what my doll is up to.

BECCA

J wish this bitch would just leave already. She doesn't even want to
be here. She's digging for information. I can practically feel her
claws. Her eyes keep looking all over the room, as if searching for some
evidence of *anything* to bring back to her bitchy cabal.

Her daughter, Ava, is freaking adorable, but she's not the least bit interested in playing with Jax. Not that it really matters when they're three. But
seriously, just fucking go home already. I watched Ava for an hour, fed them
dinner – pizza since I didn't have time for anything else – and Cindy was just
supposed to pick her up. Just scoop up your tyke and go.

I've had some really fucked up long days today and yesterday. I need to
crash. Or go to a freaking mental institution. I'm not sure which.

Cindy's hand reaches out and touches my arm, bringing my focus back to
her. It's fucking cold. I should start referring to her as the ice bitch.

She looks at me with a tilted head and a sad frown, feigning actual sympathy. I should hate this woman. She was friends with the woman I caught Rick
with. She knew! But then again, they all knew. Everyone but me. "How are
you *really*, Becca?" she finally asks.

How am I? I'm fucked. That's what I am. I'm seriously fucked in the head. I
hate Rick, yet I miss him. More than that, I feel guilty about my dead husband.
Ex-husband. I don't even know how to refer to him. I'm drowning in work.

And I'm fucking a criminal who knows where I live. I'm not fucking okay. Nothing feels okay. My perfect world has been torn apart, flipped around and is practically unrecognizable.

But I'm not going to tell this bitch that. I don't even tell Sarah that. I mean, she knows. She figures shit out on her own. Like when she dropped the kids off. She knew something happened. I could see it on her face that she wanted to ask questions, but she didn't. I bet one of these days she's just going to drive me to a fucking shrink. The thought isn't as funny as I wish it would be. Rick wanted to take me to a shrink. He said I was unstable, and therefore should not have custody of Jax. Fuck, am I unstable? No. I close my eyes and turn my head away. I'm handling all this shit as best as anyone possibly could. I'm doing my best. I really am. My hands cover my face. I have no idea if it's good enough though.

Cindy's hand squeezes my thigh. "You can tell me; I'm here for you."

I give her a tight smile. "It's really hard working through the grief and anger. But I know everything will be fine with some time." I pat her knee and say, "Grief is a journey; I'm just moving through it." It's the truth. Well, a partial truth. The slimmest fraction of the truth. But the truth nonetheless. I'm not going to open my heart for this woman. I'm not going to do it for anyone. Not anymore. Just as the bitter thought creeps up on me, Jax squeals and Ava starts crying.

"Jax!" He's got her baby's blanket in his hands. I shake my head at him and say, "Sweetheart, give that back to Ava, please." Calm tones, display behavior you want to be reciprocated. I nod my head and smile. Positive reinforcement. I think about all the books I read when I was pregnant, and it all fucking goes out the window as Jax grins at me and takes off.

Little shit. I smile, chasing him down the hall and scoop his butt up. He lets out the sweetest laugh; it's the best sound in the world. I carry him back into the playroom, lifting his shirt and blowing raspberries on his stomach. I set him down and easily take the blanket away from him. Ava and Cindy are watching us. Poor little Ava has tears in her eyes still.

"Jax, say you're sorry to Ava." I grab his hand to keep him from running. I say a silent prayer that he just says sorry. I don't want to fight him. I don't want to have to sit him on the naughty step and go through all that bullshit.

"Sowry!" Cindy's got her hands on her hips, and her lips are pursed. What the hell? Does she want me to crucify him?

"Sweetheart," I say and hand him the blanket. "Help Ava tuck in baby..." Shit, I forget what she was calling the doll. "What's her name, sweetie?"

"Missy Jane," she pouts, but she's not sad anymore, now it's just for attention.

I smile at her and walk them over to *Missy Jane.* "Let's put Missy Jane to bed." I hand Ava the blanket and she tucks one end under the doll while Jax puts his finger over his lips and shushes. "Good job, you two! You make such a good team."

It feels like a workout, but at least they aren't screaming at each other and pulling each other's hair. Next year, maybe. I've heard of the terrible twos, and the fucking fours. Not looking forward to that one. I put a hand on Jax's back to keep him there.

"Time to say bye to Ava." I smile at the two of them and then Cindy, who's texting on her phone.

I can't help but wonder what she would think if I told her about *him.* About Dirty Dom. I don't know what he wants from me, but my heart clenches at how I kicked him out. I think he came to use me, but ended up being used instead. My smile broadens, not that Cindy would notice since she's still furiously texting.

I wonder what she'd think about him, and then I realize I really don't give a shit.

DOM

*L*ooks like I got here just in time. Play date's leaving. That sounds
fucking awful. At least the parents aren't outnumbered. Two women,
two kids, it can't be that bad. The little girl shrieks as her mother tries
to buckle her in. She's got a voice on her! I wince at the ringing in my ears. I
guess it can be that bad.

At least my doll has a boy. Boys have gotta be easier than girls. I scowl
watching the car leave. What the fuck am I even thinking about this shit for? I
just came to check on my doll and make a few things clear.

She's mine now.

I guess that's only one thing, but still. I need her to agree to that. And then
I can play with Becca and see just how rough my doll likes it. I palm my dick,
thinking about that ass. Fuck yeah, I'm definitely getting in there tonight.
Women don't usually get to me, but this one has. I gotta fuck her out of my
system, and she's definitely down to fuck.

I walk up the sidewalk to her house and stand next to a car, pretending to
look at my phone. I've never stalked a person before. That's not what I do. I
know a guy to call if I need someone found. But I'm feeling a little awkward at
the moment. She kicked my ass out a few hours ago; she's probably giving her
son a bath, or reading stories, or just fucking watching Rugrats with him. I
don't fucking know. I'm not going to knock.

Fuck that.

I grimace, not knowing what to do. I always have a plan of some sort. But I'm flying by the seat of my pants over this broad. When she puts the kid to bed, that's the time to pay her a visit. But I don't know his bedtime. I don't know any of that shit. I run my hand down my face. Am I really going to creep around her house to figure out if she's putting him down for bed? I think about knocking on the door and imagine her standing there with the little guy on her hip. Yeah, I'm gonna fucking peek. I need to take a look and see what's going on in there. I'm not into playing Connect Four with the little guy. Not when all I want is to get some pussy. She's really gotten under my skin. I need to fuck this broad out of my system.

I walk to the backyard. No fence, so that's easy enough. I slink around the corner of the house. I'm probably looking conspicuous as fuck, but I can't fucking help that. I don't think anyone saw me though. It's pretty dark, but I stay in the shadows.

She's got a nice deck. Real fucking nice. A sunken hot tub, although the cover is carpeted in leaves from the oak trees lining her property. They look like they've been there for a year.

There's a giant trampoline in the back that's covered with netting. I huff a laugh.

She seems cautious. Protective. I like that, but she also seems uptight. Except when it comes to fucking.

My chest rumbles with approval, and I have to readjust my hardening dick. I have to admit she brings out a virile side of me. A primitive need I don't think I've ever felt before. I fucking love it. I'm not sure how long it will last, but I'm sure as fuck going to enjoy it while I can.

The stairs to the deck are on either side - not smart. Anyone could sneak onto her deck and get to the glass sliding doors to her kitchen easy. Someone like me. I keep my steps even and stay quiet as I move up the stairs. I take a peek inside. I don't want to startle my doll, I just wanna see if the coast is clear.

Her kitchen is pristine. Other than a pizza box sitting on the blue speckled marble counter, there's nothing out of place. Steel pots hang above a massive island. Her gas stove is large enough to cook for a dozen people, easy. This woman is serious about her cooking. That reminds me about her restaurant. I'll have to head over tomorrow and check it out. I was too busy today at the office. I cringe, remembering how a jerk-off tried to convince me he needed more time. What he needed to do was stop wasting his wife's hard-earned money on gambling. That's what he needed to do. I'm sure he won't be doing that shit anymore. Not after today.

I take a few steps in front of the glass. I can see the living room from the kitchen, and there are stairs on the right that lead downstairs.

I can't hear or see either of them though. I look at the handle to the glass door and wonder if she'd leave it open. She better not. She seems too smart for that. I take a tug and sure enough, it's locked.

Good girl.

I press my ear to the door, but I still can't hear a damn thing.

I almost leave, but then I see her. I stand perfectly still. I can't even fucking breathe.

What the fuck am I doing? It hits me this very second that I'm gonna look like a psychopath if she sees me. I push my grin down, afraid even that will alert her to my presence. She's making me fucking crazy. But I fucking love it. I never have to work this hard for anything.

A broad smile appears on her face as she raises her hand and wags her finger. Her eyebrows raise, and I can clearly understand the mouthed word "bedtime" as she disappears from view.

Fuck yeah it is. Time for me to take her to bed. As soon as she's presumably gone back to her son's room, I sneak back around to the front and wait on the doorstep. I immediately send a text.

I want you right now. – Dom

I know I'm gonna need to wait a minute while she puts her son to bed. I'm not a very patient man though. I lean against the wall of her front porch and frown at the text. I shouldn't have added Dom. She's already got my number programmed in her phone. I should know, since I put it in there. I roll my shoulders and crack my neck before crossing my arms over my broad chest. Any minute now. I look down, waiting for the delivered text to be seen.

What the fuck is wrong with me? She's got me all tied up over her. I shake my head at the thought, feeling like a little bitch. This isn't me. I don't sneak out to women's houses and second-guess my text messages. Fuck no! I send them a text, and they come running to me. What is it about this broad that has me wrapped around her little finger? Just as I push off the wall and consider leaving, my phone beeps.

I shouldn't. I'm sorry.

I stare at the text. That's interesting. She doesn't want her dirty little secret anymore? No, that's not it. She wants me. I fucking know she wants me. Before I can respond though, another text comes through.*I really can't. I'm sorry for earlier.*

Sorry for earlier? What the hell does that mean? For kicking my ass out the second she came on my dick? That better be what she meant. I think about how to tell her she's going to be apologizing for that shit on her knees while she chokes on my cock, but she sends another text.

We just aren't good for each other.

I know it's just sex to you, but I can't do that.

It's just that I've just lost my husband.

Well... you already know that.

This broad really doesn't care about excessive text messages. I run my hand down my face. What the hell am I doing?

I don't mean that as a bad thing – it's just too soon.

I finally message her back before she can continue this one-sided conversation.

Stop overthinking it. I wanna fuck. Now.

She responds immediately:

I'm sorry, I can't.

I smirk at the phone. The fuck she can't. She was pretty quiet earlier. We won't wake up her son. I'll just cover her mouth while she cums.

Yes, you can.

I didn't come all this way not to get laid. And I want that ass. I decide to make it easy on her.

I'm here. Come let me in.

I'm not taking no for an answer. She's obviously uptight, used to being in her own little world. And I'm not the type of guy she usually dates. That's fine. I don't mind. She's not my usual type either. But this is just sex. Hot sex. I palm my erection. I want it. She wants it. She's just got to get out of her own head.

I grin at her as she opens the door. She must've changed after putting her son to bed. She's wearing a robe now. Black cotton. It's simple and ends at her knees. She's clutching it to her chest as she opens the door for me to come in.

"What are you doing here, Dom?" I don't like her tone.

"I told you, I want you."

She bites her lip and closes the door as I stand in her living room. I take a good look at her. Her makeup's been removed, and she looks tired as hell. Still fucking beautiful, even more so. She doesn't wear a lot of makeup, not that I remember, but without it her natural beauty shines through. Her hazel eyes are a little larger, while her lips look rosy and plump from scrubbing her lipstick off. Her cheeks are flushed, although that could be for a different reason.

She swallows and runs her hand through her hair, looking fixedly at the floor. She looks uncertain. She looks like she's coming up with excuses. I'm not gonna let that happen. I'm not done with her. She walked into my office, into my life. I'm not letting her leave so easy. Not when I've only had a small taste of her.

"Don't say anything." My voice interrupts her thoughts, and her eyes spark with desire as she licks her lips. Her mouth parts, but my doll is obedient. She presses her lips together and nods.

"Good girl." I step closer to her and grab her hip in my right hand, pulling her body to me and wrap my left arm around her back to fist the hair at the nape of her neck. It won't hurt when I tug it. But it'll give me the control I need to make this perfectly clear to her.

"You're mine, doll. When I want you, I'll have you." She knows the word to say to stop this. But she won't. She wants this just as much as I do. The question is, just how fucking dirty does she want it? I smirk at her and pull her hair back so I can kiss her neck. I run my teeth along her neck and up her throat before squeezing her lush ass. Her breasts rise and fall with her shallow breathing.

I loosen my grip and take her lips with mine. Her plump lips are soft, and mold to mine. She parts them easily, and I take a moment to massage my tongue along hers. She moans into my mouth, and that's all I can take. I pull back and smack her ass. "Bedroom."

She leads the way down the hall and up the stairs quietly. Very quietly. I can tell when we get to her son's room because she looks back at me with hard eyes and clenched fists, and walks with slow, deliberate steps. "Relax mama bear, we won't wake him up," I whisper in her ear and give her hips a squeeze. "I'll just have to find something to put into that loud mouth of yours." Her cheeks flush a beautiful red hue, and her pace speeds up at my threat.

59

That thought turns her on. I smirk at her back as we near the last door on the right. I bite my lip and come up with a plan. Her panties. I'm definitely going to shove her panties in her mouth. That's fucking happening.

Instead of opening the door, she hesitates and looks back down the hall. I give her ass a pat and open the door myself. At first I'm confused. This can't be her room. It's too dark, too masculine. I just can't see my doll in here. But whatever, I guess if there's a bed, it's good enough.

"Strip, now." I don't waste a fucking second, and I start unbuttoning my shirt and ripping off my clothes.

A robe and panties, that's it. Fuck yes. The simple robe drops to the floor and pools around her feet. She looks anxiously at the bed.

"Uh-uh, doll," I admonish her. "Panties, too. Then get up there and get on all fours for your punishment."

Her mouth parts with a gasp, but she's so fucking obedient. Even while she's stunned by my words, her thumbs hook into her panties and drop them to her feet. She steps out and climbs onto the bed. I groan as she lifts her milky white ass into the air. It's firm, but I can tell a hard pounding will get it to jiggle. I stroke my dick, fuck yes. First I've got to spank that ass for her being so rude earlier.

I climb up behind her and push her back down with my hand. She presses her cheek to the bed and looks back at me. Waiting for her next direction. She's so fucking good. I loved her fight earlier. But her submission is even better. At least right now.

"Are you going to take your punishment like the good girl I know you are?" I'm so fucking condescending with this tone as I gently stroke and then squeeze her ass. She moans a yes into the pillow. She's turned on and primed already. Her pretty pink pussy lips are just barely visible between her thighs. "You wet for me?" I ask as I gently run two fingers along her lips. My eyes nearly roll back in my head. "You're fucking soaking."

I squeeze her ass firmly rather than spank it. Shit. I forgot about the kid. How the fuck am I going to spank her without making any noise? It's not going to happen. Fuck.

"You were a bad girl today. Do you know why?" I bet she gets this wrong. I bet she says she was bad for fighting me. But that wasn't bad at all. I fucking loved every second of that.

"For kicking you out." I'm fucking floored.

"That's right, doll." I run my fingers down her back and leave a trail of feather-light kisses down her spine.

"I'm sorry, Dom. I'm ready for my punishment." Fuck, she's so good. I line up my dick with her hot entrance and slam in, not at all in punishment. Fuck that, this is all reward. I stay deep inside her, buried all the way to the hilt and give her tight pussy a second to adjust to me. Her tight walls wrap around the head of my dick and beg me to fucking pound into her wet cunt as it squeezes me. It takes everything in me to stay still. Her face is hidden in the sheets as she muffles her scream.

"Quiet, doll." I grip her hips with both hands. I wanna be rough. I wanna fuck her raw and hard into the mattress. It won't hurt her knees now like it would have earlier on the carpet. Although maybe my Becca would like to have the reminder of me pounding into her tight little pussy. I wrap her hair around my wrist all the way to the nape and pull her head to the side, my dick still deep inside her cunt. "Don't make a fucking sound while I punish this pussy," I hiss into her ear. She lets out a small whimper and closes her eyes. I grip her hair tighter. "Open your eyes and watch."

There's a dresser to our left with a big fucking mirror attached. She can watch as I destroy her tight little cunt. My other hand targets her throbbing clit. I smack it a few times and watch as she opens her mouth in a silent scream. Her eyes watch me in the mirror. I lean down and whisper in her ear with one more smack against her clit. "Watch me own this pussy."

With that I pull back and slam into her. Her body jolts forward, her heavy breasts swaying with the harsh movement. But I don't stop. I push in harder, making her back arch. Her fingers clutch at the sheets as she closes her eyes and bites down on the mattress. Nope. That's not watching. As if hearing my thought, she quickly opens her eyes and stares, transfixed on the image of us in the mirror.

I dig my fingers into her flesh and rut into her heat. She's drenched in arousal, making the movements fluid and easy. The smacking sounds of me punishing her pussy fill the room and fuel my need. I grunt as I hit the opening to her cervix with each thrust. Her body trembles, and a look of pain crosses her face. I know she's got to be on edge with a mix of pain and pleasure. The intensity heightening her need to cum. It'll make it that much better when she does. She takes it though, she takes every blow like a good girl.

I keep up my steady pace and reach forward to grab her breast. My fingers squeeze and pull her nipple. I slowly twist her hardened peak, feeling her pussy clamp down my dick. Fuck yeah, I know she fucking loves that. She thrashes and fights her need to pull away while also needing to push back for more. I fucking love that this is torturing her. Her eyes never leave the mirror though. I switch hands, still slamming into her welcoming heat, and twist and pull her other nipple. A small squeak escapes her lips, and she bites down on her arm in response. She's trying so hard to listen. To take me fucking her while being quiet and watching. Her pussy tightens as a cold sweat breaks out along my body. I'm going to cum any minute, and so is she.

"You don't cum till I tell you to," I snarl. She whimpers and shakes her head. "Don't you fucking dare." Her body heats and shakes beneath me, needing its release. She struggles to hold on and obey. I make it even harder. I reach around her hips and run my fingers along the side of her clit. I need to get them nice and wet with her juices for what I'm about to do next. She bites her lips, and barely keeps her half-lidded eyes focused on the mirror.

"I can't." Her voice cracks as she moans her words. I feel her tightening around me. She better fucking not. I gather her juices on my fingers and move to her puckered hole.

"Yes, you can. And you will, doll; you won't disappoint me." Her eyes flash from the mirror to mine. "Eyes back on the mirror." Her eyes immediately go back to the mirror. She's so fucking good. I speed up and love how she has to hold in her screams, how her body fights for pleasure, but she's denying it, waiting for me to allow it. I push my finger against her asshole and slam into her cunt. "Cum, Becca. Cum for me." I slam in again and push my finger against her forbidden opening, waiting for her to cum. Waiting for it to relax, so I can slip it in. I slam into her once, twice, three more times and then she does it. Her mouth hangs open in ecstasy as her body shudders and heats with waves of intense pleasure.

My finger slips in, and she goes off like a fucking firecracker. The most delightful noises I've ever heard are ripped from her throat as pleasure rocks through her body. Sweat forms on my brow as I fight the need to cum. But I'm not blowing my load just yet. I twist my finger and fuck her ass as she relaxes around me, aftershocks rocking through her limbs.

I slowly pull out of her, both my finger and my dick. I'm so hard it hurts. I need to cum. Her eyes are closed, and she's slumped on the bed. Her cheeks and chest are flushed. She so relaxed, so beautiful. I smile as I look down on her. That's a good thing, because she's gonna need to be relaxed for me to fit my dick in this tight little hole.

"Eyes on the mirror, doll." I kiss the small of her back and gently press my dick against her tight rosebud. I give her a moment before really pushing into her. She knows what to say if she doesn't want this. Her eyes spring open, and her hands grip the sheets as she realizes what's about to happen. Her entire body tenses. I pet her lower back. "Relax, doll. Push back and relax." She nervously bites her bottom lip and watches with a mix of apprehension and desire flashing in her eyes. More than anything though, excitement is written on her face.

She's so tight. I push the head of my dick a little deeper and try to sink in, but she's so fucking tight. I know I must be the only one to have taken her like this. Pride makes my chest swell, thinking I'll be her first. I'm going to take her just like this. "Your husband never fucked you like this, did he?" I don't need her to answer, but I still want to hear it. I want to hear I'm her first.

Her back arches and twists, and her body pulls away from me.

I hadn't even gotten the head in, but maybe I was rushing it. I pull her hips back, and she resists me slightly. "You're giving me this ass, doll." I pull her hips to mine and watch as she buries her face in the covers. It doesn't seem right. Something's off. I don't like it. Fuck it; I'll have to wait for her ass. That's fine. I got in a finger today, and I know she loved that shit. She just needs to work up to it. My fingers run along her pussy lips before dipping in. "Your greedy cunt wants more, doll?" I fuck my fingers in and out of her swollen, sore pussy, making sure to hit that front wall and stroke her G-spot.

I don't get the reaction I expect. There's no moan, her eyes aren't on the mirror and she pulls away from me. I still, and my chest tightens. Fuck, she's hurt. What the fuck happened?

I gently place my hands on her hips and try to pull her toward me lightly, but she doesn't budge. My heart clenches, and adrenaline pumps through my veins. Anxiety floods my system. She didn't safe word. I know she didn't. I would've heard her. "What's wrong, doll?" I keep my voice calm and even, but inside I'm freaking the fuck out. I don't like to see women cry. And sure as fuck not because of me.

"I hate you." Her breathy words barely register as she lifts her head from the sheets. Her eyes are red-rimmed and glassy from tears. Her chest spasms as she takes in a shuddering breath. She may as well have punched me in the gut. What the fuck happened?

"I hurt you?" I just don't see how. I don't know what I did. "I didn't mean to hurt-"

"Get out!" she screams with tears leaking from the corners of her eyes, and then covers her mouth with her hand. She winces as her son lets out a wail from down the hall.

I don't know what the fuck happened. I open my mouth to protest, but she moves past me to get off the bed and immediately puts on her robe. She leaves the room without taking a look back.

She hates me? Did it really hurt that bad? It couldn't have. I didn't even get the head of my dick in. I slowly climb off the bed as I walk myself through everything that happened. She was loving it.

Your husband never fucked you like this, did he? I close my eyes and let my head fall back. Fuck! I groan out loud and grab my shirt off the floor. Fuck! How could I be so fucking stupid? I lean my forehead against the wall and close my eyes. I'm such a fucking asshole. She's not some bitch, looking for a night of fun and running around on her husband. She's a widow, for fuck's sake.

I bend down to put my underwear on, trying to think of a way out of this shit. I need to backpedal fast. As I reach for my pants, I catch a glimpse of something under the bed. I sink to the floor and cover my face with my hands. There are boxes under the bed with his name on them. I look on the dresser and see pictures of them. A cute fucking family photograph catches my eye.

I feel like such a prick. He just fucking died. I shake my head and scowl. She doesn't need this. She doesn't need some prick bossing her around and using her like I am. I swallow the lump growing in my throat and pull my pants up. I need to get the fuck out of here.

She deserves better than this. Better than me.

I huff a humorless laugh and push my emotions down. She's too good for me anyway. And I have no place in my life for her. I start to open her bedroom door, but I can hear her humming a lullaby to her little boy. My heart clenches, and tears prick at my eyes. I don't fucking cry. She said she hates me. Told me to get the fuck out. That's fine. I can do that for her.

I take a peek down the hall. The door is only cracked. I clench my fists and walk silently past the door and keep going. I don't look back or even wince when the floorboards squeak on the stairs. I don't stop moving until I'm at the front door. I hesitate, but only for enough time to hear her words in my head over again.

She hates me.

I take one last look at the house before opening my car door. Her picture-perfect home that I forced myself into. I climb in my car and leave her behind.

It's only after I'm halfway home that I realize I forgot my tie. At least she'll have a piece of me to hold onto. Sadness overwhelms me.

I'm sure she'll just throw it the fuck out. I would.

BECCA

J wake up to the sound of Jax squealing into the monitor. My hands fly to my eyes to rub the tiredness away. They're so sore. It hasn't been that long since I've cried myself to sleep. Divorce and death will do that to even the strongest women. So I'm not ashamed of that.

But I am filled with shame.

I roll over onto my back and stretch my sore body. My pussy hurts from last night. Evidence of what happened. I let it happen. I wanted it to happen. My throat closes, and my chest feels hollow. I can't cry over this. I don't even want to believe it happened. I wish I could just forget him.

What's even worse though is how sad I was when I heard him leave last night. It fucking hurt listening to him sneaking out and hearing the door close. I held Jax longer than I needed to. Long after he'd fallen asleep in my arms, I just couldn't let him go.

As if on cue, he screams, "Mommy!" and my room fills with the sound of his little voice. The hint of a smile graces my lips, and I climb out of bed. Time to get ready. I way overslept. But it's Tuesday, so at least there's no weekend rush. I can get him ready and off to preschool before heading in to the restaurant. Sarah will pick him up, and I'll make spaghetti. Jax's favorite. I shake my hands of this numbing anxiety racing through my body.

It's over. I ended it. My heart pains as it twists into an unforgiving knot in my chest. It shouldn't hurt this much to do the right thing.

Why does it hurt so much? I'm so tired of being in pain.

* * *

I HATE the start of the week. There's always so much shit that needs to be done. I need to make sure everything is correct with inventory first. I've got to order everything by two to make sure I'll have it all by lunchtime on Friday. I breathe in deep. I have my checklist on the laptop. I'm supposed to interview managers and another assistant manager today. But I don't have the time.

I know I should make the time because it would really lighten my load to have the extra help, but there's just so much to do. And I really try so damn hard to be home every day by five, six at the latest, so I can be there for Jax. Of course, I almost always have to go back to work using my laptop as soon as he's asleep. But as long as I'm there for him when he's done with preschool and at soccer practice, that's what matters.

I can't miss this time with him. They don't stay kids forever.

I park my car in my spot. The same spot I've parked in every fucking day for the past four years, and a heavy sigh leaves me. I really wish I could take a break. I wish I didn't have to run myself ragged every damn day. I could sell out. I could take the money and try to invest it so it would last for us. But fucking Rick got us into so much debt digging his way out of financial ruin. And then I was saddled with all the lawyer's fees from our divorce. And then of course when he died I had to pay his lawyers that tried to take Jax away from me. That bill fucking hurt like hell to pay. I take the key from the ignition. I can't stop now. Just one day at a time will get me through. And at least I still have my little man. I'll be strong for him.

Grabbing my laptop bag and my purse, I swing both over my shoulder and get out of the car. I click the button for the alarm and turn toward the restaurant.

A scream tears through my throat as a large hand concealed in a black leather glove covers my mouth and a large body wraps around my frame. No! I scream and flail my arms. No! This can't be happening. For a moment, I think it may be Dom. But this isn't him. I know it's not him. Tears sting my eyes as my throat burns with a shrill scream. I stumble forward as the man pushes his chest into me and crushes his heavy weight against my body, pinning me to the rough brick. My head bashes against it, and it scrapes my cheek.

The stinging cuts hardly register as he twists my arm. The pain shoots up my shoulder. The black sleeve of the man's sweater slips up his arm and reveals a dark, detailed tattoo of a green dragon wrapped around a red shield. Another man comes out in front of me with a rag. I struggle in the man's hold, trying like hell to get away.

But it's no use.

The rag covers my face, and I try not to breathe.

I hold my breath for as long as I can, but I can't keep it up much longer. I inhale the chloroform into my lungs.

The last thing that goes through my mind as the darkness takes over is Dom. I wish he were here to save me.

* * *

MY HEAD FEELS SO HEAVY. I'm so groggy. My vision swirls, and my chin touches my chest. I groan and lean my head back. "Agh!" That was a mistake. My temples pulse with pain. I try to move my aching shoulders, and then I remember. I struggle against the abrasive rope digging into my arms, wrists, thighs and ankles.

A scream tears through me. My eyes open wide, but all I see is black. I'm tied down to a chair and blindfolded. My heart races, and my breathing comes up short. No. I shake my head frantically. This can't be happening. "No!"

Smack! A hand lands hard across my face and whips my head to the side. The sound echoes through the room. I cry out in pain. My shoulders burn from the harsh movement. How long have I been here? Jax. Tears stream down my face. I bite my tongue. I don't know if they have him, whoever they are. I don't know if they even know he exists. I keep my mouth shut. Who the fuck took me? What do they want?

Dom. The air stills in my lungs. Did he do this? My body shudders in agony, and my chest aches with betrayal. I shake my head. He wouldn't do this. But how the fuck would I know? I don't know him. I should've never talked to him like that. My shoulders try to turn inward; I try to close myself in, but I can't. I'm stuck like this.

"Is she finally awake?" My head lifts and turns toward a distant voice on my right. I don't recognize the thick Italian accent.

"Yeah, boss." A very deep voice sounds like it's right in front of me, and I instinctively try to get away. My feet scrape against the floor. Bare feet. It's to no avail. Two large, cold hands settle on my shoulders and squeeze. It fucking hurts.

A deep, menacing chuckle is followed by the stench of foul breath and cigarette smoke. "You're not going anywhere... doll." My stomach drops, and my chest hollows. *Dom.*

"That's right. We know all about your boyfriend." The large hands try to pull me forward, which only causes the searing pain to shoot up my shoulders and make me wince.

The other voice that sounded so distant before rings out very clear and very close, "Just answer our questions and we'll let you go." A hand reaches out and cups my face. I flinch from the sudden touch, and I'm rewarded with another hard slap. I scream out again, against my will.

"He's not my boyfriend." I barely get the words out. They have the wrong person. I don't know him. I only know where his office is, and his first name. Shame floods me again. I feel like a fucking whore. A stupid slut about to get murdered because some asshole made me hot and I gave into temptation. This is what happens when you're bad. This is where you end up.

I try to keel over as a solid fist lands hard in my gut. The need to vomit floods my system, and pain radiates from my stomach to my back. Holy fuck that hurt.

"Don't fucking lie to us!" The other man, Distant Man yells at me. Tears fall freely as I gasp for air.

"Be a good doll, we need to know where Dom keeps the files for his daddy."

My head shakes vigorously. "I don't know. I swear I don't know." My heart hammers in my chest, beating furiously as if trying to escape. I wait in the silence for something, for anything.

A hard punch lands on my jaw. My bones crunch, and I swear something cracks. I sob uncontrollably from the pain.

"You do know. There's no reason to keep it from us. Just be a good doll. We saw you bring him the money. When he took it, where did he put it and where did he write down the drop? Where does he keep that pad?"

A loud ringing noise sounds in my head. White noise. It's so loud it nearly drowns out their words. I don't fucking know. I swear to God I don't know. I think back to what happened. I try to remember. There was no pad. I think he just tossed the money on the table. I don't remember. I open my mouth to plead with them, but it burns with pain. I shake my head and plead with them, "I don't know. Please. Please let me go."

I whimper through the pain and prepare for another blow. And it comes almost immediately, landing hard in my gut again. I try to crumple over from the agonizing pain, but I can't. Blood spills from my mouth as I cough it up.

They're going to kill me. I don't know what to say. I don't know how to save myself.

Tears burn my eyes as my head starts to sway. *Dom. Dom, please save me.*

My head hangs low as my breathing comes in ragged pulls. He's not going to save me. Knights in shining armor don't exist. And even if they did, he wouldn't be one of them.

DOM

I wake up to my fucking phone going off. I feel like hell. I drank a bottle of Jack last night, and I'm really feeling it. But I don't even fucking care. I feel like shit. Maybe if I drink enough I'll convince myself the hangover is why my chest aches and the fucking scowl won't leave my face.

I swallow hard. I don't give a shit about Becca. I just wanted to fuck that sweet ass of hers. I probably only wanted her because she was such a challenge. I shake my head, slowly so I don't make myself any dizzier than I am. That's all it was. She was just a bit harder to get. That's the only reason I wanted her. The only reason she got under my skin.

"This better be good." I answer the phone with a pissed off tone clear in my voice. I don't feel like doing shit today. I half hope that someone comes without their money. No, fuck that. I'll just go to the gym. It's been a while since I've really pushed myself with the punching bags.

"Boss." I jackknife off the bed at Johnny's tone and wait silently. Something's wrong. I don't like how long he pauses. I can hear him taking in a heavy breath.

"Spit it out." I can only imagine it's about Vince. They must've got him on some fucked up charge.

"We gotta message, boss. I don't know how they found her." My heart drops like a fucking anchor. He quickly adds, "I swear there was nothing on the tapes. I don't know how they got her." His voice raises with anxiety.

"Tell me everything, Johnny." I'm calm. Deadly calm. Suddenly, I don't feel a fucking thing from my hangover. All I see is red.

"I got a text with a video. They have your girl, Rebecca."

"Who and where?" That's all that matters. I just need that info, and I'll get her back. She's mine. I don't give a fuck what she said last night in the heat of the moment. I don't give a fuck if she pushes me away again.

She's mine.

"De Luca." I hear Johnny swallow, and that pisses me off. I wait for more while I climb out of bed and throw on the first clothes I find. Sweats and a white tee.

I snarl into the phone, "Where!" He better fucking know.

"We're on it now." My hand tightens around the phone, and I have to close my eyes. My shoulders rise and fall with my angered breaths.

"Someone decided to send us a message. To send *me* a message. And they didn't give any instructions? You aren't able to track the message?"

"It-It's just a video." My blood turns to ice. I glossed over it earlier in my haste when he first mentioned it, but a video means there's something to see. Fuck, no. I wait for more. I don't want to ask.

"They roughed her up, Dom." I can't breathe. I swallow down my heart, which feels like it's trying to climb out of my throat.

"She alright, Johnny?"

"She'll be alright. I promise you, Dom. We'll get her back, and she'll be alright." I wanna ask, but I can't. I just need to get to her. I need to see for myself.

"What about her son?" A panic spreads through every inch of me. He's just a child. They better not have touched him.

"Preschool. He's still in class."

"Get him out now. Give him to Ma, and don't let either of them out of your sight. You hear me, Johnny?"

"I got you, boss. I'm on it." Damn right he is. No harm is coming to her son. No one's hurting him. Over my dead body.

"We've got to find Becca now, Johnny. How long ago did the video come in?"

"Fifteen minutes." He's quick to answer.

"How long does Tony need?" I ask with a calmer voice than I thought I could manage. I shove my shoes on and walk out the door with my keys in my hand. I don't know where to go. I don't know where she is. But I can't fucking sit around just waiting. I need to do something.

I'm the reason she's in this mess.

"Any minute. We'll know any minute now," he answers.

"I'm calling Tony. Call me the second you hear anything."

"I will, boss."

I hang up the phone and quickly dial Tony's number. As I listen to it ring, the full weight of everything crushes my chest.

It's my fault.

I led them to her.

I must have. I couldn't stay away. I ruined her.

My eyes close as the phone goes to voicemail. Because of me, she may be dead right now.

* * *

"You sure this is it?" I've got two guns on me in holsters, and another in my lap. I chamber the round and lean forward in my seat, looking at the rundown warehouse. They better fucking be in there. It's been forty minutes. That's too fucking long. I watched that video over and over, looking for any kind of clue. My gut sinks, and my fists clench. My poor Becca. She doesn't deserve this shit. I got her into this mess, and I'm gonna get her out.

"This is it, boss," Johnny answers. Vince leans between the two front seats as the car behind us parks.

"Time to kill some De Luca fuckers."

"Let's go." I'm the first out of the car. If they've got eyes on the parking lot, they're gonna see us coming. There's no way around it. It's a warehouse in the middle of nowhere on a huge concrete pad with a runway for planes. There's no hiding. No getting in or out undetected.

I hear the guys get out and come up behind me as another one of our cars pulls in. I don't wait though. I've waited long enough. All of us will come. The entire family is coming to kill these fuckers. You don't mess with one of us and get away with it. We'll find you. We'll hunt you down, and make you pay.

That's what we do.

Jack is the only one not here. But he'd be here if he could. I know he would.

We form a V, with me leading the way to the large steel double doors. There's a chain and a lock on them. Anthony comes up behind me with the bolt cutters while we all keep our guns raised. The heavy steel chain drops to the ground with a loud clank, and he quickly bends and pulls it away so I can pull the doors apart. They open with a loud groan.

They definitely know we're here.

A cold sweat breaks out across my body. They better not have touched her. That image that flashed through my mind yesterday, of her cold and dead on the ground, flashes into my vision again. I try to blink it away, but it won't disappear. I shake my head and grind my teeth, keeping my gun held high. The huge room is empty, with concrete floors that are rundown, but bare. No place to hide. Which is good and bad. It's two stories with a thin hall lining the upper level. It's made of rickety wire mesh flooring so each inch is visible. Six doors are on each level, with two on each side and the back wall.

She's behind one of them. Twelve doors to look through.

My gun moves to each door, each corner. Empty.

"Start at the left. Bottom floor," I call out with determination and confidence.

"We splittin', Dom?" Pops' voice rings out, but I shake my head. I'm calling the shots. My problem, and my girl. I'm grateful Pops is ready to back me up. I don't know how many of them there are. I want our numbers high.

I lower my gun as I reach the first door. I look back at the crew as I test the handle. Locked. I bet they're all fucking locked. They're steel doors. Not fucking easy to break down, but we got this.

I put my gun up to the keyhole and fire. Once, twice, three times. I give it a hard kick, and it jostles slightly. Another shot, and another kick. Everyone has their guns ready to fire as the doors open. They swing open with a bang, crashing into the walls. Boxes are piled high, nearly to the ceiling in several rows. I take a step in with caution, keeping my gun in front of me as I sweep the room. But a faint muffled sound from a distance makes me stop.

I motion for everyone to be still. I swear I heard something. I swear I did. I almost move forward, but then I hear it again. She's not in this room. I hustle my ass past everyone and move on to the next door. My Becca. I hear the sound clearer as I reach the door in the back left corner.

Locked.

Bang! Bang! Bang! I kick it open with no mercy, making my leg scream in pain. Again I fire, and then so does Johnny. We fire together, kick together. The door swings open, and my heart stops. My Becca is hanging upside down, tied up by her ankles over a sink to the right of the room. Her head has her just barely balanced on the edge of a sink that's overflowing. Her hair is soaked.

They left her to drown. They tied her up, and put her head in a sink and filled it. As I take in the sight of her, she slips and her head falls back into the water. I run to her as her body thrashes, and she tries to swing herself to the edge again. I pull her head out as soon as I get to her. Guns fire around me. I don't even know where mine is. I don't bother looking up. A bullet whizzes by my head as men shoot. My family and others return fire. Footsteps ring out on the steel stairs at the back of the room. More gunshots. But all I can really hear is my doll breathing, gasping for air.

My fighter. My survivor. I rip the soaked blindfold off her eyes and turn off the faucet.

"It's alright. I got you."

"Dom!" she screams out, and sputters up water.

"It's me, doll. I got you." She shudders in my arms as I lift her weight up and try to cradle her body as best I can. My entire body is trembling. Loud, heavy footsteps race toward me. The screaming has stopped. The guns aren't firing anymore.

"They got away, boss!" I barely hear Johnny yell. I don't care.

"Jax?" Becca's head falls back, heavy against my arm. She shaking from the freezing water. Her skin is ice cold and pale. Her teeth chatter, and her eyes refuse to focus on me.

"He's safe, doll. You're both safe. I got you."

At my words, her body goes limp. Her eyes close. Fuck no. I jostle her in my arms, but she's still.

"Help her!" I hold her closer to me and shake her body to try to wake her as I scream. "Somebody help me get her down!"

DOM

"*Y*ou sure, Dom?" Jack's voice echoes in my head, and I scowl.

I want to smash his fucking teeth in. I get that his woman, his wife, was ready to rat on him. I fucking understand that. But this isn't *his* woman. Becca isn't a rat. I got her into that shit. She's not at fault in any way.

And what he's implying is unforgivable. My voice is low and deadly as I turn to face him and stare straight into his eyes with my hard gaze. I want what I say to be heard and understood. "If anyone touches her, or implies that any harm should come to her or her son, I will slit your fucking throat open."

"Just calm down, Dom." I look at my father like he's the one who said it, because he's keeping me from destroying Jack. My fists are clenched so tight my knuckles are white. How could he fucking imply that we should kill her?

"She's just seen a lot is all." He leans back against the bookshelves in the office, and I turn my head slowly to stare him down. Vince, Pops, Jack and I are in the office. Pops' office. It's a dark room with thick curtains and dark chestnut bookshelves lining the walls. They're filled to the brim. Pops loves to read, but he also likes to hide shit. I know some of the books are for his secrets. I just don't know which books, or which secrets.

Vince paces by the door with his hands in his pockets, head bowed, staring at the antique rug as he walks. He doesn't look up to respond to Jack, "She hasn't even come to. We don't know what she's seen."

"She was conscious when we were shooting. It doesn't matter that we saved her. She could blab. She could sell us out."

My father's hands come down hard on my chest and then move to my shoulders, shoving me into the seat in front of his desk. My breath is caught in my throat, and adrenaline courses through my blood.

"That's enough, Jack!" he yells at Jack, but his eyes are on me. I can feel them boring into me, but I'm not looking back at him. My eyes are shooting daggers at Jack. I fucking told him to shut his mouth. I don't give a shit that he's the underboss. Pops knows it. Jack's days are numbered. I won't allow it. I won't allow anyone to keep breathing if they so much as think of touching my girl.

I shove Pops away and sit back in my seat, crossing my arms. I can't turn my face neutral. I look pissed 'cause I am pissed. But I'll bide my time, I'll wait. But I'm not going to let De Luca live.

"You need to calm down, Dom; just think this through." My father's voice is calm and even. My brow furrows, and I glare at him. He can't be fucking serious. A look of shock crosses his face as he says, "Between you and Jack. Just calm down, think it through."

My tense shoulders relax slightly. I nod my head. He means me fucking up Jack. Thank fuck. I don't know what I would do if he was talking about my doll. I swallow thickly and spear my hands through my hair and then grip it while I lean back in my seat. I stare blankly at the office ceiling.

I just can't get the image of her hanging there out of my head. Her face is bruised. Her eye, her cheek. She obviously hit her head more than a few times trying to balance herself on the edge of that industrial steel sink. But it's more than that. The bruises, the blood, they really fucked her up. All because of me.

She's in my bedroom. My old bedroom at my parents' house. Just a few doors down from Pops' office. She hasn't woken up yet, and that scares the shit out of me. Her skin was ice cold and pale. When the doctor stripped her down I saw the stab wounds on her legs. They didn't show any mercy. Tears prick at my eyes, but I will them down. It's all because of me. 'Cause I couldn't keep my dick in my pants.

Jax is downstairs playing with Gino. I'm glad the two of them hit it off. Jimmy brought some remote-controlled monster trucks over, and the kids are crashing them into each other. He keeps asking for her, looking around all worried. Ma's got it taken care of though. I'm sure as hell not letting him see his mom like that. I don't want to scare him. I have to protect the little guy as best I can. Luckily Paulie's the only one those fuckers managed to hit, and it was only his leg. Doc took care of that with some quick stitches. A few days off and some whiskey will have Paulie good as new.

"What you need to be worrying about is De Luca and his gang." Pops' voice rings out through the office.

They fucking got away. They were waiting, ready to ambush us. But they didn't expect the numbers. They fled like the cowards they are. We got one of theirs. But you can't question a dead body. We know their territory though. We know where they hang out. It's fucking over.

"If I'd been there I would've told you guys to split." Jack decides to chime in again. Silence greets him. He's not the boss. He knows it, and so does Pops. But for some reason, my father lets him get away with that shit. "Someone always needs to be outside."

"If we'd split up, they wouldn't have run. But then we wouldn't have had the numbers." I finally look back at him. "I made that call, and I'm fucking good with it." I sit forward in my seat. "Pops was there," I look at my father, "and if he wasn't good with it, he would've said so." My father nods once in agreement. "If we're going to go in for the kill, it'll be on our terms. We were only there to get Becca. Nothing else."

Pops squeezes my shoulder and walks around to sit at his desk. He sinks into the leather wingback chair and then clasps his hands and rests his elbows on the mahogany desk. His fingers steeple and the tips rest at his lips. "We had to lay low because of you, Jack. We don't now."

I shake my head. "I'm not ready. I'm not going anywhere until I know she's alright."

"Since when do you come on hits, Dom?" It's not a question. Well, that's not quite the question he's asking, anyway. He knows there's no way I'm not going after them. But I never have before. I don't work the streets. I have my own business. I'm only in this family because he runs it. I have my bookie business, and that's good enough for me. I work the *familia*'s books and that keeps me in, but that's it.

"Things change." I can't look him in the eyes.

A knock at the door interrupts us. "Enter," Pops says, pausing a conversation I'm not really sure I want to have.

The doctor walks in and gently shuts the door behind him. He's an older man with short white hair and pale blue eyes surrounded by well-earned wrinkles. His glasses make him look distinguished even if he is wearing faded jeans and a thin V-neck sweater.

This isn't the first time he's been here, and it won't be the last. Nearly a decade ago, his son got into problems with a gang on the west side. He begged my father for help. Pops knows a good man when he sees him. That, and it's nice to have a doctor available for house visits on short notice for cash payments.

"She's stable and from what I can tell, her injuries are purely external."

"Is she going to be alright?"

"She'll be perfectly fine."

"Did they-?" I can't finish the question. I swallow thickly and search his eyes. He knows what I'm asking.

"The rape kit came back negative." I cringe at his answer but nod my head and let out a breath I didn't know I was holding. I'll never forgive myself for what they did to her. But I am relieved to know they didn't abuse her like that. She deserves better. She sure as fuck deserves better than me, but after what happened, I can't let her go just yet. They know where she lives. Where she works. The doctor and Pops have a few words, but I don't listen. I'm just focused on the fact that she's alright.

Right now she's alone though. I don't like that. I want to be there when she wakes up. I stand up, ready to go see her. "Where are you going?" Jack asks me as I grab the door handle.

Where the fuck does he think I'm going? I stare at him for a minute, just so he can squirm under my gaze. I didn't forget what he said. And he sure as shit better not forget what I told him. After a moment I leave, shutting the door a little harder than I should.

I wish Jack's fucking head was between the door and the frame. I shake off my anger and try to calm myself. If she's awake, she's not gonna like me storming in there with a temper.

I open the door slowly and walk into my childhood bedroom. Not that it looks like one. Statistics books and other textbooks line the back of my desk, lined up in a neat row. Other than the books, the desk is cleared off. Exactly how I like it. The desk is solid maple and stained dark espresso in color. It's modern, and reflects the rest of the furniture in the room. My sheets and comforter are perfectly white, and the walls are a cool grey. The only personality is provided by a simple framed, enlarged photograph on the wall. It's an abstract shot with bursts of colors. I don't know why I like it. But I do. Other than the framed photograph, my room displays order and discipline. It's how I grew up. It's how I stayed out of the mafia.

Lying under the sheets is Becca. The white sheets bring color to her complexion. I'm grateful for it. She's completely still with her arms placed at her sides, and her eyes are closed. Without the color, she would look dead. I pull the desk chair to the side of the bed and sit next to her, taking her hand in mine. She's warm. I watch her chest rise and fall gently. My heart seems to slow to beat in time with hers.

Bruises still cover her face and arms and the rest of her body. Even worse, the rope burns on her wrists may actually scar. On the nightstand next to the bed are ointments and bandages. The doctor applied them before he left, but I'll take care of her from here on out. I'll make sure this doesn't scar her. Not in any way. She inhales a deep breath and winces in pain. I know she's on pain meds, but maybe not enough.

"Becca?" My voice is hopeful, just as I am. I need her to wake up. I need her to tell me everything. And I need to apologize.

Her eyelids slowly open in a daze, either from a concussion or the meds, or maybe just exhaustion. I take her hand to my lips and kiss her knuckles, keeping my eyes on her face. Watching her every movement.

"I'm here, doll. You're alright." Her eyes blink slowly and she turns her head, rubbing her cheek against the pillow. It takes a moment, but her eyes find mine. They seem to widen slightly, but she's still dazed.

"Jax?" She barely breathes his name.

I give her a reassuring smile. "He's downstairs playing. He has no idea." She closes her eyes and lets out a long exhale before slowly opening them again.

"Thank you." Her hand weakly squeezes mine. Her head turns, and she winces in pain again before staring at nothing. "I'm sorry."

"You have nothing to be sorry for." My throat starts to close, so I grunt a cough and clear my throat. "It's my fault, doll. I'm sorry." I fucking hate that I'm apologizing. Not that I shouldn't be, but that I've hurt her again.

She shakes her head slowly and then takes a deep, shuddering breath. She rubs her eyes and tries to get up, but I gently push her shoulders down.

She looks at me like I punched her. "I need to get Jax."

"He's downstairs." She's fucking crazy to think she's going anywhere.

"I need to take him home." Fuck that. That shit's not happening.

"You'll come home with me tonight." I'm already dreading the drive, but we aren't staying with my parents. I have a house and a room for her and Jax. I'll take care of them.

She pushes me away, but then seems to consider my words. "Are they going to come back?"

"They will never hurt you again. I'm going to find them. I'll take care of this." Tears well in her eyes.

"I can't just stay here." Her voice is pained.

"Don't worry, Becca. I'll take care of everything."

She shakes her head and says, "You don't understand. I have work; Jax has school and soccer. I have a life." She takes in a strangled breath. "I had a life." Her knees pull into her chest, and she rolls over and buries her face in her hands. She sobs, and I don't know what to do. I don't know what to tell her.

She can't just go to work. She wouldn't want to if she got a look at herself anyway. She can't go home. I can't let her out of my sight. I'm not going to give them another chance to hurt her.

"Phone!" She pops up too quickly for me to stop her.

"Doll, lie back down." I try to get her to lie back, but she's on her feet and looking around the room for her clothes. She's holding a sheet draped around her.

"I need my phone and my clothes." What the hell is wrong with her?

"You need to relax and take it easy."

She shakes her head, but at least she stops in her tracks. "I need my phone." She just keeps repeating herself. I finally pick it up off the bedside table and hand it to her.

"Where are my clothes?" she asks with her eyes on her phone.

"Trashed." Her eyes shoot up at me. "I'll get you new ones."

"You don't need to do that. I can get my own." The way she says it makes my chest hurt. "I just need to get back. I have so much I need to catch up on."

As I stare at her like she's crazy, the doctor knocks gently and walks in immediately after. His bushy white eyebrows raise when he sees Becca out of bed.

"Mrs. Harrison?" he asks with skepticism.

She stares at him with wide eyes until her phone beeps in her hands and she starts typing away. There is obviously something very fucked up with her head right now.

"Do you mind if I ask you a few questions? I need to do a small physical as well now that you're awake."

"I'm fine. Really, I'm fine." I quirk a brow at her. Who the fuck says she's fine after going through that shit? And who the fuck is she texting? I stand up and grab her by the waist to pull her back to the bed. She goes rigid in my arms, but she doesn't fight me.

"You need to lie down, doll. You're not fine." I lay her on the bed and she immediately sits up, covering herself with the sheet, phone still in hand.

"Who are you texting?" I finally ask, and she looks back at me with defiance.

"Sarah. I needed to make sure everything is running smoothly. And it's not!"

"Mrs. Harrison-"

"Stop calling her that!"

"Stop calling me that!" We snap at the doctor in unison. Well at least we're on the same page about something.

"Rebecca, then?"

"Becca." I correct him before she opens her mouth.

"Ah. Becca, may I take your vitals and ask you a few questions?"

She keeps her lips pressed together and nods slightly. Why is she acting like this? She just got abducted and beaten, almost murdered. Is she hiding something? She's got to be holding something back. She lays the phone on the bed and I immediately snatch it. A click of the home button takes me to her security code screen. I start to ask her, but then I remember her son's birthday from the info Tony gave me. The day after my mother's birthday. I click 0405 on the screen, and it opens. Her eyes widen, and her jaw juts out.

"Don't text her back yet. I'll figure out why." She starts breathing heavy. "I'll come up with a lie."

I read through the few dozen texts from "Sarah PA." Holy shit. Who the fuck has this many questions in only a few hours? The last one is, "where are you?!?" And Becca's already responded to all of the other requests.

"You're not going to tell her anything." I put the phone in the pocket of my sweats and cross my arms. "You're going to lie there and get your physical and then rest so you can get better."

"I'm fine." Doctor Koleman's busy reading her pulse and ignoring us.

"You aren't fine." I don't want to recount everything that happened today, but how the fuck could she think she's fine?

The doctor takes the stethoscope from around his neck and instructs her to sit and breathe. At least she's listening, even if she's ignoring me.

"Becca, how are you feeling?" he finally asks, taking a seat in the chair I left by the bed.

"Don't say fine." I cut her off with a hard glare as she opens her mouth.

"I feel sore, especially my ribcage." She speaks calmly, but the doctor cuts her off.

"Two of your ribs are fractured. You'll have to rest up to help them mend." She stares at the doctor with a look of confusion before shaking her head.

"No, I'm fine." Her voice is small and laced with disbelief.

His brow furrows. "I'm certain they're fractured. You're on pain medicine at the moment, codeine. It's going to take at least six weeks to heal properly. You don't have to rest in bed all day, that's fine. But you do need to take it easy and make sure to do some deep breathing every two hours to prevent any further damage to your lungs."

She breathes in deep, as if testing his words. Her eyes fall to the floor.

The doctor continues, "Other than the fractures to your ribs, you have some serious abrasions on your ankles. I've left ointments here. You're going to want to keep them covered when you shower, but gently wash them after and apply the ointment and bandages to keep them clean until they heal."

Becca stares at the floor with a blank expression before slowly raising her head to look at Dr. Koleman.

"Becca, do you remember what happened?" he asks.

She noticeably swallows before answering, "Yes."

"Would you mind sharing what you remember?" The room is so fucking quiet I can hear every breath, every small squeak from her shifting on the bed.

"It doesn't matter. The past is the past for a reason, and it can stay there. I will continue to move forward." What the fuck? Is that a public relations response?

"Becca, your blood pressure is very high. Are you currently on any medications?" She blinks slowly before answering with a nod. "I need to know what they are."

"I'm on Valium," she answers while her fingers intertwine and pull on one another. Her eyes flash to me before finding the ground.

"Anything else?"

She bites the inside of her cheek and says, "The morning-after pill." I cock a brow at that answer, and then she continues, "Klonopin as well." She twists the sheets in her hand. "Just at night though. The Klonopin helps me sleep."

"How long have you been on these?"

"Almost three months. I was hoping to wean off of them, but it didn't go well," she answers with a hint of trepidation.

"What happened when your doctor lowered the dose?"

"Just an anxiety attack." She says it casually, like it doesn't even matter. "It's been working very well."

"I can see that. Your blood pressure is very high at the moment though, Becca."

"I see." Her words are sharp.

He leans forward and speaks with gravity in his voice. "I'm worried that you may be in a bit of shock."

"And what can I do to fix that?" She looks expectantly at him, and I can't fucking believe it.

"We'll know more tomorrow. I'd like you to take your pills if you have them on you."

Her eyes find mine as she answers with a bit of irritation, "They're at my home."

"No need to worry. I'll be back soon with new medication."

"No need. I need to go home to get a few things." She starts to stand, and I move directly in her path.

"I'll get everything you and Jax need; you aren't going home."

Her eyes flash with anger. "I think you've done enough." Her words are designed to hurt me, and they're effective, but I ignore them.

"You would really put Jax in danger?" That gets her attention. She clenches her jaw.

84

"What am I supposed to do then? Nothing? Just let life roll over me?" Her breathing picks up as her voice gets louder. "Just lie there and let life fuck me over time and time again?" Her hands shove against my chest, surprising me, but I stand still and hardly budge. "What do you want from me?!" Tears burn in her eyes as she waits for a response, keeping her gaze firmly on mine.

This is the emotion I expected. More anger than I thought. But this is more of what I had anticipated.

"You just need to come with me, and I'll take care of everything."

A humorless laugh slips past her lips. "No you won't." She doesn't say these words with anger. They're simply stated as fact. "No one's going to take care of me except for me. And I take care of Jax," she says as she sidesteps me and mumbles under her breath, "no one else."

She opens the door barely an inch before my palm slams on it and closes her in.

"You need to relax for just a minute and think things through, Becca. You don't really have any options."

She shakes her head and tries to pull the door open, even though she can clearly see I'm pushing against it. "I'll just go to the police; they'll be able to do something."

My blood freezes, and I stare hard at the doctor. She's still trying to open the door, completely unaware of what she just said and what it means to say those words.

I gentle my hand on her back and lean in close to whisper. "I'm going to pretend you didn't say that. But those words better never come out of your mouth again."

Her hand falls from the door, and her eyes go round. She turns quickly, shaking her head. "That's not what I meant." She swallows and puts her hands on my chest, still frantically shaking her head. "That's not what I meant." Her breaths come in short pants and she repeats herself for a third time. "That's not what I meant."

I rub my hand on her back in soothing circles, shushing her. "I didn't hear what you said, doll." I place a soft kiss on her forehead. "What was it you said you were going to do?" I give her a hard look with narrow eyes, and fucking hate myself for it. She needs comfort right now, but she keeps pushing me away. I'll do what I have to do to make this right, even if that means being a prick right now.

A frown mars her face, and sadness clouds her eyes with defeat. "I said I'll do as you say, Dom." Her voice is small as she pulls her hands away from my chest.

"Good girl. I'll take care of you." She swallows thickly and doesn't look at me. Doesn't answer me.

Becca's a strong woman. I knew that the day she stepped into my office, but she doesn't have to be right now. She can't be strong all the time. It's not possible. Right now she needs someone to lean on, someone to take the lead. Her small hands are still on my chest as I pull her into me. She's resistant and stubborn. I smile and kiss her hair. She's gonna have to learn to let me take care of her. I'm not gonna give her any other option.

DOM

$\mathcal{B}$ ecca looks back at herself in the mirror with hollow eyes. I watch her pupils shrink and focus on every tiny mark on her face. Every bruise. She looks beat to hell, because she was. Looking at the marks makes my blood boil. I can't wait to get my hand wrapped around their throats so I can beat them to bloody pulps.

"I'm going to need better concealer," she says with no emotion whatsoever. Her fingertips gently touch her face. She's tracing a cut over her eye and hovering over a large bruise on her jaw.

"I'll get you everything that you need."

"We could just make a stop at my house for most of the things I need."

I shake my head and don't wait for her to continue her thought as I say, "I sent Clara out a bit ago to get you new things." Her eyes dart to mine in the mirror.

"That's very kind, but I don't need-"

"It's not about need. It's about you pleasing me. I seem to recall you saying you'd do what I asked?"

Her face falls, and I feel like a prick. But she fucking needs this. She won't let me in any other way.

"I wanna see Jax."

"You should shower first," I say and as soon as the words are out of my mouth, I wish I could shove them back in. Who am I to keep her away from him? He's her son. But she really looks like hell. I can only imagine how he'd react seeing his mom all beat up. "If you wanna-"

"You're right. I'll shower first." She turns around with her back to me and looks at the shower. It's nothing like what I have at home. I have a state of the art shower system with rainforest shower heads and a solid bench to relax on with the steam going. It also happens to be good for fucking, too. But we're not at my house yet. I wanna get her put together before she sees Jax, and he's staying with Ma till then. So instead she's gonna have to settle for a simple tub and shower setup with a plain white curtain. I mean, it'll do the trick, but it's not going to feel nearly as nice, especially on her sore muscles.

"I have a steam room at my house. Just clean up here, and you can relax tonight."

She turns her head slowly to look at me. I wish she'd fucking talk to me. A tight smile pulls at my lips. Really though, how much has she said to me since I've met her? Nothing, really. She's barely said anything to me. Other than her texts on why we shouldn't be fucking. I may have looked her up and practically stalked her, but she doesn't know much about me at all. And I was just doing what I needed to so I could get her in bed.

It's painfully obvious that I don't know this woman. I almost got her killed, and I don't even know her. And she sure as hell doesn't know me.

"Go ahead and hop in, doll. I'll sit here and keep you company." I try to lighten my tone.

She slips off the baggy shirt I put her in and pulls back the curtain with one hand while covering her body with the other. My eyes linger on every bruise, the bandages around her wrists and ankles.

I need to get my mind off this shit. I take a seat on the bench by the towel rack and sit back with my ankles crossed.

"Remember the bandages-" I start, but she doesn't let me finish.

"I know. I'll leave them on until I get out." A moment passes in silence.

"You like sports, doll?" It's my go-to conversation starter. For all occasions. It's something I know enough about to dominate the conversation, so I just run with it.

"I was raised a Dolphins fan, so I'm used to hating football by now." Her sarcastic answer isn't what I expected. I chuckle and grin with my eyes on her vague silhouette behind the curtain.

"Dolphins? How the hell did that happen?" I ask with the smile still on my face. It's a rare day when I suggest betting on Miami. But if that's what she likes, so be it.

"My dad liked them. I liked dolphins. It was an easy choice. I mean, they're like the only team to go into the Super Bowl undefeated, right?"

I huff a laugh. "That was like two decades ago."

"Still counts." Her upbeat reply makes me grin. "I like watching the games. I used to go out to a bar and watch them every Sunday. Beer, pizza, wings. You know the way it is. It's a nice escape."

"Used to?"

"Life got busy." She answers with less enthusiasm, making me wish I'd prompted a different question, like who she used to go with. But I know she met her husband in college, so I can guess that answer, and I don't like it.

I smirk at the curtain. "So you know something about football?"

"I know a little. Like I know the game. I just don't know the players."

"What about other sports?"

Her voice noticeably changes. More engaging, more excited. "Jax plays soccer."

"Isn't he three?"

"Well, you know, he likes to kick the ball on the field."

"So your little man is an athlete?" I ask her, but she's quiet. Her hands have fallen to her sides. It's silent for a moment; the water spray is the only noise I can hear. And then I watch as her hands move to her face, and a sob comes from the shower.

"Doll, you alright?" My stomach drops. I wonder if it's finally catching up to her now. If she's going into shock like Doctor Koleman was worried about.

"Dom?" she finally asks. Her words are muted by the flow of the water. "If something happens to me, please don't take it out on my son." My heart clenches, and my vision blurs. The smile vanishes off my face. "I have money. I'll do anything-"

"Stop it, Becca. Nothing's happening to you." I'm hard with my response, but I don't fucking like the way she's talking.

"I'm not stupid, Dom." Her sad voice carries a heavy weight. "Please just don't hurt him." I have to take a deep breath and cover my face with my hands. She thinks I'm gonna hurt her son? I can't fucking believe it. "We don't have family, but I have a friend in Texas." Her voice is tight and full of tension. "It's been a while, but-"

"Doll. I'm gonna need you to knock it the fuck off before I lose my self-control." That at least gets her to shut up. "I'm not gonna hurt you, or your son."

"You're just going to let me go?"

No. My internal answer is immediate, but I don't voice that. I don't know what I want from her. I know I feel like shit about what happened, and that I want to make it right. But that's all I know for certain. "You can't go until we have De Luca."

"Is that who took me?" she asks with a hesitant voice. We don't talk business with women. They stay out of it. Always. I don't know what to tell her. She's just standing still in the shower. The water's going to get cold fast if she doesn't hurry her ass up.

"Doll, wash up." After a moment, she reaches for the body wash. I want her to be at ease; I want her to relax. Letting women know about the business isn't a smart thing to do. But then again, she's involved already. "De Luca's a dead man for what he did to you. I promise you that."

BECCA

I let my eyes close for a moment, just feeling the heat on my skin. Calming, relaxing. I focus on the positive. I breathe in deep and slow. It makes my chest hurt, but I ignore it. My entire body feels like it's throbbing. The bandages around my ankles and wrists are soaked, and the heat stings my wounds.

Focus on the positive. We're safe. My eyes pop open. That's a lie. I'm not safe, and I haven't the faintest clue if Jax is safe right now. My son is downstairs, *supposedly*. If I don't do what Dom wants, I have no reassurance that Jax will be alright. Tears slip from the corners of my eyes. I'm at the mercy of the mob. I need to get us out of here. I need to get away. I can't believe I let this happen to Jax. I've dragged him into this by being careless. By recklessly falling for Dom, for his touch.

Something deep inside me is soothing my worry, telling me it's alright. Wanting me to believe everything will work out, and that Dom is telling the truth. But I've listened to that voice before, and I've been fooled. I refuse to listen to it now.

I should've called the cops the moment Dom showed up on my doorstep. Instead, I was foolish. Again. I lose all sense of judgment when he looks at me with those sharp lust-filled eyes. But I can't afford to be weak. Especially not now. I just need a moment to figure something out. There has to be a way out of this. But my mind is blank. They'll kill me if I run. Either the assholes who fucked me up before, or Dom and his mob.

My heart won't stop racing. It's trying to beat out of my chest or climb up my throat. My body shudders, and I realize the water isn't quite as hot. It doesn't feel relaxing anymore.

"De Luca's a dead man for what he did to you. I promise you that." I hear the threat in Dom's voice, and it chills me to the bone. I know he saved me, but at what cost? What does he want from me? A shiver runs through my body. I know exactly what he wants. But for how long? How long will that keep me safe?

I hear a faint knock at the bathroom door, and it makes my entire body jump. My blood is coursing with adrenaline, my heart's racing, and I'm struggling to breathe. I need my medicine.

No, I don't! I can do this. I've done it before. I can get through this. I lean against the tiled wall and try to keep myself from having another panic attack.

"I'll be right back, doll."

Dom's confident voice and use of that little pet name makes my body calm. A sense of ease and peace flows through me. I hold onto that for as long as I can. The door opens and a small gust of chill goes through the room, but then it's gone. I wait for him to speak. I wait for something. But he doesn't say anything. I stay in the shower for as long as I can. Until the water has lost nearly all of its heat.

The faucet turns off with a screech, and I peek my head out from behind the curtain.

The room is empty, save a small bit of steam clouding the mirror. He left a fresh towel for me on the bench. I walk out of the stall and quickly wrap it around my body. The bandage on my right wrist is falling. So I slowly and gently unwrap it. And then the rest.

My chest hardens as I look at my body. Quick flashes of memory appear before my eyes and I fold into myself, crumpling onto the floor and bite down the scream threatening to hurl itself from my mouth. A cold sweat forms on my body, and my hands start to shake. My body trembles and rocks. I lie against the tile floor, needing to cool down and focus on my breathing. It's black. Everything is black. But I can hear them. I think I know what they look like. I see his fist coming for me, and a small whimper escapes.

No!

I will not let this hurt me. I have to be strong. I push it down. I push every-thing away. It's only a memory. It's only a memory. So many times I've had to remind myself.

This isn't the first time I've been hurt, and this will not break me. I won't let them. I grind my teeth and will the anxiety down. Just as the calmness washes through me, I remember the crash. I see the large oak tree. I hear the screeching tires, my mother screaming. I see my father's arms fly out. One in front of his face, the other to the passenger seat.

My eyes fly open, and I force myself to sit upright. I will not go back. I will not go back there. It won't be of any use. I should know. Giving into fears and false hopes only makes the pain grow.

I stand up and walk to the sink and countertop. The ointments are waiting for me along with a few Q-tips, courtesy of Dom. At least he seems to be taking care of me. I'll feel better once he lets me see Jax. I feel hopeless knowing he has the ability to keep Jax away from me right now. He has control over me. I'm not sure he means to use it like that. But it doesn't change the fact it's true. I can't disobey him and risk my son.

A chill goes through my bones, remembering how I said I'd go to the cops. I bend down and gently rub more ointment into the cuts on my ankles. They're an angry red. Anger is appropriate. I'm angry at myself for being so stupid.

Stupid to say that to a man who holds so much power over me, and power in general. And stupid to be reliving the past. It's been years since I've remem-bered that night. The night my entire world changed, and the only family I had died. I look down at my wrists and examine the scratches and raw open cuts. This is nothing. This will heal.

Shards of glass cut deeper than rope, and that healed. A sickness grows in my gut; it's not the physical pain that causes the terrors and anxiety. It's the memory of when the pain happened. I won't let them haunt me. I can't. I can't go back to being useless, all at the mercy of a memory.

An image of the tattoo flashes before my eyes. A bright green dragon and a red shield. It's burned into my memory. That memory, that one I will remem-ber. I won't forget the men. But I won't let them continue to hurt me. They may have tortured me and left me to die. But I won't give them any more of me. I close my eyes and remember Dom's promise. I nod my head.

They need to die.

BECCA

"*W*hat's all this?" Dom's bed is covered with bags. I hold the towel close to my body. He's seen me before, but it's different now. I feel really fucking uncomfortable with his eyes on me.

"I was going to put it all in the car, but you should take a look at it first." He runs a hand through his hair. "I don't really know what you like."

"All this is for me?" What the hell?

"And Jax."

"This isn't necessary." I shake my head in disbelief. Everything I need is at home.

"I don't want you going back to your house." His voice is hard and unmoving.

"I don't understand."

"Doll," he says and walks to me and places a hand on my chin. It takes everything in me not to pull away from him. "You need to learn to not ask questions. Alright?" Fuck that! Who doesn't ask questions? Although I don't open my mouth, he must read exactly what I'm thinking all over my face. I'm not all that good about being subtle with my emotions.

"We're having a few ex-SEALs check out your house and set up some surveillance."

"What the fuck for?" I almost rip the towel off my body, throwing my hands in the air. "I don't want strangers in my house. I don't want this!" I scream and give him a vicious look. I was perfectly okay before him. Everything was just fucking peachy before him.

"First off, I told you to stop asking questions." He grips my chin and stares into my eyes with a menacing look. "Second, you should really watch that smart mouth of yours." The heated look in his eyes as he scolds me sends a throbbing need to my clit. My anger instantly dissipates, replaced with desire. A very unhealthy amount of desire, considering the circumstances.

The way he controls me, commands me, makes me want to submit. My lips part, and my eyes soften as he leans down to mold his lips to mine. He pulls back and gentles his hand, moving it to the back of my neck.

"I got you into this, babe. I'm gonna get you out. I'll make them pay and take care of you. *Both* of you." My heart stutters in my chest. I love that he thinks of my son. It's so easy to fall for this. For him. The thought snaps me out of the lust-filled haze.

His hand tightens on the nape of my neck and he says, "Uh-uh." His eyes narrow. "Don't you dare shut me out again." My eyes widen slightly. "Yeah, I know that look, doll." A cocky smirk pulls his lips up. He rests his head on my forehead. "You can't hide from me, Becca." His voice is low, but it's reassuring, not threatening.

It scares the fuck out of me.

"Can I see Jax now?" I ask in a timid voice I don't recognize. I clear my throat and square my shoulders. He's my son. And I want to see him now. It feels like it's been days since I've seen him. It's a feeling I don't like. I look around the room again for clothes. "I need to get dressed."

"Of course, doll." His fingertips lightly play along my jaw. "You wanna cover this up? Just so it doesn't scare the little guy?" I stare into his light blue eyes with a heavy heart. I wonder if that's on his mind because he's used to this kind of thing. Women covering up their bruises. The thought makes me turn away from him. I swallow thickly with my back to him, facing the bed.

"Did you happen to grab any makeup?" I ask quietly. It feels wrong to ask for things from him. But there are so many bags on the bed. I see a few names I recognize – Nordstrom, Clinique, Gymboree, J. Crew. A Cartier bag catches my eye, and I inhale a sharp breath. You've got to be fucking kidding me. What would I need jewelry for? Surely that's not for me. And it sure as fuck isn't for Jax.

"Clara did. I gave her the black Amex, so I'm sure she just went crazy with it," he answers casually, and I just try to take it all in.

I pick up the Clinique bag and spot a few skincare items, but no makeup. I sift through the bags and underneath a La Perla bag with perfumed tissue paper is a bag with Lancome makeup. A shit ton of makeup. I pick it up along with the Clinique bag and take it to the bathroom.

"Take your time, doll." I give him a tight smile with my head down. I don't like this. I feel... cheap. At the same time, my lack of gratitude eats away at me.

"I'll pay you back for everything," I manage to get out as I turn the handle to the en suite.

"You can afford all that?" he asks, his voice laced with disbelief. I look at the bed and try to take it all in. Yeah, I guess if I sold my restaurant today. Maybe. I bite the inside of my cheek. "You're not paying me back, Becca."

I let his words sink in. They dig at my pride. I don't need his help. Fuck. Yes I do. I have to accept that. But I wish I didn't.

* * *

I'M COVERED from head to toe. A cream, boatneck cashmere sweater covers my wrists and the bruises on my arms. Dark burgundy yoga pants and a pair of comfy socks cover everything from my hips down. I don't think I've ever worn such luxurious clothing. It *looks* the same as some clothing I have and it's definitely my style, but it *feels* like heaven.

I haven't met Clara yet, but I like her. Or at least her taste in clothes. Although the scrap of material she calls underwear is not my taste. It's cute though. Lacy and delicate. Dom would shred it easily. My thighs clench thinking of him ripping through it and taking me again. I bite my bottom lip and scold myself. I know I'm trying to distract myself from everything that happened today, but that kind of behavior wouldn't be wise.

The doctor left Dom my pills. I took another codeine and a Valium and I'm not in much pain at all now, other than my ribs being a bit sore as I make my way down the stairs. I have to wince through the pain, but other than that, there's nothing. I feel too relaxed. I wish I hadn't taken the Valium; it makes me tired.

A small smile plays on my lips as I hear Jax laughing. We round the corner of the hall to a large open living room. And there he is, with a monster truck in hand, standing on the back of the sofa, about to push it down a ramp of cushions. It warms my heart all the way down to my toes. My little man. Relief floods through me. Thank God.

In that moment I feel so much gratitude for Dom. Emotions well up in my chest, and I push them away. My hand reaches for Dom's, and I squeeze. I don't know why. But it's all I can do. He gives my hand a squeeze back and looks at me with curiosity.

I know I'm in this shit because of him. I'm painfully aware of how fucking stupid I was. And even more so of how Rick is why I'm in this shit in the first place. But he didn't have to help me. He didn't have to make sure Jax was safe. He didn't have to come rescue me. I can't fucking help the tears running down my face. It's just too much for me to handle. Too much for me to accept. I push my back against the wall and try to calm myself. Jax is just around the corner, after all; I don't want him to see me like this.

"You alright, doll?" Dom brushes my tears away with his thumb. He looks like he doesn't know what to do. And that makes me laugh. I must look fucking crazy. Crying out of nowhere and then laughing at him. Maybe I am crazy at this point. Maybe this was all I could take. Judging by the look on Dom's face, he may be thinking I've lost it, too.

"I'm okay. I could be better, but I'm okay," I finally answer. I wipe my tears and look down at my fingers to make sure I haven't fucked up the concealer. Nothing. They're clean. This is some good shit to be able to withstand tears.

I push myself off the wall, and to my surprise, Dom wraps his arm around my waist and pulls me into him. His embrace is warm and comforting. I shouldn't like it so much. He's practically a stranger and definitely a dangerous man. I lean into him knowing all of that. I just need it.

As soon as I round the corner and Jax catches a glimpse of me, I kneel down and open my arms for him.

"Mommy!" he yells out, dropping the truck and running to me. It hurts when he slams into my chest, but I don't care. It feels so good just to hold him. I kiss his forehead and just hold him until he starts to push me away.

"Do you see trucks?" He runs back over to the pile of cushions and collects a truck to hold it up for me to see. "So big, mommy!" I can't speak; just looking at him has me too emotional to function, so I nod my head and make sure I'm smiling.

There's another little boy jumping on the cushionless sofa with an olive complexion with dark brown eyes and a faux Mohawk. He's grinning from ear to ear like he can hardly stand the anticipation of the drop.

"That's Gino," Dom huffs a small laugh at the little boy.

"Is he your nephew?" I ask.

"Basically." I think that's all I'm going to get, but then he continues. "Jimmy's my cousin, but we grew up together. We're all close." I nod as though I understand, but I don't. I don't know what that's like. "You'll meet him tonight. Clara's gone already, and Vince only comes home for Saturday and Sunday dinners."

An older woman, maybe in her fifties, walks into the room from the kitchen. Her dark black hair with grey streaks is pulled into a chignon bun. Trailing her is the sweet smell of white wine and shrimp. I can only imagine she's cooking up shrimp scampi or something else that smells just as good. My mouth waters as I lick my lips.

"Hi, Becca. I'm Linda, Dom's Ma." She wipes her hands on a small kitchen towel and walks over to us on the other side of the room. I expect a handshake, but instead I'm greeted with a gentle hug. She looks over my face with a sad smile. "Would you like anything to drink?" It's not the question I anticipate. But then I remember Dom's warning about not asking questions.

I gently shake my head and reply, "I'm fine, thank you."

"You say that a lot, you know?" He looks down at me with a quizzical look on his face.

Linda interrupts our moment. "Shrimp scampi for dinner, it's almost ready." *I knew it!* She says the last bit with a teasing tone. We have shrimp scampi at my bistro. It's one of my favorite dishes. The reminder of the restaurant makes my gut sink. Dom still has my phone.

"I need my phone." I'm blunt, and I hope he doesn't push me on this. I have a PA that theoretically could handle everything, but in reality she constantly relies on me.

"Who are you going to call?" At first I'm pissed off at his question. and then I see the threat in his eyes. *The cops.*

"Not calling anyone; I just want to check on my business." He reaches into his pocket and holds it out for me. As I reach for it, he pulls back.

"Kiss first." He turns his cheek to me. I roll my eyes, but stand on my tiptoes and plant a kiss on his cheek. For some reason his playfulness makes me feel lighter. And then I look at the phone and see all the messages. Four missed calls and thirty-two unread messages. Fuck. I sigh heavily and start with the texts, but the bottom one catches my eyes.

All taken care of. No worries. Just feel better!

I stare at the screen with confusion until Dom answers my unspoken question.

"I texted her and told her you'd be out of commission for a bit and gave her the number of our manager in case she needed help."

"Thank you." I can't imagine it's that easy though. I read through the messages, searching for anything indicating she still needs help. Nothing. She did everything without me today.

He holds out his hand for the phone back.

I purse my lips. "I don't like that."

He leans in close to answer, "After what you said upstairs, I'm nervous that you're going to do something stupid."

I shake my head and insist, "I won't. I don't know why I said it."

"I do," he says while taking my phone and putting it back in his pocket.

"What the hell does that mean?" *I do.* Like he knows me like that.

"I told you to watch that tone, doll. I'm trying to go easy on you, but you can only push so much." The threat in his voice does all the wrong things to me. So I simply turn away from him and focus on the two little men playing with their toys who are completely unaware of what's happened today.

* * *

DINNER HAS BEEN... telling. Jax is happy and playing with Gino. The men, Jimmy, Dom, and Dom's father Dante, have been joking and carrying on and playing with the kids. Even Linda's been poking fun at her husband. It's almost like today never happened. Like they weren't at a shootout. I'm not sure it's perfectly healthy, but I like it. I appreciate it. I don't want to wallow. I want to move on as quickly as possible.

I lean back slightly in the chair and lick the last bit of white wine butter sauce from my fingers. Linda knows how to cook, that's for damn sure. I've been quiet all dinner except for the dozen times I've commented on her food. Jax likes it too, which makes me happy since he hardly ever actually eats anything. I swear he lives off fruit snacks and apple juice.

Dom puts his hand on my thigh and squeezes. A sense of family and belonging that I haven't felt in so long overwhelms me. I watch him as he smiles and makes a face at Gino. Is this what it would be like, if what was between us was more? Is that even an option? I never gave it a thought. Never considered it. A man like him doesn't settle down. But this feels so right.

No, what am I thinking? I could've died today because of him. A lump grows in my throat as I look at Jax smiling and bumping shoulders with Gino. I could never let this happen. As soon as Dom gives me the chance to leave, I'm going to take it. I can't allow Jax to grow up like this. Not with mobsters.

The lump grows thicker, threatening to choke me so I reach for my glass and try to calm myself.

"You look a little shaken." A sweet, low whisper of concern comes from my left.

I give Dom's mother a tight smile and say, "I'm fine."

Dom looks at me from the corner of his eyes with a frown and runs his hand down my thigh.

"I know I shouldn't ask, but if you'd like to talk, I'm here for you." I half expect the room to go silent, but Dom and the guys continue to joke and talk in the background. It's almost like white noise. Linda's light blue eyes are the same color as Dom's and they draw me in, offering me a place to confide.

"I don't know how you do it."

"Do what, dear?"

"This." I barely speak the word. *I don't know how you can be married to the mob.* I can't just come out and say that, but after a short moment she seems to understand.

"Some days, I don't either. But I love my family. We're all good people." I stare at her as she takes another bite of shrimp. Are they? I highly doubt it, but then again I know nothing about it. I chance a question.

"What do they do?" I ask her with a low voice. The men continue their conversation, and a bellow of laughs surrounds me.

"What do you mean?" She tilts her head in confusion.

"I mean, like, what is it that they *do*?"

Her eyes widen, and her eyebrows raise. "Well, now. I don't ask those kinds of questions, and neither should you. *But*, I do happen to know that the bistro pulls in a hefty amount of money." I stare at her, considering her words. She can't possibly believe that owning the bistro is all they do. Drugs and guns and murder. That's what the mob does.

"When you love someone, it's amazing what you'd do for them." She gives me a warm smile and says, "One day I'll have to tell you how Dante and I met. I'm sure you haven't heard a story like ours before." Her blue eyes twinkle with happiness. "I love my family."

I consider her words. There's no doubt she does. There's obvious warmth and love in the room. But I could never raise my son like this. I feel like an asshole for judging her. And a hypocrite for fucking Dom and feeling so much for him so quickly. But this could never be my reality. Jax deserves a better chance at life. A good life. Not a life in the mob. This is temporary. I have to make sure this doesn't last.

DOM

I thought things were going well. And then she started talking to Ma. Her little boy is in the back, so I'm not going to question her on the drive back to my house, but as soon as we get alone, I wanna know what's gotten into her head.

She looks so beautiful, leaning her head against the car door, sleeping. So peaceful. Peaceful is the right word. She's got faint wrinkles around her eyes, and I know it's from her stressing out. She's a type A personality without a doubt. I am too, but I don't let it run me into the ground like she does.

But then again, I didn't have the shitty luck she's been having. It's hard to believe a man would cheat on her. If I had to guess why, my guess would be money. His business had just failed. That, and she was making more than him. Maybe he felt emasculated. I don't know, and I don't really give a shit why. He was a fucking idiot for cheating on her. And for leaving her.

I turn the wheel up the drive and park in the garage as usual. It feels different though. I take a peek over my shoulder, and her little boy is passed out just like her. I don't want to wake either of them, so I silently slip out of my seat and gently close the door. I go around to Jax's door and carefully pull him out, letting his head rest on my shoulder. It's odd carrying a sleeping child. He's light and limp. Probably drooling on my shirt. I stifle my chuckle and carry him into the house.

I have a guest room upstairs that'll be perfect for him. It's right next door to my room, so I'm sure we'll hear him if he wakes up. I lay him down nice and gentle, and hold my breath while he readjusts and snuggles into the mattress. I really don't need this kid waking up and freaking out.

I turn around, and Becca nearly scares the shit out of me. My heart tries to jump up my fucking throat, and my blood shoots up with adrenaline. She's standing there, rubbing her eyes in the doorway. I'm happy she has them closed too, because my first instinct was to reach for my gun. I tuck it back into the holster and casually walk toward her like she didn't almost give me a heart attack.

"Bedtime, doll." I wrap my arm around her waist and pull her out of the room, but she resists me. I look down at her wide, frightened eyes with a confused look.

"I don't want to leave him alone." Oh, fuck that. She's sleeping with me. He sleeps alone at her place; he'll be fine here.

"He's already passed out, doll." I tug on her waist again. She takes a look at him and then back to me before pulling away from me. She strolls over to him, and I wait in the doorway. I hold back on everything until I know for sure what she's doing.

She leans over him and pets his hair before giving him a small kiss on the forehead. "Good night, my baby boy; I love you." I just barely hear her.

She rises slowly, not taking her eyes off of him before coming back to my side. "Good girl."

As soon as we get to the bedroom, she looks around like she's lost. Like she's a nervous virgin. I like that she's a bit frightened. I like that I can take her control away. She'll learn to love it. I'll show her how good it can be when someone else is in charge.

I stroll to my dresser and grab a white tee shirt for her to wear for the night. I should go downstairs and grab all her shit. But I don't feel like it, and she'll look good in my shirt anyway. It's that, or she can go naked. I'm fine either way. When I look up to toss her the shirt, she's standing by the nightstand, digging through her purse.

"Whatcha looking for, doll?" I ask, walking up behind her.

"My pills." Her answer makes my body go cold. I don't like that she takes medication. I understand she's wound tight and going through some shit, but I don't like it. She grabs a bottle and pops the lid.

"Which one is that?" It wasn't my business before, but now she's in my care, so I want to know everything.

"Codeine," she says while palming a single pill.

Shit, I feel like an asshole for thinking like that. Like she shouldn't be taking medicine. Given what she's been through, it's amazing she's doing everything that she is.

"I'll get you a glass of water, babe." I jog down the stairs so I can get back to her quickly. Guilt weighs down on my shoulders. She wouldn't be in pain if it wasn't for me.

When I get back to her she's sitting on the bed, looking down at her bare feet and wearing the shirt I gave her. She has a sad look on her face. I can't even begin to guess what's causing it. There's so much shit she has to deal with.

She takes the glass with a grateful smile and quickly swallows the pain meds.

I sit on the bed next to her and take a deep breath. I've been holding off on talking. It's what we do in the family. You don't talk about shit. It's done and over with, and you move on. And we sure as shit don't discuss any business in front of women. But this is different. She's involved. She's hurt. I need to understand what's going on in her head in order to help her.

"Tell me what hurts, doll?" I start with an easy question.

She gives me a weak smile and says, "I'm f-" She stops her word and bites her bottom lip while smiling.

"You think that's funny?" I shake my head. It's a little funny that she always says she's fine, but not really. 'Cause she's not fine.

"I'm alright, Dom." I turn my body toward her and run my finger over the small bruise showing through her makeup.

"Take all this off so I can look at you." I know she's roughed up. And that there's more to her injuries than just the physical component. I'm gonna start with the bruises, then work my way to everything else.

She stares back at me for a minute with a blank look, like the one she gave me earlier and for a second I think I'm gonna have to remind her that she needs to listen to me. She swallows and gets up, heading for the open bathroom door to my en suite. I follow a few steps behind her. I'll set her up with the steam room as soon as I get a good look at her. It'll help her muscles. I should know. I've gotten the shit kicked out of me a few times, and the steam always helps relieve the soreness.

I hear her gasp when she turns on the light, and that makes me smile. My place is pretty fucking sweet. I didn't hold back on the upgrades. Her bare feet make a soft padding noise as she walks across the travertine floor to the floating marble vanity. The sink itself is carved out of the marble, and I can tell she's impressed. She turns to take in the rest of the room. The river rock shower takes up the back half of the room, with glass doors that separate it from the rest of the bathroom. There's a comfortable bench inside where she can lounge while the steam goes to work on her body. In the center of the room is a rustic bowl soaking tub also made of stone. She walks slowly to it and runs her hand along the dark grey edge.

"You wanna soak a bit, doll?" She startles when my low voice seems to echo off the walls of the large bathroom. She looks at me with wide eyes, and then stares at the tiled floor. "I thought you might wanna lie down in the steam room, but a soak in the tub would be nice, too." I still have some of that sea salt for healing. Not the shit that stings, but the good stuff. I take a step toward her, and she takes a step back.

"What's gotten into you, doll?" She's wearing that same guarded expression from dinner. I don't fucking like it.

"How…" She struggles to ask whatever's on her mind. Whatever her question is, it can't be good. There's a reason we don't like the women asking questions. We don't want them involved in this shit, it makes them targets. There's usually an understanding about this. Women stay out of it.

But that's not how shit worked out for her. She can't just go along with things and leave the business to the men.

"Ask it, doll; whatever you want to know. I'll tell you right now." That's partially a lie. I know it, but I don't want to tell her there's shit I'm not going to answer. I'll let her ask whatever's on her mind. Hopefully it's nothing too specific. Something I can talk around.

"How many people have you killed?" she asks in a voice so low, it takes me a moment to actually understand her question.

Red fucking flags shoot up in my head. Cops ask questions like that. I run a hand through my hair and watch as her knuckles turn white gripping the edge of the tub. I need to get her ass in the tub first. It's not like she's a cop.

She's not. Tony would've figured that out if she was. And she's not wearing a wire. Even if she was, I've got the blocker set up in every room of the house. No way a rat is getting shit out of me in my own home.

I take a step toward the tub, and she reacts with fear. Taking a sharp inhale, and another step away from me. She's scared to ask me questions, and I don't like that. I don't know how Pops does it. I don't know why Ma doesn't ask, and never has. But it sure as shit isn't because of fear.

I push the stopper down and lean over and turn the faucet on, letting the water warm before dipping my fingers into it. I turn the heat up a bit and walk to the shelves for the salt. It's pink. Maybe she'll like that. I scoop out a bit and drop it right below the running water and dip my fingers back in. That should be good for her. Maybe it'll help her relax some.

"Get in, babe. Relax a bit, and then we'll talk." I sit my ass on the edge of the tub and grip her hips, pulling her in between my legs. Her lips part, and her small hands brace herself on my chest. I pull her closer and gently kiss under her ear, on that tender spot below her neck and it works like a charm. She relaxes slightly, leaning into me. A soft sigh leaves her as I leave another open-mouth kiss on the crook of her neck.

I love that sound, the little moan of satisfaction. I want to push for more; I want to run my hands from her thighs up to her ass, and squeeze. My dick hardens thinking about fucking her against the tub. The tub is solid and I could pound into her and force her to take the intensity of each thrust. But there's no doubt it'd leave bruises. And she's so hurt already.

I pull away from her, remembering her current state and place a soft kiss against her lips. I take her hand in mine and gently unravel the bandages. She did a shit job of putting them on. I should've done it earlier. My thumb brushes lightly over the raw skin on her wrists. She struggled against them. The abrasions from the rope piss me off. A deep hurt settles in my chest, and it takes everything in me to keep my face from showing my anger.

They hurt her to get to me. They tried to kill her. And they wanted me to see.

As adrenaline pumps through my blood and my heartbeat picks up, her small hands land on my shoulders and rub soothing circles. A satisfied groan rumbles through me. My hands find the small of her back, and I rest my forehead against her chest. She's so warm and comforting. It takes a moment to notice that her arms have wrapped around me, and her head is resting on top of mine.

I tilt my head up and catch her bottom lip between my teeth. I pull back slightly at her whimper before letting her go. Her half-hooded eyes stare back with a spark of lust.

My doll fucking loves it rough. Her thighs clench in between my legs. I want to fuck into that hot, tight cunt so fucking much. My dick roars back to life as her eyes stare into mine, waiting for me to take her. "You want me to fuck you, doll?" Her fingers touch her lips and her eyes stare at mine as she slowly nods her head once.

I want it too, but not right now. I need to get her to tell me what's going on in her head. I need answers. And so does she.

"Be a good girl and strip." I watch her body as she pulls the shirt above her head and lets it fall onto the floor. Her breasts are full and lush, and I lean forward and take a nipple into my mouth. Teasing me, teasing her. She gasps as I bite down and pull back. She has one hand on my head, and one on her other breast. Her fingers pinch and pull her hardened nipple while her other hand tries to push me closer to her. *Naughty girl.*

I let her nipple go and love how her mouth forms a perfect "O" and her eyes close in pleasure. "Bad girl. You don't direct this show, doll." I set a bad example the last time we fucked by letting her lead like that. But damn, it turned me on. My dick jumps, remembering how fucking good it was. My breathing is picking up, and my fingers are itching to play with her body. My eyes trail down her skin, and then I see the bruises.

"You need a salt soak." I have to keep my mind focused. Her ass isn't topping from the bottom anymore. She just wants to fuck me. Other than that, she's scared of me. Which isn't necessarily a bad thing. But for some reason, I don't like it.

"Are you a fucking sadist?" She takes a step back and gives me a bewildered look. Well, she's obviously not that scared. I guess when her sweet cunt's begging for my attention she's not so afraid.

I smirk at her and push off the edge of the tub, putting my body right in front of hers. I let my lips barely brush up against hers and respond, "It's not gonna hurt." My hands grab her ass and I squeeze her cheeks before lifting her up. She wraps her legs around my body and lets her heat rub against the bulging erection covered by my sweats. "I promise I'll make it good for you." I rock my dick against her heat and smile when that small moan parts her lips again. I turn with her in my arms and slowly put her in the water. She tries to hold onto me for a moment, and her legs tighten around me as her ass hits the warm water.

"Be a good girl for me, doll. I don't want to have to spank that ass tonight." Her eyes shoot to mine and search my face, trying to figure out if that's an empty threat. She's such a kinky bitch.

She slowly unwraps her legs and hesitantly sinks her hand into the water. As soon as one leg's submerged, she drops her weight and relaxes, a look of pure bliss on her face. The steam from the bath rises around her. The salts leave a thin layer of translucent white on the surface of the water. Her breasts barely peek out just enough to tease me. Her nipples are hard, and they're begging me to suck them. But not right now. I have to keep reminding myself.

She leans her head back against the tub and looks at the open door to the bathroom, a slightly worried look on her face.

"What's distracting you, babe?" I sit on the edge of the tub, wiping the water from my arms onto my sweats. She tilts her head and narrows her eyes, wondering how I knew her mind had gone somewhere else. "You're very easy to read."

"Jax." Her answer spreads warmth through my chest.

"What about your little man?" A gentle smile plays at her lips for a moment before she sighs.

"I just want to check on him." She swallows and brings her hands out of the water to pull her hair from her shoulders and off of her face.

"I'll go." I start to get up. That's an easy thing to check. Just make sure the little dude's still knocked out. She sits straight up and grabs my hand with hers, stopping me.

I look back at her, wondering what the fuck that's about. She swallows thickly and looks between me and the door. "It's a new place, and he doesn't know you." She gives me an answer to my unspoken question.

"He'll be asleep." I hope he's fucking asleep. "Do kids get up throughout the night?" I thought that was like a *baby*, baby thing.

She shakes her head and answers, "No, not usually." Her eyes are still wide and they're pleading with me, but I'm not sure what it is that she wants. It's fucking hard figuring out this broad.

"Alright then, I'll be back in a sec." I pull my hand away and she lets me, settling back against the tub. "If he's up, I'll bring him in the bedroom for you."

She seems to relax a bit and says, "Thank you." But that look is still in her eyes. I don't like it. I'm not going to bed until I figure out what the fuck's going on with her.

BECCA

"*P*assed the fuck out." Dom strolls into his bathroom like nothing's wrong and squats next to me by the tub.

I give him a forced smile as I say, "Good." I take a deep breath.

"What's bothering you, doll?" I look back at him like he's lost his damn mind. Am I taking crazy pills? I was kidnapped by a group of men who wanted and tried to kill me, and now I'm being held against my will with my son by a man that's no good for me.

My arms splash the water as they rise up and cross over my knees to pull them into my chest. The movement of the hot water on my wounds makes them sting slightly, but it's instantly relieved by the salts in the water. It feels so fucking good. "What are the plans, exactly?" I like order; I like plans. More than that, I like knowing where my life is going so I can direct things to an appropriate path. Right now I have none of that. I have no control. And I don't fucking like it. But I also don't have a choice.

"De Luca's a dead man."

I'm quick to answer, "He wasn't when he took me." Hearing that name makes my body cower in the water. I hate it. I hate that I can't control how much my body hurts thinking of what he's done to me.

He shifts on the edge of the tub. "I'm sorry for that. I really am, babe. But I'm gonna make sure he pays."

"Is he the one with the tattoo?" I close my eyes, remembering the vibrant green against his tanned skin.

"I thought you didn't see anything?" He leans closer to me with his eyes narrowed. As if he suspects I lied to him. I should be scared, but I'm not. Instead I'm pissed.

"Don't fucking look at me like that. When they took me, that's all I saw."

His hand shifts up to grip my chin. "That mouth of yours. I swear to God it's going to get you into trouble."

"Why'd he...?" I try to push the words out, but my teeth grind together and my body stiffens. I don't want to think about it. I don't want to go back to what happened.

"His dad used to be a big deal, but he got busted and De Luca just got out of prison. He's playing fast and loose. Targeting the big guys, and being sloppy about it. He's only been out for a week, and there's already a target on his back. Him and the few people he has following him around will be dead by the end of the week. No one gets away with the shit he's pulling. Not in this business."

I pull my knees further into my chest. I want to ask him again. I want to know everything. But I keep reminding myself that curiosity killed the cat.

"Talk to me, doll," Dom says then gets up from his seat on the tub and walks behind me. I look over my shoulder as he gets something from the wooden shelf in the corner and then drags a bench from the stall over to the back of the tub. I turn and face the wall as his hands come down on my shoulders. *Massage oil.* It smells so good, like chamomile and some kind of citrus. His thumbs dig into my sore muscles. It reminds me how much my body hurts.

The punches I could take, but being hung up like that, fighting my restraints? My head hurts remembering how I smacked it over and over against the edge of the sink. But it worked. I saved myself. If I hadn't fought... My heart stills, and my body tenses. I force my body to relax and close my eyes. There's no reason to think like that.

"Ask me again, and I'll tell you. You just relax and talk to me." I don't believe him. He's not going to answer a damn thing.

I take a deep inhale as his hands work my shoulders and then glide up my neck. Fuck, it feels so good. My head goes limp, and I struggle to think of a question. I remember asking him earlier and not getting an answer, so I settle on asking that one again. "How many men have you killed?"

"A lot. I can't tell you how many, doll." My eyes pop open at his confession and my shoulders go stiff, giving away my fear. "Relax, babe. They all knew it was coming; they all had a gun aimed at me, too."

"If I hadn't had the money, would you have killed me?" He huffs a laugh.

"First of all, dead men can't pay you. It does set a bad example letting people get away with not paying you, though. The first thing, the *smart* thing to do, is to not let a man make a bet he can't afford." His hands stop, and I hear him swallow before he continues. "I knew... your ex could pay. If he hadn't shown up with the money, then we would've had a problem."

"What kind of problem?" I have to ask; I need to know.

"I'd have drained his bank account." I look up at him in absolute shock. "Yeah, doll. I have my ways." He pushes my shoulders enough to get me facing the wall again, and his hands continue rubbing soothing circles over my body. "But that wouldn't be enough. I'd have to make an example of him."

"What..." I want to ask what he'd do specifically. I try to push it out, but I can't.

"What would I have done? Do you really wanna know, babe?" I hesitate to answer. "I would've hurt him really bad, but it would've ended with him. Johnny should've told you that when you answered your ex's text. His debt wasn't on you."

He places a small kiss on my neck and says, "Don't worry about it, doll. The money's already in your bank account."

His words shock me. My body splashes the water as I turn to face him. "For real?" I ask.

"Yeah, doll. You didn't owe me. You never did." A small smile pulls at my lips as I settle back against the tub.

A moment passes in silence while he continues to rub my sore body.

"What if I was the one who owed you?" I want to know.

"If you owed me and you couldn't pay?" he asks.

"What would you have done to me?" I ask to clarify and again his hands pause, but then they continue to rub along my back, moving deeper and lower. His breath tickles along my back.

"Doll, I would've never hurt you." He kisses the crook of my neck and I find myself relaxing into him, but I don't believe him.

For some reason, my lips open and the words tumble out, "I don't believe you. You would've hurt me."

He chuckles, and his hot breath on my neck sends shivers through my body, but heats my core. His arms dip into the water and wrap around my body. "What do you think I would've done to you, doll?" His hands run down my stomach and then lower, rubbing my hips and then massaging my upper thighs. My legs part, giving him access to my heat. My clit throbs for his touch. I'm so fucking hot for him. My chest rises as I breathe in deep and tilt my hips for him.

His hand cups my pussy as he asks, "You think I would've made you pay with this, babe?" His fingers play along the folds of my pussy and circle my clit.

My head falls back; my mind is consumed with the thought of him fucking me in his office. Taking me on the floor. Forcing me.

"Would you have liked that?" He lets out a deep, low and breathy laugh. "I know you fucking liked it when you paid that way for the interest. How many times do you think I'd have taken you for owing me that much?"

"Hmm." I can't answer. I just want him to keep touching me while I think about how he took me against the wall.

He laughs again and then moves forward to push a thick finger inside me. "You would've loved to pay your debt to me with your pussy."

His finger moves in and out of me, pushing against the front wall and forcing soft moans through my lips. A tingle grows through my body, making my legs tremble. "I don't do that though, babe. I don't make bets with women." He adds another finger and rubs along that hot bundle of nerves, sending a radiating fire spreading through my trembling limbs. "I don't take pussy as payment." I hardly hear his words as my back bows, and he pushes against my clit with his thumb.

"Only you; I couldn't resist that temptation." His words set me off, and my orgasm rips through me. His fingers continue to pump in and out of me roughly. He fucks me without mercy as my thighs close tightly around him, and my body twists. His other arm wraps around my chest, holding my body still while I thrash with my release riding through my body in waves. He draws my orgasm out, forcing me to take it. As I scream out my pleasure his lips cover mine, sealing my moans in our kiss.

My body settles as the aftershocks slow. He slips his fingers out of me, and

I miss his touch immediately. He gently places me back against the tub and leaves me to lie limp in the warm water. My eyes close, and I nearly fall asleep. I'm so relaxed and exhausted.

His arms wrap around me, one under my bent knees and the other behind my back as he lifts me out of the water. He dries my body off, and I make a weak attempt to help. He pushes my hands away and continues patting my body dry, then leaves the towel on the ground to carry me to the bedroom. I try to sit in his arms, but he whispers in my ear, his voice a little more than a murmur, "I got you, doll." With his breath on my neck and his lips placing gentle kisses on my neck, he lays me on the bed and I drift off to sleep.

BECCA

My body falls forward. But it can't. I need to go forward; I need to block the punch that's coming, but I can't. I'm held back. My face slams against something hard, forcing my neck to whip to the side and sending a jolt of pain through my body. It hurts. It all hurts. My body is sore and my wrists and ankles are rubbed raw. It hurts so fucking much.

Slap! A hard smack to my face from the other side shoots a throbbing pain across my face. I try to move my arms, but they're tied. Ugh! I try to lean forward after another punch to my stomach. The air leaves my lungs, and my chest tightens with pain. I'm pinned by hands. Pinned back by restraints... the belt.

I'm pinned back by the seat belt. The tires screech. The car crashes forward. My body jolts forward. The metal twists and groans. The glass shatters. My mom screams. I can't see her. Only my dad. My vision focuses on the tree. Heat overwhelms my shaking body. And then nothing.

No sound. Shards of glass stick out of my trembling arm. I carefully lift it and grasp the broken glass. My shaking fingers slip, and the pain makes me moan in agony. My voice. It's the only noise. I try to move; I need to help them...

"Becca!" Who's screaming my name? They can't. They can't yell for me. "Wake up!" They never yelled for me. "Babe, wake up!" My body shakes, and I struggle to move.

My eyes slowly open. "Becca?" Dom's face is pained; his light blue eyes look so sad. I blink back the tiredness overwhelming me, and that's when I feel the pain.

"Dom." I wince. Fuck, my body hurts.

"Shit." He lays me down on the bed and crawls to the nightstand. He leans over, still on the bed and reads the back of the bottle. Yes, please. My chest fucking hurts, and these damn abrasions on my ankles and wrists sting like a bitch. I want to climb back into the bath.

"Thank you," I manage to say before opening my mouth to take the pill. He tilts the glass of water to my lips and I take it with a trembling hand. Fuck, it hurts.

"Are you alright?" he asks with a wary look. His brows are pinched together, making a deep crease in his forehead.

"I'm fine," I answer, handing the glass back.

He takes the glass and sets it on the table. "I fucking hate that you do that," he says, crawling back to lie next to me. He pulls my body into his gently. "You're not fine." He kisses my neck. "You weren't fine."

I have a vague memory of being in pain before waking up in his arms. "I still hurt, but it will take some time to heal."

"That's not what I'm talking about." His voice is hard.

"I don't understand."

"You were begging for it to stop." His voice is pained. I turn in his arms and watch as he pinches the bridge of his nose. "You kept saying 'no'." I turn back on my side with my back to his chest and stare across the room.

"It was just a dream." It's the only answer I have for him.

"It was a memory."

"What do you want from me?" I ask him with contempt. His grip on me tightens.

"I just want you to talk to me." He pulls me into his chest and kisses my neck. His tender touch makes me relax.

"I don't know what you want me to say." What can I say? They hurt me. I'm still getting over it. There. What more can I offer?

"You can't just hide from this." His voice is just barely more than a murmur.

"It's not hiding; it's moving on. That's what you do. You move on."

"How can you move on without giving yourself any time to grieve?"

"You want me to be sad?" I turn in his arms and keep far enough away to

116

look straight into his eyes. "Not everyone grieves the same way. Some people take time to really grasp the reality. Others seek out humor and positivity. Then there are people who'd rather just leave what can't be undone alone, and move forward with what they can change." I search his face for his reaction, but he gives me nothing.

"I can't change what happened to me. I'm only in charge of the present and my future. I learned that long ago. And I'm happy with that."

"How can you move on so quickly?" His voice is laced with disbelief.

"I haven't. Grief is a journey. It never ends." Shock sparks in his eyes, and then understanding. If there is an end, I have yet to find it.

"How bad does it hurt?"

"The medicine is already working." It is. My body already feels less tense, and the sharp pains have turned dull.

He shakes his head gently. "Not that pain." My chest hurts from his words. My heart clenches, and tears prick behind my eyes.

"Some days, a lot. And some days I don't even feel it."

He nods his head. "Tell me."

"I don't want to," I say and my throat's hoarse, making my words crack. I don't. I've tried to talk about it before; I just can't.

"Well, there's what happened because of me. That's adding to it."

"Yes. It is." I can't lie. I'm not fucking okay. What they did to me was horrific, and I'm shocked I survived it. But I survived because I fought. And I'm damned proud of that.

"And your ex," he says softly, and guilt eats away at me. I should be grieving more for him. I turn away from him and settle my back against his chest. I'm not responding to that. I don't want to.

"Doll?" he asks before kissing my neck. "You really think you'll be alright?" I consider his words.

"Some days I'm overworked and high stressed, and I can't seem to figure anything out. But I only need to make it one day at a time. Some moments I remember, and it's too much. But most of the time I'm alright. I can be okay. I can live through this. I can continue to live through anything, I suppose."

He's quiet for a long time. So long I think maybe he fell asleep and I close my eyes, waiting for sleep to take me.

"I wish I could take it all away." His chest vibrates against my back as I register his words.

"You do more than you know." It's true. I feel… alive. I haven't felt so much in months. So much desire. I mostly just run through to-do lists. Other than that, there's just Jax. Jax has kept me sane. "Jax makes it all worth it, you know?" He makes me want to smile. And I read somewhere that if you smile enough, it will make you happy. You can't help it. It's biology or something. "If I didn't have Jax, I don't know that I would've survived it all."

"I hope you know how strong you are, Becca." *Strong?* I wouldn't call myself strong. Tears prick at my eyes again. I don't ever feel strong. I feel so weak. I feel like I'm holding on to nothing, grasping for a thread that's taunting me. Tears leak from the corners of my eyes, and I try to wipe them without him knowing. But he sees. He rises from behind me and kisses away the tears on my cheek and chin.

"I didn't mean to make you cry, doll." A heavy sob wracks through my body. I don't know why I'm crying. I don't want to cry. My throat closes as another sob leaves me, and I bury my face in my hands. "Let it out, doll. It's okay, I've got you." I turn in his arms and cry into his chest. His strong arms wrap around me and hold me close.

"You're alright, doll. I've got you." His hands run up and down my back in soothing strokes as he kisses my hair. His loving touch is so unexpected. Everything about him is unexpected.

His hot breath on my neck makes my entire body shiver. Another kiss, this time on the tender spot just below my ear. I feel wrapped in his presence. Secure in his embrace. Something in me cracks. My armor falls. I feel myself melt into him.

I feel a need to be comforted by him. A need I only caved to once years ago. It's haunted me and left a deep hurt in my chest that I've grown used to. It tightens and twists, threatening to consume me. A mix of loneliness and insecurity. It fucking hurts. And feeling his arms around me, soothing me, the familiar pain pangs in my chest. I need this. I need him.

I feel a spark ignite deep in my core, and a haze of lust comes down around me. It's the same sensation when we first met in his office. My lips part at the memory of when he took me against the wall. I turn and push my breasts against his hard chest. My hand cups the back of his head, and my lips press against his gently. He moans into my mouth as his tongue tastes mine. His fingers spear my hair before fisting it at the nape of my neck. He pulls back, and his light blue eyes look deep into mine.

My breath hitches, and my body's overcome with a feeling of ice pricking my heated nerve endings. A chill goes through me as he searches my face for something. *Please don't reject me.* I need this. I whimper as he pulls my hair back and leaves open-mouth kisses along my jaw and down my neck.

Relief washes through me, and the heat in my core rages with need. I rock my pussy against his thigh for relief. His firm hand pushes my hip down onto the mattress as he climbs on top of me. He never lets up the kisses on my neck. His hands roam my body, down my waist, my hips. He parts my legs and settles between them and pulls back to look down on me.

"You're so fucking beautiful." I close my eyes and drop my head against the pillow. I'm in dangerous territory. My heart is begging for more. I'm only going to end up hurt. I know it. But I want it. I want him. I need him.

I open my eyes and find him shirtless, his ripped abs and corded muscles enhanced by the shadows in the dark. His hands grip my hips before traveling up my belly, his thumbs pulling my shirt. I lift my back and let him pull the shirt over my head, baring myself to him. His mouth immediately comes down as he sucks a nipple into his mouth and palms my other breast. His hot tongue massages my hardened peak and my back arches, pushing more of myself into him.

His deft fingers twist my other nipple. The hot sensation is directly linked to my clit. A whimper escapes me. I brush my heat against his hard cock. Too much fabric between us. I need more. My heels dig into the mattress, needing more friction. His teeth bite down gently as he pulls away from me. His grasp on the other breast becomes nearly violent as he pulls back, giving a hint of pain that only adds to the intense pleasure. A wave of heat travels down my body.

His other hand steadies my hip, and then I hear a tear and feel the pull of the lace fabric against my skin.

I force my eyes open as his fingers slip through my slick folds. His broad shoulders and heated gaze portray him as a man of sheer dominance and lust. He stares deep into my eyes as his fingers dip into my heat and his thumb presses against my clit.

My body shudders beneath the pleasure of his touch. His fingers pump in and out of me relentlessly, and his thumb pushes down harder. A tingle of heat travels through every limb in an instant and I convulse underneath him, held down only by the weight of his hand splayed on my hip. I hold in my scream, opening my mouth and throwing my head back. The sheer intensity of my orgasm nearly paralyzes my body. My body goes limp with pleasure, and I finally breathe.

Dom's lips take mine with passion as he lies on the bed, pulling my back to his chest. He sucks and nibbles my bottom lip while I try to breathe, my chest heaving for air and breaths coming in pants. He pushes into me, slowly and deep. His girth stretches my walls. One of his arms wraps around my shoulders and his hand massages my breast, while the other cradles my leg, parting my legs for him further. He pushes in and out of me deliberately slow, but deep. All the while kissing me. My moans are trapped in his kiss.

My head falls back as my pussy clamps around his dick and that hot wave travels through my body with a vengeance. A strangled cry leaves my lips. His hand grips my chin and tilts my lips to his. But they only touch as he stares into my eyes and pumps into me. Faster and harder, forcing the numbing tingles through my limbs, building with a crippling intensity at my core. His hand moves to my clit and he brushes his fingers on the sensitive nub without mercy, sending me over the edge. His gaze keeps mine as I cum violently, my body trembling in his arms while he continues to pump into me, rutting with a primal need until he finds his own release.

My chest warms, and my body opens to him as he gently settles my body and continues to kiss me with a passion I'm not sure I've ever known. I turn in his embrace as best I can, just wanting to be held.

I try to calm my breathing. My trembling hands rest against his corded arm wrapped around my waist. He gently kisses down my jaw, down my neck. His open-mouth kisses leave a warmth that quickly turns to chills as the air hits them.

My breathing finally slows, and I turn in his arms. He holds me close against his chest. My eyes open as I watch his chest rise and fall as he calms his own breathing. I hear his heart beating loudly, yet with a steady rhythm. It's hypnotizing.

A mix of relaxation and security warms my chest; my heart makes me weak. I swallow the lump growing in my throat and try to push down the emotions threatening to overwhelm me. I press my forehead to his chest as my back shudders from the cool air.

Dom reaches down and grabs his shirt from the floor for me. I give him a small smile and quickly put it on.

This is dangerous. Too emotional. I'm too weak to be playing these kinds of games. It's not like it was before, where I could just walk away. Where I could live a fantasy and then return to my reality. My heart beats louder and chaotically against my chest. It doesn't trust me, and I don't trust it.

His brow furrows, and his eyes narrow. Just as he asks, "What's wrong?" I hear Jax in the other room.

"Mommy!" he calls out as though he's lost.

Dom slides easily off the bed and reaches for his pants. "Stay here; I'll get him," he says as though it'd be alright for him to go to my son. Jax pushes the door open as I open my mouth to stop Dom.

"Hey little man, Mommy's tired right now, can I read you a bedtime story?" he asks in a sweet voice I didn't know could be uttered from his lips.

My heart beats faster and tries to climb up my throat as he bends down so he's eye level with Jax. Jax's sleepy eyes focus on Dom as he runs a hand through his hair. He lets out a small yawn and nods his head.

The word escapes my lips and echoes off the walls, "Red!" The two look up at me, both with confusion. And then the realization dawns across Dom's face. My heart crumples in my chest. My throat dries, and a soreness leaks through every inch of my body.

I press my lips together and hold back the sobs threatening me, hating myself. Tears leak out of the corners of my eyes as I climb carefully off the bed, keeping the shirt down and walk silently to Jax. My hands shake as they go to his shoulders.

Guilt consumes me.

My heart may believe that what Dom and I just shared was something more than a quick, dirty fuck. But logically, I know better. I swallow thickly, avoiding Dom's gaze. I know it was one-sided. And it was stupid. I keep doing stupid things around this man.

But not when it comes to Jax.

"It's alright baby, I'll read you a story." I'm almost surprised how easily and calmly the words flow from my lips. But then I remember I've been doing this for quite some time now, hiding the pain and being strong for my son.

Only I don't remember it ever hurting this much.

DOM

I can't fucking sleep. She ripped my fucking heart out. How the fuck am I supposed to react to that? I'm trying real fucking hard not to take offense to that. That's where she draws the line? I can fuck her all I want. Talk about using her pussy as payment, and fucking make love to her in my bed. But I can't read her kid a bedtime story?

She had no fucking underwear on. My cum was probably leaking down her thigh. But she'd rather that?

She fucking safe worded me. I've only been safe worded a handful of times when I first started playing. I know limits. I know what women want. I'm good at reading their body language. But I can't read her, my doll. Just thinking of my pet name for her has my heart clenching in agony.

I'm a fucking fool for thinking she's mine. She's not meant to be with a man like me, and it's obvious she wants it to stay that way.

I thought she felt it. How could she not? I gave her everything. I feel raw and broken. And now she's lying next to me right where I fucked her, on her side with her back to me, pretending to sleep. I know she's awake. Her breathing isn't even close to steady.

I'm not gonna do this. I'm not going to put up with this shit.

She wants to act like that, it's on her. But my heart is fucking open, and I'm not going to let her pretend I didn't just make love to her. That I didn't just see right into her fucking soul as she came on my dick. It was fucking beautiful. I'm not going to let her disrespect that.

"Why are you pretending to sleep, doll?" I ask, doing my best to keep the contempt out of my voice.

"I'm not pretending." Her voice comes out confident, and then lowers. "Just trying to sleep."

"You don't want me to hold you after tonight?" That fucking hurts, too. I should be all over her. Making sure she's alright. I know better than to let her be on her own. But fuck, I'm hurting after that shit.

"It's alright if you don't want to." Her voice breaks at the end. My brows raise in surprise.

"Babe?" I lean over and turn her so her back is on the bed. Her cheeks are tearstained. Fuck! "Doll, what's wrong?" I pull her into my embrace, and she fucking loses it. "Have you been crying this whole time?"

"No." She shakes her head into my chest and barely gets the word out.

"Let it out, babe." I gently rub her back and feel like a fucking prick. I've been lying here pissed because she doesn't want me around her son, yet she's been crying right next to me and I didn't even know. "Tell me what's wrong." I speak gently, but firmly. I know she's gonna try to find a way around telling me what's bothering her. My heart twists in agony; she didn't want me to know she was crying.

"I know this is going fast babe, but you gotta try to trust me."

A sob leaves her as she shakes her head. "It's alright babe, just let it all out."

"I can't." She pushes away from me with tears in her red-rimmed eyes. Her plush lips are turned down, and I still think she looks so damn beautiful. I don't know how I ever looked at her before as just a piece of ass. But something's different now.

"You can, babe. Just let it out."

She shakes her head and her chest heaves with a sob, her shoulders bowing inward. "I can't with you." She sucks in a strangled breath. "This," she says, motioning between us, "I can't." Her voice chokes on the last word. And it may as well have choked me.

My chest hollows and I let out a heavy breath, wrapping my arm around her shoulders and letting her cry into my chest. I don't think I've ever felt pain like this. I don't fucking like it.

"You don't wanna be with me, doll?" I need her to say the words. I don't want to hear them, but I need her to say them.

"That's not it." A spark of hope flares in my chest until she adds, "Jax." My breath stops short. "I can't do this to Jax," she cries into my chest.

"Because I'm in the mob?" I ask clearly somehow.

"I can't give him that life." She shakes her head, and I hardly hear her words through her tears.

I swallow the lump growing in my throat. "You don't think I'd be good for him?" I'd be great for him. I don't know much about kids, but I'd learn. I'd treat them both better than her shit husband did.

She pulls away from me and looks at me with disbelief. "How could you?" She wipes the tears away with the back of her hand and tries to get off the bed. I snatch her wrist and pull her closer to me. I take her lips with mine and push her back onto the mattress. One hand on her throat and one beside her head, bracing my body. I cage her in and kiss her with everything I have. Her fingernails dig into my back.

I bite down on her bottom lip and pull back until she whimpers. I whisper in the air between us, "I'm good enough to fuck, but that's it?"

A sad look of regret crosses her face. I wish it hadn't. I don't want to be a regret. I know I gave her what she needed. "Is that it, doll?" I search her pained expression for anything other than regret and remorse. "You don't want me, babe?"

Her lips part, and the saddest noise sounds from her lips. I can see in her eyes that she wants me. I know she trusts me from the way her hand gentles on my forearm. My hand's wrapped around her throat, and she doesn't even react to it. I lean down and kiss her again, closing my eyes and gently sucking. I brush my tongue along the seam of her lips and she parts them, opening herself for me and moaning into my mouth.

She fucking loves me like I do her. It's not supposed to be like this, but what really ever happens like it's supposed to?

I gently rest my forehead against hers. My body heats, and my dick hardens with a desperate need to be inside her again and show her how much she loves me.

"Don't fucking act like you don't want me." My hips push her legs apart, and she opens them obediently. "You just don't want to believe you do." I rock my dick against her heat before reaching down to push my pants down. "Stop lying to yourself."

"I do." She struggles to say her words. Relief washes through me, but it's only temporary. The look on her face tells me everything. She'll never be with me. It fucking hurts. She didn't even give us a chance. She must see my pain, because her hands grab my neck and she pushes my lips onto hers.

"Please," she whispers. But I don't know what she means. I can't ever figure her out. I look deep into her hazel eyes. "Please," she asks again, her breathing shallow. She bites her bottom lip and rocks against my hard dick.

She just wants me to fuck her. A sharp shot to my chest makes me almost get off her, but her words stop me.

"Like you want to. Like I'm yours." I barely hear her words. I search her eyes and then I hear the sweetest sounds whispered from her lips, "Punish me."

It won't take the pain away. I know it won't, but I'll be damned if I don't want to pin her down and make her love me.

I narrow my eyes and look down at Becca. "Take your shirt off and get on your knees."

I'm going to take her exactly how I've wanted to since I first held her ass in my office. It may be the last time I ever get to. In the morning I know she'll want to leave. And I don't think I have it in me to stop her. So I'm going to make this night count. I sit back on my heels and stroke my dick as she obeys me.

My hand comes down hard across her ass, leaving an angry red print. She yelps, and her body jolts forward with the blow. The slap echoes through the room, and then I remember her son. Fuck! I need to be quiet. A small voice inside me says she's right. But I push that shit down and shake it off. I reach into the nightstand for some lube with my right hand while my left rubs the mark on her ass. I can have her tonight. Every way I want, and every way she wants.

I lean forward, my dick nestled between her heat and take her throat in my hand. I squeeze lightly and whisper into her ear, "You want me to fuck you like you're mine to do what I want, how I want."

I stroke the lube over my dick and use the excess over her puckered hole. I don't waste any time slipping my finger in knuckle deep. "Good girl. Arch your back," I say and she immediately obeys. "Push back, babe." I fuck her ass with my finger until she's moaning into the pillows, and then I add a second. My left hand strokes my dick, and I wish it was in her mouth. Her lips are parted, and soft whimpers are falling easily from them. Her eyes are closed, and I know she's enjoying this. I pull my fingers out and line my dick up; her eyes fly open, and it makes me smirk.

"This is what you want from me, babe?" I keep my hand on the small of her back to keep her steady, and I watch those lips turn into a perfect "O" as I pump shallow thrusts into her ass. Her hot walls feel so fucking good. She clenches her heat as her head thrashes on the pillow.

"You want me to fuck you like I own you," I say and lean down and push my dick deep into her, all the way to the balls. "Guess what, doll?" I pull back, almost all the way out. My dick begs to be back in her warmth. Her ass looks so fucking perfect with my dick in it. I grab her chin in my hand and pull her head back so she has to look at me. "I do own you."

I slam back into her and watch her beautiful lips part with a cry of pleasure. I keep up a steady pace, holding her eyes. My breathing comes in pants as I fuck her exactly how she wants. She wants it brutal; she wants to believe that's who I am. I'll give her that. I won't deny her. I thrust into her, and I don't hold back. Her breasts bounce with my movements and I reach forward to cup one and squeeze it and pull to give her the added sensation. Her mouth hangs open, and her eyes squeeze shut as I keep up my pace. Her whimpers turn to squeaks, and I know she's getting close. My hand flies to her clit as a cold sweat breaks out on my body.

"Cum for me." Her back bows, and her head falls to the mattress as she does exactly what I told her to do. My balls draw up, and my spine tingles as I find my own release with hers. I pump into her with every wave until the aftershocks have passed.

I gently pet Becca's back and kiss her shoulder. "Stay here, doll." I plant another kiss on her shoulder and grab a hand towel from the bathroom to clean up. I wipe both of us off and lay her gently on the bed. I wasn't gentle with her. Not like I was planning to be at her place.

I lie down beside her and pull her into me. None of that crying on her own shit. Tonight she's mine. "You alright, babe?" I ask as she backs her ass up to nestle between my hips. It makes a soft smile form on my lips.

"Hmmm." She's so exhausted she can't even answer. I rub my hand down her arm and kiss her shoulder before settling behind her. Her warm body against mine feels so right.

A pang pains in my chest at the thought, and just as I close my eyes and pray for sleep to take me, I hear her say it. "I love you, Dom." It's mumbled from her lips. I prop myself up on my elbow and look at her. She's peacefully asleep, but I know I heard her say it.

I lie back down and kiss her hair. "I love you, doll." I whisper the words and pray maybe that will be enough.

DOM

I can't stop watching her fuss over her little boy. They're in my kitchen, sitting at the island eating breakfast. I lean back against the granite, gripping it to keep me in place. I could see myself with them. I could see myself with one arm wrapped around her waist, and my other hand messing up Jax's hair. An asymmetric grin pulls at my lips as she leans over to fix his hair. It makes me want to mess it up even more.

I can see the three of us together. But she can't. Or won't. I don't know which.

I push off the counter to walk over to her, but my phone goes off. It catches Becca's attention, and she looks at me with anxiety in her eyes. She's been asking to go home since she woke up. She's been avoiding me, and not letting me touch her.

Well, she doesn't move away from me, but she stills in my arms. She doesn't mold to me and thrive in my embrace like she did last night. I knew it would be like this. I just didn't know it would hurt this much.

"Yo." I answer the phone how I always do, but when her eyes fall to the counter and then to Jax, I wish I hadn't answered it at all.

"Got 'em," Johnny says, and I know exactly what he's talking about.

"How many?" He got De Luca and his crew. My fists clench, and my blood runs cold. I'm gonna beat the fucking piss out of them and make them suffer for what they did to my girl.

"All." An evil smirk forms on my face, and I have to walk out of the kitchen to hide it from her.

I remember what Becca said so I ask, "Is a dragon there?"

There's hesitation on the other end. I know I'm not supposed to ask detailed questions. It can always come back around if shit on the other end is heard.

"It's here. All of 'em." I nod my head and let out a sigh of relief. Her house is fine, untouched. I got that message when I woke up. And now De Luca is done. That's everything. Everything that's given me a reason to keep her to myself.

"Later."

"Later, boss," he answers quickly, and hangs up. Short calls, that's the way they have to be.

My brow furrows as I pocket my phone and walk back into the kitchen. I grip the back of the chair that Becca's sitting in at the island. As soon as these fuckers are gone, there's no reason for me to keep her here.

My eyes travel to her son who gives me a happy smile before picking his bowl up and slurping the milk out. I know why she doesn't want me and it hurts, but she's right. I can't put her son through this life. I couldn't guarantee her safety, and I can't ask her to risk her son. A frown pulls at my lips, and I can't help it. It hurts. I don't want to say goodbye.

"Who was that?" I smirk at her. She's gotta learn to not ask so many questions. The smirk fades as I realize she doesn't. She doesn't have to learn shit; she's leaving me.

"That was what I needed to hear this morning." That's all I can really say to her. She's already seen too much. I won't risk her knowing any more.

"We can go home?" Her eyes widen with hope. It fucking shreds me.

"Yeah, doll. As soon as Jax is done with breakfast, I'll let you two go."

BECCA

*E*verything hurts. Every last bit of me aches. But I won't take the pills. I want to feel the pain. My chest hurts the worst. The knot where my heart used to be just won't go away.

"Mommy!" Jax yells through the hall.

"Jax!" He's butt naked, and his towel is on his shoulders like a cape. I shake my head and try to hide my smile. This kid. "Baby, I told you to get your PJs on."

"I want sleepover." He's giving me those puppy dog eyes he always gives me. But that's something I can't cave on. That'll never happen again. I'm grateful he isn't anything but happy about everything. He has no idea. Thank fuck he's only three.

I squat down and hold back the wince from the slight pain in my ass. "We'll do another play date with Ava soon, okay?" I gently push the hair out of his face and wrap his towel around him.

He purses his lips and narrows his eyes at me, and I can't help but crack up laughing. "Bedtime, mister." I use my mommy voice, and he doesn't like that.

"Daddy never made me go bed." He pouts, and I have to hold everything back and try to think about what I read online. I'm coming up short. How to handle divorce. How to handle death. I don't remember. I can't think. I don't know what's best. My body heats with anxiety, and I have no idea how to respond to him.

"Fine!" He stomps his foot and crosses his arms. As soon as his back is turned, I stand and wipe the bastard tears from my eyes.

Fucking hell, could today get any worse?

Work was a disaster; I wish I'd just stayed away. Who the fuck am I kidding? Work was just like every other day. That's not what hurt about today.

I force myself to straighten my back and pick out a book to read for his bedtime story. "This one, baby?" I ask.

"I'm not a baby, Mom." He huffs and lies back on the bed. "I'm three." He holds up three fingers and speaks with exasperation. I wish I wasn't so fucking emotional, because that really hurt. I want to scream. I want to cry. But instead I ask, "Okay *Jax*, this one?"

He smiles and nods his head, and it takes everything in me to sit on his bed and pretend like I'm not falling to pieces. I read him the fairytale with the same peppy voice, although my throat feels hoarse and raw. The only thing keeping me together is hearing his little voice tell me he loves me as he hugs me before I get off the bed. He may not think he's my baby boy, but he is. I hold him longer than I have in a long time, and he lets me. My heart clenches, and I have to give him a kiss and turn out the lights quickly before he sees what a mess I am.

As soon as I shut the door, I let it all out.

I cry harder than I have for years and I stumble into my room, exhausted and wishing I could change everything.

* * *

THREE LOUD KNOCKS at the door stir me from my sleep. Shit. I'm still fully clothed and lying on my stomach over the made bed. I wipe under my eyes and slowly climb off the bed, feeling exceptionally unsteady.

Bang! Bang! The knocks pound on the door. I practically jog to the door so the banging doesn't wake up Jax. Who the fuck is banging at this hour? Anger gets the best of me, and I almost swing the door open without looking. It isn't even locked. I grind my teeth and nearly snap when whoever it is bangs on the other side again. I need to get a grip and be smart. I stand on my tiptoes to see clearly out of the peephole.

It's a cop. Fuck!

My heart sputters, and my fingertips go numb. I shake them out and open the door before that fucker decides to knock again.

"Rebecca?" he asks with concern apparent in his voice.

"Yes, that's me." I want to correct him, but I don't; technically that's my name. I just fucking hate not being called Becca.

"I'd like to speak with you if you have a moment." His eyes search my face and then behind me. I almost look over my shoulder, but stop myself. I know there's no one there.

I nod my head and say, "Sure." But I don't move an inch. We can have this conversation right here, and real fucking quick.

"We had a call this evening that you and your son were kidnapped and held against your will," he says far more calmly than I would imagine possible.

I huff a humorless laugh. "Well obviously that's not true. I'm standing right here." My fingers itch to touch my chin. To make sure the makeup is still covering the bruises.

The officer shifts uncomfortably in front of me. "Where were you yesterday?" My mouth stays shut as I look him in the eyes.

"I was with a friend."

"Could I have that friend's name?" He takes out a pad and a pen from his back pocket and I want to smack it away.

"Am I being charged with anything?" I make sure that my voice echoes annoyance. I'm not annoyed. I'm scared shitless. I don't want him here asking questions.

"Not unless you're lying. Are you withholding any information?" The officer's strong jaw juts out, and he looks past my shoulder again.

"No, I'm not. I'd like to go to bed, officer." My grip on the door tightens as I add, "I'm fine. There's no reason to waste either of our time. I'm exhausted and just want to go to bed." That last part is the truth at least.

"May I come in to take-" I don't let him finish.

"I'd rather you didn't. My son's asleep." There's no fucking way I want him in here.

"I completely understand, Mrs. Harrison." Hearing that name makes anger course through me.

132

"Bartley now."

"I'm sorry?" he asks.

"Rebecca Bartley. Harrison was my married name."

"Oh. My apologies. Have a good night now." He seems sincere, but that doesn't damper my anger. Or my sadness.

I give him a tight smile. "You, too." I'm surprised the overwhelming emotion I'm feeling is anger. It's followed closely by a deep aching hurt in my gut.

I close the door, turning both locks and lean my back against it. My eyes fall shut, and I try to breathe.

I can't do this shit on my own.

I wish Dom were here. I wish he could hold me. I wrap my arms around my shoulders and walk slowly to bed, feeling lost and unsure and very much alone.

DOM

I clench and unclench my hands to get rid of the numbness. It makes the cuts open, and it fucking hurts like hell. But I don't give a shit. I'm glad it hurts.

"You alright, boss?" Johnny keeps fucking asking me the same damn question every hour. No. I'm not alright.

"I'm fine." When I register what I've answered, I snort a laugh. That's what she'd say.

I take a seat at the desk in the corner of the office. It's on the opposite side of the room, across from the pool table. It's a sleek-looking glass desk with steel trimmings. I don't think I've ever sat here. My fingers tap along the glass top, waiting for our next drop.

It's so fucking tedious. So damn boring. I don't need to do this shit. I've got more money than I'd ever wanted, and nothing to spend it on. What the fuck did I even use to do sitting here?

"Boss?" I look up with a scowl, and then feel like a prick. It's not his fault. But then again, I am a prick.

I take in a deep breath and manage to sound somewhat normal. "What?"

"Just wanted you to know you still have those requests."

"What requests?" I ask.

"To sell out if you wanted to." My forehead pinches in confusion. What the fuck is he talking about? He answers before I have to ask. "I know you said to stop bringing it up, but I just thought you might like to know."

That's when it clicks. Give my business over to those thugs? I'm always getting shit offers. They don't want to pay the right amount to take my clients, and they'd ruin this shit anyway. They don't know what they're doing like I do. "Pass." That's an easy decision.

Johnny gives me a tight smile and nods. "Just thought maybe you'd rather do something else now." He takes a seat on the sofa, staring at the field. A few players are out running gauntlets; fucking sucks to be them.

Do something else. Like what? Just run the books for my Pops? That'd be boring as hell. I never really wanted to do anything other than make a name for myself. Get laid, and get paid. That was my motto for the longest time. But now I don't fucking want it anymore. I don't want this. Maybe I will sell the business. Maybe she'd want me then.

I shake my head and rap my knuckles across the glass tabletop; no she won't. It doesn't change a damn thing about who I am. I know it, and she knows it.

But I'm the boss' son. He tried to keep me out of the life, but I demanded my way in. You can't leave the family. Sure as fuck not when you're the boss' son. My chest hurts just thinking that. I'll never be the kind of man Becca deserves. I was born into the mob. There's only one way out, and I'm not ready to die.

A knock at the door distracts me from my morbid thoughts. I sigh and click my phone on. Ten a.m. Too fucking early. This day needs to get going so I can get home. I'll figure out a reason to be there when the time comes. I just don't want to be here.

Johnny opens the door, and my pops' voice booms through the hall.

"Johnny!" I raise my eyes to watch, although I don't lift my head. Pops pats him on the back and gives him a warm smile. But it's off. He's waiting to hear about Clara. I know he is. Something's going on between the two of them. Not my business though. Not unless he hurts her. Then I'll make it my business.

"Good to see you, boss." Johnny makes eye contact and returns the smile. Ballsy. Johnny is most certainly ballsy. He's been a friend of mine for years, and I sure as shit couldn't do this business without him. But I don't like that he's sneaking around with my sister. And I sure as shit know that Pops doesn't like it. He better give it up soon and put a ring on her finger.

"Hey Pops." I lean back in my seat and then stand to greet him. "Didn't know you were coming."

We share a quick hug and I motion to the liquor, but he shakes his head.

He takes a casual seat on the sofa, and I relax in the spot next to him. He's come here a few times, usually because we're meeting up for a family event... or a *family event*. But I always know about it ahead of time.

"What's going on, Pops?"

"I just wanted to make sure you're doing alright." He looks me in the eyes, and I almost look away. I lean forward and rest my elbows on my knees and set my chin on my clasped hands. I take a moment to answer him. I don't know what to tell him. I'm not okay.

I settle on what I hope is the truth. "I'll be alright."

"That was intense, Dom. Never seen you like that." I gaze at the floor and take a deep breath in, followed by a long exhale.

"Yeah, well." What's he want me to say? My memory flashes back to a few nights ago, to my fists beating the piss out of them. They were tied down when I got there. Just like they tied her down. I saved the one with the dragon tattoo for last. I wanted to make sure he knew what was coming. I wanted him to watch the rest of them die. De Luca was second to last. No one gave a fuck that I took the lead.

I needed to. I had to. For her.

"Sean went to see her the other night. Rebecca." Hearing her name brings me back to the present.

"It's Becca. And I know." His brows raise in surprise, and his lips turn down.

"She called you?" he asks.

"No, I went over there. Just to tell her she was safe." My gut churns, and my heart freezes in my chest. I wanted to go up there and talk to her, to convince her to just give it a chance. But I'd be a fucking asshole to do that to her and Jax. They deserve better. So I stayed in my car. Thinking about what a prick I am for wanting her. "I saw him walk up, and I waited."

"Well, what'd she tell you about it?" Pops leans into me.

I shake my head. "Nothing." I swallow the lump in my throat and lick my lips before sitting back in my seat. "I didn't talk to her."

"Ah." Pops looks to the left at Johnny and then sighs. "Well," he turns back to me, "she didn't give away anything. So she's cleared. I told Jack to back off."

"What the fuck is Jack saying now?" My blood heats, and anger stirs inside of me hearing that shit. Back off? He better fucking back off.

"Nothing, Dom." Pops puts his hand on my shoulder. "He's just paranoid as fuck. He's happy now."

I search his eyes and nod. "He better be fucking happy. She may never be mine to claim, but she's off limits."

"I don't understand, Dom." He lowers his voice and looks at me with a sad expression. "Is it 'cause she's got a kid? He's a good little guy, and he's-"

I rear my head back to look at him. "That's not it. That's not it at all."

"I don't get it, Dom. What the hell's a matter with you?" It's been a while since my father has talked to me that way.

I chew on the inside of my lip not wanting to say it, but he asked. And he's the boss. "She's got to protect her son. She can't be messing around with me."

"I didn't say anything about messing around, Dom. I saw the way you two looked at each other. What you did for her. I know what she means to you. And you're just going to let her go?"

"I have to. She can't live this kind of life." I wave my hand in the air and sit back with a heavy weight on my chest. My hand runs down my face.

"Then give it up. If you think she's worth it."

"Give up the *familia*?" I can't believe what he's saying.

He purses his lips and sucks in a deep breath. "That's not what I meant. Get outta this here. Lay low. Get a boring ass day job with your degree. Do what you gotta do."

"Do what I gotta do?" I swallow hard. I don't like subtleties. I'd rather be smacked hard in the face with a blunt answer.

"I can't tell you any more than that, son. I will say Sunday dinner will always be at our house with the family."

"What's that have to do with anything?"

"Just make sure she knows that's a condition." *The only condition.* I stare at my Pops for a moment.

He gives me a smile and rises, fixing his suit jacket. "Your ma liked her. That's a huge victory there."

"I don't think it's as easy as you think, Pops." I stand up and give him a quick hug with a firm grip.

"If you want her to be yours, then you take her; what's so hard about that?" He smirks at me and then turns his back and leaves.

I watch the door close shut. If only it could really be that easy.

BECCA

*T*he dishes in the large steel sink crash together, and it draws my eyes up to the busboy. He's new. His arms are skinny as twigs. His eyes dart to mine and then back to the dishes.

"Break any?" I ask lightheartedly to put him at ease. I try to muster up a smile, but I can't.

"Don't think so." He pulls them out carefully, one by one.

At least it wasn't at the bar. That would've been a pain in the ass. Like yesterday. I close my eyes and breathe in deep. I wish I still had Vicky here. She was one of the managers Dom put in charge while I was "recovering from a fall." I roll my eyes and rub my shoulder as I walk out of the kitchen to the back room. I had to dump her though. I didn't trust her or the others. I felt like they were always watching me. Like they were going to report back to him.

Just thinking about him has my chest tightening with pain. I haven't heard a word. Nothing. Tears prick my eyes. I know I didn't want it, well I didn't want to want it. But fuck, I do want *him*. I shake my head and try to calm myself down. My throat seems to close up every time I think about him. It physically hurts me. I can't explain it. It wasn't supposed to be this way. I lean against the wall of my office and lay my head against the wall. I can't fucking breathe in here.

After a moment I push open the door to go outside. It groans, and the bright light makes my eyes squint. But at least it's fresh air. Or as fresh as it can be for a tiny ass alley between my restaurant and the gallery next door. I prop the door open with a brick and take a seat on the crates a few feet down, closer to the empty street and away from the dumpsters.

I wish I was over this by now. Over him. Everything seems so much harder since I left him. Exhaustion weighs down on me. But it's not just physical; I'm emotionally overwhelmed.

"You alright, doll?" My body jumps at the sound of a deep, masculine voice in the silent alley. A small scream of shock forces its way out of my mouth and my hands fly up to hold it in. *Dom.* He walks toward me down the alley with a sexy ass smirk on his face.

My heart swells in my chest, and the tears flow. I can't hold them back. Fuck my hormones. Fuck my emotions. I don't care.

He takes another step toward me, and I fall into his embrace. My body feels weak; my wretched heart hurts. "Don't cry, doll." His strong arms hold me tight, and I want to pretend I can have this forever. Just the thought combined with his masculine smell and his soothing strokes on my back has my heart beating calmly and my body relaxing. It feels so right, so natural.

This is what I've needed.

"What's wrong?" He pulls back slightly to look down at me. I don't even lift my head; I keep my chin firmly against his chest and just breathe. My fingers dig into his back, holding him to me, but also fearing he's going to leave. I've never felt so weak and vulnerable. I don't know why I can't stop, but I just don't want to let go.

I shake my head against his chest and press my lips together. After a long moment, I answer, "You shouldn't be here."

"I want you, Becca." I finally pull away and stare into his eyes. I want him too, but I can't.

"You know I can't." I whisper the words. I know he understands. He has to understand.

"But you want to. I can make it right, doll. I'm just asking for a chance."

I want to. He's right about that. My breathing grows shallow. I open my mouth, but nothing comes out. A chance. Just one chance. Could I risk that?

"Let's make a bet," he says with a grin.

I snort and reply, "I'm not stupid; you're a bookie."

"It can be anything you want, babe." His smile softens, and he kisses my lips tenderly. "Just bet me." His lips barely touch mine.

"What do you get if you win?" I ask him with clear hesitation in my voice.

His hand travels to my ass and squeezes as he says, "You know what I want." I repress my moan and try to ignore how my core heats at his playful touch. I shake my head and bite down on my bottom lip to restrain my smile.

"Well, what do I get if I win?" I finally ask, looking up at him through my thick lashes.

My voice is breathy, and I wish it wasn't. I wish I wasn't so desperate for his comfort, but I am.

Dom's hand cups my chin, and his thumb runs along my bottom lip. His body brushes against mine as he takes a step forward, backing me into the brick wall. "Exactly what you want." My hands go to his chest, and I push him back slightly.

"Not here," I whisper into his mouth as his hands push my blouse up my waist. The cool air feels so wrong against my heated skin.

"You don't want me to fuck you against this wall, doll?" My pussy clenches with need, and moisture gathers in my core. Fuck yes I want it. "I need you, babe; it's been too long since I've had my dirty girl."

"I can't." I tilt my neck farther as he kisses down my throat to my shoulder. This is so bad, so wrong. But I want it. His breath, his kisses, his touch – they're everything I want. I want him to take me however he wants, whenever he wants. I want my back to scrape against the hard brick as he pounds into me. I can picture it so clearly. His hips keep me pinned with his hard-as-steel erection digging into my belly.

And then he stops. I nearly fall over from the loss of his touch. My body tilts forward, and I stumble in my heels and barely catch my footing. I hear Dom's hard steps on the pavement, his body slamming into something. Another man. I hear them barrel into the wall and fall hard on the ground. Fuck! Someone saw us! Shit, shit, shit.

I adjust my shirt and try to see what's going on. What the fuck is going on? I try to catch my breath.

"Dom, stop!" I yell out as I watch him push the man down on his stomach and twist his arm behind his back. I don't know him. No one fucking comes out here. My body heats with anxiety.

Dom grips his arm and shoves it up in an unnatural way. The man's face distorts with pain. Holy fuck! Fuck, he's really hurting him. "Stop!" I screech with a hoarse voice. My hands cover my mouth when I spot the gun falling from the stranger's grasp. Then I see what he's wearing; leather gloves, all black. *A gun complete with a silencer.* My heart drops to my gut. He was going to shoot Dom. My body goes cold and numb.

My feet naturally take a step back, and my body bumps into the brick wall. I can't turn away. I can't stop watching. I feel paralyzed as Dom relentlessly smashes the man's face into the concrete. The crushing sound of his bones crashing against the unforgiving ground makes me sick to my stomach. Oh my God. My breathing comes in short, shallow pants. I can't. I can't watch this.

"Not you! Wasn't you!" The man tries to speak. His face is distorted, covered in dark red with more blood bubbling from his busted lips.

"Who? Tell me who." Dom speaks hard and low into the man's ears, but I hear it as though he screamed it.

"The girl." *The girl.* Me.

"Who hired you?" Dom asks. My head goes dizzy watching the scene play out.

"Jack." The man's head sways, and then he takes in a hiss of breath as Dom pulls his arm back even further. And then Dom lifts the gun to the back of his head and pulls the trigger. The man falls forward, the raw bullet hole open and spilling blood onto the pavement.

My vision flashes before my eyes over and over again. No sound. No warning. He was alive, and now he's dead.

My eyes widen as I watch Dom shove the man behind the dumpster. There's blood everywhere. Holy fuck. Holy fuck. Holy fuck. Time passes in slow motion. It doesn't feel real. This can't be real.

The bang of the thin metal walls of the dumpster brings me back from the haze.

He's dead. I stare at the limp body. He was going to kill me. But Dom killed him first.

My throat closes, and I struggle to breathe. "What are we going to do?" my voice croaks. He's dead. Dom just shot him. "It was in self-defense." My voice raises, "You were only defending me!"

"Hush, doll." Dom walks to me with ease, gripping both of my arms at my side. "You don't have to worry about anything. The next people who come down this alley will be my clean-up crew. I already sent them a message."

What the fuck? I'm shaken and on edge. My body shivers as though I'm freezing. This is why we can't be together. *But if he hadn't been here...* My shaking hands cover my mouth. I would've died. I cry into my hands and barely realize Dom's dragging me away.

DOM

*T*hat motherfucker! He's dead. And if they knew, if any of them knew – they're all fucking dead. I should've known better. My heart's still beating frantically in my chest. My blood's pumping with rage, but more than that, fear.

What if I hadn't been there? I was going to wait till she was done with work, till she'd put Jax to bed. I didn't want to risk her getting so damn worked up over me until she was alone. But then I saw her. I just had to go to her.

She was going through the motions; that's all. Her beautiful plump lips never turned up into her gorgeous smile. Every time her head fell in the slightest I swore she was crying. How could I not go to her, knowing how hurt she was?

And it's a good fucking thing I did.

My hands grip the steering wheel, making my knuckles turn white. He was going to kill her. He didn't even fucking know her. A kill for pay. I saw him over her shoulder. Waiting. I fucking know who that bastard was, JD. He never asked questions, just got the job done. He wasn't family; he was an outside hire.

Well now he's fucking dead.

My body tingles and then heats. I need to beat the piss out of something.

Like I did De Luca and his crew. I need to do that to Jack. He's probably at the bistro with my father.

Sitting together. Maybe my father knew. My heart crumples in agony, and I shake my head slightly in denial. My eyes peek at Becca, but thankfully she didn't notice. I don't want her to know how fucked up I am over this. That's not the way it's supposed to work.

My poor doll is staring out of the window wide-eyed. She hasn't fucking moved. Hasn't said a word. I wish she hadn't heard that, that she was the one he was supposed to kill. I wish she didn't know. It fucking kills me.

I grab my phone and dial my father. I can't wait to ask him in person. I need to know. I have to know right fucking now. The thought that he'd do that kills me. I just saw him yesterday. I don't understand why he'd do this to me. I shake my head again harder as the phone rings, and this time she sees. Her eyes are wide with worry.

"It's gonna be alright, babe." I breathe in deep and give her a forced smile. Her eyes fall, and she leans her head against the headrest, seemingly staring at nothing. Her lack of a response worries me.

"Dom. What's going on?" Pops answers like it's a normal call.

"You alone?" I want to make sure there's no one around to hear. Just in case. I don't want Jack to know I'm coming.

Pops talks over the phone to someone and the line is muffled for a moment, and then he comes back on and says, "All clear, Dom. What's going on?"

I swallow the lump in my throat and push the words through, "Did you know?" That's really what it comes down to. It's what I need to know.

I hear Pops move around on the other line, and then he speaks lower. "Dom, what's wrong? Where are you?" I stay silent for a moment and take in another deep breath. "You alright, Dom? You need something?"

"Did you know about the time on her?" Time is code for hit. The code varies, but right now that's what it means. His questions and his tone make me believe he didn't, but I want to hear him say it. I look at Becca with sad eyes; she's confused for a moment, and then tears fall down her cheeks and she quickly wipes them away. I know she understands.

"On your girl?" The sadness in his voice is mixed with disbelief. Then his anger comes through. "We'll find them, Dom."

"I know who." The callous words leave my lips without permission. I grind my teeth, waiting for him to ask.

"Who? We'll collect now." There's a moment of silence. "Is-" He pauses, and it's quiet for a second. "Is she alright, Dom?"

"Yeah. I was there."

"She's good?" The hope in his voice relaxes every doubt I had.

"Yeah, I got her."

"Thank fuck. Dom, you are one lucky son of a bitch. You know that?" I can hear the relief in his voice, but still there's pain.

"You all at the bistro now?" I ask.

"We're here, Dom. We'll get 'em."

"It was Jack." My father's silent. It fucking kills me to say it. We grew up with him. He was always there. The last few years, not so much. But growing up, he was like a second father to me and Vince. Tears prick at my eyes. I feel so fucking betrayed.

"Are you sure?" Pops' voice is deadly and low.

"That's what the fucker said. It was him." I straighten in my seat and brush it off as best I can. It's not the first time someone in the family has done some stupid shit. But it's the first time it's been directed at me.

"Jack's here. I'll question him and take care of it." I shake my head. That's not good enough.

"I wanna see him. I wanna look him in the eyes and know why."

"You know why, Dom; she knows a lot of shit." Before I can respond, he adds, "Doesn't make it right in the least. He had his orders. He'll pay the price. I can't guarantee I'm gonna wait for you, Dom."

"I gotta get her home first." I can't bring her there.

"I know. You go take care of her."

"I wanna be there," I say one more time. I feel like he's not going to listen. Like he's gonna take him out himself.

"I understand. But I can't give you that right now, Dom. Just get her home and safe, and then call me. If I can, I'll come over."

I nod and say, "Alright," and hang up and try to relax somewhat. But I can't. I can't relax. A kill is a kill. It fucking sucks, and I've seen it over and over again. This one is different. This one's personal. That fucker was going to kill my girl. And Jack arranged it.

A long moment passes with silence. Jack's a dead man, and my Becca's safe. That's what matters.

"Babe, we're going to get through this." I reach across the console and grab her hand. I rub soothing circles on her soft skin. She keeps alternating between looking at me and out the window. I can tell she's scared, but other than that I have no idea what's going on in her head.

"The piece of shit that called the hit had no right." I try to keep her gaze, but she doesn't hold it. "Babe, you're safe. No one's ever going to hurt you again."

"You said that before." She barely speaks her words, and it shreds me. 'Cause it's true.

I wanted to go there and win her heart back with the promise of safety. And look what fucking happened. "It's over. I promise, everything will be fine, doll." Raising her small hand to my lips, I plant a small kiss on her tender wrist.

Her beautiful hazel eyes find mine, but all I can see in them is disbelief.

BECCA

"*W*here is he?" Dom's furious. His corded muscles flex, and his voice echoes in the foyer. "You brought him here?" he asks incredulously as he slams the door. My body jumps from the loud bang. I don't even know how I got here. I feel like I just woke up from a dark clouded haze.

"Calm down, I wouldn't bring him to your home." His father's voice is calm, but it doesn't match his appearance.

I'm frozen at the door. I've only known this man for a week, and already two people have tried to kill me. One to get back at him, and one to protect him. My limbs feel limp and weak. The reality weighs heavy on me.

I wanted him. I was willing to try, to give it a chance like he asked.

"I just wanted to tell your Becca that she has nothing to worry about, regardless of whatever happens between you two." Although Dante's talking to Dom, his eyes are on me. He's obviously concerned and I suppose that's nice of him, but it just makes me feel uncomfortable.

I take in a staggered inhale and try to walk to them in the center of the foyer, but I can't. My feet are planted firmly in place. I'm stuck. Everything's so fucked.

His father takes heavy steps toward me, eating up the space between us. He's dressed in a suit with no tie. He looks distinguished, like a CEO. Nothing like the mob boss he is. "Everything's alright now. I promise you, no harm will come your way."

"Is he dead?" The question falls out of my mouth. I want to know. I *need* to know. I feel like there's a target on my back.

His eyes dart to Dom, and Dom gives a quick nod. "He will be."

"I'm gonna make him pay, doll." Dom's voice is hard and determined.

Make him pay. The images flash before me. The bullet hole, his bloodied face. I look away and cross my arms.

I change my mind.

I don't want to hear. I get it now. I understand why they keep their women out of it. I want out of it. I can't handle this shit. My mind keeps replaying the vision of the man's head smashing against the ground and falling limp with a bullet hole in the back of his skull. My body heats, and I feel faint. I swallow thickly and put my hand on my forehead.

I'm not okay. Ice pricks my skin, and my vision goes fuzzy.

"She's going into shock."

I shake my head. "I'm fine." Dom mumbles something under his breath, but I don't hear it.

He lifts me in his arms and carries me away. I don't even try to protest. "Just relax, babe; I got you."

* * *

I FEEL SO FUCKING GROGGY. I rub my eyes and sit up in Dom's bed. Fuck, my head is killing me. I rub my temples as the pain radiates.

I rub my eyes and take a look around, and then I remember. My fists grip the sheets, and I sit up straighter with wide eyes. *Dom.* I need Dom.

"Relax, doll. I'm here." Dom walks into the room with a glass of water in one hand. "How are you feeling?"

"I don't know." I feel like shit. Everything feels like shit. I take the glass of water and take a sip, and then another. I greedily drain it, feeling a million times better.

He sits on the edge of the bed with his body turned toward me as I tap my nail against the glass.

"I can't do this, Dom. I can't run and hide. I can't put Jax through this shit." It physically hurts to say the words, but it's true. I need to end this.

"Tough, you need me now." His hard gaze dares me to disagree.

"That's not fair." My voice breaks.

"Life's not fair, babe."

"You got me into this shit, and now I can't leave." I shake my head and cover my face with my hands.

"That shit is over and done with." He grips my wrists and wraps my arms around his neck and pulls me into his lap. "That's not why you need me. You fucking love me, doll. You need me to love you, too."

I can't deny it; I love him. "But I can't."

"I'm not letting you go." Hearing his conviction eases my pain. He's making this decision. "No one's gonna fuck you the way I do."

A sad smile plays at my lips, and I huff a laugh as I wipe my eyes with the sleeve of my shirt.

"Can we leave? Please?" If he could take us away, I'd leave right now.

"You can't stop being family, doll." Fresh tears prick at my eyes, and my face heats. I should know better.

"I can't have Jax around this." I can't. I won't. That's not going to change.

"He won't be." Dom's answer is quick. "I'm selling the business and getting a real job. I'm backing away from all of this shit." His fingers grip my chin, and he forces me to look him in the eyes as he says, "You want me to stop working for my dad, then I'll do it. If anyone can leave the *familia*, I can."

I shake my head. I know that's not how it works. "I have to go." I need to leave him. Before he leaves his family, before he risks his life.

"I'm not letting you leave. I told you; you're mine." I love how determined his words are. But it's not enough.

"I can't." My heart clenches and hollows with pain.

"You can. And you will. We'll do this together. And after today, I can't let you go. I refuse to let you leave me, doll."

My head shakes uncontrollably. "I just can't have Jax raised like this." My chest heaves for air as heat washes through my body. "I don't want this for him." Hot tears leak down my face.

"I know, doll." His thumb brushes a stray tear away as he looks at me with a sad smile.

"You know when I knew my family was a mob family?" he asks. "I found out when I was ten." A humorless laugh leaves him. "The journalists from the papers waited for me outside of school." A sad smile pulls at his lips. "I thought my pops ran a restaurant, that he was an entrepreneur."

His smile vanishes, and his hand leaves me. "The reporters told me he was a crook, a murderer." He says the words with distaste, practically spitting them. His eyes fall, and he swallows thickly. "I had no idea until then." He shifts and looks uncomfortably at the door as he adds, "Ma cried her eyes out. She couldn't even talk to me. Pops had to take me aside and tell me he had a business and when I wanted to know about it, he'd tell me." He forces a tight smile. "I never asked." He shakes his head. "Kids were always a little afraid of me at school, but other than that I think most things were normal. As far as I know."

He takes a deep breath and says, "The only time I thought my father was disappointed in me was when I told him I wanted to go to college for statistics. He never said it, but there was a look on his face. I asked him about it later, and he said he was so ashamed of himself in that moment. That he'd planned something else for me, and that it never occurred to him I deserved better."

"Got into Stanford, got my degree and a respectable job, and I fucking hated it. I can't lie, doll, I don't fucking like working." His tone makes a small laugh leave my lips. "So I came home, and Pops told me no. He told me I was more than a gangster. He told me I'd be better than him." A wicked grin grows across his face. "He was pissed when I told him I was a bookie. Didn't tell him for nearly a year. But I was having some problems and needed his help. That's when he let me in and gave me the books."

"What I'm saying is," he takes my hand in his and kisses the back of it, "I'm not the boss, doll. Our kids aren't gonna know until we tell them. And they don't have to be a part of this." His eyes plead with me to believe him. "They don't. I promise you." He kisses the back of my hand again and his sad eyes return to mine as he adds, "But if you want to leave, we'll go. Ma and the rest of the family will understand. You've already been through too much." He shakes his head with his eyes on the floor. We don't let our-" I crush my lips against his, and they're hard at first, caught by surprise, but he molds them to mine and then parts my lips with his tongue. I push my chest against his, needing to feel him. Needing his love more than my next breath.

I break our kiss and gasp for air. "I love you, Dom." Tears fall from the corners of my eyes. "I'm scared, but I fucking love you." I shake my head as he gently grabs my face with his hands.

His forehead rests against mine as his lips come down to meet me. "Tell me you'll stay with me. I promise I'll love you till the day I die."

"Yes, Dom. I love you. I just want to love you." His arms wrap around my body, pressing my breasts against his hard chest.

"I love you, doll. I love you and your son, so fucking much." My heart swells and pounds against my chest.

I know he does.

EPILOGUE

Becca
Three Years Later

My house smells like heaven. I dip the wooden spoon into the sauce and blow lightly. I don't want to burn my tongue again like I did last time. I'm so damn impatient. I hesitantly taste it. Something's off. My lips purse, and my tongue clucks against the roof of my mouth.

"Your mother is a liar." I narrow my eyes at Dom, who smirks at me. "This is definitely not right." He walks over to me, looking hot as hell. Bare feet, jeans and no tee shirt. His muscles ripple as he strides toward me. I don't even bother trying to hide the fact that my eyes are glued to his body. Why should I give a fuck? If I wanna stare down my husband, I'm going to do exactly that.

His large hand wraps around mine, and he takes a lick of the sauce seductively. Watching his tongue take a languid lick makes my pussy clench. I bite my bottom lip to keep in the moan as his hand travels to my hip. He gives me a cocky grin. That bastard. He knows what he's doing. We had a quickie this morning… and this afternoon.

"It's perfect, doll, your taste buds are just all fucked up with your hormones." He rubs my swollen belly and leans in to kiss me. I part my lips and moan into his mouth, greedily accepting his kiss. He pulls back and I'm slow to open my eyes, I'm just so tired. Not tired for sex though. My libido is ridiculous.

"Gross!" I smile and look over to the doorway of the kitchen, seeing Jax sticking his tongue out.

"Oh, yeah? I'll remind you that kissing is gross when you get older. Only six years old, guess kissing is pretty gross to you, huh?" Dom walks back to the island, leaving me with a view of his perfect ass. He puts his hand out and Jax gives him his homework, just like he does every day.

"That's my boy. Math is on point." Dom shuffles through the sheets before turning to look at Jax. "Where's English?"

"We had a substitute today," Jax answers with his chin resting on the counter. "Did it all during free period." I smile and turn back to stir the sauce and take another taste. I'm gonna tell Linda I lost the recipe and see if she gives me the same one. I smirk at my thought as Jax gathers his homework.

I dump the sauce over the meatballs and put them in the oven. I'll fry them at the end. Just like she does. They're the restaurant's best dish now that we fry them. I don't do much now that we have the managers, but I want our sauce to be the best. And I have the final say when it comes to the details.

I brace my hands on the small of my back and stretch. This little one better drop soon. It's getting hard to breathe.

"Alright, you hanging out with Mickey tonight?"

"Yup!" Jax answers, shoving the papers into his backpack.

"Just remember-" I start, but Jax cuts him off.

"I know, Mom! I'll call when I get there."

"Hey there, watch it." Dom scolds Jax even though he has a smile on his face. "You be respectful to your mother."

Jax sighs, "Sorry, Mom. Sorry, Dad. I just must be going through some-thing." I have to turn and face the stove before I crack up laughing.

"Yeah, okay. Get outta here." Dom sends him away with a smile, and I finally turn around and lean against Dom.

His hands instantly go to my swollen belly, rubbing soothing circles. "How you feeling, doll?"

"Like I want this baby out." I do. I'm so done with being pregnant.

"Two more days." He kisses my belly. "Then finals will be done, and I won't have classes." I smile and let out an easy sigh.

"I know, Professor Valetti." I lean down and give him a slow kiss on his lips. "This little one is already a daddy's girl. She's listening to you, not me."

The baby monitor goes off on the counter; Ethan's up. I check the clock and yup, it's been two hours. "That was a good nap." I yawn and pick it up and see our two-year-old rolling around and playing in his crib.

He laughs a low, deep chuckle against my lips. "Thank you, doll."

I pull back with a questioning look. "What'd you do that you're thanking me?"

He laughs and shakes his head. "Thank you for loving me."

My heart melts, and I mold my lips to his. He's so fucking sweet. "Always." I rub my hand along his stubble and give him a chaste kiss. "Love you."

"I love you too, doll."

The End

* * *

Keep reading to start His Hostage, Vince Valetti's story.

HIS HOSTAGE

SYNOPSIS

From *USA Today* bestselling author Willow Winters comes a HOT mafia, standalone romance.

I was innocent before him, and he wanted nothing more than to ruin me.
    And if I'm honest, I wanted him too, even knowing I shouldn't.

I knew he was a bad man, it doesn't take more than a single look to know it.
    Dark eyes and a charming smile that's made to fool girls like me.
    Still, I caved; I gave into temptation.

And then I saw something I shouldn't have.
    Wrong place, wrong time. The mafia doesn't let witnesses simply walk away.

Regret has a name, and it's Vincent Valetti.
    He won't let them kill me, but he's not going to let me go either.

PROLOGUE

* * *

*E*lle
    I already regret this. I walk farther into the office as he shuts the door with a loud click. Everyone must've seen me walk back here with him and they're going to know what we're doing. I feel like a cheap whore. His hands wrap around my waist and pull my ass into him. His hard erection digs into my back. My core heats as he leaves an open-mouthed kiss on my neck. His hot breath runs chills down my body, and I cave. I *need* this. My body molds to his, and my hands reach behind me and around his neck. My fingers tangle in his hair. I don't care what they think. For once, I just want to feel good.

VINCE
    Good girl. I knew if I just got her alone I'd be able to loosen her up. She's in need, and I know exactly what to do. My fingers tease her skin as I pull the camisole over her head. I have to pull away for a moment, and she takes the chance to turn around. She stands on her tiptoes to crush her lips against mine. I part her lips with my tongue and taste her, sucking on

her bottom lip while I unhook her bra. I break away, and drop to my knees to unbuckle her shorts and pull them down. Lace panties. They'll be easy to tear right off.

MY BREATHING IS LOUD, nearly frantic, and my heart beats wildly in my chest. I can't believe I'm doing this. He tears through my panties with his thumbs and tosses them carelessly to the side, not taking his eyes off me. Another wave of arousal soaks my core as I clench my thighs. He grins and grips my hips, forcing my pussy into his face while he breathes in deep. I'd die of embarrassment, but his loud groan and languid lick make my eyes close, and my mouth part in ecstasy. He stands up and pulls my bra off of me, and the straps tickle my arms as I watch his eyes focus on my breasts. My nipples harden under his lust-filled gaze.

So fucking hot. I knew she was beautiful, but damn, I have to take a moment to appreciate just how gorgeous she is. I grip her thighs and lift her up so I can put her ass on the edge of the desk. I lean down and suck her hardened, pale pink nipple into my mouth. Her head falls back, and a soft moan falls from her lips.

HE PULLS BACK and lets my nipple pop out of his mouth before getting onto his knees. Holy shit. He's gonna go down on me. My breath stills in my lungs and I try to close my legs from mortification, but his hands on my inner knees stop them and he pushes me wide open to stare at my pussy. My cheeks flame and I can't look because I'm so fucking horrified.

"You want me to stop, sweetheart?" I know she doesn't. I bet she's never been taken care of like this before. She's in for a treat. She bites her lip and shakes her head. I smile at her, and then focus my attention back to her needy, delicious cunt. Her pussy lips are glistening with arousal and I fucking love it. I lean down and take a long lick from her entrance to the clit. So sweet. I flick her throbbing clit with my tongue and she finally relaxes under me. I smile into her heat and grip her ass tight, angling her into a position that's good for me.

. . .

OH MY GOD. It feels so good. I have to focus on staying quiet. My teeth dig into my bottom lip as I shamelessly rock my pussy into his face. His tongue massages against my clit as his fingers dip into me and curl, hitting my G-spot and making my back arch. Holy fuck!

She's loving what I'm doing; her body is so damn responsive, just like I knew she would be. I can't wait to get into that pussy and watch those tits bounce. They aren't the biggest breasts I've ever seen, but they're perky and fit in my hands just right. I bite down on her clit, not hard, just enough to send her over the edge as her pussy clamps down on my fingers. She's so fucking tight. Her pussy is going to feel like heaven on my dick.

MY THIGHS SQUEEZE around his head. I want to stop, but I can't control my body. A cold sweat breaks out along my skin and I feel paralyzed as my body ignites with waves of pleasure.

Her arousal soaks my hand. I keep my fingers in that tight cunt, stroking her front wall and sucking her clit to get every bit of her orgasm out. I don't stop until she's lying limp on the table. I smile and gently place a hand on her trembling thigh. That should calm her ass down.

That pussy's soft, hot, and wet. And waiting to be filled. I unzip my jeans and let them drop to the floor while I stroke my cock. It's begging to be wrapped in her heat.

THE SOUND of his zipper makes my eyes pop open and pulls me from my sated daze. Oh fuck! My heart pounds in my chest, and my breathing comes in shallow pants. I push the hair out of my face and swallow thickly. I'm going to lose my virginity. I don't want it to happen this way.

She props herself up and closes her legs. My brow furrows with confusion and my body heats with anger. What the fuck is she doing? She leaving me high and dry? That'd be a fucking first. I know she enjoyed me feasting on her pussy. She'll fucking love what I can do to her while she's impaled on my dick.

I CLEAR my throat and nervously try to reach his gaze. A violent blush reaches my cheeks and burns my chest. I just don't want it like this. My pussy is begging to let him fuck me, and my dark fantasies want to come to life. I want him to take me and pound into me until I'm screaming. But I can't pull the trigger.

"You all right, sweetheart?" His question holds a hint of admonishment. My mind goes wild with the thought of him holding me down and fucking me exactly how he wants. Punishing me for refusing him. But I don't want to refuse him. I want to give him pleasure, too. I bite my bottom lip to steady the need to tremble. I scoot to the edge of the desk and drop easily to my knees.

She immediately takes me into her inviting mouth and sucks the head of my dick. I groan and let my head fall back and spear my fingers through her hair, putting easy pressure on the back of her head. Her hot, eager mouth feels so fucking good. She takes me in deeper and massages her tongue along the underside of my dick. Her head bobs on my cock and her cheeks hollow out from how hard she's sucking. I let her go at her own pace, but I really want to shove myself down her throat. I hold back though. She wouldn't like the things I wanna do to her.

A SICK FANTASY of him skull-fucking me flashes before my eyes, and I find myself taking him deeper than I'm able, trying to choke myself on his dick. My throat closes around his thick length and he pumps his hips in short, shallow thrusts. I pull back and breathe quickly while his hands clench into fists in my hair. As soon as I have air I take him in my mouth and do it again.

She's acting like she fucking loves this. She pulls off again and licks the underside of my dick, stroking me with her hand while she licks my length. Her wide, blue eyes stare up at me. She's looking for approval. "Baby, you keep doing that, and I'm gonna cum." Just watching her, my balls draw up and my spine tingles, but I hold back the urge to cum. I'm not done with her yet.

I'VE NEVER DONE this before, but I've read so many romance novels and articles... and watched so much porn. I know I need to shove him deep into my throat and swallow. I do it again and choke a little, but as soon as I can, I work him into the very back of my throat until I can't breathe at all. My hands rest at my thighs. I want to massage his balls, or push against his taint searching for that little spot I read about that's supposed to make a man go off, but instead I dig my fingers into my thighs. I pull back and take a deep breath. I feel spit drip down my chin and I quickly wipe it away.

She's too fucking good. I want in that hot pussy, but it's not going to happen. "Baby, I'm gonna cum." I get ready to pull away; I'm sure she's not the type of girl who's gonna want to swallow. Although, I didn't peg her to be so good at giving head either. The idea that's she's had practice pisses me off. I don't get jealous, but I don't fucking like that idea. Then my sweetheart does the sexiest fucking thing. She closes her eyes, sticks her tongue out flat under the head of my dick and pushes her breasts together.

I OPEN my eyes when I hear the sexiest groan I've ever heard and feel his hot cum on my breasts. I watch as waves splash against my breasts and it gives me the deepest satisfaction. I smile shyly and calm my breathing. I did this to him.

I open my eyes and see her cute little smirk. "Lick it clean, sweetheart." My dick's still hard as her tongue darts out to lap up the bit of sticky cum left on my dick. She sits back on her heels, far more relaxed than she was before, and then she reaches for her clothes. I frown, and my heart drops a little in my chest. She's ready to leave? Already?

I FEEL a little sick knowing he's gonna want me out of here now that our little fling is over. Only a little though. That's what I'm telling myself, at least. I feel so dirty, but I love it. I watch in my periphery as he leans over the desk and then hands me some tissues to wipe off my chest. I give him a tight smile and quickly clean myself off. I want it again, but I don't think he's the type of guy that sticks with one girl. And I'm not going to give myself to someone who isn't going to want me after. I don't know what I was thinking. Regret starts to consume me, but I shake it off. I wanted this. I got exactly what I wanted.

"You got a lot of studying to do?" I ask, as I pull up my boxers and jeans. I know she's in a rush to get out, but I'll at least stay with her while she's out there. I'm sure they know we were back here fooling around, but I want them to give her the respect she deserves. I'm not gonna leave her for them to stare down and judge.

. . .

No way I'm staying here. I spot my bag sitting next to the door. I'll just sneak out the back. I shake my head at his question. "I'm pretty tired. I'm just gonna head home." The high I felt just moments ago is already waning, and I'm feeling more and more uncomfortable as I stand and adjust my shorts. I have no clue where my panties are. Not that it really matters since he destroyed them.

My eyes close as the denim push against my sensitive clit. Damn, I want him again. I want him inside of me. But not like this. I'm not going to lose my virginity like this. Not to someone I don't even know. The thought makes my gaze drop to the floor, and I try to swallow the shame creeping up on me.

Shit, I can see the regret. I don't fucking want that. I wanna see this girl again. I _need_ to have her cumming on my dick. I barely got a taste of her. "I'll drive you home, sweetheart."

I bite my bottom lip and grip the straps of my tote. I put it on my shoulder and nod. I wince as the straps bite down on my tender skin. Fucking hell, why'd I pack so damn much and walk the entire way here? He's quick to reach out and take it from me. It's a sweet gesture, and I don't expect it. I assume he's hoping to get into my pants when he drops me off. That sure as shit is not going to happen. I think about what's waiting for me at home and get all pissed off. I can't fucking believe how shitty my life has become. The reminder makes me close my eyes, and I try to will away the anger.

I don't like wherever her head has gone. Gently, I place my hand on her shoulder and squeeze slightly. "Stop it, Elle." Her eyes shoot up at me with daggers as she shoves my hand away.

"Just because we just did that," I say with anger as I motion to the desk, "does not mean that you have any right to tell me what to do." Immediately I regret my outburst. It's not his fault. Shit. I ruined this. Whatever this is. Was. Whatever, it's over with now.

What the fuck has gotten into her? I have half a mind to throw her ass on the desk and fuck that snarky attitude right out of her. I know just how

to do it, too. Deep and slow. I'd fucking torture the orgasms from her until she quits being like this. So damn defensive.

THIS WAS SUCH A FUCKING MISTAKE. I swing the door open and walk out as quickly as I can, leaving him behind. I keep walking, past the opening for the dining room of the bistro and straight ahead. There's got to be a door to get the fuck out of here where no one will see me. I twist the knob to what I think will be an exit and push the heavy door open.

I finally get a grip and go after her, determined to have her smart little mouth wrapped around my cock again. I take one step out of the office and bolt after her. Not that room! What the fuck is she doing?

HOLY FUCK! I gasp as my eyes widen at what I'm seeing, and instinctively take a step backwards, but my back hits a brick wall of muscle. Strong arms wrap around my waist and face, and a hand covers my mouth to mute the scream that's ripped from my throat.

God damn it. I can't believe this is happening. I hold her tight to me as she struggles in my grasp. I can't fucking believe she walked back here. Tommy and Anthony are staring back at me with looks of outrage.

I TRY TO SCREAM. I try to pull away. I need to do something, anything. Tears burn my eyes and my body heats, then goes numb with fear. Fuck! It's useless. He won't let me go. "Please!" I try to scream, but his hand stays clamped over my mouth. Tears fall helplessly down my heated cheeks as my body racks with sobs.

I wish I could let her go, but if I do, I know the family will have to get rid of her.

IF HE'D JUST LET me go, I wouldn't say anything.

She'd swear up and down not to talk, but it wouldn't be enough.

. . .

167

I'LL PLEAD WITH HIM, he has to believe me. I try to speak, but his hand pushes harder against my lips.

I wish I could believe her, but there's no way I can risk it. I tilt my head to the door, letting them know I'm taking her away.

MY FEET DRAG and stumble as he pulls me back into the office. I'll offer him anything. There has to be some way to convince him.

She hardly struggles against me as I close the door. I don't think there's any way I could convince the *familia* to let her go. Maybe there's a way.

I'M GOING to have to keep her until they're convinced.

She's my hostage now.

ELLE

Earlier that day...

$\mathcal{I}$ shift my weight and groan. This bag is freaking killing my shoulder. I don't know why I packed so many textbooks. I shoved all three in to my bag along with my laptop before I took off. Barely 15 minutes later, the straps are digging into my skin, making it feel raw and destroying my resolve to study. Part of me just wants to drop the bag and go to a bar. I'm so fucking pissed off. I shake off the bitter resentment and walk a little faster. I shouldn't have brought so much grad work. It's not like I'm in any mood to do it anyway. Not after fighting with my mother *again*.

I wish I didn't have to pay her fucking bills, so I could move back to my shitty little apartment. Her poor decisions keep fucking me over. I can't afford to live anywhere but with her now. Why the hell did she get a mortgage? Did she have to fuck me over like that? She had to know she couldn't afford it. I told her not to do it. I *knew* this would happen. And now I'm stuck here helping her ass out *again*, while she gets sober ... *again*.

I'm tired of sacrificing everything for her, but I just can't say no. I can't abandon her. Even if it's draining the life out of me. I'm just lucky I was able to transfer to a local university so I could move back in with her. I need to get my shit together so I don't fail. Playing catch-up is a bitch though. And I'm struggling to find the motivation.

I leave for not even three months and she ups and moves for some loser she met online. And then buys a house for *both* of them. I shake my head and bite the inside of my cheek while tears burn my eyes. I won't cry again. I push them back and concentrate on the anger. Mom has so many problems. It's fucked up.

I don't care that she thinks he's going to change and pay her back all the money that he squandered. It's not fucking acceptable. I don't trust this guy, just like I didn't trust the last, but does she listen to me? No. Not unless I'm rattling off my bank account number.

I know I saw a little place down the street on the way in that looked like a good spot to park my ass and attempt to relax. I just need to get out of that house so I can study without being so pissed. I groan and swing the tote over my shoulder to try to ease the pressure of the weight. After a few minutes of walking I calm down and smirk, remembering what bag I picked for today. The text on the tote reads, "My book club only reads wine labels." A smile grows on my face and I can't help it. I may have a completely new life now, a really shitty one, but at least I still have my old sense of humor.

After a few minutes I nearly consider turning back to get my car, but then I pick up the pace remembering that asshole is still there. She'd better kick his ass out. I told her I'm not going to help out financially if he's there. My fists clench harder as a long, strangled breath leaves me. Her words ring in my ear. "But you're on the mortgage!" She's such a bitch. And technically, a criminal for forging my name. But am I going to do anything about it? Nope. I always keep my mouth shut and do what's best. At least what's best for others. I don't even know what's best for me anymore.

I clench my jaw, and feel anger rising inside of me. It's not fucking right to be angry at her. Or is it? I just wish she were more responsible. I wish she weren't a fucking alcoholic. Why do I feel so remorseful for hating that she puts me through this? More than anything else, I feel guilty, like her being so unhappy is all my fault.

The place I saw on the drive to the house, Valetti's Italian Bistro, is just another block away. Hopefully they'll have some booth in the back that's empty. And alcohol. I could really use a drink. It's a little late for dinner, so maybe it'll be deserted and I can get my studying done in peace. I walk up the brick paved walkway and admire how rustic the place looks before opening the front door. This entire area has a small-town feel. I like it.

I'd like it more if I wasn't forced to be here though. As soon as I'm done with graduate school, I'm gone. I'll give Mom an allowance, maybe, and leave to find a place like this that isn't tainted. A nice, small town with family-owned restaurants just like this. I smile and let out an easy sigh. Everything's going to be alright. I just have to push through everything and work a little harder. And figure out a way to stop being a freaking enabler.

I take a quick glance around the place. It's dark for a restaurant, with a few dim lights placed symmetrically around the dining area. The walls are a soft cream, and the chairs and booths are a deep red. It's just my style. A little grin forms on my face as I spot an empty booth in the back on the right. It's directly across from another booth in the narrow room, almost like they belong to each other, but there's an obvious separation. I take quick strides to claim it.

I scoot into the seat and let the back of my tote hit the cushion before sliding the straps off my arm. Holy hell, that feels so much better. I rub my shoulder and look down to see two angry red marks from the straps. My lips purse. Next time I'm just bringing the laptop and my notes. And my car.

I lick my lips and pull out my laptop to bring up the syllabus. I downloaded it before I left, but I'm hoping this place has Wi-Fi. I breathe in deep and click to see. It's password protected. Damn. I don't like that. That means I have to talk to someone. And I really don't like that. I prefer to keep to myself. My eyes look past the brightly lit screen and search the place for a waitress, but there isn't one readily apparent. My shoulders sag with disappointment. Where the hell is the waitress? My eyes drift to directly in front of me and catch the gaze of one of the men sitting across the aisle in the opposite booth.

I quickly break eye contact, but I got a good enough look at him that heat and moisture pool in my core. He's fucking hot. Dark hair that's long enough to grab, and dark, piercing eyes to match. His tanned skin and high cheekbones are emphasized by the dim lighting.

I swallow thickly and hope the heat in my cheeks isn't showing as a violent red blush on my face. My eyes hesitantly look back at the man in question, and judging from the smirk on his face, he did see. Shit! I rest my left elbow on the table and attempt to casually cover my face while searching again for a waitress. I'm gonna need a drink to calm these nerves and focus on my work.

"Would you like a menu?" I turn to see a young man, very Italian-looking, with olive skin and bright green eyes waiting for my response. He seems nice enough and obviously still in high school.

"No thanks, just a drink please?"

"What can I get you?" he asks, and then gives me a forced smile. *Well, damn. I'm sorry me being here has rained on your parade.* I shake off the snide inner remark. Maybe he's just had a rough day. Like me.

"Citrus vodka and Sprite, please." *My favorite.* I smile brightly at him, hoping maybe a little sunshine will rub off on him, but it's a no-go. He gives me the same tight smile with a short nod, and leaves.

This place is odd. I never would've guessed that guy was a waiter. He was only wearing black jeans and a black tee. It's not the uniform I'd expect from a nice place like this. Or the service. A small, self-conscious part of me thinks maybe it's me. Maybe they don't like that I've come in here just to drink and study. There's a long bar on the other side of the room though. I close my eyes and shake my head slightly. It's not me. I'm always thinking that. I need to stop that. It's a bad habit.

I stretch out my shoulders and look back at the computer screen. I mumble a curse under my breath. The guy across the aisle distracted me, and I didn't even get to ask for the password when the waiter finally came around. Damn, I'll have to remember to ask when he comes back with my drink. I click my tongue on the roof of my mouth. He didn't even ask for ID. I wonder if I'm starting to look old. I purse my lips as I consider this thought. No fucking way. He's just a shit waiter.

Satisfied with that, I return to my syllabus and pull out the corresponding textbook and a yellow highlighter. I've got three chapters from this one to highlight, and then I'll write my notes down. I nod my head. That's a good plan. I may have transferred schools two years into my PhD, but I should be able to bang out all three classes this semester and be back on track. I've got Molecular and Cell Biology up first. I cringe a bit. It's all just so much fucking memorizing that I'll never ever use again. This may be a long fucking study hour. Correction. Hours.

My heart sinks in my chest at the thought of wasting the night like this. I'm so tired of late nights in the lab or studying. I've alienated everyone in my life. My "social life" consists of bailing my mom out of jail and talking to my primary investigator about our research. I don't even want to pursue the summer internship I was offered. I thought I'd love doing cancer research, but my only choices at this point are working with either cells or animals. And neither one is tempting. I have no clue why I'm still working my ass off for this. But if I let it go, what do I have left? Without my career, I've merely wasted years of my life hiding from reality. The thought depresses me to the core.

"Whatcha doing, sweetheart?" My body jolts as I hear the question, and I turn my head to stare at the Italian Stallion that sneaked up on me.

Hearing his masculine voice and watching his corded muscles ripple as he moves to sit across from me in my booth brings back that initial desire, full fucking force. My pussy heats and I clench my thighs. Holy hell. His muscles are rock fucking hard, and there isn't an ounce of fat on his body. His dark eyes pierce into me. I break away from his gaze and curse my hormones for making me so horny. Not fucking fair. I feel a deep urge to just fuck my frustrations away.

I don't need sex. I've never had it, never done the dirty deed, but no one *needs* sex. I bite my lip and feel my shoulders turn inward as doubt creeps in. How the hell would I know if it would help? I've never had the courage to go through with it.

I can't believe he's sitting with me, but at the same time, I don't want to be hit on. I'm sure he's just trying to get lucky. I don't have time for this. I have to catch up on my studying so I don't fall behind even more. But I find my eyes drifting down his body the way I imagine his would trail down mine. His white tee shirt is pulled taut over his muscles. My eyes dart to meet his as I belatedly realize that I'm blatantly staring. A blush blazes in my cheeks, and my stomach drops.

I nervously tuck my hair back behind my ears and lick my lips. I drop my eyes, and focus steadily on the white tablecloth for a moment. I clear my throat and gather the courage to look Mr. Hunk in the eyes. "I have to study." I'm surprised I had the courage to say anything at all, and that my voice was mostly steady. I wish I weren't so dismissive though. It came out a bit shorter than I would have liked. I don't want him to think I'm some bitch. It's not that. I'm just awkward, and I really do need to study.

"What's your name?" he asks.

"Elle," I respond quickly, and try to keep my voice steady. But it yelps slightly because of my nerves. Fuck! I sound like a damn squeaky mouse. I am a grown woman, damn it! I clear my throat again and wish my drink were here. My hair cascades down from behind my ears, and I nervously reach up to tuck it back into place and take a breath.

This is a bad idea. I'm not stupid; I need to stop this shit. He's trouble with a capital T, and I'm not in any position to handle him.

"I'm Vince. What are you studying, sweetheart?"

Vince. I like that name. It suits him well.

I consider answering him, but he just wants into my pants. And I need to study. I know this, yet I can't help getting so wound up and hot for him. All fucking week I've been miserable. Hating my life. Hating how I let my mother pressure me into giving up everything I had going for me so I can be her rock. Just like she always fucking does. I haven't done one thing for myself in so long. Not one reckless thing *ever* that I can think of. Nothing I wanted to do purely out of desire.

Would it be so bad? Would it really be so wrong to just flirt a bit? Flirting. My lips press into a line. I don't even know how to flirt. So yeah, it would be a bad idea.

VINCE

I'm so fucking bored. I haven't done a damn thing all day. I sit back
in my seat at the bistro and stretch my legs. I love sitting here at
the booth – at my booth – just relaxing. But only when I've earned it. Today, I
haven't earned a damn thing. I may need to run by the shipping docks to make
sure everything is set up to run smoothly, but other than that, my to-do list is
short. I pull out my iPhone from my jeans and sigh. I can at least check the
stocks.

Joe leans over to look at my phone and laughs. "Thought you were
checking out those nude pics again, not that stupid shit." I smirk at him, not
bothering to give a verbal response, and get back to my portfolio.

First off, Leah's pictures are no longer on my phone. And they never
should've been there. Fucking nosy prick saw them the second they came
through. I deleted them without even looking, but he hasn't forgotten.

She knew it was only for one night. Desperation doesn't look good on
anyone, and I'm not the kind of guy who commits. I frown, thinking about
how she should have more respect for herself. I told her I didn't want a relationship. It was a quick, dirty fuck and that's it. It was months ago. Thank
fuck she finally let it go and moved on to someone else.

Secondly, my portfolio isn't stupid shit. It's a moneymaker. A real fucking
good moneymaker that rivals what I get from the *familia*. But Joe's not gonna

get that. Most of these guys will never understand. They don't want any responsibility, or have any ambition. They want easy work where they don't have to learn a damn thing, just listen to orders. And that's why I'm the underboss, and not any of them. If you're not hungry for success, you'll never get it.

A grin grows across my face as I watch the door open and see a beautiful blonde walk in like she belongs here. This is a small town, but she's not someone I've seen around town before. I let my eyes drift down her body in absolute appreciation. She's wearing a thin, cream colored camisole and tight jean shorts. There's a sweet innocence radiating from her. Her waist is narrow, but her hips are wide. She's got one hell of a cute little pear-shaped body. It's a body that could take a punishing fuck. My dick hardens just thinking about gripping onto those hips.

I readjust my cock and take a look around the room. The other guys notice, but they don't show it. It's only us and the sweet little blonde here now. Technically this restaurant is a public place. People come here to get an inside look, but it's not like we'd actually do some shit here. We hardly even use the freezer room anymore. Hardly. There's some shit going on in the back room right now, and that's why I'm forced to sit here and make sure it doesn't get out of hand. It's not as if my cousins can't handle the job on their own. I know they can. But I have to wait here till they're done.

She smiles looking around the room, and her eyes light up as she quickly strides to take a seat across from me. It prompts a small chuckle from me. She obviously takes delight in the little things. I like that.

The people in this town don't come in that often anymore. They know my Pops is Don. Everyone *knows* it, but no one can prove it. I look to my left and see Joe smile as he watches the sweet little blonde scoot into the booth across from us. Joe can back the fuck off, that pussy is mine.

I grin at her being so damn cute and shy. She obviously has no idea that she's walked into the mafia headquarters. A low, deep chuckle vibrates my chest as she blushes and covers her face. Sweet. She's a definite sweetheart; I like it. *Sweetheart.*

She's looking around like a waitress is gonna come and give her a menu. I look over to Brant. He knows the drill. He should be getting his ass up and playing the part. It takes a minute for him to put down his phone and walk over to her with a forced smile. Little shit. He's only 17 and doesn't do much for the family, for obvious reasons. He should be thrilled to wait on a woman like that. Maybe the prick's hormones haven't hit him yet.

I give her a minute to get adjusted. I nearly laugh when I see her disappointed expression viewing the laptop screen and then watch her eyes search the room. She's upset about the Wi-Fi. How freaking cute. I can practically hear her every thought. She's so easy to read. So expressive. I bet she'd be that way in bed, too.

At that thought, I stand up and walk over to her. No time like the present. I know I'm going to be interrupting, but I don't wait. I'm an impatient prick. When I want something, I go for it. And I sure as fuck want her.

"Whatcha doing here, sweetheart?" My little prey jumps upright and her hand flies to her chest. I restrain myself from laughing and slip into the seat across from her, watching her face to make sure I'm welcome. She smiles slightly, and that beautiful blush rises to her cheeks again. She gives off an innocent vibe that makes me want to test her. My arm rests on the back of the booth, but it's a good distance away from her. I don't want to come on too strong. Not yet.

I'm surprised my sweetheart isn't drooling. She obviously likes what she sees. Which makes me real fucking happy, and more eager than I should be to get into her pants. It's been a while, but the need to fuck her senseless is riding me hard. Her pouty lips beg me to nibble them. I can practically hear her panting while I rut between her legs. Her chest rises and falls as her eyes find mine, and a look of embarrassment crosses her face. She shouldn't be embarrassed, not at all. She's obviously a woman with needs. I could take care of those for her. It'd be my fucking pleasure.

"I have to study." She looks nervous, like I'm about to devour her. She's smart, 'cause that's exactly what I'm going to do. It's obvious that she's a good girl who knows better. But I've learned that good girls happen to love bad boys. And that's exactly who I am, so she's in for a treat.

"What's your name?" I ask, completely ignoring her statement.

"Elle." She's quick to respond. I like that.

"I'm Vince. What are you studying, sweetheart?" I deliberately lick my bottom lip and watch her eyes dart to my mouth as her own lips part slightly. I know how to play this game. It's exactly the kind of game that hard to get types like to play. Although, I don't have to play it often. And she doesn't really come off as that kind of girl.

I pick up her textbook and my brow furrows when I see the cover. She's really fucking smart. "Biology?" I keep my voice even as I set the book back down. My confidence takes a small hit though. She's a good girl, and she's in school. Judging from the book, she's taking some pretty fucking hard classes. I never went that road. Not like my brother Dom. I mean, I still know my shit. I never wanted to sit in class and try to be the teacher's pet. But I'm damn sure this broad isn't wanting a man like me.

She's not going to want the bad boy who's only going to derail her plans. At most, maybe she'd consider me someone to go slumming with. But my read on her isn't giving me that vibe; she's not the kind of woman who'd go to a dive looking for a dirty fuck to get her off, the later tell her girlfriends what she did. Her soft blue eyes stare back at me with lust, but she's holding herself back. I can tell. And I'm finding the challenge alluring.

"Yup! Bio." Her voice squeaks a little and it makes me grin. I love that I'm getting to her. I can tell she thinks this is a bad idea, and she's right. Just like I thought, smart girl. "I--" She starts to speak, but I cut her off.

"You want to be a biologist, or a teacher?" I ask her, knowing she'd be too polite to talk over me. She blinks a few times, proving me right. "I just ask 'cause my brother went to school, but he decided to teach." I take a deep breath, then sit back in my seat as I run a hand through my hair. "Seems like a shit deal, though. That degree cost a lot, but teaching doesn't pay dick."

My jaw tics as I realize I let a bit of profanity slip. I don't know why it bothers me. It's who I am, and this is how I talk. All I'm looking for is a quick fuck, and I think she'd enjoy my filthy mouth. Or at the very least, she'd enjoy it on her pussy. But something about cussing in front of her seems off. She's too sweet to taint.

"I have no fucking clue, to be honest," she says, and I smirk at her response. I love her blasé attitude and that her sweet little mouth can say naughty things. I've always wondered why people spend so much of their lives doing things that don't thrill them. I need the high I get from my line of work. I don't get people who work themselves to the bone for something their heart isn't into.

"Then why do it?" I ask, and I honestly want to know. Her hesitation makes me think she doesn't know how to answer. Then her eyes fall to the table, and her lips tug down into a frown.

Damn. That's not what I was expecting. I feel like an asshole for putting that sad look on her face. "Didn't mean to upset you, sweetheart." She shakes her head and looks back at me with a pained expression. She swallows and takes a deep breath. She's so easy to read, and the only thing coming off of her right now is sorrow. I don't like it. It's not the read I got on her when she walked in.

"I'm just tired," she says. Her lips press into a sad smile. It's a lie. She may be tired, but that's not what's eating her. This is where I usually steer the conversation back to the direction of my dick, or just leave. But the fucking words come out of my unfiltered mouth with concern. "Tell me what's wrong," I say imperiously. I demand, rather than ask her for an answer, because I don't want to give her the option not to confide in me. I want to know. Some sick, twisted part of me feels like I could fix it all.

Her eyes narrow like she doesn't want me prying. I get that. To be honest, I'm surprised the question popped out of my mouth. Finally, she answers, "I'm just not happy with the decisions I've made for people who don't appreciate them." Vague answer, but a bit of relief washes over her. Like she's happy just to get it off her chest. Surprisingly enough, she continues opening up.

"I keep moving my life around for my mother, who only seems to date shitty assholes who take, take, take until she's spent. And then she runs to me when she has nothing."

My heart fucking hurts for this broad. She's intelligent, beautiful, and sweet, yet she's hurting like this over her own mother? That's a damn shame. "Why do you do it?" I ask her. I sure as shit wouldn't. Not that Ma would ever put me in that position.

She shakes her head and just like that, the walls come up. My fingers itch to touch her. I want to soothe that bit of sadness. I've never felt something like this before, like I could make her life better. Like I *want* to make her life better. It makes me feel uneasy. But I can't fucking stop it.

"Because she's my mother." She gives me a tight smile and reaches for the drink I didn't even see on the table. At least Brant's good at keeping a low profile.

I'm really out of my fucking element here. I'm an expert on getting laid, but this sure as shit isn't it.

I raise my eyebrows and take a deep breath. "I can see wanting to help your mom, I guess." I should give her some time to study and get out of this shit mood. "You want me to leave you alone so you can study?"

179

I feel like an ass, asking like a little bitch. I'd rather she didn't waste her time doing shit that makes her unhappy when I could have her bent over moaning in ecstasy. I should just drag her to the back room and give her what she needs. My dick is so fucking hard for her. I haven't had any ass for a while now, and the barest hint of her breasts is peeking out through her tank top, taunting me.

But, if she wants to bury herself in her work to forget about that shit, I can wait until she's done and then make sure she gets what she really needs. That, and I know she can read me like the back of her hand. She's smart. If I pull a move now, then she'll know what's up and just push me away. If I give her this, there's a better chance of me getting that ass later. I can wait. Usually I don't have to, but I'm willing to deal with a bit of blue balls, for a little while at least.

"Yeah, thanks. Sorry to be such a downer." Her words drip with disappointment and sarcasm. What the hell? She's blowing me off? Nope, not gonna fucking happen. I look like a bad influence, because I am a bad influence. It's real cute that she thinks I'll just go ahead and leave her to do her work after that smartass answer. I'm not that kind of guy though.

"I don't like the way you talk about yourself," I say with a hard edge to my voice, because I really don't fucking like it. Being honest and open like that takes courage, at the very least. She shouldn't be putting herself down. I also don't like her attitude, not one fucking bit. She's pushing me.

She squares her shoulders and looks me straight in the eyes. She speaks calmly, but her voice is strong. "I can do what I'd like." Her defiance makes my dick hard, and I ache to turn her over right here in front of everyone and show her what a good punishing fuck she needs right now. Then she adds, "And right now I'd like to study." With my blood boiling and my agitation growing, she grinds her teeth and turns her shoulder to me, effectively dismissing me.

"You could really use a release, sweetheart." I can't stop myself from saying it. I shouldn't. I should let her finish her work, and I sure as shit shouldn't get involved with her problems. But her being so short and snippy with me has me wanting to spank her ass and pound that tight pussy. She's wound up so damn tight. "A quick fuck will do you good." I tap my fingers against the glass holding her drink. "Much better than this."

I watch her squirm in her seat under my gaze. I know I'm turning her on. She wants me just as much as I want her.

She bites her lip and swallows loudly before she says, "At least you're being up front about it now. I knew you just wanted to fuck me." Her voice cracks at the end and betrays her confidence. I fucking love it. She's so damn innocent. I bet she's only done missionary before with some uptight, nerdy boyfriend. She's never been fucked like a woman deserves to be fucked. She tries to play off her desire by moving her book closer to the edge of the table and pretending to ignore me. That shit's not happening. I'm hard and we both need this. I shut her book and wait for her to look at me. She blurts out, "Why are you being such an asshole?" I have to stifle my grin.

"Because you keep denying yourself. Do us both a favor and stop trying to push me away." I don't understand her anger, but at least anger is something I can work with. You need passion to be angry. So I'm gonna fucking run with it. "You'll forgive me when I'm deep inside that tight pussy of yours. You need this, sweetheart, knock it the fuck off and let me take care of you."

Her breathing picks up. "I *need* this?" She huffs a humorless laugh. "What I *need* is for you to stop harassing me."

"Sweetheart, I've never seen anyone who needs a real good fuck as much as you do. Tell me you don't want me. If you can look me in the eyes and tell me to leave, I will. Cross my fucking heart." I lean forward, daring her to tell me off. I know she wants me, just like I know she needs this. I just hope she doesn't disappoint me. As she stares into my eyes searching for something, an uncomfortable feeling settles in my chest. She had better not deny me.

"Who do you think you are?" She's still playing at being offended, but I can tell she wants this. "I'm not some whore." My jaw clenches at her words. I don't like that. First a downer and then a whore. She really doesn't speak highly of herself.

"I never said that, sweetheart. I never even once had that thought. So, are you telling me to leave, or are you ready to get out of here?" Her eyes look back to her computer, breaking my gaze.

She answers with her eyes still on the screen. "I don't have my car with me." Her breathy words give me deep satisfaction. I've got my sweetheart right where I want her.

"You don't need one. We can go to the back." She gapes at me in surprise, but then her eyes widen in anger. "Relax sweetheart, this is my family's place. No one's gonna fuck with us here." Her cheeks flush pink and she turns away from me. Shit, she's embarrassed. She probably thinks I do this all the time. And I don't. I've never fucked anyone here. But I need to get inside her as soon as fucking possible. She's so damn indecisive I can't give her the chance to change her mind.

"No one's gonna know," I tell her, as I see her internally debating over what she should do. She should let me help her get this edge off. That's what she should do.

"Okay." The desperate word leaves her mouth with a primal need. She stands up and starts putting her things away, but I put my hand over hers to stop her.

"I got it, sweetheart." I put her shit in her tote as quick as I can and grip the straps in one hand. With my other hand, I take her hand in mine and pull her closer to me as I walk her to the back. I don't look around as we walk, and I'm glad she isn't looking around either. The guys may see, but they won't know for sure what I'm up to. Even if they do, they'd better not say a damn word to her. I won't let her regret this.

ELLE

I hear a loud bang, then someone yells. The sounds are faint, and distant. What the fuck happened? I try to move my arms, but someone's holding me down. A small moan escapes from my lips. I'm so sleepy. Why am I so drowsy? I feel groggy as I turn my head slowly from side to side, and then I remember. I remember his mouth on my body. The heat between my legs makes my body want to turn and my thighs clench, but I'm pinned down. A strangled groan leaves me as I try to move my wrists, but I can't.

"She's fine." A distant, masculine voice that I don't recognize has my forehead creasing with confusion.

"If you lay another fucking hand on her, I'll--" He sounds so angry. Why is he so angry? I struggle to remember. Vince. His handsome face and cocky smile flash before my eyes. *"I'm Vince."* I hear his words in my head. It feels like a faint memory.

"Calm down. It had to happen, Vince. This is the better alternative. For now, this should work." I hear a third voice as I start to feel slightly more alert, but I keep my eyes closed.

"I didn't fucking touch her. It's a roofie, for Christ's sake. It was either this, or off the broad." *Roofie.* That word triggers something within me, and makes me move involuntarily.

I try to jackknife off the desk, but someone's still holding me down. I open my eyes and focus on the man holding me down. I recognize his face. Vince. I struggle against him. His large frame towers over me as his dark eyes search my face. Betrayal hits me hard, and tears prick my eyes. He drugged me. Did he...? I can't even finish the thought. I struggle to breathe as a sob rips through me.

How did I get here? I'm in an office and it seems vaguely familiar. I shake my head and try to shake the sleep away. How long have I been here? I remember his face, I remember his name, I remember this room. I remember it all, but only in brief flashes. I shake my head again.

"Vince?" I ask in a wary voice. Please let me know him at least. I need to remember something.

"Shit, she remembers," one voice from over my shoulder says, and then he curses under his breath.

"She won't remember it all. I promise you this is going to work," the third voice sounds out with confidence. Remember what?

I turn to my right to avoid looking at Vince. Fear washes over me like ice against my skin. Two large men stare back at me. Their tanned skin is stretched tight across their bulging muscles. One man is much less muscular compared to the other one, but he's still jacked. It's only because he's standing directly next to a guy with a truly beastly physique that he seems even a hair less intimidating than he actually is. Their dark hair and eyes make them a frightening sight. Mostly because they look back at me like I'm a threat. Again I try to move away, but Vince's grip only tightens on my wrists as his forearm digs deeper into my hip. My wrists burn as I continue to struggle.

Their words finally start to register and sink in. I don't know who they are or why I'm here, but I know they want to kill me. Or did. I open my mouth to scream for help out of pure instinct, but Vince is faster. He covers my mouth with his hand. I take the arm that's suddenly free and push against his hard, unmoving chest in a feeble attempt to push him away. It's useless.

Vince leans down with his lips barely touching mine. "Don't fucking do it, sweetheart." His voice holds a threat that leaves my chest hollow as fear consumes me. Who is this man? The weight of the situation crashes down on me. What the hell did I do? My eyes dart to the other men in the room. I'm surrounded by criminals, predators who've drugged me. I close my eyes and try to will away the depressing helplessness. I'm not okay. I'm not going to be okay.

"Get out." Vince's hard voice has the two men walking slowly to the door. I concentrate on my breathing and watch them leave.

The larger of the two men looks back at Vince with a hand on the door, standing just inside the room, and holds his gaze. After a moment. Vince says softly, "I'll let you know if I need you."

Something about his tone, the somberness of it, sends pricks down my chilled skin.

The second the door shuts, I try again to get out of his grasp.

"Stop struggling." I hear the dark threat he whispers in my ear through his clenched teeth, but I don't listen. I can't listen. I saw those men. I saw the look they gave me, and then the ones they gave him. I'm fucked. I'm so fucked. They're going to kill me, and I don't even know why. I need to get the fuck out of here. I try to scream again, and the hot air and spit cover my chin as his hand presses even harder against my mouth.

"I said to stop it!" he yells. His strong arms wrap tighter around my body, and he easily lifts me up and against the wall. My heart beats frantically as I search for a way to escape. Adrenaline rushes through my blood. "Don't make me gag you." I hear his threat in my ear as tears streak down my face. I try to calm down, but all my body can do is stay tense. My muscles scream for me to move them. They want me to fight. Everything in me wants to fight. Against a man like Vince, it's hopeless.

But I can at least beg.

I stay still and try to calm my breath. My chest rises and falls with sporadic hiccups from my sobs. I need to calm the fuck down. I close my eyes and just try to breathe. He won't hurt me. I need to believe that. I need to believe there's a way out of this other than death.

As if reading my mind, he says in a calm voice, "It's going to be alright." His deep, baritone voice soothes me. It shouldn't, but it does. I shouldn't believe him. And yet, I do.

"I'm gonna take my hand away, Elle. And you're not going to scream." I attempt to nod, but his grip on me is so tight that I can't move. His hand slowly pulls back and the cool air makes it painfully obvious that I have spit all over my chin. I want to move my arms, but I'm pinned against the wall.

I turn my head slowly and see his stern expression, daring me to scream. I

185

swallow thickly and I can't help the need to do just that. I have to try. I won't be a good little victim for him. I have to try to get the fuck out of here. My body lunges away from him without my conscious consent. The movement makes my head spin.

His large hand tightens around my throat. I struggle to breathe as my feet lift slightly off the ground. His blunt fingernails dig into the back of my neck as he shoves me against the wall. His force stuns me. But even more so, I'm shocked by the dark look in his eyes. It's a deadly look that tells me I shouldn't fuck with him. I'll regret it if I do.

I don't understand. I'm so confused. I remember glimpses of passion between us. What the fuck happened?

My hands want to reach for my throat. It's a natural instinct as my breathing comes up short. But they're pinned at my side by Vince's hip and his other hand. My eyes water, and I look back into his gaze to plead with him. I don't want to die. Not like this. Not now.

He leans into me, and the scruff on his cheek rubs against my jaw. His lips are practically touching my ear. "I don't want to hurt you, sweetheart." His breathing is unnervingly even. He's calm. Too calm. "I don't want to, but I will. I won't hesitate if you keep this shit up."

I try to stay still. With everything in me, I try to obey him, but the need to fight against his hold wins out as my vision fades and my throat seems to close.

Just as I think he's really going to end my life and choke me to death, he lets go. My feet stumble against the hard ground and I nearly roll my ankle, heaving air into my lungs. My hands feel around my throat as I land hard on my knees. I let my body sag to the ground and just breathe.

It's only then that I realize I'm crying hysterically. My face is hot and wet from the tears.

I see him bend down, his worn, dark wash jeans just an inch from me and I fall back on my butt and kick away, scrambling backward as fast as I can until I hit the wall. I restrain the scream crawling up my throat and wait as still as I can.

He's still in a squatted position, his hands resting on his knees as he looks back at me as though contemplating what to do with me. The need to fight is suppressed for now. Attempting to run would be useless. All I have left is to try and beg for mercy.

"Please let me go," I plead with him. My words are slurred. My head spins slightly as I feel the full weight of my body. I'm not okay.

"Not until I know everything you saw." His words confuse me. I don't know what he's talking about.

I shake my head violently. "I didn't see anything."

A cocky smirk graces his lips. "Sorry sweetheart, but lying isn't going to get you anywhere with me. You remembered my name."

"What did you give me?" The question comes out slower than I intend as I move my arms sluggishly and realize my motor function is off. My body heats with anxiety.

"It's a heavy sleeping pill." My head shakes. *Liar.*

"A roofie?" I ask accusingly. I remember someone saying it earlier. He drugged me. Betrayal washes through my body once again.

"It's *similar* to Rohypnol." He doesn't even have the decency to look away as he admits that they drugged me.

"Why?" I ask, in a small voice that I hope expresses my hurt.

"You saw something after we were in here, and I didn't have much choice." His jaw clenches and he faces the wall for a moment before his gaze focuses back on me. "It was the best option at the time."

"I don't remember anything, I swear." My breath and voice both hitch in my throat. If only he'd believe me.

He sighs heavily. "It's gonna take more than that, Elle." My lips tremble and my throat dries up.

"What do I have to do?" I ask, my voice shaky.

"You need to come with me."

"Am I even going to remember this?" The thought occurs to me as I really think about what a roofie does.

"I don't know," he answers calmly. "I hope not, 'cause that would really fuck this plan up. You should still be asleep."

"I won't tell anyone." The words fly out of my mouth. I whisper hoarsely, "I swear to God, I won't." I don't care that he drugged me; I just want to get the hell out of here.

His eyes are full of remorse. "That's something we just can't risk."

"Who are you?"

He answers easily. "The mob, sweetheart." My blood chills at his confession. "You just happened to be in the wrong place at the wrong time." His eyes narrow and turn angry. "You should've waited for me." His words have a tone of accusation, but I don't even know what he's referring to.

Even with the fear from his threat still hanging over me, I manage to spit out a response in disbelief. "What did I do to deserve this?" I slam my mouth shut at the pissed off look on his face.

"That mouth, sweetheart, that mouth of yours is going to get you into trouble."

I close my eyes and pretend it's all a dream. "Please, just let me go," I whisper. After a moment, I open my eyes and find him standing, looking down at me. His broad shoulders and air of power make him the epitome of intimidation and domination. This man owns me. I am completely at his mercy.

"I'm sorry, sweetheart. I really am." He presses his lips into a straight line and shakes his head slowly. "But I'm not letting you go."

"What are you going to do with me?" My heart thuds against my chest, yet my lungs seem to freeze as I wait for his answer. He walks around the desk with his back turned to me. The sinewy muscles of his arms ripple with his movements.

He opens a drawer, and my eyes widen as I whimper and shove my body even harder into the wall. I want to look at the door. I want to search for an escape. Instead, my eyes are zeroed in on him, waiting to see what he's pulling out of the desk. I'm assuming it's a gun. I fully expect for him to shoot me.

I don't expect him to pull out thin, twined rope. It's the coarse kind that's used in kitchens. "You're going to listen to me, Elle. And I promise if you do, I'll do everything I can to keep you safe."

A mix of emotions washes over me as he pulls out more rope and wraps it around his wrist. Surprisingly, confusion is one of the strongest ones I'm currently feeling. "Why?" I can't help asking the question. "Why are you doing this to me?"

Vince pauses his movements as his eyes find mine. His cold gaze keeps my eyes locked on his although I desperately want to look away. He responds after a long moment of silence. "Trust me, Elle. It's better this way." For the briefest second, some sick part of me does trust him. But then I quickly come to my senses.

I don't trust him. I won't.

VINCE

What the fuck am I doing? I run my hand down my face as I hear her bang against the trunk. Again. I keep hearing her muffled screams and it's pissing me off. She doesn't listen for shit. The cold sweat that I can't kick runs through my body as I gently move the car through the intersection, past the familiar weathered stop sign. She can keep kicking and screaming for all I care. These back roads are deserted this time of day. No one is going to come save her. For now, she's mine. And that means no one's going to hurt her either.

I'll take her to the safe house in the country. It's a good 30 minutes away from here, and at least a 10 minute drive to civilization. I used to go there to hunt. Back when I thought I'd like that shit, anyway. Turns out waking up before the crack of dawn is not my thing. So now it's the familia's. Only Dom and Pops know about it though. She'll be safe there. I run my hands through my hair and let out a heavy sigh. I'll keep her there until I know what to do about this. Until I know for sure I can save both our asses.

I wish she hadn't woken up. If she'd just stayed asleep it would've been so much better. I would've been alone, maybe told her she hit her head. I have no idea. I've never been in this situation. But I wasn't going to let them kill her. It was my fault. My fuck up. And I'm going to fix this.

The memory from earlier flashes before my eyes. Her shrill scream as she saw my cousins Anthony and Tommy hovering over the brutalized body. Blood covered nearly every inch of that poor bastard's exposed skin.

My grip tightens on the steering wheel, and suddenly her relentless banging is more annoying than it was before.

I grind my teeth remembering how they came in to the office while I was trying to calm her down.

* * *

I DRAG her back to the room, her small body pushing against mine. Her feet barely touch the ground as I lift her squirming body to hold her tighter to my chest. Her nails dig into the skin of my forearm that's pressed hard against her chest, until I can pin her up against the back wall in the office. Her breathing is heavy and so is mine. Adrenaline courses through my blood. One hand covers her mouth to keep her screams muffled.

Fuck! I grit my teeth and keep my voice low as I speak through clenched teeth. "Stop. Screaming." She doesn't listen. She keeps it up as though I haven't said a damn thing. I slam my body up against hers, then move my hand to her throat and squeeze.

"Listen real good, you had better fucking stop." That gets her attention, but then the office door opens and two sets of heavy, even strides are heard in the silence. The door closes and locks with a loud click.

"I thought it was locked, Vince." Anthony speaks, but I don't turn around. I keep my eyes on hers as they dart to my cousins behind me.

"You want me to do it quick, Vince?" Anthony asks. "I'll make it painless."

My blood chills as I watch her eyes widen in fear. My poor sweetheart. I can't. I can't let that happen.

"No." It's the only word I can say. I don't want to explain it to them. Because I'm their boss, I should know what to do, but I haven't got a clue.

"You need her to talk or something, Vince?" I can hear the confusion in Anthony's voice. She should be dead by now. I shouldn't be toying with her like this. Thing is though, I don't want her dead. She whimpers and her eyes finally meet mine. I know I must look like a cold-blooded killer. My jaw is clenched and my eyes are hard.

She struggles again in my grasp and then I remember my forearm on her neck. Her head is pushed back in an unnatural way and she's taking in ragged breaths. I let up on my grip.

I place my lips at her ear and whisper, "Don't you make a fucking sound."

"Vince?" At Anthony's question, I turn my shoulder to Elle. And she acts like a fucking idiot and takes off behind me. My hand reaches out to snatch her but I miss. Tommy's right fucking there, though. Did she really think she'd make it? Watching Tommy wrap an arm around her waist, bringing her body up against his pisses me off.

He speaks clearly, and I can hear the remorse in his voice as he says, "I'm sorry, I really am."

I know exactly what he's gonna do. He's planning on snapping her neck. Quick, painless, but it's not going to fucking happen. I take three strides and I'm on him. I land my fist on his jaw like a fucking asshole. He doesn't see it coming, and it sends him flying into the wall. His shoulder blade hits the drywall, leaving a large dent. Elle tumbles to the ground and I step over her, fuming with rage.

"No one touches her. No one!" I scream so loud I know they all hear it. Everyone in this place. But I don't give a fuck. It's not going down like this. I know the rules, just like I know I'm breaking them right now. But I don't care. I'm not going to allow anyone to hurt her.

I hear her shriek, and I turn to see Anthony holding her just like Tommy was. But he's quick to respond. "Just keeping her from running, boss." I give him a quick nod and turn back to Tommy. He's looking up at me with equal amounts of shock and aggression.

I reach down and offer my hand and help him up. His eyes stay on me, waiting.

"I don't want her dead, Tommy." He looks at me for a moment and then nods.

"One second, boss." I don't know what he has planned. But I do know this is all fucked.

* * *

IT'S ALL MY FAULT. All of it.

What the hell was I doing letting her leave on her own? Fucking careless. I was sloppy. I'm not fucking sloppy. Never. That's not how Valettis do business. I grind my teeth and look out of the window as we finally leave the outskirts of the city. Pops is going to be pissed.

Just the thought of his disappointment makes my heart sink. I don't really give too much of a shit what anyone thinks of me, except for Pops and Ma. Sometimes my brother Dom and sister Clara. But my father's opinion matters the most. He's always been proud of me. But this shit I've gotten us into--this is not good. He's not going to fucking like that I risked the family to get my dick wet at our place of business.

I don't know what it is about this broad that has me making poor decisions left and right. I don't know if it's her curves, that little pout she has that shows me she's hurting, or that snappy little attitude that comes out of nowhere.

I fucking love the spitfire my sweetheart is. I can't fucking wait for her to go off on me again so I can spank that ass of hers. Next thing I know my dick's hard, pressing against my zipper. I let my head fall back, but keep my eyes on the road. And then I hear her thumping away in the back. What the fuck is wrong with me? I'm never getting in that pussy again. I'm the fucking enemy now.

She probably doesn't even remember that hot as fuck pregaming session we had. Shit. She'd better not. She'd better not remember anything more than my name. I shift uncomfortably in my seat and let out a deep sigh. This is so fucked.

At that thought I realize I have no fucking clue what I'm gonna do with her now. I could bring her to my room and pretend we had a one-night stand. That makes sense. I took her out to the bar, we got drunk, had a great night together. Boom, it's done and over with. My chest pains at the thought. I don't want it to be over with. I don't like that option. But I'm sure as shit not bringing her around the family after this. Tommy and Anthony are the only ones that know. They know better than to tell Pops. That's my job. My responsibility.

I look down at the watch and see it's been two hours since she woke up. That means she's gonna need another dose soon. She shouldn't remember any of this shit with that drug in her system.

Calling it a sleeping aid was a shit thing to do. It wasn't a blatant lie, but it's not like I'm gonna tell her I roofied her. I don't want to give her the impression that we do that kind of shit on vulnerable women, 'cause we don't. It comes in handy when you wanna take out someone high up though. It's much easier to take a knocked out fucker to the pits than having to fight him on his own territory. Of course she didn't get the same dose we use for that kind of thing. It's hard to know how much even got into her system though. Tommy just shoved it in her mouth, and as a result she nearly bit his finger off.

My stomach knots and twists. I'm kidnapping and drugging this woman. What a fucking low point in my life. I really hope this fucking works. Anthony swore by it. He's real fucking good at getting information from people, and when he asks what happened right before he drugged them and they still don't know even after spending an hour on his table, then they really have no fucking clue. And that means the drug works. It had better work. But she remembered my name. Tomorrow morning, I need to determine everything she remembers.

I put my hand on the seat of my Audi just like normal, and that's when I realize Rigs isn't with me.

Fuck. I look into the rear-view mirror and there's no one there. I can't risk going back to my place with her in the trunk though. I'll have to go back later to pick up my dog. I'll drop her off at the safe house, and then I'll go back to my place in the city to pick up his furry little ass. I sure as hell can't leave him at my place by himself. He'd probably chew up the coffee table just to spite me. I really hope he didn't shit in my house though. I swear puppies are worse than babies. They have to be. Dom's little one just chews on the toys they give him and he can't move, like a little sack of potatoes.

A small grin kicks my lips up, but it vanishes when I hear another bang from the trunk. Fucking hell. I wish she'd calm her ass down. She's gonna think we had some real rough sex last night and that I tied her ass up. I groan and adjust my cock as it twitches with need. I'd love to fuck this woman. I want inside her more than I've ever wanted anything before. But there's no way that's happening, not with all this shit.

I really fucked this up.

ELLE

*M*y wrists burn as the rope chafes against them. But I don't stop struggling. I won't stop. I know if I can just get my hands free then I'll be able to untie my legs. There's enough room for me to wiggle around and search for the latch. There's always a latch in these cars.

I take a deep, extremely unsteady breath and focus on loosening the knot. My shoulders hurt so fucking bad. Every bump we go over sends my body bouncing and I land hard on my side. I have nothing to brace my head against either. My neck hurts from trying to brace myself every time we hit a bump.

My throat is killing me from screaming and my eyes feel raw. It's a horrible feeling, knowing you're going to die. I just don't understand why he hasn't done it yet. He's not going to let me go. More tears prick at my eyes. My hand covers my mouth to hold back the sob. He's keeping me. My body shivers and I pull my legs up to my chest and rock myself.

I can't believe this is what I am now. A prisoner. He's going to do whatever he wants with me. I'm completely at his mercy. The tears fall down my face. I rub my cheek on my knee, to wipe the tears away, and try to steady my breath. Maybe that's not it. Or maybe I can appeal to that side of him. A flicker of hope lights inside of me. I just need to get out of here. However I can.

I'm so god damn tired. I feel dizzy and my head is killing me. I just want to go to sleep, but I can't. I want to fight this. I don't want to fall asleep. I can't just lie down and let him do whatever the fuck he wants with me. I'm going to fight as long as I can. Confusion overwhelms me again. I just don't understand why my memory is so passionate, giving me a feeling of comfort and safety, but my reality is the exact opposite.

The brakes slow again, and this time the car stills and I hear the click of him parking the car. My heartbeat picks up to a frantic pace. I failed. I couldn't get out of these fucking ropes or find a trunk latch anywhere. Fear cripples me as he pops open the trunk. I try to scream through the gag, but it's useless.

"Come on sweetheart, did you really think I'd take you to somewhere you would be heard?" He looks at me like he's disappointed. I don't know what he expects from me. "Be a good girl for me and make things easy for us both, alright?" Is he out of his god damned mind?

I try to scoot away from him, but it's useless. It's not like there's a ton of extra room in the trunk. I don't even realize he's untying the rope around my legs though until he starts massaging my calves. A moan of satisfaction leaves me. I didn't realize how sore they were until he brought more circulation to them. His large, rough hands move to my wrists and as the ease of comfort coupled with slight pain hits me, he rubs my shoulders, bringing them back to life.

"I'm sorry about that," he apologizes, and he sounds truly sincere. His thumbs move in small circles on my back, and then travel up to my shoulders and down my arms. "But you weren't really cooperating."

His excuse pisses me off. What he's doing is not fucking okay. I can't remember a damn thing. Ergo, there's no reason for me to be here. They should've just let me go. I close my eyes as his soothing touch relieves the ache. I try to remember.

I recall that moment when he introduced himself with his handsome smirk after I heard his deep masculine voice state, *"I'm Vince."* That moment flashes before me and sends a warmth through my body. That memory is followed by the feeling of my back arching on the hard, cold desk while his mouth licks and sucks at my clit. Fuck! I force my heavy eyes open as his arms wrap around me, bringing me close to his hot, hard body. I push away from him and snap, "I can walk."

His pissed off expression makes me want to cower, but he slowly puts me down and lets my feet find purchase on the ground.

I hate that I gave myself to him. I clench my thighs again. I don't feel any different. I'm not sore at all. More than anything, my clit is swollen with the need for his touch. I have no idea what all we did, but it's more than I've ever done before, at least on the receiving end. I've never had anyone go down on me. My cheeks flame with embarrassment.

I take one step forward with his hand resting lightly on the small of my back. I look up at the house. It's not large, but it's not small either. A country home, with light blue shutters and a porch swing. It looks like a picture-perfect home, out in the middle of nowhere with a dirt driveway. My eyes dart to the left--nothing but a flat field. My eyes dart to the right--woods.

Seeing the woods and knowing we're alone terrifies me. My body turns to ice.

He's going to kill me. My feet stumble and I nearly lose my balance. I take a ragged breath. I can't do this. Anxiety makes my blood race and adrenaline pumps through my veins. I can't handle this shit. My throat closes.

"You okay?" Vince asks me, and again I'm confused by the concern in his voice. I don't know what's going on. I wish I could remember. I swallow thickly and nod my head, righting myself. I wish all this were over with. I close my eyes and remember how he choked me against the wall. I can't. I can't go in there with him. I won't make it out alive.

I may not be strong, but I don't have to be. Not physically, anyway. I push my heavy body forward and shove my elbow right into his spleen. I saw someone do it in a movie once. I hear a gush of air push out of him and his groan of pain as he topples forward, but I don't waste a second. I force my body to move and sprint toward the woods. Everything is a blur. My heart isn't steady, and my ankle nearly rolls, but I push forward. I lose one of my flats, but I don't spare a moment to even consider it.

My bare foot pounds against the grass as I race to the edge of the woods. I can hear him getting up. He'll catch up to me in no time. If only I can get into the woods far enough to hide. It's dark out. I can hide. I need to be able to hide. My feet slam against the ground. I feel the cold dirt on the sole of my bare foot. My heart hammers faster. Branches whip by my face. I duck to avoid as many as I can. I brace my body against a thick tree trunk and try to keep my balance. The rough bark scratches against my skin.

I heave in a breath and then scream as Vince's body slams into mine, knocking me to the ground. His large body pins me down. His hips spread my legs apart and his knees land on my thighs, pushing my body open and forcing me to stay beneath him. He pins my wrists above my head with one hand, and his other hand wraps around my throat. I let out a scream, but he doesn't put any pressure on my throat. Instead, he's just merely gripping it. I try to buck him off of me, but it's hopeless.

He growls into my ear. "You can't fucking listen, can you?" I close my eyes and whimper.

"I don't want to die." My murmur is barely more than a whisper.

"You're not fucking acting like it." His hand tightens on my throat, and his hips push harder into mine.

For a moment my eyes flash to an image of him on top of me, pounding into me, ruthlessly rutting between my legs. My body heats at the thought. I can see us just like this. I turn my head to the side and refuse to think about it. My body flames with need, but I deny it. I'm so ashamed. So confused.

"You need to fucking listen to me." He clenches his teeth and slowly lets go of my wrists. I don't move. I stay as still as possible. He grips my chin and forces me to look at him, but I keep my eyes closed. He squeezes tighter and I instinctively open my eyes. His sharp, dark gaze stares back at me.

"Don't fight me," he commands. "You will obey me." His words send another shot of arousal through me, but thankfully he's already on his feet and pulling my nearly limp body up onto his. He slings me over his shoulder to carry me away like some kind of primitive caveman.

I don't know what to think. I don't understand why I feel this way.

I don't have a choice in any of this.

VINCE

I can't believe she fucking ran. My blunt fingernails dig into a
tender part of her waist as I drag her body back to the house, with
my hand gripping her hip. She's not walking fast enough, not making this
easy, but at least she's not fighting.

"That wasn't a smart thing for you to do, sweetheart," I mumble under my
breath. I'm pissed off. I'm really fucking pissed off. I'm trying to help this girl.
I'm going out of my way and risking my own ass for hers. If she got out... My
blood runs cold thinking what would happen. For a split second, the choice is
obvious. I can't allow it to happen. There's only one way to make sure she
never talks. I don't trust that she got a high enough dose. And neither will the
familia.

I shake my head and pull her closer to me. "Walk with me, Elle. Stop
making this so fucking hard." My voice reflects my anger. She quickens her
pace and I take a look at her as we near the porch. Her face is red from panting, her cheeks stained with tears. Her shirt's ripped from falling down
earlier, and there are scrapes on her knees.

My heart sinks in my chest. I'm such a fucking asshole for being angry
with her. I'd run, if I were in her shoes. First chance I got, I'd fucking bolt.
How can I blame her? She has no idea what's going on. Other than the fact
that I'm not letting her go, and that some people in the *familia* want her dead.

I look down at her feet. She lost one shoe somewhere back there, and her bare foot is dirty and bleeding from running through the forest. My poor sweetheart. I stop at the door and sigh. "Are you going to listen to me?"

Her wide, frightened eyes dart to mine. She slowly nods her head. She's fucking lying. I can see it written on her face. "Don't make me chase after you again, sweetheart." I move my hand up to the nape of her neck and fist her hair. I pull slightly, which gets me a small whimper, and lean down to let my lips barely touch her ear. "Next time I won't be nearly as nice." I whisper my threat and let my hot breath send a shiver down her body. I let go of her and open the door with my back to her, giving her the chance to fucking defy me. Again.

The sound of her heavy, shaky exhale make my chest hurt. I feel like such a fucking asshole. But what the hell am I supposed to do? It'll be better tomorrow. As long as she doesn't remember what she witnessed earlier at the bistro, everything will be better. If she remembers though, I'm fucked. She can't remember any of this shit. And that reminds me about the tablets in my pocket.

I unlock the door and walk in, holding the door open for her. She sways slightly on her feet and looks behind her. A low growl vibrates through my chest, making her head snap back around as she looks at me with wide eyes.

"Come on in, sweetheart." I can't help my narrowed eyes and threatening stare, but at least my voice isn't completely menacing. She swallows loudly and slowly walks in. I can see she's tired. She's fighting this shit, even though it should've knocked her on her ass. That makes me worry even more. She walks in slowly and at an angle. She keeps her eyes on me but keeps her distance, staying more than an arm's reach away.

I shut the door and lock it. The loud click of the lock makes her eyes dart to the doorknob. I practically see her heart beating out of her chest as her breathing picks up. I can tell she's on the verge of a panic attack. If only she'd just sleep. Just go to bed and make this easy on both of us.

My heart twists with agony as I watch her eyes dart around the foyer like something's going to come out of a dark corner and attack her. I need to help put her at ease. As much as I can, anyway.

"Are you hungry?" I've got this place stocked with food, no fresh stuff though. I'll pick some up when I get Rigs. I clench my jaw. I'm gonna have to tie her up to do that. She's not going to like it. But there's no fucking way I'm risking anything at this point.

She's quick to shake her head no.

"Did you eat before you went out tonight?" I ask calmly. She tilts her head to one side as though she's thinking. "Do you remember?" I prompt.

"I'm not hungry." Her voice is small, but even.

"That's not what I asked." I manage to keep most of the irritation out of my statement.

"Yes I remember, and no I didn't eat," she responds quickly.

I nod and take a step towards her, but she takes a step back. She's cornering herself in, but she has nowhere to go anyway. She won't be getting away from me now.

"I want you to eat something, and then I have to leave for a bit." I watch as her eyes light up at the thought of being alone. It pisses me off. All of this pisses me off. If she hadn't been so damn eager to leave earlier at the bistro, I could've had her cumming on my dick right now. Instead she's scared of me, when I'm the one busting ass to keep her alive.

"Stop running from me," I practically snarl. I take in a deep breath through my nose as my anger rises. I reach out and grab her waist before she can back away, pulling her small body to mine. Her hips press against mine. "Let's get one thing straight, Elle." I wrap my hand along her upper neck and use my thumb to push up her chin so that she's forced to look me in the eyes. "You fucking wanted me, before all this shit happened. You wanted me, and then you left me. You got yourself into this shit, and now I'm saving your ass."

Her eyes widen as though she's surprised. And I'm not sure which part triggered that response. I lower my lips closer to hers. "The least you can do is make this easy on me."

Her light blue eyes stare into mine. She parts her lips and all I want to do is take them with my own. I want to make this easy. I want to make it right. But when she speaks, it ends that desire.

"I don't trust you." The softly whispered words hit my chest like fucking bullets.

It fucking hurts, but I can't say that I'm too surprised. It takes a lot for me to trust a person, too. "Fair enough. Maybe you can make it easier on yourself then and stop pissing off your captor." My stomach drops as I refer to myself that way. But that's exactly who I am to her. Not her fucking savior, that's for damn sure. I'm the enemy.

"Does that sound like a smart thing to do, Elle?" I ask her as I tilt my head.

"No." Her plump lips stay parted as she answers me, and her eyes fall to my throat. A sadness washes over her. Her eyes stay on the dip of my throat as she asks, "What are you going to do to me?" I can hear the obvious defeat in her tone. I suppose in a way that's good, but it crushes me. I don't want to kill the bit of spitfire she has.

"I'm going to feed you." I tilt up her chin again to make sure she gives me her full attention. I repeat, "I'm going to feed you, but then I have to tie you up again so I can leave." She takes a quick inhale and her nostrils flare, but she keeps her mouth shut before nodding at me.

I pull back and walk away from her towards the kitchen. I turn to look over my shoulder. "Come." Her feet move obediently at the command.

"When you wake up tomorrow, this will all be over. Everything will be perfect," I say, trying to sound reassuring. I listen to her feet moving slowly behind me as I enter the modern kitchen. I turn to look at her as I reach the pantry. "You won't remember anything, and everything will be just as it was." I fill a glass with water and set it on the counter. I debate against showing her what I'm about to do, but ultimately I decide to show her. I don't want to trick her.

I reach in my pocket and pull out the bottle with the tablets. I pop the top off and drop one of the tablets into the glass.

I pick up the glass and watch as the tablet quickly dissolves into nothing. Her full, plump lips frown as I take a step toward her. "Drink this, sweetheart." I hold out the glass and her small hands reach out to accept it from me. Her fingers overlap as she lifts the glass to her lips. I'll have a good hour to hour and a half with her before she should pass out with this dose.

She stares at the glass for a moment and I consider pushing her, but I don't. Thankfully she puts it to her lips and downs the water completely. With the glass empty, she gently places it on the counter, with her eyes on the floor and drenched in defeat.

Her mouth opens as her fingers toy with the loops on her shorts. But she slams it shut and instead focuses her gaze on the slate tiles on the kitchen floor. She looks so beaten down. She looks hopeless. She's covered in dirt and scratches. I'm going to need to bathe her. She can't wake up like that.

Her eyes reach mine with sadness and her mouth opens and then closes again. "What is it?" I ask, with patience and comfort.

"Please don't touch me." Her shoulders rise and her body trembles as she swallows thickly and moves her gaze back to the floor. She clasps her hands in front of her. My forehead creases with confusion, and then I realize the meaning of her words. I close my eyes and give myself a moment.

When I open them, her hands are covering her face as she stands there in the middle of my kitchen. She doesn't belong here. It's so fucking obvious to me that this is fucked up.

"Elle, sweetheart..." I walk over to her and wrap my arms around her so that she can lay her head against my chest. She's stiff at first, but I rub up and down her back with comforting strokes. "I would never do that to you." I kiss her hair and continue rubbing soothing circles on her back.

"I promise you. I won't hurt you."

ELLE

"I'm not leaving you alone again, and I've already seen you naked, so just strip." I stand with my back to Vince as I face the shower. I can't believe he's serious. I can't believe any of this. He tried to get me to eat, but I'm so sick to my stomach. And now he wants to bathe me. I can't wash myself, thank you very much.

"I can--" I start to say the words in the softest, most respectful tone I can manage, but he cuts me off.

"I'm not leaving you for one second." I turn around slowly. His muscular arms are crossed, pulling his tee shirt tighter over his chest. It makes the muscles in his shoulders and arms bulge.

I look up at him through my thick lashes. "I promise--"

"I'm staying right here." His words are absolute. "You're going to be tired soon. You could pass out in the stall. I'm not leaving."

I take in a deep breath and close my eyes, and pull my tank top over my head and unhook my bra, removing them both quickly before I hurriedly shove my shorts down. I step out of them and quickly walk underneath the hot cascade of water. I wince as the heat bites into the small scrapes on my body. They aren't that bad. Tomorrow they'll start to scab over and not look like much of anything. I open my mouth and let the water hit my face.

Tomorrow I won't remember. I hope I don't.

I feel like a coward for thinking that. But I really don't want to remember this. I've given up. If I do remember, I'm going to pretend like hell that I don't remember.

"Here." I jump at the sound of Vince's voice and nervously watch as he hands me bottles of cheap shampoo and conditioner. They're small bottles like you'd expect to find in a hotel bathroom. I reach out and take them both with one hand. I have to close my eyes as our fingers touch. I feel so alone. That must be why I want him. It's the only reason I can think of as to why I'm feeling this way.

I don't know which emotion is stronger. The fear that he's going to kill me, or the desire for him to fuck me. My conscience is raging war within me. One moment I want him to use me. Yet the next moment, I'm afraid he's going to touch me. It's as though my fantasies and nightmares have combined into a reality. And I'm not sure which is which anymore.

I open my eyes and I find him staring at me. He looks like a caged beast. His hands grip the edge of the stall and he leans in just slightly. "Do you need anything else?" he asks. I know exactly what he's asking, and the answer is no. I quickly shake my head no and open the first bottle. The other I set down on a shelf. He pushes off the wall and steps backward, but I can feel his eyes on me.

I clean off as quickly as I can. I've already submitted. I can only hope tomorrow I'll forget. Tomorrow I'll wake up, and he'll take me back home. Then all of this won't even be a nightmare.

It simply won't exist.

I close my eyes again and feel a fog set in. I welcome it.

I lean my back against the cold tile wall and vaguely hear Vince's voice speaking. But it fades in the distance, and suddenly his face is in front of me with that handsome smirk. *"I'm Vince."* I hear his confident, masculine voice. I see him lift his head away from my heat and stare up at my body as a wave of heat rolls through me. Another flash, a mix of memories. And then my body seems to go weightless.

Darkness sets in.

The last thing I hear before I pass out gives me a sense of peace and calm that I'm not sure I've ever felt. "I've got you, sweetheart."

VINCE

*J*park in front of my house and sit in the car to take a quick mental inventory of everything before I go in there. It took a good bit to get over here, but I still haven't had enough time to process all this shit. Pops' car is out front. I know he's waiting for me inside. I sent him a text letting him know I had something I needed to talk to him about, and I know he's gonna be sweating his balls off with worry. I grip the wheel with both hands, remembering how I left her at the safe house.

She's only in an old Henley shirt of mine. Both wrists are tied to the bed frame. I think she's comfortable. I hope she is. I hate leaving her like that, but I have to get my dog. I already picked up some food for breakfast, and some clothes for her to wear. But right now I have to talk to Pops. The Don. I tap the wheel a few times and finally get the fuck out of the car. I might as well get this over with.

He's standing in the living room, and I see him as soon as I walk in. His eyes are on me as I toss the keys on the table and bend down to greet Rigs. My black lab is all muscle, with a long-ass tail that thumps onto walls as he wags it. He licks my face and I try to smile. But I can't.

"You alright, son?" My father's words wipe my pathetic attempt to smile right off my face. A thick feeling of sickness settles in my stomach.

I stand up and head to the living room. "I think everything's going to be alright. I just have something to tell you."

His facial expression doesn't change when he hears this. There's a hint of worry in his eyes, but other than that, nothing.

"What's going on, Vince?" His voice is hard, like it always is. Pops is old now, with grey in his hair, and wrinkles around his eyes. But he's still got a hard edge. Anyone who's ever met him wouldn't find it hard to believe he's the boss, 'cause he looks like and acts like the boss. I've always looked up to him. But right now, I'm finding it hard to look him in the eyes.

"It's basically taken care of, but I fucked up." I take a seat on the sofa, and Rigs hops up next to me and tries to sit in my lap. He's 6 months old or so now, not exactly the little puppy he was when I first got him. But, I really don't mind it. He can still keep thinking he's a tiny lapdog when he's 80 pounds for all I care. I give Rigs a few pats, then look my father square in the eyes.

"I fucked up and because of me a broad walked in on Tommy and Anthony." There, it's out. My father's expression stays flat.

"I see. That's very disappointing." His jaw is clenched tight and he keeps his eyes on me as he takes a seat to my left. "And it's *basically* taken care of?" He cocks an eyebrow at me.

"I couldn't let them fix it the way we normally take care of that." Witnesses don't exist to us, because if they see anything that could threaten the *familia*, they're dead. That's just how it works.

"What do you mean?" His eyes narrow. "What all did she see?"

"She walked in at the end of an interrogation."

"And where is she now?" Although his words are calm, I can practically hear his heart racing and waves of anger rolling off of him.

"At the safe house. The cabin." The look of sheer disappointment from my father crushes me. He leans forward with his head resting in his hands and his elbows on his knees. "Pops, she's not going to remember. Tommy gave her some of the roofies we use."

Pops looks pissed.

"What was I supposed to do? Kill her? It was my fault, I know, but I'm taking care of it." My voice raises in anger, and I almost regret it. Almost.

"Are you fucking kidding me?" he asks with disdain.

I press my lips into a tight line and shake my head. "What were you doing,

Vince? What was so important to you that you let a broad back there to see that?"

"I said I fucked up." I'm getting more and more pissed off listening to him tear me a new one. Yeah, I know what I did was wrong. I shouldn't have taken her back there, back at the bistro. I fucking forgot what was going on.

"And if she remembers? When she wakes up, if she remembers, are you going to kill her?" I look over his face and I have no clue what he wants me to say. My gut roils and I know I wouldn't want to kill her. But what choice will I have?

"All this, just to get your dick wet, Vince?" He asks sarcastically. God damn, does he have to twist the knife?

"Pops, you don't understand."

"Explain it to me then. I'd love to know what was going on in that head of yours that you failed to do the one thing you were in charge of."

I lay my head back against the sofa and stare at the ceiling. I run a hand over my face in exasperation. "I can't tell you. I just felt like--" He cuts me off.

"Like what? Horny? Is that it?" He's still pissed and I get it, I really do. I'm pissed, too. But give me a fucking break. I didn't let it get out of hand. I'm fixing this shit.

I open my eyes and stare back at my father with daggers in my eyes. "It was more than that."

His brows raise in disbelief. "Oh? Is that right?" He looks at me expectantly and still I don't know what to tell him.

"I told you, I fucked up. But I'm taking care of it. Tomorrow she'll be gone."

My father stares back at me with a look of contemplation. I wish he'd just give the okay. That's what I need from him, but instead he pushes me further. "How are you going to know for sure that she doesn't remember?"

I don't. That's the fucked up part. If she's a really good actress, I could be fucked. But I'm not going to tell him that. I can't. I don't want her dead. But I know I shouldn't be taking risks like this.

Pops looks at me like he can read my mind. "Bring her to dinner tomorrow."

"Pops, I don't want to hurt her."

"Sounds like you already did, Vince." He stands up and waits for me. I have to move Rigs to get up, and he doesn't like it, vocalizing his displeasure with a soft whine.

"I feel like shit."

He smirks at me. "That's exactly how you look, too."

I roll my eyes, but he's probably telling the truth. "I'm going to make this right."

He nods his head and then looks out the window. "I hope she forgets, Vince. I really do." He gives me a quick hug, coupled with a stern pat on the back. His hand goes to my shoulder and he squeezes. "If it means anything to you, I think you made the right decision." He releases me and breathes in deep. "It's not her fault." His eyes find mine again. "Let me know before dinner if she's coming." He purses his lips thoughtfully, but then he frowns. "If not, and you need help, you can call me if you need."

My blood chills. I know that's the only other option. But I fucking hate it.

I finally answer, "She'll be at dinner." He nods his head with a grim smile as he walks me to the door.

He watches me leave, and it's not until my house is out of sight that the true weight of the situation settles heavily against my chest.

I'll go back and untie her ass, but I'm staying close. I just have to wait until she wakes up. Then I'll know what I have to do.

If she remembers, I'm going to have to kill her. I don't have a fucking choice.

ELLE

O h. My. God. My head is fucking killing me. I roll over onto my side
and throw my hand out to my nightstand for my water. Every night
I put my glass in the same spot, right after taking melatonin to help me get
some rest. When my hand falls onto nothing, my heavy eyelids open slowly. I
jackknife off the bed. Oh shit, I forgot I'm at Mom's. I rub my eyes and then
look around. This is not Mom's.

My heart races in my chest. I look down at myself and see small marks on
my wrists that burn slightly to the touch. There are a few small scrapes on my
knees. Most importantly, I'm wearing a very large grey Henley shirt that's not
mine. What the fuck did I do last night?

My eyes dart across the bedroom. Judging from the décor, I'd guess that
this is a man's bedroom. The walls are a dark grey. The comforter is a slightly
lighter shade of grey, while the bed sheets are white. The furniture is modern;
a mix of clean lines and dark, stained wood. There isn't a single thing out of
place. Nothing that really denotes any personality, either. No picture frames,
nothing. There's a gun safe in the corner. It's taller than me.

Where the fuck am I? I pull my knees to my chest as I scan around the
room some more, searching for my purse or clothes. I don't see anything. My
gut churns with nausea. What the fuck happened last night?

I close my eyes and try to remember. Ugh. Mother. I'm so fucking pissed at my mother. The very thought makes my head hurt. My temples throb with pain. I remember being pissed off and leaving, but that's it. I wanted to study.

That's a fucking lie.

I wanted to get away. Just like I always do. Run and hide away in my books.

Shit! Thinking about work and studying reminds me that I have to study those chapters for my presentation in class. Where the hell is my stuff? I remember leaving, but I can't think of anything else.

The sound of the door opening startles me. I watch as the most gorgeous man I've ever laid eyes on walks in with a silver tray in his hands. His eyes stay on the cups on the tray while he kicks a foot behind him to shut the door. He takes a few steps toward the bed and my mouth falls open as I stare at him.

He's a fucking sex god. He's wearing blue plaid pajama pants that are slung low on his hips, revealing how cut his body is. That sexy "V" at the hips that I've only ever seen before on porn stars or male underwear models is on full display, and right smack in the middle is a thin happy trail of hair. His broad chest is very impressive, but it's his shoulders that get me. Holy fuck. I have a thing for shoulders. His dark eyes meet mine, and he grins at me.

"I'm surprised you're not drooling, sweetheart." His deep, masculine voice makes my clit throb with need, but more than that, it triggers a memory. A cocky smirk, then his handsome smile. *"I'm Vince."* I hear his voice in my head.

"Vince?" I feel awkward asking, but I really don't remember a thing.

His smile falters for a moment and it makes me feel guilty for forgetting whatever happened. Oh. God. What did happen? I clench my thighs and I don't feel any different. I feel horny as hell. But not... sore. Another memory flashes in front of my eyes. Oh fuck. He totally ate me out. My cheeks flame with embarrassment.

"You alright, sweetheart?" He sets the tray down on the nightstand. "You're acting a little off."

I swallow hard and look at him, and then down at the tray. Aw. He made pancakes and cut up some fruit. There's orange juice, plus the distinct smell of coffee. Thank fuck! My head is killing me. I could really use the caffeine. I hesitate to tell him I don't remember last night. Instead I crawl on the bed toward him and quickly grab a cup of coffee. I make sure my ass stays under the covers, though. For all I know it's just my hormones that are making me so horny over this guy, and he doesn't want me like that. Although the way his eyes follow my body as I move, suggests that he does.

I sit back and get settled. I have to tell him. I feel awful for practically forgetting his name. Obviously *something* happened between us. And that flicker of memory warms my chest, so it must be something good.

"I have a really bad headache right now."

His eyes look over my face. "You want an aspirin?" When I shake my head gently and blow on the coffee, he sits down on the bed. "I brought up sugar and creamer too if you'd like."

I smile into the steam rising off the cup and take a small sip. Damn, that's good coffee. "No thanks, I like it black."

He grins at me. "Low-maintenance, I see."

A nervous laugh leaves my lips. It's quiet for a moment while he grabs his cup.

"Hey Vince?" I ask. My questioning tone has his eyebrows raising in response.

"Yeah, Elle?" He sets his coffee down without taking a sip. "What's up, sweetheart?"

God I feel like an asshole. He's so sweet with the breakfast and the nickname. I just blurt it out. "I kinda think maybe I drank too much last night?" I've never been blackout drunk before, but my friend from undergrad Viv drank till she was shitfaced all the time. It scares me that I was so reckless last night. I was so pissed off. I should be smarter than that. But at least I'm still alive and I didn't get into any trouble. I clench my thighs again. At least I don't feel like I did, anyway.

He let out a sexy chuckle that shakes the bed. It makes me smile, then he smirks back at me. "Yeah, you were keeping up with me, and I drink a lot." He lies across the bed, propping himself up with his elbow. "At least tell me you remember something specific about last night."

I blush and suck down the rest of the coffee in a rush. "I mean, of course I remember *some* things." I nervously set the coffee mug down on the tray again.

"Tell me baby, I wanna know what I did that was so memorable." Oh my god, I'm practically swooning from his charm. His handsome smile makes me blush even more. I bite my lip and shake my head.

"You *know* what I remember," I say as I roll my eyes at him playfully. I see

211

the marks on my wrists again, and then my throat seems to go dry. I don't remember how those marks got there. "How did I get hurt?"

His eyes travel to my wrists and then he looks back up at my face. "Not sure, sweetheart. I didn't notice them until just now." That makes me feel a bit uneasy. I wish I could remember.

"Did we...?" *Have sex.* I can't even say it out loud. God, I'm such a child. I don't know why I avoid this shit. Thank fuck I've been on birth control since I was 16 for acne. I try to remember if I took my pill yesterday morning, and I'm sure I did. I bite my bottom lip, knowing I need to take today's pill some-time soon.

"Did we what, sweetheart?" He grins at me. "I wanna hear you say it."

I roll my eyes again and pretend to blow him off. But my heart twists in my chest. Did I really have sex last night? And I don't even remember?

"We didn't," he says after a few seconds. Relief floods through me.

"So we didn't have sex?" I ask, just to clarify. I clench my legs again and I'm certain I don't feel any different. Horny as all hell, but not like I got myself fucked for the first time last night.

He pouts and it makes me wanna kiss his plump lips. "We did fool around though. I happen to enjoy that mouth of yours." That sexy smirk is back and if I wasn't so shy, I'd crawl forward and nip his bottom lip. In my head it'd be sexy, but in reality... Nope, not going to make a fool of myself in the first five minutes of talking with this guy.

A violent blush rushes to my cheeks. I look around the room again. I don't see my clothes or my bag.

"Do you know where I left my stuff?" I change the subject to avoid thinking about sex some more.

"Uh, yeah. Your laptop is downstairs, and since I ruined your clothes I went out and got you some new ones." On his last word the door pops open, and a dog comes barreling into the room.

"Rigs, down!" Vince yells in a commanding tone, but the dog hops on the bed anyway and runs straight toward me.

I let out a squeal as the puppy rushes forward and puts both of his large heavy front paws on me. He's not quite a fully grown adult dog yet, but he's gotta be getting close, judging from his size. It's hard to hold him back as I laugh and he slobbers all over my mouth. I have to keep my lips pressed tightly shut so he doesn't accidentally French kiss me.

"That's it, Rigs!" I hear Vince's voice boom over my laughs, and suddenly the dog is gone. I watch him put Rigs outside the door and close it.

My cheeks hurt from smiling so hard. And as he turns and gives me the sexiest grin I've ever seen, I feel a blush rise up my chest and into my cheeks.

I don't remember last night, but this morning is looking like it's going to be good.

VINCE

God damn, she's so cute. There's not a doubt in my mind that she's forgotten everything. The only scars from yesterday are the small marks on her body. And fuck me, but I want to put more on her. Her sexy laugh and her rolling her eyes at me make me want to jump into bed and fuck her. I never had the chance before. I debate on getting into bed. I know I'm gonna have to leave this broad. I can't bring her around everyone. It's best if she just stays away.

But she did want me yesterday. And now that all this shit is done with, maybe it's not so wrong.

She crawls toward me like a cat, and it makes her ass peek out slightly from the hem of my shirt. That's the final straw. She wants me, and I want her. Nothing else matters right now. I lift her hips up with both hands and toss her onto her back. She lets out a sexy squeal that makes Rigs bark and paw at the door. But he's gonna have to stay outside for this.

She laughs again, but then seems to remember that she doesn't remember last night fully, and her shyness comes back to her. She tries to right herself and pull the shirt down farther. She's so damn sweet. I fucking love it.

"You don't want me to see your pussy, sweetheart?" I tease her as my hands land on the outsides of her thighs and slip up her shirt.

Her eyes widen, and I guess she's just now realizing that she's not wearing any underwear.

"You weren't worried about that last night." Her head falls back slightly as she props herself up on her elbows with her eyes closed.

"Mmm. I remember." Her words stop me short of slipping my hands up and onto her bare hips.

"What do you remember, sweetheart?" I ask her in a whisper, trying to keep the anxiety out of my voice. She smiles brightly, but turns her head to avoid my gaze and rolls her eyes. It eases some of my worry, but I want to hear her tell me exactly what she remembers.

"Tell me," I command.

She bites her bottom lip and rocks her hips a little. "You." Her eyes go down to her waist. "Doing that."

"Eating you out?" That blush that suddenly appears on her cheeks is adorable. She nods her head, not losing any eye contact. I push the shirt up her body and she gasps as I pull her ass closer to me. "What else do you remember, baby?" Fuck, I'm so hard, remembering the taste of her on my tongue. I look down between her thighs and her lips are glistening with arousal. Fuck yes! I'm definitely getting in that pussy. My cock starts leaking and begs to be buried inside her.

"I remember... tasting you."

"You sucked my dick." I focus my eyes on her. "Say it."

Her lips part and her breathing quickens. Yeah, she wants me. And this time it's going to go down like it should've last night.

"I sucked your dick."

"Yeah you did, and you're going to do it again after I cum in this pussy." I smack her pussy hard enough to make her jump. "You're going to lick me clean, aren't you, my dirty girl?"

I watch as her pussy clenches around nothing. She's so fucking turned on right now. I dip my fingers into her heat and curl up to hit that sweet spot.

"Oh!" She falls back on the mattress and her back arches. I smirk at her. I forgot how damn responsive she is. She's too fucking good. I keep pumping my fingers in and out of her quickly, but I keep my pumps shallow, focusing on that sweet spot. I just want to get her off real quick to soften her up. "Get wet for me, Elle."

My words send her off and she trembles beneath me with the sexiest moan coming from her lips. I feel her cum on my fingers and quickly pull them out and shove my pants down. I take them off and toss them to the floor. She's panting with her head turned to the side. And then just as I line my dick up, she does the same thing as last night. She closes her legs and pushes away from me.

"What's wrong, sweetheart?" I don't understand the look she's giving me. "You want me to grab a condom?"

She clears her throat a little before settling back down on the bed and relaxing slightly. "Umm..." Her blue eyes find mine and she continues. "I don't know."

"I'll get one, sweetheart. It's alright." I move to get off the bed but she pops up and grabs my forearm to stop me.

"No!" she yells out, a little too loud, and seems to be embarrassed by her own reaction.

I give her a questioning look. "I don't mind. I'm clean. So if you're good, I'm good. But I can get one."

She gives me a small smile and then settles back down, releasing my arm. "No, don't." She swallows and opens her legs for me.

Her submission is fucking beautiful. I don't waste any time and settle in between her hips, lining my cock up. Her eyes close, and her head turns to the side as her breathing picks up.

"Uh-uh, sweetheart." Her eyes open. "I want you to look at me while I'm fucking you."

Her mouth parts, and I can feel her pussy clamping down on the very tip of my dick. I can't believe how turned on she is even though she's already cum. I grip her hips with both hands, tilting her just right and slam into her heat.

Holy fuck, she's so fucking tight. She's strangling my dick. Her head pushes into the mattress and her mouth opens for a silent scream. Her pussy pulses around me as the head of my cock pushes against her cervix.

"You alright, babe?" I have to ask, because she looks lost in a mix of pleasure and pain. But closer to the side of pain, and that's not what I want.

I rub her clit with the rough pad of my thumb and wait for her walls to loosen around me. I rock in and out with shallow strokes and feel her moisture pull between us.

"Yeah." Her head turns to the side, but she keeps her eyes on me. "More," she pants with half-lidded eyes, and I fucking love it. Her lust and pleasure are evident. Thank fuck. I almost thought I was too much for her.

I watch as a cold sweat breaks out on her skin and I lean down, pushing my cock even deeper and kiss her jaw. I feel her body start to shake and her breathing pause, and I know she's close again so soon. I fucking love how easy it is to get her off. I pinch her clit to push her over the edge. Her eyes are dazed as she thrashes under me, cumming on my dick. Her tight walls try to milk my dick, but I'm not even close to being done with her.

"Look at me while you cum." She obeys immediately, and I'm half-surprised she's still so coherent. I wrap my hand around her throat and start pumping her with deep strokes. She's so wet, making my movements easy. I pound her pussy again and again, each stroke harder than the previous, and love the moans of pleasure I force out of her mouth. She moans my name and struggles to keep her eyes on me as her body trembles. Fuck yes. I want another. "Cum for me." And she does. Three fucking times already.

I feel like a king. Her king. I'm her entire world right now. I rule over her body. I *own* her. The thought has me rutting recklessly between her legs. She lets out a strangled cry, and I keep up my pace. My balls draw up and my spine tingles. YES!

I keep my eyes on her as I tilt my hips so each thrust smacks against her clit. I pound into her heat without any mercy, and as soon as I hear her scream my name in complete ecstasy as her body bows with her release, I cum deep inside her heat. She's still so damn tight that our combined cum leaks out from her pussy and down my thighs. I push as far in as I can and love the wet smacking noises I'm making with my deep, hard thrusts.

Waves of heat and pleasure roll through my body. YES! So fucking good. I close my eyes as her body relaxes and just enjoy this moment. Our heavy pants are the only thing I can hear. I fucking love it.

I open my eyes and find her watching me, as though she's waiting for my approval. Such a sweet submissive. I lean down, slipping out of her and let the cum drip on the sheets. I don't care. I'll wash them after I take her home.

The thought of taking her home hits me as my lips gently brush against hers. I kiss her with more passion than I've ever kissed a woman. I hate that this is the first and the last time.

She kisses me back with the same intensity and I know it's real. This broad can't hide shit from me. I break our kiss and smile down at her.

She winces as I move from between her legs and she closes them.

I look down and see a wet spot on the white sheets crumpled up under us and it's pink. Ah, damn. It's a good thing I didn't go down on her with her time of the month coming.

I slide off the bed and quickly grab a washcloth from the en suite and wet it with warm water.

When I get back to the bed, she's still laying on her side, exhausted and trembling from the aftershocks of her multiple orgasms.

"Open your legs for me, sweetheart." She turns onto her back with her eyes closed and winces as I wipe her off.

My poor sweet girl. I know I was rough, but I didn't think I was *that* rough. She is tight though. I wasn't expecting that.

"You alright sweetheart?" I ask and kiss her cheek.

"Mm hm," she says, nodding her head.

"You sure?" I bend down and kiss her thigh that's still shaking slightly and then her hip.

She shakes her head no. "It's a good hurt."

VINCE

I watch her move in the shower, her hands moving over her skin as she lathers up her body. I'd get in there with her and fuck her against the wall, but she's too sore. I feel like a prick for being so rough. Every time she looks at me she smiles sweetly, so she can't be hurting too bad.

"You sure you don't want to go out for lunch?" I raise my voice enough that she'll be able to hear it over the sound of the water. She didn't eat anything for breakfast; I should at least take her to lunch.

She sighs heavily. "My mom wants me to go home. She thinks I'm mad at her."

"Aren't you?" She *should* be mad at her.

"Yes. But I don't want her to feel bad." I rub my jaw, deciding on how involved I want to get with this. Fuck it. She's too sweet to watch her being used like that.

"Tell me what happened." She stops washing her hair and looks at me with surprise. "I wanna know."

She goes back to doing her thing and sighs. I almost have to get up to spank that ass for ignoring me, but then she starts talking. "She likes to move around and latch onto men. As long as I can remember, it's what she does." She rinses her hair and the lather washes down her curves. Her nipples are hard and it takes everything in me not to go to her. I want her again so

219

fucking bad. I have to concentrate on how she couldn't walk straight. She's too fucking sore.

If I'd known that would have happened, I would've gone easy, so I could have her again.

"She always picks losers who are drunks like her or have some sort of problem." My eyes snap up to her face and I have to try to remember what the fuck she's talking about. Oh yeah, her mom.

"So what's this guy's deal?" I ask.

"Well, Patrick is a gambler and lost his house because of it. So my sweet mother bought them one after a whopping two months of chatting online."

I huff a laugh. "And now what? She needs you 'cause he lost this one?"

"Yeah, that, and my name's on it."

"What?" All humor leaves me and I lean forward on the bench. Anger rises in my blood. That's fucked up. I don't know why I feel so defensive, but I do. No mother should do that kind of shit to their daughter. "Are you serious?"

"Yeah, she forged my name on the paperwork. Luckily, whatever bet he made he couldn't use the house as collateral, but she drained her bank account bailing him out, and now I have to come save the day."

"You don't *have* to do a damn thing." It takes a moment for her to look at me. "Except get your name off that mortgage."

She watches me for a second and then nods her head. "It's just..." She trails off as she turns off the water and grabs a towel to dry off. I keep my ass planted firmly on the bench so I don't get any more ideas about fucking her. "She's my mom," she finally concludes.

"So?" I ask, like I don't understand. I do, though. I really get the sympathy. But there's a point when you're being used where you have to put your foot down.

"If I don't help her, no one else is there for her."

"There's a reason for that. There's a reason she's alone." I say.

"I don't want her to be alone though. I want her to be happy." She sounds so sad.

"That's real sweet of you, babe, but sometimes you have to stop letting people use you."

She shifts uncomfortably and then sits down on the bench next to me. I grin when I see her mouth open, and her eyes close in ecstasy. She likes that little hint of pain and I'm pretty sure her clit is still throbbing, priming her for my dick again.

"Vince?" Her tone is off and I don't like it.

"Yeah, sweetheart?" I keep my tone neutral until I can figure out what's wrong this time.

"I was just wondering what all this means to you."

Oh. Fuck. It's one of *those* conversations. I'm not too sure how I want to answer that. So I play dumb. "What do you mean?"

"What's going on between us?" I know it takes a lot for her to be so straightforward, and I respect that.

"We're having fun, babe." The sadness that swarms in her eyes fucking kills me. I have to admit I want to keep seeing this girl. I really want to do all sorts of things to her body. I'd love to test her responsiveness, but it wouldn't be smart. I run my hand through my hair. Fucking her this morning wasn't smart either.

Her eyes fall to the floor, but she nods her head slightly. "I like just having fun. No strings or anything, that's okay," she says. I can see she's hurt and that she wants more. She's just saying what she thinks I want to hear. It tears me up inside.

"You sure you don't want to go to lunch, sweetheart?" I pull her to sit on my lap, still wrapped in her towel. "I'll take you wherever you wanna go." Just one more moment with her, before I have to say goodbye.

She gives me a forced smile and shakes her head. "That's alright. You don't have to do that." Fuck she looks so sad. Like it's just a pity date.

"I don't have to. I want to." I don't realize how true the words are until they leave my lips.

"I have to get back." She pushes off of me and reaches for the bag of clothes from Neiman Marcus and turns her back to me as she begins to get dressed. I know she's upset, and it hurts.

I wish I could tell her I'll see her tonight, but I'm not fucking inviting her to dinner. I've got one of her textbooks downstairs and I'll text her later tonight to swing by and come pick it up at my parents' house. That way Pops sees her, and I don't get my sweetheart wrapped up with my Ma. That shit's not happening. Ma will have all sorts of ideas going through her head if I bring her home.

"Take your time." I give her a small smile that grows as she turns and smiles back at me. She's not that upset. Something's off, but she knew what this was. I take a few steps towards her and kiss the crook of her neck. Her hand comes around the back of my head to hold me there and I admonish her by nipping her earlobe.

"I'll see you downstairs." She bites her bottom lip and nods with that blush staining her cheeks.

* * *

"You alright, sweetheart?" She's been quiet since she came downstairs, even after we left my place. Maybe the high that was keeping the regret from her is wearing off. I don't know what it is. But her sweet smiles are gone now. I hope her memory isn't coming back to her. Seeing her anything but happy makes me nervous and uneasy.

"Yeah, I'm fine." she answers with a forced upbeat in her voice.

"It was fun hanging out with you." I rest my hand on her thigh. We're parked in front of a decent enough house in an average neighborhood.

"Yeah," she says. Her smile falls and she noticeably swallows. "It was fun for me, too." My heart drops looking at the sadness in her eyes. I don't get it. I don't understand why she's so upset.

That's a fucking lie. I know she wants more. But she can't have it. It's over between us. It's better this way. She can't be coming around after the shit she saw. Even though she forgot, I'm not bringing her around the *familia*. I can't.

For fuck's sake, I want her, too. But I can't have her.

Her small hand grips the handle to leave before I can get out of the car. That's not happening. "I'll walk you up." I don't give her a moment to respond. I'm out and around to her side before she can swing the door fully open. I offer her my hand, but she's hesitant to accept. Finally, she does. She gracefully steps out and we walk in silence.

This fucking sucks. I don't know if I want her more because I can't have her, or if what I'm feeling is more than that. It doesn't fucking matter though.

I can't have her, and I need to end this in a way that she knows that. She turns to face me as we get to her door.

But I can't go through with it. Her wide blue eyes focus on me and I find myself leaning forward and wrapping my arms around her waist. She moans into my mouth and kisses me back.

I shouldn't be doing this.

My tongue dips inside, tasting her. My hands find her ass and grip her cheeks. She pulls away from me. Her breathing comes in pants. She wants me. I nip her bottom lip and give her one more kiss.

I may not be able to see her after tonight. But I'm not going to crush her heart until I absolutely have to. I don't want to see her sad. I don't want her angry at me. Not like she was. I fucking love this side of her. I love that she wants me.

"See you later, sweetheart."

She hums in satisfaction and watches me as I walk to the car.

I wait to leave until after she's in the house.

I've gotta get some shit done and then I'll send her a text. My heart hardens in my chest. The *familia* comes to Sunday dinner. I don't want her around them. I know by now everyone will know. An intense urge to protect her makes my muscles tight as I drive away.

I'll just show them she's fine. Let her wait in the foyer or something where they can see her. Then she can go.

And then I'll really have to say goodbye.

ELLE

"*I* said I'm sorry, Elle."

I hear my mom's voice, but I ignore her as I look through the bills again. I can't fucking believe this.

"I can't afford this!" I yell, interrupting whatever she was about to say. I'm sitting at my desk chair, and I finally turn to look at her. She's pale and gaunt looking. She hasn't taken care of herself. Not recently. Not ever. And it's noticeable. Her blonde hair is pulled tight into a ponytail which makes her skin look even more wrinkled and her face more sunken in. I don't even recognize her.

"Of course you can. They wouldn't let me take out the loans if you couldn't afford them."

"No! I can't!" I can't help the anger heating my blood. I'm going to have to drop out of school. There's no way I can afford to live on a grad student's wage and only work part-time in the lab in order to pay this shit off. My heart sinks in my chest. I shouldn't have to. I shouldn't have to do this.

"How many more?" I ask her. She's done this shit before. I know she's hiding some. Ones that she isn't *that* overdue on.

"Those are the only ones with your name on them." Her eyes widen as she puts her hand over her heart. Her voice lowers as she cries. "I only did it because I had to."

"You didn't *have* to do it!" I'm still angry and still screaming, and that's not what she expects. I can't help it though. It's so true. "You don't have to make my life hell."

She shakes her head and starts to speak, but I stop her.

"Don't! Don't you dare. I'm going to have to quit school now. You know that?" Oddly enough though, quitting school seems like more a relief than anything else.

"You have to know I didn't mean for this to happen. I promise you, Elle. I'm going to fix this. I kicked him out. I did. It was stupid of me. I'm going to my AA meetings, I swear!"

Her eyes plead with me to forgive her as her hands clasp in front of her and tears fall down her face. It melts my anger and just makes me sad. I feel pathetic believing her, but I really do. I can help her. I know I can.

"I'll figure this out, Mom."

She practically runs to me and wraps her arms around my shoulders, crying as she says thank you and sorry over and over again. I pat her back and try to comfort her until I can send her away.

I stare at the closed door and feel sick to my stomach. She hasn't paid a single dime on the mortgage. So there's a couple grand that I owe there. But what's even worse are the credit cards. Cash withdrawals of thousands of dollars at 22%. I'll consolidate. I don't know who's going to give me a loan for that amount. But I'll find a way. I sift through the papers and mentally calculate what I need. A little over 26k in total. My heart sinks. I made 22k a year at my old college, and a measly 14k being the night shift part-timer in the lab. I have nothing saved up because of her last "situation". And I make 26k at this university and haven't found a job here yet.

My head falls into my hands. There's just no way. I don't see how anyone would loan me the money.

I'll try. The least I can do is try. I stand up from the desk and breathe in deep. I'm not going to cry because that accomplishes nothing.

I take one step and wince. I can still feel him inside of me. I feel raw and sore, but I love it. It's a strange feeling, finally giving myself to someone.

I shake my head and sigh as I lay down on the bed. It's not even made. All my stuff is still in moving boxes, along with my sheets. I don't have much. But it'll feel better once this room looks like my old bedroom.

I close my eyes and remember his hands on me. The heated looks he gave me as he fucked me. I moan and clench my thighs, loving the soreness. I want him again and again. I loved the way he fucked me. I've really been missing out.

I pop up and and dig in my purse for the birth control pills. It's a few hours late, but it'll be alright. I bite the inside of my cheek. Maybe I should get the morning after pill too. I feel my cheeks flame and I start feeling ... dirty. I don't like the tightness in my chest. I wanted the whole experience and I got it. Maybe I'm naïve or stupid. I don't know, maybe I'm a slut for wanting that. I swallow the lump in my throat and grab my bottle of water to swallow down the pill. It doesn't matter now. I got what I wanted.

My heart hurts. I don't know what to think. One moment he's noncommittal, the next he's kissing me like he needs the air in my lungs to breathe.

I understand it probably seemed like a hookup last night, but I can't help wanting more.

I roll my eyes. Of course I'm being a clingy bitch. No man wants that. And that's not what this was. It may have felt like more to me, but I'm sure that's only because he was my first. I wonder if I told him that last night. I'm too embarrassed to ask. I pick up my phone and scroll through the contacts. Before we left he called himself from my phone so he'd have my number. I like that. I like how in charge he is. My eyes widen as I look at the screen and see it light up with a text from him.

Shit! I didn't press send or anything, did I? I stare at it for a moment trying to figure out what the hell I did before I realize he's the one who sent me a text. My heart beats rapidly and I find my body heating with nerves.

What the hell? I feel like I'm in high school again. I calm my nerves and realize the reason he's texting is just that I've left one of my textbooks back at his place.

That was stupid of me. Also... I'm gonna need that so I can sell it. These books aren't cheap.

As I'm debating how to reply, another text comes through:

MEET ME AT MY PARENTS' *house, it's closer to you and I'll be there tonight at 5.*

THE TEXT IS FOLLOWED up with an address. I wonder if I should wait a few minutes before responding, but I'm pretty sure he can see that I've read them anyway. I cringe. I wonder if that looks clingy. I don't want to look that way. I wanna seem laid-back. Eh. Whatever. I shrug my shoulder and send a reply.

THANKS. *I'll see you then.*

AND THANKS for the orgasms this morning. May I have another? I laugh at my inner thought. I am not sending that, although it's exactly what I want to say. He's sweet and funny. And fucks my body like it was made for his dick. My thighs clench again.

Damn, one time and I'm a sex addict. I put down my phone and sit up, ready to get my mind on something else. But then I remember the shit my mother left me saddled with, and my heart sinks. I bite the inside of my cheek. I need to get my ass up and go look for a job. Make that jobs. One for myself, and one fit for a recovering alcoholic. I'm not going to waste my life taking care of her. She needs to get her shit in order. I nod my head with anger as I pull my laptop from my bag and open it up on the desk.

Everything's going to be just fine. Even as I think the words and try to believe them, something deep in my gut is telling me it's a lie.

VINCE

I put the phone back in my pocket. She's quick to answer and agreed to meet me tonight, just like I knew my sweetheart would. She's giving me a clingy vibe--usually that turns me off, but on her, I like it.

I blow out a long exhale and face the docks. If only the rest of my day could be this easy.

"Boss, we got another problem." Tommy walks up behind me. I turn to look at him and see his chin is bruised up nice. Seeing it almost makes me feel like a prick. Almost. I know he was doing what he thought was best for the family, but fuck that. I'd do it again if I had to.

"It's all fucked today." I shove my hands in my pockets and stare at the water, listening to the waves beat against the dock. Three orders came in, but all three were only partially filled. "What's wrong with this one?"

"Supposed to be 50 pounds." I nod my head. I know how much we should be getting from the Marzano Cartel. It's the same we've been getting for nearly 7 months now. "We've only got 42 here."

"Someone is skimming. Who is it that counted? I want all the names, Tommy."

"I was there for this one, boss. I saw it opened."

"And the container?" It's possible someone fucked with them on the ship.

In which case we have all their names and addresses. Someone would have a real rough night if it came down to that.

"Locked and untouched." He's confident, and that tells me everything I need to know.

"So it's their end that's fucking with us." That's not good. It's never good ending business relations in the line of work we do. But I'm not putting up with this shit. "Did they think we wouldn't notice 8 pounds were missing?" Not to mention the guns. They were light, too.

"Could be someone in packing on their end." Tommy's got a point.

"I'll send a message to Javier. We need this shit dealt with immediately." I have to walk back to the docks to get the phone we use for that shit. Tommy walks with me.

"How's the other situation going?" he asks. My hands flex and I crack my neck trying to keep my temper at bay. I know he's concerned, but I don't like him asking about her.

"It worked. She doesn't remember shit."

He nods his head and grins. "That's fucking fantastic." He doesn't sound as thrilled as he'd like me to believe he is. "You sure about that?"

"Positive." He shuts his mouth and nods his head, walking silently beside me. I'm the underboss, he knows not to question me. I can see his worry though, so I decide to put him out of his misery. "She's easy to read, and she's gonna come over tonight for a quick second to grab a book I took from her." I open the heavy door and grin at him. "You can see for yourself, Tommy."

"So what'd she think? You two just had a wild night together?"

I give him a smug look that lets him know that's exactly what she thought and that I got some this morning too.

"Are you fucking for real? You tapped that ass?" He's grinning from ear to ear, but shaking his head in disbelief.

"Damn right." I hesitate to say more, but I figure why the hell not let him in on it. "I want her again, too."

He cocks an eyebrow at me. "Going back for seconds isn't your thing."

"Wasn't. But this girl is real sweet." I don't usually brag, but this broad is different. I want everyone to know I had her. More than that, I want them to know she's mine.

"Good girls like bad boys. I want me one of those." He says.

"A good girl?" I ask.

"Yeah."

"Then go get one." I park my ass at my desk and unlock the desk drawer. I reach in and grab the right cell phone and flip through the info on my notepad. I appreciate Tommy's distraction, 'cause this shit fucking sucks.

"They aren't all that easy to find, not with how often you've got me working." He sits at one of the opposite seats and stretches his legs out in front of him. He nervously runs his hand on the back of his neck and opens and shuts his mouth a few times.

"What's going on?" I just want him to say whatever the fuck is on his mind.

He spits it out without the need for further prodding. "I'm real fucking sorry, Vince." His eyes turn sad. "You know I didn't want to. I was just doing things according to protocol."

I look him directly in the eye. "Witnesses don't live to be witnesses." That's still protocol. It was stupid of me to risk this shit. Everyone knows it. I worry a bit that they think women make me soft. Specifically, this woman. After all, I'm going to be the one taking over. I can't have them thinking that. "This was a one-off, Tommy. You did what you should've."

"Alright boss." He taps his hands on the armrests and looks like he's getting ready to take off.

"Everything else good for going out tonight?" I ask him, while I have his attention.

"Everything is set. Unless you want to add anything in the shipment going to the cartel."

I smirk at him. "Not yet, let's make sure we play this smart." Sending a message like what he's thinking would be bad for everyone. I gotta make this call and let our business partners know what's up. Eight pounds missing is over 200 grand of our money gone, but it's over a million in gross after it's cut and sold. Whoever took it wanted a reaction from us. They're going to get one. I just have to figure out exactly who it was that tried to fuck us over and what they thought they'd get from pulling this shit. Stealing some product to profit on the side is one thing. Skimming off the top--I've seen that, too.

But fucking with a shipment to start a war is also a possibility. The thought gives me an uneasy feeling. War is something we've dealt with not too long ago, with my brother Dom. And his woman got caught up in that shit. An uneasy feeling settles in my gut. I'm not gonna let that shit happen again.

ELLE

I'm feeling more and more pathetic as I scroll through my phone. I literally have no one to talk to. I want to tell someone that I lost my V-card. *Anyone.* But I feel a bit pathetic that it took me this long, and who am I going to talk to anyway? I just realized I've essentially lost touch with all my friends from undergrad. We like each other's FB posts, but I haven't had a real conversation with Michelle or Amy in almost two years. Michelle is married now, and I think she's pregnant. Yeah, she's definitely pregnant. I remember seeing a picture of her with a huge belly, opening a box of blue balloons. Damn. I'm really out of touch.

That's alright though. I'm going to start today. After all, I need to meet people in this town so that I can find a job. I applied for 20 positions, everything from waitressing and working at the hardware store, to working as a library assistant at the university. I'm almost out of gas now, too. I picked up a few applications for Mom, but she needs to get her shit together first.

The more I think about it, the more I realize I need to get mom to just sell this house. I can get a part-time job and still go to school, just like I did back in Maryland. I can do it again here. Only this time I'll have Mom live with me so I can keep an eye on her.

I shove my phone into my clutch and take a look at myself in the dresser mirror. I have to back up and stand on my tiptoes to see my outfit fully. I like it. I think I look pretty in this yellow and white, striped cotton sundress, but still laid-back. The dress flows out from my hips in an A-line shape, but hugs the little dip in my waist. If only my boobs were bigger. I scrunch my nose wondering if I should grab my padded bra. My lips purse as I decide no, I don't need that. He knows they're little. It's too late to fool him now.

I'm guessing he just wants me to run in and grab the book, which is fine. I want to look good though. *And* I'm not going to be clingy or anything like that. I'm going to play it cool. He doesn't want strings, and I get that. I don't need strings or a commitment. It's not like I have my shit together anyway. But I don't like the idea of it being just a fling.

I'm sure that's what I was thinking last night, trying to hook up with him. I bet I took an extra shot or two so I'd have the courage to go through with it this time. It's not like I've been saving myself. I just haven't gotten around to it.

Each step down the stairs makes the soreness between my legs obvious. I can't hide from what I did. Part of me is feeling ashamed. Like I should have saved myself for someone who would've loved me. But I keep shoving that feeling down. My father never loved my mother. Most of my friends growing up were the products of divorced parents. Love is something that comes and goes, I suppose. I don't know if I'll ever even fall in love. I don't know if I have it in me.

But a quick fuck with no strings attached was something I thought I could handle. I always chickened out though. I'm not sure if I was more afraid that I'd fall for the guy and get hurt, or that I would be sorely disappointed afterward. I wince at the bottom step and try to bend down to relieve some of the ache between my thighs. So far, so good on both fronts, although the possibility of falling for Vince is high on my list. A sexy man who knows how to fuck, with his own house and an adorable puppy? Yes, please! But there's always a catch. So I'm going to hold back. I'm not going to put my heart out there to be stomped. And everything is going to be just fine.

I look straight ahead and see my mother passed out on the couch. I close my eyes and take a deep breath to calm myself. It will all be fine. Everything will be fine. I walk over to her and brush the hair out of her face. One of her arms is hanging off of the side of the sofa and she's drooling on a pillow. She doesn't even have any pants on. Just a saggy old tank top and her underwear.

I bet if I looked in the kitchen, I'd find the bottle. I lean down closer and smell gin on her breath. Tears prick at my eyes. How can she keep doing this to herself? And to me, too? I spent all afternoon searching for a job while she got drunk. Deep down I know I can't stand for this. I need to do something. I just don't know what. I don't know how to say no to her without hurting her. And more than anything else, I don't want to hurt her. I put a hand on my heart and try to relieve the ache. My throat dries up, and I will the emotions away.

I'll go to AA with her. I will help her like a daughter should.

I take a step away and reach down for my keys, and I hear her mumble my name.

"It's your fault he hates me." I barely make out the words she speaks in her sleep.

I know what she's talking about. It's not the first time I've heard it either. I was the mistake that ruined my mother's chances at a real life. At least that's what she says when she's drunk. Angry drunk perfectly describes my Mom. But I'm going to help her.

I'm extremely quiet on my way out. I haven't lived here long enough to know where all the creaks in the floorboards are just yet. I wish I knew though, so I could make sure to avoid them as I leave. I don't want to wake her up. Not when she's thinking those thoughts. I don't want to get into another fight with her. Not over that. I don't even breathe until I've shut the door.

I twist the handle as I shut the door to avoid the loud click it would make otherwise, and then lock it. When I turn around, I lean back against the door for a moment. I take a deep breath, and my eyes catch sight of a plain, white car. It looks old and I've never seen it before. It's really out of place parked on the opposite side of the street. I see two women sitting in the front seats, each on their phones and any anxiety I had about the car is washed away.

I try to remember what I'm supposed to be doing. What I was so scared to hope for.

Vince.

I shake my head and feel stupid for even thinking about him. He's just giving me the book back. It was just a fling. I get in my car and look at my makeup. This is all so pointless and stupid. Just like this dress.

He's just going to give me the book, and then I'll leave. I'll probably never even hear from him again. That would be best anyway.

VINCE

"*How* much is gone?" Dom asks as soon as I walk in the dining room. Becca's in the backyard picking basil leaves or some shit. And she's getting big. She looks like she's going to pop any day now even though they've got a few months left before their little one is supposed to be here. Apparently I'm an asshole for saying that. Next time I'll keep my mouth shut or say she's glowing or some shit like that. The kids are with Ma and Anthony. So it's just Tommy, Pops, Dom, and Becca for now, and everyone else will show up later. No one ever misses Ma's Sunday dinners.

"We're off by about half a mil on this shipment." I answer him and Dom's eyes go wide, then the anger settles in.

"You've gotta be fucking kidding me." He's pissed. He's "lying low" with his fancy professor job, but he's still in charge of the money. I knew he wouldn't want to hear this shit.

"It's a setup for sure." I say.

"The cartel?" he asks.

"No. Javier had no clue. Said everything is monitored and would check it out. Right now I'm just waiting to hear back, but my money is on someone in packing. Someone with connections here who wants the territory."

"Who's trying to fuck with us? You think it's Shadows MC or the Cúram crew?" Dom's stayed in the loop more than I thought he would've. Shadows

Motorcycle Club has been itching for territory, but I don't see them pulling the trigger. We'd easily take them out. Cúram family is Irish and on their own turf. We aren't friendly, but they're not stupid. No one that I can think of has been wanting to fuck with us.

"We'll find out once I hear back from Javier with a name."

"What about the money?" he asks.

I frown and I suppress a groan. "They're waiting to make sure it's on their end, and then we'll talk."

"Best for business relations I guess." Irritation colors his voice, but he's right. I fucking hate waiting though.

Thinking about waiting reminds me that my sweetheart should be here soon. I have a bit of anxiety over her coming here. I'm worried something's gonna set someone off. I just want her in and out. And then on my dick again. I can't help that last part. My stomach knots thinking about how I'm gonna have to end it. I don't fucking want to though.

Tommy comes into the room and he must read my mind, or see me shifting my hardening dick in my pants. He busts out a laugh from his gut. "Your girl staying for dinner, Vince?"

"Girl? Since when did you settle down?" The look of approval in Dom's eyes makes me want to smack it away. I didn't settle, and I'm not settling down.

"I didn't, and I'm not. A broad's coming by to pick something up so Pops can see her and then she's gone."

"Thought you wanted to see her again?" Tommy asks.

"I do, but that'd be stupid."

"What's stupid is not taking something you want." Dom starts and I'm quick to cut him off.

"It's done, Dom. I can't have her, and I won't. I'm ending it as soon as she gets here." The absolution is firm in my voice, but I don't want it.

"What's wrong with her?" Dom asks, and it makes me angry. Not a damn thing is wrong with her.

"She's a witness, that's what's wrong," Pops says as he comes into the room, and Dom seems confused for a moment, but then pissed. Calling her a witness makes my blood run cold.

"A witness to what?" Dom asks.

"Doesn't fucking matter, because she doesn't remember shit," I say, putting an end to the conversation. "She's not a witness." My words come out hard and everyone looks at me like they'd like to disagree, but they're smart enough to keep their mouths shut. "Pops just wants to be sure. And I'm gonna show him she's good, and then she walks. No one fucking touches her."

Dom's eyebrows raise and I stare at him until he concedes. "Whatever you say, Vince." He throws up his hands in surrender. "I don't have a problem with it if you say it's all good." Pops nods his head and slaps a hand on my shoulder.

Before he can speak the doorbell rings, and we all look at the door. My heart clenches, knowing I'm gonna be saying goodbye to my sweetheart. It's going to break her heart, but she shouldn't be with a man like me anyway.

She's too good for me. I'm sure she knows that.

I walk quickly to the door, knowing the book is on the dining room table. I'll walk her in so everyone can see her, and walk her ass right back out.

Nice and easy.

My chest tightens as I twist the doorknob. I'm not sure if it's because I think something's going to go wrong, or because I won't be able to let go.

VINCE

*S*he looks beautiful in her little dress. I like it more than those tiny-ass shorts she was wearing when we first met. She looks like the sweetheart she is. That, and no one can see how perky her ass is in this dress. She should wear dresses like this all the time. I give her a tight smile even though seeing her puts me a bit at ease. My nerves are fucking killing me. I swear to God everyone can hear how fast my heart's beating.

I need to get my shit together. Everything's gonna be fine. And then I'll end this, and she'll be safe. My heart drops in my chest knowing she won't be mine. She'll never be mine. But at least I know she'll be safe.

"Come on in, sweetheart," I greet her, and open the door good and wide for her to enter. My parents' house is a nice home, but it's old. Family pictures line the wall of the foyer. All of the picture frames are different, and there are a couple dozen of them in total. Ma doesn't like taking any photos down, just adding new ones over time. The newest are the pictures of my nephew, Ethan. Dom's little boy looks just like him.

She smiles, but it seems just as forced as mine. My heart sputters in my chest. She didn't remember, did she? Her eyes linger on the pictures, and her lips soften and pull into a genuine smile. Good. I want her to be happy. I want them to see how happy and at ease she is. My eyes focus past her and land on

Tommy. If she remembered what she witnessed yesterday, there's no way she'd be alright in front of him.

She turns, and the dress flutters out at the motion. Her ponytail sways back and forth in time with her hips. My eyes focus on those hips. I want to flip up her dress and fuck the shit out of her. The need to claim her is riding me hard, but I need to shake that shit off.

"Hi there, beautiful," Tommy says to her as she walks into the dining room, making a beeline for the book that's on the edge of the table. I don't like his tone. I know he's just testing her, but I don't like him calling her beautiful.

"Hi there," she answers in a peppy voice and grabs her book, hugging it to her chest. The pressure makes her breasts bulge slightly from the top of the sweetheart neckline of her dress and gives them a fuller look. She's not doing it on purpose, but I wanna spank her ass for it all the same.

Fuck this broad has gotten under my skin. All I can think about is nailing her, but now is not the time or place.

"How are you doing? Elle, is it?" Pops asks. He's across the room still, pouring himself a scotch from the old bar in the corner of the room.

"I'll take one of those, Pops," I say over Elle as she starts to answer him, and feel like an ass for interrupting. My nerves are getting to me and this isn't good. The *familia's* here. Pops is here. I need to get my shit together and keep it cool. I can't fuck this up. "Sorry, sweetheart." I gentle my hand on the small of her back and give her a kiss on the cheek. "Elle, that's my Pops, my cousin Tommy, and my brother Dom." They nod at her in turn as I introduce them one by one. "Dom's wife Becca is out back."

"Hi everyone." She looks timid and shy, and rocks a little on her heels before turning to me. "Thank you for this." Her big blue eyes meet mine and I can't speak. I don't want to walk her to the door and say goodbye.

"No problem," I finally answer, and then clear my throat. I turn, ready to walk her out, but Pops' voice bellows from across the room.

"So, how'd you two meet?" he asks.

I meet his gaze as Elle answers. I wish he wouldn't do this shit. "At a bar last night, I left my book," a blush rises in her cheeks, "in Vince's car." Her shoulders hunch inward and she fidgets with one of her heels on the ground. She's a fucking horrible liar. "He was nice enough to take me home. I drank a little too much." She can't even look Pops in the eyes. A chuckle rises up my chest and I can't stop it. She looks at me with wide, pleading eyes. She's fucking adorable.

"No problem, sweetheart." I turn my body again to lead her out. I know it's rude to be ending it so short, and I can see the hurt in her eyes, but it's for the best.

"You don't want to stay for dinner?" Dom asks, and I want to beat the shit out of him for it.

"No--"

"No--" We both answer at the same time, and then exchange glances. Why the fuck doesn't she want to stay for dinner? My eyes narrow on hers searching for an answer. I mean it's not like I invited her, but still. She's fucking quick to get out of here. She breaks my gaze and turns to walk towards the door.

She smiles over her shoulder, still holding the book like it's her lifeline. "Nice to meet you all."

"I'll walk you out, sweetheart." I open the door for her and place my hand on her back.

"That's alright," she replies, and her tone is sad. "It's fine."

The way she says it's fine makes it obvious that she's not fine. "I *want* to walk you out." The words come out of my mouth before I can stop them. I don't like the look on her face. I don't like seeing her so unhappy. But should I walk her out? No, no I shouldn't. I should let this end already. End it quickly and cleanly. Ignore her texts. That's what I should do.

Her eyes fall to the floor as she gives me a weak smile and relents. "Okay." My heart fucking hurts. I guess she can sense what's going on. Fuck, this sucks.

I open the door all the way and take a step to push the screen door open for her, but a loud bang from the dining room makes both of us jump. Tommy cusses with both of his hands raised, broken glass and bourbon at his feet. Clumsy fuck dropped his glass. I raise my eyes and look around the room as Tommy swears and wipes his hands down the front of his shirt. They focus right on Pops, but his eyes aren't on me. They're on Elle.

Her eyes are wide, and her chest rises and falls dramatically. At first I think the loud bang and Tommy cussing scared her. But this is more. This is bad, really fucking bad. I remember right before she woke up in the office. I grind my teeth in anger. He dropped something then too. The loud bang, him cussing. Fuck! Could it really be triggered that easily? She was almost gone. Almost in the clear. Her feet back up with small steps, pushing the door into the wall. Her knuckles turn white, clutching that damn book.

She swallows thickly and then looks at me. Her eyes dart from me, to each of the men in the room who are all staring at her now. She reaches for the knob to the screen door, and lets out a small scream as I pull it shut and pull her into my chest. I back her ass into my crotch and push the front door closed behind us.

Dom looks at Pops, who says something I can't quite make out. Guessing by how fast Dom takes off through the kitchen to the backyard, it must be about getting to Becca. Sure enough, I hear the sliding doors open and slam closed.

No one moves, and the only sound is Elle crying softly. She shakes her head in my arms and I find myself shushing her. She's not fighting me. But she knows something. She remembered *something*.

"Sweetheart, tell me what's wrong," I say calmly into her ear. She's facing the dining room. Everyone can see her and I hate that, so I turn her in my arms, but she tries to back away from me. She wants to get out of my arms and I don't like that. She's not going anywhere.

"Nothing. Please just let me go."

I give her a small smile and brush the tears off her cheeks. Her skin is so soft. So perfect. "I can't do that now, can I? Something's wrong, and you need to tell me what."

Her breath comes in chaotically as she frantically looks around the room like she's trapped. Which she is.

"Sweetheart, you need to calm down." I try to pet her back to calm her ass down, although I'm not sure what the point of that is.

Tommy comes up to my right side with those fucking pills in his hands, ready to shove them down her throat again. "No! Get that shit out of her face."

"You sure, Vince?" Fuck. It didn't work. I'm not doing it again. It didn't fucking work.

I look around the room and feel like a failure. I failed my Pops, Tommy, and especially Elle. It's all my fucking fault.

"Please don't hurt me," she whispers.

"What do you remember, babe?" I ask.

"Nothing." She's quick to answer while shaking her head.

"Don't lie to me." My words are cold, and my grip on her tightens. "I've got all night sweetheart, but I'd rather you just tell me now." It hits me in that moment, as I look past her to my Pops, she's dead. Doesn't matter what all she remembers. She's dead.

"I remember," she gasps and holds the book tighter. She tries to speak again, "the woods." I wasn't expecting that.

"What about 'em?" I ask.

"How we," she swallows and keeps her eyes closed tight, "how you." She breathes in deep trying to settles her breath, "took me in the woods."

Oh, fuck that! Anger consumes me and adrenaline rushes through me.

"Took you?" I raise my voice. "As in, fucked you?" She visibly recoils at my anger, and she tries to get out of my arms again. "No, no, sweetheart, that shit did not happen." This is not fucking happening. Her memory comes back and it's some shit that makes me a god damned villain. Something I didn't even do!

"I--" she tries to speak, and then finally meets my eyes. Hers are red-rimmed and filled with tears. "I think I remember."

"Sweetheart, your memory is wrong. We screwed around a bit, but that's not what happened in the woods."

Her eyes look to the wall and then back to me. Her hand raises to her throat. "Did you hurt me?" As she asks, her eyes drift to the faint marks on her wrists, and her eyes widen.

"It's not what you think." I try to keep my voice even, but my skin is on fire and I can feel their eyes boring into me, thinking I hurt her.

"No, we didn't. I know we didn't. This morning was the first time." Her voice is small as she stares at her wrists and then closes her eyes.

"That's right we didn't. I wouldn't fuck you when you were like that."

She raises her eyes to mine. "But you did hurt me. I remember. I remember you, and I remember them. You were angry with me."

Her breath comes in shallow pants and then she looks behind me at Pops and Tommy. She hesitantly steps closer to me, but then looks at the door. "Please let me go. I won't say anything." Her small hand settles on my chest and her eyes plead with me. "Please."

"I can't let that happen, sweetheart." It fucking kills me to say it. I see Tommy leave the room, but my father stays.

"I won't say anything. I don't know what to think. I'm not okay," she says.

241

"No, you're not okay," I answer back. Truer words have never been said.

She swallows thickly and then looks back at the door again with tears running down her cheeks. "I'm scared, Vince." She's huddling next to me like I'm going to save her.

I tell her the only thing I can think of to say. "You should be."

ELLE

"*I* don't want to hurt you, sweetheart. I don't want to, but I will." I hear Vince's cold, hard voice in my head over and over again. A chill washes through my body. I push my body into his chest as though it will make it go away. I don't know what's real. My mind is fucking with me.

Flashes of scenes play before my eyes. His handsome smile as he introduces himself to me. *"I'm Vince."* The heated look in his eyes as he looks up at me from between my legs. But then, there's more. More that I didn't remember this morning. Him choking me, pinning me against the wall. Then his cousin and another man. Smaller in size than Vince, but both with threatening looks on their faces. It makes my heart skip a beat.

"Vince, what happened?" I whisper into his chest, afraid to know the answer. But I need something. Something is very, very wrong.

"I can't tell you, sweetheart." His calm voice forces a sob up my throat.

"Please don't hurt me," I beg him. I know he will though. I can sense it in the thick air, in the way they all looked at me. I'm answered with silence. "I'm not supposed to remember, am I?"

"I'm sorry, Elle." His words are more sad than anything else. He's truly remorseful, and that makes me sick to my stomach. He doesn't have to hurt me.

I push the words through my hollow chest. "I promise--"

He cuts me off. "That's not good enough."

"What can I do? Please," I cry into his shirt and drop the book to the floor. I was just with him this morning. "Please, Vince. I swear."

I feel a strong hand on my back and Vince turns his body, taking me with him and pushing my back against the wall.

"Don't fucking touch her," he growls above my head, looking over his shoulder.

My body stills with fear and I can't breathe.

"No one touches her!" he screams above my head.

I grip onto his shirt tighter. He'll save me. He has to save me.

He grips my hip and throws the front door open. "Vince, what are you doing?" It's his father's voice.

"I'm taking her to the cabin." I nearly trip trying to keep up with him. Everything flies past me in a blur from the tears and from how quickly he moves my body outside to his car.

And then he opens the trunk. My feet dig into the ground, and I try to push away from him, but he picks me up and tosses me in like I weigh nothing. My head bangs against the floor of the trunk and I scream out. When I open my eyes, I see his hard gaze.

"None of that, sweetheart. Be a good girl and stay quiet." I don't dare disobey him. I know he's my only hope.

ELLE

*T*he entire car ride, I'm silent. I close my eyes and try to remember. I think I remember being here before, being tied up. My fingers graze over the faint marks on my wrists. I'm quiet. I'll do as he says for now, but I know that will only get me so far. How the fuck did this happen? I concentrate on breathing and then I remember about a secret latch in the trunk. Well, not secret. But there's a latch in here somewhere. My hands run along every surface looking for it. But there's nothing. I spend the entire ride looking for it, only to come up short.

My breathing hitches the longer the car stays still. My body jolts as the car door slams. A whimper escapes me and I cover my mouth. The light burns my eyes as he opens the trunk. It's not that bright, but compared to the darkness in the trunk, it kills my sight. He reaches in and picks me up easily by my waist. I cower under his touch as he sets me down. My feet land softly, and that's when I remember. Like deja vu.

I remember running.

My eyes follow the path I took. I remember his hard body knocking me to the ground. And then I have flashes of memories of him pounding into me, both of us naked as he ruts between my legs, pushing my body into the dirt.

As if reading my mind, Vince growls out, "I didn't." His tone is defensive and hard. I swallow the lump growing in my throat. I know he didn't. I would have felt it this morning. But I remember it. Why do I remember it happening that way? More importantly, why did he want me to forget?

"I know." The words catch in my throat and come out much higher than I intended. I clear my throat and cross my arms to grip my shoulders. "I don't understand, Vince."

He takes a deep breath, but doesn't meet my eyes. "You need to go inside, Elle."

I look at the house. It's the same country home I thought was so cute this morning, but as I look at it now, fear makes my legs collapse. We're in the middle of nowhere. I can't go in there. In the movies, a secluded place like this is where they kill you. No one will hear me scream. My body begs me to run.

Vince grips my elbow and leans into my neck. His hot breath sends chills down my shoulder and back as he warns, "Don't you fucking dare run from me."

A whimper escapes my lips. He pulls me toward the house and I move with him. This has happened before, and I was still alive this morning despite everything. Maybe it will happen again.

"Will I forget in the morning?" I can only hope I will.

"No." He swings the front door open as the hope dies in my chest. "It didn't work."

"I don't understand," I plead.

"Stop whining!" he yells at me as I walk inside with him. His anger forces me to rip my arm from his grasp, but it's a clumsy, uncontrolled motion, and my back slams against the wall just inside the door. My hands cover my mouth and I try to stifle the need to cry.

"Fuck!" he screams into the air, and kicks the door. I hear Rigs barking upstairs. His paws scratch against a door. I back away slowly and find myself cowering in the corner. Vince's fists slam into the wall, leaving dents and a trail of blood on the white walls. His knuckles are bloodied but he keeps doing it over and over. Each time his fists pound against the wall my chest jumps and a scream threatens to escape. Rigs barks and growls and Vince yells at him to be quiet.

I'm fucked. I'm so fucked.

He finally stops and takes a deep breath. The only sounds in the room are the dog barking and Vince's heavy breaths. His large shoulders rise and fall with power. He turns slowly towards me and stares at me for a long time.

When he finally opens his mouth I let out a heavy breath I didn't realize I was holding. "I'm supposed to kill you," he says.

My body turns weak and I fall to the floor. I want to plead, but I can't. I can't do anything. I'm paralyzed. *I don't want to die.*

"I'm going to figure something out, sweetheart." He walks slowly toward me and picks up my trembling body. Half of me wants to push him off of me and try to run, but the other half is too terrified to consider fighting. The terrified side is the side that is winning. He carries me up the stairs and I remain as still as possible in his arms.

He speaks calmly. "You need to be good for me. You need to make this easy." I can't respond. But if I could, I'd tell him to go fuck himself. I'm not going to make it easy for him to kill me. I can't speak the words, but he must sense my disobedience. "Don't you fuck with me, Elle."

I shouldn't make him angry, but I can't answer. Fear has crippled me.

He kicks a door open, and I recognize the room. It's where we were this morning. I look at the messy bed, still unmade, and see a pink stain on the sheets.

I hear him shushing me; I feel him trying to comfort me. It just makes me feel even worse.

My chest has never felt so hollow or painful before. I never knew I could feel this much physical pain from emotional damage.

VINCE

*W*hat the fuck am I going to do? My phone keeps going off in my pocket. I know it's the guys or Pops. I can't answer it. I know what they're going to say. I know their argument. I really believe her, I do. She's not going to say shit. But I can hear them shooting back the next logical question. *What if she remembers more?* I still don't have an answer to that question.

Not only that, but she's been seen with me now. Twice. If someone happened to be watching, which happens every now and then--if they're watching and saw her, they can take her in. They can put pressure on her. And even the best of people collapse under that pressure. I look down at Elle and try rubbing her back again. She's curled up on the bed. They'd get to her for sure. She couldn't tell a lie to save her life.

Rigs barks again and I know my poor pup wants out of the spare bedroom. I left him in there so he wouldn't chew up all the furniture while I was gone. He wants to make sure everything is alright. But it's not. He's gonna have to stay in there until I can calmly let him out. This is so fucked. It's all just fucked.

I try pulling her back to me, closer to me. My hand is fucking killing me, but I need to comfort her. I shouldn't have done that. I know I scared her. Now she won't even look at me. I just want to hold her. But she's scooting away. I don't like it. I don't want to let go of her, but I need to figure this shit out. And realistically, the only thing I can come up with, is that she has to go.

I knew it back at my parents' house. I could see it happening, one of them coming up from behind her with a syringe filled with a lethal injection cocktail trio. It would feel like a pinch, and then it'd be over with. She'd go quickly and painlessly. But the image of her dead and limp in my arms is something I can't handle. I don't want that. I want her to live. I want to see her happy.

I need to figure this shit out, but I haven't got a clue how. We never let witnesses live. I've got nothing but our standard protocol to go on.

I wrap my arms around her waist and pull her to me, forcing her into my lap. Her hand whips out and pushes violently against my chest.

"Don't push me, sweetheart," I grit through my teeth. You'd think she'd be doing whatever she could not to make me angry. I'm her only fucking hope.

"Fuck you!" she screams out, and I grab her mouth to silence her.

"Watch your mouth, sweetheart."

"Don't touch me!" She yells.

"Sweetheart, watch that mouth-"

"Fuck you!" she yells again.

"Oh yeah?" I pin her ass down on the bed. Both of her tiny wrists fit easily in one hand, and I shove them above her head and dig them into the mattress. My hip pins hers down. "You really think you should be talking to me like that, Elle?" I keep the threat in my voice. I have a soft spot for this broad. Everyone's gonna know it. But not her. She can't know that, not yet. She needs to be afraid until I can figure this shit out. And right now, fear is not the dominant emotion that I sense.

"Just kill me!" she screams in my face. Her words hit me like a bullet to the chest. Her face is red and her cheeks are stained with tears. Her eyes glassy with more unshed tears. Her voice lowers. "I know you're going to kill me, so just do it already."

"I don't want to kill you, Elle." It's true. I don't want to. The fact that she's telling me to kill her makes me sick to my stomach.

"So you're going to let me go?" Her voice doesn't hold any hope; she already knows the answer will be no.

"No." She closes her eyes at my answer and turns on the bed to face away from me as best she can with me still pinning her down. I loosen my grip and let her go. I run a hand down my face and look around the room. It's a safe house. So there's no way she can get out of here. I need to go. I've got to get out of here for just a minute and figure out just how badly I've fucked up. And let my dog out before he tears the door down.

I open the door and check my key in the lock to make sure she can't lock me out. She can't. So that's a plus, I guess. I look back at her lying limp and in the fetal position on the bed. "I'm not going to hurt you." I say it just loud enough for her to hear and take a step out into the hallway.

I shut the door and my fucking heart breaks as I barely make out her words. "You already have."

ELLE

I have no fucking clue where I am. Obviously this is Vince's house, but where this is located, I have no idea. I didn't pay attention this morning either. I just know it was a long drive. But I'm getting out of here. There's no way I'm staying here. I don't know how long he's going to keep me here. I know they want me dead. They can't risk me remembering whatever the fuck it is that I saw. But I really need to get the fuck away from here as fast as I can.

I finally get my ass off the bed and wipe the tears from my face. I need to do *something*. I can't just wait here to die. For all I know he's going to come in the room with a gun or something and kill me, or however the fuck they do it. I can't just wait around. I won't. I don't want to die.

I walk as quietly as I can to the curtains in the room and open them wide. The windows are large. Really fucking large. Like they were meant to be used to escape from the bedroom. Good. 'Cause that's exactly what I'm going to do. I run my hand along the top of the sill, searching for a latch, but I don't find one. My forehead wrinkles with consternation, and my heart beats faster. I push against the top. I try pushing it up with everything I have in me. But it doesn't budge. Fuck! What the fuck is the point of this window being so damn big then? I want to pound my fists against it, but that would be stupid. He'd hear. I have to be quiet. I have to figure out something else.

I tiptoe to the door. My heart's trying to leap up my throat, but I keep moving. I have to try. I push my ear to the door and I can hear his voice, but I can't make out the words. He must be downstairs. I twist the knob, but it doesn't budge. I try again with both hands and it doesn't give. I look at the knob and see it's not locked, but then my eyes travel up. There's a second lock. Motherfucker!

I want to scream at that asshole. He locked me in! I'm locked in here like a bird in its gilded cage. I huff in a staggered breath and walk backwards slowly until I'm against the wall. I lower myself to the floor. I have to wait. I raise my head and cast a glance around the room. I need to find a weapon. I'm quick to get up with this thought in mind.

I may not be able to run, but I'll fight. I'll do whatever I have to. I pull open the drawer of the nightstand. It's empty except for a stack of papers. I go through his dresser, one drawer at a time. Nothing. Not a damn thing. I stare at the gun safe in the corner of the room. I can't imagine he left it unlocked, but I have to try anyway. I pull the door, but it's no use.

The bathroom. I race to the en suite, but keep my steps light. There has to be something in here. My eyes catch sight of a razor. It's not much, but it'll have to do. I grab the plastic handle and tilt it on its side on the counter. I need to crack the plastic so I can get to the blade.

My eyes search for anything that's hard and heavy enough to do the job. I finally see the tumbler by the sink. The bottom is stainless steel. I grab the towel from the hook and lay it on the counter to absorb some of the noise. I smash the tumbler on top of the razor, hard, but not hard enough to make much noise.

My heart stills and my blood rushes faster, waiting to hear anything from downstairs. Nothing. So I hit it again and again until the plastic cracks. I try pulling the plastic back, but I need more give. I tilt the razor and try to angle it so it'll be more effective. I raise my arm up and smash it down.

Yes! The plastic cracks even more, and I'm able to wiggle the blade out carefully. I raise the blade up to my eyes to look at the shiny, metal weapon. It's small. Really fucking small. But maybe if I can catch him by surprise, I'll be able to hurt him enough to escape.

"Whatcha doing, sweetheart?" I jump at the sound of Vince's voice and nearly drop the blade.

I stare at Vince from across the room. He sneaked up on me. How long has he been watching me? I don't answer him. Instead I make a fist and position the blade in the space between two of my fingers so it'll cut him when I swing.

We both know what I'm doing. My blood heats and rushes in my ears. My heart feels like it's trying to escape my body. It's beating that wildly. But I ignore my heart and blood both. Vince's gaze is hard and focused on me.

"You planning on hitting me, sweetheart?" He takes a step toward me and as much as I want to stand my ground, I instinctively take a step back. "You wanna hurt me, Elle?"

No. I don't. I don't want to hurt him.

"You wanna kill me baby, is that it?" I shake my head, but keep my eyes trained on him. I take another step back as he steps even closer. My back hits the wall. I'm cornered. Sweat covers my body with a chill.

"That's not very nice. Here I am trying to help you." He lunges for me and I try to hit him, but he grabs my wrist and forces my hand above my head. I scream and try to push him away as he twists my wrist and the blade slips through my fingers. Faintly, I hear the thin metal hit the tiled floor.

My body sags as he pushes his hard chest against me. I close my eyes and push my head against the wall. Sadness weakens my body.

He grips my jaw and forces me to face him, but I keep my eyes closed. I can't look at him. "You were going to kill me, sweetheart? You wanted to kill me?"

I try to shake my head but I can't. I try to speak, but with his hand on my jaw, I can't.

"Look at me!" he yells into my face, and it forces a whimper out of me, but my eyes stay closed.

Without any warning, he leaves me. My body falls limp to the floor and my knee slams down against the tile. Fuck! I grab it and lay on my side as the pain shoots up my body.

"Fuck, Elle!" He bends down beside me and picks me up off the floor. I expect his anger, not for him to take me gently into his arms. I bury my head in his chest. I can't take this. I'm not a person who can handle this kind of situation. I'm just breaking down. He walks me back over to the bed and sits down with me limp in his lap.

His hands pry my grip from my knee, and I watch his face as he looks it over, examining my injury. It'll bruise, but I'll be okay. It hardly hurts anymore. He's looking at me like I got shot. The concern on his face just doesn't make sense. He runs his fingers over the mark that will be a bruise. And then his dark eyes find mine. "You shouldn't have done that, sweetheart." There's a trace of a threat in his voice.

But there's something else, much stronger. Something that makes my breathing pick up. My fingers itch to run along the prick of his stubble. I want to grab his hair and push his lips to mine. Maybe I just want comfort, maybe it's something else. I don't know, but I want him. I *need* him.

I may die any minute now. I'm not going to hold back. I reach up and grip his hair, pulling myself to him and crushing my lips against his. His lips are hard at first and he pulls back, looking shocked, but also guarded.

"Please," I whisper. He answers by pushing my body against the mattress, keeping his lips on mine.

He pulls back and takes a shallow breath before asking me, "You think you can manipulate me with your pussy?" I shake my head. That's not it. That's not why.

"It's not going to work, sweetheart." He tries to pull away from me. And I can't stand the distance. I need this. I need to feel his hard body against me.

"Please," I beg again. If he denies me I don't know what I'll do. I feel sick with myself. But I won't refuse this need. I have for so long. Not again. I can't.

His hard body cages me in, and I find myself wanting more. Wanting to push him harder. His eyes spark with an unvoiced threat, but more than that-- desire.

Yes!

"Please," I say again, and pull his lips to mine. His tongue dives into my mouth. I suck his bottom lip. His hips spread my legs and I part for him. I still hurt, but I need this. I need to get lost in his touch. I need to feel something other than this hopelessness and despair. His hands move to my thighs and push the hem of my dress up to my waist. I moan into his mouth as his erection pushes against my clit.

He breaks our kiss to look down at me. I'm panting beneath him, my fingers digging into the mattress. He pulls his shirt above his head, his muscles rippling with the movement.

"Take it off." I immediately obey him and pull at my straps and shove the dress off my body. I watch as he kicks his pants off and takes his hard dick in his hand to stroke it. He's the epitome of lust and power as he pushes my knees farther apart and runs his fingers down the thin fabric against my pussy, before pulling the panties down my thighs. I shudder under his touch. My body feels cold without his warmth. I need him.

"On your knees." I turn over and hate it. I don't want him to take me from behind like this. I feel him run the head of his cock from my entrance to my clit. The velvety feel of his head on my throbbing clit makes my back arch and I moan into the air. I want him to hold me while he fucks me. I want to feel like there's more than just lust, but before I can say anything he slams into me.

Fuck! I clench at the sheets, grasping handfuls of the fabric as I scream into the mattress. Holy fuck. That's intense. More than earlier. Much more. My legs tremble as he stills deep inside me. I'm so close to the edge of pain. The mix is a dark delicacy. I don't know how to handle it. I want to move away, the feeling too intense, too much. At the same time, I want to push back. I need more.

"Are you okay, Elle?" Vince whispers in my ear, and it's only then that I realize tears have leaked down my cheeks. My head shakes back and forth on its own accord.

He quickly withdraws, causing a bit of pain, and leaves me feeling empty and raw. He pulls me into his chest. "I'm sorry, sweetheart." He kisses my hair. "I didn't realize you were hurting." I brush the tears away with the back of my hand and try to pull myself together. I'm such a fucking mess.

"Do you always get this sore?" he asks me, and I huff a humorless laugh.

"I wouldn't know." I manage to push the words out while I lean down to wipe my face with the sheets.

"What do you mean?" he asks.

"You were my first." I bite the words out and regret admitting it immediately. I'm met with silence, and I don't dare look up at him to see his reaction.

His hands grip my hips and flip me onto my back. I gasp in shock and then stare wide-eyed as his head dips to my heat and he sucks my clit into his mouth. My fingers spear into his hair and my head falls back against the mattress as my eyes close. I push him further into my heat and try to rock my pussy on his face. I feel needy. I *am* needy. And he gives it to me.

His hot, wet tongue laps at my pussy, nibbling and sucking along every sensitive part. My clit is throbbing and in need of his touch. My pussy clenches around nothing. Finally, he satisfies both at the same time, massaging my clit with his tongue while dipping his fingers into my pussy. His fingers curve and rub the sensitive bundle of nerves at the front wall.

I close my eyes and moan into the air above me. My thighs start to tingle and my toes go numb. My body stiffens and I know it's coming. I know he's going to shatter me into a million pieces. His head lifts between my thighs with his fingers still inside me.

My mouth opens to object, but before I can utter a single word, he pinches my clit and pushes his tongue into my pussy, fucking me with it. The forceful-ness of his deft fingers on me pushes me over the edge. Waves of heat and pleasure crash through my body.

Wave after wave of heated pleasure rocks through me.

I barely register him pulling away from me only to cage my body in.

He leaves hot, open-mouthed kisses on my neck, down to my collarbone. His hot breath tickles my neck, causing my nipples to harden. My head turns to the side as my breathing settles. I feel the head of his cock push into me. He moves deeper and deeper, slowly stretching my walls. His thumb pushes against my clit, making my entire body heat as a radiating pleasure builds in the pit of my stomach, threatening to take over my body. My head thrashes as I absorb the intense waves of pleasure mixed with the hint of pain from his large girth.

He kisses and licks his way down to the pale peaks of my breasts and sucks them into his mouth. He rocks in and out of me slowly as he keeps one hand massaging my clit, while the other hand roams over the rest of my body. The combination of his expert touch and practiced motions overwhelms my senses. I tremble beneath him feeling the slow build of pleasure rising higher and higher, threatening to consume me. Fear paralyzes me. I don't know if I can handle this. It feels too high, too intense.

And then all at once, he pushes deeper into me, all the way to the hilt. As he thrusts, he pinches my clit while biting down on my nipple hard enough to cause just the tiniest hint of pain. With his free hand he pinches my other nipple between his fingers, and I explode beneath him. Overwhelmed with heat, every nerve ending in my body lights aflame. My back arches and my body stiffens.

As my orgasm crashes through every limb, Vince pounds me harder and harder, pushing the edge of my release higher up. His hands grip my ass and angle me to his rough pubic hair brushing against my clit with every violent thrust. My fingers claw at the sheets as my mouth hangs open in a silent scream of pleasure.

His head dips to the crook of my neck, and he nips my earlobe as he growls, "Mine."

He thrusts harder and faster, pistoning into me, the gentleness completely gone as he owns my body. "Mine," he says louder in my ear. His hot breath mingles in the suffocating air between us. His lips crash against mine with a primal need and I meet his passion, pouring everything into our kiss. His hands move to my thighs and spread me even wider for him.

I moan from how deep he enters me, hitting the opening of my cervix with every thrust. He's so deep, almost too deep. I feel the need to pull away, but each time he leaves me I want more. Again and again he thrusts mercilessly into me.

I feel the rising tingling through my body. My breathing comes in heavy pants. My lungs seem too empty, not filling fast enough. The need to breathe barely registers as he forces himself deep inside of me and hot waves of cum splash inside me. I feel him pulse as his eyes go half-lidded and his mouth hangs open in ecstasy. The sight of him in complete pleasure and the feel of his cock pumping inside of me sets me off. I shatter beneath him yet again.

The heat, the tingling sensation along every inch of my skin is too much. I want to thrash and move against the overwhelming feelings, but instead I'm paralyzed. My body bows, and the heels of my feet dig into his ass. My pussy clamps hard around him and I scream his name as I cum violently around him.

As my breathing slows and my heart settles, the hot, numbing feeling on my skin begins to subside. But every small movement sends a jolt of pleasure through my body.

Vince moves me, picking my small body up in his arms and spooning beside me, my back pressed against his front. He plants small kisses on my neck and runs his hand down my side, over my hip, ending at the top of my thigh. Once my breathing has calmed, he pulls the blanket over me and wraps his arm around my chest, molding my body to his and holding me tight.

It's everything I thought it would be like. I close my eyes and try to keep reality from coming back. I can't avoid it. The second I try to resist, it floods back to me and I stiffen in his arms.

He tries to soothe me, to mold my back to his chest, but I resist.

After a long while, Vince finally speaks. "I need to get out of here." He lets me go and moves off the bed.

I sit up to look at him. "Where..." I start to question him, but I stop. I'm fucking stupid for thinking there was something there between us. That I felt something for him. I close my mouth and try to gather up the courage to ask to leave again. I just want to go. The thought is like a brick in my stomach.

"I just want to leave. I'm not going to say anything about anything." I try to cross my legs on the bed, but fuck, I hurt so bad. I'm so sore. I wince slightly and a look of pain is reflected in Vince's eyes.

"You're not going anywhere, sweetheart. I need to figure this shit out."

"You're just making it worse!" I yell at him.

"You don't understand." His cool response makes me angry.

"Explain it to me then!"

He grips my mouth with one hand and grabs the nape of my neck with the other. He lowers his head and kisses me hard on the lips. "Sweetheart, I swear to God, you really need to shut your mouth and trust me."

I want to. I want to trust him, but I can't.

"I need to tie you up." No. I don't want that. I shake my head, no.

"Why?" I ask in a hoarse whisper.

He stares at me like I'm an idiot. "You just tried to kill me."

"You just fucked me," I spit back.

"It was a lapse in judgment." That fucking hurt. That's a damn blow to my ego. Shame replaces any possible positive feeling I have.

He must see the hurt on my face. "Not like that. I didn't mean it like that."

I can't look at him. He tries to touch me and I push him away.

It was a mistake. All of this is such a mistake. I'm a mistake. I've heard it all my life, but I never thought it was true until now. I don't want to die, but part of me wishes he would just kill me.

VINCE

I don't fucking want to be here. I shouldn't be here. Instead, I should be making sure that she's staying put. But I tied her up so tight, there's no way she's getting out.

She was a virgin. She lost her virginity to me like that. No wonder she was so fucking sore. I tilt my head back and slam down another shot. So fucking tight. So fucking good.

I don't know what the fuck I'm doing. Billy lines up another shot for me. His eyes are full of pity. I'm sure everyone knows. Everyone's avoiding me. I'm guessing they think I killed her. The occasional pats on the back and squeezes of my shoulder as they walk by tell me that's what they're thinking.

They feel sorry for me that I'm so fucked up over having to kill her. Or having killed her, depending on whether they think I went through with it already.

I take another shot. I'm so fucking drunk.

What was I thinking? Like I could just keep her, and that would solve the problem? She saw. They saw. She has to die. It's as simple as that. But I don't want that. And I always get what I want. It's not fucking happening. I won't let it happen.

"Did you take care of that issue?" Anthony asks looking at my mangled hand. Everyone keeps looking at it. I know what they're thinking. And I fucking hate it.

"Which issue?" I ask sarcastically. I know he's talking about Elle. But the fucking cartel is a pain in my ass, too.

I put the edge of another shot glass against my lips and shake my head before throwing it back. My body starts to tingle, and my teeth seem to go numb. Good. I want to be fucking wasted. My phone stopped going off in my pocket a little while ago. I take it that means someone told Pops that I'm here. I wonder what he thinks. Specifically, what he thinks of her. Not to mention what he thinks of me and my fucked up decisions.

"It's not like she's yours, Vince. It fucking sucks." Anthony puts a hand on his chest. "She was just in the wrong place, at the wrong time. I fucking hurt for her, I do." I can see it in his eyes that he doesn't like it, that he does have remorse. "But this is the entire family we're talking about." I nod my head solemnly. "If she talks, we're fucked." He takes a drink of his beer. "She's not one of us. She's not a *comare*. They'll make her talk. You know how they harass anyone who comes in here. If they saw her, they'll make her talk."

I take another swig and almost choke as the perfect solution hits me. I need to knock her up. I need to marry my sweetheart. They won't touch her if she's mine. No one will touch her if she's mine. And if I get my way, she's going to be mine. And the police can't make her testify against me if she's my wife. No one will be able to threaten her.

She. Is. Mine. I repress the need to scream it into everyone's face. I want them all to know. She's not going anywhere. I push away from the bar and slide off the stool. It wobbles, then tips over as my feet hit the ground. I walk forward and reach for my car keys in my pocket.

"Whoa, Vince. What the fuck, dude?" I hear Anthony pick up my stool, then come up behind me, grabbing at my elbow to make me stop.

"I gotta go," I say simply. I do. I need to get back to Elle. He walks in front of me to stop me in my path.

"You're trashed, man." I shrug my shoulders.

"She needs me, Anthony." I'm vaguely aware that the bar is quiet. I can feel their eyes on me. I know everyone in here. It's all familia. And they're all watching.

"Hey, calm down. Let's talk this out, Vince," he says. I shake my head and take a step closer to him.

"She's mine," I growl in his face. His hands come up in a gesture of surrender.

"Alright. I get that. No one's taking her from you."

"Damn right no one's going to touch her!" I scream it as loud as I can. I feel like a fucking fool. It's not smart to yell. It's not wise to lose your cool. But I can't fucking help it. I want everyone to know she's mine. I run my fingers through my hair, then take a deep breath. "I'm gonna make her mine and no one's going to hurt Elle." I stare at him as I speak calmly, but everyone here knows I'm talking to them, too. From my periphery I can see my men nodding.

"No one's going to touch her," Anthony says, and I feel Tommy come up to my right side and lay a hand on my shoulder.

"You need a ride, boss?" he asks.

"Yeah, I need to get back to her, Tommy." My words slur a bit and I pinch the bridge of my nose as we walk towards the doors.

"You know, I feel bad for your girl, Vince," Anthony says from behind me loud enough for everyone to hear. I turn to face him. "She's gonna have to deal with your whiskey dick tonight."

I grin at him and laugh. After a split second, the rest of the bar joins in on the joke.

A calmness settles in my chest. For the first time since all this shit happened, I feel like it might be alright.

I may get to keep my sweetheart after all. I just need to knock her up first.

VINCE

I don't remember why I'm so fucking horny for her. But I am. It takes me at least four tries to get the key in the lock to the door. But I fucking did it and I feel like a champion for getting into the house. Rigs is barking and barreling down the stairs like a good boy. I bet he was laying outside her room. I feel like an asshole as I watch him squatting in the yard. I gotta get up there and make sure she's still alright. I close the door after he gets his furry butt inside and we make our way up the stairs. I leave him out in the hall and ignore his little whine when I don't let him in. I gotta get him a giant ass bone for dealing with this shit. I huff up a laugh as I walk, I'm fairly certain, straight to the bed. Right where I left my sweetheart all tied up.

Her wrists are bound with a silk tie and it's wrapped around a rod on the headboard. It doesn't look very comfortable, but she appears to be sleeping. I grip my shirt and pull it over my head, then shove my pants down. I palm my raging erection and stroke it up and down while my eyes travel over her body. She's in one of my tees. It's bunched around her hips and there's a nice red mark still on her thigh from where I was gripping her earlier. I groan and stroke my dick again before climbing on the bed.

Mine. All mine.

The creak of my movements and the dip of the bed gets her attention and she stares back at me with her lips parted. I take it she's surprised to see me.

Her legs scissor as she tries to turn and lift herself up. But with her wrists bound she can hardly move. My dick bobs up and down as I crawl across the bed. I grab her ass with both hands and push her up higher so she can sit how she'd like.

Feeling her bare ass in my hands only makes me want her more. I remember that she's not wearing any panties. My cock gets even harder.

I feel lightheaded and groggy as I crawl closer to her.

"I got it figured out, Elle." I move her ass up higher on the bed again so there's less pressure on her arms.

"Vince?" she asks in a tired voice. She looks a little out of it. I know she's gotta be tired.

"Yeah, baby?" I rub her shoulders to help ease the tension.

"It really hurt me, what you said before you left." I love how straight forward she is. I kiss her shoulder to reward her.

"I wish I could take it back. I wish I could take it all back. You don't deserve this."

She looks at me with those big blue eyes and pleads for an answer. "What are you going to do to me?"

I finally have an answer for her. I smirk at her, "I'm going to keep you."

Her eyes widen and her lips part. "I'm gonna make you mine." I kiss down her body and settle between her legs. A small pant comes from that gorgeous mouth of hers and her thighs clench. I don't know if she loves the idea, but she sure as fuck seems turned on by it.

"Spread your legs for me, sweetheart." I'm sure some of those words are slurred, but she obeys. I drop to my elbows and push her thighs further apart. I run a finger from her sensitive clit, which makes her body shiver, all the way down to the entrance of her pussy. She's hot.

And red.

Too red. My poor girl's gotta be sore. I wanted to be gentle with her earlier. But knowing I had this virgin pussy all to myself broke a wall inside me and let out a beast that I didn't know I had in me.

I push my thumb against her throbbing clit and grin as her back bows and her arms pull against the restraints. She's still primed for yet another orgasm. What a greedy little pussy. I lower my head and push her legs apart further with my shoulders, then take a languid lick of her heat. I wiped her off after I tied her up, but I can still taste some of our combined cum on her pussy. I don't give a fuck. My tongue dips into her pussy. I keep my movements easy and gentle. She's too sore. I just want to soothe her.

My dick jumps in disagreement. Maybe not. That's right--I need to knock her up. That'll keep everyone away from her. I groan into her heat and suck her clit into my mouth. My sweetheart tries to ride my face and I fucking love it. She's not afraid to ask for what she wants. She just goes for it. I suck her clit hard and push a finger into her to rub her G-spot and push her over the edge. She's too fucking easy to get off. She's so damn tight I feel her clamp down on my finger as her orgasm takes over. I let her clit go with a pop and lick my lips.

So fucking sweet.

I crawl over her trembling body and reach up to untie her wrists. I want her on top, riding me. I want to watch her tits bounce as she fucks herself on my dick.

And then I remember.

It's a shock to my system remembering how she tried to run from me. How she wanted to get away. Just hours ago she was going to fight me to try to leave. I can't blame her, but fuck me if it doesn't hurt. I look at her face, eyes closed in rapture as she bites down on her bottom lip. Right now she's being my sweetheart. But I can't untie her. What if she up and runs? Fuck! I can't let that shit happen. I can't be sloppy.

Tomorrow she's going to learn she belongs to me now. Neither of us has a choice. I flop down on the bed beside her and pull her ass against my dick. I take a deep breath in the crook of her neck, loving the way she smells. My eyes feel heavy and my body sags deeper into the warmth of the bed. I haphazardly grab the comforter and pull it over our bodies.

Tomorrow. I hug her body close to mine and splay my hand over her belly. I'm going to make her mine tomorrow.

ELLE

J wake up to the bright light coming in from the window. It hurts my eyes, but I can't block it. My arms won't move over my face. Vince's heavy and so hot, laying against my body. His chest is molded to my back and his arms are wrapped tight around me. His weight puts more pressure on my arms. Fuck it hurts. His scent fills my lungs, a woodsy pine and masculine smell, mixed with the faint odor of whiskey. I moan softly, loving how he smells. And then I get angry from my reaction.

I hate that I want him. He stirs behind me, and I hold my breath. I feel his grin on my neck. "Elle, sweetheart, you keep fucking me up, you know that?" His words are slurred and full of sleep.

"Vince?" I ask in a voice loud enough for him to hear, but not so loud that it would wake him.

"I'm gonna put a baby in you. Then they won't hurt you, sweetheart." He whispers his words against the side of my neck. *A baby.* "No one's gonna lay a finger on my girl." He pulls my back up against his chest again and rocks his dick against my ass.

"Vince?" I ask again, a little louder. I get no response.

Holy fuck. He wants to knock me up? That's his plan? I can't help the fact that the very thought of being pregnant with his child makes me want him inside me.

I feel alive in his arms. I want to get lost in his touch.

But a baby? It's life-changing.

Once I'm pregnant though, I'm sure he won't hurt me. Hope lights inside of me. I can have his baby. If that's the cost, I'll pay the price. I'll be a good mother. I've always wanted a child, but never thought it would happen. Maybe this is a blessing. Everything happens for a reason.

I calm my racing heart. Maybe I don't even need to really get pregnant. I can just go along with the plan.

His phone goes off from somewhere in the room and interrupts my thoughts. My body stiffens as Vince turns away from me and groans.

He rolls to the edge of the bed and presses his palms to his eyes. His broad, muscular back ripples with his movements as he stretches and reaches down to pick up his jeans to retrieve his phone.

"Hey Pops," he answers only a little drowsily and then yawns, holding the phone away from his ear.

"What's going on, Vince? I'm worried over here." Ever so faintly, I can hear his father's voice.

"Everything's good," Vince speaks into the phone, and then looks back over his shoulder at me. He moves quickly to my side and starts untying the knot on my wrists with one hand. *Thank fuck!* My shoulders are killing me.

"You still got her?" his father asks.

"Yeah." Vince props the phone between his ear and shoulder so he can use both hands while he's untying me. "It's all good." Hearing him say that makes my heart swell with hope. But I know why he's saying that. I know what he's planning, and that makes my heart harden.

"Good. I'm coming over." Vince stills for a moment and then pulls the tie away. My shoulders sag as I'm released, and I wince with pain as I move my arms down to my side.

Vince is quiet, but then he answers his father, "Alright Pops. You bringing breakfast?" He answers lightheartedly, but the look on his face doesn't match his tone.

ELLE

"That feel any better?" Vince asks, as he sets the heating pad on my shoulders. Once he was off the phone with his father, he spent a good 20 minutes rubbing feeling back into my arms and quietly apologizing. The heat and his touch feel so good. My shoulders and arms are still sore, but I give him a small smile and nod. I lean back in his dining room chair and bring my cup of coffee to my lips. He hasn't said much this morning, and neither have I. Things have changed. Drastically.

I remember what he said in his sleep, and while part of me is terrified of him really wanting to knock me up, the other part is worried he's changed his mind. Or that it was just a dream. That he doesn't want to be tied to me, and it'll be easier to just kill me. So I've behaved. I've listened to everything. I'll do whatever I have to in order to survive.

"We need to have a talk, Elle." He rounds the grey granite countertop and walks into the kitchen. The open concept design of the space gives a light and airy feel, but I'm practically suffocating from nerves.

"I'm listening," I say, and take another sip of coffee. My eyes stay on him so he knows he has my attention. He's wearing those pajama pants slung low on his hips again. He gave me an identical pair to wear, but I'm drowning in them.

"I need for you to be patient with me." He looks out of the window and shoves his hands in his pockets. "I believe you, sweetheart, but they won't. Even if they do, they won't risk it."

"Won't risk what?" I ask.

"Rule one." He holds up a finger and walks back over to the dining room to take a seat at the chair next to me. He leans forward in his seat as he looks at me intently. "Don't ask questions."

I open my mouth to ask why, but then I close it and purse my lips. An asymmetric grin grows on his face. "Learning already."

"No questions. Understood." I really don't like that. I like to ask questions so I can know things. But then again, I already know too much.

"What do you remember, baby?" he asks.

I take a deep breath and set the mug down on the dark maple tabletop. "I remember--"

He cuts me off. "Nothing. Rule two, you don't remember a damn thing, and you don't know what anyone is talking about." My eyes dart to his. His face is all hard lines and seriousness.

I pick up my mug and take a sip. "I don't remember a damn thing."

"That's right--you don't." He leans down and picks my feet up to put on his lap. His thumbs dig into the soles as he massages my feet. I moan into the cup. It feels so good. "I'm going to take care of you until things settle down. Everything is going to be fine, alright?"

I meet his soft gaze and nod. "Mmm hmm."

He gives me a tight smile. "That brings us to rule number three." He keeps rubbing my feet and holds my gaze. "Who do you belong to, Elle?"

I feel my eyes widen and my heart skips a beat. I know the answer, but it's caught in my throat. I swallow the lump in my throat and answer him with a whisper. "You."

"That's right. And you're going to listen to what I say, aren't you, sweetheart? You're going to do as you're told."

My pussy clenches at his words. He obviously doesn't realize how fucking hot that makes me. I'm fucked up in the head for wanting him like that in this very moment, but I do. I nod my head to try to keep the lust from coming through my voice.

"Answer me, sweetheart." There's an admonishment in his tone and he stops rubbing my feet.

"Yes. I'll do as I'm told." My voice comes out breathy and a smirk kicks up his lips. He drops my feet to the floor and moves closer to me, but a hard knock at the door interrupts us.

He stands up, then bends at the waist to cup my jaw and plant a kiss on my lips. It's forceful and full of need. "Stay here, sweetheart."

My heart races in my chest. I've agreed to be his, and I fucking love that idea. But I have no idea if it'll be enough to save me.

I hear Vince open the door and I grip the mug with both of my hands. Surely anyone in my position would say they'd listen. They'd do whatever they could to stay alive. I just hope he believes me. Because it's true. I'll listen to him. I *want* to listen to him. Some sick part of me wants to be his.

Heavy footsteps bring my eyes up past the kitchen to the foyer. His father has an arm braced around Vince's shoulders and he's talking in his ear. I don't like it. It makes me feel uneasy, like he's trying to convince Vince to get rid of me.

Vince must feel my eyes on him, because he looks over in my direction and stares back at me. He smiles at me and turns to his father. His warm expression relaxes me some. My shoulders feel heavy with weight of the heating pad so I pull it off and stand on shaky legs.

"No need to stand for me, Elle." Vince's father gives me a tight smile. His hair is peppered with grey and his eyes are a light blue. The laugh lines on his face make his age apparent, but his body is still muscular. There's no doubt in my mind that he's lethal.

I swallow thickly and try to smile up at him, but I can't. My mind keeps racing with the memory of yesterday. My hands grip the back of the chair.

"Sweetheart, go grab yourself another cup of coffee." Vince places his hand on the small of my back. My eyes are focused on the table as I try to will my fingers to just let go. I nod and as soon as I release the chair, I grab my cup and walk quickly to the kitchen. I stand with my back to them trying to listen to their whispers. I can't make out what they are saying.

Tears come to my eyes and my heart races. This is stupid, so fucking stupid. He isn't going to keep me. They're going to kill me. I walk to the sink and dump the lukewarm remains of my coffee down the drain. My hands grip the front of the sink, and it feels like my legs are going to collapse. I close my eyes and try to steady my breathing. My back is still to them.

If they're going to kill me, I wish they'd do it like this. During some mundane activity like washing the dishes or something. That'd be an okay way to go, I guess, if I didn't see it coming. I squeeze my eyes shut and then jump and scream at the feel of hands on my waist.

"Sweetheart." There's a note of warning in Vince's tone. "Whatever's going on in your head, knock it off."

I force my eyes open, but I can't turn to face him. "If you're going to kill me, please do it when I don't see it coming."

"Elle, stop it." Vince pulls my body close to his so that my back is right up against his chest. He kisses my neck. I don't know if he knows how comforting and at ease it makes me for him to hold me like this right now, especially in front of his father. It makes his claim to me that much more real.

"No one's going to hurt you." I hear Vince's father and a sense of calm moves through my body. I dare to take a look at Vince's father. "I promise you, we have no intentions of hurting you."

"I told you you're mine, didn't I?" Vince asks me. I nod my head against Vince's shoulder and try to stop my nerves from getting the better of me.

"No one touches what's mine."

VINCE

"*Y*ou wanna pick some stuff out or something?" I push the laptop to Elle across the table. Pops left after having a private conversation with me about the shipments. I have a small list of names I need to handle to get shit back on the up and up on that front. They've got to know it's coming though, since Javier made sure to take care of his end as soon as he found out who was stealing from him. Their partners getting murdered is a good sign that we're coming for them. The Locos Diablos MC is gonna be short a few members real fucking soon. They're an offshoot of Shadows MC, essentially their rejects. They're fucking stupid to think they'd start a war between the *familia* and the cartel by stealing from us.

And then there's the issue of Elle's mother, Sandra Hawthorne. She's got to be dealt with, but I don't feel like handling that issue right now.

"You're letting me go online? What if I emailed someone?" she asks with disbelief. Leave it to her to give me a reason that I shouldn't let her go online. She's questioning everything she's doing, which is good, but I want her to get comfortable. I want her to just act natural, like how she was when I took her for the first time. That moment in time is what I want every day.

"Don't. I'm going to be right here. Just pick out what you need." She reaches for the laptop and slowly opens it.

"I could just get some things from my house," she offers.

"Your mother already tried reporting you missing. You can't leave." I'm short with her, but it's for a good reason. All she has to do is listen to what I tell her and everything will be fine.

"What?" she asks, looking at me with her eyes opened wide.

"Rule one, sweetheart." She opens and then closes her mouth. I can tell she's going to have a hard time with that one. It can't hurt to let her know what's going on with her mother though. I'm gonna have her give her mother a call sometime soon, but right now it's too soon. "We have a guy on the inside, a police officer. Luckily he's the one that got the call."

"I'm surprised my mom gave a shit." Her voice turns sad and her eyes focus back on the laptop. I don't like it.

Apparently someone saw Elle with me and went to her mom's place to try and question her about me. Sandra didn't say shit to the police, which is good. It means my sweetheart really didn't remember anything that happened at the bistro until she came to my parents' house yesterday. It didn't piss me off that Sandra tried to file a missing person's report. But the fact that she attempted to make a will for my sweetheart today really fucking pisses me off.

"I don't understand why you put up with that shit." I'm not going to keep my mouth shut anymore. If she's going to be mine, her mother's going to have to back off and get her shit straightened out. I can tell this is going to be a fight, but I don't want it to be one.

"And what'd she do that got you so pissed off, huh? I mean on the night I met you. You were all bent out of shape." Elle doesn't have to tell me though, because I already know what she did. I got the report from Tony. It has everything on my girl. And there's a ton of shit there. A ton of debt, to be specific. I know her mother took it out, too. She tried to file for loans a few times with just Elle's name on the paperwork. Fucking bitch. I had to call Dom to have his guys transfer money from my account to Elle's and wipe her debt. I know Sandra's gonna do it again soon. As soon as she realizes she can. And I'm not looking forward to having to shut that shit down. I'll throw her thieving ass in jail. That's what she fucking deserves.

"She's my mother." I shake my head and bite my tongue. I know all about family. For fuck's sake, I have the entire *familia* to worry about.

"You're a strong woman. I hate to see you being taken advantage of." It's true, but she gives me a disbelieving look and I swear she almost rolls her eyes. I'm glad she's finally getting over that shit from earlier today, but my little sweetheart isn't gonna walk all over me.

"Don't look at me like that." I lower my voice to a threatening level, but she ignores it.

"You don't want to see me taken advantage of?" she asks without any sarcasm in her tone, but I know it's there.

"What the hell am I supposed to do, Elle?" I ask her, but I don't know why. I should really end this conversation. We shouldn't be talking about this shit.

"Just let me go." It fucking hurts that she's asking that. Even if I could, I wouldn't.

"They'll know. Then we're both dead." My blood freezes. If I fuck this up and she talks, I probably am dead. The family can't risk weakness like that.

"We can run," she whispers.

"We?" She wants to run away with me? It fills my chest with hope for us. But I'm not fucking running. I love this life. She'll learn to love it, too.

Her eyes fall and she focuses them on the screen.

"Answer me. You wanna go away with me?" I ask.

"I don't know. I don't have anyone else." I want her to want me, plain and simple. But not because she has no one else. That means someone could get between us and I don't like that.

"Get over here, sweetheart." I push my chair out and pat my thigh. She obeys immediately, walking quickly to me and sitting down on my lap.

"You would run away with me?" I wrap my arms around her waist.

"Yeah, I would. Does that make me stupid?" she asks.

"I care about you, Elle. Do you believe that?" My heart sputters in my chest. She better believe it. Because it's true. I don't know how or why, but I do care about her. I want her to be happy with me.

"I do." I love those words on her lips. I groan as my dick hardens and I rock it into her ass. I'm gonna hear those words again. Real fucking soon.

VINCE

*F*uck, today was a hassle. I can't find those MC pricks. They're in hiding now that they know we're gunning for them. And I know they'll be gunning for us, too. At least the shipments came in right this time. I toss my keys down on the table and bend down to let Rigs to lick my face.

"Good boy." I pet behind his ears for a minute. But my eyes are focused on the stairs. It feels good to have my sweetheart in my house. Not the safe house, but *my* house. Even though she's making it look more like *our* house with all the shit she has.

It's been two weeks. Two weeks of filling her greedy, needy cunt with my seed and trying to knock her up. The guys know we're together. They've backed off entirely on the issue of her being a witness. Now they wanna meet her, get to know my girl. I'm just waiting for the right time. I want her ready. I want her to know without a doubt she belongs to me.

She called her mom like I told her to. Did everything the *familia* wanted and asked of her to make them comfortable with her being mine. There's nothing standing between us now.

I smirk as I walk up the stairs. Rigs follows me and I let him, but I put my foot in front of him to stop him from coming into the room. he's used to it now.

I shut the door and turn to face my sweetheart. She's tied up on the bed.

She tells me she hates it, that I can trust her and don't have to tie her up when I leave. But that pussy of hers is always soaked when I get home. Her pussy knows it belongs to me. She's ready for me every day. I know it's 'cause she's tied up. She says she hates it, but I know she's lying. She fucking loves it.

She's gagged for being a naughty girl this morning. Her panties are in her mouth for talking back to me. I need to get more ties. I've got one around her wrists, one keeping her panties in her mouth, and two more around her ankles, keeping her spread open for me. I went all out this morning since I knew I wouldn't be long. I wasn't gone for even an hour. And every minute was fucking torture for me. I kick my pants off and walk closer to the bed.

I stare at her pussy that's just waiting for me. It's glistening with her juices and my dick jumps in my pants with a desperate need to be inside her.

My eyes lock on hers. "Did you learn your lesson, sweetheart?" She nods her head obediently. She's fucking perfect. She's my obedient sweetheart. All fucking mine.

"I'm not sure you did." I shove two fingers into her tight pussy and pump them in and out. She pulls against the restraints, but her ass isn't going anywhere. Her moan is muffled by the panties in her mouth. I pull my fingers out before she can cum and remove the tie from around her mouth. She spits out her panties and pants. Her eyes are on me, just waiting to hear what I have to tell her. So fucking perfect.

I smack a hand down on her pussy. Slap! Her head falls back, and she moans again with pleasure. It's music to my ears. She's so fucking close already. I love keeping her on the edge. "Now, whose pussy is this?"

"Your pussy," she's quick to answer, and I reward her by pushing down on her clit and rubbing small circles. She struggles against the pleasure.

"Damn right it's my pussy." I push against her front wall with my fingers and smile as her walls tighten and her cum soaks my hand. She's been waiting for a full hour to cum. I should give her another.

I pull the ties free from around her ankles, but keep her wrists bound. My hips keep her legs open as I line my cock up. I lean down and kiss my sweetheart and she kisses me back with passion. I slam into her all the way to the hilt and fuck her mercilessly. She pulls her lips away to scream out my name.

That's right. My name. This pussy is mine. She's mine, all fucking mine. I pick up her legs and place her calves on my shoulders. Her eyes go wide as I slam in deeper and deeper, taking her to a new edge of pain and pleasure. Her pussy is so fucking tight like this. She's squeezing the hell out of my dick.

"Vince!" she yells out, as her legs start to tremble. Fuck yeah. Keep screaming my name.

My balls draw up watching her chest rise and fall, and her eyes nearly roll back in her head. My spine tingles as I push my dick as deep into her as I can. I cum violently as the head of my dick butts up against her cervix. A shudder goes through my body as her pussy spasms just as violently, matching the intensity of my orgasm, and she cries out in pleasure.

My lips crush against hers, silencing her moans and I reach one hand up to untie her wrists. It doesn't take long. I've had plenty of practice.

Her hands grip and tug my hair and she kisses me harder. She fucking loves me. I know she does. I wrap my arms around her body and roll her onto my chest. She pulls back with her eyes closed, lips slightly swollen from our bruising kiss. Her hair's a mess, looking just-fucked and her skin is flushed. The sight of her in complete rapture makes my heart swell.

All that shit was worth it.

* * *

"You got some boxes, baby," I call out over my shoulder as I pick up a box. She's been getting a shit-ton of packages. Books, makeup, clothes, art supplies, all sorts of shit. It makes me happy that she's finally feeling more comfortable with me buying her things. Not to mention that now she's got her painting hobby to have something to focus on.

I look suspiciously at the box in my hands and then at the remainder of the packages on the porch. They aren't marked or labeled in any way. I don't fucking like it. At first I assumed they were something she ordered, but there's no indication that these were sent through the mail. Someone left them here. I hear her coming down the stairs and I hold an arm out to stop her from coming any closer. I don't know what's in the boxes, but she's not going to be around when I open them.

"Elle, don't--" She pushes past me and screams out.

"Fucking bitch!" Elle cuts me off, and I turn to her in shock. That kind of language doesn't come out of my sweetheart's mouth. Her eyes are glassy with tears, but her facial expression reads that she's pissed.

"They're mine. I didn't get a chance to unpack them. My mother must've brought them over." I can feel her anger brewing. All over her mother. Sandra. What'd she do now?

"What'd she send you?" I can only guess that whatever's in the box, it's not wanted or needed, based on how Elle kicks the box and storms away. I debate on taking the boxes inside, but I'll wait till I find out what they contain.

"Sweetheart, answer me," I call out for her across the hall. She falls into the sofa looking defeated. Sandra really pisses me off. The only time my sweetheart is unhappy is when she hears from her mother.

"They're my boxes of things that were at her house. At *my* house. I didn't even get to unpack them." She pauses and then continues. "I told her she could come for a visit." She presses her lips together and crosses her arms over her knees, pulling them into her chest. She's a mix of hurt and anger and I'm not sure which is going to win out.

"Okay?" I don't understand. I must be missing something.

"I told her I couldn't give her any money since I wasn't working, but she could come see me if she wanted." I know all of this already. She asked me what I thought about that arrangement beforehand, and I agreed that would be wise. Elle's a smart girl. Plus, she enjoys this arrangement as much as I do. She hasn't done a damn thing suspicious and asks for permission before doing anything. I get the feeling she really enjoys me having the control in our relationship, which I fucking love.

"I'm missing something," I say. The tears in her eyes fall down her cheeks and she wipes them away angrily.

"I didn't tell you what she said," she answers.

"She said I was a selfish bitch for abandoning her, and that I could come get my shit."

I keep my voice light and don't let it show how pissed I am. I have to work real fucking hard to keep my anger out of my expression. I've never wished ill on a woman before, but I can't stand that bitch, Elle's mother or not. "Well at least she saved you the trip." Elle rolls her eyes and doesn't even crack a smile. I know it hurts her. If she could, she'd give her mom everything and I know her mother would take it all, too. Now that Elle's mine, it's not happening.

I have to do something to make her smile. I don't like her being so upset. "Do you have a nice dress to wear, sweetheart?" She looks back at me, tilting her head with a questioning look on her face. I raise my brows, waiting for an answer.

She shakes her head slowly. "Only my sundress." She hasn't been out of this house in two weeks. She's got to want to get out of here. I'm surprised with all the shit she's bought lately that she hasn't ordered another dress.

"Well, go put it on--I wanna take you out tonight." Her eyes brighten and a wide smile grows on her face. She hops up and runs to me to wrap her arms around my back, planting a small kiss on my lips.

"How much time do I have?" she asks, all peppy like. I've been afraid to take her out. A small part of me questions her loyalty to me, as though this has all just been an act. Like she's just waiting to get away from me. A deep pain shoots through my chest at these thoughts, but I ignore it.

"Take as much time as you need, sweetheart. We can go wherever you'd like." I'll spoil her to the point that the thought of leaving me doesn't exist for her. If she leaves me, I don't know what would happen.

The guys have been hounding me to bring her around. They all wanna meet her. I know what they must think. I'm sure they can't believe she really *wants* to be with me. Part of me doesn't believe it either. That doubt creeps up on me while I'm away from her.

But every time I get home and find her waiting for me, that doubt vanishes. When she yammers on about some recipe on the cooking shows she watches, there's no doubt in my fucking mind that she wants to be with me. Either that, or she's trying to kill me with domestication.

It's time the guys met her. We'll all go out. They'll see her, and she'll see them. It's gotta happen at some point. A part of me wants to keep her here with all this tension between the MCs and the *familia*, but it'll be alright. We haven't gotten those fuckers yet and Javier's breathing fire down our necks, but I can't keep her locked in here forever. She needs to get out and have some fun.

"Let's get out of the house, baby. I wanna show you off."

ELLE

*M*y nerves are shot. My palms are sweaty, and I can hardly breathe. I'm going to meet the *familia*. The Don is Dante, Vince's father. I don't know much about anyone else, though. Well, except that Dom and Tommy were the two that I ... met already. I breathe in deep and shake out my hands as we stand in front of the restaurant doors.

"They're going to love you." I hear Vince's voice and my heart hammers in my chest. I just don't believe it. I swallow thickly. They want me dead I'm sure. It'd be stupid for me to think otherwise. I see my reflection in the mirror and I cringe. I can't get this stupid panicked look off my face.

I turn to face Vince and try to bail. "I changed my mind."

"Stop it, Elle." He opens the door and puts his hand on the small of my back. "Just be yourself." I take a deep breath and try not to freak out. Everything's going to be fine. Vince won't let anyone hurt me. That thought soothes me. Every part of me calms, because it's true. He won't let anyone touch me. *I'm his.*

I look around the table, and the only people I know are the three I met. The two men, Dom and Tommy, I haven't seen since the incident. It chills me to the core to set eyes on them. But when Dom sees me, he stands and smiles. "Vince, I'm happy you finally brought her out!" Dom walks to me with quick strides and kisses my cheek. Vince loosens his grip on me and leaves my side to give his mother a kiss on the cheek. Without him beside me I feel vulnerable.

The last two weeks have been the same every day. And I'm almost ashamed to say I've enjoyed it. I don't fear Vince at all. I know he wants me. In his eyes, I belong to him, and he takes care of me in a way I desire. It's a sick fantasy come to life. Well, some of it. Our days are almost normal until he has to leave for work. Every morning we wake up beside each other, exchange small talk, and drink coffee. We joke around like a normal couple, banter like a normal couple. It's almost easy to forget that we're anything but normal.

When he leaves is when everything changes. Or at night, before we go to bed. I like to pretend it's a fantasy, a game we like to play. It makes it that much sweeter. I don't want it to stop. I know that's bad. I'm sure it's not healthy. But I fucking love when he ties me up. I know he's going to reward me and fuck me like he owns my body. Just thinking about it turns me on. But it's wrong. It's so wrong.

I haven't left his house in two full weeks. I've barely spoken to anyone but Vince and my mother. Vince wanted me to call her since she filed a missing person's report. It fucking killed me to think she was worried, but when she answered the phone she seemed more pissed than anything. I almost asked Vince to let me go see her. Almost. But I'd rather stay inside the house with him. It's all so wrong. But it feels so good. I don't worry about anything. I enjoy being his. I'm sure a shrink would tell me I'm insane. And maybe I am.

Being here in this restaurant with these people emphasizes how fucked up this situation is. He's told me about each of them. His brother Dom, and Dom's wife Becca are on the right side of the table. I know Dom's a professor and that Becca owns this restaurant. His father is seated at the head of the table on the far end, and Vince's mother is seated next to Becca. His cousin Joey's here. I know he has a son, but I don't see him here. An older man is sitting next to him, that must be Uncle Enzo. And then there's Tommy and Anthony, Vince's cousins, sitting together on the left side of the table. Looking at the two of them reminds me of my memory. Of them looking at me like I'm a threat. I still don't know what I did or what I saw. I just remember Vince pinning me down and them staring at me like I had to die. My palms grow sweaty and I wipe them on the sides of my dress.

"You want a drink, Elle?" Tommy asks me from across the room. He gives me a smile as he takes a sip of his wine.

"Please," I respond as normally as I can, given the situation and my nerves, and take a step closer to the table.

"Everyone, this is my girl Elle. Ma, no questions. Don't scare her off." Everyone laughs at Vince and I pretend to laugh also. But fuck me, my nerves are shot.

"I'm so happy to meet you dear," Vince's mother, Linda, says. "Dante has filled me in on how you two met." I struggle to keep the smile plastered on my face. I'm certain there's a hint of truth in whatever he's told her.

"I'm a lucky girl," I say back as sweetly as possible. I may be scared and intimidated, but I want them to like me. Is that so wrong? If they like me, then maybe Vince will trust me more. Maybe he won't tie me up every single time he leaves the house. I wonder if I would leave though, if given the choice. Should I leave him? I'm not sure I would. Maybe I really am fucked up in the head.

"There's no doubt in my mind that he's the lucky one," Dom says to my left as Vince pulls out a chair for me. I smooth out my dress and take a seat.

"So, what do you do, Elle?" Becca asks. The swell of her pregnant belly touches the table even though she's leaning all the way back in her chair. I sure as fuck can't answer that question. What do I do? I do your brother-in-law. That's not an appropriate answer. Let's see, so far I've quit school, which essentially ended the career I've been busting my ass for years at. I don't have a job, and I'm not sure I'm going to get one. I've been painting which I love, and Vince thinks I should sell online. But I'm nowhere near confident in my work to even think about showing it to anyone. Not yet. Maybe someday.

I decide to circumvent the question and change the subject. "Oh my goodness! You look beautiful. Congratulations, you two." It's easy to compliment her. She really is radiant with her swollen tummy. "When are you due?" I ask to continue pushing the conversation along.

"Two months." Dom answers for Becca as he rubs her stomach. The look in his eyes is one of pure devotion. I find myself reaching for Vince's hand. I wonder if he'll look at me that way when I'm pregnant with his child. *If. If* I ever get pregnant with his child. Again, if I could run, maybe I would. I know I'm not pregnant now though. I just got my period before we came out for dinner. For some reason that hurts. Maybe I could justify staying with him if I was carrying his child, but I'm not.

"We're all so excited for another baby in the family," Linda says with a smile on her face. "Three grandbabies. I'd love a dozen of them!" Dante rolls his eyes, and Dom snorts.

"You'd better get on Clara and this one then," Becca points at me, "because after our little girl, I'm getting Dom fixed." The table roars with laughter, but my face heats with embarrassment and my fingers nervously tighten on Vince's hand. It's all too real.

"Damn, Becca, give them the chance to get to know one another before Vince has to knock her up," Anthony says, and grins at the two of us. I'm trying to relax, but just being around them has my fight or flight instincts on high alert.

Vince wraps his arm around my shoulder and kisses my cheek. He whispers in my ear, "Relax, sweetheart." His words instantly calm me. I close my eyes and take a deep breath. I don't care if it's sick. I can keep up this fantasy, whether it's right or wrong.

The conversation continues as two waiters bring large bowls of chicken alfredo and spaghetti with meatballs to the table. Ah. Family style. Becca licks her lips and reaches for the bowls, but can't quite get to them with her belly. I stifle a small laugh. It's pretty adorable watching her struggle. Dom smacks her hands away playfully and dishes out a large helping of both entrees onto her plate.

Tommy and Anthony start talking about bets and making wagers with Dom. Dante cracks a joke, and the entire mood seems to lighten and flow naturally. Laughter and chatter fill the air.

I start to relax into my seat, and think I can actually eat without feeling sick to my stomach with worry. When the tension finally leaves my shoulders, and just as I start to think I can do this, I hear a loud bang. And another and another, as glass shatters and people scream. I feel the air whiz by my head. I hear it over and over--a mix of screams and bangs. It's surreal.

Vince's hurls his body in front of me and pushes me out of my chair. I land hard on my back with his body caging me in. I look to my left and see Becca screaming and crying. Dom's holding and protecting her the same way as Vince is holding me. Tommy and Anthony are screaming at one another, but their voices are muffled. Each of them is down on one knee with their guns extended, propped up on the backs of the chairs for extra support. They're firing. Some of the bangs and bullets are coming from them.

"Get her out of here! Get them out!" I can barely hear Vince screaming as he lifts up my body. The sound of tires screeching echoes in my ears, and strong arms pull me away from Vince. I find myself running, my heart beating out of control as adrenaline races through my veins. My feet trip on a fallen chair and I land hard on the ground.

Dom doesn't give me a moment to right myself. Instead, he picks me up, tucking my body under his left arm, and carries me as though I weigh nothing.

"Vince!" I scream out as I see him jumping through the shattered large bay window. He doesn't stop. He doesn't hear me. He's gone and I'm being carried away.

* * *

I LOOK around me behind the restaurant. It's a small alley. There are dumpsters at the end of it and the other side leads to the busy street. Dom is holding Becca, who's crying hysterically. No one else is here. I'm alone. I hear him shushing her. I hear the ambulance and the sirens from the police cars.

Reality hits me in the face. I can run. I can get the fuck out of here and save myself. I turn to look over my shoulder and Dom is staring me down. His face is all hard edges and his eyes hold an edge of a threat. But I doubt he'd leave his crying, pregnant wife to chase me down. But then again, I wouldn't get very far. I'm not a fast runner. I settle my back against the brick wall and sink down until my ass hits the pavement.

I feel far too sober. What the fuck am I doing? Who is this woman I've become? I wish Vince were here more than anything. I feel like that thought should be alarming to me. That it should send up red flags, but instead it offers me comfort. I'll feel better once he comes to get me. My gut twists. He better come get me. He better not get hurt. I don't know what I'd do without him.

The door to the right of me slams open, and Dante comes out. I rise to my feet and look behind him. Vince isn't there. My heart races faster. What if something happened to him?

"He'll be alright." I jump at Dante's words. He puts a hand on my shoulder, but I move away from him.

"This doesn't happen," I hear Becca say as she tries to calm her breathing. Her hand rests against her belly and she looks me in the eyes. "I don't know how long you've been with Vince, but I promise you this is *not* normal." She swallows and breathes in. She's sitting in Dom's lap and he's rubbing her shoulders.

This is not normal.

"Let's get you to the hospital, doll." He stands and helps lifts her up.

"I'm fine. I'm fine," she says, pushing him away. Dante walks closer to them, leaving me alone across the opposite side of the door.

"You should go to the hospital just to be sure. Get a look at my grand-daughter and make sure everything's okay." He gives her a reassuring smile and Dom whispers something in her ear.

I can't handle this. I turn and walk to the door.

"I have to go to the bathroom." They all turn to me and I wait for a response. No one says anything. Both men look at me like they aren't sure I'm telling the truth. If I'm honest with myself, I'm not sure that I am.

"Make a right outside of the office," Becca answers with her eyes closed. I nod my head once, and walk through the door with my eyes on the ground. The commotion in the dining hall makes me walk faster. I get to the bath-room, shutting the door behind me and the noises are muted. It's quiet. I walk quickly to the faucet and turn it on. I take a moment to splash some cold water on my face, then run my wet hands down the back of my neck.

I breathe in and out. What am I doing? What am I going to do? I swallow thickly. I don't know the answer to either question.

"Miss Hawthorne? Elle Hawthorne?" Hearing my name startles me and I turn around to face two women, each holding a badge out for me to see. It takes me a minute to realize what's going on. Two cops. Blood drains from my face and my hands go numb. Fuck. Fuck, this cannot be good.

"Yes?" I ask weakly.

"You're coming with us."

VINCE

My feet pound against the pavement, my eyes focused on the red Honda ahead of me. Multiple car doors open and slam shut, then the tires squeal as they peel out. Someone fires a gun out of their window as I duck into Tommy's car.

He starts it and hits the gas. The tires spin, and my back presses against the seat as we take off after those fuckers.

They hit us on our home turf. With my mother there. My pregnant sister-in-law. My sweetheart on my arm. They're going to fucking pay for this shit.

"Don't lose 'em, Tommy!" I yell, leaning out of the window. I line up my gun and fire, aiming at the fucker in the passenger seat.

Bang! Bang! Bang! The third shot gets him. I see the asshole lean down in the seat and the driver turns the wheel but the motion is too sharp, and the car swerves into the intersection. They go over the lines and almost lose control of the car. We're closer now.

Tommy hits the gas, trying to get closer. But there are so many fucking cars out this late at night. My heart slams in my chest. They could've got my girl. Adrenaline fills my veins.

I look up and see we're closer. I need to get my head on right.

The driver keeps one hand on the steering wheel, then points his gun out of the window, spraying bullets. I duck behind the dash as a bullet hits the windshield. Tommy swerves, but stays on that fucker's ass. A car honks a warning, another to my right swerves to avoid us, and all hell breaks loose. A car behind us crashes into a parked car, and the traffic light turns red. Brakes squeal and my hands push against the dash.

Fuck! They speed through the intersection and several cars speed by us as they run the light. Tommy slams on the brakes, just barely avoiding a crash. Tires screech and the smell of burning rubber floods my lungs. My head slams down on the dash, and my palms push against the leather.

"Fuck!" I yell, slamming my fist into the dash. The cars finally start moving.

"Take me back. I need to get back to my girl," I tell him, feeling sick to my stomach. The fact that those bastards got away from me pisses me off. But I know who they are. And they're going to fucking die. Every last one of them.

* * *

JUST AS WE park in front of the restaurant, my phone goes off.

"Vince." Dom sounds somber and I don't like his tone. My heartbeat slows and my vision seems to blur.

"Becca alright, Dom?" I ask first. I know my sweetheart's okay. I stayed with her until those cowards took off. I close my eyes and pray his baby's alright. I hate that I think the worst. But the way he said my name has my mind going crazy.

"She's alright."

"The baby?" I ask.

"She's good too. Got a good view of her sucking her thumb right now." I feel a little bit of relief at this. "Your girl..." He trails off, as if he's unsure how to say what comes next.

My heart skips a beat, and my lungs feel empty. That's what he called about. Elle. My sweetheart. She's okay. I know she is. She'd better be safe. I told him to take her. "What about her?"

"She's been picked up."

"No." I shake my head. No fucking way.

"We tracked her phone, Vince. And it was on the cameras. Two undercovers, not ours." I lean back against the side of the car. The sound of sirens is getting louder and louder, but I can't begin to process what that means.

"Vince, we gotta go!" Tommy's screaming in my ear, but his words barely register with me.

I look at him jumping in the driver's side as Dom talks away in my ear. I don't know what he's saying, and I don't care. I thought we had something. I thought she loved me. Loved what I did to her. Loved being mine.

The red and blue lights flash down the road ahead of us. They'll be here soon.

I turn off my phone and put a hand over Tommy's, stopping him from moving the car. We won't make it. They're gonna be here before we can get away. They'll see us. It'll be a chase. They don't have anything on us right now. Questioning. It's gotta be questioning about the shooting. *It's not my girl*, I say over and over in my head. *Not Elle*. This isn't about my sweetheart. My world feels like it's collapsing around me, but I refuse to believe it. There's been a mistake.

"Get out, and get low." I hand him the gun in my hand and push his shoulder toward the door of the car. Tommy doesn't waste a second, and I hop over the console to sit in his seat. As the cops roll up and park their car in front of mine, blocking me in, I get out of the car through the driver's side, making it appear as though it was opened for me. The fucking sirens and bright lights piss me off.

"Good evening, officers." I shut the door and walk to them as the uniformed men get out. Another car pulls up and Detective Anderson gets out. I narrow my eyes at him. I fucking hate that prick. He'd lie, cheat and steal to see us all behind bars.

"Vincent Valetti, you're under arrest."

My brows shoot up in surprise, but I don't fight them. It's foolish to put up a fight. That would just give them something they can actually charge you with. I mentally check off every possible thing in my head. No concealed weapons on me. Nothing they can pin on me. I can't think of a damn thing that they would be able to find in the car.

I try to breathe in and out calmly as I turn around and put my hands on my head. I know the drill. I lean my stomach against the car door. This isn't the first time it's happened. As they slam my head into the roof of the car, I see

Tommy walking down the alley. He catches my eyes and nods. He knows the drill, too. My lawyer will be there faster than I will.

I'll be out in no time.

As long as this isn't about my girl.

ELLE

"Elle, my baby!" My mother stands in the brightly lit front room of the police station. The place is mostly deserted, save for me, the two cops behind me and the one at the desk. And my mother.

I don't answer her. I don't know what to say. I'm still pissed off about how she dropped me from her life the second I had no money to give her. Her nose is bright red, and her eyes are watery. I'd say it's from crying, but it's not. She's drunk. I bite my bottom lip as the cops walk me closer to the front desk. They leave me standing there as my mother comes closer.

"Baby girl, are you alright?" she asks, with both hands grasping for mine. *Baby girl?* My mother has never called me that. I pull my hands away from her.

"What did you do?" I snarl at her. She backs away slowly, looking to her left, then her right. Her hand comes up to her chest and if she were wearing a necklace she'd be clutching it.

"They called to tell me they found you," she answers.

"Found me?" I practically yell. "You knew where I was!"

"It's okay." She reaches out for me again. "We're going to get you out of this mess." I stare blankly at her as she continues. "I know he kidnapped you. I was so worried."

I sneer at her. "Were you worried when you called me a bitch for not giving you more money?"

She looks to her right and lowers her voice. "Just calm down. The police are going to give us a place out west. We're going to go into the witness protection program. Everything is going to be worked out. Just as long as you tell them whatever they need to know."

I look at my mother up and down. Does she think she's getting a fresh start? Is that what she sees this as? A get out of jail free card where her past mistakes vanish, and she can use this to her advantage?

"I love you. I really do." My voice cracks because it's true. I do love my mother, and for some reason it makes me sick. But I deserve better. I raise my voice and harden it. "I told you that you could call me. And you called once, for money. You really were 'so worried,' weren't you?"

"Elle." My mother tries to make her voice sound stern.

"You're drunk, mother. Go home and take care of yourself."

"I can't afford it on my own!" she yells at me. That's really what it all comes down to. It's always what it all comes down to.

"Then get a fucking job!" The officers come between us, and one pushes me toward the back, while a third comes behind my mother.

"You ungrateful bitch!" she screams at me as the officer pulls her away. She's drunk and being stupid and she tries smacking the officer away. I can't watch. She needs to get her shit together. I keep moving and try to ignore my mother's screams as the cops lead me to a back room. My heart fucking hurts. I can't help her if she doesn't want it though. I just can't put up with her shit anymore.

They open a door on the left and I walk through and almost laugh. It's just like the movies. A mirror and everything. I guess they're going to interrogate me. I choke on the ball forming in my throat.

At least they didn't handcuff me. I sit down and take a shaky breath. I'm not going to give them anything. Not a damn word. As soon as they close the door I say, "I want a lawyer."

"Miss Hawthorne. There's no need for a lawyer; we just want to ask you a few questions." My eyes dart to theirs. They have to give me a lawyer, don't they?

"I want a lawyer," I say without confidence. My heart beats louder in my chest. The weight of the situation comes down hard on my shoulders. I'm in the police station. Even if I don't say anything, they're going to know I was here. The *familia* will know. I close my eyes and for the first time in a long time I wonder if Vince will be able to save me.

If I don't say anything, they won't be mad at me, right? They can't blame me for being taken here against my will. I stand up quickly, and the chair tips over behind me. I look at each of them as though they've cornered me. "I want to leave!" My body heats, and anxiety overwhelms me. A man walks in. He's bald with bushy eyebrows, but he doesn't seem old. Maybe it's his broad build. His eyes are sharp, and his teeth are perfectly straight and white. He gives me a tight smile as he takes a seat across the table. He places his badge on the table.

"Hi there. Miss Hawthorne, I'm Detective Anderson, and I've been assigned to your case."

"Hello," I answer back.

"Try to calm down. We just have a few questions to ask, and then you can leave if you wish."

"We'd like to make you a deal," one of the female officers says. I forget her name. She told it to me, but I forgot. It all seems like a blur. The other woman picks up my chair and motions for me to sit. I sit down calmly and put my hands on my thighs. I stare at the table.

"We know you've been held against your will, Elle," the sweet blonde who looks about my age says. It's the first time she's really spoken. She sounds kind and she puts her hands out for me to hold, but I don't take it.

"I can't imagine everything you've been through. But we're here to help," she adds.

"We know you were abducted by Vincent Valetti on Sunday, May 16th." How do they know that? As if hearing my unspoken question, the blonde answers. "You were seen being forcefully pushed into the trunk of his car."

I feel shock first, then anger. I remember the unmarked white car I saw outside of my mother's place. They were watching me this entire time? Holy shit. They saw me being taken, and they did nothing!

"We need you to answer a few questions for us, and then we'll be able to give you a way out of this, Elle." I look at the man as he speaks. That's why. Bastards.

As I stare between the three of them, all I can think is that I wish Vince was here.

Rule two: I don't remember a damn thing, and I don't know what anyone is talking about. "I want a lawyer."

VINCE

"*We* got you, Vince. You want to give us your story now? You got anything you wanna work with?" Detective Anderson sits back in his seat with a smug look on his face. I've been sitting here for a good half hour, just biding my time while they make me sweat it out.

I stare back at him with my mouth closed. I'm not saying a damn thing until my lawyer gets here. And then I'll be thanking them for their time and walking the hell out of here.

"Miss Hawthorne's already given her statement. You're going away for a long time Vince. The only way to ease up on your sentencing is to give us something. Something worth my while."

"Not saying a word." Cops will lie, cheat, and steal to get a statement. It hurts that she sold me out. But she's only got shit on me and no one else in the *familia*. And what do I care if I go away anyway? It's not gonna be the same, not after her. Not with her leaving me. My jaw tics and my fists clench. I wonder what she told them. I wanna know what my sweetheart really thought about me. About everything we went through together.

"She told us how you forced her into the trunk of your car and took her against her will." Fuck! I feel a sharp pain in my chest, like he fucking stabbed me. I can't believe she'd talk. Not my girl.

Even knowing she sold me out, I don't regret it. I love the way she made me feel. Even if everything that was real between us was only on my end. I can't stand the hurt in my chest. I fucking loved her. I still do. Tears prick at my eyes. I really thought she loved me. What a fucking idiot I was. I push down my emotions. They still aren't getting shit from me.

He's been babbling on with threats, but then he says something that rings clear in my ears. "She told us how you smacked her around and threatened her mother."

The tightness in my chest fades as his words sink in.

I smirk at them. Fucking liars. They were doing real good, too. I thought they had me. My girl wouldn't lie. I know she wouldn't. And I never said a word about her mother.

"You charging me with anything, officers?" I cock an eyebrow.

"We'll keep you in holding--" he starts threatening me, but I cut him off.

"And piss off my Pops as a result? How's that restraining order faring on your record, Detective Anderson?" He'd better not have upset Elle, either. She hasn't been through this shit before, so I can't imagine what she's feeling. "You better being treating my sweetheart good too. If you threaten her with anything, I'll make sure you lose your fucking badge."

Detective Anderson's nostrils flare with anger, and he slams his fist on the table. He takes off and slams the door on his way out. I know they'll keep me here for a bit longer. That's fine. So long as she's alright. My chest tightens with pain. The family knows she's here, but they don't know shit about her. A cold sweat breaks out on my forehead. I need to get to a phone. I need to get out of here. I start feeling fidgety, sitting in this chair. I've been at the station before, but I've never felt like this. Never felt the need to get the fuck out immediately. But knowing Elle will be out soon? Knowing they'll be waiting for her? I need to get out.

ELLE

I walk down the driveway with my arms crossed and my hands gripping onto my shoulders. I didn't have an address to tell them to drop me off at. I can't go back to my mother's, even if my name's on the mortgage, I don't want to be there. And I don't know Vince's address, even though I've been living there for the last two weeks. So I gave them the only address I had, which was Vince's parents' house.

I could run, I know that. I could go to a shelter and wait for the *familia* to eventually take me out. I could go into witness protection and give them everything I have on Vince. But I won't. I don't want to.

The blonde officer looked at me with pity, while the brunette one like I was a fucking idiot. And maybe I am. I know I could go to a women's shelter. They tried to convince me that's where I should be while I get back on my feet. But that's not where I *want* to be. I want to be with Vince.

Dante opens the door with an aggressive look directed at the cop car. He looks pissed and it takes me by surprise, but it's not directed at me. Still, I struggle to breathe, and my gaze falls to the floor. Fuck, I knew I shouldn't have come here. This was a mistake.

I move to turn away and go anywhere other than here. I don't care where, but his strong hand comes down on my shoulder, stopping me from leaving.

"Come on in," he says calmly. I look over my shoulder and see the female offi-cers watching me. They look like they're waiting to pounce.

It's my last chance to decide. I know it is. I can go inside and risk whatever plan the *familia* has for me, or I can turn around and take my chances with the witness protection program. I look up at Dante and ask him the only thing I want to know. "Is Vince here?"

He gives me a tight smile as he answers, "Not yet." As soon as I hear his answer I walk inside quickly, pushing my body against the doorframe to get the fuck away from the cops. My arms are still wrapped tight around my shoulders.

"Elle!" Linda yells from the dining room. She strides toward me and wraps her arms around me. "Are you alright, sweetheart?" she asks me, pushing the hair out of my face. A soft smile forms on my lips. *Sweetheart.*

"I'm scared," I answer honestly. I really am. My body starts to tremble.

"It's okay, we've got you now." She pulls me in for a hug and gently pats my back. She doesn't understand that that's why I'm scared. I feel like a sheep that's walked into a lion's den. I open my eyes and see Anthony and Dante watching me closely, mumbling something to each other.

Dante walks toward us, and I pull away from Linda. I give her a tight smile as Dante tells her to go upstairs. She says something to him, a protest of sorts, but I can't hear. It's like white noise in my ears. I turn toward the window and look outside, only to see the cop car leaving, driving away to leave me to this fate I've chosen.

Dante stands next to me and puts a hand on my arm. "Come sit with me, Elle." I look up at him and try to speak, but I can't. The knot in my stomach grows larger and my skin turns to ice with fear. I nod since the words won't come out.

He leads me to his office. Anthony falls in line behind me. I'm convinced it's a sentencing. I'm being led to my death. Tears leak out of the corners of my eyes as I sit in the chair in front of his desk. Dante's quick to come to my side as I put my hands over my face and sob.

"I swear I didn't--" I try to speak, but a hiccup interrupts me.

He shushes me and pats my back. "It'll be alright, Elle. We're just waiting for Vince." Hearing his name helps calms me down. Vince will take care of me. He'll protect me. I know he will.

After a moment my breath evens out, and my head seems to clear. I feel tired and emotionally drained as well. "When will he be here?" I finally manage to ask.

Dante searches my face for a moment, and I see Anthony sit in the chair on the far side of the room. "That depends on what you told them," he finally says.

"I didn't tell them anything," I answer back. A smile grows slowly on his face.

"I believe you." He sits at his desk and pulls out a bottle of some brown liquid. "Would you like a drink, Elle?"

I scrunch up my nose. "I don't like whiskey." He laughs from deep in his chest.

"Good thing this is bourbon then. I'm sure you could use a drink." He pours three shots, and gives one to me as Anthony reaches for his.

"Throw it back and I'll get you a chaser." He winks and tosses his shot back, so I do the same with mine. Ugh. It tastes awful.

I put the glass on the table and look at him straight in the eyes. "The chaser?" I ask. I could really fucking use it. I want to lick my dress to get this taste out of my mouth, but then I'd have to lift the hem up to my face, and that wouldn't be ladylike at all.

Before Dante can answer, the door opens behind me and I turn in my seat to see who it is.

"Vince!" I get up from the chair, knocking it into the desk and run into his arms. He holds me tight, and I melt into him. Everything is better now. I nuzzle into his arms. The heat from the liquor intensifies the warmth in my chest.

I pull back and look up at him with wide eyes. "I didn't--"

He kisses me on the lips, cutting me off. He pulls back and a small grin pulls at his lips. "I know, sweetheart."

"Do they have anything?" I hear Anthony ask.

"Nothing. They were reaching." Vince answers over the top of my head. He leans down and gives me a peck on the lips. I grip him tighter, and he rubs my back in soothing strokes.

"You did good, sweetheart. You did real good." Hearing his praise makes my heart feel light. He holds me for a moment and then they start talking behind me. I try not to listen as I shut my eyes and just focus on how good he feels.

"We need to get those MC bastards," Vince says, and it makes my eyes pop open. I want to ask who they are. I want to know if they were the ones who shot at us. But I remember the rules. I turn in his arms and look to the door. I'm afraid to ask if I can leave. I shouldn't be here listening. I know that much. But he pulls me into him, my back against his front, and he kisses my neck.

"We got 'em waiting for you, Vince." Anthony's eyes travel to my face and then back to Vince. "We figured you would want to do the honors."

"Damn right I want the honors. All of them?" he asks.

"Still looking for two of them." Anthony answers in a tight voice. It makes my stomach churn. Judging by the look on his face, that's really fucking bad. I try to ignore it all. I need to forget.

His hands grip my hips and he leans in to talk to me in my ear, "Sweetheart, you stay here."

I turn around and plead with him, "No. Don't leave me." I don't want him to go. I don't want to be left here.

"They put a hand on you, baby?" he asks me. "Who hurt you?"

I gently shake my head. No one's hurt me. "No one."

"That's 'cause you're mine." He kisses me on the lips. "I'll be back."

"Please, Vince. Just wait till I'm asleep. I need you." His face softens and he leans down to kiss me.

"I can do that, sweetheart."

"Good man," Dante says from behind me. "Take care of your girl, and then you guys take care of that shit tonight." Vince nods his head as Dante walks to the door and opens it. "Don't be late for dinner tomorrow," he adds before crossing through the door. Under his breath, he mumbles, "I gotta take care of your mother."

Vince smiles at his father and leads me to the door with his hand on the small of my back. "Let's go home, sweetheart. I'll take care of you."

VINCE

*B*oth men stare back at me. Only two out of four, but I'm giving them the full treatment. I want to send a message. These are the bastards who opened fire on me. On my family. On my sweetheart. My fists clench in anger. They're screaming through their gags. I wanted to make sure they were awake for what comes next. Tommy beat the shit out of one of them, and it was nearly 40 minutes before he woke up. It made it easier to tie his ass up to the truck though. The other one put up a fight, not that it was of much use against all of us. I stretch my jaw, feeling the slight bruise there from the shit punch he landed. I suppose if I knew I was going out, I'd fight like hell, too.

"Any last words?" I ask, knowing they're trying to say something. I don't give a fuck though. They scream louder and fight the ropes that are chafing their skin.

"You ready, boss?" Anthony asks, as he tosses the container into the bed of the truck. It smacks against the one guy's leg and I swear to God he shits himself at the touch. The whole front yard of the Locos Diablos MC club house smells like gasoline, so I just take a few steps back. I hope the two fuckers we didn't find are in there right now or hiding somewhere watching. I want them to see this. I want them to know what's going to happen to them.

"Light it up." I don't turn my back as Tommy lights a match and tosses it at them.

I stare at the flames as they rise higher and higher. Their screams get louder and louder. I know the cops will be here soon, and I need to get my ass out of here. The smoke will rise and someone will call it in. I gotta get out of here in case it explodes, too. Everyone on the streets will know, though. You don't fuck with the Valettis. A chill runs through my body as I turn and get into the car. Tommy's in the driver's seat and Anthony's in the back.

"Am I taking you home, boss?"

"Yeah." I need to get home and feel her writhing under me. I'll need her every night until I die.

No one touches what's mine. No one but me.

ELLE

I purse my lips as I look at the canvas. I set it up in the dining room so I'd get more natural light on it while I worked. There's just too much darkness. It's supposed to be a man's lips on a woman's neck, with his hand around her throat and her mouth parted. It was too realistic though, initially. I wanted to make it more abstract, so I added a black gradient to make them look like they were fading into it. But, I overdid it. I think I really fucked it up. I take a step back and put the brush on the easel as I take a deep breath in, and then out.

"They're going to love it, sweetheart," Vince says from behind me, and I smile. I keep my eyes closed as his arm wraps around my waist and he kisses my neck, just like I knew he would. He holds me to him and I open my eyes. We both stare at the painting.

"You think they'll really like it?" It's my first exhibit. The gallery next to Becca's restaurant is featuring me in their exhibit. I'm scared shitless. Painting is a lot of fun, and relaxing as well, but I never thought it'd be a viable career. There's so much risk and no stability. But Vince is right. It's the next step for me. It's been a few weeks since the shooting, and everything has finally calmed down. I've even gone out a few times with Becca. Vince didn't like the idea at first, since there's still something going on with the MCs, but he relented. I'm fairly certain him and Dom just sat outside of the restaurant every single time. I know they did at least once. Becca and I kinda of love it. How protective they are. The only place Vince has taken me is to family dinners and the gun range. I *need* to get out and do something. Thank God for Becca. I call her almost every day. She's going to pop sometime soon. Having her as a friend really helped me to take painting seriously. She calls me an artist, but I haven't earned that title yet.

My vow to be more social could be going better. I was going to take my mother to her AA meeting. But when I showed up and found her drunk and heard her excuses... I stormed off and haven't been back since. It wasn't worth cussing her out. I'm tired of putting the energy into helping her. I really do want to try; I want to help her. But I can't take her bullshit anymore.

I tilt my head and get a wave of inspiration as I look at the canvas. I need to make more of it black and white, and have the red lips saturated in comparison. That and more contrast on his hand. That would really make it pop.

"I've got it!" I yell out, and move to pick up the paints on the table.

"I gotta get going, Elle. Are you sure you wanna open those now? They'll dry up by the time I get back."

Arousal shoots from my chest down to my heated core. The thought of him leaving turns me on so damn much. He still ties me up when he leaves, and fucks me so fucking good when he gets back. I love it. I live for his touch. I clench my thighs and close my eyes trying to hide my desire. Not that it matters. He knows how depraved I am. And he loves it, too.

But playing during the daytime has waned a bit. I've been busy with shopping dates and luncheons. The women in his family are so friendly and open, I can't possibly say no to their invitations. He always ties me up at night though. And I fucking love it.

My eyes shoot open and I stare at the canvas. This is supposed to be done tonight, and it needs at least two days to dry completely. I bite the inside of my cheek contemplating what I should do.

"You need to get this done, don't you?" he asks, picking up his mug off the table. He grabs mine as well and walks to the sink.

"I really should," I say, as I take in more details of the painting. I should take advantage of this inspiration while I can.

"When I get back..." Vince walks over to me, and reaches under my night-

302

gown to cup my pussy. He breathes on my neck and puts his lips up to my ear, "...you'd better be ready for me."

His words send a shiver down my back. My lips part and a small moan of lust escapes me. He turns me to face him and gives me a sweet kiss on the lips. I deepen it. I want him now. I always want him.

"Did you hear me, sweetheart?" he asks with a slight threat in his tone.

I look up at him through my thick lashes and place my hands on his chest. "Yes." I plant a chaste kiss on his lips. "I'll be waiting for you."

He smiles down at me. "That's my girl. I'll be gone for a few hours." He gives me another kiss, then gives my ass a squeeze before leaving me in the dining room.

I watch him as he leaves. I'm not sure what he's doing tonight. But I don't ask. He told me if anyone asks, that he plays the stock market. I sigh, feeling a little empty inside. I don't like lying, but luckily for me, no one has asked in the half a dozen times I've left this house.

I shake off the ill feelings and get to work. I add a little white paint, and then some black onto the easel. I need a really faint shade of grey though. As I dig though a mason jar of brushes for my favorite thin one, my phone goes off.

Becca. I grin from ear to ear. Baby time!

I answer the phone and have to refrain from asking if her water broke. She told me she'd stab me if I asked one more time.

"Hello?" I answer in a playful, singsong voice.

"I need a trampoline," she says as clear as day on the phone.

"What?" A trampoline?

"I need to get this baby out! My fat ass needs to get on the trampoline and have gravity do its thing." I bust out laughing. I freaking love her. I smile as Rigs barrels into the room, wagging his tail that moves the back half of his body. He looks ridiculous. This dog is going to be huge when he's fully grown. I walk to the back door and let him out while she talks.

"I need to get this painting done and then have a nice glass of wine," I sigh into the phone as I shut the door, leaving him out to play in the fenced back-yard. It's a large backyard. It's the perfect size for a trampoline or a swing set. I rub my belly, thinking we could have a little one someday. I could be complaining about heartburn and backaches like Becca does. I think I'd go with a swing set though. Trampolines seem a little scary for little ones.

"Well, have an extra one for me," Becca says with a laugh. I smile at Becca's playful tone, and then my heart stops.

I can hear Rigs snarling and growling, and then all of a sudden he's barking like crazy. My blood freezes, and my body goes numb with paralysis. I'm not okay. I turn to race to the backyard to get him. I need to get to Rigs. I don't make it two steps before the front door smashes open, and I scream and drop the phone. My body nearly falls to the ground, I just barely catch myself, and I cover my head with my arms before staring at them with wide eyes.

There are three or four men, all dressed in long-sleeved black shirts, wearing ski masks, covering their faces. One of them is pointing a gun at me as the others move around him, walking toward me with determined steps. One barks orders at the others. He sounds Hispanic. The responses he gets sound like American accents though. I try to pay attention to the details. I scream it out, hopeful that Becca will hear. "Four men! One is Hispanic! Gun! Al--"

A hand whips across my face, knocking me to the ground. A metallic taste fills my mouth. I see my phone on the ground. My heart sinks. It's off. It must've hung up when it fell from my hands. She didn't hear. My eyes close with failure. I know they're going to take me. I know there's nothing I can do. My body goes limp. I won't fight them. Not here. Not now. Not when I don't have a chance. I didn't just start living for them to come and kill me. It's not going to happen like this. I won't let it.

Someone kicks me in the stomach. I try to curl inward, but they grab me. The last thing I see is a fist coming at my face as one man holds my arms to my side and pins my back to his chest. The fists lands hard on my jaw, and the world fades to black.

I don't fight it. I'll wait.

And when I wake...

I will make them pay for taking me away from Vince.

VINCE

I tap the small, black velvet box in my pocket as I get out of the car and shut the door. I can't wait to ask her. Well, I'm not going to ask. I'm going to tell her she's marrying me. It's been enough time that Ma will approve. She calls me after their lunch dates. I'm glad the two of them get along. Nothing at all like the relationship Elle has with her mother.

I cringe remembering how she reacted when I told her Sandra went to rehab. Maybe once she's out and stays sober Elle will believe she's changed. It seems like the more time she spends with the *familia*, the more resistant she is to forgiving Sandra. Which isn't necessarily a bad thing, it just hurts me thinking she won't have a relationship with her own mother.

My phone's going off again. I know it's Dom. He's been calling to get my ass down to the docks, but I told him yesterday, today, they would have to wait a while. Right now it's all for her.

I gotta pull the trigger on this. She deserves this for putting up with me. For fitting so perfectly into my life. That, and Ma will kill me if I don't put a ring on her finger before knocking her up. Part of me still thinks the *familia*'s waiting for her to run. But putting my baby inside her is gonna change all that for them. And this ring on her finger.

As soon as I see the door, I know something's off. Adrenaline pumps through my blood and my heart races. The door's cracked. It's been kicked in.

The wood is splintered from where the door was locked. I always lock it behind me. Fuck. Fuck! I take the steps up slowly and pull out my gun. I want to call out for her. I need to know she's safe. But, I have to be smart.

I already fucking know who did this. I know it was Shadows MC. They're a bunch of fucking liars. They've been working with the Locos Diablos. They set them up to take the fall. But Tony got all their transfers and finances. I grind my teeth as I walk silently through the house. Rigs barks and paws at the back door. I walk to the dining room first. Two chairs are turned over and her canvas is on the ground. Broken. The paint is smeared on the tabletop. Her phone's on the floor.

Mine goes off in my pocket again and I answer it. I know they're gone. Looking around the room, it's obvious they took her and ran. They want war.

I answer it and hold the phone to my ear.

"Vince! 'Bout fucking time! Becca's been--" Dom yells through the phone. I keep my eyes on the entrance to the dining room, just in case someone's here, hiding and waiting to jump me. But I know they're gone.

I cut him off. "They took her." I swallow the lump in my throat.

"Elle?" Dom asks after a quiet moment.

"Yeah." I bite back my emotions and let the anger come through. "Tony has their info?" I swallow the lump suffocating me and clear my throat. I put the phone back to my ear to hear him rattling off something in my ear.

"I don't want to risk going to the wrong place. We need to split it up."

"You sure that's smart, Vince? We could be outnumbered easily. They've got at least 10 of 'em at any given time at either the clubhouse or the warehouse."

"Well we'll have the advantage of coming up on 'em. They don't know that we're on to them. They have no fucking clue. But if we all show up to the wrong place, we're fucked. They'll know. They'll…" I don't say it. They'll kill her. I know they will. My chest pains and I struggle to take a breath. I can't even imagine what they're doing to her now. I don't want to think about it. But I can't help it. "I swear to God, Dom. I swear I'm gonna kill them."

"I know. I know," he says solemnly.

"I gotta go now. Text me the address."

"You need back up! Don't be stupid, Vince!" he yells back.

"Tell them to meet me there," I tell him. I can't wait. I won't.

"You won't do her any good if they kill you first." Fuck. I hate how right he is.

"I can't wait." I can't just stand here. She's most likely at one of those two places. And if she's not, someone there will know where she is. And I'll make them talk. I'll find her.

"I'm on my way. I'll call the guys now. I'll split 'em."

I nod my head. I can't talk. I try to, but my throat dries out and closes. If they killed her... If they put their hands on my sweetheart... I shake my head and focus on getting her back. I have to believe it's possible.

"Hurry up, Dom. And text me that address."

ELLE

"We need to get her out of here." I wake up groggy, to a voice I don't recognize. My back is to them. I know they're behind me. I'm lying on my side, and I can feel a cool breeze on my face. I remain still and silent, and I'm sure to keep my breathing even. My face is killing me. My temples pound with pain. But I ignore the painful throbbing. I do a mental check. It's only my face and my side that hurt.

They didn't bind my wrists. I try to keep the smile off my face. Thank fuck they're behind me so they can't see my relief. Vince was wise to tie me up. These fuckers have underestimated me. My heart pounds in my chest, but I keep forcing myself to breathe evenly. I listen to them. I'll wait until I can strike. I couldn't do anything back at the house, with all of them on me at once. I just need to wait until I have a chance.

I'm sure Vince will come. But right now, I can't rely on him. I don't know if he'll get to me in time. I also don't know how much time I have. I listen and wait.

"You really think this is going to work?" someone behind me asks. His voice is deep and throaty, like someone who's smoked his whole life.

"It's their signature move. They'll definitely believe it's a message from the cartel." Another man, one who's closer to me.

"They're a bunch of pussies." I can hear three men in total laugh. So I'm up against three of them. Those aren't good odds. I don't think I could take out three. My heart sinks. I won't give up hope though. I just need to try to take them on one at a time. I can manage that. I *will* manage that.

"Thought they'd have already gone after them. They move slow." My eyes slowly creep open as I continue to take stock of my situation. I'm facing a cinder block wall, lying atop cardboard boxes. My arm is above my head and it fucking hurts. I want to move it but I don't. I lie still and wait. Smoke fills my lungs with the smell of cigarettes and I hear a drag being taken.

"I want at her first." My eyes open wide, but I keep my breathing steady.

"You'll wait your turn."

"You sure they won't be able to get anything from the video?"

"Yeah, we'll edit it to cover our voices. It'll look just like the cartel's threats. Vince is a fucking stupid hothead. I know they'll go in for the kill as soon as it's sent."

The men laugh again, and I try to keep the sickness I'm feeling from creeping up my throat. But I can't. I nearly vomit at the image they've put in my head.

I'm fucked. I know it, too. A hand grips my hair and yanks my head back. I scream out with tears creeping out of the corners of my eyes.

"Our little bitch is up." I want to close my eyes, but I can't. A bald short man with yellow-stained teeth stares back at me with a menacing look. He's got a sick grin plastered on his face. From his voice, I recognize him as the one saying their plan will work. I decide to think of him as the planner in the group.

His nose is nearly an inch from mine and I take the opportunity to spit in his face. He wipes his face off with the back of his arm and then backhands me so hard I hit the cement ground with enough force that I nearly go unconscious.

"Get her ass up here." I hear him move around as I hear more heavy steps come from behind me. "We can all have a practice round." A sick, disgusting chuckle fills the hot air as I'm pulled up onto my feet. I turn around and kick the fucker as hard as I can right in his balls. The second hurls himself at me from my left side, and I ball my hands into fists, and draw back to punch him, but the first man's arms wrap around my front and hold me back. Fuck! No!

"No wonder he kept this cunt. I hope she fights us every time." A tall, thin man with oily black hair smiles and walks closer to me with his hands out to reach for me.

I don't care that I'm being held back. I'm not going to stop fighting. Vince would want me to fight. As soon as this bastard's close enough, I push my weight back and throw my legs up to kick him. The bald man holding me tilts backwards as he's knocked off balance, and my foot gets high enough to knock the guy square in the face. His head flies back as I fall to the ground and when I look up, blood's pouring from his nose. I don't waste a second, but the man behind me is faster. He wraps his arms around me and pins my arms in place. He holds me close and I'm trapped. I struggle against him, but I'm trapped in his hold.

The door to the room flies open.

"They're here!" A man barges into the room, completely out of breath.

"Who's here?" the bald fucker asks, his vile breath filling my nose and I try to push away from him again.

"Valettis!" the man yells, and the men all exchange quick glances.

"I'll tie her up. You three go now!"

They run out of the door and the bald man reaches into his jacket and I know what he's getting. I lunge at him. I'll pry it from his hands if I have to. I'll scratch, bite and claw. I latch onto his wrist while it's tucked at his side, gripping the gun, and sink my teeth into his arm as he fires a shot that hits the wall behind him.

He screams from the pain and pushes me away, but I bite harder, until his flesh rips from his arm and I spit it out, digging my nails and fingers into his arm and back.

The man looks down at me with a twisted snarl on his face and tries to shove me away. It gives me enough room to elbow him in his ribs and as he hunches over, the gun falls to the ground and goes off.

This is my chance. My only chance.

VINCE

The tires screech and I jump out before we even come to a stop. I know they have cameras here. If there's anyone looking, they'll see us coming. I don't want to give them time to hide her. Or worse.

I hear Tommy and Anthony call out from my right as they each pull out their guns and run up to my side. Uncle Enzo and Pops are coming, too. Dom has Tony and Joey going with him. A few of the soldiers should be there waiting for them, too. Every last motherfucker is going to die.

I stand in front of the large doors and Anthony opens them up, staying behind the doors as a barrier. Not me. I'm planted right in front with my guns raised, one in each hand. As soon as I see those fuckers I fire.

They don't even see it coming. Immediately I take out three MC assholes. Got one in the chest. Bang! Another in the head. Bang! Bang! Another tries to run, and I shoot that fucker in the back. Bang! Bang! Bang! I walk into the larger room. Stacks of coke and pot are on my left. Bricks of each of them, wrapped in plastic. A bagging station is on my right. Their operation is shit. And now, it's fucking over. As I walk in a gunshot goes off to my left and I fire. Bang! Bang! Bullets fly by me from my right. They whiz past me in what seems like slow motion. Anthony gets a kill. Another MC fucker in leather drops behind a counter. He was counting the cash. With the doors open the wind blows the money off the table.

I walk over to the fucker who got a shot off. Looks like a gunshot caught him in the neck. It must've hit an artery, judging by the way blood gushes out from the wound as his heart pumps. He's clutching the wound with both hands as blood pools around his head and soaks his hair. His eyes focus on me. He tries to speak, but blood coughs up his mouth. I point the gun at his head and pull the trigger.

I keep walking at a fast pace with my guns raised. My heart beats frantically, trying to jump out of my throat and the only sound I can hear is the blood rushing in my ears. But on the surface, I'm a cold-blooded killer, walking with purpose, moving with a deadly calmness that would frighten sociopaths. I have one goal in mind. Only one thing that matters.

My girl. My sweetheart.

Three men run out with guns firing, and a bullet hits me right in the chest. I fire off both guns. One man's downed immediately but the other two move off to the side to take cover behind an old rusted car. Tommy and Anthony go up the right side and duck as the guns come up and fire aimlessly. I take a step forward and aim. I hit the hood right where the hand was and hear the bastard swear. That's not good enough. If he's talking; he's breathing. I walk forward and watch my guys go up the right side, sneaking behind. I'll distract them. I run up close and fire continuously. Four more shells each. Bang! Bang! Bang! Bang! They sound off one after another, after another, until I'm firing blanks. I keep pulling the trigger, letting the empty clicks fill the air. I want them to know I'm empty. I'm counting on them to stand up and fire at me. And they do. As soon as they're visible, shots fire from behind them and both men only get a single shot off. One just misses me. But the other lands on my chest, close to the first shot that hit me.

It hurts like hell.

I look down and make sure the Kevlar held up and there's no blood. I'll fucking live. But not without my girl. I take the pain and keep moving as I reload my guns. I need to find her.

I know there are rooms in the back. She's got to be in one of them. My phone's in my pocket. It's silent. I don't know how they're doing at the clubhouse. But until it goes off, I've got to assume she's here. My eyes raise and my guns point at a door as I hear bullets firing in the distance, somewhere in the back, and a terrifying scream.

Elle!

All at once we run down the hall, my only focus on the door. I need to get to her. She's here. I heard her.

Gunshots fire over and over. Three shots, four shots, five shots. No!

I kick the door and it flies open. I run through ready to fire, and instead I stand in shock.

Anthony and Tommy stop behind me. I hear Uncle Enzo yell something from the back, but I don't know what. All my focus is on my girl.

She's got blood on her face. A nasty bruise on her chin. And she standing, breathing heavy, with her arms straight, holding a small gun. It's pointed down at a short, bald man lying face down on the floor. His leather jacket is speckled with bullet holes and blood. So much blood, pooling around his body.

"Elle," I call out to her, and lower my guns. I see Anthony and Tommy searching the room. I hear a yell clear outside the room, it sounds like Pops. But I'm not paying attention like I should. I walk to my girl. She hasn't moved, except for her chest rising and falling with each heavy breath as she keeps the gun still pointed at the dead man.

"Sweetheart?" I try to get her attention, and it works. Her startled eyes find mine, and her body relaxes finally. She drops the gun to the ground. It falls to the cement floor with a loud clank and she runs to my arms.

Her small body wraps around me and she holds onto me tight. I hold her to me, loving how she's clinging to me. But hating that she had to do this. Hating that she went through this.

"Are you alright, sweetheart?" I finally ask her. She doesn't pull away and doesn't answer.

"We gotta go, Vince," Tommy says to my left. I turn, still holding her to me and see all the guys looking at us. I nod my head and kiss her hair.

"Sweetheart, are you alright?" I ask again. My heart won't beat right until I hear her talk. I know it won't. I just need to hear her say it. I need to hear her voice to really believe I'm holding her in my arms.

She nods her head in my chest and pulls back. Tears run down her face. "I'm okay," she answers me, and then wipes her face. My lips crush hers in a passionate kiss. Her hand wraps around my neck and she kisses me back with the same ferocity.

"I was so scared, Vince," she whispers with her eyes closed as she pulls away.

I kiss the tip of her nose. "I got you now, sweetheart."

She hugs me close, molded to my side, as we walk over the dead body and leave the room. "I won't let that happen again. I promise you," I murmur into her ear. I see my men nod and walk around us. They've got us covered so I can just hold her and give her the comfort she needs.

She looks up at me with tears in her eyes. "You'd better not." She gives me a small laugh, but it's accompanied with tears.

"I promise you, baby. No one's ever going to hurt you again." She buries her head in my chest and wipes her face on my shirt before looking back up at me. I wait until her eyes are firmly on me. "I love you."

"I love you too, Vince." She reaches up to kiss me again as we exit the warehouse and I have to stop to wrap my arms around her and kiss her back. "I love you so fucking much."

EPILOGUE

Elle

"You look beautiful." Vince's mom mouths at me as I walk down the aisle of the church. I smile at her and mouth back a thank you.

The church is gorgeous. It's more beautiful than anything I've ever imagined. St. Rose. The family church. The large stained glass windows and intricate frescoes on the walls give it an old-world feel. It's a traditional wedding, during Sunday mass. So I don't know everyone, but all eyes are on me.

My hands tremble and I hold the bouquet tighter. I love my wedding dress. It has a sweetheart neckline, with an A-line silhouette and it's covered in expensive lace. The gown hugs my baby bump and my curves before flaring out at the top of my thighs. My eyes focus straight ahead. Vince is waiting for me. His hair is styled neatly and he's clean-shaven. His suit is perfectly fitted to his muscular form, and emphasizes his broad shoulders. His eyes travel down my body with lust, and I find myself walking faster. I have to really work to slow my walking to match the pace of the bridal chorus.

Everyone's here. Even my mother came. She's in the back, and I'm not sure if she'll speak to me, but it's a start.

I take a step up the stairs and feel my heart swell with happiness. It overrides my nerves and I take another, to stand with him in the center of the room in front of everyone.

"You look beautiful, sweetheart," Vince says, as I turn and pass the bouquet to Clara. I feel my cheeks heat with a blush. Behind Clara, Becca's holding her little girl. I insisted she still stand up here as my bridesmaid, even if Cloe was being a little Velcro baby. My heart swells and tears prick at my eyes.

I can't wait for the vows, or any of the readings. I'm so overwhelmed with emotion.

"I love you, Vince." I lean forward and give him a quick peck on the lips.

Vince smirks at my impatience. His hand wraps around the back of my head and the other around my waist and he pulls me in for a kiss. A real fucking kiss. My lips mold to his and my body bows under his touch. The cheers and catcalls from the members of the church make me wanna pull away, but I know better.

"Alright, alright, you two," the priest says, and Vince finally loosens his grip on me. I know my cheeks are bright red and I'm slightly embarrassed, but Vince takes my chin between his thumb and his forefinger and makes me look him in the eyes. I'm lost in his look of pure devotion.

"I love you too, Elle," he whispers, and plants another kiss on my lips before taking my hand in his. My heart beats louder in my chest. There's not a doubt in my mind. I know he loves me. And I love him.

The End.

* * *

Keep reading for the next book in the series, Rough Touch.

ROUGH TOUCH

SYNOPSIS

From *USA Today* bestselling author Willow Winters comes a HOT mafia, standalone romance.

I thought I was safe.

I still remember smoothing my dress and putting on my earrings the day it all happened.
  The day my family was murdered and I was taken.

The chain around my neck won't ever leave me, but I won't stop fighting.
  I'll have my revenge at any cost so long as I can remember the girl I used to be.

But I didn't expect Kane. A man of power and fear, yet he shows me kindness.
  Kindness I desperately need.
  Kindness that will break me.

PROLOGUE

Ava
Kane

I was the mafia princess. I thought I was safe.
I was the muscle and moneymaker. I was supposed to be
untouchable.

I STILL REMEMBER SMOOTHING my dress and putting on my earrings the day it all happened.
I remember wiping the blood off my face and feeling the heat of the fire the night it all went down.

I PULL at the chain around my neck and hate what I've become.
I wrap my knuckles with tape before laying hit after hit, hating what I have to do.

. . .

THEY'RE ALL DEAD. Now I have no one.
> They're all dead. Now I have no one.

I FEEL SO ALONE, but I won't stop fighting.
> I feel so alone, but I won't stop fighting.

THEY WANT me to be scared of them, so I'll play the part. I can use that to my advantage.
> They're terrified of me, and that's good. I'm going to need that fear to survive this.

THE PLANE DESCENDS and lands with a loud thump that shakes the cargo hold, but I keep the sick feelings at bay. I hope that bastard's here.
> I hear the plane land and I know it's almost time. I hope it's him this time and not just another shipment.

HE'S the reason I'm shackled and beaten. Used and degraded. I won't stop fighting to breathe until I have my revenge.
> He's my chance at redemption and a new life. I'm not gonna lay down and die; I'm making a name for myself.

THEY KEEP SAYING I'm a good girl.
> They think I'm a bad boy.

NONE of them really know who I am.
> None of them really know who I am.

THEY CAN KEEP CALLING me a good girl though, right up until the moment I slit their throats.

KANE

*M*y fist slams against the bag. I see my uncle's face. I throw a right hook. Next, a left jab. Over and over I slam my fists into the leather until my muscles scream with pain. And then I push myself harder. I feel my knuckles crack under the weight of my hits. The sound of my fists making contact with the heavy bag doesn't do anything to relieve this tension, though. I want to hear the crunch of his jaw. Fucking rat. That coward destroyed my family, and ruined my life. And I can't do shit about it. I can't turn back time.

I hit the bag again and again, trying to get this weight that's crushing my chest to leave me. I hear my father's voice, the screech of the tires. The gunshots. I grab the bag and slow my racing heart. A deep breath fills my lungs, but it only serves to fuel my anger further. They hunted us all down because of my fucking coward uncle. And I can't do shit to change any of that.

"Kane!" Marco shouts; his voice echoes in the empty room. I hear the door swing shut and his boots smack against the concrete floor of the warehouse. I wipe the sweat off my face.

I needed to get out some aggression, but I have to be presentable for the meet, so I grab the towel on the pile of boxes next to me and wipe down quickly. I hear Marco walk toward me as I pick up my shirt and slip it on. I button it up, concentrating on keeping my anger at bay. Aggression would not be good right now. Not when I'm on my own, completely outnumbered, and about to meet the new boss of the Marzano Cartel.

Abram Petrov. He's become notorious for taking over the industry quickly, and with lethal force. Recently he's acquired the lead cartel in Mexico as well as heavy hitters in France and Russia, where he's from. He's a new force that's not scared to play dirty, and now he's on my doorstep.

"I'm ready!" I yell over my shoulder, and stalk toward him. Time to meet the new *famila*, or Bratva as the Russian fucks keep calling it. Or whatever the fuck he calls his crew. I have to try to earn a position with a mob that's willing to take in the nephew of a rat. I swallow thickly. I've been waiting for a few weeks for this meet-up, staying in the warehouse and lying low with a target on my back. This place used to be a safe house for my family. Now it's my bargaining chip to get the attention of Petrov.

His crew came and set up yesterday, but I kept my distance. They know it's my place and they came to do business here, which is great. But I'm not a part of their crew. I'd rather give them the space they want and a warm welcome without getting involved in their shit. I can't fuck this up.

"This is gonna be great. I know it will." Marco grins at me and slaps his hand on my back. His arm has to reach up to hit me square on my shoulders. I'm six-foot-five and all muscle. Next to Marco I look like a fucking beast. I was the top earner in the *famila* for a reason. I'm a terrifying fucker to go up against. People tend to pay up rather than piss me off. But even with all the money I was bringing in, they tried to have me killed. They tried, and they failed.

"Boss's already impressed with everything you did to those pussies." My gut twists and my chest tightens with pain. They should've known better than to come for me. That shit with my uncle had nothing to do with me. Or my father. And they sure as fuck knew my sister and my mother didn't have shit to do with any of it. They fucking came for us all the same, though. They should've made sure we were all dead. Those fuckers left me alive. And they paid the price. Even if they were the only people I had in this world.

I grin at him and huff a laugh. I need the boss to like me. I need somewhere to go, someone to be. I grew up in this life. And everyone I knew turned their backs on me. If I hadn't been so fucked up, I could've started the business myself. I have contacts. A few I still trust. But I made this call too soon. Now I need to go through with it.

I breathe in deep and walk through the hall to the hangar. The meeting's going down here. I'm ready for this. It's not an ambush, but they could easily kill me. It's just me against all of them. They're not here for that. No one's touching me after what I did. Revenge will make a man crazy. Unstoppable. Untouchable. But it's also left me alone. I'm ready to move on and get back to work.

There are a few small planes in the relatively empty hangar. Stacks of cocaine bricks wrapped in plastic are sitting on a folding table. It's not what I'm used to. I'm more of a blackmail-the-politician type. But shipping and selling will have to do in the beginning, I suppose. Onward and upward or some shit like that. I'll prove my worth.

Four men in black and grey suits surround the table, watching the two workers weigh and bag the product. As they hear our footsteps, they turn to face us. The boss, Abram, walks toward me. His underboss walks next to him, but a step or two behind. The other two men with them are obviously soldiers, judging from their broad shoulders. One has a scar across his face. It looks like it came from a slash that should've taken his eye out. The other has a tattoo scrolling up his neck. Both of the soldiers read as highly dangerous, nothing like Abram himself. Their dark eyes stare back at me as they put their arms behind their backs and square their shoulders, waiting for orders. Marco walks behind them and back to the table. He's just a soldier. And he's completely happy with that. He's a dumb fucker.

"Kane," Abram greets, as he extends his hand to me. He's a tall, slender man, with black hair that's slicked back with oil. I shake his hand firmly and stare into his eyes; they're so dark, they appear black as well.

Abram's a deadly boss. I heard about what he did to the cartel in Mazatlan. I'm not all that happy seeing how he cut ties purely for business reasons. And by cut ties, I mean demolished their businesses, stole everything they had, and murdered them. To call him ruthless would be putting it lightly, but beggars can't be choosers. I know there's a target on my back. I need to find a place and lie low. And this is the only option I have right now. So I'm making a deal with the devil.

"Abram. Or should I call you Boss?" I ask, with the hint of a grin on my face.

He smiles back broadly. "Boss, I think." Hearing that allows me to breathe, but I don't show my relief. He turns and wraps his arm around my shoulders, guiding me to the group of men. It's an awkward hold on me, because I'm so much taller than him, but I allow it. "Thank you again, for making this transition easier on us. I appreciate the gesture."

"No problem." I nod my head and take a look at the product lined up on the table. That's a lot of coke. No doubt using my hangar was a decent option for them. And a sign of trust that they accepted my offer.

"I'd like you to meet Vadik, my second-in-command," Abram says. I reach out my hand to the underboss and he's quick to take it with a smile. Another good sign. This man is older. Vadik looks to be somewhere around my father's age, whereas Abram can't be any older than 35. Abram's face has the hint of wrinkles around his eyes. This man, however, has earned his age. Grey hair that's slicked back the same way as Abram's and deep-set wrinkles on his face. His pale blue eyes are like ice. So fucking cold. This man reads as deadly. Abram could easily fool you into thinking he's less dangerous than he is, lulling you into a false sense of security. Based on everything I've heard about him, he's succeeded in doing that multiple times in the past with former rivals. But this man, Vadik, looks like a killer.

"Nice to meet you." I shake his hand. He puts his other hand on top of mine.

"It is indeed, Kane. I've been anxious to meet the man who took down the entire Armeno family in one night." He smiles wickedly as he says, "You've made quite an impression."

"I'm happy to hear that." I say the words, but I'm not happy at all. I did what I had to do. I didn't want to. I had to.

"I've considered your proposal to join me," Abram begins, while looking me in the eyes. I can feel a "but" coming, and I don't like it. I keep my expression impassive as he continues. "I like it. I like it a lot. I think we'll work well together." My brows raise slightly and he registers my surprise.

"We're going to have some more guests in a moment," Abram says, motioning with his hand and guiding me to the front of the hangar. The doors are open, and the sun is shining through. It's a bright, beautiful day. The breeze is refreshing. Too fucking bad there's so much adrenaline pumping in my blood that I can barely breathe.

"More guests?" I ask, with a bit of curiosity in my voice. I'm not curious though--I'm pissed. I offered my place to him to use for entry into the US. Not for him to use as a base for his operations. And definitely not so he could invite more people. But I'm sure as shit not going to tell him that. Not right now, anyway. I may be fueled by anger, but I'm not a hothead.

"Now that our competitor is no more, we have a few business meetings to conduct." He stops in the open tarmac, looking toward the road. "Have you heard of the Valettis?"

I nod my head at his question. The Valettis are a tight pack. They're nearly the only *famila* left that has an actual family related by blood heading up their organization. At least around these parts. I've heard good things about them, promising things. But we've never met personally. They stayed in their territory and we stayed in ours.

"Well, they did business with our former competitor and now they're coming to meet us regarding our new terms."

"New terms?" I question. I'm surprised to hear that. I know they *can* raise their prices now that they're the lead exporter. But I'm not sure it's the wisest to do that at the beginning of a business relationship.

"You'll see," Vadik says from my left side with a crooked grin and a twinkle in his cold eyes. I don't like the way he says it, but again, I don't give them anything. Instead, I nod my head and stare at the two black Range Rovers driving up the dirt road to the landing strip. My heart beats faster in my chest and it's harder to keep the anger from showing.

I don't appreciate the secrets. Nor the sudden company. I don't like being at the bottom and not knowing shit. Not controlling shit. But I have to remind myself that I'm in a tight spot. I need to take it easy and make myself valuable. I'm not valuable to anyone right now, and that's not good for my chances of survival.

The Valettis park and get out quickly. I want to walk to them and meet them halfway, but Abram's feet are planted. I take notice; I stand and act appropriately. It's a rude gesture if you ask me. But what the fuck do I know? If I'm going to be working for him, I'll have to put up with this shit. Regret is already pumping through my blood. I grit my teeth and wish I could take out this anger on something. On someone. I fucking hate the position I'm in.

"Abram Petrov," Vince says, as he stops in front of us. I recognize him immediately. He's the new Don of his *famila*. His father retired and word got around fast that Vince had taken his place. Three more men come up behind him and then two more exit the second vehicle.

"Vincent Valetti. Nice to finally meet you." Abram smiles and extends his hand in greeting. Vince is calm and collected as he accepts the gesture, but he doesn't return the smile.

"It's quite a drive to get out here, Abram. I've heard you're a man who gets these sorts of business arrangements done quickly. Is that so?" An asymmetric grin pulls at my lips. I like how quickly Vince gets to the point. I would also like to get this shit done promptly. The two men standing behind Vince and the others from his *famila* are armed and showing it. Which isn't that big of a deal since the men behind me, the two I've yet to be introduced to, each have a hand on their guns, too. It's not a display of a threat, or of violence. It's simply business. It's how things are done in this life.

I'll still feel better when it's over. I don't particularly enjoy being surrounded by men I don't know who are all armed. I have to start some-where, though.

Abram laughs from deep within his chest and nods his head. "Quick works for me, Vince." He walks forward with a smile and gestures with his arm to a plane that landed an hour or so ago.

More shipments.

The pilot stands outside of the cargo hold smoking a cigarette. He's in jeans and a black tee shirt. Tattoos cover both of his arms and his brow is pierced. He's got a Mexican look to him. I imagine he was the contact Abram must've had in Javier's cartel. Someone was a traitor. But no one knows for sure who it was. Maybe it's wrong of me to assume. Not that it matters anyway.

"I'm ready to do business, and I'd like for things to go smoothly. So, the prices are exactly what they were for you before. Everything the same. The only difference is you'll be going through me, rather than your former contact." Abram talks as we walk closer to the plane. Sickness churns in my gut. I don't know why, but I know I'm not going to like what I see.

"That makes me a very happy business partner," Vince says, but there's hesitation in his voice. He's skeptical. And so am I. There are reasons for meets. But keeping terms the same is not one of them.

"We need your docks for other business ventures. So I'd like to add more to our arrangement," Abram says, as we stop in front of the plane.

"What are you looking to export?" Vince asks, with his eyes narrowed.

"Felipe, bring it out here," Marco says to the pilot. Felipe tosses the cigarette on the ground and walks to the very back of the plane.

I watch with wide eyes as a woman is dragged out from the cargo hold. She's quiet the entire time. Not fighting, simply moving as fast and as best she can to keep up with the man. I'd like to kill that fucker. I struggle to keep my exhalation even. There's a metal collar with a chain around her throat, but he's pulling her along by her hair.

Blood rushes loud in my ears and my body heats with anger. Sex slave trafficking. I had no fucking idea they were into this shit. And judging by Vince's face and the matching looks on his crew's faces, neither did they. When I made contact with Marco, I thought I knew what I was getting into. This wasn't it. This is new, and I don't fucking like it.

The woman doesn't make a sound as she's forced out. Her blue eyes stare at the ground. Her wrists are bound. She isn't wearing shoes, just a filthy and tattered dress. Her pale skin is bruised, but clean. Her brunette hair is a mess around her face, but I can see a red mark from recently being slapped. She walks with her lips firmly pressed together as though she's trying to remain expressionless, although she's showing a hint of pain. The man pushes her onto her knees in front of us and she doesn't react. I know it fucking hurt, and I want to break his fucking kneecaps for pushing her around like that. But she doesn't make a sound, doesn't show that hurt. Instead she maintains the pose he put her in.

"We'll need half a dozen or so to go through the docks every month. We'll have them all coded and chipped so they're easily accounted for." Vadik reaches down and grips the woman's wrist. She doesn't fight him. She stays still and allows him to twist her arm so we can all see a tattooed barcode on the underside of her forearm, just below her wrist. His fingers point to a reddened bump on her skin. I assume that's where they implanted the chip.

My fists clench by my sides and my breathing threatens to pick up. But there are too many fuckers here. I don't have a gun on me. I'd be dead if I tore him apart like I want to.

"They'll be fairly broken in, although not all respond as well as Ava here has. She was the Russian princess when her father had the territory. She was a keepsake and a bit of a trial run for how to handle this product. So we've had a few weeks to teach her proper behavior." The woman, Ava, doesn't flinch or react as he drops her arm and kicks her legs. She merely bows and lies flat on the ground with her arms at her side. Her face is turned with her cheek lying against the concrete.

"That's where my associate, Kane, is going to come in." My skin prickles, and a chill runs down my spine as Vadik slaps my back. I'm supposed to do this shit. That's not what I signed up for. I stare straight ahead and grind my teeth rather than responding. I can't say no. I'm dead if I do.

"He'll have the product ready and ensure they're packaged nicely for shipment." I glance down at the woman and look into her eyes. I'm surprised to see a flash of defiance in them that leaves so quickly I almost start to think I imagined it. Her body tenses, as though she's preparing to take a hit. I swallow the lump in my throat and force myself to look away. I can barely stomach this shit.

"We don't partake in this area of business," Vince finally responds. He's firm in his words, but there's no emotion behind them. None of his men seem to hold an attitude toward the fact that a woman is bowing on the ground in chains. Part of me wishes they'd act on the disgust I saw on their faces earlier, but they don't. So I'm left standing here with no fucking options.

"I understand this would be a new venture." Abram walks forward as he talks to Vince, leaving Vadik and me standing next to the girl. Next to *Ava*. "I'd like to give you some time to consider the amendments to this business opportunity." He gestures back at me and adds, "Kane will stay on your territory and get a feel for your operation."

Vince clenches his fists and interrupts Abram. "We don't allow that."

"You *didn't* allow that." Abram corrects him with a grin. "Just know that I don't do partial orders. It's all or none, and all on my terms."

Vince narrows his eyes at this. He seems to weigh his options and then looks back over his shoulder toward the men behind him. "I need a minute to discuss this over with my men."

"Take two weeks. We'll need that long to gather the first shipment. And Kane will need time to learn your protocols and how to handle this particularly *fragile* product."

Vince's eyes flash toward me and I want to punch that judgmental look off his face. I don't do this shit. More than ever I feel backed into a corner. I don't mind being a prick to assholes. I think of it as part of the bad karma they have coming their way. But this shit? I don't fucking like this.

"Kane De Rocca?" Vince asks, and I nod my head. His eyes flash with surprise and then he gives me a knowing look. Just as I knew about him, I'm sure he knows all about me and the shit I've been through.

"Kane," Abram turns to me, effectively dismissing Vince and his crew. "Take this one and head on down with them. I'm sure they have somewhere you can stay." He motions toward the girl on the ground next to me. "Hold on to this one until the others are collected." He points to my hangar as he says, "This will be perfect for housing them." He speaks loud enough for everyone to hear as Vadik walks behind him, ushering Vince and his men back to their vehicles. He's thanking them and talking about how great this business will be for everyone involved. His voice gets lost as I watch them walk down the landing.

Abram leans forward and grips my shoulder tightly, forcing me to awkwardly bend at the waist to his level so he can speak directly into my ear. "Learn everything. I expect a full report." He leans away from my ear, still gripping my shoulder. I meet his eyes and give him a tight nod in return. "Consider it your first test." He pats my shoulder. "We'll be back in a few days to see how you're handling this one. Don't disappoint me."

I can't respond verbally, and I don't even try. He walks away, back to the hangar, as I stand on the tarmac next to the woman bowed at my feet. The rest of Petrov's crew walks back inside. The Valettis get in their cars. I meet Vince's gaze and I know there's trouble waiting for me in his territory.

The pilot in the black tee shirt walks over to me and reaches down, yanking the chain around the poor woman's neck. She lifts her head quickly and stands before the chain can force her movements. She's used to this. She knows how to avoid the pain.

He looks down at her and huffs a quick laugh. The wicked glint in his eyes makes my stomach revolt and my muscles coil. "I'll doubt she'll give you much trouble." He smiles, revealing his stained teeth. "Shame, really. I enjoyed the fight."

He hands me the chain and I reluctantly take it. The woman stands quietly at my side, her hands clasped in front of her and her head slightly bowed.

"We'll be back to make sure you've got a good handle on her." He nods with a smirk and walks toward the hangar.

My body is tensed and ready to fight, but I have no choice. I'll be dead if I do anything other than what I've been ordered to do. I grit my teeth. I'm really not fucking liking the position I'm in. As the Valettis leave, the cars kick up dust and vanish in the distance.

I look down at the chain in my hand and follow it up to her throat with my gaze. The chain is locked on her and that pisses me off. They didn't give me a key, but I don't fucking care.

I'm breaking it off as soon as I have her alone.

AVA

"Come." I walk quickly, expecting him to pull the chain. I still have a raw cut on the nape of my neck from the last prick who yanked it just to get a reaction from me. I was as quick as I could be. But that didn't matter. It wouldn't have mattered if I'd been fast enough. He would've found a way. For him, it wasn't about being obeyed; he just wanted to hurt me. He got pleasure from tormenting me.

I've learned there are two types. The first type just wants to inflict pain. They're the worst, because even if I do everything right, they'll find a way to trap me. They just want to punish me. Then there's the type that wants perfection. It's difficult to live up to their expectations, but I try so fucking hard. I have to if I don't want to be beaten.

In the beginning I fought. And I paid the price. I couldn't help but to fight against them. They held me down and brutalized me in front of my father. He was an asshole and a vile human being. But still, it hurt to have him watch. I close my eyes and try to will away the image. Everything hurt. So much so that I'm sure parts of me are dead. I'm only slightly aware that I hardly bear any resemblance to the strong woman I used to be.

They raped me, took my innocence. There was no way I couldn't fight. But then I realized how much of a waste it was. I needed to play the part. I needed to fool them into thinking I'm broken. That they've trained me to be the perfect pet. I'm just waiting. I'll bide my time until I can have my revenge, although there are moments. Moments where I forget why I still want to live. Why I have to be good and try to continue to live.

This new arrangement throws me off. Not that I had much of a plan, other than to survive. I'd hoped when we landed that there would be fewer men. I just need for there to be fewer, so I can pick them off one at a time as they come for me. There are three I keep being given to. I'm recognizing their pattern now. Or I was. But now I'm all thrown off.

I need to get my hands on a gun. I'll wait. There's always been something stopping me. I almost had a chance before we left. But I didn't take it. Abram and Vadik were gone. I want them there. I need to make sure that bastard pays the price for what he did to me and everyone I loved. I want him to die last. I want him to truly suffer.

I'll have my revenge, at any cost. I won't be sold off. That's not their plan for me. That'd be too easy for the mafia princess. I hope their guard will be down. Just one moment is all I need. My body begs me to rest and a small voice whispers, *but you need the strength to do it.*

"In." The hard word dropped from Kane's lips brings me back to reality. Kane De Rocca. I recognize the last name, but I'm not sure why.

This isn't going as I planned. I don't like this. Fear makes my knees go weak. His large hand steadies on the small of my back and my body tenses in anticipation of the blow. I close my eyes and bow my head waiting for it. I've earned it. I wasn't paying attention. I was stuck in my head. What's wrong with me? I can't do that.

It gets me punished. I don't want to be punished. I want to be a good girl. I need to be good.

I need to pay attention and follow orders.

"In," he commands louder and my shoulders shudder, but my body is quick to move. I open my eyes and realize I'm in the back of his car. Not in a trunk or a crate. He shuts the door and I look around, although my head stays forward. I'm careful not to actually move. I can't show my surprise either. No emotions. I sit silently. My back is ramrod straight and won't relax against the leather.

It's been days since anyone has laid a hand on me or even seen me. Traveling is a blessing. But now I'm back to being given to someone else. A new master or keeper or sir. I'm terrified and my gut fills with a wretched acid that creeps up my throat. Tears threaten to well up in my eyes, but they don't. I won't let them. Maybe I've forgotten how to cry. I'm not sure. But I know crying will get me punished. My face is set in stone. Expressionless, just as they like. Well, as the second type desires. The first type wishes for something else.

I have to remind myself what I overheard Abram say earlier. He said they'd be back. I'll have another chance at him and Vadik. I just need one chance. This is only temporary. Just like the other times.

I want to turn in my seat and look at the man. At Kane. But my heart hammers in fear. I'm expected to sit, so I will. I stay still and wait. I'm careful to keep my breathing low and my body still. I've learned that's the best way to handle it. It's as though I've disappeared. If only I could.

My eyes close and my body begs to sleep, but I can't. I'm exhausted from staying awake during the flight, though. I was worried that they would dump me at any point. That their threats weren't hollow and they were truly going to kill me this time. I couldn't sleep. I haven't been able to sleep soundly since I was taken.

My body shudders, and it makes my eyes widen with fear. I moved. I made a movement. It's bad. I want to look around, but I don't. I listen, and after a long moment, I hear nothing. It's silent in the car. He still isn't here. He isn't waiting behind me to punish me. I wonder which of the two types he'll be. I hope it's the second type. They're easier to survive.

My heart slows, and my head yearns to fall against my chest. My body craves rest. But I resist. Until he comes back and gives me an order, I won't do anything that will give him a reason to punish me.

As my heavy eyelids slowly close, I hear the door open. I lift my head to attention, my eyes staring fixedly at the floor. I can feel his eyes on me. I know he's looking at me, maybe deciding what to do with me. But I stay still and wait for his orders.

"I need you to lie down." I quickly obey, and fall to my side. My wrists immediately feel the comfort of the position. The heavy weight of the shackles is relieved as my body sags into the seat. The shackles don't irritate me as much as they used to. I've grown used to them. But I still look forward to the relief when I'm given it. I see a movement in my periphery and I almost react. But instead I only tense slightly for the blow I'm sure is coming.

The soft fabric lays on my body in a gentle wave. I expect it to cover my head, but instead he tucks it under my chin, covering the collar. I close my eyes as it moves against my neck. The collar digs into the cut, but I don't say anything. I don't react. I'm not sure if he's aware, but it doesn't matter. I can't do anything that would anger him.

I won't put myself in a position to be punished. I don't know this man, but I'd rather stay obedient than risk his irritation. I tuck up my legs, knowing he's going to shut the door, but beyond that I make no other movements. After a moment, he stands at the door, watching me. Waiting for something; I don't know what.

But after that long moment, he shuts the door and I finally let out a breath I didn't know I was holding. And then the driver's side door opens and the car roars to life. I don't know where he's taking me and I don't ask.

But I know they'll be back for me. And I'll be ready for them.

I won't break until I've had my revenge.

* * *

I WAKE UP, pinned against a rock hard chest. My eyes pop open and my breathing stalls. But I don't move. I stay still and pretend to be asleep. I can hear his steady heartbeat and his shoes crunching on gravel. I inhale his scent and resist the urge to bury myself into his shirt. A masculine woodsy pine fills my lungs. His strong arms are wrapped around my back and under my legs. I peek past him and see nothing but a field. A flat field.

I rock in his arms as we climb up a step, one and then another, and then a door opens with a creak. We're on a porch. There's even a porch swing out here in the middle of fucking nowhere. He turns his body and to the left I make out what appear to be endless woods before he carries me into the house.

"I tried not to wake you." His deep voice jolts my body slightly. I don't know how to respond. I'm quick to answer with an apology. Apologies have never stopped the beatings in the past, but I know I have to respond. Being quiet is much, much worse than saying the wrong thing.

"I'm sorry." I speak clearly. I know I must. When I started to pretend, when I decided submitting was the best way to survive until I had the opportunity to escape, I learned that whispers and mumbles are often accompanied by blows to the face. I'd like to avoid that as best as I can. *If* I can. I'm still not sure which type this man is.

He sets me down on the sofa and I'm not certain if I should lie down or sit. When I switch owners it's the worst in the beginning. Their expectations always change. He walks across the foyer and hallway to an open living room. It adjoins a large kitchen and dining room. Modern and clean. This place is dark. It looks like it hasn't been used in years. I settle down on my side, facing the room.

I want to ask if this is his home. But that would be stupid of me. I know better. I won't be foolish like I used to be. Instead I lie still and simply wait for instructions.

"Stay there," he says, as he turns his back and leaves the room. My heart beats wildly in my chest. It's horrible when they leave. It terrifies me. They always seem to come back with more anger and ammunition. The faces of my previous owners flash before my eyes. I'll never forget them. If I can, I'll kill each one of them.

But *his* face is the one that persists in my mind. The leader. The one who made sure that my father saw everything. He will die a slow death. The memory is vivid. I can still see the way my father looked as they came from behind me. It must have been hours before they finally beat him to death. I'd hoped they were going to kill me after. But that wasn't enough for *him*.

Tears don't even threaten to fall from my eyes. I can't feel them. My eyes almost feel itchy with dryness at this point. Crying is pointless and only gets me beaten. The more I cry, the harder the blows. So I hide the sadness; I hide every emotion, because it's safer that way.

It was one thing to be beaten, raped, and humiliated in front of my father and then have to watch as they murdered him. The image of his throat being slit is still clear in my mind. It was one thing to have that happen just before my death. I was waiting for it. Praying for it. It was another thing entirely to live through that nightmare and then be taken by my father's enemy. Someone who wants to make sure I suffer.

I'll make sure he suffers as well.

My eyes dart to the hallway Kane left through. I'm not chained to the ground. I'm not tied to anything, or locked away. I can see the front door. *I could run.* I bet I could even get the door partially opened before he gets back to me. The old me would've taken the risk. The old me would've ended up scarred and bruised. Now, I'm a good girl. I'll wait.

Why am I a good girl? Because it may be a test. I've failed so many times before. I won't fail. I won't disappoint him. At least not in this way.

Even if it's not a test, if I leave now, I may never find *him* again. And I can't let that happen. I won't run. I'll simply wait. My chance will come. I only need one chance.

I hear Kane's heavy steps coming down the hallway and I focus my eyes forward. I would school my expression to be impassive, but it's already set. I haven't dared to show emotion in so long. I don't know how long it's been actually. Now that I think of it, it's a strange feeling to realize I have no idea how much time has passed. I spent a very long time in a basement and then even longer in *his* bedroom. Learning proper technique.

I can tell Kane's entered the room, but I force my eyes to stay straight ahead and my body to be still. It's only when he comes closer that I want to move away. Only when I see the pliers in his hands do I want to run, hide, or show fear. But I resist. I can't do that.

I can only imagine what he's going to do with the pliers. I remember their threats, to cut me up and ship parts of me one by one to different family members. But I thought they were all dead. I know some are. They showed me pictures. Or simply took me with them as they hunted them down. Maybe this is just for enjoyment though? My eyes want to close, but I force them open. I know if I try to hide, he'll force me to look. I can practically feel him fisting my hair and shaking me until my eyes are wide open. It's happened before. I've learned.

I wait for orders as he stands above me. The large pliers are in his right hand; his muscles corded. His left hand reaches down and he firmly lifts my hands up to the pliers. They're bound by a shackle. It's the same type as the one on my neck. The leash has always been on the collar though, so there's not much bruising on my wrists. I want to close my eyes as he opens the pliers, but I don't.

I stare straight ahead and expect the cold metal to clip around my finger. That would make sense. Maybe I still have family alive. Maybe I've angered Felipe more than I thought and this is the price to pay. I thought I was more valuable whole, though. That's an argument I've heard before, when they wanted to leave more marks. But they weren't allowed to do anything permanent.

Perhaps after all this time I no longer hold that value. I hear the snap of the pliers and feel my right arm fall. Snap! The metal clicks again and then my left arm falls as well. The muscles in my arm scream. It's been so long since they've had the freedom to move at this angle.

I steady my breathing and try to make sense of what's happening. I wish I could ask, but I can't.

"Hold still," he says, as he moves the pliers to my neck. I don't want to, but my eyes close. I try to resist, but I pray he's only cutting the lock on the collar. My heart hammers in my chest, and when I hear the loud snap and feel the metal give from around my throat, I can't help the emotions that wash over me. I hear the chains clinking and open my eyes. I watch his back as he leaves the room and walks into the kitchen. I shouldn't, though. I know better. As he drops the chains into the trash and turns, my eyes snap forward. I stare straight ahead and resist the desire to put my hands to my throat. He walks back to me and stands over my body.

I wish I knew what he wanted. I wish I knew how to react.

His hand slowly lowers to my neck and he squats down in front of me. His finger brushes along a cut on the side of my throat. I try not to, but I wince from the pain. I know better! I shouldn't have winced. I knew the pain was coming. I school my expression and wait. He lays his hand on my shoulder and lets his eyes travel down my body. I wish I could hide. I used to be beautiful. Now I'm thin and bones poke through where they shouldn't. I'm scarred, although they did try to keep the whips on skin that's normally hidden by clothing. Most of the bruises have faded and not many are new.

He stands up slowly and continues to watch me. "I want you to look at me." At his command, my eyes reach his. My heart stops and for a moment, the world tilts on its side.

Kane De Rocca. I heard his name earlier. I make sure to listen. I know I shouldn't, but I do. And I know that's this man's name. Kane. He's stunning. His jaw is stubbled and hard against the sharp lines of his high cheekbones. His shoulders are broad and his chiseled chest pulls the crisp, white dress shirt he's wearing taut against his body. His dark eyes stare into mine with such passion and emotion that I feel a pull to look away.

But he commanded me to look at him. And I'm a good girl. I will obey him. For now.

I wish I knew what the look in his eyes means. But I don't.

"What's your last name, Ava?" he asks.

I'm quick to respond, "Ivanov." I will never forget. That name is why I'm here. Why all of this has happened to me. I didn't choose this life. I didn't want it.

"I see. You're Alec's daughter?" he asks. Hearing my father's name causes a stir of emotions in the pit of my stomach. I've heard his name before, over and over. Accompanied by hateful slurs, or laughter and cheers of his death. But not like this. Hearing his name spoken calmly. With respect. That's something I haven't heard in a long time.

"Yes," I answer, still holding his gaze.

"Ava Ivanov," he says, with reverence in his tone. He repeats it in a murmur I almost don't hear.

"Come, Ava," he says, and turns his back to me. I stand quickly to obey.

As I watch him move with dominance and power through the hallway, I feel a stir of emotions I haven't felt in some time. I feel hope.

I know I shouldn't, though. Hope will destroy me.

KANE

I don't know shit about this house. I fucking hate this. Vince sent me here. This is where I can stay on *his* territory. I feel like this is a fucking trap. Like this place is wired and they're watching me. I know a safe house when I see one. And this is definitely the Valetti safe house. I looked for bugs when I got here, but I couldn't find shit.

Ava was passed out, but I still didn't want to leave her alone for too long though. If I lost her… fuck. That'd be bad. Who the hell am I kidding? This is all fucked. I'm not a member of Petrov's crew. I don't belong on Valetti soil, and I know I'm not fucking wanted here. Even worse, this job is a fucking nightmare. I don't want to do this shit. I can't stand the fact that this is what I'll be doing.

Anxiety races through my blood. I don't like this insecurity. I never should've gotten myself into this shit.

Fuck it. It's not going to happen. I'm not doing it. I'll hold on to her until they come back. But I'm not doing this shit. It's not what I did for my *famila*. This is fucked up and wrong.

The thoughts fly through my head, but I know better.

If I tell Petrov no, I'm a dead man.

I need to figure something out. The Valettis didn't look so keen on doing business. Not this kind of business, anyway. Maybe I can get in with them. My gut churns. Would they take in the nephew of a rat? I can hear it now. The disrespect. The dismissal. No one takes in the last member of a tainted name. I'm on my own and that means I'm at the mercy of these fucks.

I climb the stairs and listen for her footsteps. For *Ava Ivanov's* footsteps. She was practically royalty. Untouchable. And now she's in chains and being sold as a slave. Passed around. She's so fucking scared. I know she's trying not to show it. She's doing everything she can to obey and disappear into the background. I can sense it though, deep down.

She's terrified.

There are so many scars on her body. Multiple small scratches over her hip and her shoulders. There are bruises of all different colors on her thighs and arms. A silvery bite mark on her shoulder. The sight of it infuriates me. Worse is the large cut on the nape of her neck. The metal dug in and rubbed her skin raw. It has to have been like that for a while to look so fucking bad.

I need to stay calm and think of this as just another job until I can get through it.

I stop at the top of the stairs. I look to the left and there's a small hallway with a large door at the end. To the right is a hallway with more doors. The left has the largest room, so we'll stay there.

I don't care what they say about the chains being gone. I know they're going to be pissed about it. I don't give a fuck though. I'm not doing that shit. She's in my care, so she's mine for now. I'll do what I want with her. A shudder runs through my body and I'm sickened by the thought that ran through my mind. She's gorgeous, but it's wrong to imagine her as mine.

I open the door and walk into a fairly barren room with a decently sized bed and a dresser. The closet doors are open and the closets are empty. The room is light and airy, with a soft pale blue paint on the walls and a grey bedspread. There are black and white abstract paintings scattered around the walls of the room. It's not too bad for a safe house. There's a door to the right and I'd guess that's the bathroom. Good. She'll have everything she needs in here.

I start thinking about how I have to go and get supplies, and then I curse under my breath. I've got nothing to make sure she stays put. I just cut off the chains and it's not like I have anything on me to make sure she stays here. If I was her I'd take off the second I could. And if she does that, I'm fucked.

Fuck! How did I already mess this shit up? I sigh heavily and walk farther into the room. There's gotta be something in here. Maybe I can use the closet. I can put something in front of the door. My heart sinks in my chest. I don't want to do that. That's so fucking shitty. But I have to make sure she doesn't leave.

I don't know how to do this shit. I turn around and run a hand down my face as I shut my eyes briefly in exasperation. "Ava?"

"Yes?" she answers quickly. When I open my eyes, her light blues stare back at me. Thank fuck. I couldn't stand her looking at nothing, avoiding my gaze and looking as though she's trying to fade from existence. I'm glad she listened.

"How does this normally work for you?" I ask, and cross my arms across my chest. I don't really give a shit that I'm asking her. I'm sure as hell not calling up one of those sick fucks and asking them. I know a bit about this. I'm not proud to know, but I do. I can be her caretaker for a few days. I can do that. But I'm not fucking training women. Breaking them into submission. That shit's not for me. I don't want any part of that. But for now, I have to deal with Ava.

I'm not giving her the upper hand and giving her an option to take off. I can't let that shit happen. I can't piss off Petrov by losing her, even if I fucking hate what he's doing. I'll figure this shit out. If worse comes to worst, there's the option of the closet.

Her mouth opens, but then closes quickly. Her eyes dart to the floor and then back to my face. Her fingers wrap around each other nervously. "I'm not sure how to answer," she says in a calm voice that doesn't match the anxiety she's showing at all. Fear and apprehension wash off of her in waves.

I don't like it. I fucking hate how hurt she is. "How about we take a seat?" I cock a brow at her and walk forward. I keep my movements slow. I half expect her to take a step back, to flinch. But she doesn't move. She lets me place my hand on the small of her back and guide her to the bed.

I pat the comforter with my right hand. "Hop on up." I sit my ass down and the bed dips with my weight as she climbs on and settles herself. Her shoulders turn inward, but she looks back at me expectantly, waiting for another order.

Jesus. I hate this shit. I know they trained her to behave like this. But I can't handle this shit.

I'm staying far away from her. I can't get attached. Can't lose her, either. I'll do what I have to so I can survive this, and then I'm cutting my ties. This shit isn't for me.

"I need to head out and grab some things. I want you to stay here."

"I understand," she answers immediately. Like it's that fucking easy.

"I'm thinking I should tie you up or put you in a room." I don't say it like a question, but that's exactly what it is.

She nods her head slightly. "I understand," she repeats. I take a deep breath.

"Which would you prefer?" I ask. I guess that's the least I can do.

Her hand wraps around her wrist and a sad look crosses her face. "I would rather be locked in a room."

"It'll have to be the closet." Her face falls at my words. I'd put her ass in the bathroom, but I can only imagine the trouble she'd get herself into. I could see her shattering the mirror and trying to stab me with a shard of glass. I've seen a lot of shit over the years. I'm keeping her ass away from anything that could be used as a weapon. And that means it'll be the closet.

"I think I'd rather be tied up, if you'd allow it," she responds. She swallows thickly and adds, "Please, sir."

"I don't like you calling me sir." The words fly out of my mouth before I can stop them. They come out hard, but she doesn't flinch. I probably shouldn't have done that. I don't know if they trained her to do that or not.

"I understand. I'll call you whatever you wish," she's quick to respond.

I search her face, but I find nothing. "When they get here, call me sir. If anyone comes over, you call me sir. But for now, just call me Kane." It's probably a bad idea. All of this is a bad idea though.

She nods her head again and answers, "Yes, Kane." Hearing her say my name makes me feel more at peace than it should.

I take a moment to absorb everything. She's so obedient. It's surreal. My brow furrows, and I have to wonder what all she's been through. My chest hurts thinking about how much she has to be hurting. I swallow the lump growing in my throat and get off the bed.

I can't think about it. I can't go soft. I can't help her. I'm only one man and she doesn't belong to me. They'll be here soon enough and then I won't have to deal with this.

Guilt weighs heavily on my chest at that thought. I know she doesn't deserve this. No one does. I pinch the bridge of my nose and try to get out of my head.

This is a job.

My phone goes off in my pocket and I'm quick to answer it. Not because I really give a fuck who's on the other line; I just need to think about something else.

"This is Kane." I answer like I always do, and I fucking regret picking up the phone when I hear the voice at the other end.

"And this is Abram." I'm surprised he called, but I'm also pissed. I fucking hate that I got myself in this mess. Why is he calling me though? I would think he has more important things to do.

"What can I do for you?" I ask. It's hard to keep the irritation out of my voice. I'm so fucking pissed off that I even thought about working for this prick. I've felt regret before. But this is something else. I need to figure out how to get out of this situation and keep my ass alive.

My eyes drift to Ava. If I can...No. I stop that train of thought. It'll just get both of us killed. She's not mine. I'm doing a job.

"I wanted to make sure the Valettis are playing nice."

"They set me up in a safe house. I have my first meet with them tomorrow."

"Good. And the girl?" he asks.

"What about her?" I feel defensive and protective. I don't like it. But more than that, I don't like that he's asking about her. She's in my possession right now.

"Are you enjoying her company?" he asks, and I can practically see his sick smile. I don't know how I want to answer him. He expects me to fuck her. To degrade her. To enjoy *owning* her. He's going to have to learn to manage his expectations. I suppose it's better to lay the groundwork for that now.

"No. This isn't my thing, Abram. I didn't anticipate this either." I should watch my mouth. I should be smart about this. I'm having a hard time with that as I look at Ava. Her head is bowed. Her eyes are on her hands, which are resting on her thighs. I fucking hate how she tries to hide like that.

She was untouchable. And now she's been reduced to this. I don't fucking like it.

"I see." His answer is short and I can sense that he's unhappy with me. "Is she not being good for you? She has her shots and she's clean." There's a pause, but I don't respond. I'm sick to my stomach. "She's been trained exten-sively." The sickness in my gut threatens to climb up my throat.

"She's been very obedient."

"I'm happy to hear that. You'll grow to enjoy your new role, Kane. I'm sure you'll be very good at it."

"I'm not sure I'm cut out for this, Abram. It's not what I had in mind." I'm careful not to tell him no. I know I'm pushing my limits with him. If I piss him off, I could be dead come morning. I don't have a fucking death wish, so I keep most of my thoughts to myself. This is business, after all. *Supposed* to be business.

"Tomorrow, someone with more experience will come down to help you handle her. Get some information about the export procedures. We'll need the names of the workers and the space limitations. We'll need to ship this type of cargo in large containers. Make sure they have them. If they don't, they'll need to be ordered." He's talking about shipping off women in metal boxes like they're nothing. I bite down on the inside of my cheek so hard I taste blood.

"I'll be sure to get the details." I clench my teeth after pushing the words out. I have to remind myself that I want to live. That I can't fuck with a man like Abram.

"Wonderful. I'll see you soon, Kane." I don't answer. I just hit end and shove the phone back in my pocket.

I haven't had a fucking moment to even think about any of this shit. I need to tie her ass up and get out of here. Then I'll really figure out what I need to do. How I'm going to handle this shit. I turn my back to her and walk to the door.

"Alright Ava, stay right there." I don't turn around to look at her. I can't. The reality of the situation is coming down hard on me.

Abram's man is coming tomorrow.

I'm going to have to treat Ava like a submissive, like a slave. Whether I like it or not.

AVA

The bed is so comfortable. So warm. And Kane covered me with a blanket and gave me a pillow to rest against. It feels so good. It's been a long time since he left. There's no clock in the room, but I think it's been hours. My muscles relax, but then I remember who I am. I remember why I'm here. My body tenses and I sit up and push my back against the headboard. I can't let my guard down.

I thought of Kane while he's been away. My new owner. Temporary owner. Bad thoughts, things I shouldn't be thinking. I don't know if it's because of what I've been through or something else. But I want him to take me. My thighs clench together and a wave of arousal heats my center. I've been a good girl. And when I'm good, they're nice to me. They're still rough, and sometimes it hurts. But they make sure it feels good for me, too. When I'm good.

But Kane hasn't.

I wonder if I haven't been good enough. If I haven't earned my reward. Usually they establish it quickly. I shake my head. This isn't right. "No." The word slips past my lips as a mere breath. Something's wrong. I shouldn't be thinking these things. I shouldn't be fantasizing about him pinning me against the wall. My back arches at the thought.

I can't help it.

I crave his touch. I need to know I'm being good. I've worked hard to be a good girl.

At least I know I haven't angered him. I would definitely know if I had. The thought sends a chill down my spine. The warmth in my core and my heated thoughts vanish.

I still don't understand Kane. I don't know what to think about him.

He's not like the others. Not yet, anyway. I don't remember what's normal and what isn't. I used to think they'd be nice, they'd be different. But they're all the same.

Except Kane. This is very, very different.

I want to believe he's a kind person. He doesn't seem so bad. He's not rough with me. Not at all. And he's given me freedom from that fucking collar that kept digging into my neck. But I'm afraid to think that. I'm afraid that he's merely setting me up. He wants to test me. That must be it. This is all an act. He's waiting for me to be bad.

I look down at my wrists at the shitty knot that's binding my hands together. I could get out of this. I'm sure I could. I haven't tried, but I know I could. He's either not used to this, or he's testing me. I'm not sure which one it is, and either way I would end up with the same result.

I settle my back against the headboard and square my shoulders. I will be right here when he returns. I close my eyes and picture *his* face. I will not do anything to compromise my opportunity. I know I'll see him again soon. He'll come to check on me. He said he would. I need to be good. I need to make sure I live to see him again. Memories flash before my eyes that harden my heart and strengthen my resolve.

My eyes pop open at the sound of the door opening. I have to remind myself Kane is the enemy. His comforting touch makes my body weak. The cravings I have are from the sick way I've been conditioned.

Kane is not good. I'm just fucked in the head. I need to remember that. I've already forgotten so much about myself. But I have to remember that. None of these men will help me. None of them are good.

He walks through the door with fistfuls of bags. I feel a pull to go help him. But I stay seated. After all, I'm tied to the bed. *Kane* tied me to the bed.

He drops the bags on the floor in the center of the room. He looks tired. He turns to me and gives me a tight smile before walking closer. I stay still and make sure to look at him. I've only had one other owner who wanted my attention. And he only kept me for a day.

"Sorry it took so long," he says, as he starts untying the binds. He must see how easily they come undone, but he doesn't say anything. Instead his face displays a quick look of worry and then confusion. But then it's gone.

He doesn't look back at me. He avoids eye contact altogether and that makes me worry. My heart sinks in my chest and I start to think I've upset him. My heart races and adrenaline flows through my veins. I stay still and wait. I need an order. Some kind of a command that I can obey.

He walks back to the bags and finally looks at me as he says, "I need you to go through these things and put them away."

I move quickly to get off the bed and to the bags. "Yes, Kane. I understand," I answer as I kneel on the ground. I open the first bag and I hesitate. It's full of women's clothes.

"Make me a list of the shit I forgot," he says, as he walks toward the door on the other side of the room. I turn my head to face him, but all I can see is his back. I don't have a pen and paper. I also don't want to assume that I know everything he wanted. I go through each bag, pulling out the clothes and try not to assume they're for me. A few bags are white plastic; Walgreens is written on the side of those. A few of the other bags are from department stores I recognize.

I hear him put a few bags down on the counter in the bathroom and he walks back into the room, avoiding my gaze once again. He told me to look at him. Didn't he? My heart falls in my chest. I'm sure of it. I continue to move as doubt creeps in. Kane walks back into the bathroom and I hear the water running as he washes his hands.

I'm being good. I'm listening. I stack the clothes neatly next to me on the floor. There's another bag with Advil and warm and cold compresses. There's a tube of ointment and bandages. My heart swells in my chest thinking they may be for me. I push it down. I can't get my hopes up. No one has ever offered me comfort like this. Even if he is, he's not good. He's working for *him*.

He walks out of the bathroom and looks down at the pile of clothes. My body tenses for a moment, but I continue my work. I haven't finished. I'll go quicker though. I can be faster if he'd like.

"I'll get the rest," he says, bringing my attention to him. "Is there anything you didn't see that you'll need?"

Yes. There's no underwear that I've seen. I don't have a hairbrush, but I can use my fingers. No deodorant or toiletries. But I'm not sure if I need them. I don't want to make an assumption, but I don't want to give the wrong answer either. I feel like he's testing me on what my expectations are maybe. I'm not sure and anxiety starts creeping in.

I set down the bag I was emptying and swallow before answering, "I didn't see anything to wash with. If that's something you'd like me to do."

He looks at me for a moment and then down at the bags with his brow furrowed. "Must've left it in the car," he mutters after a moment. He starts to walk to the door, but then turns around. He looks at me and then the bathroom door, like he's not sure about something. I feel frozen in place, waiting for an order. I give him my attention, but every second that passes without me unpacking a bag or doing *something* makes my anxiety peak. After a moment he finally says, "Stay here and be a good girl for me."

I feel a weight lift off my shoulders. I nod eagerly and put my palms on my thighs. "Yes, Kane." I know how to be a good girl.

KANE

*I*f she breaks that mirror or something else and tries to attack me, so be it. Rightfully, I fucking deserve it. I could've tied her up again, but I don't like it. I walk up the stairs feeling a bit apprehensive. It was fucking stupid to leave her alone and give her a chance to arm herself. But at this point I'm feeling lower than low. I fucking hate this. If it was anyone else, I would've told them to fuck off.

Abram's been known to slice a man's throat for merely looking at him the wrong way. I never should've gotten involved with him. If I'd fucking known that's who Marco was talking about, I would've thought twice.

Her handler, Felipe, called me while I was out. Apparently he thought I needed pointers about how to keep her in line. I don't like being micromanaged. I know Abram's behind this. I don't fucking like it. I know this is a test. And I'm not willing to fail because failure is the equivalent to death, but I'm doing this my way now. They want me to take her, fine, but she's mine and I'm doing this shit how I want.

I stop outside the door and place my free hand on the butt of my gun. The plastic bags I'm holding in my left hand shift and crinkle. She knows I'm coming. If she's gonna put up a fight, now would be a good time.

The door opens and I find her in the corner of the room, neatly stacking a pile of clothes on top of the dark stained wood dresser. She drops quickly to her knees and pulls her hair forward, exposing her back. Her wrists cross in front of her and she stays still although her hips are slightly raised. I breathe in deep and calm my racing heart.

I only know a little about this sort of shit. And what I do know, I'm not comfortable with.

I need to figure out something though. I can't have her keeper come here tomorrow thinking I don't have a handle on the situation. I don't need Abram to have me on his hit list, but I also don't want her going back to him or in someone else's hands. And he'll take her from me if she's not being "handled properly".

I have everything I need to handle her now. Including a proper collar and leash that won't hurt her. I don't want to put it on her, but I can't fuck this up.

I'm going to have to do this, but at least I can do it my way. She's mine now.

I walk closer to her and she stays perfectly still. I put the bags on the dresser and run a hand down my face. I need to do this. I breathe out heavily and then regret it when I see her thigh start to tremble.

I lean down and pet her hair. "Good girl." Her body relaxes slightly at my praise. Thank fuck she's so damn obedient. I couldn't stomach the shit I'd have to do if she wasn't. If she can be this good the entire time, then everything will be fine.

My heart clenches and sinks in my hollow chest. I don't know what will happen to her once they take her from me. I don't want to think about all the possibilities. I close my eyes and focus on the present. For now, she's with me. And that's all that I need to focus on.

"You need to shower." I put my hand under her chin and lift up her head to face me. Her beautiful blue eyes meet mine and for a moment, I forget it all. I forget she's a slave. I forget she's not mine. The world seems to tilt and I lose all sense of reasoning. My thumb gently brushes against her jaw and her eyes close as a small sigh of contentment leaves her plump lips. I feel a pull to draw her into my arms.

And then I snap out of it. My hand falls, and her head drops a bit from the loss of my touch. I pull back and turn around, facing the bathroom door. I don't know what the fuck that was, but it can't happen. What kind of sick fuck would that make me? She's obviously beautiful, but she's hurting. She's been used and degraded, and I have no right to let a fantasy like that run through my head.

I walk to the bathroom and listen for her behind me. She's quick to get up and walks at a steady pace to follow me. I walk straight to the shower and turn it on. I peek out of the corner of my eyes to the mirror. My back is still facing her as I put a hand under the cascade of water, waiting for it to warm for her. She stands facing me with her legs shoulder width apart, and slips one strap off her shoulder and then the other. The scrap of a dress falls to the floor, exposing her skin. Her breasts are firm and plump. Her nipples are small, pale pink buds. They harden as the air touches her tender flesh.

I close my eyes and try to will away my erection. This was not something I planned on when I decided to man the fuck up and take on this role so I didn't get my ass killed. If I acted on my body's urges, I'd be taking advantage of her. I won't fucking do it. I may be a prick, and I may be a criminal. But I would never do that. I don't give a fuck what Abram expects from me.

I hear her walk closer to me. Her small feet pad softly against the tiled floor. That and the sound of the water cascading into the shower stall are the only sounds. I lick my lips and turn to face her. I'm her keeper and I need to act like it.

I move out of her way and watch as she enters. I could leave her, but that wouldn't be intelligent. My eyes look back at the mirror. If I was her, I'd shatter it and try to slice my throat with the largest piece I could get my hands on. I've seen it before. If you're lucky, there's not much glue holding it up, so large chunks will fall. If I was her, I wouldn't even hesitate. I peek at her from the corner of my eyes as the sound of the water changes. She's washing herself quickly with a nervous look on her face.

"You can take your time. No need to rush." I say the words calmly, hoping to ease some of the tension I can see coming off of her. She's been worried from the second I saw her. I don't like it. She doesn't need to worry. So long as she stays in line and obeys me, she'll be safe.

For as long as she's mine, anyway. I clench my jaw not liking the thought, and decide to walk over and lean against the edge of the counter.

"Ava?" I ask, to get her attention. My eyes stay on the floor, but I monitor her in my periphery.

"Yes, Kane?" she's quick to ask, pausing her movements. Her muscles are coiled. She's waiting for an order.

353

"I don't like this, Ava." I just want to get this shit off my chest. I'll be honest with her. As much as I can be, anyway. "I don't know if you can tell," I begin to say as my eyes find hers, "but this isn't what I usually do." I wait to hear her response, but I don't get one. She's still waiting. I take a deep breath and grip the counter while looking back down at the floor.

"I'm your keeper for a while, and I know things are going to be different with me than they've been with your other..." I trail off and pause. I don't fucking know what to call them.

"Masters." She says the word for me. Masters are what they call them. Masters and Slaves.

"I don't want you to think of me as a master, Ava. That's not what I am."

"Are--" she starts to ask a question, but then she seems to jolt and stills in the shower. I look up at her and nod.

"I want you to ask me questions. I want you to listen to me." I point a finger at her to emphasize what I say next. "But talk to me." I almost say, *it hasn't been that long, you must remember what it's like to be normal.* But instead I bite my tongue and feel like a fucking asshole. Yeah, it's only been weeks of torture and countless times being passed around, used and degraded. I'm such a fucking dick. She's obviously fucked up from all of this. How could she not be? I grip my hair and lean back against the counter with my eyes closed. I have no fucking right to ask her to do a God damn thing.

What the fuck am I even doing? She's gonna be gone in a week or two. I'll never see her again, and not treating her like a... like a *slave* could get her hurt when she goes back to them. *"She's been trained extensively."* Abram's words echo in my head. I fucking hate him. I hate him for telling me to do this. I hate him even more for hurting her.

"Are you my new keeper?" Ava asks, and it breaks me from my thoughts.

I look back at her, not knowing how to answer. I don't want any part of this shit. But I don't have a fucking choice.

I say the only words I know that are true. "You're mine. I'm going to take care of you."

Her eyes widen slightly in shock, and her bottom lip trembles. She asks with a shaky breath, "Are you going to save me?"

My heart sinks in my chest. I want to save her. I feel a pull to protect her...and I will, for as long as I can. But I don't know how long that will be.

And I won't lie to her and give her false hope. I press my lips together and shake my head no.

Her head drops as she noticeably swallows and fights the urge to cry. Her shoulders turn inward as she pulls at her fingers. I feel like absolute shit. I've never questioned being a part of the family. Never in my life. It was the way I grew up, and the way we got shit done. Yeah we did some fucked up things, but in the long term, everything made sense.

But this? Fuck this. I don't want any part of it. There's not a damn thing okay with this shit.

But I can't save her. Abram hunted her family down. He did that with all his competitors. They fucking took off and went into hiding, but he found them. If he wants you dead, you're dead. There's no other way around it. Right now she's alive at least. But if we took off? If I decided to be her knight in shining armor? We'd both be dead. It would only be a matter of time. Shit. I might be dead regardless. I'm not looking forward to turning his job offer down. I rub the back of my neck and let out a heavy sigh as she straightens her shoulders and tries to compose herself.

"Finish up. It's getting late," I tell her, once she seems to have settled some.

My eyes travel down her body, not at all in a sexual way. She's beautiful, but she's not well. She's thin and the light shines off of several small scars on her body. One is noticeably larger though, and looks like a bite mark on her shoulder. There are more small scratches on her hips and shoulders, and some look like they were left by fingernails--from digging in and piercing her skin while holding her down.

I have to close my eyes and look back to the floor. I can't imagine everything she's gone through. I can't imagine what she expects from me. But I'll do everything I can to make this easy for her. I want to protect her from that shit and take away the pain she's in. I don't know if I can, but I'll at least try.

There's no doubt in my mind. If I could save her, I would.

AVA

$\mathscr{I}$ look at the cuff on my hand and then back to Kane. He locked one cuff around my wrist, and the other around the bedpost before going into the bathroom to shower. He takes another step into the bedroom, drying off his hair with a towel. Boxers hang low on his hips and my eyes stare at the deep "V" carved from his rock hard abs that taunts me. His muscles are still faintly covered with droplets of water and my fingers itch to feel his body. To run my hands along the smooth lines. If there's no other truth in this world, Kane is the epitome of man candy. My cheeks flare with a blush and I have to look back down at the bed, then to the cuff.

I'm not sure why I have these feelings toward him. I shouldn't. I haven't had them before with the others. But the thought of being his--the idea that he can protect me? It has my body aching for his touch. The need to please him is stronger than I've ever felt before.

But he can't save me.

My eyes close as I hear him walk to the dresser.

No one can save me.

But for now, I'm his. And the thought sends a warmth through my body. First from a sense of security, but then I feel something else entirely deeper in my body. Lower. Heating my core. I feel so ashamed. I must really be broken, to feel this desire for someone I should loathe. I should fear him. I do, in a way. But not like the others.

There were five. First him. And then Felipe finished my training, as they called it. And then there were three more. He gave me to them. He used me as a bargaining chip. I was nothing more than a temporary toy to be used and given back once they were finished.

And now Kane.

But Kane isn't like them. He's not like any of them. I believe everything he said earlier. Maybe I shouldn't. Perhaps it's all lies. But something inside of me craves him in a way I've never felt before. Something is telling me to trust him. A soft voice buried deep in my chest whispers that he will save me. I need only be his.

There's no doubt in my mind that I'm a fool to believe it. But the very thought that it could be true makes me want to give him all of me.

My eyes widen, and fear quickly drowns out all the other feelings. That's not what I'm supposed to be thinking. That's not what my focus should be.

Revenge is my purpose. I can't forget. I won't let the past lay in silence. I will make them all pay. And this man, whoever the fuck he is, he's only a temporary stay. I can't lose sight of where I'm going.

My eyes snap up at him as he walks closer. He has a stern look on his face that's been there ever since our conversation ended. I never should have asked questions. He said he wants me to, but I shouldn't have. It didn't do me any favors. Instead my focus is distant and my mind is fogged with thoughts I shouldn't be having.

I asked him if he was going to save me. A shudder runs through my body as I close my eyes and try to keep myself composed. As if this man could be my savior. Shame and disgust run through me.

No one is going to help me. I thought I'd come to terms with that, back when I decided I'd fight to live solely for the chance to kill them. *Him* first. He needs to die. So long as I watch the life leave him, I'll die with contentment in my heart.

My body stiffens as Kane walks over to me. I'm clothed at least. I don't think he's going to want to fuck me. He doesn't look at me like the others do. He hasn't taken from me. But I'm still on high alert. I don't know if I believe him. I shouldn't. I shouldn't trust anyone that works for *him*.

I hate that I did for a moment. It was a mistake. I won't do it again.

He stands over me as I sit on my heels on the bed.

He leans over and unlocks the cuff with a tiny key, and then places both of them on the nightstand. It's so quiet. The only sound is the clinking and loud clunk of the metal handcuffs. I swallow thickly and look up at him. Waiting for his orders. Waiting for him to use me. I have to work hard to keep my eyes open and stay still.

"Don't make me regret uncuffing you," he says with a low, threatening tone to his voice.

"I won't." I'm quick to respond.

"You're going to have to lie with me though." He walks to the other side of the bed and lifts the covers. "I'm a light sleeper. Just know that." He stares at me as he gets in and lies down. "Lie down, Ava. It's alright; I'm not going to hurt you."

I release a breath I didn't know I was holding. My heart swells and shatters in my chest and tears prick at the back of my eyes. But they don't surface. They never do. Even though this is the first time in a long time that the tears are from a man's kindness and not his cruelty.

"Thank you," I whisper. My body stiffens as I realize I haven't spoken clearly. I clear my throat and look him in the eyes, as he told me to. "Thank you." I repeat the words with confidence and slowly slide under the sheets. I lie on my back, staring at the ceiling, although I can feel his eyes on me.

I lie still and close my eyes, focusing on my breathing. It's coming in ragged breaths as I try to calm myself. How odd that my breath is failing me when I believe I may be safe from harm. At least for the moment. The other times, when they rape me, beat me, humiliate me or leave me to starve or lay in filth--those times my breathing is just fine. It's as it should be. But right now, I don't know what to think. I'm frightened of the unknown.

My body jolts as a heavy arm settles across my lower belly. Kane drags my body across the bed and into his arms. I struggle to move, to speak, to breathe. I thought he said he wouldn't hurt me. My body trembles as he kisses my jaw. I keep my eyes closed, although I shouldn't.

"Sleep well, Ava. I'm here. I won't let anyone hurt you." He speaks quietly into my ear, his lips close enough that they just barely touch my skin. His hot breath sends a warmth through my body. As he settles along my side, my entire body relaxes.

An overwhelming urge to sleep suddenly makes everything heavy. For a long while, I listen to Kane's breathing. It's steady. The grip his fingers have on my waist loosens. I think he's fallen asleep.

My eyes slowly open. I don't dare turn my head. Instead I look at the ceiling, at every imperfection. Time ticks by. I can't sleep. The bed is heaven on my sore and aching back; the sheets are warm and welcoming. It's the first time I've been allowed to sleep in relative comfort.

But I can't.

I've been given an opportunity. I could run, although I probably wouldn't get far. Kane could wake up and come find me. But I could kill him. He's asleep. I'd do it quick. It'd be relatively painless.

Once that's over I'd have to cut the tracker out of my arm. I thought about doing it before. But they'd know. They'll know the instant the temperature changes, and then they'll come for me. I'd have a little time to get a head start, but that might be all I'd need. I could run and hide. My body lifts slowly off the bed without my consent. Kane's arm drops onto the bed beside me and my eyes dart to his.

He's still asleep; his breathing is steady and his eyes are closed.

I scoot slowly to the end of the bed and gently lift my body up. I shouldn't be doing this. This is bad. It's wrong. I close my eyes as anxiety and fear weigh down my limbs. But I move against them. I hear my feet pad across the wooden floor.

I open my eyes and find myself at the dresser. Staring at his gun. I saw him leave it here earlier. I don't know why I've walked here. I didn't want to. But maybe I did? I'm so confused. So terrified. But I slowly raise my hand and let my fingers wrap around the metal. My head whips around as I hear Kane move against the sheets. I wait a long while, watching him, anticipating that he'll wake. He moves to lie on his back, but other than that, he's still. I watch his chest as I lift the gun, bracing the butt of it and holding it steady as I walk back to the bed.

I look back at Kane with the cold gun in my hand and my finger on the trigger. His broad chest rises and falls in a steady rhythm. He's at peace. I study his face. His hard jaw is covered in stubble. His plump lips are slightly parted. My heart pangs in my chest. I feel a pull to him, a desire to be at his side. I must be fucked up from everything that's happened. It's not right to feel this way, to want to be with someone whose purpose is to torment me.

Someone who's only going to ship me off to someone new. Or worse, give me back to them.

I swallow the lump growing in my throat and lift the gun. My finger barely reaches the trigger. I have to steady the cold metal with both of my hands. I look past it at Kane's sleeping form and breathe in and out. Time passes as I stand there, trying to pull the trigger. Trying to set myself free.

I can't. I can't do it. I won't hurt him when he hasn't hurt me. I can't bring myself to run from him either. I need to stay. My resolve hardens. I can't run now. I need to stay and face *him*. Otherwise I'll never be able to stop running. I'll never be able to rest until I watch him die. I drop the gun and breathe in deep.

I won't leave Kane. Even if he's one of them. Even if he can't save me. I'll save myself. But I won't be able to do that by running.

I return the gun to the dresser, then I walk back silently to the bed and carefully lie just as I was. The bed dips slightly and I make my movements slower. I ease my way back down, right where I was earlier and breathe a little easier once my body has settled back onto the bed.

My breath stops short with panic when Kane moves next to me.

"You made the right decision, Ava." My body stiffens and my eyes pop open. My breath stills in my lungs. "I thought you'd be alright without the cuffs at night." The bed dips as he leans over my body. The intensity of his large frame hovering over my small body makes a knot form in my throat.

"I'm sorry, Kane." I'm barely able to speak. Fear paralyzes my body. I'm not okay. I wasn't good. I'm not okay. He takes my wrist in his hand and I let him. My body is weakened and I know I need to obey. I need to be a good girl. I shouldn't have done that.

"I understand." He clicks a cuff shut around the bedpost and then the other around my wrist and runs his hand along my arm and down my body. "But you must know that I have to do this now." His breath tickles my ear and sends a chill down my body as he speaks. "I didn't want to."

I nod my head slowly, hating what I've done. I've caused myself pain. I ruined it. I've upset him. I've disobeyed him. My body trembles knowing what's coming. I swallow the lump growing in my throat and say, "I'm sorry, sir." I choke out the words. He was going to let me sleep, and I destroyed that.

My body jumps at his hard response. "Don't call me that." He's angry, and I need to make this right.

"I--" I try to speak, but my throat closes and I struggle to respond.

"Shh. Shh. I'm sorry." He strokes my hair and pulls me close to his body, gentle enough that he doesn't pull the cuff against my wrist too much. "It's alright, Ava."

"I'm sorry." I heave a deep breath and push out my apology. "I'm so sorry, Kane."

"It's alright, Ava. I would have done it, too. It's okay." I shake my head, but he pushes me into his chest. My left arm twists slightly, nearly to the point of pain and makes me wince.

"Fuck," he curses under his breath. "God damn it!" he yells, as he gets up and leans across my body. I hear him pick up the key and struggle with the lock.

He pulls the cuff apart and I slowly rest my arm down by my waist. I lie on my side, curled inward. I'm frightened and unsure of what he wants.

"I don't know what to do with you, Ava."

"I'm sorry, Kane." I speak with my eyes closed and my chin tucked to my chest.

"I know why you're fighting me, but please," he holds me tighter to him, "please be a good girl for me. I don't want to hurt you. I don't like this."

"I'm sorry, Kane."

"I don't want you to be sorry." He kisses my neck and sighs. "I'm sorry too, Ava."

I cuddle into his chest. His arms wrap tighter around me. I'm so confused, but for the first time since all this happened, since I lost everyone I loved...for the first time I don't feel alone. I close my eyes and lean into him as he kisses my forehead. I'll be good for him. I can do that.

As my body calms and he continues to shush me, all I can think is that this isn't going to last. I've behaved badly. Very badly. Yet he's holding me and consoling me. I could've tried to kill him, but he's not punishing me in the least. I nestle deeper into his chest and clench my fists into tight balls to keep from gripping onto him. I'm afraid to hope that he can hold me forever. But it's too late.

I wish he would keep me. Maybe if I'm good for him, he will.

I take a ragged breath in as my body heats with anxiety.

"It's alright. I'm not going to hurt you." He kisses the top of my head. I believe him. I trust him. My lungs fill with the hot air between us.

It's a mistake, but I can't help but hope that he'll save me. Even though he said he won't. Some dark part of me wants me to believe that he will. So I close my eyes and I let that part consume me. It may be the last wish I ever have. But with everything in me, I pray that he'll keep me.

KANE

J didn't sleep. Not for one fucking minute. I couldn't cuff her back to the bed, not with the way she is. But I sure as fuck wasn't going to let my guard down. Even if the gun wasn't loaded, she had it pointed at me for a long fucking time. Part of me wanted her to run. I don't know if Abram's going to let me live when I reject his offer. If she had run, at least one of us would have gotten away.

But she didn't try to run. Instead she decided she'd try to kill me. I'm not sure why she didn't pull the trigger. But I'm sure as fuck happy that she didn't. Not because I want to live. I was never in any real danger. Some twisted part of me wants her to want me. The fact that she thought about killing me is like a bullet to my chest.

I understand it. I'd do it too if I were in her position, but that doesn't ease the pain. I take a look at her from the corner of my eye as we pull up to the red light.

She was surprised when I told her to sit in the front seat. I wish she'd fucking act normal. Her hands won't stop shaking and I fucking hate it.

If I keep pretending that everything's alright, maybe she'll settle down. I hope she will. She's so fucking broken. She's so scared that I'm going to hurt her.

I had to bring her with me. I didn't trust leaving her alone. Not after I came back yesterday and saw what a shitty job I did tying her up. I'm used to zip ties. But I'm not tying her up like that. I've seen it go wrong too many times. I don't want to risk hurting her.

She's staying with me. Every waking moment, I want her right next to me. But I don't want her to be the shell of a human she was when I first saw her. I know I can bring her out and help her heal.

My hands grip the steering wheel tighter, making my knuckles turn white. I fucking hate how she tries to fade into the background or trembles with fear. I loosen my grip and ease up off the gas as we make our way closer to the docks.

I gently lay a hand on the console, getting a bit closer to her, but not touching her.

"Just relax, and everything will be fine." I repeat the words I told her when we left and she acknowledges me with a nod.

"I will. Thank you, Kane." I don't know why the fuck she's thanking me, but I shove my annoyance down. I don't want to yell at her, not like I did last night. She doesn't deserve that. I need to go easy on her. After everything she's been through, it's a miracle that she's as functional as she is.

I move my hand down to her thigh, just below her jean shorts and give her thigh a gentle squeeze. Her skin is so soft. "Everything's going to be fine, Ava." I turn my head to meet her eyes. "No one's going to hurt you." I'll fucking kill anyone who tries to fuck with her. I'm not playing around. Right now she's mine. It may not be the smartest thing for me to be handling her like this, though. The thought makes me grind my teeth and I turn to look out of the window. I don't want her to sense my anger at all. She's mine, and I want her relaxed and to be able to blend in. Not some trembling slave, chained away and devoid of life.

I know I can get her there. I will get her there.

So long as everyone stays out of my fucking way.

They better not fucking hurt her. I got a call from Vince this morning with the address for the meet-up. I've never liked the docks. That's where we dumped the bodies. I've seen plenty of men led to the docks, only to be shot on-site and discarded. But that's where the shipping containers are, so it makes sense that we'd meet there.

I take another look at Ava. She's nervous still, but at least she's looking around a little. A small smile plays at my lips. I wonder if she knows she's not staring straight ahead, looking at nothing. I fucking hate that, so if I've broken that habit I'll be happy with that little bit of progress.

"You ever hear of the Valettis?" I ask her, as I follow the directions from the GPS and turn into a gravel driveway right off the bay and drive to the far end. There's a large building and then a smaller one that looks like it's obviously comprised of offices. Undoubtedly that's where Vince told me to meet him. My eyes travel to Ava and I question bringing her along. It's an impossible situation, leaving her alone versus bringing her with me.

"I haven't." She shakes her head and her large blue eyes shine with sincerity. "My father didn't talk much about business." Her eyes stay on me, waiting for an answer.

"I'm sorry about your father." She visibly flinches from my words and it makes me feel like an asshole. I put the car in park and turn in my seat to look at her. "I really am, Ava. I know what it's like to lose someone you love."

"Thank you, Kane." The way she says the words seems different than before. The words are softer and have more meaning. I reach into the backseat and grab the bag with her collar and leash. I imagine I need her collared when everyone's around, just like I need her to call me sir. I want the collar on her neck, too. I want to cover the bandage over her cut. It's a large fucking cut, too. The fact that they didn't do shit to help it heal pisses me off. I lean over and push the edges of the Band-Aid down.

"This'll cover that up." I have to lean across the console to put the thin leather band around her neck. It looks good on her. It's an off-white color and makes her skin look brighter around it. The leather should feel good compared to the metal. There's a loop at the front, for a tag or a leash.

I adjust the collar so it fits nicely and covers the bandage. Most of it, anyway; a small bit peeks out. It makes me scowl. I don't like seeing it. I hate the evidence of what those fuckers did to her. My eyes involuntarily travel to the large, silvery scar on her shoulder. The indentation of each tooth from the bite is visible. I have to force myself to look away and calm my breathing.

"That feel alright?" She nods her head at my question and I shove the bag into the backseat. I'm not putting a fucking leash on her. I won't need it.

"You'll stay to my right. Do you understand?"

"Yes, Kane."

"If anything happens, you stand behind me." She hesitates as her eyes widen slightly; it's the first time she's ever waited even a second to answer. I raise my eyebrows, waiting for her to acknowledge what I said. If guns come up, we're probably fucked. But I still want her behind me. I need to know she's alright.

"Yes, Kane," she replies as she nods her head, keeping those beautiful blue eyes on mine.

"Kane?" she asks.

"Yeah, Ava?" I meet her kind gaze and it takes me by surprise. Her eyes have such life in them.

"I'm sorry for your loss as well." I'm shocked to hear that from her. My eyes search her face. If her father didn't talk about business, then Abram and whoever else had her must've been running their mouths. Adrenaline courses through my blood and I struggle to keep the anger from my expression. Not because they were talking about my family, but because they had her.

I open my mouth to ask her more about what she heard, but also about the shit they put her through. Before I get a word out though, a knock on my window surprises the shit out of me.

Fuck! Fucking sloppy of me to let a Valetti sneak up on me like that. I should fucking know better. I open the door and step out. The man who knocked on the window takes a step back with a smirk. Behind him is another man. Both are dressed casually, sporting jeans and tee shirts. They resemble each other quite a bit--both Italian with dark hair, and dark eyes. Most likely they're true-blooded Valettis.

The smaller one, toned and broad-chested, but not nearly as muscular as the fucker to my right, smiles up at me like it's a big fucking joke that they walked up on me. His hand is on the butt of his gun and as my eyes settle on it, he pulls his shirt out a bit and hides it away. I've got mine, too. But I'm not fucking ready to pull it out. Not without reason.

"Just a precaution," he says with a smirk.

"I'm Tommy, and this is my brother Anthony," says the one closest to me. I nod my head. I was right. Valettis. I know a bit about them. I know Anthony is the fucker who gets people to talk. His methods are known to be extreme, but effective. Looking at Tommy I don't have to wonder what his job is. He's almost as tall as I am, with just as much muscle. His shirt is stretched almost too tight across his chest. He should start investing in some that actually fit.

"Nice to meet you two." Not fucking really. I lean into the car with the door still open. I put my back to them. It's a deliberate move on my part. I want them to know I'm not scared of them, although I'd be a fucking liar if I said I wasn't the least bit anxious. I also want them to know I trust them not to fuck with me with my back turned.

I look into the car and give Ava a small smile. I fucking hope she's alright being here. I don't know when was the last time she was around anyone without being in chains. She's still sitting there, wide-eyed and looking like she's waiting for a shootout to start any second.

"You ready?" I ask in a soft voice. "Just stay by my side and everything will be fine." I hope that she's reassured, but if she's smart, then she knows I can't guarantee a damn thing. Judging by the look on her face, she's definitely doubting my words. I reach out my hand and cup her chin. "Just be a good girl and stay with me. I'll protect you."

Her shoulders relax slightly and her eyes soften as she replies, "Yes, Kane." My heart warms at her words. It shouldn't, but it does. I like that she trusts me and that she's associating me with safety. My heart twists in my chest. I won't be able to give her safety for long. But as long as she's mine, I will.

KANE

"Stay. I'll come around and get you." I give her the order then quickly shut the door. I don't turn around to face the Valettis, but instead I immediately walk around the car to get her. I had her slightly relaxed, so I want to make sure I keep her that way.

When I open the door, she stands gracefully. My hand rests on the small of her back to steady her, but also to give her guidance. I rub my hand in small soothing circles as we walk around the car to face Tommy and his brother. I fucking wish I had her in Kevlar, too. It's standard attire for me now, after all that shit that happened. It's the only reason I lived.

I clench my jaw and try to settle the churning in my gut. She'll stand behind me if anything happens. It'll be alright.

"This is Ava." I introduce her and give them a hard stare. I know they saw her before back at the hangar. Back when she was in that dirty dress, bowing on the ground in shackles. But this is different.

Anthony gives her a tight smile and a nod. Tommy's eyes stare at her collar, at the little bit of bandage peeking out from underneath as he gives a curt hello. I fucking hate them for it. She shifts slightly as she swallows and quietly, yet confidently responds, "It's nice to meet you."

I pull her waist closer to me and put my lips to her ear to whisper, "Good girl."

Tommy and Anthony walk ahead of me, with their backs to us and it gives me a little security. Ava's walking with her hands clasped in front of her and I know it's because she's used to the chains around her wrists. My arm slips off the small of her waist and I take her left hand in my right. Her footsteps falter slightly, and Tommy must hear it because he turns to look back at us and I watch as his eyes stare at our hands.

A jolt of anger races through my blood. He doesn't fucking know anything, yet he's judging me. I can see all the shitty emotions on his face. He's judging *us*. I don't have a fucking choice in this, and neither does she. What the fuck does he expect from me? At least she's not in chains and crawling on the ground like Abram would want.

A quick panic washes through me. If they told Abram about this, I don't know what he'd say. I push that shit down. I don't fucking care. I'm doing this my way and he gave her to me. He'll have to get over it if he doesn't like it.

We get to the front of the building and Anthony pulls open the large glass door and holds it for us. I press my lips into a slight smile and nod.

"Thank you," Ava says, stepping in front of me to walk through the door, but not letting go of my hand. It's such a natural move. It makes my smile turn more sincere. As she steps into the large waiting area she seems to realize something and stops in her tracks. She looks back at me with a flash of fear on her face. Her wide eyes stare at mine as she waits for a reaction from me.

"Good girl." I'm quick to give her praise. A look of relief washes over her, but my eyes travel to Tommy who continues to walk in front of her, but shoots me daggers. My nostrils flare with anger and I grip her hand a little tighter. Her eyes fall to the floor as we walk behind Tommy and I wish I could take it back.

That's strike two as far as I'm concerned. One more shitty look like that and that fucker is getting what he has coming to him. I stare at the back of his head as we walk down a narrow hall, trying to will my anger down but doing a shit job of it.

He opens the door to an office on the right and waits for us to enter. He braces the door fully open with his foot, and I want to push it open farther to crush his foot with it and punch his fucking face in. She may be a sex slave and I may have to watch over her, but she doesn't need those fucking looks from him. Every look is a reminder and I don't fucking want that for her.

"Ava." Vince gets up from his desk with a wary smile, looking at me and then back to her. He holds out a hand for her in welcome. That's better. That's the greeting I want for her. She quickly but unsteadily places her hand in his, and looks up to me quickly. Her constant need for reassurance makes me sick, but I give her a small nod.

"Hello," she greets Vince as she visibly swallows, and looks back up to me as she takes her hand away.

Vince looks at me although he speaks to Ava when he says, "Women don't usually come to these meetings." He gives her another smile and looks at her face, and then her neck. His eyes focus on the bandage like Tommy's did. "I wasn't anticipating you being here."

On one hand, I'm happy he's speaking to her. I want her to interact with people. But on the other hand, I'm the one he should be talking to about this shit.

I speak up, getting his attention. "I want her with me."

He narrows his eyes as he replies, "Women usually stay at home."

"Forgive me, but I don't want to leave her somewhere I don't know is secure." He seems shocked by my answer. What the fuck did he expect? I don't know him or his *famila*. And I don't trust the safe house we've been staying in. He must be able to read that from my hard expression.

"We'd never hurt her." Ava takes a small step backward, away from him and moves closer to my side. Her hand brushes against mine and I'm quick to take it. The tension in the room is thick. I rub soothing circles on the back of her hand with my thumb.

"I don't know you, Vince. So you'll understand that I'd like to have her with me."

"Yes," his eyes dart to her neck again before meeting mine, "I imagine Abram would be upset if anything were to happen to her." Ava noticeably cowers at this and scoots closer to me. It pisses me the fuck off.

The hot air seems to suffocate me, and the only thing I can hear is the blood rushing in my ears. I'm surrounded by three armed men with Ava at my side, and all I want to do is take out my anger by beating some fucking sense into them. I focus on my breathing instead.

"Let's get to business, Vince." I bite out the words with only the tiniest bit of aggression apparent. His eyebrows raise and he exchanges a glance with someone behind me. I don't turn, I just stare back at the asshole with a hard look.

"What is it that you'd like to know?" he asks, walking back around to his desk and gesturing to a chair to my left. There's only one chair there. I look to the far corner of the room where Tommy's standing and there's a chair behind him. I think about moving it over so she can sit with me, but then I think twice about it.

I don't feel like sitting anyway. I guide her to the chair with my hand on the small of her back and motion for her to sit. I move to stand behind her and grip the chair. She looks uneasy and she has every right to be. I do my best to comfort her by placing my hands on her shoulders so she can feel me there.

"Would you like the other chair?" Vince asks, as Tommy pulls the chair across the floor. There's an awkward tension in the room and I don't know how to get rid of it. It's making Ava tense, it's pissing me off, and if I turn down the seat it's only going to get worse. I turn around and look at Anthony who's standing behind me and in front of the door.

Regret settles in my chest as I clench my fists. I wish I hadn't brought her. I wish I had somewhere safe to take her. But I don't have anyone. I turn back to Vince and give him a quick nod before gripping the chair and pushing it to butt up next to Ava's.

I take a seat and hold out my hand for her. She's quick to take it and turn her body toward me.

"We don't deal with this aspect of the industry, so you'll have to excuse me, but I find this..." Vince looks between the two of us, "...odd."

I crack my neck to the left and stare back at him debating what all to tell him. Fuck it. I might as well lay it all out there. "I don't do this shit, and I won't be the one working between you and Petrov." I take a steady breath knowing I may have just triggered my death sentence. When this gets back to Abram, he's not going to be happy. But I'm sure as shit not going to be doing this. "I'm here to learn the ins and outs of your business and report back."

Vince narrows his eyes at me. "That's not the impression I was under. I thought you were in charge of this..." he trails off, looking at Ava and then quickly averts his gaze as he concludes, "...this kind of handling."

"I'm not, and I won't." My words come out hard and I'm glad they do.

His brows raise in surprise before he schools his expression. "Is there anything else I should know?"

My brow furrows in confusion. I don't know what he's hinting at. "Subtlety isn't a strength of mine, Vince." I lean forward, but keep my hand back so Ava doesn't have to change positions. "If you want to know something, you should just come on out and ask it."

"Is she yours, then?" Vince asks, and I swallow thickly as I settle my back against the seat.

I don't know how to answer that. If I could take her away, I would. It's one thing to turn down Abram, I'm probably already dead for that. But to steal from him, that would most certainly put me six feet under.

"For now." I answer as honestly as possible. All eyes dart to Ava as she takes a ragged breath in. When she notices how much attention she brought on herself, she cowers in her seat and looks to me with a sad expression. Her lips part, but I quickly shake my head, stopping her. I don't want to hear her say she's sorry. She's said it too much already.

I brush my thumb along the back of her hand. "It's alright, Ava." I try to reassure her quietly before turning back to Vince. "The circumstances are different today than they will be in the future. I just need to get a handle on how you run this operation." The questioning look on his face vanishes and is replaced with a hard, no-fucking-nonsense look. He gives a nod and rises from his seat. I do the same and Ava quickly follows suit. Her other hand covers the back of mine and she walks closer to be by my side.

She's scared and obviously unwell. I would give anything to ease her pain. I wish I could say she was mine and that I was taking her away from this shit. But I can't. And I won't lie to her.

"I have a shipment coming in any time now. We'll wait outside." He walks around the front of the desk and meets my eyes, before walking toward the doors. "I'm not sure what all could possibly be different on our front that Abram would need to know. But I'll let you have a look." I give him a tight nod as my muscles coil.

He's right. It's a simple operation. I don't know what Abram has planned, but I can't imagine there's anything the Valettis do that would be a surprise to him.

I walk behind him with Ava gripping onto my hand like she's afraid I'll let go. I won't. I pull her closer to me and just barely resist the urge to kiss the temple of her forehead.

Abram already knows everything except simple numbers. He must want something else.

I hadn't thought of it before, but now that the realization has hit me, I don't fucking like it.

KANE

I watch as the last forklift moves across the ramp with the container
secured. I've seen this shit a million times. The waves crash against
the dock and beyond that it's relatively quiet. A few men are shouting in the
distance. Vince is quiet next to me with his hands shoved into his pockets. Ava
is somewhat settled in a folding chair a few yards from us. It took her a while
to feel comfortable after the shit that happened in the office, but she seems to
be okay now. Although, her eyes have lost the bit of vibrancy I saw this morning, and a small frown mars her beautiful face. I wish I could take her unhap-
piness away.

"She's fine, Kane." Vince's words distract me from my thoughts and I turn
to face him. "She's not gonna fucking dive in."

My face contorts with anger, and I have to bite my tongue.

"What? Is that not what you were thinking?" He huffs a humorless laugh
and looks over the bay. "I'd fucking jump before I'd go back to that fucker."
My heart stops beating and my throat closes. It's so fucked up, but it's true.
She's such a sweetheart, such a good girl, and the fate she has is such fucking
shit. It's a nightmare.

I feel tears pricking at the backs of my eyes thinking about the hell she's
been through. It's not fucking right. My jaw tics as I stare off into the distance

and watch the waves form and crash along the beach. I want to save her from that shit. But I don't want us both to wind up dead.

I open my mouth, ready to tell Vince what a fucked up position I'm in. I might as well. Maybe I'll die for it, but something about him makes me think I can trust him, even if I don't fucking like him. The sound of fast-paced, heavy footsteps coming closer makes me turn away from Vince and toward the men walking toward us.

I practically growl in anger when I see that bastard Felipe stalking toward us with his gaze firmly locked on to my good girl. That fucker shouldn't even be allowed to look at her. I clench my teeth tighter to stop myself from saying shit that'll get me killed. I have to remind myself that I'm on my own, and I'm the only thing standing between all these fucking pricks and Ava. I can't do something stupid.

"You got this one, or is it on me?" Vince asks, with a touch of humor in his voice. If I was in a better position I'd find it funny, but I don't.

"What the fuck is she doing here?" Felipe yells out loud enough so Ava can hear as he stomps closer to us and it pisses me off.

I don't like that he knew where I was. My eyes drift to Ava. He was tracking her with that fucking GPS chip in her arm. My jaw clenches and my hands ball up into fists.

Like he fucking owns her. She's mine.

"She's right where I told her to sit." I keep my voice low and even, then cock a brow at him. "What the fuck are you doing here?" I ask.

Vince stares Felipe down with daggers in his eyes. All traces of the humor that was there previously are gone now. Felipe doesn't seem to give a fuck. He's acting like he's untouchable. And in a lot of ways he is. But I don't give a fuck. Ava was finally settling down, but now that he's here and his eyes are on her, she's all fucked up again. The men trailing Felipe are Vince's, which means this prick came alone.

She looked nervous and a bit sad before, but now there's nothing on her face. She's staring at the ground with her hands on her trembling thighs. On her face is that blank expression that I fucking hate. I can tell she's debating on whether or not she should get down from the chair and bow on the ground.

"Stay right where you are, Ava!" My command comes out hard as I yell, and I almost regret it. But she doesn't belong to Felipe, and I'm not going to let him turn her back into the shell she was when I got her.

Her eyes dart up to meet mine, although her body remains tense and still. Her shoulders rise as she takes in a heavy breath.

"Answer me," I yell out to her. I fucking hate that I'm giving her a command, but I want the fact that she's mine and only mine to be made very fucking clear. I'm not going to let her think Felipe's in control here.

"Yes, sir," she calls out. My teeth grind against each other and I can feel the eyes of every man out here on me. I know I told her to call me sir when other people were present, but I changed my mind.

I shake my head slowly as I walk closer to her, and her eyes widen with fear. "Be a good girl. Call me Kane." At my words, tension leaves her shoulders and her eyes soften.

It soothes my heart that the mention of my name can have such a profound effect on her. "Yes, Kane," she says, with a soft touch in her voice.

I walk up to her and cup her chin in my hand. "Stay here while I handle this." She nods slightly and closes her eyes as I rub my thumb along her jaw. I can sense her trust in me. I only hope I don't fail her.

"Good girl," I say to her, and then stare at Felipe who looks pissed off. His eyes are on her, but her eyes are on me. I smirk at him. He thinks he can control her, but he can't. I won't let her be used like that.

"What do you need, Felipe?" I ask, and walk closer to stand between him and Ava. It's not really a question though, since I'm more or less telling him to get the fuck out. I know it. He knows it. And Vince and his *famila* know it.

Finally, the fucker looks back at me. He narrows his eyes and smirks as he says, "I saw the bitch had moved and I was informed that you may not have a firm grasp on her."

"Everything's under control here, as you can see."

"Where the fuck's her collar?" I watch as his fists clench and he leans to one side to look around me. I turn my head to find Ava looking out at the waves like she was earlier, ignoring us. A smile widens on my face. That's my girl.

"I like the one I got her better," I say lightheartedly. I watch as Anthony and Tommy walk toward one another with their hands on their guns and their eyes on Felipe. I don't like this shit, because behind Felipe and me is Ava. I don't want this to turn violent. I just need her to get the fuck out.

"It wasn't yours," he bites back.

"Wrong. She's mine, and everything on her is mine."

He cocks a grin and takes a step closer to me. "Not for long," he says with a smile. Every bit of confidence and happiness leaves me. My heart drops in my chest, leaving it hollow.

"She's mine right now, and she'll do as I say."

He just smirks at me and turns to look at Vince as he clucks his tongue. He looks back at me with his eyes traveling up and down my body like he's sizing me up. "I guess I'll be seeing you shortly. We have a meeting arranged for tomorrow. I'll check in with Abram about your *unique* handling methods." His words make my stomach churn with sickness. I can't fucking stand it.

He brushes by me and I almost turn around and knock the fucker out, but Vince grabs my arm and silently shakes his head. I debate on doing it anyway. I know what he must've done to her. The thoughts flash before my eyes and I see red. All I fucking see is red.

As Felipe continues to walk off, Vince starts talking business again. Trying to diffuse the situation, I guess. But it's not working. I watch Felipe as he veers off his path to make a sharp turn, heading for the exit behind Ava. I don't like how close the fucker is to her.

"As long as he doesn't touch her," Vince speaks quietly so no one else can hear, "don't fucking make a move."

I don't acknowledge him. I keep my eyes steady on that prick as he walks by Ava, slowing his steps and staring at her. She cowers in her seat with her eyes staring straight ahead.

I don't give a damn about the docks, or the shipments. I couldn't fucking care less. Instead I'm watching as Felipe walks even closer to her. He stands a few feet away, but just by him being there her entire body is stiff and she's not okay. I know she's not.

The water splashing against the docks is drowning out what he's saying. I know he's talking to her though. And I don't like her reaction. Her face is mostly expressionless, save for the slight frown on her lips and the flash of fear in her eyes. And then I just barely hear him say, "You're going to regret it, you fucking cunt."

Every ounce of control inside of me snaps. My poor Ava goes pale, and I fucking lose it. He's not going to do that shit to her. I'll make sure he never fucking touches her again. I'm quick to pull out my gun and shoot him right in his fucking kneecap. Before I'm aware that I've even moved, I'm on him, standing over his body as he's clutching his leg and cussing rather than reaching for his own gun. Fucking stupid shit.

"Motherfucker!" he screams, as blood covers his hands and pools in the dirt under his knee.

"You'll fucking die for this, Kane." I smirk back at him as I hear the Valettis come to stand around us. I'm sure they have their guns drawn and pointed at me, but I don't look. I won't take my eyes off this fucker until he's dead.

"Not before you." He makes a move for his gun and I shoot his hand as it reaches his belt. I'm a good shot. The bullet goes right through his hand. Blood pours from the wound as he curls inward and covers it with his left hand.

"Fuck!" He screams and winces as blood soaks his clothes and pools around him. It's gushing from his hand, but also his knee now that he isn't keeping pressure on it.

Everyone around us is silent and still. I can feel all eyes on me. Waiting for my next move.

A small gasp and slight movement in my periphery bring me back to why this prick needs to die right now.

"Ava. Come here." I keep my eyes on Felipe and he flashes me a nasty look. He reaches toward his belt, and I shake my head. "Don't fucking think about it."

"I got it." A man's voice to my right sounds out and I watch as Tommy leans in and takes Felipe's gun away from him. Felipe lets go of his injured hand to grab Tommy's wrist, but Tommy shakes him off and pulls away. Felipe sneers at him as he's dragged across the dirt, struggling to retrieve his gun before finally giving up and letting go. He curls up on his side, still cussing and grabbing his hand. His face is distorted in rage and pain, but then he sees my face. He swallows and looks around me. I don't follow his eyes. I know we're surrounded.

Felipe goes pale, all blood drained from his face and his expression shows the realization that he's about to fucking die. Good. I'm glad he knows it.

Ava skirts around Felipe slowly and he stares at her with daggers in his eyes. "*Puto coño,*" he cusses under his breath and then spits on the ground.

Ava's eyes are closed and her shoulders are trembling as she stands to my left. She's terrified. I feel like a fucking asshole for not ending him the second I came over here. But I want to give this to her. I think she *needs* this.

"Ava, baby, open your eyes." She doesn't hesitate. Her blue eyes stare up at me, pleading with me to make this stop. "Take his gun." I tilt my head toward Tommy, although my eyes are still on Felipe. His nostrils flare and he's cursing in Spanish under his breath. I can't hear whatever he's saying due to the loud crash of the waves.

I see Tommy hesitate to give her the gun. I look to him with impatience and he relents, passing her the gun in front of me. She takes it in both hands and points it at Felipe. She steadies her stance and squares her shoulders as though she's at the gun range. I imagine with her father being the boss, that she should know how to shoot. But she's probably never actually killed anyone before.

"What did he tell you, Ava?" I ask her. I want her to know this is what happens to men who threaten her. I want to give her this power.

She closes her eyes and I see hope flash on Felipe's face as he leans forward. I'll make sure he never orders her around again. I point my gun at his other leg and fire off a shot. Bang!

It hits his shin, and judging from the sound of impact, the bullet is lodged in the bone. "Fuck!" he screams out, grabbing his leg. He leans on his side, whining like a little bitch.

"Eyes open, Ava." She opens her eyes and takes in a ragged breath.

"Did he say he'd hurt you?"

"Yes," she speaks, barely above a whisper.

I lean closer to her and whisper in her ear. "He's never going to hurt you again." I see her fingers tremble on the trigger. She's reluctant to pull it. I remember my first time. I was only 17. The prick had raped a *comare*. He had it coming. I wanted him dead, but I still couldn't do it. My father put his hand over mine and helped me. It was the only time I needed that support. Maybe she needs that now.

I stand behind her and keep my movements slow. I brace her arms with mine and rest my chin on her shoulder, staring down the barrel of the gun with her. I place my hand on top of hers and steady my fingers on hers, holding her hands loosely.

Felipe tries to move, but Vince points his gun at him, followed by the rest of the Valettis. The corner of my lips kick up into a smile. Felipe's phone goes off in his pocket. An annoying ringtone is the only sound other than the waves and Ava's ragged breathing.

Just as Felipe opens his mouth to yell out to her, her finger pulls the trigger. The bullet hits his right pec, shoving him violently onto the ground. She points the gun down, with shaking hands, but I help to steady it and she fires again. Bang! It hits his throat and blood bubbles out as his hands fly up, reaching for the wound. And again, bang! His head falls back forcefully and his body goes limp. Blood seeps into the dirt, turning black. The phone stops ringing as I slowly lower Ava's arms and take the gun out of her hands.

It's Felipe's, so I'm gonna need to dispose of it. Tommy walks up to me as I debate on what to do with it. He holds out his hand and I'm happy to pass it to him. I don't feel like dealing with this shit. We used to put them in acid. Along with people's fingertips and teeth. I turn to look at Vince, with an arm still wrapped around Ava. I need to square this up with him. I know I fucked up. I directly disobeyed him. It only hits me right now how fucked this is. Felipe is one of Abram's close men. This isn't good. And it went down on Valetti property, with witnesses.

"You sure do make a mess for someone who doesn't have backing." I turn to face Vince, letting go of my hold on Ava. I stand between the two of them and take a look around. There are at least 10 men standing around, with everyone looking at the two of us.

I take a deep breath in through my nose. I feel like I've got their support, but I didn't have the go-ahead. I know for a fucking fact I didn't. I noticeably swallow and square my shoulders. "I'm sorry, Vince. I know better." I return my gun to the holster on my belt and run a hand down my face. As soon as the gun is tucked away several men shift and put theirs away, too. "I fucked up." Vince gives me a hard look. It's real quiet for a moment, except for Ava, who's heaving in air. I clench my fists and resist the urge to go to her. Not until he gives me the go ahead. I already directly disobeyed him in front of his *famila*. I can't disrespect him like that again.

"Yeah, you did. You're lucky I didn't like that fucker." He turns to his right and calls out, "Tommy!"

"Yeah, boss?" Tommy walks up to my right with a grin.

"Get the cleanup crew." Vince looks over his shoulder at the rest of the men. "Get back to work. You didn't see shit here."

"I can clean it up, Vince. It's my mess."

"No offense Kane, but I like to do shit my way. And where the fuck are you planning on taking the body?" His eyebrows raise, and I press my lips into a line.

"I'd figure it out. I won't get you into any shit."

He smirks at me. "You killed Abram's man on my turf in front of me." Fuck, I fucking hate that he's laying into me. I have it coming, though. "You already got me into shit."

I keep my eye contact with him as I state, "Just let me know what to do." I'll make this right. I always do.

He looks at me for a long while, searching for something, and then he looks over my shoulder. I hear Ava take in a deep, ragged breath and it breaks my heart.

"Just take care of your girl." As Vince says the words, his phone goes off.

Ava's right behind me, staring at Felipe's body. Her hands are clasped in front of her. She doesn't look like she's doing alright. She's pale and trembling, like the fucker's still alive and going to beat her.

I hear Vince answer his phone as I pull her into my arms and against my chest, turning her so she can't see Felipe's body. "It's going to be alright."

"Abram, nice to hear from you so soon." I hear Vince talking behind me and I turn around with her in my arms. His eyes lock with mine as he speaks. "Yeah, he was just here, looking for the girl." My heart drops and my blood chills. This is bad. Real fucking bad. He's quiet a moment. I can't hear what Abram's saying on the other end, but judging from the look on Vince's face, it's not good. "Kane's got a good handle on her...Felipe just left. Kane? No, he took off a few minutes after Felipe did."

I feel the faintest bit of relief. Vince covered for me. He nods at me and then tilts his head to the parking lot. I give him a stern nod in return and start walking in that direction.

I pass Tommy and Anthony on the way out. They both look smug and happy. Probably because their family has me under their thumb now.

I open Ava's door and gently push on the small of her back for her to get in, but her grip on me tightens. She looks up at me through her lashes like she's waiting for something.

"You alright?" I ask, and kiss her hair.

She nods her head and asks, "Am I still a good girl?" She's tense, and waves of anxiety are rolling off of her. It takes me by surprise. I can tell she needs

381

reassurance. She's worried, and I don't like that. I'd hoped that Felipe's death at her hands would help her, but the only vibe I'm getting from her is that she's scared.

"Of course you are. And he'll never hurt you again."

She's still a bit tense but gives me a small smile and says, "Thank you, Kane." Her fingers twist in her hands and she gets into her seat.

It leaves me with an uneasy feeling in my gut. Something is very wrong. Maybe I shouldn't have done that. I should've just shot him myself. I spear my fingers through my hair and stand outside of my door, looking back over to the docks. A few men are shoveling dirt into a wheelbarrow right where his ass was lying when I shot him. They're cleaning up my mess.

Maybe it was wrong of me. Maybe I shouldn't have made her kill him. Fuck. I did that. I *made* her kill him. I didn't give her a choice. I made her a murderer. It never occurred to me that she wouldn't take it like I did. She's a woman, a sweet girl. She's not like me. Fuck. I don't know if I made things better or worse for her.

I finally open the door and sit in the seat. My hands twist on the steering wheel as I look straight ahead and ask, "Are you sure you're alright?"

"Yes, Kane." She's quick to answer and it's in that tone she used to use. I turn to face her. "Tell me what's wrong." I stare into her eyes, willing the truth from her. I don't want her to wall herself off. I need this to be beneficial for us both.

"Abram's going to kill you if he finds out." She chokes on the last word.

"Baby, you don't have to worry about me." My lips pull into an asymmetric grin. "He has no idea."

"He'll find out. I've seen what they do." She struggles to breathe, and I reach across the console and wrap my arms around her. I pull her into my lap. She pulls up her knees and lays her cheek against my chest. Her eyes are closed and she's shaking her head. I wrap my arms around her and rock her gently. After a moment, she calms. I keep rubbing her back to soothe her.

"Ava, sweetheart, everything is going to be alright." I pull back a bit to look at her and brush the hair away from her face. I tilt up her chin and she opens her eyes to look back at me. She's not crying, but she's obviously not okay. "I want you to forget about this. I don't want you to worry, alright?" She nods her head and parts her lips to say something, but I press a finger against them.

The move is more intimate than I intended. A heated spark lights in her eyes, and her lips stay slightly parted. Her chest rises and falls, and the air between us changes. I pull my hand away and resist the urge to kiss her. I search her eyes for a moment, trying to calm my own needs. My dick is hardening in my pants and the urge to fuck her is riding me hard. I push it down.

"Ava, forget about this." I clear my throat and add, "All of this. I want you to disregard everything that happened today." She nods her head once and pulls away slightly, the meaning of my words sinking in. My heart falls as she pulls away from me completely, righting herself. I help her move back to her seat and ignore the fact that my dick is digging into my zipper.

I put my hands on the wheel, but before we take off, I have to apologize. "I'm sorry about that, Ava. I shouldn't have made you do that."

She slowly shakes her head. "Please, don't be."

"I shouldn't have made you do something you didn't want to."

She looks straight at me as she says, "You have no idea how much I've wanted to do that." She looks forward and adds, "He's only one of many."

AVA

I can't get over this sick feeling I have, like I'm going to heave up the tiniest bit of water I'm able to swallow. I need to force it down, but it's hard. The food smells amazing. Chicken carbonara, with fresh Parmesan. I want to devour it. My stomach rumbles for it. But as soon as it touches my lips, I have the urge to throw it up. Kane keeps looking at me. He wants me to eat and I want to eat too, but I'm going to be sick. I've felt like this ever since the ride home. Kane was silent; he didn't even look at me once.

I don't know what's wrong with me. I killed him. And I'm so fucking happy I did. At the same time, I'm scared to death that it's not real. That it's fake. I'm convinced it's a setup, and he's going to walk in here any minute and punish me. I keep picturing him over and over, clutching his throat and then nothing. Completely gone.

Is it possible? I saw them kill so many people. But I never had this feeling. The feeling it wasn't real. I'm terrified he's going to come back.

I also want to do it again. I need to do it again. I've never killed before, but he was only the first. I'll handle this sick feeling every day for the rest of my life in exchange for the rest of them lying in the dirt with bullet holes in their heads. An image of him flashes before my eyes. His face covered in dirt, his hair a mess. Laying lifeless with his eyes open and a neat hole right in the center.

Kane sets the fork down on his plate and the clinking of metal on ceramic makes me jump in my seat.

"I need you to talk to me," he says from across the table.

I nod my head and swallow the lump growing in my throat. "What would you like to know?" I gently set my own fork down and stare at him with my hands clasped on my lap. I need to be sure I give him my full attention.

He's angry. I don't think he'll hurt me, but with the others, the slightest thing set them off when they were angry.

"I hate it when you do that," he says, and it makes chills go down my spine. My breath falters, and I struggle to respond. I don't know what I've done. "Fuck!" he says under his breath, as he pushes the chair back, and the legs drag loudly across the floor. He walks over to me with determined strides, and I resist the urge to cower.

I don't know what I've done, but I've obviously displeased him.

"We were doing good earlier. Before it all happened." Is this a test? He told me to forget. I don't know how to respond.

I open my mouth to respond, but I have to cover it. Sickness climbs my throat and I just barely push it down. A wave of heat rolls over my body. I'm vaguely aware that I'm in his arms as he moves through the house to get to the nearest bathroom. He sets me down on the cold tile floor and pulls my hair back as I lean against the toilet. I focus on pushing the urge down. I don't want to be sick. I hate the feeling of throwing up. He stands behind me holding my hair, and patiently waits while the nausea settles.

After a long while, I try to move.

"Are you okay?" he asks quietly behind me.

I nod my head and apologize, "I'm sorry." He lets go of my hair and holds me against his chest. My face still feels hot, and every bit of energy has left me. I brace my hands on his chest, but I don't push away. I lean into him instead. His arms wrap around me and he rubs my back.

"Are you sure?" he asks.

"Yes, Kane." I answer as I should, even though everything feels different between us. Lines have blurred and I'm not sure what's expected of me. I like answering him though. I want him to know I am alright. I swallow and push away slightly.

"Do you want to go lie down?" His dark eyes look down at me, and I find myself mesmerized. I shake my head no and then force myself to look away. I bring a shaky hand to the back of my neck and then we both look down as my stomach growls.

"Can you eat?" he asks.

I'm quick to answer, "Yes." I'm starving, and I really do want something. I'm not sure I can handle what he's served me, but I'll try.

"Maybe soup?" he suggests.

My eyes itch with the need to cry. I feel so overwhelmed with emotion. "Please," I answer.

"I saw some in a cabinet in the kitchen. I'll heat some up for you. Head upstairs, and I'll be up in a minute. Alright?" He pushes the hair out of my face and I lean in as he cups the side of my head.

He leans in and kisses my forehead. I find myself wanting more. But I'm grateful with what he's given me. "Go upstairs and lie in bed. I'll be up soon." I nod my head, but as I start to say "Yes, Kane," his lips brush against mine in a soft kiss. I close my eyes, needing more. But I feel the air shift and hear him walk away. When I open my eyes, I'm alone.

It's a long walk up the stairs. I brace myself on the railing. I feel slightly sick and lethargic. I've never felt like this before. I'm just so tired. It must be everything weighing down on me.

I felt something like this before, although it was different, the first few weeks of this new life. My life of imprisonment. I crawl onto the bed and lie down. I can't help remembering how everything was supposed to be that day.

I was going to help Marie with her calculus. Summer break was nice, but that's only because I didn't take summer semester classes. My sister did, though. She had to retake it. It was a Thursday, her final was the next day, and then we were going to celebrate. I can still hear myself scolding her for not studying like she should have. My dry eyes itch with the need to cry, but the tears don't come. *Do you want to fail? 'Cause you sure as fuck aren't acting like you care!* I was so pissed. So angry that she wasn't trying.

I know we were handed a life of luxury. We'd never have to work a day for the rest of our lives if we didn't want to. But I was so angry that she'd pissed away another semester. I mean, fuck calculus, but don't sign up and then waste it. My heart thuds painfully in my chest. It never mattered. I never should have yelled at her. I swallow thickly as I see her face down on the table, bullet holes in her back. I hear myself screaming as the men surround me. At first I wished they'd killed me instead. But after all this time, I'm grateful.

I never would have wanted her to go through this. I would have rather died than go through what Felipe did to me.

He was the first, while Felipe held me down. They tied me to a chair and each did what they wanted to me. I close my eyes remembering how much it hurt. Remembering the pain on my father's face.

At first I blamed him. He did this. He's a bad man, and they came for us because of him. But that's not true. I spent weeks watching them hunt down my family. But then there were more. Innocent people who they took just for their own pleasure. Other families who were afraid to say yes equally as much as they were afraid to say no.

They're horrible men who deserve to die a thousand agonizing deaths. I hate them with everything in me. My fists clench at my side. The three of them need to die. A small, wicked smile grows on my face. One down, two to go.

I was never this person. I would have never felt happiness at another's misfortune. But there's nothing about me that's remotely the same as before. I was their prize. A gift to lend out to help seal deals.

They've made me a different person.

And they'll die because of the monster they created.

Anger lights inside of me. It's been so long since I've felt this need. My forehead creases with confusion. Why does it feel like it's been so long? This is my one goal. My one reason to live. As the thought registers, I hear the door open.

The anger dissipates and a soothing balm runs through me.

Kane.

He's going to make me better. I just need to be his good girl. He'll make everything better.

KANE

*a*nxiety races through my body as I climb the stairs. I feel like a sitting duck staying here. But I'm fucked if I leave. I shove my nerves aside. I killed a man today. Not just any man. I've killed before and felt next to nothing. All of them were bastards who deserved to die. Each time I pulled the trigger and never looked back, unless it was to make sure he wasn't still breathing.

But today I killed a man that could haunt me. A man who Abram's going to be pissed about losing. It's only a matter of time before he finds out. Or before the Valettis tell him. I'm almost certain they won't, but it'd only take a single man to tell. Just one lowly soldier in their *famila* could bring about my death sentence.

Between the two of them, the Petrovs and the Valettis, I trust the Valettis more. But I'm not fucking stupid. I've trusted men before and gotten shot at from behind. I need to figure something out. I half expected a call by now from Abram. If Vince was going to make a move, he would've by now. He could've easily taken a shot today. He didn't though, and I'm not exactly sure why. I imagine they're displeased with the current business arrangement, but I need to find out exactly what's going through his head.

Right now I feel the need to run.

I need to get the fuck away from Petrov and all that shit. I'm not going to do this shit for him, and I know that telling him no isn't going to go over well. I could run on my own and take Ava with me. But I fucking hate that idea. I'm not a little bitch. I didn't run when my own *famila* came after me, but back then I was fueled by anger. I'm using my fucking head with this one. And going in there by myself against his powerhouse; that'd be fucking stupid.

If I had the backing of the Valettis though…That's a different story. Right now I don't know what to think about Vince and the rest of them, but I'm going to find out. I need to do it quick before Petrov gets wind of what happened. I'm sure it's only a matter of time. When he finds out, I'm fucked.

All because of Ava. And it was fucking worth it.

She's quiet when I open the door, lying on her side and curled up like her stomach is hurting her. Her back is to me. My eyes travel the length of her small body as I walk into the room.

I feel like shit that she's sick over this. I know she said she's happy that he's dead, but I still shouldn't have told her to do that. She would have done anything I told her to do. And I had her kill a man.

Felipe was her keeper though. He was her tormentor. I can only imagine the fucked up shit he did to her. I'd want to see him dead if he'd done that shit to me. I set the bowl down gently on the nightstand and sit on the edge of the bed. It creaks and dips with my weight. She starts to get up, but I place my hand on her hip to stop her. She needs to rest.

I need to know. It's killing me to not know what she went through. I want to understand. I need to help her.

I clear my throat and ask, "You feeling any better?"

"Much," she answers with a small smile. She looks so sweet and innocent. Her face is still pale though. I was afraid she was having a panic attack at the table. This is too much for her. I'm a fucking prick for putting her through that.

"I'm sorry, Ava." I take her hand in mine as she scoots closer to me, giving me her full attention. She shakes her head, but I don't give her the opportunity to make excuses for me.

"I never should've told you to take the gun." I press my lips into a straight line as I remember standing behind her, steadying her hands. "I thought it would help you. I didn't think you'd get sick over it."

"I'm alright," she states, as though everything is perfectly fine. It's not.

"You almost had a fucking heart attack at the table." I squeeze her hand tighter. "You're just a woman. You shouldn't even see things like that."

Her eyes flash with anger so briefly, I question it. I can see she wants to say something, but she's holding it in. I fucking hate that. "Tell me."

"It was because you told me to forget everything that happened. I wasn't sure if you were testing me or not." Her eyes dart to the door and then back to me. "I didn't know what to say."

My forehead wrinkles with confusion. And then it hits me. She thought I was testing her? "Did you think I was going to hurt you, Ava?" My blood boils, and I resist the urge to show how angry I am. Not at her, but at the fact that she expected that shit from me.

Her lips part and her eyes fall as she admits, "I wasn't sure." Her tone is so sad. It fucking breaks my heart.

"I wouldn't do that to you. I wouldn't set you up." I cup her chin in my hand and tilt her head. "I'm not like them." I fucking hope I'm not. I don't know what she's been through. But I hate that she thinks I'm some sick prick like the fuckers who got their hands on her before me.

I have to change the subject. I'm getting too fucking worked up. "Can you eat?" I ask, as I drop my hand.

She nods her head and answers with a confident, "Yes."

That makes me happy. She needs to eat. I give her a small smile and reach over for the bowl as she sits up.

"I'm glad you're eating. Did they feed you?" I need to know. After seeing her reaction to killing that prick, I want to know what all that fucker did to her. I wish that bastard were still alive, so I could take out this anger on him and make him suffer for what he did.

"Yes. I was always fed something." She says it simply. But it's a veiled answer.

"Something? Be more specific?"

"Some fed me whatever it was they were eating." Some. My throat closes and my eyes fall. How many men have hurt her? I swallow thickly and turn to her with the spoon held out. I want to feed her. She doesn't hesitate to lean forward slightly and part her lips.

"Good girl." She swallows and smiles with a small blush. The color looks beautiful on her cheeks. I like seeing it. But I know my next question is going to take her happiness away. I need to know, though. "Tell me what happened,

Ava." I dip the spoon into the hot broth and keep my eyes on it as I add, "I want to know." I bring another spoonful to her lips.

There's not a trace of a smile on her lips. Or any other emotion. A bit of disappointment, maybe.

"What would you like to know?" she asks warily.

"I want to know the names of the men who hurt you. All of them." I raise the spoon again, but she shakes her head with a small frown.

"I'm sorry; I can't." Her answer pisses me off. I know she owes me nothing. I grit my teeth knowing I'm still waffling on what I'm going to do when I finally see Abram again. But a very large part of me doesn't want to let him ever see her again. I'd rather lie and say she was dead. I need to think of something and let her know.

"I don't know their names. Not all of them." I give her my attention and try to control my anger.

"How many? Tell me what you can." I clench my jaw realizing I've given her a command. Just like I did earlier with Felipe. What the hell is wrong with me? I set the bowl on the nightstand and get off the bed with my back toward her. "I'm sorry. You don't have to tell me anything." She doesn't owe me anything, and if she doesn't want to talk about it, she doesn't have to.

"I think I'd like to talk." I turn to look at her and stare into her blue eyes. I nod and clench my fists. I look at the bowl and then the bed. I don't think it's smart of me to sit next to her. This shit is getting to me, and she doesn't need my aggression. But when I look back into her eyes, she's begging me for comfort. She leans forward slightly and adds, "If it's alright, I want to talk." She noticeably swallows and looks back at the bowl of soup on the nightstand.

"Do you want more?" I ask. I quickly reach for it and climb on the bed to give it back to her.

"There's more downstairs if you like it." It's just a can of homestyle chicken noodle. But it does smell good.

She takes the bowl eagerly and smiles. "I do like it. My mother made us chicken noodle when we were sick, too." She spoons out the broth and blows on it before taking it into her mouth.

She seems happy with the memory, but the mention of her mother makes me sick. It reminds me of my own mother. Both our mothers were slaughtered.

"My mother did, too. Never from a can though." I grin at the memory. "My mother loved cooking," I say matter-of-factly, and settle on the bed next to her. This is better, I think. Besides, I'd rather talk about this.

She chuckles into the spoon and takes it greedily into her mouth. "My mother hated cooking. We had a chef. But not when I was little. Back then it was different."

I try to recall what I know of her father, but it's not much. I suppose her *famila* made more money later on in her life and that's why things changed for her. With the right setup and connections, there's a shit-ton of money to be made.

"A chef sounds nice." She shrugs her shoulders and takes another bite.

"I like cooking. But it's nice every once in a while."

I huff a humorless laugh. "I can grill, and I can bake, but I tend to burn shit on the stove."

She looks at me with a wide smile as she asks, "But it's harder to bake, isn't it?"

"Nah," I lean farther back and rest my back against the headboard, "Baking is just mixing up a simple recipe and you pop it in the oven."

"Oh, do you mean like Betty Crocker?" she asks, and I look at her with confusion.

"Of course, what did you think I meant?"

She sets the empty bowl down and tries to cover her mouth with her arm as she laughs while shaking her head. As I watch her shoulders rise and fall slightly with the sweet sounds of soft laughter, I realize how easy the atmosphere is between us.

This is Ava. I like this side to her.

"What kind of baking do you do?" I ask. I just want to keep the conversation going. I want this feeling to last.

"Like, fresh morning biscuits--" She looks reminiscent, and I interrupt to be an ass.

"They have those in a can. They're called Pillsbury." She outright laughs and swings her hand at me, playfully smacking me on the arm.

It triggers her, though. Her face falls and all sense of humor is gone. It's as though I had the real Ava to myself, if only for a small moment. But now she's gone. Replaced by the shell of a woman.

"Ava," I say, as I reach out to her. Her eyes dart to mine, but her body is tense and I can feel waves of anxiety pouring off of her. My hand lands on her thigh and I decide to keep things light. "You have to know what Pillsbury biscuits are, don't you?"

She quickly responds, "Yes. I've seen them before." Her body stays tense as though she's expecting a harsh reaction. It brings me back to reality. She's so fucking hurt.

It breaks my heart. I clear my throat and lean back against the headboard, patting the seat next to me. She obediently scoots closer.

"You're hurting. I want to help you," I say simply. I know the only way to help her is to make sure she never goes back to them. I know that. And I want to make sure that happens. I question if she'll ever be alright, but a feeling deep in my gut tells me I can heal her. I can take away her pain and make everything alright.

"Tell me what I can do, Ava." It's a command. It may be fucked up to take advantage of her submission. I don't feel comfortable pushing her to talk. But I have no problems pushing to find out how I can help her.

Her sad blue eyes look up at me as the corners of her plump lips tilt down. Her lips part and then close as her eyes fall. This is my Ava. I know this is her because she's giving me emotion, even if it is sadness. I pull her small body into my lap, wrapping my arms around her waist and she melts in my arms. Her hands grip my back, and she holds onto me tighter as I run my hand down her back with soothing strokes.

I hear her say something, but I'm not sure what she says since she's so quiet. I pull back to look at her, but she keeps the side of her head pressed to my chest and her fingertips dig into my back.

"I've got you, baby. Just tell me what to do." I run my hand along her back, hoping this is helping her. I was wrong before, with Felipe, but this can't be anything but good for her.

"Please," she barely whispers, "keep holding me." Hearing her plea breaks my heart. I kiss her hair and rest my chin on her head. I hold her close and keep rubbing her back.

If she wants, I'll do this all night.

Feeling her in my arms reminds me of the last time I held my mother. She didn't hold me back, though. They'd already killed her. The memory flashes before my eyes.

The car slams into another vehicle. The bullets fly past me, barely missing me. But my father clutches his chest, each bullet jolting his body as they pierce his back even through the thick seat. It happened so fast. We were driving to the drop, and then all of a sudden we weren't. The acrid smell of gas is still vivid in my memory. So is the sound of the bullets. My father's eyes stayed open even as he stopped breathing. I can hear my own voice screaming.

I remember reaching for my gun. I only got one shot off as the tires screeched, and I saw them drive off. I saw Paul and Cory in the back. They didn't see me stand back up as they slapped the front seats, urging whoever was driving to go faster. Unlike my father, I'd been wearing Kevlar, and it had saved my life.

I saw red. Nothing but red. But fear crippled me. I was barely coherent. I stood in the middle of the road as a car drove toward me. I walked toward it, forcing the driver to stop. My hand hit the hot hood. The thud sounded so loud.

"Are you alright?" the woman asked, as she clutched her chest. Panic was written all over her face. I remember how pale she looked, how frightened she was for me, but also *of* me. She wanted to help. Her eyes darted from me to our car. I saw them grow larger as she registered the bullet holes. I still feel like a fucker for pushing her to the right and getting in her car. She didn't try to fight, just backed away as I stole her car and took off.

It took fucking forever to drive home. It was only 15 minutes away. I drove like hell, laying on my horn and running red lights. It was surreal. I knew they would be headed there next. All I could do was try to get there first.

But I didn't. I couldn't save them. I got there too late.

My mother wasn't breathing. I remember holding her, waiting for her to react. Instead she was limp in my arms. I held her close, just wishing she would breathe. I rocked her just like this. Waiting for a breath. Some sign of life.

Ava pulls herself even closer to my chest and I realize I've stopped rubbing her back. I tilt my head down to kiss her forehead and whisper, "Good girl."

AVA

I lean against the table with both hands braced and my elbows locked. I stare at Marie with daggers in my eyes. I know she didn't study. She smells like coconut rum. She never takes things seriously. She's only two years younger than I am, but she's so fucking immature. She takes everything for granted. She doesn't remember what it was like before Dad got in with the mob and took over. She doesn't remember how hard it was. Fuck her arrogance. I can't stand it.

She's going to go through life wanting for nothing. Taking advantage of everything. Even if she fails, it doesn't matter. They'll still hand her a degree with smiles on their faces. All because of her last name and how deep our pockets go. And she's happy with that. She's completely content with her ultimate life goals amounting to nothing more than having an hourglass figure, long blonde hair and long legs that she's more than happy to spread.

Everything about her pisses me off. I fucking love my sister, but the person she's become her freshman year of college is horrific. She needs to get the fuck over this phase. My anger boils at the surface.

I open my mouth to lay into her again. But I can't. Her body jolts, and the wicked grin on her face vanishes. Then she's shot again. This time the bullet hits her chin. I see her head whip to the side. There's blood everywhere. I still don't register what's happened. I don't believe it. Not until I feel their hands on me. Even then I can't take *my eyes away from her. Her face is flat on the table. Blood is slowly soaking into her hair.*

No! It's not real!

But it is.

Thick, heavy arms wrap around me. I don't struggle. It's not real.

"What about this one, boss?" Felipe asks, with his sick, hot breath trailing down my neck. I struggle and try to scream out as I realize what's happening. I scream, but they don't hear me. I kick, but they don't flinch. I fight, but it's useless.

A hand wraps around my throat and squeezes. I can't breathe. I try to reach my throat, but I can't. My face turns hot as I struggle. I need to breathe.

"No, don't," I hear him say. The hand around my throat loosens, and my body sags forward in Felipe's arms as I heave in a gasping breath. "Let's get some use out of her."

* * *

"Ava!" Hands hold down my shoulders, and I struggle to move against them.

"No!" I scream out. I plead with them. My body tries to push them away.

But they'll only hurt you more when you do that, I hear the small voice say.

"Ava, wake up!"

I should listen to that voice. I don't want to be hurt. They're nicer when I listen. I go limp, letting him pin me down.

If you behave, he'll make it good for you. I gasp for breath and try to forget. It's wrong to feel this way. I need to listen, though. I need to live.

Why? Why do I need to live?

"Ava, please!" My shoulders shake and it makes my head slam against the pillow. Fingers dig into my skin.

Why do I want to live? What was the reason?

"Ava, wake up!" I hear Kane cry out so loud it hurts my head. I wince and slowly open my eyes. I feel dazed and my head hurts.

What have I done? He's upset with me. Kane's dark eyes stare down at me. His large shoulders cage me in. He's shirtless, and his breathing is heavy. I stay still and try to think. I don't know what happened.

"Are you alright?" He speaks softer than I expect. His eyes soften as his hand gently cups my face. I close my eyes, loving his touch, his affection. I just want him to hold me. I need him.

I lean forward and press my lips to his. *Please. Please touch me.* His lips are hard at first, since I caught him by surprise, but they quickly mold to mine. He leans into my kiss and I slowly lay my head back down. I reach my arms around his muscular body and pull him toward me. My blunt fingernails dig into his shoulders. I part my legs as his body comes closer to me. I need him.

He pulls away, breaking our kiss and leaving me wanting more. I don't know why I need his comforting touch. But I do. I need this pain to go away, this hurt in my chest. And Kane can do that for me. I need him.

"Please," I whisper. My chest heaves as his lustful eyes look down at me. He tries to back away, and tears threaten to burn my eyes. He doesn't want me. Why would he? I'm tainted. I've never been touched by a man before, other than raped. They took my innocence. Tears prick at the back of my eyes, and I have to close my eyes to stop them from falling. They took everything from me. But I could give my body to him. I want to. I want to feel what it's supposed to be like.

I risk his anger and plead again, "Please." I don't know how I'll be able to live if he denies me. I can't stand this pain. It feels like my chest is caving in on me. My throat closes, and I swallow the lump in my throat as he sits up and shakes his head.

"I won't take advantage of you." His denial chills my body. My arms cross and I turn to the side. I struggle to breathe.

What's wrong with me?

I'm ruined.

"Please, please," I whisper into the pillows. My eyes burn, but the tears don't come. I need to feel something other than this. I'm ashamed and humiliated to beg like this and be denied. But I should've expected it. If he wanted me that way, he would've had me already.

A shadow covers my body as Kane moves to lie behind me. He pulls me to his chest, but I stiffen. He feels sorry for me. But that's all he feels. He pities me, but there's no attachment. I tense as he kisses my neck.

And like a fool, I beg again. "Please, Kane."

"I don't want to hurt you." His lips tickle my neck as he breathes his words.

I roll over and brace my hands on his chest as I lean against him. His dark eyes are a storm of sadness, but I can still see a spark of desire. I push myself into his chest and crush my lips against his.

Please don't deny me. I moan as he kisses me back with passion. Yes! He rolls me onto my back and hovers over me.

I break the kiss and reach lower, needing to feel him. His hand catches my wrist, stopping me. "Please, Kane. I need you." His gaze is haunted, but I see that same spark of desire growing stronger. "I need you to take their touch away."

As soon as the words leave my lips his hands grip my hips, pinning me down. His lips push against mine. My hands tangle in his hair as I deepen my kiss. His fingers tickle my skin as they slide up under my shirt. A shudder runs through my body as his fingers just barely graze the sides of my breasts. I break our embrace as he pulls my shirt over my head.

I open my eyes and take in the sight of him, and see him doing the same with me. His muscular body ripples as he leans forward and takes my nipple into his mouth. His hands roam my body and stop at my hips. He gently bites my nipple and pulls back before letting it go. My pussy heats and my back arches, loving his touch. He pushes the pajama bottoms down my hips and kisses my lower belly as he takes them off of me completely.

He slowly pushes his own pants down with his eyes focused on my body. His plump lips are parted. His breathing is heavy. And the only thing sparking in his dark eyes is lust. His cock springs free and my eyes are drawn to it as he strokes it once.

Fuck. He's big. Holy hell. My thoughts must be evident on my face, because I hear him chuckle as he moves forward. He crawls toward me on the bed and I part my legs for him. My pussy clamps in anticipation. But the feeling of nothing makes me roll my hips and moan with need.

As he hovers over me, the rough pad of his thumb gently strokes my throbbing clit. My eyes widen, and my lips part in a silent scream. Fuck yes! My head thrashes to the side as waves of building pleasure threaten to crash down on me. Fuck. I breathe out heavily. I'm so close already.

"Cum for me." He whispers his command as his deft fingers pinch around the hardened nub. And I obey.

His lips push against mine and trap my scream of ecstasy. My body heats and tingles. The pleasure is almost paralyzing.

He pulls back as he lines up the head of his dick at my hot entrance. "Good girl." My body cools as my pussy tries to clamp around the tiniest bit of his large erection. I can feel how smooth and velvety the skin of his dick is as he slides it up my folds and pushes it against my sensitive clit.

I push my hips forward. I want him in me. I need him.

My lips part as he pushes in, stretching my walls. Absolute pleasure mixes with a slightly painful feeling as his dick moves deeper inside of me, pushing against my cervix. I breathe in through my nose as my mouth hangs open. It feels so good. I want more. At the same time, I feel the need to get away.

A cold sweat breaks out along every inch of my skin as he pushes in even deeper. "Fuck," I moan into the hot air, as my head falls back. He pulls out slightly and my head whips forward, my eyes locked on his.

"More." I push the word out, needing to feel that again. He bites his lip and leans forward, settling his forearm next to my head. His chest brushes against my sensitive nipples, and I want to move from the heated sensation that's directly connected to my clit, but his hand grips my hip and pins me down.

His lips brush against mine in a passionate but quick kiss. He takes my bottom lip between his teeth and gives me what I want, rocking into my heat slowly and pushing the head of his dick deep into my pussy. Filling every inch. Every nerve ending sparks with need. My body heats and cools too quickly.

"More," I moan, tilting my head to the side. He takes my lips with his and does the same. Over and over he thrusts into me with a slow, torturous, steady pace. My release rises higher and higher. The building sensation is so intense. I nearly fear the crash of my imminent orgasm threatening to consume me.

"Harder," I beg. "Faster." The words escape my lips in a desperate murmur.

But he hears them.

And he gives me what I ask.

His hips thrust hard against mine and he buries himself to the hilt. My nails claw at the sheets as I scream my pleasure. Again and again. Faster and faster he thrusts into me. His hand pushes against my leg, opening me up to him even more.

Pushing his hard length deep inside of me, his lips barely touch mine as he says, "Cum for me." His hand smacks hard against my clit, and my pussy spasms around his dick. Wave after wave of pleasure rocks through my body as he kneels back on his shins and grips my hips with both of his hands as he pumps in and out of me relentlessly.

Every inch of my skin is alive and tingling with infinite pleasure. He pounds into me, ripping through my orgasm. He pistons his hips all the way in and almost all the way out, over and over. My breasts bounce with each pounding fuck and my mouth opens with a silent scream.

I watch his muscles ripple with each thrust. The dim light shining through the windows leaves a contrast of shadows on his rigid, muscular chest. His dark eyes look down at me as he fucks me like he owns my body. The thought makes my pussy soak with arousal. He is the definition of power and lust. And I am his.

Fuck! Heat swirls deep in my belly. My body seems to ignite, and the tips of my toes and fingers go numb.

"Good girl." He continues to pound into me. "Cum on my dick again." His low baritone voice commands me as he mercilessly thrusts into me. I lose all sense of feeling. And then everything crashes down on me. My body thrashes beneath him and he thrusts all of himself deep inside of me. Hot waves of cum fill me as my body tenses with the overwhelming sensation.

I struggle to breathe as my orgasm hits me with near violence. My fingers dig deep into the sheets and mattress, and my heels dig into his ass, holding him there. I'm loving the intense pleasure.

His strong arms wrap around my sensitive body as he pulls out of me. He lies on his side and pulls me close to him. My body shivers without my consent as he kisses my hair. He pulls the covers around me and then kisses my cheek. I look up into his eyes and breathe slowly. He closes his eyes and leans down, pressing his lips to mine.

My heart clenches in my chest. A different kind of pain I've never felt before rises to the surface as his thumb gently brushes against my jaw. I feel the tears coming, so I break away and bury my head into his chest.

Just as quick as the unfamiliar emotion came, it leaves me. And I'm left only with exhaustion. I tilt my head and kiss Kane's jaw and then his lips, keeping my eyes closed. I can't look into his eyes. Fear nearly cripples me. There was something there--a spark. It gives me hope. And I can't have that.

Reality threatens to bring me down, but I push it away and wrap my arms around Kane. Whatever this is, I want to keep it. I don't want to lose this.

But I know I will. I can't hold on to hope. I won't.

KANE

I brush her hair away from her face. Ava's still asleep. She looks so sweet. So innocent. Guilt and regret make my chest hurt and my heart sink. I shouldn't have taken advantage of her. I'm holding her against her will. She's forced to stay with me.

And yet, she begged me for it.

It took everything in me to turn her down, every ounce of control I had. But I couldn't resist when she asked like that. I clench my jaw remembering her plea. "Take their touch away." The desire to kill every one of those fuckers rides me hard. I'm up against all odds, but there's no fucking way I'll ever let them touch her again.

She stirs in my arms and it brings me back to the moment. I held her all night, her back to my chest. I fucking love the feel of her soft skin against me. My fingers itch to trail along the dip of her waist. As my eyes travel her body I see her ribs and my desire falters.

She's still hurt, still suffering. I need to make this right for her.

The sound of my phone ringing on the dresser makes my eyes dart across the room. Ava stiffens in my arms, and it fucking kills me. She's scared. She's so used to waking up in fear that even after the night we shared, she still wakes up tense and full of apprehension. I quickly pull her body to mine and kiss her shoulder. My lips linger on her skin.

"Good morning, my good girl." I know that little pet name makes her relax, and it does the trick once again. Her body molds to mine as the phone rings again. I look from the phone down to her and see her baby blues looking at me, and a soft, small smile is on her lips. I give her a quick kiss and leave her warmth to walk across the room to my phone.

It stops ringing just as I get there, and I grind my teeth when I see the name. Abram.

Fuck.

It's not a good sign that he's calling. It doesn't have to be about Felipe, though. I fucking hope it's not, anyway. I breathe in deep and hit "call back". I put the phone to my ear and watch as Ava sits up in bed, covering herself with the blanket.

She's so fucking beautiful.

"Kane," Abram says flatly as he answers.

I don't want to respond as he expects, but I should. He needs to think everything is just fine while I figure out what my next move is. I can't let him onto anything. I don't have a plan, and I don't know who I can trust. I can't fuck this up and let him in on anything, so I answer like he wants me to, "Boss. Sorry I missed the call. What do you need?"

Ava stills on the bed as she realizes who I'm talking to. I make eye contact with her and put a finger over my lips. I look to the door thinking maybe I should get out of here so she can't hear what's going on. She's not going to like this conversation. But I want her to know everything. I want her to know what I'm telling Abram, and then I'll let her know what's going on once the call is over. I need to tell her she's never going back to him. I'll die before I let him take her from me.

"I'm not going to lie, Kane. I was worried for a minute. You're always quick with your phone." There's a moment of silence. He's waiting for me to answer and I don't fucking like it. I feel like I'm being tested. Something's up. Maybe he's heard about Felipe.

"Sorry boss, it was across the room and I was a bit busy."

"Is that so?" he answers, with a bit of humor in his voice, but that could be to throw me off. "Busy with my gift, I presume?" I fucking hate how he says that. She's not an object to be given.

Pain radiates in my chest as I answer, "Yeah, I won't lie. I've been enjoying this role." I enjoyed watching Felipe meet his death, so it's not a complete lie. He laughs on the other end. It's a short, robust laugh that comes deep from his chest. Ava's eyes fall. I fucking hate it. I walk closer to the bed and stand at the side next to her. She's motionless and looking unsure of herself. I grip her chin gently and tilt her to look at me. "It's okay," I mouth to her. I lean down and plant a kiss on her plush lips.

"Good. I was worried I'd made a mistake bringing you on," he says.

I smirk as I talk into the phone. "No mistake there, boss."

"You know you don't get to keep that one. But I'm willing to let you have whichever you want from each shipment. As long as you leave no permanent damage, of course." His words make me sick to my stomach, but I push it down.

"Of course. That's very generous of you." I decide to suck up to him like the little bitch he wants me to be. "I appreciate that."

"That's good news. Very good news, Kane. But we need to get back to business." He clears his throat and I straighten my back preparing for whatever's about to come through on the other line. It hasn't even been 12 hours since Felipe's been killed, but I have a bad feeling that this is exactly what the call is about.

"Have you spoken with the Valettis?"

"I had a meeting with them yesterday, boss. I think you'll be happy." I take a deep breath, ready to rattle off the shipping times that would be best to send the larger crates. I have to pretend it's for a different reason than sex trafficking. I can't stomach the thought of what's really going to be in those crates. "So there are--" I start to speak, but he cuts me off.

"I don't need to know any of that just yet," he says.

"Alright. Whenever you're ready."

"What I want to know is if Vince is fully on board with this?" I know I need to be smart about that answer. He saw Vince's face. He knows Vince was less than happy about this shit.

"I'll give it to you straight, boss. I think it's hard for him to stomach this shit. But..." I pause so he gets the feeling I'm working on his side of things for this. "...I think there's a way to make it a bit easier on him."

"I'm listening," he answers. I take a deep breath and look back at Ava, who's wide-eyed on the bed, listening. I don't want her to hear this. I'll have to tell her this is all horse shit. I'm sure she'll believe me, though. She has to know that everything I did yesterday was for her.

"I brought Ava along with me yesterday. I had to tone it down a bit for him, but I think he just doesn't enjoy seeing it. We'll just have to keep them out of sight, I think."

"You brought her out in public?" he asks disbelievingly. His voice is raised, and Ava can hear his words. Her eyes widen with fear, but I'm quick to pet her back and calm her.

"I think you underestimate me, Abram." It kills me to say the next words, but I have to. "She's very well-behaved. Vince was impressed, but I could tell he was still uncomfortable, so keeping it on the quiet side would suit him better."

"Was Felipe there yesterday?" he asks, with a hint of distrust in his voice. I know what Vince told him yesterday at the docks, that Felipe had just left, so I answer honestly.

"He was. He wasn't happy about her new collar."

Abram's voice carries a hint of relief. "Yes, I can imagine. He's rather fond of those." He clears his throat. "You do realize that Ava is special? The others won't be as trained as her. They'll be newer, and not broken in."

Fucking sick bastard. I have to bite back my disgust. "I figured that much."

"We'll keep them drugged though, so they'll be easy to handle." I want to ask him about Ava. About his plans for her, but he cuts me off.

"I haven't heard from Felipe since he told me that he was going to the Valettis' shipyard." He states it simply, without a hint of emotion.

"I haven't either boss, but if you'd like me to give him a call, I will."

"No. I'm certain he's dead, Kane."

His words chill me to the core. "The Valettis?" I ask.

"I can't imagine it would be anyone else. We'll have a meeting tomorrow."

"A meeting?" I have a real fucking bad feeling about that. "Is this staying between me and you, boss?" What I'm really asking is, is this an ambush?

"No. I need you to set it up. Let's do it at the docks so I can have a good look around."

"You really think they took him out, boss? That's not at all a good sign."

"I agree, Kane. But I've had better men killed for no reason. He's replaceable." He pauses and I think he's finished, but then he adds, "And so are the Valettis."

"I see." I answer simply, unsure of what he's looking from me.

"I'll decide tomorrow. I'll bring enough men to make sure that if I decide we'd rather go forward without them, it'll be easy to handle right then and there." I nod my head imagining the fucking bloodbath it would be. I can see it happening, and I don't fucking want it to.

"So you think it will work, then?" he asks, and I'm completely thrown off by the question.

"Taking them out? Of course, boss, there aren't many of them there at a time. Maybe six total yesterday." I'm sure as fuck giving the Valettis a heads-up. I'm not letting this shit go down like that.

"No, no. Working with them. I'm not certain I'm ready to take them out just yet."

"I do," I answer quickly and confidently. "Also, I think everything will be ready soon. If you decide to do business with them, that is."

"Even if I don't, we'll continue as planned."

"How many do you have ready?" I ask.

"Nine right now, but we're gathering the other three tomorrow." No. I need to stop that shit. I can't let that happen.

"Oh, boss." I have to think fast. "The boxes may not be able to carry more than eight." I'm met with silence.

"The other end can do 12. There's no reason the Valettis shouldn't be able to meet the same requirements."

"We can't do the large crate, boss. They'd only be able to fit the large crate one day a week. But that's not going to work 'cause of the guards that day." That's absolutely true. Or at least it's what Vince told me.

"Ah, shit." He sounds pissed. He starts cussing in Russian and I have no fucking clue what he's saying beyond the basic profanity. Part of me is worried Vince did lie to me and that he's in deep shit now with Abram because Abram knows better. Another part is freaking the fuck out that Abram can tell I'm trying to save those other girls. I just need a little time until I can figure out what I have to do to stop this shit. I can't let it happen. I won't.

"There's no way, Kane?" he asks, after a moment of calming his shit down.

"We could split the shipments," I offer. I need this to sound unappealing. "We could do eight on Monday, and then try for the other four the following Thursday."

"Only twice a month." I grit my teeth wishing I could lie and say yes. But I can't. He'd know. I'm sure he already knows this answer.

"Technically there are four. But like I said, the one is the verification day. I wouldn't risk that, boss."

"What about the fourth?" he asks.

"It's a longer trip, two stops before hitting Russia. It has more risks in getting caught, but also in losing some of the shipment." Some of the shipment. By that I mean the women will die. Being trapped in a box, sleeping in your own filth. Jesus, the others are only 10 hours. But even that thought makes me fucking sick.

"Losing?" He wants me to clarify. As if he doesn't understand how horrific that would be.

"It'll be days with no water," I say simply.

"Hmm. And they'll need another dose." He seems to be weighing the risk in his head, and it pisses me off. I look down at Ava. Her eyes on the blanket. She looks hopeless. I fucking hate it. I wish he'd let me get off the phone so I can talk to her. I need her to know I'm not going to let this happen.

"Alright, Kane. We'll go with your plan for now, but we're going to have to shake things up and get more women sooner. The timetable has changed. I'll have to dump one of the girls before Monday."

Chills run down my skin and I speak without thinking. "Bring them."

"What's that?" he asks, with irritation in his voice. He doesn't like that I made it a statement and not a request.

"I can take one with me. To practice." I clench my fists and restrain the sickness threatening to climb up my throat. "And we should test the Valettis on how they'll handle them. I think that will be a good gauge on whether or not this will really work with them."

"Smart thinking, Kane. And to think I wasn't sure you'd do well with this role." I press my lips into a thin line. "I'm proud of you, Kane."

"Thank you, boss. I want to make sure you know how seriously I'm taking this position."

"I can tell. And Kane?" he asks.

"Yeah, boss?"

"Don't fuck up this meet tomorrow." His words come out hard.

"Of course not." Anxiety shoots through me.

"If they aren't on board with the shipment, we'll simply end the relationship there. So make sure you're ready for that."

"Got it. I'll be ready."

"I'll see you tomorrow, then. I'm looking forward to it." I can practically see the wicked grin on his face.

"Me, too," I answer, as I hear the click on the other end.

Tomorrow. It's going down tomorrow.

KANE

My fist bangs on the front door with a hard knock that echoes in my head. Anxiety and adrenaline are coursing through me. It was different on the phone. I was calm. I was calculated. Now I need to figure shit out. This setup is fucked. I have no one. My best bet is to trust the Valettis.

I need someone. I need backing. I can't go in there guns blazing and take out Petrov's entire crew by myself. That's a fucking death wish. I'm not stupid. I'm going to need help, but I have no one.

I kept thinking on the drive over, what if I'm reading Vince wrong? What if he's set with doing business and Felipe was a one-off? Like maybe he gets his kicks from randomly knocking off pricks. He could have the same feelings as Abram. That same nonchalant attitude that fuckers are gonna die in this business, so it doesn't matter.

I'm not sure how Vince is going to react. I'm not sure how much I should tell him, either. I guess I'm about to find out.

As I hear someone walking toward the door, I take a glance at Ava. Her shoulders are squared and her eyes are forward. I reach down and take her small hand in mine. She faces me with a small smile, but I can see she's worried. I lean down and give her a small kiss. I know the conversation this morning was upsetting for her. I told her everything, though. And I promised I'd get her out of this shit.

She's a smart girl though. There's no doubt in my mind she's questioning whether I'll be able to make it happen or not.

I debated on whether or not I should bring her with me. But I want her to hear. I want her in on this. It's not good to have women involved. But she's a part of this, and she deserves to know.

Besides, this is just me and Vince. Maybe another man or two. If they try anything, if I think anything is going to happen to her, they're fucking dead. I can't take out 20 men on guard, but I can sure as fuck kill two or three pricks if I have to. I told her to just stay behind me if she's not feeling safe.

I'll protect her. As far as I'm concerned, she's mine.

The door swings open and a man I recognize from the initial meet at my hangar answers. He's a bit taller than Vince. Looks just like him though. If I had to guess I'd say he's Vince's brother, but I don't have to. He introduces himself right away.

He smirks as he says, "I'm Dom, Vince's brother and the bookie."

"Nice to finally be introduced to you, Dom." I give a tight smile back.

"Come on in." He opens the door wider and takes a look at Ava. She's wearing the collar I got her, and I watch the smile on his face falter as he sees it. I wasn't going to put it on her, but the thought of running into one of Petrov's men without something that displays what she is to them...well, that shit wouldn't end well.

"Ava, come on in." His eyes soften some as she smiles up at him.

"Thank you, Dom," she says in a soft, sweet voice. I place my hand on the small of her back and lead her in front of me. Dom's eyes harden and narrow as he watches me. I know he's wondering what the fuck is going on. Quite frankly I'm wondering, too. There's something between us. Given the situation, it wouldn't be right of me to say she's my girl. But that's exactly how I feel. She's mine.

We walk in relative silence through a large foyer and down a hall to an office. The first thing I do is count how many men are in the room as Dom shuts the door behind us.

All eyes are on me when I walk in. Dom's behind me. Vince is at the desk. I recognize Tommy to the right, leaning against the wall, and I assume the older man in the chair to my left is Mr. Dante Valetti, the former Don, and Dom and Vince's father. I give them each a nod in greeting.

"Mr. Valetti," I say, extending my hand to Dante.

His brows raise and he shakes my hand firmly. "Kane. It's nice to have you here. I'm sorry for your loss."

My chest tightens with pain. I respond with a small, "Thank you." I walk Ava over to the chair and settle her in the seat. They're the only two, but I don't mind standing.

"You want Ava to stay?" Dante asks. Before I respond, he addresses Ava directly. "No disrespect, Miss Ivanov. We usually try to keep women away from business matters." It gives me pride that they're talking to her, but she goes still at the question, and looks to me rather than answering.

"She's involved to an extent that I feel she deserves to know everything." I gently place my hand on her shoulder. I look down at her as I add, "But only if you want to, Ava." I should've asked. I feel like an asshole for assuming she'd want to know. Shit. I need to stop doing that.

She turns her eyes to Dante and answers, "I'd like to stay, if that's alright." She looks so small and vulnerable sitting beneath me.

"Let me grab another chair," Dom says, as he opens the door behind us.

"If that's what you want, that's fine with me," Vince says, exchanging a look with his father and then giving Ava a sad smile. "I'm sorry you're in this situation, Ava."

He looks at me and starts to speak, but the noise of the door opening and Dom carrying in another chair stops him. I'm quick to take it, but it makes me feel weak. Both hands are on the chair, and I'm in a room with four men who could kill me at any time. I quickly set it down to the right of Ava and take a seat. My heart beats heavy and fast in my chest.

I clear my throat a bit and take a deep breath. "Vince, I need to know where your head's at."

His eyes search mine as he places his elbows on the table and forms a steeple with his fingers. His chin rests on his hands and he deliberately looks at Ava's collar. My fists clench, but I give him a moment to fucking say whatever's on his fucking mind.

"I think I'd like to know where your head is first, Kane."

"Fair enough." I push out the words and lean forward in my seat. "I told you I won't be the go-between for you and Abram. I told you before I don't handle this sort of business."

"What is that you did for the Armenos?" he asks, interrupting my train of thought.

"I was in charge of..." I trail off, and look to my left at Ava before answering. I don't want her to know. I don't need her to know this shit. I don't want her to look down on me either, so I choose my words carefully. "I did the collecting mostly. Occasionally I had to help with assisting people with their memories." I fucked people up when they didn't pay, and when they didn't talk. That's the truth.

A corner of Vince's lips kicks up into an asymmetric smirk. His eyes dart to Ava and then back to me. "You sure you want her here for all of this?" he asks.

"No." I settle back in my seat and run a hand down my face. "But she said she wants to stay, so I kinda fucked myself over there, huh?"

The men in the room laugh but Ava looks at me nervously and sets her small hand down on my forearm. She lowers her voice and leans in to talk to me, "I don't have to."

I lean over the chair and give her a quick kiss. I know she likes it when I do that. "Stay right where you are. I want you to know what's going on."

"I'd like to know, too," Vince says, as I turn back to him and take Ava's hand in mine.

I give her hand a squeeze and get to the point. "Abram wants a meeting tomorrow."

"Tomorrow," he says, but it's more of a question.

Before I can tell him it's a setup, Tommy speaks up. "Told you he'd fuck us over."

"Becca's gonna be pissed. She knows there's no class tomorrow." I hear Dom's voice from behind me, and I have to turn around to look at him.

"So it's a setup then, Kane? Abram doesn't want to do business? Or is this about Felipe?" Ava grips onto my hand at the mention of Felipe.

My thumb rubs soothing circles on the back of her hand as I speak. "More than likely. If I had to guess, I'd say he's leaning toward taking over."

"How many men do you think will be there?"

"More than a dozen. He's bringing the new women, too." I have to push out the last part and readjust in my seat. "I told him to."

"You like women bringing into this shit, don't you?"

I force myself to stay calm. "I don't." Fuck. That came out sounding pissed off, and I didn't mean it to. "He was going to collect more..." I pause, fucking hating talking about this shit. "But I told him we could only take eight and to bring the nine he already has there so..." I take a breath and try to keep my shit calm with what I'm about to say next. "So I could pick one to keep for when he takes Ava back."

It's quiet and awkward for a moment. All eyes are on me and they're searching for answers to questions that are obvious. They aren't going to budge. They aren't speaking first. Fine. I'll man the fuck up and lay out the plans for them. "I don't intend on going through with Abram's plan for tomorrow."

"What was it that you're planning, then?" Tommy asks. Vince's eyes stay on me. What I say next is going to determine whether or not I live or die tomorrow.

"I'm planning on killing as many of Petrov's men as I can."

"That's suicide," Vince says calmly, with a brow raised.

"It's that, or go through with what Petrov has planned. And I'd rather die." I take a moment to let that sink in. A cold sweat breaks out along my skin. "It'd be easier if I had someone backing me."

"Someone?" Vince asks, with a cocky smile.

Dom laughs from behind me and smacks my back as he walks forward to stand at his father's side. "You coming too, Pops?"

"Of course." The old man has grey hair and tough skin with wrinkles around his eyes. But he's still toned muscle and there's no doubt in my mind that he couldn't take down a man as well as I could. He only stepped down a few months ago.

"So I can count on you, Vince?" I would feel more confident hearing him say the words.

"Petrov thinks he can make deals and then stab backs," he says, as he stands up from behind the desk. "I know all about that rat and the shit they've pulled." He walks around the desk and stands in front of me, leaning back against the front of the desk. "I knew this was coming. I just wasn't sure whether or not I'd have to kill you, too."

A smile grows on my face. "I'd appreciate it if you didn't." Vince's smile widens and Tommy lets out a laugh.

"You have my word, Kane." Vince extends his hand and I stand up to take it with my own in a firm shake.

"Can you shoot, Ava?" Dante asks to my left, taking my attention away from Vince.

"I can," she answers confidently. I remember Felipe though, and how she held the gun with shaky hands. They'd shoot her first. They'd kill her before she got a shot off.

"I don't want to bring her." Even as the words leave my lips, I know I have to. I can't react on my emotions. I have to be smart. I thought about removing her chip and giving her a head start. But according to her, they'd know. And judging by how fast Felipe was on her, having her go off with it in her wouldn't be wise either. I have no fucking clue who else is tracking her.

"You need to. You'll fuck it up if you don't." I grit my teeth and try to come to terms with this. I can't risk putting her in danger though. When shit goes down, I'm going to be on Abram's side of things. I'll be an easy target. With me gone, I don't know how Ava will make it through this.

"Promise me that she never goes back to them." I look him straight in the eyes. I need to know he'll take her if Abram takes me down before I can get her to safety.

"You have my word." Vince puts a hand on my shoulder. "I'll make sure she's safe."

AVA

"It's gonna be alright, baby. I promise you." I straighten my shirt and then look back into the mirror. It's only been three days with Kane, but the change is so significant. I'm no longer in a raggedy and soiled dress with shackles around my wrists, and a metal collar digging into my neck.

I reach up and touch the small bandage peeking out from underneath the thin leather collar. The nasty cut it's covering has almost healed, but not quite. My fingers travel along my collarbone. I can still see the bones sticking out just beneath it, but not nearly as much as before. My skin looks more vibrant now that I've slept.

I'm not the person I was before this nightmare began, but I'm healing. Slowly. My eyes spot the silvery scar of *his* bite mark on my shoulder. Some things will never heal.

My eyes catch sight of Kane in the mirror, and all the anxiety rising in the pit of my stomach settles. He did this to me. But we're getting ready to leave. I'll either leave with him, or I'm going to die. I won't let them take me back. Today is my chance. I won't risk not taking it. My fingers rest on the butt of the gun under my shirt. You can't even see it there because of the way the blouse hangs.

"Stop thinking about it. I'm sure you won't even need it." He has no idea. I know he'll be angry with me. He doesn't want me to do anything but hide behind him. I can't tell him what I have planned. I nod my head and act like I'll obey. But I have every intention of putting a bullet in Vadik's head.

After I kill Vadik though, I may not be Kane's good girl anymore. The thought makes my heart clench with agony. He may be angry with me. Even worse, he may not want me anymore.

"Just one more time, Kane. Please." I need this. I need to feel him once more. It may be the last time I ever feel his touch. I hope we live through this. But if we don't, I just want one more time with him.

He walks up behind me and wraps his arms around my waist. He pulls my body into his, and I can feel his erection digging into my back. I want to drop to my knees in front of him. I want to please him. I want him to know I can still be his good girl.

"I do want you again baby, but we have to go." His full, plump lips leave an open-mouth kiss on my neck. I close my eyes, loving his warmth. And then it's gone. He takes my hand in his.

"We need to go." I want to resist. I want to tell him no. I don't want to go. But this needs to happen. I need to end this nightmare one way or another.

I nod my head and swallow thickly.

"It's gonna be alright," he whispers, and kisses my forehead. "Just stay behind me, stay close."

I look him directly in the eyes and lie, even though it hurts me. "I will, Kane." I stop myself before more words tumble out. Three words that seem so natural to say. My heart twists and aches. I'm not sure if it's because I didn't tell him the truth just now, or because I really do love him.

* * *

THE SOUND of our shoes and the blood rushing in my ears are all I hear as I walk next to Kane on his right side, slightly behind him. A lump grows in my throat, but I do what I've done to survive since this nightmare began. I hide away. I bury myself deep down, and pretend it's not real. The pain goes away, and all the noise vanishes. My heart calms. This is all just pretend.

Kane grips my hands and I obediently respond as I know he'd like me to. I squeeze back. And then he releases me. My heart thumps painfully in my chest as he opens the door to the large warehouse. It groans and reveals the location of what I imagine will be my death. I've resigned myself to that fate. I can only hope that *he* dies first.

Everyone is already inside. A natural division separates two groups of men. I don't count the numbers, but it seems relatively even. On the left are Petrov's men. I recognize most of their faces. Shame overwhelms me as memories flash before my eyes. Their sick, twisted smiles, their stale breath in my face. Their hands on me. And then that shame is replaced by rage. My fingers itch to touch the gun. But drawing attention to it would be useless.

It's relatively quiet, save for the soft laughter from Petrov's lips over something one of the men behind him said. There are a few other laughs that echo in the large storage room of the hall.

"Are all of them there?" Abram calls out from behind him to someone else entering the large space. The walls are made from drab cinder blocks, and the ceiling is at least two stories high. I don't look around more than that though, I keep my head forward and my eyes on the floor.

We walk closer, keeping between the two groups of men. I'm closer to the right side, where the Valettis are, and doing my best to stay close to Kane like he told me to.

"Yeah, all nine of them," someone calls out to my left. I can see Vince out of the corner of my eye. He's talking to someone I've seen before in a low voice, but his body is positioned toward the rest of the men.

"Good," a deep Russian voice says. I know it instantly. My eyes whip up to find Vadik, standing directly next to Abram. He always is. He likes to pretend Abram's the one making the moves. But I know better. I've seen the way Vadik orders him around when I'm chained to the floor, being as still as possible so they forget I exist.

This is my chance. I don't waste a second. The moment I see *him*, my hand is on the gun. I know Kane told me to stand behind him, but I can't. I have to do this. I have to free myself of him.

"Fuck!" I hear Vince call out to my right just as I grip the gun and point it at Abram. One shot. Bang! I don't waste any time I move the gun slightly as Vadik tries to grab Abram to shield himself.

Bang! The second shot grazes Vadik's arm, and other shots and screams ring out. I hit the arm he had wrapped around Abram. Abram's limp body falls to the floor as two shots from someone else hit his chest.

Bang! Bullets whip past me, but I get off my shot and hit Abram in the chest as he aims his gun at me. Bang! A bullet skims past my thigh, slicing it. Maybe worse, but I don't look. I don't care. I'm prepared to die.

I run past Kane as he yells out for me to stay behind him. "No!" he screams, but his voice sounds distant. I'm faster than him, though. Both his hands are on his gun when he yells as I pass him, but he quickly reaches out a hand for me. He nearly grabs hold of my shirt to pull me back. But he misses. Bang! Bang! The bullets fly through the air as I get closer to my target.

I see everything in a blur. And then I only see him. He's gripping his arm on the ground and reaching for a gun nearly two feet away from him. Bang!

His body jolts and he screams out as his hand flies to his chest. Bang! A bullet flies through the center of his throat. Bang! A headshot, and he lies motionless on the ground.

I fire again, but there's no bang. Only a click. I watch as blood flows from the neat hole in his throat. It spills onto the concrete and pools around his neck. Again I pull the trigger. And again there's only a click. Again. Again. Tears sting at the back of my eyes.

I need to kill him. But I'm out of bullets. His dark eyes stare back at me unmoving, threatening me. Like they did that night that he took me. After they'd all had their turn. After he'd killed my father. When I thought he'd end my life, instead he took me. He took Viagra so he could make sure he got everything he wanted from me. He tortured me. He trained me to be nothing but a toy for him. He used me to broker deals. He made sure I felt like a whore. Like I was nothing but a slave to him. Like I owed him for not taking my life.

Those eyes stare back at me. I point the gun, but nothing happens. Click. Click. Click. I hear screaming and bullets flying around me. Men run past me in a blur. Click. Click.

I can't let him live. I drop to the ground. My knees slam hard into his chest as I smash the butt of the gun against his face. I do it as hard as I can. The gun stings my hand as the metal crunches bone. I raise my arm higher and slam it into his face again. And again. Hot blood splashes against my chest. I do it again, and instead of crunching bone I'm met with the sick sounds of soft flesh.

I look down at what I've done. I'm breathing heavily. My hand is covered in blood, still gripping the gun. My face and chest are splattered with blood. I look for his eyes in the mess beneath me. I gasp and hardly take in the sight before strong arms grip me from behind and pull me into him.

"Don't look," a voice whispers in my ear. *Kane.* The gun falls from my hand and I turn in his grasp.

"Kane." I hold onto him. My fingers dig into his back. Kane. He'll save me. He'll fix this. Shock and horror grip my heart, stilling it and freezing my blood. "I'm sorry." I pull away from him and look him in the eyes. My bottom lip trembles as I apologize again. "I'm so sorry."

"Shhh. It's alright. It's alright."

"Am I still your good girl?" I ask. He looks at me with a pained expression. I'm still good. I can be his good girl. It was only once. I'm still good. I can still be good. I need him to forgive me. I need to be his good girl. If I'm not, then I'm nothing. Images of Vadik's eyes and his yellow teeth flash before my eyes. I hear his voice taunting me in my head. "You're nothing but mine." I bury my head in Kane's chest and shake my head, willing the images to go away.

No. I'm not his. I'm not his. I'm Kane's. I'm Kane's good girl. I'm his good girl. I'm still good. "Please," I whisper into his hard chest. Tears sting at the back of my eyes, threatening to fall, but not coming. "Am I still your good girl?" My voice cracks, and my throat dries with a harsh scratch on each word.

"Shh. You're still my good girl." His hand comes down on my back and runs soothing strokes over my tense body.

Everything's alright. I lean into his embrace and breathe in deep. I take comfort in his warmth. I'm Kane's now. The thought soothes a sick part of me. A darkness within me wanes, but it's still there.

KANE

"*Y*ou're alright, baby." I kiss her hair and look around the room. I can't fucking believe she's the one who fired first. She put herself in danger. She put the rest of us in danger. To be fair though, we all knew. Every fucking one of us was wearing Kevlar. They weren't. Cocky fuckers.

Dead bodies are still lying on the ground. Two have been removed. Their blood left streaks across the floor as they were dragged out of the room. Valettis. It fucking hurts my chest. Two lost. But that's two too many. The cleanup crew sprays something on the ground. They're almost done cleaning up the evidence they don't want found.

One's a young boy, maybe in his early 20s. He wasn't here when this shit started. He's not one of the group that flew in here when bullets started flying. Vince was smart. The numbers were stacked in his favor, but they were hidden.

I need to take her out of here. I walk us to the back quickly and spot an open door with soft voices coming from beyond the jamb. At this distance I can only make out incoherent murmurs. I know it's the women, though. The shipment. I walk to the open doorway and take a look inside.

Nine women are lying on their sides in the middle of the room. They're strung out on something so fucked, they couldn't even sit in the chairs.

They're normal women. Wearing I'm guessing whatever clothes they were taken in. The entire room smells like piss. Most have scratches or bruises somewhere on their bodies.

One woman is leaning against the wall. Her eyes are vacant and her body is swaying. Two men are beside her. One is holding her up, while the other is kneeling on the floor. The one kneeling digs through a small black bag. When he looks up at her, I recognize him as Anthony. He stands up, opens her eyes, and flashes a small light into them.

Fuck. That poor woman. All of them.

I force myself to look away. They're safe now. But they wouldn't have been. I wish I could've done something more. I wish I'd done something sooner, before any of this shit happened. Maybe this sick feeling is why my uncle turned to the feds. Regret consumes me. I know I'd be dead if I had acted earlier, though. And then where would those women be? I hold Ava tighter and keep walking.

Vince is straight ahead. I have to ask to make sure. "You call them yet?"

"Not yet." We're just waiting on Anthony to give the okay to leave them so we're gone when the LEOs get here.

"They need to remain in the room." His eyes dart to Ava. "Just so they'll be easily found." My grip on her tightens.

"I understand." I say it simply, but my tone is hard.

"We're all set, boss. She's gonna make it," Anthony announces from behind me. He walks past me to Vince. As he stands at his boss's side, he also looks at Ava and then at me.

I won't fucking do it. She needs me. I won't leave her with the Valettis. And they aren't taking me away from her either. I struggle to come up with an excuse. I know she's not okay. The way she looked after she fucking mutilated Vadik. I know she's not alright. But I can help her. I need to be there for her. I know they won't let her go when she knows as much as she does. She's a mafia princess. She should be respected and she knows the rules to keep her mouth shut. But I don't know if they'll live up to the unspoken rules. I'm not letting her go. Not with them. Not with anyone.

Vince stares at me as he answers Anthony. "Alright, time to call 'em." He finally looks at Anthony and says, "Let's get the fuck out of here."

The two of them walk past me and Vince glances over his shoulder. "You'll hear from me later tonight."

I nod my head and stay right there, holding onto my girl. The thought warms my chest. That's exactly who she is. My girl.

I hear the men yell as Vince turns the corner and tells them to get the fuck out. I take that as my cue and walk her out of the back. I quicken my steps to get to my car as fast as fucking possible and get her in the passenger side. The other cars are in front of me, but the Valettis aren't there yet. I look to my right and there's no one there. As I walk around the car to my side I look to my right, still no one.

And then I open my door and slide in, my heart beating wildly in my chest. I feel like a fucking thief. I need to get her out of here. I put the car in reverse and look in the rear view mirror.

Vince looks at my car, and I swear he makes eye contact with me. But then he turns around and walks to a black Range Rover in the back.

I know he saw us.

I don't know what he's going to do about it.

But I don't fucking care. She's mine.

AVA

"*I*'m sorry, baby," Kane says, as the blade slips out and blood runs down my arm. I wince at the sight, and seethe through my teeth. I turn away as he uses the tweezers to get the tracker out before wrapping a towel around my arm. It doesn't hurt right now because of the drugs I'm on, but I know it's going to catch up with me later. Fear grips me, but then I remember. They're all dead. No one is going to know it's out of me. Even if they do, they don't have the backing to come for me. All of them are fucked with the data Tony found and sent to the police.

I'm happy and grateful that Kane told me. I want to believe I have no reason to be scared anymore, and knowing that helps. But I'm still terrified. We have no one. It's just the two of us hiding out in an abandoned safe house. If the Valettis are planning on screwing us over, we're fucked.

I look back at my arm as the towel grazes my hand. He takes the towel away and I'm surprised to find only a small and neat cut where the tracker used to be. He's quick to put a small bandage over it. His hand travels the length of my arm and stops at my wrist where a small barcode is tattooed. Instinctively, I itch to touch the scar on my shoulder. These are two marks that will forever stay with me, and they'll never let me forget.

He stands with the bloodied tracker wrapped in the towel and walks to the front door. He grabs the hammer that's sitting on the stairway banister before going outside. I close my eyes and listen as he smashes the tracker to nothing.

I wait in the silence for him to tell me what to do. There's no plan; I'm not certain he'll keep me. If he doesn't want me, I'll have nowhere to go. I grew up in the States, before we moved back to Russia, but I have no family here. I have no family at all anymore.

My chest feels hollow and rings with pain. If Kane doesn't want me, I have no one. I have nothing. I hear Vadik's vicious words in my head as he sneers, "You are nothing."

I shake my head and close my eyes tightly, denying it. I can't be nothing. I cross my arms and grab my shoulders, needing to be held. I don't want to be nothing.

"Ava, baby, what's wrong?" I open my eyes and see Kane. His arms open and wrap around me, bringing me into his chest.

I'm not nothing. I'm *his*.

I hold onto him and bury my head in his chest. I need to hear him say it. I need that, but I don't dare ask. I'm too afraid to hear the answer.

"It's all going to be alright. I'm so sorry you had to go through that. I'm sorry I even brought you along." My eyes open at his words, but he can't see that. I'm not sorry I was there. I'm fucking happy I killed them. But he wouldn't be happy with that.

What kind of person am I that I revel in the fact that *I'm* the one who killed *him*?

"Ava, I'm going to ask you this once. Do you want to stay with me?" I pull away from him, eager to answer. But before I can, he puts a finger over my lips to shush me.

"Just hear me out first." I nod my head as his finger leaves my lips. I don't care what he has to say though. My answer is already decided.

"I have enough money to take us wherever we need to go. I was smart about shit, and we can get by for a long fucking time. But I don't have anything else lined up. I don't know where we'll go." His eyes look past me, and his face turns stern. "Before we leave, I have to have a chat with Vince, too." He swallows hard before looking back at me.

He cups my chin in his hand, and tilts my head to face him. He leans in with his nose brushing mine, and plants a small kiss on my lips. "But this is real for me. What we shared. I've never felt that before, and I want it, Ava. More than anything else."

His words melt my heart. A warmth floods through me. Security, desire, and something else. Something I'm afraid to admit.

"I want it too, Kane. Please." I look up at him through my thick lashes and see a sexy-as-fuck grin growing on his face.

"I'm all yours then. I'll take care of us, baby."

"Yes, Kane," I say diligently. He backs away slightly, and I have to force my expression to remain as he likes it.

"You okay, Ava?" he asks, with a slightly worried tone in his voice.

No, I'm not. I know I'm not okay. But he won't want this fucked-up version of me.

I press my lips together to keep the automatic response of "Yes, Kane" from coming through. He doesn't like that. Or he at least doesn't want it right now. So I nod my head instead and offer him a sweet smile.

He smirks at me and leans in for another kiss before saying, "Good girl."

It soothes the broken part of me. That's all I need right now. I just need to keep being his good girl.

KANE

*M*y nerves are getting the best of me. I like Vince. I like the other fuckers sitting in the room--Tommy, Anthony, and Dom. But I know he's pissed at me. I directly disobeyed him again. He's fucking pissed. I just got here. And Dom brought me back here without saying a word. We're in the same office as before. I'm sure they aren't planning on getting rid of me here, though. Mostly because there's a nice carpet beneath my feet and not a plastic tarp.

"What are you doing, Kane?" Vince finally asks. His fists are clenched and laying on the table. Pretty sure this isn't going to come to blows, but if it does, I'm gonna be pissed. He's the Don, and he has every right to beat the shit out of me. I'm not going to be able to fight back. That'd be a serious infraction. But I won't fucking like it. Technically I could fight back, but I don't want to be an enemy of the Valettis. That, and there are three other men in the room that could hold me down. Maybe it's a compliment that so many men are present.

"I have feelings for her, Vince. She needs me. I'm not going to lose her." I push the words out. I don't know if he'll understand, but he's going to have to get used to it.

She's mine. And it's staying that way.

"And how are you going to take care of her? You've got a target on your back, and no family behind you." He narrows his eyes and leans forward before adding, "What are you going to do about that?"

Is this fucker serious? Is he really questioning my ability to take care of Ava? That motherfucker. I bite my tongue and try real fucking hard not to turn my hands into white-knuckled fists. But I fail miserably.

I watch as his eyes travel to my fists and he smirks. "You don't like that, do you?"

"No, I don't fucking like what you're implying."

"The fact that she'd be better off without you." He leans back and shrugs as he says, "All of our women would be better off without us. We know it. They know it." He points a finger at me. "You know it, too."

A tightening pain spreads through my chest. I know she would be better off without me. But I'm a fucking bastard, and she said yes. That's all I need to keep her. I stare back at him with the air between us crackling.

"I'm not letting her go," I bite out, making sure he knows we're going to have problems if he tries to take her from me.

"That's fine." His eyebrows raise. "But that's not what I asked. What are you going to do, Kane? Where are you going to go?"

I try to relax some. I take a moment to think of an answer. I could go anywhere, and do anything. But I'm fucking good at being in the mob. I'm damn good at what I do. That, and Vince is right; there's a huge fucking target on my back. Now I've taken out two families that were big names. It's not good to be too well-known.

People tend to disappear when they reach a certain level of visibility. They're a threat, they're also a competitor. I don't need every fucking guy out there thinking he can prove something by getting the best of me. And that's a very real possibility at this point.

"I'm asking you what your plan is, because I need someone I can trust, and I'm not sure if that person is you." The last line comes out hard. His anger is coming back in full force.

"What can I do for you?" For the first time in a long time, hope starts to creep up on me. If I can get into Vince's good graces, things may turn out to be just fine. People don't fuck with the Valettis. It'd be a dream come true to get in tight with them. Maybe I could become a made man if I can prove my loyalty to them. My blood spikes with doubt. Ava. I doubt Vince would make me a made man for constantly going rogue.

But I can fucking try.

"Tommy's being watched. He's out on bail."

My eyes dart to Tommy in the corner of the room. I thought the stale air and tension in the room were solely because of me. I hadn't picked up on the different emotions. Vince and Anthony are pissed. Dom looks anxious as fuck. But Tommy, he just looks defeated.

"What do they have on you?" I ask him.

"My prints at the scene, on one of the women's shoes..." He pauses and looks at the ceiling before continuing. "And one of them said she recognized me." Fuck. That's so fucking bad. But they were all drugged up, so I can't imagine it's going to stick.

"So the women, and all of Petrov's dead men." His voice is flat.

"They're pinning all that on you?" Holy fuck! Tommy is screwed.

"The evidence is minimal, which is why he's out." Vince cuts in. "Well that, and we have the judge in our pocket." Even with a judge on their side, those charges aren't going to be easy to beat.

"They want him to talk more than anything. Those fuckers will pin anything they can on us to fuck us over." Vince is getting worked up again, so I stop him and get back to the conversation at hand.

"So what do you need, boss?" I ask him, leaning forward in my chair.

He gives me a small, crooked smile. "I'm gonna need for you to take over Tommy's route in the meantime. I believe you would be a good fit."

Pride fills my chest and I nod slowly, although I'm eager to take this opportunity.

"I'm happy to help however I can."

"Good," Vince says, smacking his hand on the desk.

"I won't disappoint you guys," I say, looking at each of them.

"I know you won't." Vince smirks. "That's why I asked you."

I smile back at him and get ready to take down all the information I'm gonna need from Tommy. But before I can open my mouth Vince adds, "You're not off the hook just yet, though. We're watching your girl."

"Watching?"

"Just to make sure you're the kind of man I think you are. We don't tolerate certain things like other families do."

"I've never smacked a woman around before, if that's what you're getting at."

He looks at me for a minute before taking a deep breath and finally answering, "I just wanna make sure you're the man I think you are."

I give him a stern nod. I hear the clause in there that's not said aloud. If I'm not that man, he's going to have to take me out. I hear it loud and fucking clear. But I'm not worried. Ava and I are solid.

I'm not worried about a damn thing.

AVA

*T*his is going to hurt, but not nearly as much as the pain I felt when they held me down and tattooed the barcode on.

"You ready, baby?" Kane asks, as he gently rubs my back. My ass is firmly planted on what looks like an exam bed from a doctor's office. I take a deep breath and look down at the quote I picked out. It's in a beautiful scroll with my sister's initials added to the end made to look like a small heart and it reads *forever in my heart*. The way the artist drew it, it should cover the barcode so it's not even noticeable.

At least I hope it won't be.

I bite my lip and then nod. "I'm ready." I let out a deep breath and hold out my wrist.

The tattoo artist, Aaron, is a big man made of lean muscle. Tattoos cover his entire neck and, from what I can see, both of his arms. I wouldn't be surprised if his chest and back were covered, too. But there's an air of professionalism about him. As he wipes down my wrist I can tell there are questions in his eyes, but he doesn't ask.

I'm grateful for that. I just want to forget. I want to forget all of it.

As Aaron turns on the machine and it comes to life with a loud hum, Kane takes my other hand in his and squeezes.

"Talk to me." The words tumble out of my mouth. I just want something to distract me so I can ignore the pain. The needle touches my skin and I wince, but stay still. "Please," I add.

"Did you decide on one for your shoulder?" he asks. It chills me to the bone.

I don't want one there, but he does. He thinks it would be good to cover it up. But it's already fading. I don't want to draw any more attention to it. I just shake my head. There's no point in trying to cover every scar.

I have too many scars. They'll never be gone.

He can sense I'm upset, and I know he doesn't like it. I need to stop it. He leans down and kisses my temple.

I have to be his good girl. He needs me to be happy. I'm so far from happy, though.

"I'll think of something," I finally answer, and put a smile on my face.

"Whatever you decide, baby, I'm sure it'll be beautiful." He grabs my chin between his fingers and tilts my chin up to him. He plants a soft kiss on my lips and it soothes me.

He's happy with me. I want him to be happy.

* * *

"You sure you don't want a shower?" Kane asks, as I crawl into bed. There are a few boxes in the center of the bedroom. They're mostly just packed with my clothes that Kane bought me. We're leaving tomorrow to get a place he picked out downtown. It's really homey, and I kinda love it. I know he was waiting for a reaction from me, and I'm happy I found one. I was worried I wouldn't like any of the five places he was considering. But I instantly fell in love with the fourth one.

I shake my head no and yawn before I can get the word out. He chuckles as he climbs into bed with me. My eyelids feel so heavy.

"You too tired for me, baby?" he asks in a low voice as his arms wrap around my waist. I giggle in his arms and nestle into his hold. Before I can answer, I yawn again.

"In the morning, you're all mine," he says, kissing my neck and laying me down at his side. My eyes widen with anxiety. I wasn't turning him down just now.

Everything feels normal between us, like a new couple exploring each other. Most of the time, when he's with me, I forget. Sometimes it comes back, though. Hatred and sadness. I glance down at the bandage around my wrist. Sometimes I remember the worst things, and the nightmare feels so real.

But not when I'm with Kane. He wards off all of my demons. I feel so safe with Kane, but I'm still terrified of him being upset with me. A dark voice whispers deep inside, *it's because you're broken.*

"We can--" I start to suggest, but he cuts me off.

"You're tired, baby. You're gonna pass out on me." He yawns and puts one arm behind his head.

It has been a really long day. After we picked out the apartment we had to buy everything to fill it. Tomorrow's going to be a long ass day, too. But at least the morning will be off to a good start. I cover my mouth as another yawn takes control and shows itself without my consent.

"Get some sleep, baby. Tomorrow night I gotta run out and do some things, but we'll still celebrate and break in the new apartment together." He rocks his dick into me and forces a small giggle from me. I'm excited to move in with him. My heart swells in my chest. It feels like a huge step forward for us. I lower my eyes and rest my head against the pillow as his arm wraps around me.

Confusion stirs in me as I start to think about us as a couple. He was my captor, and then my savior. And I've been nothing but a victim. At least to him. *Broken,* the dark voice whispers. I close my eyes and force the voice away. I'm not broken. I'm his. I can't be broken.

*S*MASH! *The gun falls down and crashes against his skull. Smash! I hit the butt of the gun against his teeth, cracking them. They break off and the jagged edges scrape and cut the skin of my hand.*

I pull my hand back and examine my wound. Small drops of blood fall from the cuts and I follow them as they land on Vadik's broken and bloodied face.

As my eyes land on his, they open and stare back at me.

I scream out, "Help me!" Terror strikes my heart. My blood runs cold. I scream out for Kane. He'll save me. But my voice is broken. I can't speak his name. My hand grips my throat as I try again. Kane! I want to yell, but there's only silence.

"He'll never love you. You're just playing a part. What do you think he'll do to you when he finds out who you really are?" Vadik sneers, with a wicked smile.

I shake my head in denial. "Kane loves me," I whisper, feeling as though the words are true.

"If he loved you, he'd tell you that. He doesn't even know you and your sick thoughts."

I shake my head and back away as he rises from the ground, following me. Getting closer to me. I scoot back on my ass, shoving myself against the wall. Vadik cages me in, his face just an inch from mine.

"He'd never love a whore like you. A worthless little bitch who lied to him. He wouldn't be able to stand the sight of you. You're nothing!" he screams at me, and pulls his hand back to strike me. My hands fly up to cover my face.

Kane's hovering over me as a scream is torn from my throat. He has a grip on both of my wrists as they fly through the air.

"It's okay. Ava, I'm here. It's okay." He keeps repeating himself as my breathing comes in frantic, desperate gasps, and my heart threatens to leave my chest. I try to steady myself, but I can't. It was so real. It was too real.

"Baby, what's wrong? What's wrong?" His eyes search my face with worry. I can't make him worry. I can't lose him.

I shake my head and place a hand over my beating heart. I remember the dream. I remember Vadik's words. I won't let that happen. I won't let Kane know how ruined I am.

"Just a bad dream," I whisper. His shoulders stay tense and his mouth parts slightly. He doesn't believe me. "Will you hold me?" I ask him. He likes it when I ask him to comfort me. And I like it, too. I need it. I feel so safe in his arms.

"Of course, baby." He kisses my lips and pulls me closer to him. "I've got you, baby."

I close my eyes, but I'm very much awake. He doesn't have me. He hardly even knows me. And if he did, I'd be nothing to him.

AVA

"You look beautiful, baby," Kane says, and then kisses the crook of my neck. "But I think you need a little something extra." I turn in his arms, and stand on my tiptoes to give him a peck on the lips. He grins at me as he reaches in his back pocket.

My heart sputters in my chest. Could it possibly be a ring? No. I shove down that hope even though it's clawing its way up my chest. These last two weeks have been a dream come true. We have a cute little apartment I'm making into a home. I just got accepted into the university. All the little things on my wishlist are getting checked off.

And it's all because of Kane. He's my everything, and I feel like he loves me. I feel like we're meant to be together. The doubt I had seems to dim each day. Most of the time I think we're perfectly happy, perfectly fit for one another. I almost feel whole with him.

But a ring?

He'd be committing his life to me. *To a liar.* The dark voice that's gone quiet for so long speaks up, and depression shatters the fantasy in my head.

"These." He opens the box to reveal a pair of drop dangle sapphire earrings. "I think they'd really bring out your eyes." My heart slows, and my world seems to stop. They're beautiful. He gently pries one from the box and I quickly hold out my hand, waiting with bated breath.

I put them on one at a time and then face myself in the mirror. The silver boatneck dress I'm wearing clings to my curves. It sparkles in the mirror. My skin looks radiant. I've certainly gained weight. My hand rests on my lower tummy. Maybe a little too much weight. I clear my throat as Kane's eyes catch mine in the mirror.

Déjà vu hits me. I remember what I looked like that day. My eyes drift to my neck, where the collar used to be. Where Kane's collar was that day. I look to the small jewelry box on top of the dresser. He thinks I threw it away, but I didn't. I don't want to. It reminds me of that day and who I really am. I feel the blood drain from my face as the day plays fast-forward before my eyes.

"Do you like them?"

"I love them." I force out a peppy voice and try to show him my sincerest gratitude.

I feel like a fraud. I don't know what I've been doing all these days playing house with Kane. That's what it feels like now that I'm reminded who I am. It's fake. It's all pretend.

I close my eyes and try to will away the feelings, but instead I see a flash of his face. My eyes open quickly and I instantly catch Kane's questioning expression in the mirror.

"Are you alright, baby?"

"Yeah." I force a casual smile onto my face and then look back in the mirror. My fingers touch the sapphires and I watch as they sparkle in the mirror. They're beautiful.

But I don't deserve them.

* * *

WHITE TABLECLOTHS COVER EVERY TABLE. Some have pale pink overlays, while others have a soft lavender. There are at least 20 tables in the hall, although most are empty now. Most guests are on the dance floor, leaving the tables empty. My ass has remained firmly in this chair ever since Kane sat me down. I don't know anyone here. He at least knows a handful of the men.

It's Vince's uncle's godson's wedding. So, no one I fucking know. The only people I do recognize are the few from a time in my life I'm doing my best to forget. I loved how Kane put his arm around me during dinner. He made me feel more welcomed, and more comfortable. But I still couldn't manage to contribute to the conversation.

Becca and Dom have a newborn, a son. I love babies, but I couldn't speak up. Elle is pregnant now and she looks so beautiful, but I didn't even compliment her.

This wedding is just like every other wedding. Only every wedding I've ever gone to in the past was for family.

I remember the last wedding I went to with my family. I went with my mother, father, and sister. We were the first table. Naturally. My father always got the first and best of everything. Alec Ivanov, the Pakhan of the Russian mafia, the Bratva. My father was an immigrant in the States when he met my mother. He was there on family business, but elected to stay behind when she got pregnant with me.

When I was eight, my grandfather died. We were only supposed to go there for the funeral, but that's when things changed. My father went on the warpath. He was out for blood. And he got it. He quickly became known as a threat, but instead of fighting him, they made him the Pakhan, the boss.

It didn't take long for things to spiral out of control. I don't know whether my mother and sister didn't see, didn't care, or just didn't want to admit it was true. The men my father associated with in his line of business were strange, and touched my sister and I more than they should have. I know my parents saw, but they didn't do anything to stop it. It's like my father paraded us around, saying we were untouchables, but he never did anything to actually enforce that. I never felt safe with any of the men he'd bring around, but he'd leave us alone with them and practically dare them to disobey him.

He taunted them.

He started coming home late and drugged up or drunk most nights. One night I watched as he beat my mother until her head hit the wall so hard she went unconscious. I watched as he kicked her, thinking she was faking it. Once, then again. He looked genuinely sorry he'd hurt her when he realized she wasn't faking. He got down on his knees and held her. And then he passed out.

I'd never wanted to hurt someone so much in my life. He was there, helpless. But I didn't. Not then.

I never saw him try to hit her again, but I was ready. He did leave me alone with his men again, well he tried, anyway. I was only 16. And Marie, only 14. But I knew better, and I wasn't going to stand for it again.

"You're a sick fuck!" I yelled at him as he turned his back on me. Our own father. Marie grabbed my wrist to pull me back, but I wasn't going to let him do this to us. Leaving us with men who could hurt me, men who wanted to hurt me. Tears streamed down my cheeks, but they were from anger. I remember the faces of the men in the room.

"Excuse me?" he sneered, stomping toward me. "What the fuck did you just say to me?" His face was so red, and his eyes the darkest they'd ever been. His fists were clenched at his sides.

But I stood my ground.

"You know what you're doing." I looked to my right at the three men watching me with nervous glances. "How could you do this to us?"

His eyebrows raised, and a sick smile formed on his face. It was then that I realized I no longer truly knew him. He was a monster.

"Maybe I should just leave you here." He nodded to the men in the room. "I'm sure they could teach you what this mouth is for." He gripped my face and shook my head. My eyes burned, and my heart hurt.

When he let me go, the force made me stumble back. "You wouldn't," I said, looking up at him with daggers in my eyes. "It wouldn't be as much fun to you." I sneered at the ground, not bothering to look my father, the bastard he was, in the eyes. I grabbed my sister's hand and dragged her out of the room with me. It was silent. I'd never been so scared in my life as we hid in my room. Waiting for him to come home.

I was too ashamed to tell my mother.

When he finally walked through the doors and my mother called us to dinner, it was as though nothing had happened.

As though we were the same family, not one of us broken.

I couldn't swallow a single bite; I kept waiting. But nothing ever happened, and he never brought either of us around his businesses again.

That was my family.

And now they're all dead.

I take a sip of water and try to calm myself. I need to stop with all these negative memories. I'm doing a miserable job of fitting in. The men took off a bit ago to let the women chat. I'm finding it hard to click with them, though.

They seem like wonderful people; women I'd love to be friends with. But I'm holding myself back.

At least Kane doesn't seem to notice. And everyone seems to think I'm just shy. "Oh, she's so shy," they all say. And, "You're so sweet." I've heard it over and over today. I'm not sure why. I feel awkward and like I'm failing Kane. He just keeps kissing my cheek and running his hand up and down my back.

But now he's gone.

Elle and Becca have been talking about kids and I know they don't mean to, but I feel a little excluded. Even though every time they ask me a question, I give them a one-word answer. Maybe it's better this way.

My heart sinks a little. I don't want it to be this way. I take a deep breath and notice a pause in their conversation, so I cut in.

"Where did you two meet your husbands?" I keep my tone peppy and give them a bright smile. I lean forward to show them they have my full attention.

Becca answers first. "Work." She looks to her right as if she's searching Dom out in the crowd, and adjusts the napkin on her lap. But after a second she turns back to me with a small smile. "Sort of through my ex-husband."

"Oh! I didn't know you were divorced."

"He passed away."

"I'm sorry to hear that," I respond quickly, and with a lowered voice. Dead. Death follows me everywhere.

"Where did you two meet?" Elle asks.

I blink once, then twice at them. "I was sort of lost..." I start to say, and Becca raises her eyebrows, almost comically. "In the States, I mean. I'm from here originally, but we moved to Russia when I was young. I bumped into Kane and he helped me find my footing here." I make up a bullshit answer.

"Oh! So that's where that hint of an accent comes from!" Elle says.

"Accent?" Becca looks at Elle like she just said something truly perverted.

"I think I may have a tiny accent on some words. But I was older when we moved," I answer.

Elle starts to ask the obvious question. And I can practically see the wheels turning in her head as her mouth slams shut. I wonder how much she knows. How quickly she'll be able to put two and two together.

"I have to say, you two are an adorable couple. I'm so happy we finally got a chance to meet you," Becca says, and Elle nods in agreement.

I feel a slight smile pull at my lips and say thank you, but my chest hurts.
How did they meet? At a bar and through work. Like normal people.

"I have to pee. Again," Elle says, holding her swollen belly and it's funny,
but I don't laugh.

"Do you have to go, too?" Becca asks.

I do. But I'd rather not right now.

"No, you two go ahead. I'll wait right here for you." I smile back at them.

"Are you sure?" Becca asks.

"Of course, I'll keep an eye out for the dessert tray for us." I force out a
happy tone. But I'm feeling more insecure than ever.

"You're so sweet," Elle answers, and turns to her right as someone calls out
her name. She leans closer to me with a smile and says, "We'll be right back to
talk more." She squeals at the end and it forces a smile from me.

But it's forced nonetheless.

Everyone keeps calling me a sweet girl. Kane thinks I'm a good girl, but I'm
not. None of them know me. Not the real me.

I'm not like these women. They're strong, and obviously in love with their
men. But they're also normal. They aren't ruined and broken beyond repair.
My eyes fall, and I reach for the tall glass of champagne in front of me and put
it to my lips. I taste the smallest bit on my tongue, but nausea keeps me from
taking more into my mouth.

And they may already know who I am. What I've been through. They
could be talking about it in hushed whispers in the bathroom right now.

Everyone at the wedding may know. They've been sweet to my face, but
behind my back, what are they saying?

I'm sick of who I am. I'm sick of hiding it. I'll never be okay. I'll never heal.
My eyes search the room and I find Kane by the bar. Talking and laughing. It's
genuine, not forced like me.

He deserves so much more.

Shame and guilt consume me.

He's done so much for me; how can I treat him like this? All I do is lie to
him and pretend to be someone I'm not. I can't keep doing this. I set the glass
down and lift the white linen napkin off my lap. As I place it on the table, I see
the knife.

I casually slip the knife into my clutch and stand up.

No one will notice me leaving.

My heart clenches at the thought of Kane finding out. But it'll be better this way. He deserves so much more than me. I'm so fucking selfish. I'll keep lying to keep him. It's wrong. I'm ruined and broken.

I'm not his good girl.

KANE

*W*here the hell is Ava going? I watch as a sliver of her dress vanishes behind the door. It closes slowly and I give it a moment before opening it as quietly as possible so she doesn't hear me sneaking up on her.

I can't imagine what she's up to. She's not from around here, so I don't think she'd be doing anything but taking a look around. Still, it's not wise. She should know that. You don't go snooping around on mafia territory. It's just not smart. I hear her heels clicking down the hall as I walk slowly to the corner. And then the noise is gone, replaced by the patter of her feet smacking against the tiled floor.

Maybe her feet are hurting her and she just needs some fresh air? My forehead wrinkles in confusion. She has to know I'd give them a little rubdown for her. I clench my jaw as I turn the corner. Something twists in my gut. This is off. Something's just not right.

Ava's my good girl. She never leaves to go anywhere without telling me. I clench my fists as I hear the large doors to the back entrance of the hall open with a soft creak. As my pace picks up, so does my heartbeat.

Adrenaline races through my blood. I catch the door just before it closes shut and open it as silently as I can. I peek out and see her walking into the edge of a line of trees to the left. I clench and unclench my hands. I want to pretend she's going to be happy to see me when I get to her, but I'm not fucking stupid. That's not going to happen.

Ava wouldn't have gone off by herself like this if everything was okay.

I just need to find out what the fuck is going on.

I take a look to my left and then look to my right. No one's out here. The night's dark except for the light from the full moon. The air is crisp and feels cool against my skin. I can faintly hear her steps and the crunching of leaves and branches under her feet just beneath the sounds of the night. The crickets are loud as fuck.

I walk quickly and decide I don't give a shit if she hears me as I enter the woods. I'm not gonna tiptoe through the trees to find out what my baby's doing. As a branch cracks beneath my heavy steps, I catch a glimpse of Ava.

I see her silver dress sparkle with the barest hint of moonlight. I see her raise her wrist. Then I see a bright light. A reflection, just above her wrist. I don't stop as my forehead creases in confusion. It doesn't register as I speed up my pace to get to her.

Not until her eyes catch sight of me, which is the same moment that I snatch her wrist and yank it away. Her eyes widen and fill with fear. Her other arm lowers to her side and something drops to the ground with a loud thud. Her face pales and her eyes look at the ground.

My breath catches in my throat as I pull her body closer to me. She trembles in my embrace.

No. The reality hits me slowly.

No. This isn't real. It can't be.

"Ava?" She's not looking at me. Her shoulders rise and fall as she takes in a ragged breath. "Baby, what are you doing?" Even as I ask the question though, I know. There's a serrated knife on the ground by her feet. My heart twists in my chest with agony.

No. I close my eyes and brace myself against the tree next to her. My head feels light and dizzy. She was going to slit her wrist.

"Tell me this isn't what it looks like," I say with my eyes closed. I'm answered with silence. My chest hollows and my heart refuses to beat. My lungs refuse to fill.

"Why?" I ask, as I open my eyes and see her looking back at me with regret.

"Why would you do--?" My voice cracks and my throat goes dry. I can't finish it. The thought is just too fucked up. Why would she do that to herself?

She shakes her head and opens her mouth, but no words come out. I grip her shoulders in my hands and rest my forehead against hers.

This isn't real. I keep my eyes closed, waiting for something. For anything to happen that wakes me from this horrific shit.

I love her. I would give her anything.

I thought she was happy.

I thought she loved me, too.

"I'm sorry." Her breath hitches and her arms wrap around me.

Her touch is all I need. I wrap my arms around her and pull her close to me. I kiss her hair, her forehead. I cup her jaw in my hand and tilt her head so I can push my lips against hers. I need to feel her. I need to know she's still with me.

At first there's passion, but then she pulls back.

No. No. I can't let her. She needs me.

Don't pull away from me, Ava.

Her lips leave mine as her body moves away, and I'm greeted by the chill of the night.

"I'm sorry, Kane," she says as she wraps her arms around her shoulders. I quickly rip off my jacket and wrap it around her slender frame. At first she resists, but she caves. She always caves to me.

"This is my fault, but I'll fix this, Ava. I can make it better. Whatever it is." I grip onto her hips under my jacket that's draped over her shoulders. I pull her toward me and whisper, "I can fix this." I can, and I will. Whatever happened, whatever triggered this...I'll make it better.

Her eyes turn sad and I see the answer on her face, before she starts shaking her head.

"I'm too broken. No one can fix me."

"Just tell me what's wrong. What happened?"

"Nothing. I'm just not normal anymore; I'll never be normal again." I don't understand. Where is my Ava? This isn't her.

"Fuck, normal? Who fucking cares about normal?" I try to blow it off, like there's nothing to this. But she's not okay. I can help her though.

"I'm not okay, Kane. I'm happy I killed them!" she yells out, and I find myself covering her mouth and holding her close to me. You never fucking know who's listening to this shit. This is a public place, and the fucking cops know it's a family wedding.

"Shh. Don't say that shit, Ava," I whisper in her ear, and she starts fighting my hold on her. I fucking hate it. I hate her fighting me. She never has before. Not once. She struggles in my arms, and it fucking destroys me.

I let her go to try to calm her down. I'm not helping this situation. And I fucking need to figure it out fast.

"I'm not the woman you think I am, Kane," she finally says in a calmer voice than I expected. It's a voice with resolve. I shake my head as as an uneasy feeling settles in my gut.

She tried to kill herself to get away from me.

"I thought you wanted to be with me," I say. I know she did. I gave her a chance to go. She said this was real for her, too.

"You'll never love me." She whispers her words.

I shake my head and hold onto her hips, forcing her closer to me. "I love you, Ava." I search her eyes for a reaction, but there's nothing. "Is that what you need to hear, baby? I love you so fucking much. I'm so damn proud to have you as my girl. I'll make you my wife." Tears prick at my eyes. I almost bought a ring to go with those earrings. The only thing holding me back was I wasn't sure what design she would have liked. I'm so fucking ready to have it all with her.

But I can see it in her face that she's leaving me.

Her mind is already made up.

"I can't be with you. If you love me, you'll let me go." My heart sinks in my chest as I watch tears stream down her face. "I can't be with anyone right now." She heaves in a breath and wipes her eyes, smearing her mascara. Her tear-stained cheeks and wide, glassy eyes only make her more beautiful. Everything in me pushes me to comfort her. I know she needs me. If only she'd let me help her.

I take a step forward to pull her into my arms and calm her down. She's just worked up over something. This is all a mistake.

But she steps back.

She pulls out of my arms.

I stare at her with disbelief as she wipes away her tears and bends down to pick up her clutch.

"I'm sorry, Kane," she whispers, and then sobs into her hands.

She's leaving me.

She doesn't love me. It doesn't stop me from pulling her into my arms and rocking her. I try my best to soothe her. This time she lets me, but I know as soon as I let go, she's not going to be mine anymore.

KANE

*I*t's fucking silent in the car. Vince is next to me and he doesn't like
what I'm asking him to do. He's either going to help me, or I'm
doing it on my own.

"What do you mean, 'for her'?" he asks with what seems like disbelief. I
haven't told anyone. Last night I made her stay with me. No fucking way was I
going to let her go in the state she was in. I took off with her and didn't leave
her alone till just now. No one else knows and I want to keep it that way, but I
know it's going to get out.

"I mean, I need you to set her up with a place and a job."

"You have a place." He looks at me dumbfounded.

"I mean for her. Without me." It fucking kills me to say the words. My
heart hardens and my eyes narrow. I speak clearly and look him dead in the
eyes. "I need eyes on her, Vince. She needs space, but that's all she's getting."

"She's leaving you?" he asks, and I want to knock him the fuck out. She
thinks she's leaving me. And I'll let her think that until she's feeling better.

Doubt creeps in on me. I'm the one who made her kill Felipe. I brought her
to that massacre. Even worse. My stomach churns with sickness. I took
advantage of her. I never should've touched her when she was so vulnerable.

I'd take it all back if I could. I fucking wish I could.

I don't answer his question. I refuse to believe she's really leaving me. "I need cameras in there, Vince."

"Are you out of your fucking mind?" Vince asks, with his anger coming right through. I know I need to tell him, but I don't fucking want to. I don't want him to think less of her. She just needs time to heal. I thought she was, though. What kind of asshole am I that I didn't know?

I'll do everything I can to make it right. Starting with her getting her freedom back. Freedom away from me. I fucking pray she comes back to me. She just needs a little time.

"She's not alright, Vince." I run my hand through my hair and look up at our apartment. Fuck. She loves that apartment. I told her I'd go, and she could keep it. My heart feels like it's breaking in two. She said she couldn't stay there though, not with all the memories of the two of us together. She wants to erase me. She wants to forget it all. Including me and what we had together.

I push my bitch emotions down and give my full attention to Vince. "She's not alright, she just needs some time to heal. She tried to hurt herself. I can't let her go without knowing she's okay."

"What happened that set her off?" he asks, and I wish I had something with weight to tell him.

"Nothing." I shake my head and I fucking hate the answer. "She said she'd just occasionally remember things and it hurt her. She said she wants to deal with it, and that I can't be a part of it." My bitch emotions come back as I remember her telling me I deserve better. Better than her? No fucking way. She's it for me.

I'm a lucky bastard to have her. I'm not letting her go. I'd be a dumb fuck to do that. I'd be reckless to let her have space without watching her, too. I'm worried she's going to hurt herself. I can't let that happen.

"So you want eyes in the apartment?" he asks.

"Yeah," I say, as I take another look up to our apartment. She's sleeping now. My poor girl cried all night in my arms. I kept begging her for another chance or to think of another way that we could still stay together. It just made her cry harder.

The sick feeling in my stomach is the same one I had when I took out everyone I ever knew as family. It's not a feeling of revenge, it's a feeling of being utterly alone.

I remember thinking, it'll be alright, when Vino set me up. I was wrong. It was a mistake. Vino was my best friend. We grew up together. We were so close, we were practically brothers. But he didn't tell me to run, didn't give me a heads-up. He's the one who told me that my father and I were needed for the drop. I had this twisting hollowness in the pit of my gut that it was wrong. That everything was wrong, and it was going to end badly. But I ignored it. I couldn't imagine Vino would set me up.

But he did.

And everything changed for the worse that day.

He was the first one I killed. I went straight to his house. He was there with his girl. He tried to play it off for her, like we needed bro time, but he knew what was going to happen before he even saw the gun I had pointed at him in my jacket.

I couldn't look her in the face as she left. He didn't even kiss her goodbye. I know he loved her, so maybe he thought it was better that way. If the last time she saw him he was a dick, maybe it'd be easier for her to get over him.

I kept waiting for him to reach for a gun, to plead for his life, or to at least deny everything. But when he shut the door and turned to me, he just shook his head and said he was sorry.

It fucking sucked pulling the trigger on him. The others, not so much. They didn't see it coming. They didn't even know I was still alive. It didn't feel like much of anything for them. But for Vino, it felt like the end.

And that's how it feels right now for us. But I won't let it be the end.

I can fix this. I can give her what she needs to get better.

"I know she needs this. She's got to have a little time to deal with what she's been through."

"She needs more than just a new place to live, Kane." Vince tilts his head and cocks his brow. I know that, really I do. With all the shit she's been through--it's a miracle she made it out as well as she did. I should've known something was off. I fucking hate myself for not realizing how hurt she was.

"I know that. That's why I want you to get her a job. She needs a normal routine." I pause before adding, "I got her the psychiatrist too. Anthony told me to call Mae." I had to get someone who knows what's what and is trusted. She's the familia shrink according to Anthony. I think it's the only thing that will help and she was really receptive to it. I already scheduled an appointment for today. I told her I'd take her, but she didn't want that. She wants to go by herself.

"What if," Vince pauses, "What if when she's better, she doesn't wanna stay?"

I know what he's really asking is: if once she's better and she doesn't want me, how am I going to react. What am I going to do once she comes to her senses and realizes she's the one who deserves better?

"I don't want to think about that, Vince," I tell him simply.

"It's a possibility, Kane. I like you and all. And I like her, so I'm going to do what I can to help. But when she's doing better, if she wants out, I'm out."

I nod my head and look back up at our place.

I fucking hope she still wants me after this.

I know I'll still want her.

AVA

"*My* eyes are killing me." I push the palms of my hands against my burning eyes. Fuck. The tears finally came back, with a vengeance.

"We can take a break if you need." I hear Dr. Mae pull another tissue out of the box and I roll my eyes. I need to woman up and stop crying. I know it doesn't do anything to help.

I reach for the tissue and try to calm my ass down.

"Let's switch gears," she says, as she picks up her pen to scribble something in the tiny pad on her lap.

In my head I call her the shrink, even though Doctor Amelia Mae doesn't like to be called that. It doesn't matter what I call her, she's a doctor for people with mental issues. For the crazies. For me.

I feel comfortable in her office. She has a no shoe policy. It makes me feel more relaxed. I flex my toes into the plush carpet beneath my feet. My nose scrunches as I wonder how many other people do that. I pull up my legs to sit cross-legged on the leather couch. It's a pretty dove grey and has a modern feel. Everything in the office looks modern and clean. And open. It has a very airy vibe. It makes me feel comfortable enough to talk at least. And I'm doing my best to do just that.

I fucking snapped. Out of nowhere. Well, that's not true. I had triggers, and

449

I did nothing about them. But I snapped, and I didn't come to until Kane's arms were around me.

If he hadn't come to me...If he hadn't seen me leave...

I don't like to think of it. But I'm fairly certain I would've done it. I had the blade to my wrist. I remember thinking, just one quick move and it's all over. But then I thought, I should just impale myself through the chest. It would be quicker.

Thank God that Kane grabbed me just then. He saved me. Again.

Dr. Mae pushes the thin, metal frame of her glasses higher up on her nose, quickly reading through her notes before looking up at me. "It's been a week of big changes. How are you feeling?"

It's been weeks of big changes, but I don't correct her. That'd just be bitchy of me. This week seems just like the last one. Empty and boring.

"These meds are much better." I start off with a positive. And it's true. Whatever she has me on now is a shit-ton better than the first cocktail. It's been two weeks since I left Kane to try and deal with my shit. I'm blaming the fucking meds on how god damned depressed I was the entire first week. I didn't do a thing but sob uncontrollably into my pillow.

Every time I'd cry out his name, Kane would come running through the door within 15 minutes. He has to have my place bugged. I should be offended or angry, but I'm not. Maybe that makes me more sick than I thought I was. But I feel safe knowing he's watching over me. My chest hurts, and I have to take a deep breath to calm myself.

I'd ask Kane to just hold me, and he would. No questions asked. It happened nearly every night for the first few nights. But on the fifth day without him, I cried myself to sleep alone. Waking up without him hurt so fucking much. But I need to take care of myself.

I need to do this on my own. I can't rely on him.

"So no more negative thoughts?" the doctor asks.

"Of suicide, you mean?" I just want to be sure I know what she's asking.

"Yes, or any thoughts of self-harm. Your nightmares increased on the other meds, but you didn't say anything about any desire to hurt yourself."

I nod my head as she takes off her glasses and folds them, holding them in her hands. "Right. Not since the wedding night. And the night terrors are gone now that I'm off the other meds."

"That's great to hear." She puts the glasses back on and looks back down at the pad in her lap. "Now, how are you feeling on this prescription?"

"Normal. Just like before."

"But before you were having occasional lapses? Have you had any this week?" she asks.

I shake my head. "None yet. I usually would have had a reminder or two by now." That's what I'm calling them, *reminders*.

"And how would you have reacted to those reminders in the past?"

"I would've thought I was a horrible person; thought I was undeserving. A lot of self-doubt." My heart twists in my chest.

I didn't deserve that. I wasn't okay though. I don't think I'm okay now, either. "I don't feel like that now, but..." I trail off, twisting the tissue in my hands and start picking at the ends. I look out of the bright office window and wonder how I should word this.

"I'm afraid." I swallow the lump growing in my throat. "I'm afraid that something is going to remind me about everything, and I'm going to snap again."

"That's what the meds are for."

"So I'll have to be on antidepressants for the rest of my life?"

"We could try to wean you off of them if you'd like." I'm surprised how casually she responds.

"Is that dangerous?" I ask.

"Not if you're honest with yourself and with me. You had triggers that day, but you did nothing about them. You're aware now of what could happen."

"I am. And I won't let that happen again." I won't. I don't want to die. I didn't live through all of that to end my own life.

"I'm very proud of you, Ava. Not many people are able to get a good look at themselves the way that you have."

"Thank you," I respond, although I feel awkward. I'm not proud. I'm ashamed.

"How's your scar?" she asks, as her eyes dart to my shoulder. It's a warm day outside, so my skin is exposed.

"One more treatment left to go, but I can't even see it." The surgeon said there was a small amount of scar tissue still, but I can't see a damn thing. It makes me smile. I'm happy I never got the tattoo. It would have been a constant reminder. This is so much better.

"That's wonderful." She jots something down before looking back up at me. "And your weight? Is that back to normal now?"

"I'm still finding it difficult to eat." It's been hard for me to gain weight.

She purses her lips and writes some more. I hate it when she does that. Usually I know what she's writing. But her pen keeps going and I find myself trying to read the fucking novel she's writing.

"You're looking well though, Ava. Are you feeling better as a whole?"

"I am." I started jogging again. I used to fucking hate it. My sister used to make me go with her. It's nice though. I can see why she liked it. I don't know why she dragged my ass out along with her though. I don't want company when I'm running. I just like the music, the feeling of being free. The burn of my muscles.

It wears my ass out though.

"Good. Let's move on. How about work? How has it been integrating with your coworkers?"

I fucking hate my coworkers. I need to find something other than working as a clerk at the hardware store. I can't wait for classes to start up.

I take a deep breath and think about Mindy. She's the only one I freaking talk to because of our shifts. She's a little firecracker, and I like her. But she's also a ho. She's currently sleeping with Jeremy, who's the store manager. And also the boyfriend of Tammy who works in the stockroom and orders supplies.

"It's just like any other retail job," I finally answer. I'm pretty sure that's not true. But I don't want this to become a bitch session.

Kane got me a job at a restaurant, but I turned it down. I was going to withdraw from the university too, before classes even started; he convinced me not to, though. I'm grateful for that. I'm really looking forward to it.

I pushed the chance at going back to school away at first, because Kane was paying for it. But one of Vince's men, Tony I think, tracked down my father's money and wired it to me. I half wondered if it's really my father's, but I stopped putting effort into thinking about it.

I got the money a few days ago and I want to quit this shit job, but I feel like I need to be a part of the real world again. I really fucking hate that petty drama though.

Kane told me once that I could get a job at the restaurant whenever I wanted. He also said I could move back in with him and not have to work, or do whatever the fuck I wanted.

It's so tempting, but I keep pushing him away.

I thought I needed to be apart from him. But I miss him so damn much.

I haven't cried for him in over a week. I haven't called him. I haven't even seen him in over a week. Sometimes when I'm walking to a nearby café on my lunch break, I swear I feel his eyes on me. But when I turn around, no one's there. It breaks my fucking heart every time.

"What are you thinking now?" Dr. Mae asks, and it pulls me from my thoughts.

I don't want to admit it, but I tell the truth. That's the only way I'll get better.

"About Kane." I swallow. "I miss him."

She nods her head and scribbles something in her notebook. "Any more late night calls?"

"No. I haven't seen him in over a week now." She cocks a brow as she writes more in that damn book.

"I see. And have you thought about seeing him?" she asks as though she thinks it would be alright.

The word falls out of my mouth easily. "Yes." I've thought of him holding me. Almost every night I try to remember our nights together so I can focus on a bit of happiness. The sweet moments of passion. I know he loves me. I think he loves me.

"Is it wrong that I care for him so much?" I ask her.

"You've asked me that before." She places her glasses onto the table and reaches for her cup of coffee. "I think it's reasonable to idolize him. I think it's natural that you developed feelings for him. The question is, why do you think it's so wrong?"

"I started having feelings for him before I was capable of leaving on my own."

She nods her head. "And after?"

"After what?" I ask.

"After you left him? The feelings are still there, yes?"

"Yes." My hand flies to my heart as an ache radiates through my chest. Every moment I remember I left him, it hurts. It hurts so fucking much. I know I hurt him. He saved me, and I fucking killed him by leaving him.

"What would you do if you could see him right now?"

Fuck him. I would hold him, I would kiss him, I would beg him to fuck me. I purse my lips and the good doctor smirks at me. Am I that obvious?

"Do you still think he deserves better?" she asks. I don't know the answer. I don't know if I'll ever be completely whole again. I may forever be haunted. And he deserves better than that. He's a good man.

She leans forward and looks me in the eyes. "Or maybe a better question to ask is, do you think *you* deserve happiness?"

KANE

"*How's* she doing?" I hear Anthony ask. I turn on my barstool to look at him. He's a lean fucker compared to me, not real bulky, but I've learned over the past few weeks that he's not someone you wanna fuck with. If you're doing shit you aren't supposed to be doing, having Anthony knocking on your door at night is a bad fucking omen.

But I like him. When he's not working, he's sitting down and having a beer. He's pretty chill. Everyone's still on edge about Tommy though. As I think his name, he walks through the doors of the bar with Vince. We watch as they come up to our right and sit on Anthony's side.

The bar goes quiet as they take a seat. Everyone's waiting for something to happen with this case. But it's gonna take time. There's only so much postponing and bribing will get him.

"She's alright." I answer Anthony as Tommy orders a beer. It's on the bar before he even finishes, along with Vince's Jack.

"Ava?" Vince calls out, from the far end of our row. It's a curved bar so I've got a good view of him.

"Yeah." I don't volunteer more info. I don't want to talk about it. I watch my phone every time there's an alert that she's home. I know her appointments and work schedules, too. I feel like a fucking creep at this point. In the beginning I was worried about her. We all were. But the better she is, the less she seems to be thinking about me.

I keep waiting to hear her call out for me. I prayed that I'd have a reason to help her. But for over a week, it's been nothing.

"I don't like that manager fucker either. He likes to get around," Vince says from across the bar. They think it's funny. I lost my shit the other night and they keep holding it over my head.

I grit my teeth. If that bastard makes another pass at Ava, I'm gonna knock his fucking teeth out. She's such a good girl though, she doesn't even realize it.

The guys laugh when they see my reaction. But there's no humor in it for me. I think it's time I came to grips with reality.

She doesn't want me. Why would she?

"I never should've touched her," I bite out, and grab the neck of my beer. I take a swig and then another.

"I don't think it's like that, Kane," Vince says. Tommy and Anthony nod their heads.

"I should've waited." I put the bottle down feeling like a fucking failure. Like an asshole. She wasn't okay, and I was so wrapped up in her that I didn't even see it. I took advantage of her. I don't deserve her.

That's why I'm giving her the space she needs. She genuinely needs me to be gone to get through this. Fuck. It fucking kills me that seeing my face, feeling my hands on her, or hearing my voice would remind her of that hell. I took her pain away, or at least I thought I did. I wonder if I just made it worse. I fell for her too soon. I loved her when she couldn't possibly love me. Not in a healthy way at least.

Every time I start to think she's mine and I need to go get her, I have to remind myself that it's too much like what they did to her. I need to wait until she's better. And then she'll come back to me. We'll work through this together. I'm not giving up though. I know she felt something for me. I just have to wait until it's the right time. I need some sort of sign.

"Stop pouting like a little bitch," Tommy groans out. "Jesus, I'm the one getting 50 to life."

I glare at him. I'm not a Valetti. I shouldn't even be in this bar. But I'm gonna beat the fucking piss out of him if he keeps it up.

"Just go get her, Kane," Tommy says.

"Her shrink says it's alright, right?" Anthony asks. Shame washes over me, along with a little guilt. I may have bugged Ava's purse. And I may have deliberately listened to her first few sessions. But I've been better about giving her space. I was just worried since I hadn't seen her.

But she was fine. She just didn't want me.

"The doc isn't why she's not seeing me." I roll the empty bottle between my palms and nod when the bartender asks if I want another.

"You want her?" Vince asks.

I stare at him dead in the eyes. "Fuck yeah, I want her."

"Go get her."

"What if I'm the reason for that shit?" That's what it all boils down to, really. If I'm the one triggering all her pain, how can I expect her to stay with me?

"What if you're not?" he asks back. "What if you let her go, and you never find out?"

"Look at you," Anthony says, elbowing Tommy as they snicker at Vince. "We've got a fucking romantic over here."

"Shut the fuck up!" Vince spits back with a grin. "I'm just saying, I think she'd make a great addition to the family. Mostly 'cause my wife likes her."

"What do you mean 'addition'?" I question him.

"You're not a made man yet, Kane. It's gonna take time to put in your dues." He points his finger at me and raises his voice. "But you sure as fuck are a Valetti." I hear a few guys let out a cheer and one asshole claps. Poor fucker, everyone looks at him, but he just picks up his beer and smiles.

"Thanks, Vince." I push out the words. It means a lot to be a member of the Valettis and have a family around me again. But it's all worth nothing if Ava won't be a part of it with me.

"She will," Anthony says, as if he read my mind. "Just go get her."

He says it like it's that easy. In the past it was. If I wanted something, I just went and got it.

But this is different. If she says no, then nothing else matters.

AVA

"*I*'ll see you in a month, unless you need me sooner," Dr. Mae says, as I walk to the door. I give her a tight smile and nod. I still don't know how I feel about it. Over the past month our meetings have been fewer and fewer. Now it'll be a month before I see her again. Unless I have a relapse. I haven't though, since switching meds. Nothing other than normal emotional reactions, as the doctor says.

I feel insecure, but I suppose it's normal. There aren't any guarantees in life. My eyes fall to the floor as I shut the door behind me. Like Kane. I haven't gathered up the courage to call him. I haven't spoken a word to him in weeks. When I did talk to him before, it was just sobs and pleas to hold me or leave me.

I can't imagine what his reaction would be if I called him now. If I said I was better and asked him to take me back.

He said he loved me. I feel an unbearable pain in my heart as a thought occurs to me.

I never said it back. I never told him how I felt.

As I walk down the stairs to leave the office building, I pass the clinic. I purse my lips remembering what Dr. Mae said about the nausea. I may have a stubborn bug.

Whatever it is, I need this shit taken care of. I want to eat. I'm hungry all the fucking time now. I pull the doors open and feel relief wash over me. Not a soul in the waiting room. Good, I can get in and I can get out.

I walk straight to the counter and see a young woman with blonde hair pulled into a sleek ponytail and coral painted nails tapping on the keys of her laptop. After a short moment, she looks up at me with a bright smile and asks, "Can I help you?"

"Hi there, I think I have the flu or something, and I just wanted a checkup."

"Absolutely, I just need you to fill out these forms first, please." She chomps on a piece of gum in her mouth and hands me a clipboard with a pen clamped at the top. I forgot about this shit. I just want to walk back there and get a prescription. Instead I give her a small smile and walk back to the waiting area to take a seat. I scroll through the lines and fill out the bare minimum.

I stare at the emergency contacts section for a long time. I want to put Kane down; I have no one else.

I want to call him, but I'm scared. I don't know what I'd do if he's moved on. I take in a shaky breath and calm my emotions.

I fucking love him. I can't deny it anymore. Whether it's right or wrong, I don't know.

But I do love him. I just need to gather up the courage to tell him. I pick up my phone and click it on and then off. Not now. Right now I need to get some meds to get rid of this fucking bug.

I fill out five fucking pages of the same thing and wait an ungodly amount of time before I'm called back. At least the doctor is there in the hall waiting for me.

"Miss Ivanov. Nice to meet you." He ushers me through the door to an exam room and then says, "Have a seat."

I hop up onto the exam table with crinkly paper on top. It still feels unsanitary to me, though.

"So what brings you in today, Ava?" The doctor is an old man. He has to be in his 60s, if not older. The lines around his eyes make him seem approachable and kind. He has the palest blue eyes; they remind me of my father. My heart swells with cheerful memories and then the happiness dims.

I push the thoughts away and return to the present. "I think I have a bug. I've been having a difficult time holding food down for a month or so now."

"I see. Any other symptoms with your nausea? Sore throat? Indigestion?"

I shake my head no. He takes a quick look down at my tummy and asks, "Is there a chance that you could be pregnant?"

His question steals the life from me. Everything stills and my breath halts in my chest. Those fuckers gave me so many shots, the assholes who drugged me, tattooed me and chipped me, but I know they said one was birth control. I know they did. They weren't talking to me, but it would make sense.

"Would you like to take a test?" he asks, snapping me out of the painful memory.

"Please," I answer without thinking. He reaches over to a cupboard above a small sink and grabs a small plastic cup. He's a short man so he has to stretch to reach. I hesitantly take it and exit the room absentmindedly.

Why the fuck didn't this cross my mind before? Mid-walk I'm struck with horror.

"Pills!" I yell in the hallway, like a fucking lunatic. The doctor exits the exam room and stares at me with his eyebrows raised. I dig in my purse and pull out the prescription bottle. I shove them into his hands like they're poison.

He stares at the bottle for the longest fucking time. He rotates it and takes his time reading every last fucking word.

My heart won't beat until I hear him tell me something. I need to know if I hurt my baby. If my own fucking problems hurt my child before he was even born.

Finally, the doctor gives me a smile and hands the bottle back as he reassures me. "You'll be fine. And so will the baby, *if* you're pregnant." He walks a few steps and gestures to an open door.

"Thank you," I say just above a murmur. My hand rests subconsciously on my belly.

I close the door and take a single breath before my skirt's around my ankles.

The stream hits my hand and I cuss before getting as much urine as I can into the tiny cup. My nerves are getting the best of me, but I know it's true. It all makes sense.

I wipe down and wash my hands before wiping the outside of the cup and staring at it. It's a tiny cup of pee and it could tell me that my world is about to change forever.

It only takes a minute once I'm back into the room for the colors to start showing.

Two lines.

"Congratulations! We've found the source of your nausea. It usually eases up around the second trimester." The old man gives me a smile.

"How far along am I?" I ask. That matters. That really fucking matters.

"Well, that's hard to say. You'll have to make an appointment with your gynecologist for an ultrasound for more specificity."

I nearly cringe. Technically I have one now. But I haven't gone to see them for anything other than to pee in a cup and take blood. I had to make sure I was healthy after everything I'd been through, after all. But they never said a damn thing about being pregnant.

Maybe it didn't show up at the time. Maybe I was too newly pregnant and that's why.

I fucking hope that's why.

Anxiety creeps up on me. I'm pregnant. My hands hover over my growing baby. I'm going to be a mother. Warmth and happiness flow through me. I lean back against the wall.

Everything is going to be okay. I'm going to do everything I can to give this baby the best possible life.

I don't know how Kane will react. Tears prick at my eyes. He may not want me, and he may not want this baby. There's a small chance this baby isn't even his.

I don't care.

I brush my tears away and square my shoulders. I'm not going to put this off. I'm going to make that appointment as soon as I get home.

I won't be *that* woman. I won't be weak. I won't be scared. And I'm sure as fuck not going to let Kane's reaction do anything to stop me from being the best mother I can be.

I won't let the past ruin my future. I won't do it.

I'm not broken. I'm a survivor. I splay my hand on my lower belly. I'll be strong for this baby. I'm going to give him everything I can.

KANE

*S*he's taking a really long fucking time to get out of her appointment. I know her schedule, and she should've been done almost an hour ago. I don't want to startle her by showing up unexpectedly, but calling her on the phone just didn't seem right.

I walk through the tall glass doors to the office building just in time to see her walking out of the clinic. What the fuck is she doing in there? She's got a little baggie in her hand that she's stuffing into her purse.

She looks up from her purse and stops as she sees me.

My heart skips a beat. She's so fucking beautiful. But the sight of me has her looking like a ghost. I can see the anxiety in her eyes.

Fuck. This isn't good. My heart clenches, but I walk forward.

She's going to deny me.

I know it.

"I just wanted to see you." I don't know why they're the first words out of my mouth. Not hi, how are you? None of that. I'm granted a small amount of happiness as her eyes soften and a gentle smile plays at her lips.

There's a chance. I hold onto it with a fucking death grip. If there's a chance, I'm taking it.

"Are you feeling okay?" I look up past her and she turns to look at the clinic doors, too.

"Yeah," she answers after a moment. And then she says, "No. But I will be."

"Is there anything I can do?" I ask.

Her bottom lip trembles and her eyes water. Fuck. Fuck! This isn't good. I take a step forward to comfort her, but I stop in my tracks. I can't take these kinds of liberties. I need to make sure this is what she wants.

"Can I hold you?" I ask.

She nods her head and practically runs into my arms. My heart swells with pride that I can give her this, and I run my hand up and down her back.

"It's gonna be alright, baby. Whatever it is, it's gonna be alright." I try soothing her. I hear the door open behind us and I turn to see an older man walking up the steps. I break away from her for a moment. I need to get her ass somewhere private so I can calm her down. So we can talk.

I press my lips into a hard line and see a door on the left. It's unmarked, so I turn the knob and it opens. It's an empty office with paper lining the windows. There's not one fucking thing in this room and there's hardly any light coming through, but it's quiet and she can cry in peace with privacy.

I pull her in and bring her back into my arms, but she pulls away and wipes her eyes. It's just like that night in the woods. Fear creeps up on me, but I don't say a fucking word.

If this is it, if it's the end, I'll take it like I should and leave her alone so she can find someone better. But I'll be fucking watching, and I'll destroy any fucker not good enough for her.

"Kane," she says in a pained voice. "Do you still love me?" Her voice breaks and her shoulders hunch forward. I can tell she's scared to ask, but I'm going to put that shit to bed right now.

"Of course I do. I'll always love you, Ava. Even if you don't want me, I'll always love you."

"I love you, too." She breathes out the words and wraps her arms around my shoulders. She pulls me into her small body with a force I didn't know she had. I hold her for a few minutes as she calms herself, just taking in her words. *She loves me.* I fucking knew it.

I swear to fucking God if she follows this up with a "But I can't be with you," or "But I'm not in love with you," it will rip me into fucking pieces. But judging by how she's hanging onto me, I don't think she will.

She's mine. I kiss her hair and she lifts her head back and takes my head in her hands to kiss me. It's a soft kiss and I try to deepen it. I'm rock fucking hard for her. It's been a month since I've been inside her and I fucking need to feel her cumming on my dick. We *need* this.

But she pulls away from me. She needs to stop fucking doing that. Each time it hurts.

"Kane, I have something I have to tell you." She looks at the ground and then wipes under her eyes.

I put my hands on her hips and give them a small squeeze. "Go for it, baby, whatever it is. Just tell me."

"I just...I have to tell you." She looks at me with wide, glassy eyes and then whispers, "I'm pregnant."

My entire world stops. She's pregnant.

"How long have you known?" I ask. It fucking hurts that she kept this from me.

She gives me a weak smile. "About five minutes." Worry clouds her eyes as I stand there dumbfounded.

She's pregnant; we're going to have a baby.

We're going to be parents.

Two minutes ago I thought I might never see her again.

Now she's telling me she's pregnant.

"Say something, please." She looks scared, and I fucking hate it. I don't want her to be scared.

"Are you feeling okay?" It's the first thing that comes to mind. I hear pregnancy can be a bitch.

"I'm okay," she says in a small voice.

"Are we having a boy or a girl?" I ask. That's fucking important there. What the hell am I going to do with a baby girl?

She huffs a humorless laugh and cries at the same time. "I don't know, Kane." Her hand rests on her tummy and she looks down with tears in her eyes. "I don't know how far along I am."

I let the meaning of her words hit me. My eyes watch her hand rub along her small bump. "Is he healthy?" That's what really matters. She's mine, and that means her baby's mine.

"I don't know. I think so." Her voice is slightly sad. "I have to make an appointment."

"I'll come with you." She finally smiles, but it's small.

I'll be there every step of the way for our little one. I splay my hand over her belly. That's my baby in there. I know it. Sure enough, there's a small bump that wasn't there when she left me.

"I want you to come home with me." I'm not going to order her around, not like before. But I'm going to make sure she knows what I want. "I wanna be with you, Ava. I want you back. I want you forever."

Her hands cup my chin and she stands on her tiptoes to plant a small kiss on my lips. She nods with her eyes closed as I wrap my hands around her waist.

"Yes, Kane." Hearing her say those words reminds me how fucking hard my dick is.

"Do you still love me?" she asks, her voice laced with worry.

"Of course I do. Don't ever question it." I fucking hate that she has to ask.

"I won't. I love you so much, Kane." The sincerity in her voice and in her eyes gives me security. She pushes her body against me and kisses me with passion.

I love her touch.

I *need* her touch.

I know she needs me, too.

I pull back from her kiss and stare into her baby blue eyes that are drowning with lust. "Tell me you want me, Ava."

She doesn't waste a second. Her voice is breathy. "I want you, Kane."

"Tell me you're never going to leave me again." I need to hear it.

"Never." She shakes her head.

"Tell me you love me." I wanna hear it again. Every fucking day.

"I love you, Kane, I love you so much. Please forgive--" I crush her lips with mine, stopping that shit in its tracks.

"Good girl." I suck on her lip, but she pulls back.

"I'm sorry, Kane." She gets the words out and I wish she hadn't.

"Nothing to forgive. Nothing to be sorry over. I love you. This was supposed to happen like this." My hand rests on her belly, and I lean down to give her a sweet kiss.

She deepens it and I moan into her mouth.

Enough apologies. Enough of this sorry bullshit. We've been through hell and back, but what matters is that we have each other.

"I'm never losing you again, Ava. You're mine now." I back her up against the wall and lift her ass up to the perfect height for me to slip inside her. She nods her head and answers, "Yes, Kane."

I don't care if it's fucked up. She's my good girl. I push her panties to the side and undo my zipper. "Keep your eyes on me, baby," I tell her, as I slip my rigid cock deep into her heat. Feeling her tight cunt wrap around my cock makes me want to bury my head in the crook of her neck and fuck the shit out of her.

But not in this moment.

I need her with me every step of the way. I pull out and fucking love the whimper from her lips. I slam into her and catch her moan in my kiss.

My good girl is loud as hell. This is going to have to be quick.

"Hold onto me, baby." She wraps her arms around my shoulders, all the while keeping her eyes on mine. My hands grip her ass and I move her easily on and off my dick, never pulling all the way out.

I match the downward stroke with a hard thrust of my hips, making sure I hit her throbbing clit. She bites her bottom lip to keep in the moans of pleasure as I increase my pace.

"I'll give you more when we get home, baby." I can already feel my balls drawing up.

She feels so fucking good. And it's been so long. Her back arches, and her heels dig into my ass.

I know she's close and I can't fucking wait to feel her pussy milk my dick. I slam into her faster and harder, pushing her against the wall.

"This is where I belong, Ava. With my arms wrapped around you." I crush my lips onto hers. She moans into my mouth as I part her lips with my tongue and kiss her with all the passion I have.

I thrust myself deep into her heat and feel her pussy clamp down. Her heels dig into my ass, wanting even more. I silence her moan with my kiss and pull back. My fingers rub around her swollen nub; she's so fucking close. "And you belong right here. Impaled on my dick."

Her back arches at my dirty words. Her thighs tremble. She fucking loves this. She loves *me* and what I do to her. I know she does. "Cum for me, Ava," I whisper in her ear, my lips barely touching her tender skin.

My lips catch her screams as I pinch her clit and send her over the edge. The feeling of her hot, tight pussy spasming around my dick causes a tingling sensation to shoot up my spine and I fucking lose it. I cum violently inside her. A cold sweat breaks out over my body as waves of pleasure go through me. I keep up short, shallow pumps until both of our orgasms have subsided.

Our breath comes in pants as I plant small, open-mouth kisses on her shoulder. She grabs my face in her hands and kisses me like she needs the oxygen in my lungs to breathe. When our frantic breathing calms I pull back and give her one more kiss.

"Good girl."

AVA

I scrunch my nose and purse my lips as I say, "I look like a whale."
Tears prick at my eyes and I know it's from the hormones but
damn it, I really wanted today to be fun.

"You look beautiful," Elle says from the bench in the gallery of the bridal
shop. She's literally said that for every dress I've put on. She's hormonal too
though, so I can't call her out on it. She rubs her very swollen belly.

"It's the dress, not you." Becca stands up, keeping her eyes on the mirror,
and starts walking over to me. The dress is a ball gown style, meant to hide
my baby bump, but it's making me look like a balloon and with my face a little
swollen from this baby...I'm feeling genuinely awful.

"Okay, first of all, your hair is going to be up, so let's do that." She hands
me a scrunchie and I take it reluctantly. I've learned that Becca knows her shit,
so I trust her, but I'm hesitant to believe a scrunchie is supposed to make this
better. I fasten a quick ponytail and take a look. I guess my face looks a little
less fat, but the dress is still horrible.

As if reading my mind, Becca says, "Okay. Now I think we should
emphasize your bump all the way down to your hips." She tugs the dress
from the back of it and grabs a handful of giant ass clips from the ottoman
to my right. I've needed them for the other dresses too, but not like this.
She pulls the fabric tight around my body. I smile as soon as I see the

outline of my swollen belly. My baby. My heart fills and I let out a small sigh.

"Better?" Becca asks, and I have to blink a few times to get back into bridal dress shopping. I stare at myself in the mirror and I have to say I'm shocked.

"Say it," Becca says, with a cocky grin on her face.

"You were right," I huff, and return to looking in the mirror.

"Ha! Mermaid gown for the win! There are plenty of options." Elle cracks up and a smile forms on my face. That is, until I hear the woman from around the corner.

"Sir, you really shouldn't," I hear a timid voice say as loud as possible while still being polite.

"Shit! It's Kane." I hop off the little platform and run to a dressing room as the clips fly off the back of my dress and land on the floor.

"Kane De Rocca! Get your ass out of here!" I yell from the slightly ajar door. "It's bad luck to see me in my dress!" I sound like a little brat, but I want this to be perfect. I don't want anything to go wrong. It might be stupid to be superstitious, but I'm doing it all. Something borrowed, blue, old and new. And there's no way he's seeing me in my dress.

"So you found one?" I hear him ask in a voice clear enough that it must be coming from only a few feet away.

"Kane, really?" I hear Elle as she waddles on over. A giggle is forced from me when I see her stand in front of the door with her arms crossed.

"You are not seeing her, and that is final." She even nods her head at the end.

"In her dress," Kane tacks on. "I won't see her in her dress, but I have something I need to tell her; it can't wait."

My eyes widen and my heart sputters in my chest. I push the door open and ask in a worried voice, "Is everything okay?"

His eyes look down my dress and I can tell he's having the same reaction I was. Now that the clips are gone, I'm a little...puffy.

"Yeah, baby." His brow furrows. "Uh. That dress is just beautiful." He couldn't sound more unsure if he tried. I give him an asymmetric grin.

"This is only one of them. I'm getting another with more tulle for the reception. I thought I should get that one in pink, too." He blinks at me a few times and then purses his lips.

"Is my good girl being a little naughty?" he asks in a lowered voice.

"Oh, God. Get a room." Becca rolls her eyes and plops down on the ottoman while Elle and I just laugh. Kane looks over his shoulder with a wide grin.

"No worries. We've got one right here." He walks forward and I instinctively take a step back as he enters the fitting room with me.

I push my hands on his chest but he moves in enough to shut the door. "Not here." I am so not fucking him with them in earshot.

He huffs a laugh. "Don't worry, I'll take care of that needy pussy of yours when you get home." He wraps his arms around my waist and pulls me in. The tulle crinkles and my shoulders shake with my laughter.

"Good news?" I ask. My heart swells as he gives me a broad smile and a quick kiss.

"I'm in, baby. We're gonna stay."

"In, in?" I ask. I can't believe it. He wanted this so badly.

"Valetti through and through." I give him a hug and he picks me up gently, hugging me back. It's a little awkward with my belly and the dress, but it feels so right. I'm so happy, happier than I've ever been. Everything is just perfect.

He sets me down and gives me a sweet, open-mouth kiss that instantly ignites my core. When he pulls back to look at me, he chuckles. "Not here, baby. You're going to have to be a good girl and wait."

I feel a violent blush color my cheeks and I stand on my tiptoes to kiss him.

"Yes, Kane." I say with a smile.

EPILOGUE

Ava

I spear my fingers through his hair and arch my back. "Yes!" I moan and arch my back. I rock my pussy in his face, needing more. He takes a languid lick then sucks my clit into his mouth. "Fuck! Yes!" My body bows as he pushes two fingers into my heat. He curves them and strokes my G-spot.

Heat overwhelms my entire body, and an intense pleasure radiates from my core before exploding through my entire body. My breathing comes in pants as I look down my body and see Kane rise between my legs.

His broad shoulders spread my legs as he licks his lips and then wipes his mouth with the back of his hand. His eyes are half-lidded and filled with desire.

His large hands push my thighs apart as he crawls up my body, keeping eye contact. "You need to be a good girl and keep quiet."

My pussy clenches around nothing at his words. "Yes, Kane." My response comes out breathy and he smirks at me as his large frame cages me in. I love telling him yes, just to see the spark of desire in his eyes from my submission. He grins at me and I smile back at him.

He rests a forearm by my head and reaches below him to push the head of his cock against my wet pussy lips.

"Mmm," I moan, as my head tilts back and his hand grips my hip. Just before he's able to push into me, the baby monitor goes off.

Our little girl is quite literally the world's worst cockblock.

"Ah, no. No, no, baby girl." Kane climbs over me, leaving my heat and ignores the giggles coming from my mouth without my consent. His hard dick bobs as he grabs the baby monitor and clicks the top button so the video will come to life. His wedding band clicks against the monitor, and it triggers me to look down at my rings. Almost a year, and I never tire of looking at them. It never ceases to amaze me. I'm so fucking lucky.

"I'm sorry, babe," I say with a sarcastic pout. I really do need to be more quiet. The look on his face makes me suppress a laugh. Our little girl shrieks with joy on the monitor. She's just found her feet and apparently that's the most exciting thing in the world. Especially when she can fit her little toes into her mouth.

"You and your big mouth," he mutters good-naturedly as he stands, and snatches his pajama pants off the floor of the bedroom.

"Technically it was your mouth," I say as though it's an admonishment, with a wide smile on my face.

He walks over to the bed with a handsome grin and puts his hand on my hip. "Two minutes," he says before reaching down to give me a kiss. He's not lying either, he's a pro at getting our little one back to sleep. She's daddy's girl and he has the magic touch to get her to sleep. She looks just like him, too. She has her father's eyes. We named her after his mother, and my sister. Rebecca Marie. She's a perfect little angel.

Everyone says the next one is going to be a demon because she's so easy. I'm more than happy to find out.

"Two minutes," I say just barely above a murmur as his lips leave mine. I open my eyes to see his dark, heated gaze staring back at me with absolute devotion.

As he turns to leave, to go to our babbling little girl, I grab his wrist and pull him back to me. I crush my lips against his and pour my passion into it.

Tears prick my eyes and leak from the corners. I'm so full of love that it hurts. "I love you so much, Kane."

He sucks my bottom lip into his mouth and leans back. A deep chuckle rumbles from his chest. "I know you do. I love you, too."

There's not an ounce of doubt in those words. He loves me just as much as I love him.

The End.

***

Don't stop reading! Continue to read Tommy's book, Cuffed Kiss.

CUFFED KISS

SYNOPSIS

From *USA Today* bestselling author Willow Winters comes a HOT mafia, standalone romance.

I didn't plan on stumbling into Tommy, the muscle of the Valetti crime family.
    He warns me to stay away, but holds the key to everything I need.

All of this started because I wanted the truth. I need answers to numb the pain of my past.
    It was never supposed to be anything else.

He makes me beg when I've never pleaded with anyone for a d*mn thing.
    He makes me crave something I never imagined.
    He makes me wish I could hold on to this moment and forget everything else.

He's a thug, a mistake, and everything I need...

PROLOGUE

Tonya
Tommy

I **push the cuffs together and grin when I hear them** *click, click, click,* **as they slowly tighten around her wrists. She's not going anywhere now.**

"Tommy, please," I plead with him. My pussy clenches as his hot breath tickles my neck, sending shivers down my body and making my nipples harden. I don't even know why I'm begging him. This is exactly what I wanted. He's what I need.

"I TOLD YOU TO STAY AWAY," I whisper into the crook of her neck. My hand travels slowly up her thigh, sending tremors down her body.

I rock my pussy into his hand as his fingers shove my panties to the side. I shouldn't want this, but I do. And I fucking love it. He pushes his hand harder against my pussy, letting me take my pleasure from him. Even though my eyes are closed, I know he's smirking at me for giving in to him.

. . .

"You knew **what I'd do to you if you came around, didn't you?" I ask her, even though I already know the answer.**

"Yes," I whisper as his fingers gently circle my clit, sending a hot wave of pleasure through my body.

"You deliberately disobeyed me, **didn't you?" I ask her as I slowly push two thick fingers into her welcoming heat. She arches her back and pulls against her restraints. She's so fucking wet. So ready for me.**

I bite my bottom lip and muffle my moans of pleasure. He pulls his hand away, leaving me wanting, and my eyes pop open, already missing his touch. My body sags on the bed as I pant, waiting for him.

I'm **the muscle of the** *familia*, **and under investigation. This shit isn't supposed to happen. But I want her. And I always get what I want.**

I'm a cop. I shouldn't be fucking around with a thug like him. I should know better, but my body is begging for his touch. And I can't tell him no.

Just one more time, **before I have to say goodbye.**

Just one more time, before it all comes to an end.

"You're such a bad girl, **aren't you?" I give her clit a light smack with the back of my hand before climbing off the bed to unzip my jeans, letting them fall to the floor.**

"I'm your bad girl." My voice is barely above a murmur as he climbs between my legs. It hurts saying the words, because after today, I'll never see him again. I can't. But I want to be his bad girl.

That's right, **she's mine. All fucking mine. At least right now she is.**

I wish I could just stay here in this moment. I don't want this to end.

. . .

I SLAM **my dick into her tight pussy all the way to the hilt, and stay deep inside her as her walls clench around me. She screams out and bucks against me, trying to get away, but all she needs is a moment to adjust. She feels so fucking good. Each time is better than the last. I'll never be able to fuck this broad out of my system.**

My body tingles with an icy sensation as he pounds into me. Every nerve ending feels lit up, ready to spark, threatening to go off and consume me. The bed dips with each thrust and I instinctively pull against the cuffs, needing to touch him. The only sounds are the clinking of metal, our frantic breathing, and his hard thrusts.

HER HEELS DIG **into my ass, wanting more as I rut between her legs. My fingers dig into her hips to keep her still, to make her take it. She asked for this; she begged for this by coming to me again.**

I tilt my hips as he pushes deeper inside of me. A strangled cry escapes my throat as he pushes me to the brink of pain, then leaves me wanting more. He pulls out almost all the way, teasing me, but gives me what I need before I have to beg for it.

MY EARS ARE FILLED **with the sexy sounds of her moaning. She's so loud that she's almost drowning out the sounds of my dick slamming into her hot cunt. I fucking love it. It encourages me to fuck her harder. I never want to stop hearing her cries of pleasure.**

He slams into me and groans, the sound lingering in the hot air between us. It's the sexiest sound I've ever heard. My body heats in waves, and the tips of my fingers and toes go numb. I'm so close. I moan and whimper, and stare into his dark eyes as my orgasm hits me with a force that renders my scream silent.

THE SIGHT **of her cumming on my dick is my undoing. I press my body against hers and thrust with short, shallow pumps, filling her until our**

combined cum leaks down and onto the sheets.

He kisses the crook of my neck, and I turn my head to eagerly take his lips with my own. My heart clenches in pain as I surrender all of my passion into our final kiss. Tears threaten to fall, but I push them away. I know this was our last time, but I don't want it to be over.

I KEEP **my lips on hers as I reach up and unlock her cuffs with the key. As soon as one wrist is free, her hand's in my hair, pulling me closer to her.**

I just need to feel him; I need to remember this. I don't want it to end. I wish I could live in this moment forever.

As I PULL AWAY, **I see her eyes are closed and I know she wants this, too. I wanna make her happy; I wanna keep my bad girl. And I will. Everything and everyone else be damned. I can't say goodbye to her. I'm not letting her go.**

THREE WEEKS EARLIER

Tommy

I run my hand through my hair and take another look out of the window. Nothing yet. My apartment is a few stories up, but I can see down below to the first floor from here. I'm expecting a few cop cars to show up any minute now, sirens blaring. We got word a little earlier from the judge that he had to approve my arrest. He's in our pocket, but there's only so much even he can do.

They have enough to bring me in for questioning, so I just need to keep my mouth shut. And I can do that--I've had plenty of practice.

"Quit worrying," my brother says from the other side of the living room. I turn to face Anthony as he pours more whiskey into our glasses. The ice clinks softly against the glass as he hands me my drink before taking a sip from his. "At least this will give you something to do." He chuckles at his own joke.

"Yeah, I'm bored to fucking tears." I've been keeping a low profile, which means no family business. I don't know what the fuck to do with myself. I'm used to going out and getting shit done. Instead I'm holed up, waiting for this to be over. I miss being out there and making sure the Valettis are still respected and feared like we should be.

I'm the best of the best at keeping that fear alive. I'm six-foot-two, and muscle on top of muscle. I know some fucker is going to mess with our shit. They always do. And right now I can't do shit about it. Instead I'm sitting here on my ass, being a good little boy while the judge works his magic and Kane takes over my position.

"It's not like this is your first time." He smirks at me and I grunt a humorless laugh.

Anthony does the hits, and all the shit behind the scenes. He's never been taken in, not like the rest of us in the *familia*. Lucky fucker. When you work on the streets like I do, you get hauled in every once in awhile. Usually it doesn't faze me, but this is different. I'm not gonna lie, it'd be nice to get a gig like Anthony's and not have to deal with this shit.

The first time I was taken in was back when I was 22 years old. A low-life asshole thought he could steal from us. He was a fucking idiot. No one steals from us Valettis. We're well-known, feared, and respected. More so now than we were back then. But junkies will do whatever it takes to get their next hit. The poor bastard knew it was coming, too.

I found the fucker shooting up outside of a strip joint. He was in the back alley. Couldn't even wait till he got home, I guess. It doesn't bother me much now, but back then it took a toll on me. I hadn't toughened up yet. I broke his arm first. I learned that from my pop. Grab, twist, and crack. That way it's more difficult for them to fight back. He didn't even see me coming until his arm was busted and hanging limp at his side. I had to rough him up a bit. It was one of my first errands, and I knew the *familia* would go checking up behind me to see what kind of a job I'd done.

We agreed on new terms to the deal while he sat huddled in his own piss in that dark, filth-covered alley. And by that I mean he agreed to pay it all back with hefty interest by the next day. I have no clue if he ever paid up. I can't imagine if and how he did, but then again, that's not my job. And I don't ask questions.

Unfortunately, a little old lady saw us and decided to do the right thing. She stood at the entrance to the alley. I remember how her silhouette blocked the golden glow illuminating us from the street light. She was a small, frail woman in a cardigan, and had a plastic bag from the drugstore next door hanging from her wrist. When I looked her in the eyes, daring her to reach for her phone, she looked back with no fear at all. Feisty old woman.

I didn't bother dealing with her the way we normally handle witnesses. I figured the punk would live, but his ass wasn't going to press charges. That, and I'd only killed once before. That fucker had it coming to him, but this woman didn't. I wasn't getting her blood on my hands.

The prick ran out of the alley ahead of me and knocked her to the ground as she dialed the police. Having done my part, I took off and prayed she wouldn't be able to identify me. After all, it was dark, I was clad in all black, and I never got close enough to her so she could really see me. Or so I thought.

Old bat did see me though, and the cops knew exactly who she was describing. They know we're the mob, so they're always waiting for a chance to pin something on us. And I gave it to them, like a dumbfuck. Uncle Dante reamed me out pretty good. He was the Don back then, before his son Vince took over.

Luckily, nothing ever came of it. A night in the slammer, and I was a free man. That was the first time. Since then I've been careful, but occasionally we get pulled in for questioning. It's rare to spend a night in jail, though. Not when we have the best lawyer money can buy, and more than enough cops and judges on our payroll to make up our own court system. We always know when we'll be detained ahead of time, so we're always prepared.

But this time, fuck--this time it could be the real thing for me. The uncertainty surrounding this arrest is different from all the other times, and I don't like it.

"You're gonna be fine," Anthony says, taking a seat on my sofa. He drapes his arms across the back of the grey leather couch, and I wish I were as relaxed as him. I've never been envious of Anthony. He's a few inches shorter than me, and between the two of us, I'm the bigger pussy magnet. But right now I wish I'd been smart like him and and taken a job that didn't have me risking my neck like this.

"He said there's a good bit of evidence," I point out. Those are the words I keep hearing. *Good bit of evidence.*

"What are they gonna charge you with, huh?" He takes a swallow of his whiskey and leans forward, setting his drink down on the glassy surface of the coffee table before answering his own question. "Doing their job for 'em?" He says it sarcastically with a raised brow.

We got into a tight spot with some business partners, Abram Petrov and his crew. He was a big fucking deal, along with his supposed second-in-command Vadik Mikhailov. They took over international territories like it was nothing. Then he came here and wanted us to deal in the sex trafficking industry. That's not our thing. Unfortunately, when you tell people 'no' in our line of business, cutting ties takes on a whole new meaning.

"Murder, that one's legit," I finally respond. Thirteen dead members of Petrov's crew were left at the scene, along with twelve women we made certain were safe in the back room. We had a heads-up from Kane about Petrov's plan to murder us, so Petrov and his crew went down easier since they didn't know our ambush was coming.

Now the cops are trying to pin it all on me. I was the one stupid enough to leave evidence behind. Usually the clean-up crew gets all of it. But this time, they didn't. It's not like I was sloppy--I'm never sloppy. Shit just falls through the cracks sometimes. And this time it might fuck me over real good.

"Stop sweating it. They're just trying to get something from you," Anthony points out, still trying to reassure me. I should listen to Anthony. My brother's got great intuition, and he's always right. "I'll be there to pick you up when you're done, waiting right outside." He picks up his drink again, taking another pull before continuing. "And I bet the ice in my drink won't even be melted by the time you're getting into my ride." He swirls the ice around in the glass for emphasis as he says it.

He keeps my gaze, but I have to break it. I have a sick feeling in my gut. Vince says it'll be fine, that the judge says some of the evidence is inadmissible. But *some* is not all, and something deep down is telling me they're going to get me this time. It was way too big of a scene to clean up. Too much shit on our turf. We've been laying low, but it's going to blow up in our faces. I just know it.

Tilting my head to the left and right, I crack my neck on both sides. I down the remainder of my glass, savoring the sensation of the cold liquid mixed with the hot burn of the whiskey. It slides down my throat and warms my chest. That's when I hear them. I take a heavy breath and roll out my shoulders, knowing they'll be hurting once the cuffs are on. Gotta loosen them up now. Somehow, hearing the wail of the sirens get louder as they approach puts me at ease. Maybe it's just the waiting part that irritates me.

My heartbeat steadies, and my nerves follow suit. It's just like any other day, I tell myself. I'm used to this. These high-stress situations can't faze me. I can't let them see me in any other states but calm and confident. No one ever gets to see me in any other condition than prepared. If they view you otherwise, you give them a chance to think of you as weak. And that's one thing I'm not.

"That's the brother I know." Anthony gets up and walks past me to the window, tipping the upper blinds back to get a better view. "Oh, five," he says as his voice rises sarcastically. "You're so fucking special." I chuckle and pat him on the back as I head to the door.

Him being so at ease and having a sense of humor about it all does help. I gotta admit, whenever I'm in this shit, he's always here for me, before and after. The other guys are at the bar, but I know they'll be waiting for me there when I get out, too. That's something the *familia* is always good for, buying you a drink when you get out.

"You're not gonna make them walk their asses all the way up here? Seems like a missed opportunity to me." He shakes his head with a grin.

"You just wanna watch, don't you?" I ask him with a smirk.

He pats my back again and sets his glass down on the end table. "I'll go with you."

I grin at him as I open the door and hear the sounds of them walking through the building. I decide to leave my apartment unlocked. I know they're going to search my place, and I'd rather not have to replace my door in case they decide to be assholes. "Lock it up for me when they're gone?"

Anthony nods. "You know I will." They're already climbing the stairs as we get to the landing, so I just stand there with my hands clearly visible. I don't want these fuckers to shoot my ass.

"It's all good, Tommy. Just remember that. Not a damn thing's gonna happen," he says under his breath with a straight face. His smiles and jokes are all gone. He's doing the same thing as me and putting on his mask.

I'm large and all muscle. I look like I'd fuck you up with my bare hands, and you'd be right to think that. Anthony has a different air around him, he always has. He's a little shorter than me, a lot leaner, but toned. But something about his expressions and his dark eyes lets you know not to fuck with him.

"Thomas Valetti, we have a warr--" the cop closest to me begins, as he starts pulling out a piece of paper, but I don't even need to see it.

I cut him off and don't let him finish. "Yeah yeah, I know." I turn and put my hands on the top of my head.

As a set of hands grab my wrists to pull them behind my back, and a voice starts spouting off the standard bullshit, I look up and see Anthony.

I almost don't see it, but I know I do. I see a flash of worry in Anthony's eyes. And that's the only thing that keeps playing through my head as they take me in.

TONYA

I'm fucking furious. It feels like I'm back in high school again, dealing with petty, catty drama. I didn't like it then, and I don't like it now. The only difference is that I can't meet up behind the school to put this bitch in his place. I may be small, but I could take him. It wouldn't be the first time I've had to prove myself.

"This is bullshit, Harrison, and you know it!" I slam the folder down on my desk and push off my chair so fast it almost tips over. I don't give a shit. I also don't give one fuck that my skirt is all wrinkled and riding up from sitting at my desk all day. If it was up to me, I wouldn't be sitting at this damn desk. I'm not a paper pusher; I like getting shit done, and I hate that he's trying to stand in my way.

"Is there a problem, Officer Kelly?" he asks me with a twisted smile. He's such an ass. He went behind my back to have more paperwork assigned to me. If he thinks he can wear me down until I'm his little bitch, he has another think coming. I'm a fighter. That's what I do, and I'm damn good at it.

"Oh, now I'm 'Officer Kelly'?" This angry woman, yelling at her coworker? This isn't me. But I'm so pissed. I hate my temper, and I've worked so fucking hard to tone it down. I really hate getting angry. But Harrison brings out the worst in me.

I'm fed up with this asshole. He's a crooked cop, and now he's trying to

489

boss me around. I might be new, but I want to be the lead on this case more than anything. It's the only reason I'm here, and I won't let him stand in my way. Motherfucker better back off. I don't care that he has more experience than me; what he's doing is wrong.

"Thomas Valetti is a criminal," he says from the doorframe of my office. There's conviction in his voice. I get that. I know Thomas is mobbed up; everyone knows the Valettis are the big time mafia around here. But that doesn't mean he should be going down for this.

"He didn't do this, and you know it." My voice wavers, and I hate that it does. I wish it were steady and strong. I *am* strong, but I feel like I'm on the verge of breaking.

"You don't know shit." I swear I see spit fly from his mouth as he sneers his words. "If you knew what I had to deal with from these lowlifes, you'd be chomping at the bit to get him in here and sweating in his seat." *'Lowlifes'* hits a nerve with me. I've been called a lowlife before more than once. I grew up in a trailer until my mom got clean. It wasn't my fault. If I'd had a choice, I wouldn't have lived there. I wanted real walls around my bedroom, not thin sheets of metal that barely protected me from anything that happened to bang against them in the middle of the night.

My only saving grace was my sister. I'll never understand how we grew up in the same environment, yet turned out so different. After we moved to the suburbs, she just naturally fit in. It didn't take long for me to settle down and find ways to fit in as well, but I never forgot who I was. She was a good girl through and through. It's not that I was a bad girl. I just had to tame that spitfire in me and throw my favorite sparkly pink polish on top so I could blend in better.

He walks closer to me with a scowl on his face. "He's one of the big fish in the family. We can get him to talk. I know we can."

That's what this is about. He's looking for anything he can get to put the Valettis behind bars. But not this way. I fucking hate that he's chasing a name and bending the law. What's right is right, and what's wrong is wrong. And right now what Detective Harrison is doing is just plain wrong.

I learned long ago that if you just do what's right, bad shit tends to stay away from you. Most of the time. My heart clenches in my chest and I almost reach for the locket I used to wear every day, but I don't. Sometimes bad shit just happens, but you still try to do the right thing.

Harrison and his vendetta could fuck this up for me. I don't care about past crimes. Shit, I don't even care about whatever the hell the Valettis are doing now. I care about one name, and getting the information I need to make sure he pays. I care about revenge.

Some may think it's wrong, taking revenge. But it's not. Not for me. My sister deserves justice, and I won't stop until she gets it.

I speak through clenched teeth, arching my neck to look this prick in his eyes. He might be taller than me, but he's not going to intimidate me. At least not so much that it's completely obvious to him. "You and I both know Petrov had that deal lined up with the Bratva in Kirov." All the wire transfers and cell phone activity point to it. He knows it, and I know it. It's fucking obvious, and international relations corroborated our theory. The Valettis put an end to that shit, and got a target on their backs for their troubles. Yet Detective Harrison is ready to pin the entire case on Thomas Valetti. The evidence is weak at best, but he's pushing.

"You'll stick to the script, or spend every fucking day sifting through these files, Kelly."

"I'm not your goddamned secretary." I walk past him and head straight to the Lieutenant's office. I'm done with this conversation. Since I can't kick his ass, I'll just go around him. He's not my boss, and I'm not going to put up with this.

I knock on the closed door with my white-knuckled fist and keep my back to Harrison as he stomps up behind me. His shadow looms over me. I can't fucking stand him. He crosses the line whenever the hell he wants. I'm tired of him ordering me around and threatening me when he's the one in the wrong. I know I'm new and I have to prove myself, but there comes a point when it's just him being an asshole.

I raise my fist to pound against the door again, but it flies open.

"Harrison!" Jerry Weldon is an old man who's tired of Harrison's shit, too. I have to work hard to keep the grin from showing on my face.

"Lieutenant--" Harrison tries to speak over me, but Jerry cuts him off.

"I swear to God, if this is over the Valetti case, I'm going to fucking pull you off it, Harrison." The grin slips into place, and I feel like a damn villain for enjoying this. But I can't help it.

"He's threatening to take me off, Lieutenant," I say as calmly and professionally as possible. Which is easier than I'd thought it'd be. I can play the good girl part when I have to.

Jerry's eyebrow cocks and he looks at Harrison like the fucking cockroach he is, then back at me. "I don't have time for this shit, Kelly. Ignore his ass for now and do your damn job." The blood drains from my face. Fuck. I hate that he's scolding me like a petulant child. I just want Harrison off my ass. Is that too much to ask?

Again I feel like I'm in high school. The teachers looked at me with sympathy because they thought I just couldn't help that I was always getting into trouble. It was bullshit then, and it's bullshit now. I swear to God some days I feel like I've taken crazy pills.

"He's in holding now, and you'll interview him together. Is that clear?" Jerry asks, looking between both of us.

"Yes, sir." I answer clearly while Harrison practically mumbles. I didn't bust my ass to get here so that I'd have to stand by men like him. He earned this position, and I should respect him for it. I *try* so hard to respect him for it. If he'd stop being an asshole, it'd be easier. I know the Valettis are big fish, but this is *my* case. And he needs to stop trying to shut me out of it.

I would cave and drop it if it weren't for Petrov. He's the only reason I'm here, and if Harrison knew why, he'd stop trying to push me off the case, because he'd know there's no way I'm ever backing down. But none of them know; I don't want them to. I can't let them know this is personal.

Jerry gives me a tight smile, and I can see a faint glimmer of sympathy in his eyes. I'm not sure if it's because I'm standing next to this asshole and I don't have a choice, or if it's because he thinks I won't make it.

I'm petite, I like the color pink, especially *hot* pink, and I'd rather smile and joke around than brood over something stupid. Or I used to, anyway. Now it seems like all I do is get pissed off. But that's an exception. It's because I'm forced to deal with an ass all day.

All of those girly touches I love so much make me seem young and naive. Everyone looks at me like I don't belong, and maybe they're right. Maybe I learned to like all of that girly stuff because it softened me up some. Maybe I just wanted to copy my sweet-as-sugar sister. I don't know. I'm a tough girl, but I'm still a girl. I don't understand why people don't think I can be both, like they're mutually exclusive or something. Instead I'm judged and shunned, no matter how many times I prove I have what it takes.

I stopped wearing anything remotely fashionable to the social gatherings. Even though I have palettes upon palettes of eyeshadow, I keep my makeup simple, or I just don't wear makeup at all. I don't wear any jewelry or get my nails done anymore. I have to wear my hair up in a ponytail or a bun. When it's down I look way too feminine. I do everything I can to look like I fit in, because apparently that's a requirement here. It doesn't matter that I graduated at the top of my class back at the academy. A girly girl can't survive here. Or so they say behind my back.

The problem is that they don't see my confidence and passion for what it is. My personality's misconstrued because of how I look. I'm a bad ass bitch when I need to be, but I don't want to come off that way all the time. I haven't proven myself to be strong in their eyes.

I'm pushing the bad bitch to the surface and repressing every other part of me. All that's left after getting rid of the frilly shit I love is just a tough girl trying to fit in, so I can do what I came here to do. But I'm failing, and that fucking sucks, because I don't fail at anything, and this is the only thing that matters anymore. I have to work twice as hard, to be considered half as good.

When I hear the guys talking shit about being tough, all I can think is that they're talking about tough actions, not appearances or words. Maybe they're just trying to convince themselves that a petite woman with a penchant for pink couldn't kick their asses. I'm happy to prove them wrong though.

A part of me wants to prove them wrong. I want to show them I'm a bad ass bitch when I need to be. But another part of me is tired of fighting their prejudice. I didn't come here to win their approval. They can talk shit about me. They can assume I'm going to fail. I don't give a fuck. All I need is to be on this case. It's the only reason I put up with this shit.

It hurts though. I'm woman enough to admit it. I want companionship. I want to feel like I belong. But right now, I have no one. I try to call my mom every once in awhile, but that's just depressing as hell. I'm most concerned with the fact that I don't know what happiness is anymore. I don't know what I expected. But this isn't it. I was so shortsighted with wanting to get here that I didn't think things through all the way.

The reality is a swift kick in the ass.

Harrison pushes past me just as I get to the door to the interrogation room. Fucker holds it open for me though, like he's a gentleman. I give him a tight smile and walk in first.

I almost stop when I see the hulking man in the metal chair. An air of power surrounds him. His hands are clasped in front of him and they're resting on the table. He doesn't bother to look up at us. His dark, thick hair is longer on top than it is on the sides, just long enough to grip onto. It tempts me; it excites the wilder side of me that I usually keep suppressed.

He's in a simple white t-shirt that stretches tight over his shoulders, and faded blue jeans. I've never seen a man who could make those casual clothes look so fucking hot. His arms are all thick, corded muscle, and they flex as Harrison walks in front of me and stands across from him. Dark tattoos scroll down his left arm. I find myself itching to touch them, and wonder how much of his body they cover.

The younger me would have drooled over this man, but I know better now. Men like him cause more trouble than they're worth. And he's a member of the strongest *familia* on this side of the country. He's a Valetti. He's trouble.

"Valetti." Harrison's nose scrunches as he sits in the seat across from the sexy-as-fuck suspect. I stand with my back against the wall. I don't want to go near those two knowing what Harrison is up to. I'm not afraid to get into it if I have to. I can hold my own, regardless of how big and how scary my opponent is. But I'm not fucking stupid. I avoid physical altercations if I can. And Harrison has a smart mouth and likes to push people.

He likes to take advantage of these situations and get them to act out so he can put them in the cells and threaten a heavier sentence. It's not a move I'd make. But I try not to judge other officers' tactics. I *try*. Never said I was perfect though.

The man, Thomas Valetti, raises his head slowly. His full lips tip into a slight smirk and his blue eyes hold a hint of humor. "Detective. Nice to see you again."

His voice sends a throbbing need to my clit, and for the first time since I've taken this job, I question if I really am cut out for it. I've never once been attracted to the fucked-up criminals that come and go in here. But right now, right here? Fuck. He's hot. My body can't deny that. I have to work really hard to keep the embarrassment off my face. I'm a professional. I'm a cop now. I need to put my hormones in check.

I try to ignore the pulsing need between my thighs and I clear my throat to help settle myself.

The action causes both men to look at me. Thomas' eyes roam my body, but not in a way I find rude or offensive. He's just sizing me up. I half-expect him to make some sexist comment, like most thugs do. I can *feel* my defenses go up.

His eyes reach mine and I wait for it. I wait for the dismissal. The demeaning comments I'm constantly used to getting.

Instead Harrison interrupts, "I won't stop until you go away for life."

The corners of Thomas' lips kick up slightly as he turns to face Harrison, leaving me with nothing. "Sorry, Detective. I'm just waiting for my lawyer."

Harrison looks at me from the corner of his eyes like it's my fault that Thomas isn't talking. I grab the folder from the desk and move to sit in the seat next to Harrison and square my shoulders.

I know in the pit of my gut Thomas Valetti is one of the people who saved those women. But he also has information I want. Now's my chance to make everything I've worked for up to this moment worth it.

He's my only lead.

TOMMY

"$\mathcal{M}$r. Valetti," begins the gorgeous woman who's all curves and sweetness. She's looking back at me like we're on good terms. Like she can talk to me as though I'm an old pal of hers. She's either fresh blood, or she's damn good at what she does. This good cop/bad cop routine would be easy enough with detective Harrison being the jackass he is. It's not the first time I've run into him, and I'm sure it won't be the last.

Judging by her body language when she walked in here, and the pissed-off looks Harrison keeps throwing her, I'm guessing she's new. I wouldn't mind having her try to cuff me. Wish it was her who'd brought me in, not that fuck-face from earlier.

"We know you were at the scene of the crime *after* it occurred based on the fact that your prints were found covering the prints of Lucas Mikhailov, a man found dead on sight." She reaches into the manila folder and slides a photograph of a doorknob across the table. Her small hand holds it in place. She doesn't move it, and I find myself eyeing her chipped nail polish. It's a soft cream color and it makes her appear even more dainty that she already looks. What the hell is this little thing doing trying to play cop? She interrupts my thought as she takes her hand away and asks, "Would you like to explain how that could've happened?"

I meet her gaze and love that she's not intimidated by me. Her eyes are the most beautiful shade of green I've ever seen. And they're staring back at me waiting for an answer. I'm real fucking sorry to disappoint her. But even a sweetheart like her can't get me to talk. I'm not saying shit.

I almost apologize--almost call her love, or sweetie. But I keep my mouth shut and remind myself that this is an act. These cops like to set the scene. It's all lies in here. I give her a simple shake of my head and answer, "I'm just waiting for my lawyer."

If I'm being honest with myself, this is the most nervous I've ever been, but I don't show it. I don't give them anything.

They have my prints, even though they're smudged, and so are the ones beneath mine. They have the tire tracks to the Escalade, which is in my name. They have a witness who says she saw me, although she was drugged up. At least that's the evidence the judge was willing to hand off to Vince. Three pieces of shit evidence. One piece of evidence by itself could be a coincidence. But put three pieces together, and it starts sounding real fucking bad.

"Mr. Valetti. Are you aware that a Miss Georgia Stevens was found dead in the back of the rental car left at the scene of the crime?" the sweet little thing in front of me says, and it takes me a moment to register what she said.

My heart skips a beat, and my blood goes cold. A dead woman. No. We saved those women. But we didn't check any cars. Fuck! I wanna ask whose car. I wanna know how she died. More importantly, was she alive when we left?

My eyes search hers. She could be lying. She could be fucking with me just to get me to talk. But I see her expression soften with compassion. She can tell I didn't know. I lean back in my seat and do my best to wipe every emotion off my face. It's quiet for a moment. It's been about an hour, so my lawyer should be here soon. I just need to hold on till then, and then I can look up the woman they found dead. Vince never said shit about her. At least not to me, but I've been out of the loop.

"The car was rented to a man we believe to be Abram Petrov. His prints were found in the car, although his body was never found."

None of this is throwing up red flags to me. His body was sent back to the buyers as a sign from us that we weren't willing to partake in that aspect of the business. Our hands won't be forced. If they didn't know it then, well they sure as fuck know it now.

"Do you have any information regarding Petrov's whereabouts?" She leans forward, and I have to resist looking straight down her blouse. Her body is lean and toned with a touch of color from the sun, but her tits are bigger than you'd think they'd be for a woman as athletic as her.

I give her a weak smile and shake my head no again. I'm grateful for the bit of information she's given me, if it's true, but that doesn't mean I'm gonna talk. I need to know if the woman she mentioned was alive when we left. It couldn't have been more than twenty minutes before the cops got there. But a lot can happen in twenty minutes.

As if reading my mind, she answers my unspoken question. "Drug over-dose," she says simply. My lips press into a tight line and my heart sinks. Maybe if my brother had seen her, like the other women, maybe he could've saved her. I drop my gaze to the edge of the table as I try to keep calm and not give her anything.

"She'd been dead for almost a day, judging by the autopsy." My eyes fly to hers. Thank fuck. That makes me feel better. I feel like an asshole for feeling any kind of relief. That poor woman didn't deserve to die, but at least she didn't die on our watch. We never had the opportunity to save her.

I run a hand through my hair and look at the closed door.

"Do you have any details that could help us uncover who was responsible?" I hear her sweet voice and I almost turn to her to answer, but I can't. We don't say shit except for what I've already given them. *I'm waiting on my lawyer.* That's the *familia* way.

"You don't have any fucking sympathy, do you?" Harrison starts up again with his shit from across the table. "The jury's gonna eat you alive." I resist rolling my eyes and sigh instead. This is fucking draining. Usually I don't give a fuck, but I am a bit worried. I don't like the sick feeling in my gut that keeps rising up on me.

"Are you charging me? If not, I'm gonna go ahead and leave," I say, looking at the door. I'm tired of waiting. I just want to get the hell out of here.

Harrison shoots up from his seat. I know he's coming over to get in my face. I stand up as he walks around the table. They can keep me here longer for questioning. I know that. But he's fucking lost it if he thinks he's gonna yell standing over me while I'm sitting down. That shit's not gonna fly.

I stand up and stare back at his narrowed eyes. I vaguely sense that the cute ass broad got up from her seat and is backing away. That puts me at ease.

She doesn't need to get into this. She can keep playing the good cop part and stay the fuck out of the bad cop shit.

Harrison's body bumps into mine slightly, but I allow it. I know he's pushing me. He's done it before. Sometimes I get a little hotheaded. More than I should. But when you're here, in this position, you keep your cool. Otherwise you're just giving them a reason to keep you locked up. And that's the last thing I want.

"I'll charge you with everything possible, to the full extent of the law. Your ass isn't leaving here tonight. Or tomorrow. Or the next day." I focus my eyes on his crooked smile and imagine my fist slamming into it over and over. "Your big shot lawyer isn't getting you out of this one, Valetti."

His hands knock into my chest, palms first and push me backward ever so slightly. I'm a big fucker, and that's a bold fucking move for this little prick. I make a white-knuckled fist with my hand and clench my teeth.

Before I can even think about swinging, I feel the softest touch on my forearm. Gentle, but firm. And then it's gone. I don't turn to face her; I don't make any move that I even registered her touch. Harrison's yelling in my face, but my anger is gone and instead I find myself angling my body to guard her from this prick.

Why? No fucking clue. She's one of them. But I know she's just to my right. I can sense her there, and I don't like it.

She's a cop, and as far as I know she could hold her own. But I don't want her to. I track her to my right, hoping she doesn't try to get in between us. It might be sexist, but that's no place for a woman to be.

Harrison still hasn't caught on to the fact that him screaming in my face and subtly pushing his body against me isn't affecting me.

The sound of the door opening has Harrison taking a step back and trying to maintain eye contact with me, but I break it to watch her leave. He's no threat to me, so I couldn't give two shits about keeping an eye on him. But it wasn't her opening the door. Instead, my lawyer's standing in the doorway.

"Is there a problem here, Mr. Valetti?" Scott Kemmer is the *familia* attorney, and he's good at what he does.

I give him a tight smile and shove my hands into my pockets. "Not at all. I was just asking if it was time to go." I look over my shoulder and see the pretty little thing who didn't even bother to give me her name. Her eyes are shooting daggers at Harrison. I don't waste my energy to see what he's doing behind me. I bet she thought she could get me to talk if he wasn't being a prick and doing the shit he does.

She has no idea what she's up against, though. She'd never get an ounce of information from me. She must be *really* fucking new to think she'd get anything from a Valetti.

"Are you ready, Mr. Valetti?" I barely hear the words from my lawyer and that's when I belatedly realize I'm good to go. I didn't hear all the bullshit coming from Harrison about how I can't leave, and my lawyer's response. It's the same shit every time.

"All set." I give him a nod and make my way through the doors, not giving either one of them another look. But I have to admit, I wanna turn back and see her. I at least wanna know her name.

I let myself breathe freely for the first time all day as I leave the station, and see my brother in his car waiting for me, just like he said he would.

"Told you," Anthony says, lowering his window and giving our lawyer a salute.

"Hey, you wanna do something today?" I ask him.

Wicked curiosity flashes in his eyes.

"I wanna look someone up." He tilts his head and keeps his eyes on me as I round the car and get into the passenger seat.

"Look someone up?" he asks as I shut the door and lean back, making myself comfortable.

"Yeah, a cop," I tell him. The humor's completely wiped from his face until I add, "I think she's new."

"Oh, I see." He chuckles as he puts the car in drive. "Maybe we should've left you in there a little longer."

I laugh and roll my window down so I can put a hand out and feel the breeze.

"I'm just a little bored, and a lot curious," I say.

"You know what they say about that, don't you?" He looks at me like what I'm doing is stupid as fuck. And maybe it is. But I at least need to know her name.

TONYA

I feel like a fucking failure. I sigh heavily and lean my back against the wall of the station. I run my hands over my face and feel like shit. Damn it's been a long couple of days. I got the approval to keep an eye on Thomas, so there's one positive thing that happened. Tomorrow I'll get something, even if it's just learning his routines. I have the next three days off. I can use them to get a good look at the Valettis and try to talk to Thomas. I may be off-duty, but if anything happens, I'll just say it's field work.

I really think I could've gotten information from him. I could tell he didn't have shit to do with Georgia's death. I could've fed off that emotion. I'm good at reading people, real fucking good at it. I get people to talk. There's just something about me that puts people at ease. I don't know what it is, but I love it. It's a gift, and it's always worked in my favor.

If Harrison had just shut his fucking mouth, I know I would've had Thomas right where I wanted him. I recognize the way he looked at me. I know what he was thinking. If I'd just kept it up, I would've had him talking to me and confiding in the poor, sweet girl who just wants to make things right. In some ways I'm a bitch for thinking that way. After all, I can be sweet. I just needed him to give me anything at all on Petrov. Everyone keeps saying he's probably dead. I need to know for sure.

If he's already dead and gone, it would kill the sick, twisted part of me that wants to beat him to death with my own two hands. I've spent years trying to find a way to get to him. I've come too close to give up hope. If he's dead, I *need* to know. I need to be able to let go. I can't really say goodbye to her until I know for sure.

The thought makes my eyes water, but I just blink a few times to shut that shit down. She would tell me not to cry, and if there's one person I took advice from, it was my sister. My fingers reach for my locket, the one with Melissa's picture in it. But it's not there, so instead I rub the dip in my throat. I never wear it when I'm on duty, but it does wonders to calm me down and keep me focused.

I shake my head to get rid of all the emotions threatening to consume me, and hit the unlock button on my key fob. The key itself is sticking out through my clenched fist. Just in case, I look to the right as the lights go off on my car and the gentle beep fills the air. I pass the corner of the building. No one's there. No one's out here. You can never be too careful, though. I always check. I'm always on guard. I'd say it comes with the training, but that's not why I do this. I wish I could lie to myself, but I can't. I know why I do it. And I hate the reminder.

I feel like I've felt eyes on me the last few days. So I guess being on guard like this may eventually pay off. I just can't get rid of the feeling that I'm being watched. My stomach coils into knots, and I try to shake it off. I'm just para-noid and tired. That's what I tell myself, over and over. This isn't the first time I've felt like this. And I was fine then. It's just my past that's haunting me.

I climb into my car and toss the messenger bag onto the passenger seat. I have so much paperwork to go through. I'm not looking forward to it, but if I have to work overtime to get it done and still be able to keep up with the Valetti case, then that's what I'm going to do.

I put the key in the ignition and start the car. My mind drifts as I drive back to my apartment. My sister was the only person I really had in this world. She was no one special to anyone but me. Just a nurse. No one who anyone would ever want to hurt. She never really went anywhere high-risk. She hardly went out for a drink. But one night she went out to get groceries and never came back. One night is all it took, and she was gone. Her body was found a few months later, among others, in Russia. At first I was filled with disbelief. This sort of thing doesn't happen in real life. Definitely not in America.

But it does. And it did to her. When I got over the sadness, the anger set in. I had nothing to hold me back. I was already in college for forensics, so it was a small step to get into the academy. Anger turned into determination. I read everything I could. I became obsessed.

It was almost like a graduation present that there was a position available in a town where Petrov was last seen in the US. I've never been so lucky. But since I've gotten here, the leads have gone cold. And so has everyone else I've been surrounded by.

I watch the red light as I pull up to it, waiting for it to turn green, and my eyes catch movement to my right. It's a small Italian water ice shop. A few kids are standing out front with their parents leaning into the window to order. I hear their little screams of joy as they each dig into their treats.

Their life is normal; I wonder if they do that every Friday night. We used to go to the ice cream parlor a few blocks away when we were younger. Melissa talked about how she would keep up the tradition with her kids when she bought her house close to where we grew up.

The light turns green and I slowly move along. I'll never have that again. I don't see how I can ever have a normal life. How can life go on when you've suffered that type of tragedy? My mother's doped up on antidepressants. I'm surprised she didn't go back to coke. She's barely a shell of a human being. My father took off when I was young, so I don't even know him. So now I'm just … alone. Chasing what may be a ghost. But I won't stop looking until I know for sure.

I pull into my spot and put the car in park. The street light is shining down perfectly, and the entrance to my building is only a few feet away. I make a quick exit and enter the building and only breathe once I've made it upstairs. I can't help that I feel this way. It's late, it's dark. Nothing good happens at this time of night.

I climb the stairs and make my way to my place. I take a look out of the peephole and expect to see someone watching, but I don't. There's no one there. I wish this paranoia would leave me. It's only been this bad for a few days, ever since I saw Thomas. The reminder brings me back to my sole purpose.

I lock the front door and walk calmly to my bedroom. The necklace is on my dresser. I pick it up and open the little oval locket.

I want to end this for her.

I have a feeling in my gut that Thomas Valetti is the next step. I always follow my intuition, and it's clearly pushing me to talk to him. I feel like I already know the truth, but I just need to hear him say it.

If I can just get an in with Thomas, I know he'll lead me to something.

TOMMY

"*I* mean, what's the worst they can do?" The Bratva may be pissed we took a shipment from them, but they should've known better than to assume Petrov could speak on our behalf. Apparently they *did* make that assumption though, and now they're saying we owe them. I lean back a bit on the bar stool and look around. We're in the bistro now, just chatting it up.

"They could come here, but I doubt they will. Too much effort," Kane says. Most of the guys are here, bullshitting and having a drink. I like Kane. He's new to the *familia*, but he knows his shit and he's good at what he does. Which right now is taking over my position.

"It's not the loss of one shipment, it's their entire trade structure that they have to rebuild. A few million in revenue," Vince says from across the bar. I cross my arms and take it in. They haven't threatened us, but they made it clear they were pissed.

"It's not our fault they were doing all their shit through Petrov," Joey says.

"Maybe sending his body to them instead of the women wasn't the way to go?" Anthony's question has a few of the men chuckling.

"I'm not sure it's even worth replying. It's not like we do business with these people." I offer up my opinion. We keep our trades to Mexico, and that's it. The new dealer there is low-key and reasonable. Nice and easy. None of this overseas shit.

"We need to respond with something." Vince takes another drink and adds, "I want this to be a clean break away from them, but I sure as shit am not buying them off." They want 2 million for their hardship, which is bullshit, and I know Vince isn't going to pay them. It's quiet for a few minutes.

"Fuck 'em," he finally says, "let 'em come to us. Tony's got eyes on their contacts here. We'll know they're coming before they strike." He puts his glass down and pulls out his phone. I know he's checking on his wife, Elle, and his little one. Angelo is a cutie and almost six months old now. Ever since he's made his arrival, Vince checks his phone on the hour every hour.

Marcus comes up behind me and pats my shoulder as he says, "Your shadow's out front." He says it loud enough so that the rest of the guys can hear. Anthony chuckles into his drink, "Funny how you wanted to keep an eye on her, and now she's coming to you." He smirks and throws back his drink.

I spent a couple days just watching her after I looked her up. I had Tony do a little digging, too. I can't shake this broad. She looks on edge every time she's alone, yet she's completely confident and at ease any other time. Something's off about her, and I wanna know what it is. She knows her shit though. She's a tough bitch, not quite the quiet, demure type I pegged her for. And she fucking hates Harrison. The first time I saw her mimicking him behind his back and rolling her eyes, I laughed so fucking hard I thought they were going to hear me. I like that about her, but there's something else there, too. Something that had me chasing her ass.

I'd be a fucking liar if I said something about fucking a cop doesn't have me interested. Most of the time I was watching her that's all I could think about Bending her ass over and taming that wild side of her. The taboo aspect has me getting hard thinking about using her own cuffs to chain her to my bed. I think I just need to fuck this broad out of my system.

Vince rolls his eyes and says, "You need to tell her to back the fuck off, Tommy. We have restraining orders for a fucking reason."

"We don't have them on her." I can hear how defensive I am, and it throws Vince off. I'm quick to add, "I'm being watched and on lockdown; better her than that prick."

I like her watching me. I like knowing she's close. And besides, I'm inactive until I'm completely in the clear, so there's nothing to worry about there. If nothing else, it's giving me something else to take my mind off this shit.

"Well, get her out of here," Anthony says as he looks me up and down. "And try to keep your dick in your pants." The guys laugh as I stand up.

"I hear you." I'm ready to get out of here anyway.

Vince follows me to the door.

"I don't like this talk about fucking a cop," he says.

"I'm not, so it's all good." He watches me as I look past him at the door. I don't tell him I want to, but I'm too fucking obvious.

"You're a shit liar, Tommy."

"I'm not lying." I don't even believe me as I say it. But it's the truth. I haven't touched her. Yet.

"You're not telling the truth, either."

I open my mouth to respond, but I don't. He knows I wanna fuck her. Everybody fucking knows it.

"You're looking for trouble, Tommy," Vince says in a lowered voice. "And that's what you're going to get."

"I'm not gonna do anything stupid, boss." He's gotta know I wouldn't say shit to her. I'd never breathe a word of anything.

"Women make us do stupid shit. And she's a cop." He stares into my eyes, willing me to listen to him. "Don't fucking believe a word she tells you." His hand grips my shoulder as I nod.

I know this shit looks bad. I don't know why I'm drawn to this broad. She could fuck me over in a heartbeat. I'm not going to give her shit. But the thought of playing with her is giving me a high I haven't felt before. I know she wants in, and I'm dying to find out how much I can push her.

Vince shakes his head as he warns me, "Do not fuck this up to get your dick wet."

"I won't say shit, Vince. You know I won't risk the *familia*."

He huffs a laugh and pinches the bridge of his nose. "I'm not worried about that shit, I'm worried about you fucking a cop, Tommy. Tell me you aren't trying to get into her pants and I'll feel better."

I hesitate to answer. I'm not gonna lie. I wanna fuck this broad, she's hot as shit and the idea of those lips wrapped around my cock has my dick hardening every fucking time it comes to mind. Even right fucking now.

"Jesus, Tommy," he says with exasperation. Fuck. I don't wanna piss off the Don.

"I won't," I say with regret in the pit of my stomach.

"You're fucking lying to me," he says, although he doesn't sound that pissed about it.

"I've never lied to you before." I look him in the eyes, "if you're telling me to stay away from her, I'll end this shit right now and threaten a restraining order."

"Good. End this shit," he says with relief and finality in his voice. Well that fucking sucks. I take a frustrated breath and leave the guys to go tell her she needs to stay away.

I feel a wave of disappointment as I leave the bistro. But then I see her walking toward me with quick steps. She's in civilian clothes. Jeans that hug her curves and a teal tank top that rides up a little as she walks. The color brings out her eyes.

I can play a little more. Just a little before I have to give her up.

Fuck, no. I told Vince I wouldn't, and I know I shouldn't.

I hate that I want her and that I can't go after her. But I have to listen to Vince.

TONYA

"*T*homas." I call out his name as he blatantly turns away from me and starts heading down the street. I know he saw me. He fucking smiled before blowing me off.

I have to jog to catch up to him, but before I can put my hand on his shoulder to stop him, he turns around.

"What the hell are you thinking, Tonya?" he asks with more concern in his voice than anything else. "You could get yourself into serious shit hanging around out here waiting for me."

My brow furrows with confusion. "How do you know my name?"

He smirks at me and turns his back on me once again. I don't fucking like it. I don't like being ignored.

I reach out to grasp his arm. I shouldn't. I know I shouldn't, but something is telling me he'll allow it. Probably the same something that has my core soaked with arousal.

He turns sharply and grabs my wrist. "That's not a good idea." He doesn't let go as the words drip from his mouth with a threat. He walks toward me and I find myself taking a step back. My back hits the brick wall of a building and it makes my heart thud in my chest.

"I just wanna talk." I say the words through the hint of fear I'm feeling. His eyes hold a look of hunger, but also a dark look that has me questioning my instincts. Maybe I was wrong about him.

"Well, I don't." He releases my wrist and walks away again. My heart sinks in my chest, and I hate myself for feeling like I've failed. I can't rely on Thomas alone. I know that, but somehow there's more to this ache in my chest than just losing a lead. His rejection hurts.

I watch his back as he walks away, and the hurt turns to anger. He's not going to blow me off like that. I'm not giving up that easily. I walk faster to catch up to him. I'm shorter than him, and he's walking fast, but I quicken my steps until I'm right behind him. I *need* to know. I just need him to answer one question.

I grab his arm just enough to get his attention and pull away before he can touch me again. He opens his mouth to tell me off again, but I blurt out the question I've been dying to ask him since I first saw him at the station. "Abram Petrov, is he dead?"

The anger on his face morphs into curiosity as he tilts his head, looking me up and down.

"It's a simple question." I swallow thickly as a lump grows in my throat. I already know when he says yes, I'm going to want more answers. I'm going to want proof. I clench my fists and make sure I keep my voice down as I say, "I need to know if he's dead."

"Is that what this is for you? Revenge on Petrov? Is that why you're so damn stubborn?" he asks, like I'm being a petulant child and he finds it comical.

"He's why my sister's dead, asshole. You can at least tell me if he's dead."

Remorse flashes in his eyes as he answers, "I wish I could, but I even if I knew one way or the other, I can't say shit to you. You're a cop, remember?"

"You can tell me." My eyes plead with him. For the first time since I graduated, I wish I wasn't a cop. It never occurred to me that being a cop would close doors I'd need to go through to get to him. At the time, it was the most obvious way to move forward. I never thought twice about it until I got here.

He presses his lips into a straight line and looks at me for a moment, considering. I don't budge. I won't. I need to know.

"You think I'm stupid?" he asks, and I can see that he's gearing up for a showdown, but that's not what I want.

"You're not stupid, I don't think that at all. I'm not wired or anything. You can just nod. I swear." My words fly out in desperation.

"I'd have to strip you down to make sure you weren't. Is that what you want, little miss good girl?" A wave of arousal soaks my pussy as he leans into me. My mind starts fantasizing about things it shouldn't.

"I'm not a good girl. And if that's what it would take." I say the words before I can regret them. It's so fucking wrong. Would I really do that? Would I lower myself to stripping for him? I don't know if I'd go through with it. His eyes heat with lust, and I start to think it's a real possibility.

"No, you're not a good little girl at all, are you?" His smile widens as he takes a step back. "You're such a *bad* girl." He's mocking me. Fucking prick. I bite my tongue and watch as he turns away. My ego takes a huge fucking hit.

I turn my back on him and take a left into an alley between a convenience store and a barber shop. I know my car is parked somewhere on the next street over, parallel to this one. I don't pay attention to the men at the corner when I turn, but I sure as fuck hear them walking behind me.

Fuck!

I shouldn't have gotten so damn emotional. What the hell was I thinking? I listen to the crunch of the gravel beneath their shoes as I pass a large dumpster. I'm certain there are three. Maybe four. I'm halfway through the alley when I hear their steps pick up.

My hand drops to my gun. I'm ready for this shit. I didn't graduate at the top of my class for nothing. This is the first time I've been faced with a real-life situation like this, though. The realization makes my confidence slip as I take three large strides and turn on my heels. My gun flies out in front of me as I face three men. Two are in black hoodies, and the other one is wearing a bright green t-shirt and black jeans. I take it all in. Their heights, their weights, every bit of information I can. It's second nature at this point from all of my training.

I can feel my face heating and my body needing to tremble with fear, but I ignore it. Adrenaline flows through my blood, and the only thing I can hear is the sound of my heart beating chaotically in my chest. I swear I can feel it trying to climb up my throat.

They smile at me, like they think it's cute that I've got a gun. Like they expected me to turn around with it aimed at them. It sends a bolt of fear through me. I don't like that they knew this was coming. It means they don't care and they decided it was worth the risk. Shit, maybe that's why they followed me down here. Maybe it's obvious I'm a cop because of the way I talked to Thomas. I bet they were watching. Fuck, fuck, fuck!

I rock hesitantly on my heels, not liking the situation. I'm outnumbered, and they're looking for a fight.

One takes a step toward me and moves his hand toward his waistband. My heart slams to a stop and a cold sweat takes over every inch of my body.

"Hands up!" He continues to approach me, and I yell out again to make sure he hears me clearly. At the same time, I lift up my shirt with my left hand so he can see my badge. "Hands up!" I'm surprised I'm so composed, but I have been trained for this. I've prepared myself for this situation. "I am a police officer and I *will* fire. Put your hands where I can see them."

My left hand steadies on the butt of the gun and I watch as they show no signs of letting up. They don't give a fuck that I'm a cop, or that I've got a gun. As I prepare to shoot this prick in his hand as he reaches for his gun, I see a movement in the back of the alley.

I can't get distracted, not now. I focus, and I shoot that fucker as he grips his gun.

TOMMY

I almost flinch as her gun goes off. I've been around God knows
how many guns going off, so I never flinch. It never bothers me.
But I didn't see it coming. I guess it's just something about a cute little thing
like her, I don't know what, but I underestimated her. The lowlife clutches at
his hand, blood flowing freely from the wound, and he actually drops to the
ground. Like a little bitch. She turns to face the other thug, but he's quick
enough to close the distance between them and grab her arm.

I don't fucking like it. My blood heats, and I stride quickly to get there
before shit gets out of hand. Adrenaline pumps through my veins as I grab the
third guy by the nape of his neck and slam his head into the wall. I hear a loud
thud and a partial scream as I take a swing and hit him square on the nose. I
know it's broken. His eyes roll back in his head, and his body goes limp. I wait
a second, watching to make sure his chest rises and that he's still breathing.

It does. The fucker's just knocked out, not dead. Blood leaks out of his
nostrils and pools above his lip before dripping down his face and onto the
pavement. He's gonna have a busted up nose and two black eyes, but he'll
fucking live.

My heart beats loud in my ears as her gun goes off, hitting nothing but the
brick wall and then falling to the ground with a loud bang. My surroundings

go quiet and everything seems to happen in slow-motion as I take in the scene.

She's struggling with the second asshole. The first is crawling toward his gun that dropped a few feet in front of him. What a fucking pussy. The bullet passed right through his hand. I yank him backward and lift him up so I can stare that fucker in the eyes. They widen with recognition, and then fear.

He should know who I am. Everyone here knows who we are. And they know not to piss us off, either.

"Get the fuck out of here." I toss him backward like he's nothing and watch as he scrambles off. He's still clutching his hand like it's gonna fall off if he lets go. He tries to go to his friend, but that's not going to fly. I want them all separated. I want them to feel alone and scared, so they think twice about ganging up on someone else on my turf.

"Leave him." He looks back at me for a split second before taking off. Fucking prick.

I turn back to watch as Tonya knees her perp in the gut and then smashes an elbow into his jaw, blood flying from his mouth. Damn. It looks like it fucking hurt.

I walk slowly toward them, not sure if I want to interfere or not. I admire her strength. And honestly, I'm getting pretty fucking turned on watching her beat the shit out of him. The guy scoots on his butt away from her and she crawls to her gun, picking it up and pointing it at him. She's leaning back slightly and her legs are parted. She looks hot as fuck with her hair a little messed up, and her cheeks flushed.

I can tell she's out of breath because of the the heaving movements of her chest. But she's calm on the surface. I stand back and wait to see what she's going to do. She's got this shit. She kicked his ass.

"Don't move, or I'll shoot." The fucker looks up at her with daggers in his eyes and a bloody nose; he's clearly pissed that she got the best of him. She reaches into her pocket for her phone, and I have to put an end to it. I can't let her call for backup. I look at her and shake my head no.

"Give me your wallet." I walk closer and motion for her to put her phone away. She looks hesitantly at me, but she listens and slips it back into her pocket.

I have to admit that earns her a little brownie point from me. I like her obeying me. She's a cop, she has power, she can obviously kick some ass. But she obeyed me. I fucking love that. My dick loves it too and I have to work hard not to palm my growing erection.

I watch as she slowly gets up off the ground and brushes the dirt off her ass. She doesn't look shaken up at all. She looks pissed.

The dumbfuck looks at me like he's not sure who I'm talking to. I reach down and grab him by the shirt. I pull him up and speak through clenched teeth. "Don't make me ask again."

I toss him backward and he lands hard on his ass. He doesn't waste a second as he pulls out his wallet, holding it up for me to take.

"I don't have any cash. I got nothing on me." I open up his wallet and take out my phone to take a picture of his driver's license.

"This your current address?" I ask. Fear flashes in his eyes, and the blood drains from his face.

"Answer me!" I yell louder than I should, but it doesn't make Tonya flinch.

"Y--yes," he stutters out.

"What were you planning to get out of this," I look the fucker's license and chuckle, "Earl?" I crouch down so I can look this fucker in his eyes. "What were you hoping to get from messing with her?"

"Nothin'!" He's quick to deny everything and I just tilt my head and get ready to beat this fucker to a bloody pulp. I don't have a problem getting people to talk.

I smash my fist against his jaw so fucking quick he didn't see it coming. I hear Tonya take a step back and I look at her from the corner of my eyes. She looks back at me with no fear. She's watching me. I need to keep that in mind. I straighten my back as the little prick wipes the blood from his mouth and tries to figure out whether or not he should be looking at me. The coward doesn't even try to look me in the eyes. I have to tame the animal in me that wants to rip him to shreds. I should, he earned it, but I can't, knowing a cop is watching my every move. Even if it is for her. I'm not sure I trust this broad. My jaw ticks. I *shouldn't* fucking trust this broad. Ever.

"I like this broad, and I don't like that you fucked with her. You understand what I'm saying?"

"It w--won't happen again." He stutters again, and I swear to God I smell piss.

"Damn right it won't." I toss his wallet back to him. "Get the fuck out of here."

As he walks away, nearly stumbling over his own two feet, Tonya walks closer to me and says, "I could've handled it myself."

I look at her with a bit of disbelief. My eyes roam her body. She's a bit scuffed up. She takes the hair tie out of her hair and pulls it back up, casually tying it into a ponytail. Like messing up her hair is the worst thing that happened.

When she looks back at me, I see her true emotions in her eyes. She's pushing down the fear and anxiety I know she's feeling. I know it well, because I do that shit, too. I walk over and stand close to her, wanting to hold her, but knowing I shouldn't.

I shouldn't have even come down here. I'd ended it. But I saw those pricks and the way they looked at her. I wasn't letting that shit happen.

I don't care what Vince has to say about it.

"You could have, but you didn't have to." Her eyes flash with surprise and then sadness. I try to lighten the mood by saying, "I couldn't let you have all the fun."

I put my hand on the small of her back and lead her out of the alley, onto the sidewalk. There's no one out this late. I doubt anyone around here called the cops either. I take out my phone and text Nicky about the prick we left behind. He'll clean it up. The fuckers will live, but they'll know never to do stupid shit like that in our territory again.

As soon as I hit send, she seems to come to her senses and tries to turn back.

"I have to call for backup," she says as she turns to look back down the alley. Fuck that. She's not calling anyone. I spin her around in my arms and look her right in her eyes.

"It didn't happen. Nothing happened." A moment passes between us, like she's weighing her options. Finally, she nods her head slightly with understanding, but I know she doesn't like it.

She looks past me at the passed out fucker in the alley.

"Don't worry about him," I tell her as I grab her by the arm. "He'll live."

She doesn't put up much of a fight. She just looks at me with curiosity on her face. It's not good that she's curious, but at least she's smart enough not to ask questions. I'm surprised how she lets me lead her out onto the street. She doesn't care that I'm practically manhandling her.

That's another thing I like. She obeys me, and she likes my hands on her.

Fuck, I can't help how much that turns me on. My dick is begging to get inside her. Damn it. I really was going to listen. I have to fucking listen. I try to will away my erection, but it's not doing anything but getting harder for her.

As we get to the end of the sidewalk, her eyes steady on a parking lot across the street. I recognize her car and let her lead a bit so she doesn't realize I know that's where we're going.

I push my luck a little further and wrap my arm around her waist. She doesn't lean in, but she doesn't pull away. I'm fine with that. I like feeling her body up against me. I know being out with her like this is a risk. If Vince sees it, he's not going to believe I'm not trying to get into her pants.

Shit, I can't even believe I'm not trying to get into her pants. I have enough willpower to say no though. I'm just taking a little more than I should. After seeing her take care of that asshole, though, fuck it was sexy as fuck. How could I not put my hands on her? I wanna teach her a lesson though. She shouldn't have gone down that alley.

If she was mine, I'd have her ass red by now.

I always thought I wanted a good girl, but this woman is a bad, bad girl in need. I look down at her and watch as her eyes dart around the parking lot as we near her car. It's the same shit she always does at night. I don't like it.

"You alright?" I ask.

"Fine," she says simply, and pulls away as she takes her keys from her back pocket. I let her go as she unlocks her car and turns her body toward me. I have to remind myself she's a cop, and that's not okay.

She looks up at me and I can't help but feel like a dick for holding that against her. Besides, it's fucking hot. I wanna test her, I wanna push and see what I can get away with. After all, she left that prick in the alley for my men to clean up. I wonder how far she'd let me go before she did anything.

I put my hand on her hip and push her ass against the car.

Her eyes widen as she gasps, and I swear her thighs clench. She bites down on her bottom lip, looking up at me with a hint of fear, but mostly lust. Fuck me, but I fucking want her. I lean down and take in her sweet smell, then dip my head into the crook of her neck. I want her so fucking bad, but I can't.

I pull back and look down at her again. I get a glimpse of her badge, and suddenly she's not the hot bad girl who needs a lesson. She's the woman who sat in the interrogation room. This is a woman who may be setting me up, but all I can see is a woman who needs my touch.

Her eyes close and she tilts her head just a bit. Enough that it makes me want to cup her chin in my hand and start out nice and slow. That's how I'd do it. I'd be sweet and gentle, let her lips mold to mine. I'd make sure she was relaxed after that shit that happened. I'd make sure it was completely out of her mind. And then I'd take her wrists in my hand, pin them to the car and push this raging erection that won't let up into her thigh so she'd know how much I want her. I can see it all playing out before my eyes.

But I can't have it.

I have direct orders to stay away. And usually that doesn't mean shit, but Vince is right. This broad could be playing me. I don't think she is, but she could be. All this tension I feel between us could be her doing, just so she can find something to pin against me.

My dick jumps in my jeans thinking about pinning her against her car and slipping those jeans down so I can feel if she wants me as much as I want her. My eyes roam her body in appreciation and when I look back up, her eyes are open.

She looks vulnerable and I take the chance to give her a little smirk and a pat on the ass. She may be using me and until I'm sure she's not, I'm not giving her anything. Even if my body is fucking begging me to indulge.

She pouts and then narrows her eyes. But I saw that little pout. Sexiest fucking look a woman's ever given me. Then she swings her door open and nearly punches me right in the dick. She smirks back with a tilt of her head before climbing in.

I grab the door before she can shut it and that smirk on her gorgeous face fucking vanishes. I wanna say something smart, something that an asshole would say to push her away, but there's a look in her eyes that's telling me it'd really fucking hurt her. And that's something I don't want to do. I should push her away. I know I should. But she just had three fuckers come after her and she's not showing any signs of giving a fuck when I know she is.

It's hard for me to understand. I'm not used to women taking shit like that. Not in our family. They stay out of *familia* business. It's an unspoken rule. Women are off-limits. Yet she chose a career that puts her in harm's way every fucking day.

My grip tightens on the edge of the door. I have no right not to like it. It's her decision and she's not mine, but I'll be damned if I say I'm okay with what happened.

I ask her again, making sure the concern comes through, "You sure you're okay?"

She blinks a few times as if gauging whether I really do give a shit before she answers. She nods her head and replies, "Yeah, I'm fine."

She puts her hand on the door to close it, but before she does, she looks up and asks, "Is he dead?"

She keeps asking the same question and I don't like it. Cops ask questions. And answering that particular one could mean trouble for me. The concern is wiped off my face like it was never fucking there.

"You have a nice night, Officer Kelly," I say as I turn my back on her and walk away. I get a few feet from her when I hear the car door shut and her engine roar to life.

As she drives away, the anger and disappointment settle in. What the fuck was I thinking? She could've handled herself; I could've stayed back and made sure she was fine after the fact. Instead I got shit on my hands that she could arrest me for.

But she didn't. I'm not sure I trust it though. I sure as fuck don't trust her. As I walk away with more resolve to keep my distance and listen to the orders Vince gave me, my phone goes off. It's a text from Vince.

WHY THE FUCK *did you need Nicky?*

FUCK.

This is exactly why I need to stay the fuck away from her.

TONYA

J still don't understand what happened. I park my car under the light and look up at my steps. I sit there for a moment. It's a moment too long. I should get inside. I'm quick like I always am, and I walk straight upstairs. It's not till the keys fall into the glass bowl on the end table that I realize my hand is shaking.

I take a deep breath and try to calm myself. It happens a lot. I thought it would stop eventually. It's a reaction from the adrenaline and endorphins wearing off. It's not shock, but it's not okay, either. I see it as a weakness and I hate it.

I sink into the sofa and try to calm myself down. I can do this. I *have* to do this. Other women are strong enough. Fuck, if a man can do it, so can I. Men use brute strength, while women use leverage, and brains. I truly believe that. But damn, this is fucking hard. It's so goddamned hard. I thought police academy was rough. And it was. But real-life situations are scary as fuck.

Hand-to-hand combat is its own kind of beast. It's terrifying at times. Women are worse than men. Way worse. Men sometimes only go a blow or two. They wanna prove a point. I've seen them tear each other to pieces in front of me. Even the bang of my gun going off didn't pull them off each other. But that's rare.

Women are the opposite. When they go at it, they're going for damage. They want blood. Humiliation. They want to scar their opponent and ruin them. They go for the face and eyes, their hair. Anywhere visible. I've pulled men apart on my own before. Men stronger than me. But it's nothing like pulling women apart. They go for damage and they don't give a fuck who goes down with them.

I swallow thickly, trying to just calm down. It only takes a moment to think back to when things were easier. I remember why I'm doing this. Why it's worth it to continue.

I remember playing with my sister in the front yard with chalk. Her graduation from nursing school. Talking to her on the phone. I remember the last time I heard her voice. I hear the conversation echo in my head.

"You're such a dork, Melissa. You need to go have some fun," I say to her.

"I'm seriously fine at home, you go ahead without me."

"You are truly missing out. Like you have no idea." I can't believe she'd hold herself back again; she's gotta learn to live a little. *"There's nothing wrong with going clubbing. You gotta get some from time to time."*

"Oh my God, don't talk like that!" she admonishes me with a hushed tone.

"Why?" I ask.

"'Cause you sound like a slut!" I can hear the humor in her voice.

"So?" We both laugh at my joke. *"You just need to loosen up is all I'm saying."*

"Well I'm not like you, Tonya." I can hear a little disappointment in her voice and I hate it. *"I don't have that confidence."* I want to tell her she should. I want to tell her she's beautiful and deserving of happiness and that includes meeting up with me to go out for drinks. But I don't want to upset her. I don't want to be pushy. So I don't say anything at all.

And because of that, I missed out on one more night that I could've had with her.

She really was a prude and an 'inside person' as she used to say. She didn't read the same smutty books as me or enjoy the dirty jokes I liked. But she didn't hold it against me, either. She never judged me. I'm guilty of judging her, though. I assumed she'd meet a doctor and make lots of babies and drive a minivan in just a few years. I teased her all the time about it. To her, it was a dream. To me, it's a fucking nightmare.

I shake my hands out and wipe away the stray tears as I walk to the fridge. I grab the opened bottle of wine from the bottom shelf, a cabernet. I take a glass from the cabinet above the sink and ignore the dishes. They can wait. I just need to settle in a bit first.

I close my eyes and watch the scene from the alley play out again. I did everything right, flashed my badge, said hands up. First guy reaches, I shoot him in the hand. Second guy comes at me, but I'm too slow. I play the scene over while I fill the glass about halfway. Both hands were on the gun. There was nothing I could do with the other one coming after me. I needed a hand free.

I replay it over and over, trying to come up with a better strategy. But I don't think there was one. I definitely did right by going for the armed one first. Maybe if I'd used the butt of the gun to smash in the second fucker's nose, that may have been more effective. I rewind a bit in my mind. I should've turned sooner, before I'd gone so far down the alley. Fuck me, I just shouldn't have gone down there in the first place. That was fucking stupid.

Thomas is why my head is all fucked up. He does something to me. He makes me stupid, that's his fucking superpower. He blinds me from all this shit that I've trained myself to do. He makes me feel...safe, in a weird way. I feel unstoppable around him. That's not a good thing. Maybe it's because he gives me hope. When I think about the end to all this shit, when I think about having some sort of closure, I see him there. I can see him handing it to me. Telling me Petrov's dead. That I don't have to face my demons, because he's already killed them for me. Maybe it's my way of dealing with the failure of not finding Petrov. Maybe I've made it all up.

I don't know, I'm not a fucking shrink.

I tip the glass back and drain it. Mmm, I love the taste. I set the glass down on the counter and strip as I make my way to my bedroom. Most of my things are still in boxes. I need to make time to put that shit away. I toss the clothes into the hamper. At least that's not overflowing. Score one for me.

My feet patter against the tiled floor as I turn the water on to fucking-scorching, just how I like it. I look at my face in the mirror as the water heats and steam starts to fill the stall.

I look back at a stranger.

This isn't who I used to be.

I look... tired. That's exactly how I look. And I am, I'm so damn tired. I'm lonely and angry. And fucking sad and miserable.

The need for justice. The need for vengeance. They've taken over a part of me that I miss. But they are needs. I need to know if Petrov is dead. If he's not, I won't stop. I hate that I've come to the end of this lead, all because Thomas won't give me an inch.

Suddenly, I wish I had more on his ass. I want something to make him talk. I need him to tell me. I could use what happened today. But that'd be so fucking wrong. I feel like a bitch for even thinking it. Maybe this anger that's driving me, this desire to fuck him over until I get what I need, maybe that's what fuels Harrison every fucking day.

The realization snaps me out of my thoughts. No, I can't do that. I shouldn't want that.

But I know that Thomas knows. He could tell me where Petrov is, or if he's dead. I know he can.

I step into the shower deciding I need to push him just a bit more. After all, I've given him something. I could have called it in, the scene today. I *should* have called it in.

But he didn't have to do it. He didn't have to help me.

Oh fuck, I'm such a bitch. I never even thanked him.

I let the hot water hit my skin and fucking hate the obsession that's taken me over. Who am I? I shake my head and try to shake off all these unwanted feelings, all these horrible thoughts. I don't like the person I've become. I just want it all to stop.

If only he'd help me.

TOMMY

I look out of the peephole and curse under my breath. This broad has a fucking death wish. I stand in front of the closed door and listen as the loud knock echoes in my apartment. Fucking hell. She just won't let it be.

This is what I get for wanting to find out more about this broad. Vince already bitched at me for involving myself. He couldn't hold it against me though. Not when I fed him a little lie about how she was shaken up from how they'd roughed her up.

I really think she was a bit messed up from it. But I may have exaggerated some to get myself off the hook.

I decided I was done with this that night, done with her. I should threaten a restraining order. I could do it, too. I've told her I don't want to talk.

And now she's standing outside my door.

"I know you're home, Thomas," she yells from the other side. "I just wanna talk." I roll my eyes. No shit. That's all this broad wants from me. *'Cause she's a cop.*

I need to send her away. I need to do it now.

I swing the door open and it stops her fist in the air. I look at her clenched hand pointedly until she lowers it and then I stare at her. I keep my face impassive. None of that bullshit I gave into before. This needs to end.

"You wanna talk, go ahead and talk," I tell her in a no-nonsense tone.

She opens her mouth and then closes it. She clears her throat and looks to the ground before looking back up at me. "Thank you. I just wanted to say thank you."

I stare at her, not quite understanding. I'm surprised by her sweetness. It catches me off guard. Which isn't a good thing.

"For helping me with those guys." She closes her eyes and takes a deep breath. "I never thanked you for stepping in. It would've really sucked if you hadn't." *It would have sucked.* That's putting it mildly.

I should just stare. I shouldn't respond. She'd get the message loud and clear, but I can't do that. I look past her and give a curt nod as I say, "No problem."

She noticeably swallows and asks, "May I come in?"

"No." It's easy shutting that down. The only reason I'd bring her in here is to fuck her. And that's not going to happen. My dick doesn't like that answer and starts hardening in my pants. I clench my jaw, trying to get it to go down. I'm only in a pair of sweats. She's gonna see how fucking hard I am for her. Fuck it, I still can't have her. Doesn't fucking matter if she knows I want her or not.

I need to push her away.

"You're in the wrong part of town, Tonya," I say, keeping my eyes on her with my voice low.

A smile spreads slowly across her face, making her look gorgeous as fuck. She cocks a brow and tries to suppress the laugh that I can practically hear escaping from those full lips of hers. "You're kidding, right?" She's not really asking though, and she has a point. I'm a scary fucker, but it's not like I live in the rough part of town.

"You know what I mean." She should know not to fuck with me. Maybe I've been too easy on her. I've given her this idea that I won't hurt her, and I'm her pal. But I'm not her buddy. She should be fucking careful around me. She should be scared of me.

She rolls her eyes at my words and it's the last straw.

"You think you're such a bad ass bitch, don't you?" I walk into her space, pushing her farther out into the hallway.

She seems taken aback by my tone, and it takes a moment for her to square her shoulders. I can see her changing before my eyes. Like she just realized who I am, and that she's a cop. She may think she doesn't have to take any shit from me, but I'm about to prove her wrong.

"You think you can play this good girl act with me, but I know who you really are."

She looks confused and then pissed. "I never said I was a good girl, and I'm not putting on an act." She speaks through clenched teeth with her hands balled at her side. It really pisses her off when I call her that. That's good to know. I like pissing her off and getting her riled up.

"So what? You're a bad girl then? Just like I said, you think you're a bad ass. You're not."

She huffs a laugh and rolls her eyes. She literally doesn't give a shit. I need to instill fear into this broad. I've given her too much length on her leash.

I look her in her eyes and lower my voice. "I could fuck you raw in the front of this building, and no one would stop me. No one would say shit to me."

Her lips part, and her eyes soften with lust at my words. Fuck me, that's so fucking hot. That's not at all the reaction I expected. I anticipated disgust. I would think she'd pull out the cop card. But she doesn't.

"You'd like that, wouldn't you?" I ask as I grip her hips and turn her around to pin her to the wall next to my open door. "'Cause you're such a bad girl." I lower my lips to her neck and whisper in her ear. My lips barely touch her. "You'd love it so fucking much, you'd cum on my dick as I fucked your greedy cunt however I wanted."

I shove her back against the wall. I'm not gentle, but only because I can see how much she likes it rough. I grab her ass with both hands and hold her against the wall with my hips. My hard dick pushes against her thigh, digging into her. I can see the moment she realizes she's about to get fucked. Her eyes widen and she pushes her hands against my chest. I pull back slightly, but my hands and hips keep her in place.

My heart beats wildly in my chest. My blood's laced with desire and races with a primal need to fuck her against the wall. She'd fucking love it. We both want it.

I lean forward and barely hear her say, "Ssst." She knows she should say it, but she hasn't yet. She likes me pushing her boundaries.

"Stop?" I ask with a lopsided grin. "Is that what you were gonna say?" She presses her lips together and turns her head to the side, refusing to look at me and refusing to answer. I heard it on the tip of her tongue. But she doesn't want this to stop. She wants to be impaled on my dick.

"You'd better fucking say it, Tonya." Her eyes whip up to mine with a flash of anger. She doesn't like me telling her what to do. Good. It's going to be fun getting her so worked up. I love it already.

I wrap my hand around her throat and give her a gentle squeeze. My left hand grabs hold of her thigh and she spreads her legs for me. I cup her pussy and rock my palm against her clit. I can feel how hot and wet she is. Her eyes go half-lidded, and her lips part with a small moan of pleasure. It's the sexiest fucking thing I've ever heard. I bend my head down and hesitate just a second before taking her bottom lip in between my teeth.

This is dangerous. At first it felt like a game. But the more I push, the more she gives me. I'm already addicted, and I haven't even had a taste of her yet. I should stop this before it begins, but I can't. I want her, and now that I know how much she wants me, I'm taking her.

I'm going to have to fuck this broad out of my system. Just once. Just once, so I can satisfy this beast clawing at me to fuck her into submission.

I lower my lips to the crook of her neck and bite down hard enough so she knows I won't be gentle. She rocks her hips and rubs her hot pussy against my dick. Fuck, yes. I growl into her ear, "Get your ass inside."

I pull back and stare into her green eyes. They spark with a challenge. "Thought you said you could fuck me out here." My dick jumps in my pants.

"Bad girl." I back away so I'm not touching her. "Get inside." I see the defiance in her eyes. She fucking loves this. She's coming alive with my touch, and I love that I can do this to her. She bites down on her lip and looks to the stairs. For a moment, one split second, I think she's going to leave, but then her cute ass starts walking inside, and I know I've got her.

After I close and lock her door, I grip her waist and lead her to the bedroom. I'm not wasting any time. I don't want to give either of us a second to think and realize what a fucking disaster this is.

I kick the door shut behind me and give her another command. "Strip." I fucking love how she turns on her heels and looks back at me like she's debating on giving me a hard time.

"You have this coming. For teasing me like that. You better take them off before I rip them off of you." Her mouth parts and the moan I was fantasizing about hearing finally hits my ears. "I don't give a fuck if you have to walk back home naked." Yes. Yes I really fucking do give a shit, but that gets her ass moving to obey.

Her hands slowly remove her jeans, and then her top. She reaches around behind her to remove her bra, but I can't wait any longer.

I pick her ass up, a cheek in each hand and let my knees hit the edge of the mattress. She's quick to wrap her legs around mine. Her heels dig into my ass as my lips crush hers. I fall onto my bed with her beneath me and push down my sweats. My cock smacks against her clit as it bounces out, and the force of it makes her break our kiss. She moans into the hot air and it fuels me to grip my dick in my hand and smack it against her swollen nub. I want to hear that sound again and again. Her back arches and her head digs into the mattress. I move my cock through her folds from her entrance to her clit, making sure to watch her body for her reaction. She fucking loves this. She's loving what I'm doing to her.

She still isn't looking at me though, and I don't like that. I want her eyes on me as I sink deep into her heat. I line my cock up and then grip her chin in my hand. She looks back at me with half-lidded eyes. She's already so close. My bad girl is dying to be fucked.

I hold her gaze as I slowly push into her tight cunt. Fuck, she feels so fucking good. My thick cock stretches her walls as I slowly thrust deep inside her. Her eyes widen and her lips form a perfect "o". I'd smirk at her if I could, but I can't. I'm lost in how fucking good she feels.

I rock into her once, twice, and then a third time, keeping my pace slow and steady with short, shallow strokes letting her adjust to my size and then I thrust into her hard enough that the bed slams against the wall. She screams out and I capture her screams of pleasure with my kiss. My fingertips dig into her hips, holding her in place as I continue mercilessly fucking her into the mattress. The bed groans and creaks as I pound into her pussy with a relentless pace.

Her thighs tighten around my hips as she bites down on her lip to keep from screaming out from the intense pleasure.

The bed smacks against the wall with each thrust. As I fuck her harder it gets louder, and I fucking hate that she looks up at the headboard. It was only a glance, but it's enough that I want to drag her ass onto the floor and fuck her there. She can hear the creaking and groaning and it's distracting her. It pisses me off. That's not going to fucking happen. I want her so far gone that she can't think about anything but my dick giving her the release she so desperately needs.

I pick her ass up in one hand and press my thumb against her clit. I push down hard and ignore her body trying to thrash in my arms. I don't stop. I don't let up on my ruthless thrusts as I circle her clit, taking her higher and higher. Her head thrashes from side to side as her pussy spasms around my dick. I feel her hot arousal and groan as the sound of my dick slamming into her gets louder and messier. I fucking love that I made her cum. I want it again. I want more of her.

I ride through her orgasm and push her to another level of ecstasy. I rub her clit with the rough pad of my thumb and keep up my pace. My spine tingles and my toes curl, wanting my release, but I hold it back, waiting for her to go off again. I need it again. I want to take her over the edge. She claws at the comforter and screams out as I pinch her clit.

Only when I feel her body trembling and see her back bow with her own orgasm, only then do I let the sensation wash over me. I cum violently deep inside her and groan into the crook of her next as the pleasure runs through every inch of my body. I brace my forearms above her head, and we sink into the mattress as I pump short, shallow thrusts until I'm completely spent and have nothing left.

I roll onto my back and pull her close to me while we both catch our breath. It's been a long time, a really long fucking time, but it's never felt like *that* before. More than anything, I feel triumphant. Like I've tamed the untamable.

I let a few minutes go by for my heart to calm down. You'd think I held my breath the whole fucking time. My lips travel along her shoulder and I leave a sweet kiss on the tender part of her neck, just behind her ear before getting up. She was so fucking good, better than I fucking hoped she'd be.

I need to get her something to clean up with.

When I get back from the bathroom, she's sitting up on the bed holding the comforter across her chest. Her hair's a mess, her lips are swollen from my kiss, and her skin looks radiant. She looks like she got fucked, and it looks damn good on her.

I pass her the washcloth and pretend like I'm looking away while I pull on my boxers.

She rolls off the bed and sashays her ass in my face. I know she did that shit on purpose. I smack my hand playfully across that perky, lush ass, and smile as she jumps and turns around to face me. A deep red blush colors her cheeks as she smiles shyly back at me.

That's when it hits me.

This broad is getting to me. I watch as she grabs her clothes. All the bits of happiness leave me in an instant. I didn't check for a wire. Fuck. Fuck, how could I forget she's a cop?

I didn't say anything, though. I know I didn't. I replay the scene in my head.

It's like snapping back to reality. I don't know what the fuck happened.

Shit. Maybe she wanted this. She wanted to get close to me. Fuck. Fuck. I keep fucking this up. I'm so drawn to her. I run a hand down my face in exasperation. What the hell was I thinking? I keep losing my shit when she's around.

I look at her from across the room as she pulls her jeans up and over her sweet ass. Fuck, even right now as I'm telling myself this is wrong, my dick is hardening at the chance to be inside her again.

"This shit can't happen." I say the words before I forget that I need this to be over. "It can't happen again."

She turns to face me with a look of shock and hurt. But she's quick to cover it up. It fucking kills me. A weight pushes against my chest. It fucking hurts. I hate that I hurt her. "You're right. Sorry it happened." She talks clearly, and with a hint of sarcasm, but doesn't face me. She sounds fucking pissed, but there's an undertone of sadness. She's doing what she does best, and masking her true feelings.

I walk over to her to hold her, or apologize, or something--I don't know what, but she makes a beeline for her purse and then starts heading to the door. It fucking hurts, but that's what I get. What did I expect, opening my mouth and ruining it?

We were playing house though. Caught up in something that doesn't exist.

"I'm not kicking you out." I talk to her back as she walks out on me. I may as well have kicked her out though. I close my eyes and take a deep breath.

This needs to go down like this. She needs to be pissed at me. But I don't want that.

This is all so fucked.

She turns to face me as I walk up behind her before she can open the door. I want to say something to her. I don't know what. I just don't want her to leave like this.

"Don't worry, it won't happen again." Her voice is hard and full of menace, but her eyes are glassy with tears. It fucking guts me.

"Stop it, Tonya. It's not like that." She turns her back to me to open the door, but I put my hand above hers to keep it from opening. She turns around and I cage her in. She closes her eyes to avoid my stare.

"Stop it. You know I didn't mean it like that." I talk with a gentle tone and try to calm her down. But her defenses are way up. She's not giving me anything. "You don't want this anyway. You're a cop. I'm suspect in your case for fuck's sake."

"You didn't do it," she says calmly. Her admission shocks me. If she knows I didn't do it, what the fuck is she after me for? "You're right though. This shouldn't have happened." She opens her eyes and speaks calmly, "I want to leave now."

There's no emotion left. No sadness, no disappointment, no anger. She's got her mask on, and she's not giving me anything.

I should make her open up. I shouldn't let her leave like this.

But it's what's best for both of us. She's a cop, and I'm mobbed up. This shit should've never happened.

"Alright." I stand back and let her open the door. I fucking hate that I feel anything for her. She's a cop. I have to keep repeating it in my head. I have to remember I can't have her. I've been ordered to stay away from her. I shouldn't have let it get this far. This is bad. I don't know what I was thinking.

"Can you just tell me one thing?" she asks, as she steps out into the hallway. "Is Petrov dead?" She looks up at me with nothing in her eyes, no emotion. Not a damn thing.

I bite the inside of my cheek fucking hating that she's asking that.

"You know I can't tell you anything. Stop asking me. I'm not gonna answer." I can't. I'd be a stupid prick to admit anything.

"Yeah, I figured. Couldn't hurt to ask one more time though." She walks down the hallway without looking back.

I feel fucking used. But what's worse is that I want to stop her. I want to tell her how he suffered. How a woman who he tortured killed him. But I can't.

Instead I stand in my doorway and listen to her steps. I grip the door jamb tighter as I hear the door open and listen as she leaves.

Fuck, I want to tell her. And that's not good. None of this is good.

TONYA

I'm not gonna cry. I don't fucking cry. Sure as shit not over men. I've had a few boyfriends here and there, but that's never happened to me. It's never been a hit it and quit it situation. And sure as fuck not five minutes after cumming inside of me. Asshole. He didn't kick me out, but he could've picked a better time to start talking like that.

It was a mistake. I know that. It never should've happened. I have more restraint than that. I don't know what it is about him that makes me so weak. I cave to him, when I haven't ever caved before. I don't like it. I also don't like that he brought it up first. I was thinking it, but I was pushing it down.

It just felt so nice to be held. It's been a long time. I feel so fucking deprived of human interaction. It's been too fucking long. I take a deep breath as I lie down on my bed. It's cold. But it feels good to just relax against the bed. I snort a humorless laugh.

I shouldn't be relaxing. I shouldn't even want that. I've lost sight of my purpose. I swore I wouldn't stop until I found Petrov and destroyed him and everyone who works for him. It's like I was wearing blinders all through the academy. I didn't even care about how much my body hurt. Nothing else mattered. I was just obsessed at taking a leap forward.

And then my huge break when the department had an opening was as if the stars had aligned. Like God was handing me my revenge on a silver platter. But then nothing. Not a fucking trace of him. The other names on my list are all dead. There are no leads. I shouldn't be relaxing, but I don't know what else to do.

It's as if I've been running as hard and as fast as I'm able, chasing a ghost. And now he's disappeared, and I'm finally taking a look around.

How did I get here? This isn't what I went to college for. This isn't what I wanted to do. My life wasn't supposed to end up like this. Even back then I wasn't really sure what I wanted, but the shit I was studying was at least interesting. All of this is just depressing as fuck.

But I owe it to my sister. She was older than me. Only by three years. She was reserved and polite. I was the handful child that always got into trouble. Maybe that's why I never got along with my mother. I don't know. But that relationship completely vanished when Melissa died. My mother couldn't take it. She's not a fighter like me.

The night Melissa didn't come back, my mom was sure she was dead. The next morning when I went looking for her, putting up signs and waiting for the police to actually do something, my mother did nothing but cry. I was pissed. She wasn't even trying. I think she buried Melissa that day. And what was left of her own soul.

Ever since I've been so fucking alone.

Melissa could've been trapped. She could have hit her head somehow and been unconscious. A million scenarios ran through my head. I knew deep inside me that she needed me. She needed *us*. Yet my mother did nothing but sob inconsolably.

I hated her then. It was like I could feel my sister's pain, and I tried so fucking hard. I looked everywhere I could. But I never would have found her. I was looking in all the wrong places.

It wasn't long after that when her body was discovered. I couldn't believe it. I couldn't imagine that someone would take her. After the shock and the sadness, all that was left was anger. I knew I had to do something.

I took a semester off school to join the groups that all promise to bring awareness to sex trafficking. I went to meetings, presentations, and counseling. But it didn't feel like enough. More than that, I saw my sister in the women who survived. I could see her in their place.

But I knew she'd never be there. She was dead. She wasn't ever going to sit in the chair across from me, and tell me what happened to her. She wasn't going to be making plans with me on how to handle simple, everyday tasks that now felt impossible. I had to stop going.

I needed to go after the man who'd led her to her death.

I feel like it was just yesterday that I'd made up my mind to chase after Petrov. Like I'd gone into a dark tunnel and sprinted through it blindly, only to emerge and not realize where it was taking me.

He may be dead. I may never get to face him. I may never even know for sure. But I won't stop.

The rest of the Valettis know something, and I can question them. Well, I can try. I know it's risky. But I have to try. I'll do anything to make sure Petrov never puts his hands on another woman. I hope he suffered. Tears leak down my face and hit the pillow beneath me. A sob tears through me, and I have no idea where it came from.

My anger is waning, knowing he may no longer be alive. What's left if I don't have the anger to hold onto? My chest feels hollow. And I can't stand the distant feeling of sadness.

I wish I knew one way or the other.

He could've at least told me. Thinking of Thomas makes the pain subside, if only for a moment. He made me weak. I enjoyed it though. I'm tired of being the strong one. I'm tired of fighting an enemy I can't even see. I'm tired of chasing ghosts.

I close my eyes and try to think of anything other than the dark past, and twisted obsession that's brought me here. I steady my breathing and see Thomas' face.

I feel his hands on my body. His lips against my neck.

"Bad girl." The memory of his deep, baritone voice sends a shiver through my body. I can imagine a time when I would have run off with him. When I would have gotten on my knees and done everything and anything he asked, just for the thrill of it.

That time's passed though. And now neither of us are in a position to allow what we did to ever happen again. My eyes pop open, realizing if he told anyone, I'd lose my job. I expect to feel fear, or shock, or anger at the thought. But I feel nothing. I don't think I'd care.

It would hurt though, for him to use it against me. He should. If I were him, I would. What we did wasn't right, and it would certainly add a level of distrust and uncertainty to the case if I got pulled off. It would severely compromise the case.

But the evidence is iffy as is. All we really have are the prints at this point. The tire tracks are circumstantial, and the witness deposition is inadmissible due to her state of mind.

The partial print is the only piece of evidence that's damning, according to the prosecutor.

There's no more evidence to collect, and everything we have points to the Valettis ending the deal and saving the women.

I can't even fathom why Jerry is still gunning for them, unless he's hoping for the same outcome as Harrison, just in a more professional way. I guess it's professional to leverage and threat in order to get information for other cases.

The lines are blurred so much more than I ever thought they could be.

And I'm tired of looking at black and white. I rest my head into the pillow and try not to think about any of it at all. I just want to rewind time. I want to go back to the last time I saw Melissa and hold her. If I'd known then, what I know now, I'd never let her go. I don't care if it's crazy. I would do anything I could to save her.

The tears come again and I hug my pillow. I can't save her. I'll never be able to save her. My throat closes as I sniffle and try to breathe into the pillow.

She's never coming back. And nothing I'll ever do can change that.

TOMMY

"What the fuck is that broad thinking?" Anthony walks up behind me at the bar, and I have to turn around to face him.

He looks worried. "What are you talking about?" I ask.

"Your chick, Tonya Kelly. The cop." He says, "the cop" like I wouldn't know who he's talking about. My eyes lower to the drink in my hand. I haven't had one fucking moment go by where I didn't think about her. From the way she felt writhing beneath me, to the pissed off and hurt look when I shut it down before the situation got any worse than was necessary.

I fucking hate this. I hate that I can't get her out of my head, and I hate that I can't have her. I've never had this problem before. And I don't fucking like it.

"What's she doing?" I ask, looking past him at Vince. Vince is in the corner of the room talking to his brother over a beer. They barely come in here anymore with the kids taking up so much of their time. I hope whatever my bad girl has gotten into, it hasn't found its way back to either of them.

"She's about to get slapped with a harassment lawsuit if she keeps her shit up." I look him dead in the eyes, waiting for more. "She went to Tony's and waited for him outside his house. She keeps pushing for information." He looks over his shoulder at Vince. "She's worse than a fucking reporter."

He turns like he's gonna go tell Vince, and I stop him. My hand grips his

537

shoulder. His forehead pinches, and his eyes narrow. "What the fuck, Tommy?"

"Don't tell him, and tell Tony to keep his mouth shut." He looks at me with disbelief. "I'll handle it," I say, standing up from my barstool.

"Are you fucking kidding me? You can't go around making threats to an officer. You aren't off the hook yet."

"That's not what I have in mind," I say under my breath.

Anthony closes his eyes and lets his head fall back. "You're fucking kidding me, Tommy. Tell me you're not fucking around with her."

"I'm not." I've never been good at lying, and I sure as shit don't like lying to him. But it's partially true.

"Good. That'd be a fucking mistake."

"Stay out of it, Anthony." I'm done with this conversation. I turn to walk away and he doesn't stop me. I feel like a prick, but I'm going after what I want.

Before I make it to the door, Vince and Dom approach me, and I know I need to stop and hear them out. I just hope it's not about her. She really should know better; she shouldn't be doing this shit. She's gonna get herself into deep shit, and I can't fucking have that happen.

"Tommy, you alright?" Dom asks. I'm sure they can see the stress on my face. I need to man the fuck up and play it cool.

"Everything considered, I'm doing just fine." I talk easy, but the tension in my body is keeping my guard up.

"You know we got you. It's all gonna be taken care of. Soon, too. We already got the witness stuff thrown out, the prints and the tire tracks are close to being gone too, and then they won't have shit on you."

I nod my head, not really listening. I'm sure I'm gonna get off, so I'm not too worried about that. But my bad girl is gonna get herself into some deep shit, and I need to stop that. I don't want them thinking of her like they do Harrison.

"Has that bitch cop been bugging you?" Vince asks, and it takes everything in me not to make a fist and smash it into his face.

"She's not a bitch," I manage to say back, and he doesn't like that answer. Dom seems surprised and takes a step back. He doesn't get involved with this shit. I can't help that the words come out. I don't like him calling her a bitch.

She may be a little rough around the edges. She's a little pushy, but she's not a bitch. Nothing about her makes me think that.

"She's still a cop though, isn't she?" Vince asks in a hushed voice.

"Yeah she is." I answer him quickly, wanting to get rid of the tense air between us.

"She still bugging you?"

I answer him honestly. "I haven't seen her in a few days."

"Haven't seen her?" he asks, tilting his head and narrowing his eyes. "What's that mean, Tommy?"

"Means she hasn't been around to bug me. She's not like the others, Vince."

"I don't like the way you're talking Tommy." Vince wraps his arms around my shoulder and leads me to the back room. "You talking like that to anyone else?"

"I haven't said shit to anyone about anything." That's always the correct answer to give.

"You sound like you've got something going on with her, Tommy. You talking to a cop?"

"Fuck no, Vince." My body goes ice cold. I can't have anyone think I'm talking to a cop. That gets your ass killed.

"If you were anyone other than my cousin, I'd be thinking twice about believing the shit coming out of your mouth right now."

"She's a woman, is all," I answer back.

"She's a cop, Tommy. You can't forget that shit. You can't go easy on her just because she's got tits. She'll still use anything you say against you. Isn't that one of their fucking lines?"

I press my lips into a tight line and nod diligently.

"Don't fucking talk like that around anyone else. I can't have anyone thinking you've got a thing going on with the cops. They can't start spreading shit about you talking, Tommy. There's only so much I can do to squash shit like that."

He sounds desperate for me to listen to him. And I am, but only partially.

Even as he's warning me away from her, I already know I'm going to lie to him. I already know I'm not going to listen. I think I've just been waiting for a reason to go to her, and she just gave me one.

TONYA

J shut the door, dropping my keys in the glass bowl on the end table, and drag my ass over to sink down on the couch. It's been a long fucking day. I wince as I scrape the wound on my arm against the rough fabric of the sofa. I suck in a deep breath through clenched teeth. Fucking asshole made me chase him through the woods, all for what? A couple hundred bucks he stole from his parents? Seriously? It fucking pisses me off. I'm so fucking tired of dealing with junkies and this stupid shit. What's worse is I know he'll be out soon. Only to get hauled back in later. I lean my head back against the couch.

I put my hands on my forehead, and try to let the stress leave me. This isn't what I thought being a cop would be like. I shake my head and forget that shit. I knew this was going to be hard. It's not what's eating me. I know exactly why I'm all fucked up. It's because I have no leads to the only case I really care about.

My heart twists in my chest. I don't want to think about him. I've been trying to avoid it, but he keeps haunting me. I don't know what hurts worse, the fact that he could end this pain for me, or the fact that he's gotten to me. I haven't been with anyone in so long. I don't remember it feeling like this. But then again, I've never been dumped like that either.

I snort, and force my tired body off the sofa. Like we were seeing each other. As if I mattered to him.

My gut drops, and I find myself regretting it. But I can't stand that. I don't like regret. I do what feels right, and I don't do what feels wrong. It's my own insurance policy so that I never regret anything.

At any point in my past, I know whatever I was doing was exactly what I wanted. At least right then and there. And I'd be a fucking liar if I said I didn't love every minute of Tommy fucking me. I came alive under him. I smile, remembering how loud his bed was. I shake my head and open my fridge looking for a snack or something.

It sucked though, when it was over. I look at the half gallon of milk and the rest of my practically-empty fridge and frown. I close the door and try to shake off this shit feeling. I don't hold it against him. It never should've happened. But it still fucking hurt.

I'm not going to let him stop me from getting to the bottom of Petrov's case though. I'm sure as fuck going to avoid him like the plague though. I need to get him out of my head. If anyone at the station found out what happened between us, I'd be fucked.

I feel like a bitch for judging all of them and how hard they are after years of doing this shit. No wonder they look at me like I don't belong. Fuck! I lean my head against the fridge and breathe in and out slowly. I can't shake this negativity. I can't get out of my own fucking head. I'm second-guessing every-thing, and feeling like shit as a result. I need to stop. But I don't know how.

I slowly open my eyes as I hear a loud knock at my door.

My heart stills in my chest. I have no clue who would come over here this late at night. I wait with anxiety trickling through my limbs for a voice. But I don't hear anything. I walk silently, but quickly to the end table and pick up my gun where I left it. I hold it down and walk steadily as I hear a loud knock again.

Bang. Bang. Bang! On the third, I hear his voice say, "Open up, Tonya." Relief washes through my body and I almost put the gun down, but then I think twice.

I look at it in my hands and remember how angry the other members of the Valetti *familia* were. In two days, I've managed to piss off more men than my mom has in her entire life. That's saying something.

"I know you're in there, you may be a bad girl, but I don't want you pushing me right now." His voice doesn't come out hard, but it's not playful either. It's almost a little worried. Like he's fairly confident that I'll answer him, but scared that I won't.

I like that.

I like making him wait. Not because I don't want to answer him, I do. The wild side of me is jumping at the chance to answer him. But I also like keeping him on edge.

I put the gun down on the end table. It may be stupid, but I don't care right now. I walk to the door and unlock it. I wait a second to see if he'll open it. But he doesn't. He respects that boundary. I close my eyes and take a deep breath. I can't let myself go back to how it was before. This is going to be professional.

I open the door and curse myself as my eyes land on his hard, muscular body. Fuck, I want him. I want all of him. I close my eyes and don't open them as he speaks.

"What are you doing snooping around?" He gets right to the point, and anger rises within me. Enough so that I can stare back at him.

"Snooping around?" I'm not snooping. I'm simply trying to get answers.

"You need to knock it off." His voice is stern and admonishing. It pisses me off, but also lights something else in me. Something I need to let die.

"I don't need to do anything, and as far as you're concerned, you weren't giving me what I needed, so I had to go somewhere else." I know the double meaning there. And I hate that it slipped out. I feel fucking pathetic.

His eyebrows raise, and he looks me up and down like he's sizing me up, but I can see he's angry. "Is that so?" he says with a neutral tone.

I start backpedaling the best I can and say, "I need answers for my own sanity."

"You're a cop, you think they're going to give you anything?" He raises his voice as he continues to lay into me, "They're not like me, Tonya. They aren't going to treat you like I do."

"So they aren't going to fuck me and then toss me aside?" I'm so fucking bitter I can't help but spit it out. I don't feel any anger toward him, but apparently some part of me does.

"Is that what you want from them?" he asks.

"Fuck off, Thomas." I start to close the door. I don't have the energy for this. If he's not going to help me, fine. If he doesn't want to fuck me anymore, that's fine, too.

Thomas stops the door and pushes it open so he can lean in. "What the fuck? You trying to piss me off, Officer Kelly?" I don't like the way he's saying my name. Like he's asking if he's talking to me or someone else, someone who he doesn't trust. I've never been anything but honest with him.

"What do you want?" I ask with irritation coloring my voice, but I'm not irritated. I'm hurt. I want him to say, "You." I want him to come in and take me. I want him to make everything better. And that realization makes me feel weak. It makes me feel sick to my stomach.

"I wanna come in and talk."

"Now you wanna talk?" I shake my head and try to push down the bit of hope growing in my chest. It's stupid. I shouldn't be hoping. This can't happen.

"You gonna let me in?" he asks, like I might actually say yes.

"No." I shake my head and open my eyes, making sure to only look at his face. The thought of him coming in here only makes me want to test whether or not he can make my bed creak and groan like he did his. This is bad. Real fucking bad.

"Why the fuck not?" He sounds all pissed off.

"'Cause I don't have to, that's why." I'm flippant as I say it.

"Don't push me, baby." He narrows his eyes at me as he says it.

"I'm not your baby. I'm not your anything." I at least have a little pride knowing that those words came out strong.

"With a mouth like that, right now you're my bad girl. That's all you are." My pussy clenches at his words. I can't help that it turns me on. But I have to remember that this can't happen. This is wrong.

"Bad things will happen if you come in here." I tell him the truth and regret it when his eyes heat with lust and his lips pull into a smirk.

"You want me that much? You really can't control yourself?" he asks with a cocky grin.

It pisses me off. And I hold on to that anger so I can push him away like I know I should.

"Fuck you!" I grab the edge of the door and try to slam it shut, but his boot hits the door, blocking it.

For the first time ever in his presence, I feel scared. I don't know why, but a sense of danger takes ahold of every part of me, and I race to get to my gun. I grip it with both hands and point it at him as he takes a step inside.

His eyes go wide when he sees the gun pointed at him. He raises both of his hands, "Whoa, baby, what are you doing? Put the gun down."

My hands tremble slightly, and I feel so fucking insecure. I don't know what I'm doing anymore. I don't trust anything that I'm feeling. My hand starts shaking. It's never done that. I've always had control. But I've never been in this situation before, either. I don't even know why I grabbed it.

"Hey, it's alright." He keeps his hands raised. "You really want me to go? I'll go."

I don't know what I want. I slowly aim the gun down and keep my head down. I've fucked this up so fucking bad.

"I know I push you. I didn't mean to threaten you though." I watch in my periphery as he walks toward me like one would a wounded animal. And that's exactly how I feel. I'm so fucked up. So worn out and torn.

"I'd never hurt you, Tonya." I shouldn't believe him, but I do. He reaches out slowly and grabs my gun. I think about resisting, but I don't want to. He gently places it on the end table and looks at me like he doesn't know what to do with me.

He takes his gun out, making sure to point it away from me and quickly sets it on the end table next to mine.

He cups my chin in my hand. "I'm sorry I pushed you like that. I really thought you were just pushing me back."

"I don't know what I'm doing," I say weakly, and look up at him through my thick lashes.

A soft chuckle rumbles through his chest. "I don't either, baby." He lowers his lips to mine. He whispers with his full lips barely touching my own, "I won't hurt you. And I won't let anyone else hurt you, either."

I open my eyes and see sincerity in his dark stare.

"You gotta stay away, though." My gaze drops to the floor. I try to push him away, but it's a weak and useless effort.

"Not from me." His words pull me back from the defeated place I'd sunk to. "I want you. But they can't know. No one can know, and you need to stay away from them."

His chest rises and falls, and his breathing is the only thing I can hear other than my own heart thumping in my chest.

This is dangerous. It's forbidden. But I want it. I want him.

"Tell me you want me, baby." His voice is confident, but I can tell he needs the reassurance. He needs me to tell him I want him, too. And I do. I desperately want him.

"I want you." Before the last word leaves my lips, his hands grip my hips and he pulls me under him as he falls onto the sofa.

His fingers tickle my skin as they travel under my shirt, slowly lifting it up past my breasts.

"I'll make you feel better, baby."

"Yes," I whisper. Please. I need to feel better.

"You're just too tempting. I fucking need you under me." He stares at my breasts as he pulls the cup of my bra down and pinches my hardened nubs. It sends a direct shot of need to my clit.

A soft smile plays at his lips, but he looks into my eyes with concern.

"You really thought I'd hurt you?" He pulls my shirt over my head, taking the bra with it and lifts me into his lap. His arms wrap around my waist as he leans back against the sofa.

I feel ashamed, so I try to look away, but he cups my face and turns my head so I have to look at him. "Don't do that."

"I'm sorry," I say barely above a murmur. I am. I'm so damn sorry.

He smirks a bit and says playfully, "I had it coming, messing with a bad girl like you."

He takes my lips with his, and I feel every emotion crash down around me. The only one left standing is lust. I moan into his parted lips and let his hands roam my body. I need him to take me away. I need to *feel* something else.

He tosses me backward and climbs between my legs, ripping off everything in his way. I want to close my legs, but I don't. The look of hunger in his eyes keeps my legs spread wide for him. He licks his lips and gently runs a finger down my hip bone and over my clit. My body shudders under his touch, and his lips twitch into a satisfied smile as he lowers his lips to my pussy.

His deft fingers pump in and out of me while he sucks my clit. My eyes roll back in my head as my back bows and I struggle with my composure. It's so intense. Too intense. My body begs me to move away, not knowing if I'll be able to stand the power of the orgasm he's forcing out of me. My fingers dig into the couch and scratch along his back.

He pulls away as my thighs loosen, and the sight of him is nearly enough that I cum just from looking at him. His chiseled frame is all ripped muscle, with his left arm covered in intricate tattoos. His eyes are intense with his own need, and his breath comes in pants. He stares at my pussy in awe as he curls his fingers and mercilessly rubs my G-spot. His thumb presses down on my clit and I find my body trying to turn away. It's too much. I can't stand the overwhelming sensation.

"Don't you move," he says while withdrawing his fingers. My eyes pop open and my breath finally comes back to me.

"I didn't mean to." I'm so ready. I want him so fucking bad. I was so close. So fucking close.

He smirks at me and backhands my clit. My back arches, but my pussy clamps down on nothing. I need it. I'm so close.

"Bad girl," he says with a smirk. If he wasn't so fucking hot, and I wasn't so delirious with my own needs, I'd tell him off. Instead I bite my lip and wait with bated breath for him to take me over the edge. "Hold still." He lowers his head and relief flows through me, but it's immediately replaced with the tingling sensation of every inch of my skin being lit aflame.

He laps at my pussy, and gently places his thumb against my ass. My mouth opens as the foreign sensation of him pushing against me adds to the intensity of his tongue massaging my clit. My eyes close, and my lips part. My breathing comes in ragged pants as he starts fucking my ass and sucking my clit at the same time. It's too much. So fucking overwhelming.

In an instant, my body goes numb and then immediately explodes with paralyzing pleasure.

My thighs clench around his head as I cry out in complete ecstasy. Every nerve ending heats in waves, starting at my toes and working their way up. Each wave of pleasure is higher and more intense than the previous. My body is twisted and still stiff, unwilling to move. I try to relax as I come down from the high. I try, but my body doesn't respond. I can only feel.

After a few minutes of lying limp on the sofa, I come to my senses. My body is covered in sweat, and my legs are still trembling. I try to speak and realize my throat is sore and dry.

I look down my body and watch as Thomas stands up and shoves his jeans down his muscular thighs. He grabs his thick cock in his hands and strokes it once. The head glistens with a taste of his cum. He embodies power and lust. And the sight of him is intoxicating.

"I want you on the bed next." With the heated look in his eyes and my arousal glistening on his lips, I can't deny him. I can't deny what I want either. I love the way he makes me feel. In this moment I'd let him have me however he wanted. And I do.

I'll give him every bit of me that he wants.

I can't remember how long it's been since I've felt this alive. A spark I haven't felt in years is blazing inside of me. He lifts my body in his arms and carries me to the bedroom. I lean into him. I don't want to think about anything except how good it feels.

That's all I care about. I just want to *feel*.

He tosses me onto the bed and immediately crawls toward me. He looks dangerous, he *is* dangerous. He licks his lips and climbs over my body, forcing me onto my back.

His lips crush mine, and I can faintly taste myself on his tongue. I smile and pull back as a blush rises to my cheeks. His chest shakes gently with his rough chuckle, and it warms every bit of me.

"Where are your cuffs?" he asks. My eyes widen at his question. My heart races in my chest.

"You need to learn to trust me, baby." He kisses me with such passion I have to close my eyes.

"I can help you with that. Let me."

I pull away from him and look at my dresser. They're in the top drawer. My anxiety spikes.

"I can't." I push the words out. I know there's something between us, but what that is, I'm not sure.

"You can," he says, standing up from the bed. He walks to my dresser, following my line of sight and guessing correctly that the cuffs are there. They're right on top, so he doesn't have to look very long to find them.

"You could hurt me," I state simply. It's one thing to fool around, but another to give up control and make myself so helpless. I don't want to be vulnerable. The very thought chills my blood.

He looks at me with incredulity before pointing out, "My arm is almost as large as your head. I could hurt you right now if I wanted." My eyes linger on his corded arms and broad shoulders. I know what he's saying is true, but I don't like it. I don't like how accurate his words are.

"That right there," he walks back to me and gentles his hand on my forearm, "That fear. I'm going to take it away." I stare into his heated gaze and feel too much comfort.

"Why?" It's stupid to even consider it. But I am. I don't want to be scared anymore. I don't want to be angry, either.

He shrugs and dangles the two sets of cuffs from his finger. He watches as they sway. "You look like a girl who could use a little help."

"I don't need help." I know I sound defensive, and I don't mean to.

"No, you don't need it. But you could use it." He hands me the cuffs. "Lock them around your wrists." He gives me the command and it instantly heats my core. I have to stop myself from scissoring my legs.

"What are you going to do to me?" I ask him in a breathy voice. Now that I'm holding the cuffs in my hand and he's standing so close, it's turning me on. His muscular chest ripples as he takes a step back from me.

"I'm going to watch as you cuff yourself to the bed."

I bite my lip and watch him stroke himself. "Just the thought of you being at my mercy has me almost cumming. You know that?"

I feel my cheeks heat and a wave of arousal shoots through me. I shift the cuffs to my other hand and look at them and then at him.

"Then what?" I ask. My lips stay parted as my breathing comes in short pants.

"I'm gonna do whatever I want with you." My eyes fall and the insecurity comes back. I don't like not having a plan.

"I'm going to start by getting between your legs and getting your taste back on my tongue." My eyes shoot to his as I listen. "I need to get you ready to take me." My thighs clench, and I know I'm already ready.

"Not your pussy, baby. I want your ass." My eyes widen, and I actually scoot away slightly on the bed. He chuckles and strokes himself again. My eyes focus on the bead of precum leaking from his slit.

"Not tonight, baby. But I'm gonna get you ready for me. Tonight I'm fucking your pussy like I own it. But next time, I'm taking your ass."

His words force a moan from my lips. I want that. I want all of that. But I don't want to give up control. I look up at him with apprehension, and see nothing but desire written on his face. I have to tell him how I really feel though. "I'm scared," I whisper, and it makes me feel weak.

"That's normal. But I promise you, you're going to love it."

"What if it's too much?" I ask.

He smirks at me as he says, "You have to trust me." He walks over and plants a soft kiss on my lips before I can object to anything else.

His hand strokes my hair. "All you need to do is trust me."

This is stupid and reckless, but I feel like I need this. I close my eyes and quickly tighten the cuffs on both my wrists. I bring my right hand up to the bedpost and attach the cuff to the thin metal cylinder.

My heart races in my chest. "Just tug, baby." I hear his words and it takes a second to understand the meaning of them. I do as he says. I pull against the restraint, and I can see why he wanted me to. If I struggle hard enough, the post will give. It'll fuck up my wrist, but I could get out. It would fucking hurt though.

"I won't do anything that'll make you feel like you need to. I just wanted you to realize, if you really needed to, you could take control back." He plants another soft kiss on my lips and I close my eyes and lie back against the pillow. I put my left wrist up against the post and wait for him to tighten it.

My heart races in my chest. He could do whatever he wants to me now. His grin widens into a gorgeous smile as his eyes roam my body.

"Spread your legs," he commands, and I instantly obey.

"See, you can be a good girl when you want to." He climbs on the bed and buries his head between my legs. I moan and arch my back as he sucks my clit into his mouth and massages it with his tongue. His fingers push into me and curl up, hitting the sensitive bundle of nerves. He's rough and brutal. His movements are harsh and strike my desire each and every time. My body heats so hot I swear I'm not alright and then the trembling waves start from the pleasure stirring in my center.

My orgasm hits me with a force I've never felt before. It comes so quickly, and so forcefully that I wasn't prepared. I scream and convulse as a white light blinds me and my skin turns to fire. He kisses my thigh, my hip. His rough stubble scratches gently across my sensitive skin and makes my body shudder.

I breathe heavily as I come back down and watch as he sucks on his fingers with a look of pure rapture.

He takes them out of his mouth with a pop and smirks at me. "I told you

you'd enjoy it. Now lie back and be a good girl for me. I'll give you everything you need."

* * *

WHEN THE MORNING light shines through the bit of my window not covered by the curtain, I roll over in my bed to avoid the light and reach out to nothing. My eyelids part and I sit up to make sure, but I already know he's gone. My hand rests where he was last night and it's cold.

I clench my thighs and feel so fucking sore. My pussy is slightly swollen and the movement sends a shot of need through me. If he was here, I'd want him again.

But he's not.

I lie on my back and stare at the ceiling not knowing how to feel, or what to think.

I want him, obviously, and our chemistry is undeniable, but I can't possibly expect anything to come of this. It's a bad idea to play a man who won't keep you. I pull the covers tighter around my shoulders and sink back into the warmth of the bed.

I close my eyes and try to ignore it. I'm not in any state to even think about what happened, let alone try to figure out where this is going.

TOMMY

I can't believe I'm here. I'm practically stalking a cop. She looks different today. She's wearing a cute little sundress. It's black on top, and white on the bottom, with a bright pink sash separating the two colors around her waist. It looks cute on her. Different, but cute. I watch as she takes off her sunglasses and looks into the window of a sandwich shop. She's hungry, good. I wanna feed her. I keep watching as she purses her lips and puts the sunglasses back on and walks closer to me, even though she's on the other side of the street and hasn't even seen me yet.

I'm just waiting for her to feel my eyes on her. I wanna see her reaction. I grin from ear to ear as she stops in her tracks with her head turned in my direction. A smile spreads across her gorgeous lips. That's a good reaction. I see her shoulders relax as she looks down the road, checking for oncoming traffic. She crosses the street and I motion for her to follow me into the shop I've been standing out in front of. I don't want us meeting on the street. We need to be inside for this.

Once I'm sure she knows I'm heading inside, I walk into the coffee shop and sit at a table near the back. No one should really notice us here. No one would recognize me so far from our territory. It's still a risk, but it's one I'm willing to take.

"What are you doing here?" she asks in a hushed voice as she sits down.

She looks around the restaurant and I let her. I give her a moment to realize it's alright. Her hair is in a high ponytail, but a small piece has fallen out and it tickles along her collarbone. She turns to look at the customers in line. She looks so fucking beautiful. Her skin has a faint flush to it, and I'm not sure if it's because of me, or something else. But I'd love to think I caused it.

I wait for her to look at me with those beautiful green eyes full of curiosity. "I had nothing better to do."

"Nothing better than to follow me around?" Her tone has a bit of admonishment to it. But I know she's happy. I can tell. And I like that. Her hand is fiddling with the locket hanging from her necklace. I've seen her do that before. I wondered back then what's inside her locket, or who gave it to her. It's someone important and I want to find out, but now's not the time.

"Yeah, well, my day job is on hold at the moment." I watch her eyes widen as I answer her. She didn't expect me to talk about work, but if we're planning on fucking, and I sure as hell am, then we need to be blunt and honest.

She noticeably swallows and looks toward the front of the restaurant. "Should you really be telling me that?"

"Are you wired, baby? The last couple of times I've checked your clothes, you weren't." Her cheeks go bright red, and it's fucking adorable to see.

"Thomas--" I cut her off before she can finish.

"Tommy. Call me Tommy." It feels good telling her that. Such a stupid thing. But everyone calls me Tommy. And I want her to do the same. I shouldn't. I know this is wrong, but I do.

"Tommy, I don't know about this." I can hear the worry in her voice.

"What's there to know?" I shrug, and then lean in a little. "I like fucking you." My words make her smile even though she's trying to contain it. "I want what happened last night to happen again." Her chest rises and falls. Her pupils dilate with desire. I made sure to make up for the squeaky bed last night, and I know she enjoyed herself. I bet she can still feel me buried deep inside her.

"You know we shouldn't." Her words are breathy. I know I've got her. So long as I want her, she's mine.

My lips pull into an asymmetric grin as I agree, "Yeah, we shouldn't. But we're gonna. 'Cause I'm a bad boy, and you're a bad girl."

She bites her lip and rests her elbow on the table, cradling her cheek with her hand. Her forehead pinches with worry. "I don't know, Tommy."

"You don't know what? If you wanna cum on my dick again?"

As I ask the question, a barista walks up with a pad and pen to take our orders. I watch as Tonya's eyes go wide, and she looks down at her lap like there's something there that's going to save her from embarrassment. I doubt the barista heard because she seems unaffected, but that doesn't stop Tonya from having a moment.

"Can I get you two anything?" the girl asks in a sweet voice. She's young. If she heard, I doubt she'd be so calm.

"Yeah, could I have a coffee with cream, a blueberry muffin, a slice of banana nut bread..." I lean back to look at the menu. I figure I might as well order a few different things to see what Tonya likes. "A cake pop, and a cookie too, please."

"Is all that for you?" Tonya asks.

"I think I'll share with you." My answer makes her smile shyly. I like this side of her.

"Just a coffee, please. French Vanilla, with cream and sugar." She likes it sweet. I could've guessed that, but I wouldn't have been shocked if she liked her coffee black, too.

"So, what's it going to be, Tonya?" I ask as soon as the waitress is out of sight.

She looks down at the table with pursed lips and then back up to me. "Just sex?" she asks.

"Yeah," I'm quick to answer.

My sweet forbidden bad girl. I want her so fucking bad.

"Okay," she agrees. My dick stands at full attention and pushes against my zipper. Yes! I can't fucking wait to be inside her again. It takes everything in me not to bend her over the table and fuck her right here and now.

I play it cool though, leaning back in my seat. "Good." I keep it simple and let my eyes wander to her breasts. I don't give a fuck that it's blatant. She's mine now. I remember biting down on her nipples and pulling back last night, forcing those moans from her lips. I can't fucking wait to do it again.

The barista sets a tray down in front of me, and brings me back to the present.

Tonya laughs under her breath and thanks the young girl before she walks away.

"I think you're drooling, Tommy," she says with confidence. She shoots me

553

an I-own-your-ass type of look, and I fucking love it. I love how damn confident she is around me.

"I might be." I lift her hand to my mouth and make a sweet, soft giggle
erupt from her lips. This side of her is different. It's soft and sweet. I like it.
Even more, I like that I bring it out of her.

I watch her pick off the little bits of sugar on the top of the muffin and pop
them into her mouth. She picks at it for a while and then finally bites into it.

As she takes a bite, she looks up and sees me watching her. She's quick to
cover her mouth as she chews and sets the muffin down. "What?" she asks,
still covering her partially full mouth.

I chuckle at her and shake my head as I reply, "Nothing." It's cute I guess to
watch her eat like that.

She finishes swallowing and takes a sip of coffee before asking me, "Aren't
you going to eat?"

I shake my head. "No, I just thought you may be hungry."

She smiles sweetly and takes another sip of coffee. "I'm good to go, if you
are. I have some errands to run." She wipes her hands on the napkin and
tosses it onto her plate.

I nod my head and reach into my pocket for my wallet.

"You don't--" she starts, but I cut her off.

"Knock it off, I wanna buy you breakfast."

"Thank you," she looks shy as she says it. She downs the rest of her coffee
and stands to leave.

"I'll walk you to your car." She looks at me for a moment, as though she
doesn't understand. But as I stand she nods obediently. I might call her my
bad girl, but she's so fucking good to me. She just doesn't know it.

TOMMY

a s we walk out of the coffee shop, she looks all around us, like she's just waiting to be spotted. I don't know what the fuck is wrong with her. Apparently she forgot how to play it cool.

"Relax," I wrap my arm around her waist to make a point. "No one's gonna see us."

We walk in amiable silence. I let her lead the way.

After a few minutes she says, "I just don't know about this, Tommy." I hate the insecurity in her voice.

"You weren't concerned about that just a few minutes ago," I point out as I look down at her to watch her expression. "You changing your mind?"

"No, I--" she clears her throat and walks a bit straighter as she continues. "I enjoyed last night."

"Good, then there's no problem." I enjoyed it, too. I loved playing with her body. Watching how she responded to every move. I got her off every way I knew how. She was limp and sated and I still wanted more. I'll be damned if I'm not going to keep going after what I want. I've never known real limits before. I've never wanted to venture past what the *familia* gave me. But I'm not giving this up. Now that I've had a taste, I'm not willing to let go.

"This is just so wrong," she says as I spot her car. She parked behind a little shopping center. There are a few cars in front of us as we walk in, but hers is off to the side. It's a vacant lot. I take a quick glance to make sure no one's around us, and I decide right then that I'm gonna teach her a lesson.

She walks to her door but I take hold of her hip and keep her walking to the backseat door so we're a bit more hidden. She looks shocked and a little confused until I press my lips to hers, and let my hands roam down her body.

She breaks the kiss and looks out into the empty lot, seeming to remember we're out in public. That's the shit I'm gonna punish her for. Right fucking now.

"You wanna know how wrong it is?" I grab her ass in both my hands. I give her a firm squeeze that makes her gasp, and then spin her around in my arms. I shove her front against her car. Her breasts flatten against the window, making them appear even more lush and biteable. "You wanna see how much I don't give a fuck that it's wrong?"

My hand cups her pussy and I have to stifle my groan. She's already hot and wet and ready for me. I've waited long enough for that ass, though. I push the inside of her thigh and she obliges, spreading her legs. She looks over her shoulder to look at me with a wicked spark in her eyes and taunts, "You gonna punish me?" Those words on her lips nearly has me cumming in my pants.

I'm quick to unzip my pants and unleash my cock. I stroke it once as her mouth opens and her tongue darts out to lick her bottom lip. She looks around the parking lot like there's no way we aren't getting caught. I almost change up my plans and push her down onto her knees to have her suck me off, but this isn't about me taking pleasure from her. It's about her seeing just how much we can get away with.

"Only if you're quiet." I grip the nape of her neck and pull her back so I can take her bottom lip between my teeth. Her ass backs up against my cock and she teases me, rocking it back and forth like she wants to ride me.

I let go of her and lift up her dress. The desire written on her face fades as she hears voices coming through the narrow sidewalk. She looks at me with a hint of fear. I hold her gaze as the voices fade just as quickly as they came. I'm sure these cars belong to employees of these shops. No one's coming back here. I know she's scared of getting caught. I'm gonna show her that shit's not going to happen.

"Your greedy pussy wants me, but you're gonna have to wait." My thumb probes her puckered hole, and the motion makes her moan. A rough chuckle grows up my chest as I slip on a lubricated condom. I hate condoms, but for this I need to make sure there's lube. She's gonna need it. I spit in my hand and make sure my dick is nice and wet for her. I line my cock up and slowly push just the head in. I gotta get her loose and feeling good before I finally take her ass with my dick. I've been thinking about it all day.

"Tommy," she moans my name as my fingers dip inside her heat and spread her moisture to her swollen clit. I pinch her lightly and she arches her back in response, causing my dick to slip in a little deeper. It feels so fucking good. I wanna slam into her, but this is the first time, I've gotta be gentle.

My arm wraps around the front of her so I can cup her pussy. I press my palm to her clit and gently slip my fingers into her hot cunt. I rock my hand as I pick up my motions. I keep rubbing her clit and playing with her pussy until she writhing under my touch and letting her moans slip out with no inhibition.

She's getting louder and bolder, moving her pussy against my hand to take what she wants. That's exactly how I need her. She's so fucking easy to get off. A few more rough pumps and she's biting down on her lip while her thighs tremble with her orgasm. Her pussy clamps down on my fingers and I'm too fucking excited to get my pleasure next.

"You like that, baby?" I ask her.

She tilts her head slightly and smirks as she answers, "Fuck you, you know I do." I fucking love it. I love how she pushes me.

I put my lips up to her ear and speak in a low, threatening voice. "My bad girl is really pushing it. That's a brave thing for you to do with my dick in your ass."

I take a quick look up and to my left. I've been so busy watching her I haven't been paying attention, but there's no one there.

Soon she'll be ready for me to fuck her rough and deep. I just need a few more minutes to get her ready. I keep looking ahead of us and every voice makes my heart beat a little faster. She's trusting me, and I don't want to ruin it because I was so damn set on fucking her ass.

I aim my spit and get my cock more lubed as I push in a bit more and pull out. "Push back, baby," I tell her.

She obeys me and I slide in a little deeper. It only takes a few more gentle rocks until she's moaning and pushing back to take more of me.

Finally, I'm all the way in, and it feels like fucking heaven. She moans against the window, and I take a quick look to make sure no one can see her.

Right now she's mine. I pull out slowly and push back in with just as much care. I need to be gentle until she's adjusted to me being inside her.

Her forehead pinches, and I know she's feeling a little pain. I rub her clit to make sure it's only going to heighten her pleasure. I don't want to hurt her. I want this to be just as good for her as it is for me. Each movement makes those sweet sounds fall from her lips. Her eyes are closed, and her hands are gripping onto the frame of her car. She's completely lost in pleasure.

"Tommy," she whispers my name. "Harder, fuck me harder." Her words are a desperate plea.

I grip her hips and thrust into her harder. She cries out, and I have to wrap my hand around her mouth. I lean in and growl into her ear. "You want everyone to see me fucking you, don't you?"

She shakes her head and moans into my hand as I keep fucking her ass like I own her. My balls smack against her pussy with each hard thrust. Over and over I pound into her. She struggles to keep quiet, and I have to remind her. "Shut the fuck up and take it." Her pussy clamps down on my fingers at my dirty words. She's loving this. I move my other hand away from her mouth so I can grip her hip and mercilessly fuck her ass. She bites her lip and pushes her head and breasts against the car door.

"Where's my cock, baby?" I ask her as I keep up my ruthless rhythm. Her ass is tight and hot, and I'm getting close already.

"In my ass," she whimpers, and her mouth stays open with her eyes closed tight. I know she's close again. She just needs a little more.

"That's 'cause you're a bad girl, and bad girls get fucked in their ass." I thrust in and out of her, loving the soft moans she's giving me. I strum her clit as she pushes back against me. "Do you feel like a bad girl now?" My body starts to sweat, and my breathing gets labored as I give her ass a punishing fuck.

"Yes." She's louder than she should be, and it makes my eyes dart up. Still no one.

"Say it." I push my dick all the way in and lift my hips so I'm as deep as I can go. Her mouth opens in a silent scream. I pull back slightly, and she's quick to obey my command.

"I'm your bad girl." Her words bring me that much closer to my release, and I desperately rub her throbbing clit to get her off. I need her cumming with me. Her body goes limp, and her legs tremble. Her head flies back with her teeth digging into her bottom lip. Fuck yes. I pump into her again, and fucking lose it. I hear her words over and over in my head as my spine tingles and waves of pleasure rush through my body. I thrust my hips once more to give her everything I've got.

I pull out of her gently and steady her hips. Her legs are quivering, and I know she must feel weak. She took a rough fuck. "Lean against the car, baby. I got you." She listens and rests her head on the window, catching her breath. I look to my left and right, and there's still no one there. Thank fuck. I don't want anyone to see her like this.

I remove the condom and tuck my dick back in my pants. She's still trying to regain her composure, so I pull her panties back into place as her breathing calms. I pet her back in soothing circles. Her hair has fallen out, and I have to push it away to give her a small kiss on her shoulder.

After a minute she rolls her body on the car so that her back is leaning against it and she's facing me. She gives me a small, satisfied smile and it fills my chest with pride. I knew she'd like that. I give her a kiss just below the tender spot behind her ear. She hums with approval. My lips tickle her neck as I ask her, "Did you like that, bad girl?"

"You fucked the ponytail out of my hair," she says weakly, with a bit of humor. Her eyes light with happiness, and the smile grows on her gorgeous face.

I shrug and wrap an arm around her waist as she bends down with trembling legs to pick up the hair tie on the ground. She looks around us as she stands up. "Did anyone see?" she asks with a quiet voice.

"Not this time." I grin at her.

She gives me a small smile, but I can see she doesn't like that answer. She runs her fingers through her hair and breathes deeply. "Just sex." She says it like it's a reminder. To herself and to me.

She takes a few steps to her door, looking as though nothing even happened. She's pulled herself together, the only signs that she just took my cock up her ass are the flush in her cheeks, and her slightly swollen bottom lip.

I clear my throat and answer her, "Yeah, just sex." That's all this is. I'm fine with that. And she sure as shit enjoys it just as much as me.

She nods and steps out of my embrace to open her door.

"I have to get going." Her words are weak, almost filled with regret.

"Yeah, me too." No I don't. I don't have shit to do but fuck her. Even though she's the one that's supposed to be watching me, so I could probably run errands. It'd be stupid to risk it though.

She parts her lips and looks up at me through her lashes as she settles into the driver side door. She winces slightly instead of saying whatever was on her mind. I don't know what she was going to say, but she decides on nothing. It makes an uneasiness settle in my chest. She's unsure of something.

"You good?" I try to keep it lighthearted, but she just nods and doesn't look me in the eyes.

"I'll see you later," I tell her. I lean in and plant a small kiss on her cheek.

"Okay," she says, looking up at me with a slightly confused look. I don't understand where it's coming from.

"You alright?" I ask her.

"Yeah, I'm good," she says as she puts the key into the ignition. But she's not good. I don't like it.

I want to ask her why she's being so distant, but I hold back. No questions is better. For both of us. I wanna fuck her, she wants to fuck me, we have to leave it at that. I grip her doorframe and gently close it as she lowers the window.

"I'll see you later then," she says, and I give her a tight smile.

As she drives away, I can't help but feel like I'm not going to see her again. She's going to realize what a mistake this is.

I want to prove to her it's not, but it is. Maybe I should just stay away. I run my hand through my hair and sigh. I don't know what I was thinking. It's gonna be like this every time we leave each other. And I don't like this raw hollowness in my chest.

I watch her car drive away before I start walking back through the opening to the sidewalk.

I hate how she left. But that's what this is. It's all it can be.

It didn't occur to me that I don't just want sex until right this moment. And that's not good. That's not fucking good at all.

Fuck, this was a mistake. A big, fucking mistake.

TONYA

I stare at the folders on my desk, and then back up at the computer screen. I have a ton of shit to update. I need to put all this information in the system, but I keep fucking up. I have to do this right, but my head's not in it. I just can't think straight. I'm exhausted from the last two days on the job. I'm miserable.

It's not that the work is any harder, it's just not what I want to do.

I'm on cases that mean nothing to me. I'm getting spit on and kicked while I arrest assholes I don't give a shit about. I feel beat up and abused. I know this is the right thing to do and people do appreciate it, even if I never hear it. But damn, this is hard. And it's wearing me down.

I heard back from our contacts in France and Russia, still no sign of Petrov. He has to be dead.

I feel defeated more than anything. Like the finish line vanished before I could make it there.

"How's it coming along?" Chris' voice makes me jump in my seat. He laughs at me and pats my back. "You need more coffee."

I smile weakly up at him. Chris has been a cop all his life. He's gotta be in his fifties now, but he's still smiling, and still kicking ass. I don't know how he does it.

He's not chasing a case or running toward the darkness. He deserves to be a cop. I don't. I was using this position for my own selfish reasons. I feel like fraud.

"Yeah, for real." I clear my throat and scoot back in my seat. "I'll run out and grab one, you want anything?"

"Nah, I'm good," he says. "Hey, I just wanna say, you're doing good, kid. Don't be so hard on yourself."

"Thanks." I try to look him in the eyes, but I can't.

"We can't get 'em all, and the Valettis are a big fish. It'll go on their file, so we can use it next time. Trust me, there will be a next time."

I look up at him with a deep crease of confusion marring my forehead. "What are you talking about?"

"Oh shit. I thought you were all bent out of shape because the prosecutor gave you the news."

"No, Marcy didn't tell me shit."

"Fuck, she must've told Harrison. He didn't tell you? He's supposed to be taking you under his wing."

I huff a humorless laugh. "No, he didn't."

"The judge ruled against us. We can't use the fingerprints." He shrugs and looks like he feels guilty for telling me. "There's no case." I don't answer. I don't know what to say.

"He really should've told you."

A lump grows in my throat. Tommy's off the hook.

He's going to be okay. A weight lifts from my chest, but that only makes the pain I'm feeling there grow stronger.

"You okay?" Chris asks. I look at him for a moment. I see the kindness in his eyes, and I know I don't deserve it.

"Yeah, I'm--"

"Kelly! We need to talk." Harrison interrupts us, and I swear to God I'm gonna strangle him if he yells at me.

"Yeah, I'm all ears," I say, not holding back the sarcasm.

"We lost our case, but I'm betting something's gonna blow up in their faces soon. We just gotta stay the course."

I'm surprised by his tone. It's not condescending or full of anger. He's almost excited.

"Why do you think it's going to blow back on them?"

"You can't fuck over a Kingpin and not get dealt with."

"I imagine Petrov is dead," I say flatly. It kills me to say it, but it's the truth.

"Possibly, but Nikolaev has taken over." He says the words like Petrov was no one special. After a moment of quiet he adds, "There's always going to be another one."

My heart thuds once in my chest and stops. I try to push the words out, but I can't hear them.

"You've got a lot to learn." He grins at me. "We're gonna get 'em. I know we will. They're getting sloppy, and soon enough, it's gonna happen." I've never seen him this happy and I don't know how to handle him. Or all the emotions bombarding me.

He pats me on the back and turns to walk away. "I can *feel* it. It's coming," he says as he walks off.

I try to sit back down, but I can't. I just need to get out of here. Something in my gut is telling me everything is wrong. And it's all revolving around Tommy.

It's been four days since I've seen him. I don't understand. I thought he meant he'd see me later that night. But he never showed. I guess I was presumptuous. And then I got a message. A text from his cell. I only know because I looked up the number.

I'M SORRY, Tonya. It's over. You were right.

HE TOLD me to stay away. It fucking hurt.

I know it was wrong. I knew we shouldn't have done it. But still. It was nice to be held. I feel like I have nothing. I have no one. I need something. I need *him* right now. Whether he wants me or not. That's my selfish side coming through again. I wonder if I'll ever learn.

I take a deep breath and grab my jacket to get out of here. I walk over to Jerry's office, but stop before knocking. The door's ajar, and I can hear him talking to his wife on the phone. I press my lips into a straight line as I listen to him lie to her about being on a job last night. I take a peek at him and see he's still in his clothes from yesterday. My heart drops in my chest.

It hurts to think he's cheating on her, but it's so fucking obvious. I don't ask to leave early, I just keep walking and try to ignore all this shit. My

563

thoughts are running a mile a minute, about everything, and everyone. I thought I had shit all figured out, but I didn't.

I don't have anything figured out. I'm just lost. I'm so fucking lost.

I thought I knew how all of this would play out, but now what I wanted seems impossible.

I thought I knew what Tommy would be like before I ever met him. I read his profile and looked at the evidence. I had him painted in my head as an arrogant prick who thought he could get away with whatever he wanted. And then I met one of the women. The only one who was coherent. She said she saw Tommy. She heard gunshots and shouting, but she couldn't move. She wasn't sure if it was the drugs or the fear. She was in and out of it for a while, but one of them, one of the Valettis shot her up with something. She tried to make him stop, like the other times. But they said it was to make her better. To help save her. And it did. And Tommy was the one calming her down and telling her it would be okay.

My heart clenches in my chest. The line between black and white is so goddamned blurry. And at this point, I'm having a hard time knowing what's right and what's wrong.

TOMMY

I look out of the peephole and my heart sinks. I knew this was going to happen. I'm surprised she waited. I prepared for her anger that night when I sent the text. It's not fucking right the way I ended it. I rest my head on the door and she knocks again. Right in that very spot. Like she fucking knew I was there.

It hurts, and I wince like a little bitch. Shit! I need to get this over with. I open the door and part my lips to tell her I'm sorry, but she walks right past me, brushing against my body and continuing to the bedroom like I wasn't even standing in the doorway.

What the fuck?

"Tonya!" I call after her, but she doesn't stop. I shut the door and follow her to my bedroom, not knowing what to expect.

I walk in and find her sitting on the edge of my bed, waiting for me. She's gripping the edge of the comforter and looking at the ground.

"Charges are dropped," she says to the floor.

I take in her appearance. She's nothing like the woman I was with this past weekend. Not the sweet spitfire in a sundress. She's hurting bad. I walk over and sit next to her on the bed, but I keep my hands to myself. We can't keep this shit up.

"I know." I'm not going to tell her I found out from the judge. She doesn't ask though. She's quiet for a while. I let her sit and think. I won't push her to tell me why she's here.

"I need you right now, Tommy," she finally says. Tears leak from the corners of her eyes and it breaks my heart in two. I lose my resolve and wrap her small body in my arms. I pull her into my lap and hold her while she cries.

"What's wrong, baby?" She cries harder at my words, and I can't stand it. I just want her to stop. She's a strong woman. I didn't think I'd hurt her like this. "I'm sorry." I kiss her neck. I wish there were another way. I wish we hadn't met like this. "I'm sorry it has to be this way."

She nods her head into my chest, but she doesn't let up on the tears. I stroke her back and rock her. Kissing her hair, her shoulder. I keep soothing her the best I can.

"You don't deserve this, baby. You deserve better."

She shakes her head and heaves in a shaky breath. "Don't act like I'm good enough for you. I'm not. I'm a thug, and you're a cop," I point out.

She doesn't respond. The only reaction I get is that her cries slowly stop. It takes a few more minutes before she lifts her head and wipes away the tears.

Her cheeks are tear-stained and red, her eyes are glassy. She sniffles and I reach to the nightstand for a tissue for her.

"You're gonna be alright, babe, you're going places." My heart clenches in my chest. I don't wanna do this. I have to admit, when she didn't come that night it hurt, even though I told her to stay away. A part of me hoped she wouldn't listen, and she'd come to me. Even if it was just to yell at me for putting her through that shit. But I realized it was for the best. I'm only gonna hold her back. I'll ruin her career. And just being with me puts both of us in danger with the *familia*. It's impossible.

She was right to question us being together. It never should've happened.

"I just need to feel something right now." She turns her head to look at me. Her eyes are pleading with me. And I sure as hell am not going to refuse her. I want her. Even if it's only once more.

"I'm here." I pull her into my chest and lie on my side to cradle her. I leave an opened-mouth kiss on her neck. She takes my face in both of her hands and crushes her lips against mine.

I can feel all of her emotion pouring into her kiss. She needs me right now. I can't deny her anything. In this moment, I'm only hers. She takes my bottom lip between hers and kisses me sweetly. I moan into her mouth as she parts her lips and grants me entry. My hand brushes against her hip and then slowly lifts her shirt. I let my fingers skim her skin. I smile against her lips as she pulls away and shivers from my touch.

I lift her shirt over her head. I kiss her belly, her breasts, and then the dip in her throat. I can hear her heart beating calmly as she raises her hands above her head. The tie holding up her hair loosens and slips out, letting her hair fall around her shoulders. She shakes it out gently and looks back at me with her beautiful green eyes. There's a small amount of lust and desire, but mostly need and vulnerability.

My heart swells in my chest as I grip her hips to keep her steady and lean forward, making her fall back on the bed as I kiss her. I suck her top lip and move down her body. I kiss her belly as I unbutton her jeans and slide them off. I watch as the goosebumps slowly show along her skin. My hot breath blows across her skin as my fingers slip off her thong and leave her completely bared to me.

I've never felt so powerful as I do when I look down at her. It feels like a heavy weight on my shoulders, but I want it. I want her. I want to give her everything she needs.

I take a languid lick as her fingers spear through my hair. Her thighs tremble as I blow over her sensitive clit.

"Please, Tommy," she moans into the air above me. I look up and find her staring down at me. "I need you," she whispers.

I kick off my pants and crawl up her body. I kiss her once and watch as her eyes close while I slowly push into her. I lower my head and groan into the crook of her neck as her back bows, and I slide deeper inside of her welcoming heat. I angle my hips so I push against her clit as I settle in as deep as I can go.

I brace myself on my forearms, and watch as her mouth parts with small pants and her eyes stay closed. I cup her chin in my hand and lean down for a sweet kiss. I give her a moment to adjust to my size, and then I pull back and slam into her. Her eyes open as she gasps from the impact and pleasure.

I hold her gaze as I do the same again and again, hitting her clit each time.

"More," she whispers. I run my hand over her thigh and let my blunt fingernails dig into her ass. I tilt her so she's at just the right angle and hold her there as I thrust harder and deeper. Her head rocks, and her breasts bounce slightly with each pump of my hips, but her eyes stay on mine.

I want to kiss her, I want to bury my head into her neck and fuck her with wild abandon, but I can't. I can't break her gaze. I pick up my pace and brutally fuck into her greedy cunt, again and again. A strangled cry of pleasure escapes her lips as her thighs tremble and her nails dig into my back, leaving small scratches behind. I feel her walls tighten and I know she's close. She's so close, and so am I.

I suck her nipple into my mouth and pull back. My teeth bite down enough to hold on as I pull back. Her back bows off the bed as I do the same to the other breast. My breathing comes in pants and so does hers. It's all I can hear. It's all that matters right now.

I pick up my pace and gently kiss her lips. It's soft, and our lips barely touched, but it feels like more. Her lips stay parted as she moans my name. "Please, please," she keeps begging me, and I thrust harder and deeper every time, but I know this isn't what she's begging for. It only fuels me to hold her closer and kiss her more deeply, searching for the same feeling. I give her everything I have.

Her body tries to twist away beneath me as she calls out my name. *My name.* It sounds perfect coming from her lips. I slip my hands under her knees and push them forward. Her head thrashes as I fuck deep into her pussy. My hips smack against hers with each brutal thrust. Faster and harder until I can feel the highest peak. It's so close.

"Tommy!" she cries out as her body shakes uncontrollably. My name on her lips. I'll never stop loving that. It just sounds too perfect.

My spine tingles at the base, and a cold sweat breaks out over my entire body as I pump into her three more times, chasing that high that I always get with her. And then her eyes close, and her body trembles beneath me with her own orgasm. I find my release with her, lowering my head to her neck and breathing in her sweet scent.

After a moment, when the high of our release dies, the pounding need of my heart slows, and I realize it's over.

That was the last time.

TOMMY

Tommy

I know when I let go, I'll never hold her again. She's lying still in my arms, thinking the same, I'm sure.

So I don't move. I pretend there's no reason for her to leave my embrace. That there's nothing waiting for either of us beyond these walls.

But I'm weak. I'm the weaker of the two of us, because she's the first to speak.

"Thank you," she murmurs without looking at me. She's thanking me, like I did her a favor. Like she didn't feel that. She didn't feel the same emotions I felt between us. I rest my head just above hers on the pillow.

"Don't thank me. Don't degrade what just happened like that." The words come out harsher than I intended.

Her shoulders turn inward like she's cowering from my hard words. I wanna tell her I love her. But it'll only make it harder. After a minute, she molds her body against me again and relaxes in my embrace. I kiss her hair, and just as I lose my resolve and decide I should risk it all and tell her, I hear my front door open.

My blood turns to ice. I move quickly to get to the other side of Tonya, to block her from whoever just came into my place uninvited. A million possibilities race through my mind. It could be the cops coming to get me for something, a rival prick trying to prove he's tougher than me. For all I know, I could be on someone's hit list. I open my drawer for my gun. But then I hear Anthony's voice as he calls out, "Tommy! Where are you, bro?" My heart only races faster as I look between Tonya and the closed bedroom door.

"Wait here," I whisper to Tonya as she stares at the closed door with fear.

"Coming!" I yell out to him before leaning down and kissing her.

"Yo! We gotta talk!" I hear Anthony yell, and I resist the urge to hold her longer and finally back away.

I grab my pants and shove them on as quick as I can. I can't let him back here. I can't let him see her.

By the time I get to my living room, I'm pissed and aggravated. And worried. I breathe out slowly as I see Anthony going through the liquor cabinet. He turns to face me with two glasses in one hand, and a bottle of scotch in the other.

"What's wrong? You're all good now. Why the fuck do you look like that?" Anthony's pissing me off, but it's not his fault. I gotta calm down, but I can't. My heart's banging in my chest with the fear that shit's about to get real.

"I'm fine. What's up?" I ask him flatly.

"You don't look fine," he says.

I exhale heavily and think of a way to get him out of here.

"We gotta talk about Judge Steckel. He wants his--"

I'm quick to cut him off. I know she can hear, and this shit cannot fucking happen right now. "Not now, I can't talk now."

He looks at me like I'm fucked in the head. And he's right, too, 'cause I am fucked.

"You can't talk to me?" he asks.

"Not at the moment." His eyes fly to the bedroom.

He looks confused for a moment, and then it hits him. "Are you serious, she's back there?" His arms lower and he almost drops everything in his hands. "You've gotta be fucking kidding me."

Tonya must've heard him because she comes out, pulling her shirt down and looking all sorts of pissed and upset.

"You're a fucking idiot, Tommy." Anthony sneers his words and moves to the other side of the room while she walks to the door. He intentionally turns his back to her, snubbing her, and it's the last straw.

"What the fuck is wrong with you? Don't treat her like that!" I grab his shoulder and turn him around to face me while Tonya walks past us.

"Like what? Like a cop?" He raises his voice with disgust as I hear the door open.

"You're a fucking prick." I turn away from him. I have nothing to say, and I need to get to Tonya before she leaves.

"Me?!" he yells with disbelief. He grabs my arm to stop me from going to her and I turn around and swing. I don't hold back and hit him square in the jaw.

His back hits the wall and leaves a dent in the drywall from his right shoulder and head. He winces from the pain and cradles his chin. I feel regret for only a second. But he crossed the line.

He looks up at me with raw anger in his eyes. He spits blood onto my floor and rights himself. I face him, waiting for his response, waiting for something.

He flexes his jaw and avoids eye contact. "I have to tell him," he finally says with a hard look. His eyes flash with pity, anger, and betrayal.

"You know I'm not saying shit to her." My heart beats wildly in my chest.

"I can't fucking believe this, Tommy. What have you done?" His voice cracks on the last word.

"I just wanted her." That's all this is. We just wanted each other. We fit together in some crazy, fucked up way.

"You wanna get laid, you go to the strip joint." He looks at me with a pained expression. "You had to settle on a cop?"

"It didn't happen like that." He doesn't understand.

"Fuck, Tommy." He leans back against the wall as I look to the door.

"I have to go get her," I tell him, feeling like I'm stabbing him in the back.

"How could you even think it's gonna be alright?" he asks.

"It's not, I know it's not. It's over, she just needed me."

He snorts a laugh as he sarcastically says, "Yeah, I'm sure she needed you."

"One warning, Anthony." I walk toward him and hold his stare. "Don't talk about her like that."

He holds my gaze for a moment, neither one of us backing down. And then I break it and grab my keys.

"Tommy, just think about what you're doing," he calls out after me.

I look back at him over my shoulder, with my hand on the doorknob.

I'm betraying the *familia*. I'm risking everything. But I can't let it end like this.

* * *

I HIT the gas pedal on the way to her place. She got a head start, but I wanna get there before she has a chance to think too much. If Anthony hadn't barged in there, I don't know what would've happened, but something was happening. I know we need to end this. But I don't want to hurt her. She said she needed me, and I owe it to her to at least make sure she's okay.

As I pull in front of her place, I see her car and she's sitting in it, with her head down. Her hands are covering her face, and her shoulders are shaking. She's crying. The realization makes my heart sink.

I pull in a few cars down and quickly make my way to her as she opens her door. She stands up and goes still when she sees me. Her face is red, and her eyes are swollen. I don't waste any time pulling her into my chest and hugging her. At first she's tense and stiff in my arms, but I know she'll relax. What we have between us is fucked up, but I know I make her feel good. Just like she does for me.

She molds to me and I don't hold back, leaving little kisses on her cheek and neck and shoulder.

"I'm sorry," I tell her. I don't know what else to say.

She shakes her head and sadly says, "Don't be." She wipes under her eyes and pulls away from me. "You were right to end it. This shouldn't be happening. I shouldn't have come to you."

She pushes away slightly, and I almost let her, but instead I tighten my grip on her.

"One more night, Tonya. Just one night more."

She stares at me with longing in her eyes before saying, "When I wake up, Tommy, you can't be there." The finality is evident in her voice. Her hand cups my chin, and her eyes water. I nod my head and kiss the palm of her hand and lean into her touch. It hurts like a bitch, but I answer her, "I know. I'll be gone."

TOMMY

I don't know what to expect as I walk up to Aunt Linda's. I know
Vince knows. Anthony called to apologize and told me he wouldn't
say shit. But I told him to. If anything happens, I don't want the *familia*
thinking Anthony knew something, but didn't say anything. I know fucking
around with Tonya wasn't smart. I'm going to have to take the consequences. I
just don't know what they'll be.

I grip the doorknob and push the door open. The normal sounds of
Sunday dinner fill the air. Gino and Jax are running around the living room
making screeching tire noises. The women are in there chatting away and
bouncing the kids on their knees like the shrill noise is normal.

I'm already starting to get a headache. I walk past them giving a short wave
and head to the right, to the dining room. Most of the family is already here.
Looks like I'm the last to arrive. Uncle Dante sees me and smiles. The guys
carry on with their conversation. Everything seems normal. It's not quite
what I expected. I anticipated Vince laying a punch on me the second he saw
me, but instead he keeps talking and gives me a nod to let me know he's there.

"Tommy!" Aunt Linda comes up behind me and gives me a hug even
though she's got an oven mitt on one of her hands. She plants a kiss on my
cheek and says, "You got here just in time. Dinner's almost ready."

I chuckle at her as she keeps on moving to the kitchen, "Dinner's always *almost* ready," I tease.

She smiles over her shoulder, but keeps moving. I take a seat at the table and listen in as Dom rattles off some numbers and argues with Joey about a college football game. If I had to guess, I'd bet Joey made a dumb bet. And judging by Dom's smile, that bet was with him.

"Anthony." Vince calls out my name, but so quietly, only I hear him. The rest of the conversation carries on around us as I look at him down the table.

"Yeah?" I ask.

"Help me with something outside real quick. I gotta carry this painting shit to the car for Elle." I stand up and follow him out. No one seems to notice.

My heart beats a little faster as we walk out front. This is it. I take a deep breath. I went against orders. I fucked around with a cop. Shit could get real ugly, and I'd fucking deserve it.

"Anthony told me what was going on," Vince says as we stand out on the porch.

"Yeah, I know."

"How long?" he asks.

"Not long. It's only been a few times."

"A few times is a few times too many." He lowers his voice and he leans into me as he says, "You lied to my face."

"I didn't." I shake my head. "I never lied to you." I would've told him if he'd asked. "Things got carried away." He steps back with a real pissed-off expression, and I put my hands up in surrender.

"I fucked up. I know that, Vince. It wasn't supposed to happen."

"A cop though, Tommy, what the fuck? I told you to stay away." The anger he's feeling at me comes out in his voice.

"I know. I--" He cuts me off before I can finish.

"You can fuck any broad you want, Tommy. You got 'em hanging all over your dick at the club. Why would you settle for a fucking cop? One I told you I wanted you to stay the fuck away from."

I look away, not liking how he's talking to me. I also don't like the way he's talking about Tonya. Like her being a cop is such a bad thing. She's good at keeping her mouth shut. She trusts me. It could've worked. Even though we're done with, I find myself defending her. "We have judges in our back pocket. Why not a cop?"

"She could never be with you if we had her on our payroll. It doesn't work like that. Red fucking flags everywhere, Tommy. The whole point is for us to stay far away from those people. So there's no goddamn connection."

"I'm sorry, Vince. She didn't get anything from me," I tell him.

"She could've though. You let a cop get close to you. That looks real fucking bad."

"It doesn't matter, Vince. It's over."

"You're damn right it's over. I have no fucking clue what to do with you." He runs his hands through his hair and starts pacing. "If you were anyone else, you'd be dead. You know that?"

His bold statement makes the air leave my lungs. I do know. I knew it was stupid, and it was risky. But he's gotta know I'd never say shit.

"And thank fuck it was your brother who saw. If it was someone else...If anyone else knew?" He shakes his head but his eyes aren't angry anymore. Now he just looks sad as fuck. "Don't you fucking put me in that position."

"I won't. It's over." I say the words with a defeated tone. Any thought of going back to her is gone. If they'd kill me, I know they'd get rid of her, too. I can't risk that.

"It's over, over. It's completely done with?" he asks.

"Yeah, it never should've happened." My heart twists in my chest as I say the words. He wraps his arm around my shoulder and pats my back.

"Thank fuck, Tommy." He walks us back inside and we stand in the foyer. Aunt Linda is setting dishes down on the table and Elle's strapping Angelo into his high chair.

Vince lowers his voice and reminds me, "No one can know about this. You know that, right?"

"Of course I know." I nod my head as I watch the scene in front of me unfold as though I'm not even there.

I watch in a daze as Elle sings in an upbeat voice to Angelo. "Sitting in my high chair, my chair, high chair. Sitting in my high chair, banging my spoon!" She bangs on the tray in rhythm to the words, and the little one squeals with joy.

Vince is saying something, but all I can hear is Elle. The happiness in her voice, the love in her words. I want Tonya to have that. She deserves that. I could give it to her. I should go to her and beg for her to take me back. I'd give her the world. I'd change for her. I swear I would.

She asked me for one thing, and I never even gave it to her. All this time I could've told her. I should've told her that Petrov's dead. But I didn't.

"Jesus, Tommy! Are you even listening to me?" Vince's voice snaps me out of it and I turn to look at him. I feel all choked up like a little bitch.

"You gotta get your shit together," he says.

"Yeah, I know, boss."

"I'm talking to you as family, Tommy. What the fuck is wrong with you? You should be happy. The charges were dropped. You're a free man, but you look like death."

I shake my head, not knowing how to tell him. I look back at my cousin and know that I can't. You don't leave the *familia*. Well, there's one way to leave.

I turn my head back to Elle as Vince leaves me with a pissed-off sigh.

"Bring on the carrots, bring on the peas," she lowers her voice, "Somebody feed this baby, please."

Both she and her baby laugh. My eyes drop to the floor.

I don't deserve Tonya. I won't ever be able to give her that. I'm only going to bring her more pain or worse...

TONYA

$\mathcal{I}$ feel like hell, I look like hell; I'm fucking living in hell. I'm in a meeting with half a dozen cops going over the portfolio of several suspects in the investigation. There have been three reports of missing women in the upper east side suburb over the last two months, all fitting the same description.

I can't even look at their pictures. Melissa was a tall blonde with dark brown eyes. These women look nothing like her. Yet I only see her face. She's staring back at me. And I can't face her. I have nothing. I've come this far, for nothing.

"I wish we'd known when the other women were abducted." For some reason I blurt out the words, and Harrison pauses his presentation.

"Which women?" Jerry asks from my left. "All their data is in the portfolio."

I shake my head. "The twelve. Petrov's dozen." That's what they named them at the station. It's what the media used when they released the story. I hate it. I hate the name. Each woman was her own person, with her own name. But that's how they're referred to here. And I've been trying the 'fake it till you make it' approach. So I'll do what's expected and call them that. But I hate it.

"What do you mean? We knew," Carl answers from across the table. He's an officer like me, with a few years of experience under his belt. But a nice guy in general. He's got a wife and two kids. One's in middle school and the other is in kindergarten. I stare at him blankly, thinking I must've heard wrong. We didn't know Petrov's men had them. We had eyes on two locations. We were waiting for him to be seen so we could arrest him. We had enough against the other men, three were wanted in multiple countries. We left them as bait for Petrov. But we didn't know about the women until the day we found them.

"You were a bit wet behind the ears, so you weren't in on that intel, but we had eyes on a Felipe Barros."

Harrison continues for Carl, and I look between the two of them with a mixture of disbelief, hate, and disgust. "It was important that we waited until Petrov was spotted so that we could link him to the abductions."

"You knew where the women were located?" I ask in a voice I don't recognize. It's almost like I'm watching the scene, rather than participating.

Jerry puts his hand on my forearm in an attempt to placate me, but I pull away and stare at him. "We felt it was best since you were new on the case to keep you in the dark on some aspects. We were planning on telling you, but everything just happened so fast."

They knew. I look around the table and everyone's eyes are on me.

"You all knew?"

"Not about all of them. We had reason to believe that three of the women were being held at their headquarters," Harrison says.

"But you didn't go in?" I look at him with confusion.

"We couldn't risk the operation," Harrison responds simply.

"But we could've saved them."

"We did." Harrison speaks up and I find myself biting my tongue. *We* didn't save anyone.

"What about Georgia Stevens?" I ask them with a dull voice.

"Which one is that?" Carl asks. My eyes bore into his skull.

"She was the victim in Abram's car," Jerry answers to my left. I clench my teeth and feel the tears prick at my eyes, waiting for an answer that doesn't come.

"Did you know?" I look Harrison in the eyes, and he has the decency to look ashamed.

"We knew," he answers after a moment, and it's the last nail in the coffin. I lose all sense of composure.

"You didn't look for her? You didn't try to save her?" My breathing picks up, and I have to try hard to keep it steady.

"Petrov would've been a big fish to catch. The number of crimes and murders we could've stopped--" Harrison speaks calmly and with conviction, but that's not enough for me.

I cut him off and raise my voice as I ask, "One woman wasn't enough? How many women would have been worth it to step in?" Tears slip down my cheeks.

"We were keeping an eye on their location--" Carl starts to respond and I cut him off, too.

"Oh, so was she dead before, or after he shoved her in the trunk?" The room goes silent, and the only thing I can hear is the pounding of my heart in my chest.

"We did everything that we could--" Jerry starts to give me an excuse, but I'm not having it.

"Don't fucking lie to me." I'm so angry I'm shaking. I pound both of my fists on the table as my voice cracks. They knew, and did nothing. My heart beats too hard, my blood rushes too fast. "Why wasn't she good enough?" I feel my heart twist in my chest. Would Melissa have been good enough? Would they have saved her? Tears leak from my eyes as multiple people start talking over one another to justify their actions. This happens. Sacrifices are made. I know this. But it's not okay.

I stare into Harrison's eyes as I inform him, "She had a son." I don't bother wiping the tears off my face. I'm too far gone for this. "What if it had been your mother? Or your sister?" I yell out my questions so loud it makes my throat sore. I see Jerry reaching out for me from the corner of my eye. I stand up from the table and my chair falls back. I almost stumble over it, just trying to get out of the room.

She was a person. She was a victim. She was worth saving.

I would have saved her. I would have risked everything to save her.

"You don't understand. We couldn't risk the entire operation," Harrison calls out to me as I turn my back on him and leave. I can faintly hear the other officers, but I don't listen to what they're saying. I don't make it to my office. I turn the corner and crouch to the ground. Sobs tear through my chest and I know they can hear me, but I don't care. I have to purge this sickness that's taken over my body. I feel lightheaded and nauseated.

I would do anything to go back and save her.

I can't do this. I shake my head as my face heats and my hands tremble. It's too much. I've failed my sister, but I'm just not strong enough to handle this.

I brush away the tears with the back of my hand and slowly stand, resting against the wall.

I'll find another way. I can't chase ghosts anymore.

TONYA

I look around my apartment, and it's almost pathetic how little there is to pack up. I don't know how I didn't notice. I look down at the open box next to my bookshelf. It's full of all my favorite romance novels. I used to love reading. From Fifty Shades and BB Hamel to Riley Rollins' Bad Boys and Marci Fawn's Mafia men. I huff a laugh, but it's humorless and pains my chest. I only read books with happily ever afters, but this is real life, and there's no guaranteed HEA for me.

I didn't take a single book out the entire time I've been here. I used to read every night. It's been so long. It was my stress relief. I could get lost in a book and forget the world around me. A woman with a book never goes to bed alone. But I've been alone every night and I never sought out the comfort. I never tried to get lost in a different world. Maybe a part of me was just punishing myself, like I deserved to be alone and without any happiness.

I should call my mom to let her know I'm headed home, but I don't want to. The last time I called her she picked a fight. She likes to throw the fact that I used to party in my face. She likes to blame Melissa getting taken on me. She twists it around in such a sick way that I can see her logic. And I can't take that shit right now.

I pull my hair up and into a ponytail. It's just habit now. I hardly ever used to wear my hair up, but it's nice to get it away from my face. I'll have to think of something else though, I want as few reminders as possible. I want everything about these last few months to just disappear. It hurts too much.

I feel like a failure on so many levels. I know my sister wouldn't think that, or at least she wouldn't tell me that I failed her. My chest hurts just thinking about how she would try to console me if she knew how much I was hurting for her.

I'm not sure this pain will ever go away. I'm ready to deal with it, though. I have to. With no one to blame and no one to chase, all I have are memories flooding my thoughts. I lick my dry lips and take a seat on a box. I don't know what's in it, and I don't care. I just need to sit down. I've wasted too much time and energy searching for revenge. Harrison is right about one thing at least. There's always going to be someone like Petrov.

My heart pangs in my chest. I still don't know for sure. Tommy could've told me. I think if I'd asked him, he would've told me. I've thought that before though, and I was wrong. But something about our last time together makes me think...I close my eyes and stop that train of thought. I can't possibly think that.

Love isn't something I'm used to feeling. Not for a man. But the way he held me, the way he soothed every pain. My hands cover my face and I hunch over, sobs wracking my body. I'm such an idiot. What kind of person falls for a man like him? I'm a cop, for Chrissake! Or was a cop. I could've been killed. That's all I could think when I heard his brother's voice. They're going to kill us. The reality slapped me across the face.

But what if it was love?

The thought strikes my heart and causes a lump to grow in my throat. I try to stand, but a wave of lightheadedness and nausea make me slowly lower myself to the floor in a crouched stance. I balance myself on the balls of my feet for a moment. Once I think I can stand, I slowly rise, but the nausea hits again and I sprint to the bathroom.

I dry-heave into the toilet and it fucking hurts.

I turn and sit on the tiled floor with my back against the cabinet. My face feels hot and I close my eyes. I'm so tired and feel so sick. It's almost as if I'm pregnant.

My eyes pop open at the thought, and my heart refuses to beat in my chest. Pregnant. Fuck! I frantically try to remember the day. It's the end of the month. Fuck! Fuck!

I don't remember the last time I got my shot. I get one every three months. I've lost track of time, but I know I get them at the beginning of the month. I went a full month without birth control. How could I be so fucking stupid?

Fuck, no fucking way. I put my hand to my forehead as if I'd be able to tell I had a pregnancy temperature. Fuck! We've only been fooling around for a few weeks.

It only takes once.

Panic sets in and I storm through my apartment, picking up boxes until I get to a small one marked bathroom supplies. It was still half packed up until today, when I tossed the rest of the contents back in. I dig through it and find an old pregnancy test. The kind with a + sign for positive. It's not in a box so I look on the thick foil surrounding it for an expiration date, but I don't see one anywhere.

My skin heats and anxiety runs through me. I can't be pregnant. I can't.

I rip it open and leave the foil on the floor as I dart to the bathroom.

I've never been shy or anxious about peeing before, but it takes way too long for me to get a stream going, probably because I'm so nervous. Finally, my bodily functions obey and I put the stick under the stream for what seems like a long enough time and then slip the cap back on. I wipe it off with some toilet paper and set it down on the sink to wait, but I don't have to.

As the liquid runs through the window, I can already see it. Positive.

A faint + sign shows up almost immediately.

I stare at it without breathing.

I can't believe it. I'm pregnant.

Nausea and lightheadedness hit me at once, as if my body wants to confirm what the test is saying. I fall off the toilet and turn to hug the bowl as the sickness comes up. My skin flushes with heat, followed by chills as I wipe my mouth and try to sit up.

I'm pregnant.

I never planned for this. I never even considered children or a life where I settled down. I just didn't think it was for me. That kind of life was for my sister.

My hand hesitantly touches my belly, and tears well in my eyes. She would have loved to have a baby. But not with a man like Tommy.

I stand at the sink and turn on the water to gargle it and try to feel better.

I can't be far along. The thought enters my mind quickly, that I could leave and he'd never know. He'd most likely never find out. Even if he did, he's not the type of man who'd want a child. Right? If he found me, if he ever thought to look for me and found me with his child, I don't know what he'd do.

The thought makes my chest hurt even more. I'm bringing a child into this world and I don't even know if the man I think I love would want either of us.

I've felt strong my entire life. But right now, all I feel is weak.

I slowly stand and try to calm my breathing.

I can't just leave. I have to tell him.

If he doesn't want this baby, I'll leave and never come back. But if he does...I pause my steps and lean against the wall. If he does, I don't know what I'll do. I can't stay. I doubt he'd ever leave his *familia*. As if they'd give him a choice. I close my eyes and shake my head as I walk to the bed, gripping the locket in my hand. I lie back and try to think of what my sister would do. I know what she'd do. She'd tell him she was pregnant. And she'd move on with her life, loving her child. She may have never seen herself as strong. But she was. She was so fucking strong for always doing the right thing and sticking to what she believed in.

"I need you." My fingers slowly scroll over the locket's tiny engravings. "I need you right now." I whisper my words in a pained voice as tears slowly roll down my cheeks.

Do the right thing. That's what she'd tell me. She'd smile. She'd make sure this baby was born into a life surrounded by nothing but love.

And I will, too. I won't settle for anything else. I wipe the tears away and get my shit together. I breathe in with a long inhalation, and breathe out just as long.

Holy fuck, I'm really pregnant. An hour ago I felt like I had nothing, and no one. And now, everything has changed.

TONYA

*T*he walk up to Tommy's apartment is difficult. Every step toward him brings me closer to knowing whether or not he'll want me and this baby. My hand settles on my tummy as I get to the first landing and continue walking up the stairs. The outcome is most likely going to kill a piece of my soul. He can't be with me, and a man like him doesn't want to settle down with a baby. But it's the right thing to tell him. So I have to do this.

With my resolve firm, I brace myself to walk up to his door, but when I look up, my heart freezes in my chest. Vincent Valetti stares back at me with a look of contempt.

I push down all the emotions I'm feeling and school my face. My heart pounds in my chest with fear. I can't die now. Now when I have this life to protect.

"Officer Kelly." Vince speaks with a hard voice and an even harder expression.

"Miss Kelly, now," I respond without backing down from his stare. He may be the Don, and he can definitely hurt me, but I know better than to show weakness to men like him.

"Oh, I see. Did you think that'd make it alright for you to cuddle up to my men?" he asks.

The way he says it makes me want to knee this prick in his groin. I may not be in a committed relationship, but I'm not a whore. And what he's implying pisses me off.

"No, I didn't. And if my slut memory is correct, I've only been fucking Tommy, so you can shove that bullshit right back up your ass."

He narrows his eyes and grinds his teeth. He's looking at me like he's not sure what to do with me. After a long moment of neither of us backing down he says, "I didn't mean to offend you."

"Yes you did," I'm quick to answer.

He grins at me with a twinkle of delight in his eyes and agrees, "You're right. But I'm generally not fond of cops. Please accept my apology."

My eyes finally break away from his and I feel like I can breathe. I nod and swallow thickly, looking at Tommy's door.

"You're here to see Tommy, then? You quit to be with him?" he asks.

I shake my head. "No, I quit because I never should have been a cop."

"You don't think you have what it takes?" he assumes.

"No, I think I'd be a great cop if I had the determination for it. If I had the heart for it. But I don't. I joined for the wrong reason."

"What reason is that?" He tilts his head as if he's sizing me up. He's going to judge me, just like everyone else. I don't give a fuck, though. They can all judge me if they like, but I'm not going to change for them.

"Because my sister was taken by Petrov. I wanted to find him; I wanted to kill him."

"So you wanted to know about Petrov?" he asks, and I know exactly what he's thinking. He thinks I was trying to get information out of Tommy. He thinks that's why I was with him. That may have been the reason in the beginning, but that's not why I slept with him. And I hate that Vincent thinks that.

"Yeah," I answer him, not willing to elaborate.

"And now you've quit?"

"Yes." He looks at Tommy's door with a pissed-off look. He thinks Tommy told me. I can't let him think that. I don't want Tommy to get shit for it, and I won't have to lie anyway.

"He never told me. Even after we were together and everything happened between us. He never told me, but I think he's dead." *Between us.* My walls go down and I have to work real fucking hard not to break down. Maybe it was one-sided, and I just imagined him feeling anything toward me.

"So you *think* he's dead, so you quit." Although it's not a question, I know he's asking.

"No. I've had a hunch he's been dead for awhile now. I quit because I realized revenge wasn't the answer. There's always going to be someone to fight. I'm not the person to do it. I need to find another way."

"Another way to do what?" he asks.

"To let go." Tears prick at my eyes and I feel so fucking weak. I try to keep my composure and walk closer to Tommy's door. "I just need to tell him something."

"What do you have to tell him? I'd be happy to relay the message." He takes a step closer to me, and I instantly take a step back. I don't feel the same sense of security with him as I do with Tommy. I don't think I've ever felt that way about anyone before.

"Tell me," he says, but I can't.

"I--I can't." I've never spoken to Vincent Valetti before today. And I have no idea what kind of man he is, or what all he knows about us.

"Is it about police matters, or personal?" he asks.

I stare at the door, not knowing how to answer that. I don't want Tommy to get hurt.

"That's what I thought. You know that's not smart, right? A cop, and a man like Tommy?" He shakes his head before continuing. "It's over now, isn't it?"

"I came to tell him something before I leave." A part of me just wants to tell Vincent so I can leave and avoid the rejection I feel coming.

"Good. It's a good thing you're leaving. It's for the best."

I look back at him, not sure how to respond. It fucking hurts. All of this is really none of his goddamn business.

He presses his lips into a straight line and then he asks, "You tell anyone about this little arrangement you had with Tommy?"

"No. It's over, so it doesn't matter." The words come out hard, but I stand my ground and maintain eye contact.

Vince rocks on his heels and looks to the left. "Good. So what do you have to tell him?"

"Something that's none of your concern." He narrows his eyes, but I don't care.

"Tommy's in a bit of hot water right now, sweetie, so you might want to be a little bit more forthcoming." The way he says it makes my heart stop. I don't want Tommy to get hurt because of me. My mother's words ring in my head, *it's all because of you.*

"I'm pregnant." The words fall from my mouth, and his eyes widen in surprise as he looks at my stomach. I feel the need to explain, so I blurt out, "It's early. I can't be any more than a few weeks along."

"So it's been going on for a few weeks, huh?" he asks.

"About that, yeah." I answer him and he nods his head. His eyes stay pinned on me, like he can read my thoughts. He's judging me. And along with me, Tommy.

"Are you sure it's his?" he asks me with an odd expression.

"I don't fuck around." I bite out the words with a little anger and instantly regret it. He hardens his expression and stares back at me. "Yes," I say.

"Why?" he asks me, without any indication of what he's referring to.

"Why what?" I look at him with confusion. Surely he isn't expecting me to tell him why women get pregnant. In my case it's because I'm a fucking idiot who got lost in a man's touch and wasn't thinking straight.

"Why'd you go after him?" he asks me.

"I didn't. It just happened. We didn't mean for this to happen." It strikes me that Tommy may be in deep shit. Really deep shit. "He tried to end it, more than once." I breathe in deep, remembering how he left me, how he never showed and sent me a text. Each time he tried to break things off I knew it was for the best, but it still hurt.

His brows raise in humor. "So he was that good, huh?" He huffs a small laugh and I give him a sad smile in return. That's all I can offer.

Vince puts a hand on my back and hesitantly gives me a pat as he says, "It'll be alright. I'll have him call you." His comfort is awkward, like he doesn't want me to cry, but he doesn't know what to do to make me stop.

"He's gonna be okay, right?" I ask him, before turning to walk away.

His eyes narrow, and I shake my head and wish I hadn't said anything. "I shouldn't ask questions. I take it back." He looks at me for a long time and I just want to hide.

"My wife didn't learn as fast as you. She's got a real problem with being nosy."

I look at him with a bit of worry.

"You know she tried to kill me once?" My mouth falls open in a little shock and I'm not sure what to say. "It was a horrible effort, really. But I'm just saying, shit can start out rough and end up alright."

I stare back at him, speechless.

He smiles at me as he says, "Everything's gonna be alright. I trust you'll see that soon."

TONYA

I'm still shaken up as I park my car. It's different to say I'm pregnant out loud. It makes me feel more vulnerable than I ever have before. It almost hurts, admitting the insecurity that I may be on my own and Tommy may truly want nothing to do with either myself or our baby. I take a look at my apartment building and I have to squint. Something's different. My heart pounds in my chest. The light, it's too dark. My breathing halts as I realize the street light is broken. Something's wrong. No, I'm just freaking out. It's okay. It's just a light. I tell myself that over and over as my eyes dart from my left to my right.

Something deep in my chest is telling me something is wrong. Something is not right.

I'm not safe. I hear my sister's voice screaming at me to run. *"Run!"*

Warning bells ring in my ears and I quickly turn the key in the ignition. But it's too late.

The window smashes and something hard crashes into my skull, splitting the skin on my forehead. I scream out and try to put the car into drive, but large hands reach in and grab my body. Blood drips down my face as strong hands wrap around my neck. I try to scream; I try to fight. The seat belt digs into my skin and holds me down as I hear the doors being unlocked. I open my eyes and see a large man wearing all black open the passenger side door and reach across the console. He's older, and his skin is tanned and wrinkled. His lips are thin and his eyes are deep set and dark. I try to move and get away, but I'm pinned in place by the man I can't see reaching in through the window.

The man to my right turns off the car and removes the keys. I feel hopeless and weak. I should've known better. How could I let this happen? Anxiety courses through me.

"You will not scream." The man in the passenger seat speaks in a deep, low voice. A voice I don't recognize. Maybe Vincent didn't trust me after all. Maybe they've come to kill me because of Tommy. My heart twists with agonizing pain. Maybe they killed Tommy. It's also possible that Tommy knows. My throat dries up as the man slaps his hand across my face. The slap burns my skin, and it's so forceful that it splits my lip.

"You will answer me!" I hear a faint accent as he yells at me. Russian. My eyes pop open and I stare back at the man.

His lip curls into a sick smirk. "Do you recognize me, Officer Kelly? You should. We know who you are." I do. I've seen his face before. He's a member of the Russian Bratva not far from here. One of the last times Petrov was seen was on their territory.

Revenge. They're here for revenge. But we didn't kill Petrov.

My eyes widen with fear. *Maybe he's still alive.*

A sick part of me wishes it were true. I find strength in thinking I'll see him. I want to see his face. My fear and anguish dissolve into nothing but sheer determination.

The hand over my mouth slowly moves away. I wish I could wipe the spit off of my mouth, but I can't. The arm pinning me down doesn't move.

"You're going to listen to me, and answer me when I tell you to." I stare back at the man who thinks he's calling the shots.

"Yes," I say obediently. I'm just waiting for my chance.

"You're going to call Tommy," the man says, staring me in the eyes. "We need one Valetti. And he'll come to you any time you call him. He doesn't tell anyone, just sneaks off to find his bitch in heat."

"Why?" I ask him in a calm voice. So calm it nearly terrifies me. I don't recognize my own voice.

"Why do you think, sweetheart?" He gives me a twisted smile. "We need to set an example." He looks at the man holding me and I'm released. I hear more

591

glass fall as the man to my left leaves my side and opens my door. "Be a good girl, and call him."

I look down at my purse and consider doing just that. But I don't want to lead him to his death. "Don't you want to live?" he asks. If I didn't know I was pregnant, I would never do it. But I have to do what I can to save my baby.

They'll never let you live, a sad voice whispers in my ear. My eyes dart to his. They're dark and full of excitement. I know they're going to kill me. There's nothing I can do to stop them. I turn my head, and see there are two more men standing outside the car. Four men total.

I think back to the alley. There were only three, and I had my gun in my hand aimed at one. I had an advantage there, that I don't, here. My heart stutters in my chest. I'm not going to be okay. I can't do this. And I need to. I can't fail.

I look back at the man as I take out my phone. I have to call Tommy. He's my only hope.

TOMMY

I've never been nervous going into Vince's house, never. It's a good sign that Elle opened the door and didn't seem to act any differently. It's funny seeing her with a baby in her arms. She's carrying him around like a pro now.

I open the door and reluctantly take a seat across from Vince. I know this isn't good. All his text said was that we needed to talk. I wonder what happened between Sunday and now. A million possibilities are running through my head. I don't think he'd kill me, not his own blood. Especially not with Elle around. But giving me a head start to run, or telling me to go away and never come back? That thought is a very real possibility.

I don't know how I ever thought I could get away with being with Tonya. I never should've fucked with a cop. I swallow and it hurts my dry throat. I crack my knuckles and try to relax, but I can't. If I had to take it back, I don't think I would. That's the worst part of it all. There was something between us that I'm glad I felt. Even if it left a scar on my heart. I wouldn't change it.

They may think it was wrong. But there was nothing wrong about what we did.

"We gotta talk, Tommy," Vince says from across his desk. His body is stiff. It's not a good sign. As I open my mouth, my phone goes off. Vince's eyes dart to my pants.

593

I should've put that shit on silent. I take it out quickly to turn it off and see it's Tonya that's calling. My bad girl. She sure has some real shit timing. I don't know why she's calling me. She shouldn't be. She should know I can't answer. I look Vincent in the eyes and I know that he knows who's calling. I hit the switch to turn it to vibrate and put it on his desk.

The shit part is that I would've answered her. Even though we've said our goodbyes. If I was anywhere other than here, I would've answered.

"You need to make a decision today, Tommy. If you go to her, you're leaving the family," Vince says simply. It fucking hurts. He's telling me he'd kick me out. My own blood. The *familia* is all I know. They're all I have.

"It's like that?" I ask him, not holding back how hurt I am. Fuck it, he should know what he's asking.

"We can't have a cop in our family." I bite the inside of my cheek, letting the pain consume me. My eyes settle on a dark swirl in the rug beneath my feet. "It's over. I told you that." My voice is flat, just like my emotions.

"I know you did. But you have to have one more talk with her." My eyes dart to his. What the fuck does he want from me? I'm not using her. She's staying out of whatever shit he's thinking up in his head.

"She's leaving town. She quit being a cop, did you know that?"

She quit? Damn. I wish I knew why. My brow furrows. I don't know why it hurts me to think that she quit. I should be happy. That means she's not a cop anymore. But whatever her reason is for quitting must have something to do with how fucked up she was the other night. And I don't like that. I don't want anything to hurt my bad girl. And something did, something tore her up. And I'm not there for her. She needed me. She still does. I know she does.

"No, I didn't know." She never told me, maybe that's why she called. Just as I think that, the phone goes off again. It's a gentle vibration. The screen lights up and I see her number.

We both ignore it.

"She went to your place today."

My heart stops in my chest and I lean forward in my seat. I have to grab the armrests so hard my knuckles turn white just to stay seated. "You better not have fucking touched her." I swear to God if he laid a hand on her I'll fucking kill him.

He cocks a brow at me and shows no signs of fear. That's why he's the Don, but I know my threat didn't fall on deaf ears.

"She came to tell you she's pregnant."

His words strike me with a force that makes me fall back in the chair. I stare at the phone as the words settle. She's pregnant. She's going to have my baby.

"So you need to choose between her or the family, Tommy." Vince's words smack me across the face and bring me back to reality.

"Choose? Between family and my child? I fucking love her, Vince. I'm not giving her up." Saying it out loud feels so fucking good. I love her. And I love that she's having my baby.

"I'm sad to see you go, then." He's firm in his response.

"You said she quit." He can't honestly expect that I'm going to leave her when she's pregnant.

"I can't allow it, Tommy. Do you know what kind of position this puts me in?" My anger comes back with full force, just as the phone rings, *again*.

"Fucking answer it already." He looks at me with an exasperated expression. It pisses me off, but I answer it.

"Hello," I answer her without giving anything away.

"Thomas," she answers me with my name like that, and I hate it. Just because we ended things doesn't mean that she's gotta do that shit. I loved hearing her call me Tommy.

"Talk to me, baby." I hope my answer warms her up to me. I know she's gonna tell me she's pregnant and she's probably worried. I don't want her to be though. I'm gonna be there for her. Even if Vince tells me I've gotta leave, I'm not leaving her.

"I need you to meet me," she says calmly. There's no emotion from her at all.

"Sure, baby. Wherever you want." Again I soften my voice. I want her to know I'm receptive to whatever it is she's gotta tell me. I'm also anxious though. I wanna hear it from her lips. "We could talk now, if there's something on your mind," I offer.

"It's nothing." My forehead creases. Nothing? She's carrying my child, and she thinks it's nothing?

"I just want to see you before I leave. I thought we could meet where we first met. A small smile plays at my lips as I answer her, "At the station." She doesn't laugh. Instead she replies flatly, "At Rosetti's. I know it's closed now, but it'd be nice to say goodbye by the creek in the back. Where we first met."

Something's off. My eyes bore into Vince's skull until he looks at me.

"Something's wrong." I mouth the words to him as I put it on speaker. We've never been there before. It doesn't make sense. She's trying to tell me something. "Sure, baby, you want me to bring anything?"

"No, I think it will be quick." I don't understand what she's getting at, what she's hinting at.

"Maybe a bottle of wine. I can bring those chocolates; you remember the two packages we had at your place the first night? The two on the end table before I had your taste on my mouth for the first time. How many of those are you expecting?" I'm hoping she's getting what I'm talking about. Vince looks at me like I've lost my damn mind.

"I think four would be good." She's quick to answer, and I nod my head. Four men. I knew it. Thank fuck my girl is so smart and so damn strong.

"Alright, baby. What time do you need me there?" I ask.

"As soon as you can." Her last word comes out with strain. My heart aches in my chest like it never has before.

"Hey, baby, you okay?" I have to ask, even though I know she's not.

"I'll be better when you get here." With those last words the phone cuts out.

I put the phone down and look at Vince, my cousin. The boss of my *familia*, but also my friend.

"What's wrong?" he asks as I try to compose myself. I can't help that I'm choked up. I just realized how much I love her. I just chose her over everything, and now she's in danger.

"There's gonna be shit happening tonight," I tell him. "I need you."

"You think it's a setup? She's setting you up?" Vince looks pissed.

"No. No, she wouldn't do that. But someone's got her, Vince. Four men."

He stands up and runs his hand through his hair. "Fucking hell, Tommy." Vince looks out of the window like he's debating on what to do.

"You gonna leave me to go in there alone?" After everything we've been through, too. We grew up together. He's my blood. My *familia*.

He cusses under his breath. "You go in first, but we'll be there."

TONYA

*J*can't stop my body from trembling. They didn't bother blindfolding me, but I'm gagged, and my wrists are tied behind my back and my ankles are bound. Zip ties dig into my skin. I'm on the ground, propped up against a shed to the right of the restaurant parking lot. There's a creek to my left, and I'm almost certain that's where I'll be soon. I guess they wanted to hit him with shock factor. His girl, tied up and gagged, in clear view of the dirt road that leads here. Just beyond the treeline is the highway. I can hear the cars. I can even see the headlights. But they can't see me. No one can save me.

Maybe Tommy, but I may have also led him to his death. I'm certain he knows this is an ambush, though. Why else would he talk in code? My heart stopped when he said packages. My eyes almost darted to look at the man holding the phone, almost gave me away. Thank fuck I stayed calm. Four men. The odds are against us, but hopefully with the warning I managed to give Tommy, he'll have a chance.

They dumped me here like I was a bag of trash. Tossed me to the ground and went to stand behind their cars. Two black cars blend into the dark. But they're there, and if he's looking for something off, he should see them. They aren't in their cars. They're standing behind the one closest to me, with their weapons drawn and ready.

Jagged rocks dig into my knees as I move slightly across the ground. I'm moving slowly, so they don't notice. They aren't paying attention to me. One's smoking, and the other three are talking in hushed whispers. I can barely hear though, except for the occasional laughs. They're also going back and forth between Russian and English, so even when I can hear them, I'm not exactly sure what they're saying.

I'm not certain, but I think they want him to watch me die. As soon as he drives down and sees me tied here and struggling, that's when they'll do it. Shoot me until I fall lifeless on the ground. Although one keeps saying how he wants to see Tommy run to me as they shoot us both. The others don't. They don't want to kill him right away. They have questions that need to be answered.

I don't care what they're saying. I know their endgame is to have both of us dead. I'll most likely end up in the creek, and Tommy's corpse will be sent back as a message to the Valettis.

I'm not going to let either of those scenarios happen. I need to live; I have to survive this. And right now, there's only me. If I can get free, I can run. My eyes dart to the four men who are in plain view and holding guns. My heart beats rapidly in my chest. I'll have to wait until I have a chance, but I'll try. I can't fight back without having any weapons on me. That would be suicide. But I can give Tommy a warning, and I can run. That's my only hope.

There's a broken bottle only a foot from me. If I fall over, I should be able to snag a piece. There's only a single zip tie binding my wrists, and one more binding my ankles. I can do this. Ankles first, so I can run as soon as Tommy gets here.

I scoot my knees across the dirt and they scrape against the gravel. I ignore the pain. Just another inch and then I prepare myself for the fall. It's gonna fuck up my shoulder since I can't brace for it. But I can fucking take it. I crash against the ground and hit my shoulder. My head bounces from the impact. The men look over at me while I struggle to take a piece of glass in my hand. My fingers graze across a few small pieces, but they aren't large enough. The jagged chunks pierce through my shirt and cut into my skin. Again, it's not horrible, but fuck it hurts. The fucker smoking sets his eyes on me. He tosses his cigarette onto the dirt and walks over with quick strides.

His dark eyes stare into mine as my fingers finally find a large chunk. I'm quick to make a fist to conceal it, even though it digs into the palm of my hand. I can't risk him seeing it. It's my only chance at freeing myself.

My heart skips a beat as he grabs my shoulders and drags my body back to the shed. The glass and gravel scrape my legs and I try to cry out, but the gag mutes the screams.

"Stay!" he yells, pointing his finger at me like I'm a dog. It gets a laugh from the other men. His large hand grips my chin and then he smacks my face several times—not hard, just enough to demoralize me. "Bad bitch. Stay." His accent is thick. I rest my head against the shed and pretend that I've lost all hope. I let the tears that beg to be released, slide down my cheeks. He laughs sickly and his foul breath fills my lungs as he turns to leave me, walking back to stand with the others. They're talking louder now, and in Russian.

As soon as I hear them patting him on the back and laughing, I push the glass to the zip tie on my ankle. It almost slips from my hand. The blood from my hand makes it difficult to hold. But I keep my grip and move it back and forth across the plastic. The glass is uneven and cuts into my ankles a few times, but the pain doesn't register at all. My eyes are focused on the gap in the trees, marking the entrance to this area. Tommy will be here soon; all I need to do is free myself before that happens.

It feels like forever, but it must only be a few minutes until both the zip ties around my wrists and ankles have snapped. I don't move yet. My limbs are screaming at me to take off. But they don't need me alive, they just want to make it hurt that much more for Tommy. If I run, they could shoot to kill me and there's no reason they'd hold back. Even worse, if I did run and they caught me, I don't know what they'd do to me. But I'm sure they wouldn't let me get out again.

So I wait. My skin prickles with anxiety, and the only thing I can hear is my heart beating loudly in my ears. I remember my phone in my back pocket and I struggle to keep my movements slow. Every time one of them looks at me, I freeze and try to remain as still as possible.

I should call the cops. I need help, and I know they could possibly come in time to save me, but they may also find Tommy. I don't want him to get caught in the middle of this, but I have to do everything I can to save myself and our baby. My skin feels like ice as I dial the numbers 9-1-1 behind my back. But I've done it.

I can faintly hear the dispatcher speaking, even though I can't give her any verbal confirmation that I'm on the line. I hit a button every few seconds, hoping she'll catch on.

"Are you unable to speak?" I barely hear the words. I don't hit any keys.

"If you can hear me, dial a number." My thumb presses down. I barely hear a faint beep. I keep my eyes on my captors. They show no signs that they can hear anything.

"Assistance is on its way. Is there a threat in your immediate vicinity?" she asks.

The phone slips from my hand as I try to push a number. It falls to the ground with a faint thud. I watch them, but they don't hear it. I can't hear her anymore.

There's no one else.

All I can do now is wait. There's nothing else left that I can do to save myself. I need Tommy.

TONYA

*T*ime passes slowly, yet nothing happens. I keep my eyes on the road and then on the men. My heart won't calm, and my skin sweats with anxiety. He's coming. I know he is. But what if he isn't? What if the cops come and the men hear? It'll only take a single bullet to end my life before they take off.

I'm relying on someone else to save me. And I fucking hate that.

I think I hear a car coming through the trees and closer to the entrance, and it distracts me. It also gets the men's attention and they raise their guns. No, no! I can't let them shoot. I start to stand, but the deafening sounds of guns being fired stops me in my tracks.

Bullets ring out from my left and right. But I can't see where they're coming from. They ricochet off the cars, and I instantly scramble back behind the shed to find cover.

I turn my body to run, but I slam into a hard, unmoving chest. My eyes flash to a set of light blue eyes, but before I can react, the man's pinning my arms down and carrying me toward the back of the shed. I kick out as hard as I can and land a blow to his shin. I try to push him off me as he curses and nearly drops me. I hear bullets hitting the metal of the cars. I hear men shouting and yelling. The sound of a man getting shot and falling to the ground fills my ears.

"Left, left!" someone calls out. These are the sounds of an ambush.

Fear overwhelms my body, but I force my limbs to push him away. I didn't come this close to escaping, just to be taken again. I refuse to stop fighting.

"Jesus, woman, I'm here to protect you." He pushes me against the shed with all of his body weight. I try to move my arm so I can get an uppercut in, but he leans his entire body against me, rendering both of us useless. I continue to struggle. I won't give up. "Calm the fuck down! Tommy sent me." My body stills as I hear a few men call out. "On the passenger side!" A bullet and then another.

"Tommy said stay here." He pulls away a bit. "He'll fucking kill me if you go out there."

I turn my head to face him as the sounds die down and see a kid. He can't be any more than in his early twenties. He's got shaggy hair and an uneven patch of stubble. He backs his body away slowly, looking at me like I might take off.

"Don't move," he says with his finger pointed at me. If I was in a different situation, I'd roll my eyes. But right now, I'm full of nerves and apprehension.

"Can I have a gun?" My body heats as I ask.

"Tommy said you'd ask for one." He laughs and slowly hands me a gun. The first thing I do is check for bullets. It's loaded. He eyes me warily. "You think he'd short you on ammo?"

"Not him, no," I say, taking a step toward the edge of the shed.

"Don't. He'll kill me. For real," he pleads with me, rocking on his feet. "Just stay here."

He takes a peek around the corner and grins. "They really only sent four." He shakes his head and smiles from ear to ear. "Fucking idiots." He turns to face me, leaving his body exposed, and I yank him back to the safety behind the shed.

"Take cover," I practically yell at him. Dumbass kid.

"They're done," he says defensively, with his forehead scrunched up.

"Stay back here until you hear otherwise." I feel like I'm back at the academy. This kid's gonna get his ass shot.

He smirks at me. "No wonder Tommy likes you." It's silent all around us; I think it's over. "You really a cop?" he asks.

Before I can reply, I hear the answer behind me.

"No, she's not." I turn and immediately wrap my arms around Tommy's neck. I have to stand on my tiptoes. His large arms wrap around my body as he lifts me up. He buries his head in my neck.

"Is it over?" I ask him, looking around to see something, anything, but I'm still in the back, so I can't see shit.

"It's over. Probably a little overkill," he says with a huff of a laugh.

"Really, only four?" the kid says from behind me. I lift my head up in Tommy's arms to face the shaggy kid.

"Well, they thought it'd just be me," Tommy explains.

"Dude, you should take offense to that."

"Get outta here, Brant." The kid takes off as Tommy turns me in his arms.

"Are you alright?" he asks me, as his eyes roam down every inch of exposed skin. He touches the small gash on my forehead and it makes me wince. "I'm so sorry, baby," he says in a voice so soft and sincere I can feel his agony.

I shake my head, "don't be. It's not your fault." He tries to object, but I give him a small kiss and try to distract him, but when I pull back there's still pain in his eyes.

He gently brushes the pieces of rock and glass off of me, but I fall against his chest and hold onto him. "It's alright baby, I'm right here." He pulls back from me and takes my chin in his hand. It feels so good to just be held by him. He gives me a soft, sweet kiss and it soothes every part of me. "Is the baby okay?" he asks, looking down on me with worry in his eyes.

Tears prick at my eyes as I say, "Vincent told you." My heart stops beating, and the world seems to blur around us.

"Yeah," he says, putting a hand on my belly as he asks, "Tell me you're alright?"

I push the words out through my sob, "I'm okay." I bury myself in his chest, feeling completely safe and secure. But then I remember, the cops will be here any minute. "You need to go. I called the cops."

At the word cops, the noise around us stops and I realize the other Valettis are still here.

"You called the cops?" Vince comes up to our left, and Tommy angles his body so that his shoulder is between me and Vincent. I hold onto him as my body heats and a wave of nausea hits me. I had to. I didn't know they were all coming. I never would've guessed that.

"What was she supposed to do, Vince?" Tommy asks. "We've got enough time to get out of here anyway."

Vince looks between the two of us and then says, "She has to stay here so they'll find her. Or else they'll come looking."

Tommy nods his head slowly, but he's clearly not planning on listening. His grip on me tightens. "Don't be stupid, Tommy. She'll be fine. She'll be out in a few hours," Vince points out.

"I don't wanna leave her." His words are absolute.

"I'll say I was inside the shed and I didn't see anything," I quickly say. Vince searches my face, like he's not sure if I'm being truthful or not.

"They touch you?" Vince asks. At first I'm confused, but then I realize what he's asking. I shake my head as my eyes fall and Tommy's grip tightens on me.

"You did real good. Guess they taught you something right, huh?" Vince talks to me, and I struggle to respond. I don't want to talk about being a cop with him. Not now, not ever.

I give him a tight smile in return and say, "Thanks."

"We saved your ass, remember that," he says before turning away from me. He yells out to the men who are picking up the bodies and lifting them into the back of their cars.

"I don't want to leave you," Tommy whispers into my ear.

"Go, baby, please." The danger is gone and the cops will be here soon. He needs to go. Him being here will only complicate things. It'll give the department leverage to use against the Valettis, and more ties to the Petrov case. The reminder of the case has me wanting to know if Petrov is truly dead. My eyes fly to Tommy's. I should ask him. I still don't know. The words are there, but I don't say them. The power they held before has waned. Before I can ask, I hear the sirens in the distance. "Go," I tell him, staring in his eyes, begging him to listen to me.

"I'll be watching and waiting, baby. I'll be right here for you." He kisses me again as Vince's car pulls up in front of us.

"Move your ass, Tommy! We gotta go!" he calls out, and I hear a door open.

"I love you, Tommy." I have to tell him. I can't hold it in anymore.

Before he leaves, he gives me a small smile and brushes the hair out of my face as he says, "I love you, too."

TONYA

"*Y*ou sure you didn't see anyone?" Jerry asks me, for the fourth time. He's nodding his head and trying to get me to talk. He should know I'm not going to say shit. I haven't for the last three hours. They found the blood at the scene. They ran tests and came back with nothing. All I told them was that I was taken against my will by men with Russian accents who wanted information.

I shake my head with downcast eyes. I hate lying and putting them in this position, but I'm not going to give them anything to lead them to the Valettis. I told them I was blindfolded the entire time. I hate lying, but I need to stick with the story.

The Russian mob is in deep shit, and there's plenty of evidence on them. But nothing against Tommy or his *familia*.

"Not a damn thing that could tie them there?" Jerry asks. He has a hunch it was the Valettis who came in and took the Russians out. All three of us know it was them. It makes sense. A Russian mob on their turf? It doesn't take a genius to figure it out.

"You're fucking one of them, aren't you?" Harrison sneers at me from across the table. I fucking hate the way he says it. I also hate that he's right. He doesn't buy that I was taken in order to get information on the Valettis. That's the story I'm supposed to give the cops. That the Russians wanted intel on their routines and addresses. Everything and anything I knew about them. But it doesn't make sense that I would be left unharmed. Not unless the Valettis needed me alive. Or if I meant something to one of them.

Harrison can see right through that. I'm not a good liar. Jerry can as well, but he hasn't said anything. I can see the disappointment in his eyes.

"Get out, Harrison." Jerry doesn't yell, doesn't even turn to look at him.

Harrison clenches his fists and mutters an apology before stalking out of the room. There's no love lost between us. As the door closes, Jerry leans forward and asks in a low soothing voice, "Are you sure you're alright?" Concern is written all over his face.

"I'll be alright." I cross my arms over my chest and take a deep breath. I'm still a little shaken up. A lot shaken up maybe, but Tommy's there waiting for me. I close my eyes and I can feel his lips kissing my neck and his arms holding me close to him. He's my happy place. I need him, and now I have him. I'm not letting him go. I can't. He better know that.

"If you're in any trouble, you know to come to me. Don't you?" he asks, and I know he means it.

I nod my head. There may be times I don't agree with him, but I know he'd help me if he could. Right now I don't need help though. At least not from him.

"Are you sure you wanna go through with this?" He puts his hand on the table, offering it to me in a sweet gesture of comfort.

I accept and put my hand in his, and he squeezes. "I dug into you a bit after you left the conference room and found out about your sister. You may have joined for the wrong reasons, but you're a good cop. It's not too late to stay." He emphasizes the last line. If only he knew. It's too late for so many things.

"My mind's made up." I pull my hand away and breathe in deep.

"As long as you know what you're doing," he says, leaning back in his seat.

A short laugh erupts from my lips. "I have no clue what I'm doing," I confess. I run my hands through my hair and lean back, shaking my head. "I just want to be happy."

"You deserve to be happy, Tonya. Don't let him hurt you. And when the time comes, don't say I didn't warn you."

"He's not going to hurt me, not ever." I don't know when the conversation changed, but we both know who we're talking about. I won't say it though. I won't name him.

"Not the way you're thinking." He walks to his door and locks it before shutting the shades. "What are you going to do when he gets charged with something, and it sticks?"

I shake my head, "I'll figure it out when it happens." My hand subconsciously goes to my belly. I jerk it away before he has time to see. I know he loves me; I know I love him. And he'll take care of us both.

"I hope he treats you right, Tonya. I really do. But if he ever does anything, or any of them ever do anything," he looks at me with absolute sincerity, "I'll be here for you."

"Thank you, Jerry."

"Don't thank me," he says bluntly. "You're asking for trouble." I know what he means, and I understand it, I really do. But I can't help what I want.

A sad smile plays at my lips as I say, "I'm good at that, apparently."

He looks at me for a long moment and I don't know what he wants from me.

"I'll be alright, Jerry. I promise you." I stand up and walk over to give him a quick hug.

He walks to the door and unlocks it, but before he opens it, he adds, "I just hate to see a good girl like you wind up with a man like him." I can't help the smile that grows on my face. He has no idea that I'm really a bad girl at heart.

TOMMY

*T*hat was intense. I'm shocked at how fucked up I am over that shit. I scouted it out first. It took everything in me not to run to her as that prick put his hands on her. I got that fucker. I took him down first. I've been in worse situations though. Vince brought everyone. It feels so fucking good to know he still had my back.

Those Russian pricks didn't stand a chance, and only two of 'em even got a shot off. They aimed at nothing. They couldn't see us in the dark. The one that took cover--fuck, if I was him, I would've just killed myself. Instead now he's sitting there, chained to a chair with a gag in his mouth. He should've known this was going to happen.

"Whatcha gonna do with him, boss?" I ask Vince.

"Well, we got the information we need, so I couldn't give two fucks. Figured you may wanna take some aggression out, since it was your girl he took." Vince walks over to the sink in the back room. We're in the basement of the safe house. It's fucking freezing down here. The fucker in the chair has bruises all over his face. His one eye is swollen so bad his face looks inhuman.

Anthony's drying off his tools. I instinctively look down and see three fingers on this fucker's right hand have been removed. That's usually Anthony's first move. They're easy to cut off, and it makes a pretty bold statement.

"So you got everything you need?" I ask Vince as he dries off his hands. He turns back to me.

"Yeah, they aren't going to fuck with us unless they want their entire operation shut down. Thanks, Nik!" Vince slaps a hand on the man's shoulder and he doesn't even react. He's so close to death.

"Alright, I'm good. Just kill the bastard," I say.

Vince looks at Anthony and he nods as we turn to leave. Anthony's not talkative when he's on the job. Never has been. I used to take offense to it. But now I get it; he has to be in the right headspace, and that doesn't include saying a fucking word.

"There's one more reason I called you down here," Vince says as we climb the stairs.

"I figured there was." And it's about Tonya. I know it is. I waited at the station and followed her home last night. I just held her all night; I needed to feel her. Knowing I almost lost her fucking hurts. I'm not letting her go. I can't.

"I understand that you wanna be with her. And truthfully, she's a nice broad." We walk into his kitchen and he grabs me a beer. The faint sounds of a chainsaw can be heard coming from the basement. It sends chills down my spine.

"I'm not leaving her, Vince. I can't do that." My stomach drops, knowing that what means. I don't wanna leave my family. The *familia* is all I know. But I'm not letting her go.

"I get that. I do." He passes a beer to me and shuts the fridge.

Leaning against the counter, he pops the cap off his beer with his keys. "She's still associated, Tommy." I put down my beer and shake my head as he tries to pass me his keys. I can't drink right now. "You know we can't have that shit."

"Yeah. I know." I do know. I wouldn't be a smart move to have that shit known.

"Good," he says with finality. "I'm sorry, Tommy."

I nod my head, my throat closes, and my heart tries to leap out of my chest. "What's it gonna mean, boss?"

"You can't do errands anymore. It can't happen. You can't represent the *familia*." I wanna argue with him, but I can't. I know it's true. Fuck--realistically, he should kill me. It's a risk keeping me alive. It's a risk letting her get close. "Not like that, anyway," he says, and it brings my attention back to him.

"I've been thinking about you and your brother. I think it'd be good to finally take on those contracts. We'd get a shit-ton more money from the hits. And it'd keep us in a good place with our contacts. Anthony always said he'd need another person to help. That's what I want from you two, and he agreed already. Just need you in on this, too."

My heart slows, and I swear to God I lose feeling in my hands. "What do you mean?"

"I mean, if you're gonna be taking a cop as your girl, then you're going to have to be a contractor."

"A contractor?" I ask, not understanding.

"You two will do the hits. We'll give you the names and you get it done." I nod, taking it all in.

"What about the rest of the *familia* business?" I ask.

He shakes his head and says, "That's no longer a concern of yours. It keeps things a little neater."

"I understand." I take a moment to process it as he opens my beer himself and hands it to me. I finally ask, "Does that mean I don't have to call your ass 'boss' anymore?" We both give a small laugh. I have to admit it hurts a bit, but I understand. And I'm fucking grateful to still be around.

He smiles broadly. "It's the best I can do, Tommy. She's loyal to the family, and to you. That's enough for me. She's a good girl, like my Elle. She's not gonna say shit. So long as that's the case, everything's good."

"That mean I'm not made anymore?" That'd put some bigass targets on my back.

"You're still a Valetti. And just like last night, we've got you, and you've got us, right?"

I pull my cousin in for a hug and feel like a little bitch for getting even the least bit emotional. This is better than I'd hoped for.

"You'd better fucking marry that broad, too. The sooner, the better," he says.

"Yeah, I know, so she doesn't have to talk."

He looks back at me with a grin as he says, "Well, that and Ma will be pissed if you don't do right by her." His joke fills my chest with warmth. He's right, too. Aunt Linda will kick my ass.

"Love you, cuz," Vince says.

"Love you, Vince." We both pat each other on the back harder than we should to make up for getting so emotional.

"Still family?" I ask again, not really believing it could be that good.

Vince nods his head, "Always."

TONYA

"*Y*ou gotta meet the *familia*." Tommy wants to take me to his aunt's house for dinner. To Dante Valetti's house. Dante Valetti is the former Don and father of the current Don, Vincent Valetti. I'm nervous as hell. It's been two weeks of just us. Two weeks of hiding away in his apartment while we figure this shit out. There's no doubt in my mind that I made the right decision leaving the department and doing what feels right. But then I remember his family, and I'd be lying if I said I wasn't worried.

"They know I was a cop." That's the only explanation I need. That right there is enough for them to want me dead.

"Yeah, they do. And they know you're my girl." Tommy rubs his hand over my belly and forces a smile from me. "You're a woman, Tonya, and I know you hate this, but we keep women out of it."

"But I was a cop." I've seen them all a handful of times now, and each time it gets easier. But this is different. It's not one or two of them coming over to drop something off, it's all of them in one place. And I feel like I'm going to be an outsider.

"Yeah, for under a year. And they know about your sister and why you joined. They know you're loyal to me." He stands behind me and wraps his arms around my body, pulling me into his hard chest. I feel cocooned in his warmth. I close my eyes and breathe in deep. It's not fair that he can put me at ease so effortlessly.

"Besides, there's someone there I really think you should meet."

"Who's that?" I ask.

"You should meet Ava. I think you'd really love getting to know her. She lost her sister, too."

"Ava?" The name rings a bell, but I'm not sure why.

"Yeah, she's been asking about you. She wants to meet you." He speaks his words softly, like he's waiting for something.

"Why does that name sound familiar?"

"Ivanov." He says her last name and everything clicks into place. I turn in his arms to face him with wide eyes. She's supposedly dead.

I part my lips, but I don't ask. I know not to ask questions.

He gives me a small smile and says softly, "A bad man hurt her once, but she made him pay. She's a strong woman, like you. I think you two are going to get along great."

Tears prick at my eyes, and I hold onto him with everything in me. He kisses my hair, while I try to calm down.

"I'm sorry I didn't tell you sooner, but he's long gone, Tonya. He'll never hurt anyone else."

I cry in his arms. I haven't cried in weeks, but the need to purge all my sadness has me leaning against him in tears. He rubs my back while I cry for all of them. For my sister, for Ava's sister. For Ava and the other survivors. I cry for them all. A calmness washes through me as I settle with exhaustion into his embrace. A feeling like a rebirth. Like I'll finally have a fresh start. Maybe now I can finally get the catharsis I've been striving for all this time.

My blurry eyes catch a glimpse of the picture frame I put on Tommy's nightstand. It's the same picture that's in my locket. My hand reaches up and I grab onto it. We were just young girls in middle school and high school, but it's my favorite picture of us. I can't wait until we move and make a new place of our own. We need a fresh start. And moving is the way to make that happen.

I look up at Tommy with wonder, but also a sense of insecurity. I haven't forgotten what Jerry said, and if I'm honest with myself, I'm worried about Tommy and about him staying in the *familia*.

"Spit it out, baby." His hand settles on the nape of my neck, and his thumb brushes along my jaw. It soothes me. Everything about him soothes me.

"I don't know if I can live with you doing this, Tommy. I don't--" I just want to list all the reasons this is so wrong. But his lips silence mine in a sweet kiss.

I moan into his mouth, just loving his touch. He pulls back, and looks at me with sincerity.

"I told you, I'm not working for the *familia* anymore." I know what he said, but he's too fucking happy for that to really be the case.

"Forget about right and wrong for just a moment. Just listen to your heart, baby. What does it want? Us being together may be fucked up and wrong. But it's what I want."

I struggle to respond. He's right. I do want him. He's the only thing I want.

"Just give me a chance to love you." His hand brushes along my belly, where our baby's growing.

It may be wrong, but I want him. I love him.

He must see that I've decided. He smirks and says in a playful tone, "You know you're my bad girl."

I shake my head and let a small laugh escape me. Tommy takes my chin in his hand and kisses me. My lips mold to his and I give in.

I love him, and that's all that matters.

"I love you, Tommy," I whisper as he pulls away from me.

"I love you, too."

EPILOGUE

Tommy

I'm so fucking nervous. I don't remember the last time my heart beat so damn hard in my chest. I shake out my hands again and start pacing.

"I'm telling you, she's gonna say no." I turn on my heels to face Anthony. The fucker's grinning from ear to ear.

"You fucking love this, don't you?" I ask him.

He smirks back at me and says, "You know I do. You get all stressed out about shit you shouldn't be worried about." He takes a sip of his drink and then adds, "Besides, you'll have plenty of stress when the next list comes in."

He's right. I'm not as calm as Anthony is yet. I'm doing hits with him now. I'm cut off from *familia* business, and taking the contract hits instead. Anthony's been showing me the ropes. And I have to admit I'm enjoying it, but I've got a ton of shit to learn.

I should probably be worried that I'm not really seen as a member of the *familia* by outsiders, but I'm not. Vince told me not to be. He's my cousin, my blood, and he's grown to love Tonya. All the family has.

He said things need to blow over, time to settle down. And I'm fine with that. I'd be lying if I said I was unhappy taking these hits with Anthony. It's a nice change of pace, and less risk than what I'm used to. I don't really give a shit what I do, so long as I have my family and my girl.

She's accepted, especially with the women. They've been pampering the hell out of her since she's pregnant with our little boy. She's having a difficult time now that she's so far along. But he's going to be here soon. We can't fucking wait.

"You're thinking about him, aren't you?" Anthony asks. Then he teases, "He's gonna ruin your sex life."

I shake my head and grin at him. He's got a shit-eating grin on his face. "You said her pregnancy was gonna ruin our sex life, and look how good that turned out." I can hardly keep up with her. My bad girl still wants me. All fucking day if she can. "You're so damn negative, you know that?" I tell him, as I peek out of the back doors and into the restaurant.

"Yeah, I'm a little jealous, I gotta admit that."

I look at my brother with surprise. "Of me?" He's never been jealous of me my whole life.

He scrunches his forehead as he replies, "Don't look at me like that. I can be jealous if I want."

"If you wanna girl, go get one. You wanna baby, go make one."

He huffs a laugh and downs his drink. "It's not quite that simple, Tommy."

I start to tell him, "Yeah, it is that simple," but think back and realize that no, it's not. Not for the right one. Then I hear my girl. She's laughing, and I'd recognize that beautiful sound anywhere. I open the door a crack and look out.

She's in black leggings and a hot pink sweater that hugs her swollen belly. She went out for ladies' night and looks so damn happy. Ava's hanging on her arm. The two of them are close now. Thick as thieves. I've gotten to know more about Kane than I ever wanted.

"Showtime." Anthony smacks my shoulder and gets ready to open the door.

"Not yet." I say quickly, shutting it and taking a deep breath.

"Bro, knock it off. It's in the bag." I look back at him and try to calm my nerves. "For real, Tommy. She loves you." He pats my back and adds, "She's gonna make a good wife."

I nod my head. She is. She's gonna be my wife. And I'm going to give her our happily ever after that she deserves.

Anthony smiles at me. "That's the Tommy I know. Go get yourself a wife." He opens the door and I take a few steps out into the restaurant.

She's facing away from me in her seat. They sat her like that on purpose. Ava sees me first, and lights up. She grabs a drink menu and tries to distract Tonya. The ladies look up at me one by one, and try to not make it obvious.

Aunt Linda's smile is so fucking big, though. She's gonna give it away. She covers her face with her hand and pretends to cough. I get down on my knee behind her and look to my right to see the guys coming out. We're all ready to surprise her with a baby shower. I knew I wanted to do this in front of everyone, and doing it here and now, it just felt right.

While the ladies distract her, the guys open up the back room doors where the party will be. I hear them all standing behind me. It's go time. I know it is, but I can't fucking move. My nerves are getting the best of me.

I shake out my hands with my eyes closed, and that's when I hear her.

"Tommy?" Her voice is full of shock. I open my eyes with the ring box in my left hand, get down on one knee, and see her wide-eyed and covering her mouth. She's got her hands up like she's saying a prayer.

"You're such a bad girl. You were supposed to wait till I told you to turn around." I smirk at her. Just seeing her excitement and the happiness in her eyes puts me at ease.

Her hands fly down and start flapping like she's a little kid.

"Tonya Ann Kelly, marry me." I hold up the box to show her the three carat, cushion cut diamond ring with side accents I've picked out for her. I went to three different stores, but the second I saw this one, it was all over. I knew I needed to put this one on her finger.

She flings herself at me and wraps her arms around me. I don't wait for her to answer. I slip the ring on her finger, where it belongs. Everyone's clapping and laughing. I can hear Aunt Linda crying, 'cause that's what she does. But the best sound is coming from my bad girl's lips. She's got her head buried in my neck while she clings to me, "I love you so much Tommy. I love you."

I pull back to look into her gorgeous eyes; they're full of nothing but happiness. "I know you do, baby. I love you, too."

The End.

* * *

Keep reading for the next book in the series, Bad Boy, Anthony's story.

BAD BOY

SYNOPSIS

From *USA Today* bestselling author Willow Winters comes a HOT mafia, standalone romance.

I'm a dangerous man. You may be fooled by my good looks and charm, but my eyes give it away.

I'm the hitman for the Valetti familia, and I'm damn good at what I do.
    They want men to talk, and I make them talk. They want men gone — bang, it's done. It's as simple as that.

Until her.
    She's on my list, but I want her. On her knees and submitting to my every command.
    I'll give her a simple choice — die, or be mine.

I've always wanted this. Now that I have the chance, I'm taking it.
    I can fulfill those fantasies I know she has. I'm going to make her beg for it.

ANTHONY

$\mathcal{I}$ stare at the picture from the envelope and feel so damn conflicted. I crumple the edges in my hand, not knowing if I really wanna go through with this. My eyes travel along each feature of her face, pausing to admire her large, brown eyes and long, thick lashes. She has gorgeous full lips I want to bite, but also see wrapped around my cock. Her nails are done in a classic shade of red, and her light brown hair hangs over her shoulders in loose curls. Her breasts peek out just above the neckline of her flowing blouse. I wish I could slowly strip her out of those clothes. But I can't. She's not mine. Even worse, I'm supposed to kill her.

I shove the slip of paper back into the envelope containing the other photos, those hits I couldn't give two shits about. They're for assholes who have it coming to them. One stole and ran in order to keep up with his addiction. You don't steal from a mob boss and think you can get away with it. The second killed a made man. He knows it's coming. Neither are doing a good job of hiding. They'll be easy hits.

I take another swig from my beer and debate on taking the sheet back out. But I have her face memorized already. I want her. More than that, I want to break her. My thoughts are depraved, and I know it. I think back to the last chick I had. She liked to play. But that's all it was to her. Play. I want the real thing. I want to earn a woman's submission, earn her desire to please me through training. So far, it's always been pretend. I've never had an opportunity like this. But it's wrong. It's so fucked up and wrong.

But then again, so am I.

I carve up assholes and kill them for a living. The torturing and their screams don't affect me in the least.

This broad has it coming to her, even if she doesn't know it. She probably thought she was doing the right thing by going to the cops. She probably thinks she's safe in the witness protection program. She's not. She didn't know what she was doing, and now it's my responsibility to make her disappear. She cost the Cassano *familia* a lot of money, but more than anything, they lost face. The fucker she was involved with doesn't care that she's on a hit list. He's just pissed she ratted on them, even if the charges didn't stick.

Killing her is purely about their pride and the deal they lost.

I grind my teeth and slowly peel back the label on my beer bottle. I have to be delicate so it doesn't tear apart. Patience. I need patience. With everything I do, I need patience.

I've been looking into her, and I know she'd fit the part. Poor girl didn't know what she was getting herself into when she started fucking around with a member of the Cassanos. She's a sweet little thing who thought she'd like a taste of the more dangerous things in life. I can give her more than a taste though. I can give her exactly what she was looking for and fulfill those fantasies I know she has. And she can give me what I've always wanted.

I spied on her again last night. She was reading one of her books, and I watched as it turned her on. Of course she had no idea, but I was right fucking there. The only thing separating us was a brick wall. With her window open, I clearly heard all those soft moans coming from her lips. I had to know what she was reading, so I snuck in and took a look around.

I Googled that book the second I got home. Her own dark desires sealed her fate.

She has deviant fantasies just like me. She's fucking perfect.

"Anthony, you wanna talk now?" I hear Vince ask as he pulls up the stool to my right. I messaged him earlier. I place my bottle on the bar and push it to one side as the bartender slides Vince his usual Jack.

I lean back a bit and tap my knuckles on the bar before facing him. Vince is a ruthless fucker, and he doesn't take any shit. He's also my cousin, so I feel safe with him. But this is the mob, and he's the Don. I'm never *that* safe.

"It's about the hits we got in," I tell him in a low enough voice that no one else present is going to hear. Not that it matters. It's our bar, and we know everyone in here.

"You need help? Tommy's not enough?" he asks, cocking a brow. Tommy's my brother, and he's also my second-in-command. Technically we're both contractors for the *familia*. We only do hits, and we don't bother with that other bullshit.

"No," I say with certitude. I never need help. Hits are easy for me, in addition to being good money.

He takes a sip and licks his lips. "What's the problem, then?" he asks.

"There's one that I'd rather not do," I tell him.

"Why's that?" he asks, setting the glass down to face me with his shoulders squared. He's in business mode. Right now he's not a friend, and he's not my cousin. Right now he's the boss.

"I want to make them an offer instead," I explain.

His brow furrows as he replies. "I'm listening."

"One's a woman." His eyes flash with sympathy. None of us like taking women out. It's something that rarely happens, but when it does, we don't like it. We make it quick and painless for them. Maybe it's sexist, but I don't give a fuck. I've tortured a lot of men for information. Never a woman though. That's where I draw the line.

"They won't let her walk." His words are said with finality.

"I want to ask if they'd accept a substantial monetary offer from me to buy her." I feel my blood rushing faster and hotter. No one knows about my perversions. I'm sure they can all guess. But I've never said a thing about my tastes, and they've never asked. They keep me on the edge of the social circle for the most part. I'm fine with that. It's better that way.

"Buy her, and then what?" he asks with his eyes trained on the back of the bar.

"I want to keep her." My voice is low, but steady.

"As a pet? As a slave?" Equal amounts of disgust and disbelief color his voice, and it almost makes me regret letting my dark desire come to light. Almost. But I want this. I want it more than anything.

"If that's what you want to call it." The determination in my voice rings out clearly. I'm sure my eyes look dark and absolute. I'm not ashamed of what I want. But I'm not willing to risk my position in the *familia* over it. Not yet, anyway. It's been a week since I was given the hit. Each day my obsession with her has only grown. I cleared out a room for her already. In my head, she's already mine. This is just a formality. But to Vince, this is a twisted sickness.

He looks me dead in the eyes as he begins, "After that shit Ava went through--"

I stop him right there and say, "This would be nothing like that." My voice is louder than it should be, and the dark stare he gives me in return makes that clear. I settle in my seat and continue with a respectful tone. "I would never hurt her. Not like that. Not beyond any pain she didn't want."

"Ava said some days she would've rather been dead than been in that position." My heart hurts for her. Ava's a *comare* to a member of our *familia*. To Kane. He's a good man. He saved her, and in a lot of ways, she saved him as well.

She went through a lot of shit. Her captors loved hurting her and humiliating her. She's a strong woman to have survived all that. That's not what I want though. The idea of doing that to a woman makes me angry. I'd never do that. Never.

"It's not the same." I reach for my beer and turn away from him slightly. He doesn't understand. I didn't expect him to anyway. "She's already dead. She's on their list." I take a drink and then look back to him. "I'll give her a choice."

"Death, or your slave?" he asks with a humorless grunt. I know to him she'd be seen as a slave, as a pet. That's fine. To me, she'd be *mine*. Nothing else but mine.

"Better than death with no escape," I respond flatly.

He takes a sip of Jack, looks at me, and says, "It may not be to her. You want to hurt her and abuse her, rather than carrying out an order that would give her a quick death."

"No. I don't want that. It's not like that." He doesn't fucking get it. I torture and kill people for a living. I can see how he thinks that's what I'd do to her. But I wouldn't. I don't know how much I should explain. To be honest, I don't fucking feel like explaining anything.

My blood heats with anger, but then I have a pang of worry and think, *What if she doesn't get it either?* I brush my doubt aside. I'll show her. I'll have to teach her how perfect it would be to be mine. I've looked into her. I've been obsessed with learning everything about her. She's smart. She'll learn. She'll catch on quick that I'll be a good master to her. And she's familiar with the concepts. She's read enough to have an idea of what I want from her. "Think of it as hardcore BDSM," I say. I look at him from the corner of my eye, but it's not convincing him.

I want this too fucking badly to let this opportunity pass me by. And after thinking about all the ways she'd calm the beast in me, I don't know if I could actually go through with killing her.

Vince shakes his head and asks, "What are you looking to get from me, Anthony?"

"I want your permission to offer them a deal for her." I need my proposal presented to the Cassano boss. He's the one who ordered the hit. A number of other bosses come to us for hits, and we take care of their messes. For the right price, anyway. I don't want to piss anyone off, and I want this to be a clean deal. Vince is quiet for a long time as he considers.

"You won't hurt her?" he finally asks.

"I won't. It's about something else for me." Control. Desire. Submission. I want it all from her, but not her pain.

He nods his head once and I take that as an agreement. I can't help that an asymmetric smile grows on my face. Step one is done. Now to contact the other mob head. He'll be easy to convince, I'm sure. He didn't give a fuck about the soldiers she gave up. He cares about the deal he lost, and the money that went with it.

I down the rest of my beer and nod a goodbye to Vince. I don't have anything else to say to him. I'd rather he forget this conversation ever happened.

As I turn to leave, eager to clear out the cell I've prepared for her and put the finishing touches in her room, he turns in his seat and grabs my arm to stop me.

"What are you going to do if she chooses death?" he asks as I turn to face him. The idea of her dying makes my heart stop in my chest.

"I'll make sure that doesn't happen." Chills run down my body at the thought of those beautiful eyes staring into mine, begging me for death. That's not what I want. I know she'll want this when I show her how good it can be.

"It might," he says, looking at me with sympathy in his eyes. I don't want his sympathy.

She's going to fucking love what I do to her. But I'll have to break her first.

CATHERINE

3 WEEKS LATER

I tip the edge of the porcelain cup to my lips and close my eyes as the perfect temperature of tea spills into my mouth. My eyes close and the comfort of routine washes through me. But the feeling is only temporary. That's when I register the change. Something feels off. I remember thinking that earlier as well. It's too quiet. Crickets and other creatures of the night always provide soothing background noise for my evening tea. But tonight the noises are muted. It's as though something's scared them away.

I always drink chamomile tea to help me relax and sleep. My normal routine is to sit on the porch while I finish a cup, followed by a melatonin pill. I've had issues falling asleep for the last year or so. Ever since my life completely changed. Staying asleep is never an issue, but falling asleep is difficult. In the year that I've been here, I've done the same thing every night.

Before my life changed forever, I didn't have a care in the world and slept like a baby every night. I did whatever I wanted, whenever I wanted. Then I hit my mid-twenties and decided I needed to sow my wild oats. My mother had just passed away. She was older when she had me, and she died peacefully--as peacefully as you can with cancer--but it was hard on me and I didn't want to face the pain. To say I engaged in high-risk behavior would be putting it lightly. Then I fell in love. Or rather, what I *thought* was love with an asshole named Lorenzo Passanova. I called him my Cassanova because I was a fucking idiot, high on lust and loving the risk that came with being with a man like him.

I thought being with him would be just like the books I love to read. Like I'd be living out the plot of a romance novel. I was a fucking idiot.

Meeting that asshole was the worst thing that ever happened to me. I didn't even realize it until it was too late. He sucked me out of my safe little bubble into his world, and I felt alive for the first time in my life. But it was a mistake. A horrible fucking mistake.

When you play with fire, expect to get burned. Over and over, I'd heard my mother's warning, but I ignored it. The first time it happened, I knew I'd seriously misjudged him. Lorenzo smacked me so hard across the face that I fell to the ground. Even worse, I eventually tried to sneak out and leave his ass behind, but ran into his *familia* beating the shit out of a guy. Bags of dope were scattered everywhere as they made their threats. That was it for me. I saw and heard too much. I ran like hell, but they got me. They cornered me and took me back to Lorenzo and then to their Don.

Lorenzo beat the hell out of me in front of them. He told them he'd keep me in line for now, so they didn't have to kill me right then. His *familia* were cold-blooded murderers who wanted me dead. I'll never forget the looks in their eyes. Or the disgusting joy that filled Lorenzo's dark eyes when he would repeatedly hurt me. I had one chance to slip away, and I took it. I ran like hell and blabbed to the police so they'd protect me.

That's what living on the edge got me. As a result, I've settled my ass down tremendously. And now I'm back to being the good girl my mother raised me to be. Being through that shit and getting placed in the witness protection program will do that to you.

So now I stay in my cozy house feeling alone but safe, and surround myself with comfort and familiarity. It's different now; I'm more alone than I've ever been in my entire life, but at least I'm safe. The last time the marshals checked in on me was nearly three months ago. Now I'm on my own and settled in.

This screened-in porch is now my favorite room in this snug, raised ranch house.

My toes sweep across the soft and high pile of the rug beneath the wicker furniture set. Across from me I have my antique curio cabinet. It contains my large collection of teapots and cups. When I run a load of laundry, I can faintly smell it from here. I inhale deeply and my lungs fill with all my favorite scents.

But the best part is the location. I'm nearly half a mile away from anyone. My home is set back into the woods and I'm surrounded by trees. The moonlight shines down and tonight it's full, illuminating the woods as though it's nearly dawn. Usually my ritual helps put me at ease, but tonight it's less familiar, less comforting.

The night air feels a bit colder on my shoulders, sending a shiver down my back. I wrap the cashmere throw tighter around myself, all the way up to my neck. I feel my forehead crease as I realize I feel someone's eyes on me. The sensation freezes my body for a moment as the fear I had nearly every night when I first moved here returns. I turn quickly in my seat and feel my heart racing. The sound of blood rushing through my ears is all I can hear. When I first moved here, I was terrified the Cassanos would find me. But they didn't. It took a long time for me to feel safe, and an even longer time for the nightmares to stop, but it's all over now. I breathe in deep and concentrate on relaxing.

I settle my back against the seat, thinking I'm just being paranoid. A thought occurs to me. *Maybe this is my survival instinct warning me.* The idea causes a row of goosebumps to travel down my arms. But just like all of the anxiety I've dealt with this week, I push it down and chalk it up to my nerves.

I place the teacup down gently on the table and stand up, stretching slightly and covering my mouth as I yawn. The blanket slips off my shoulders, and a chill runs through my body. I'm quick to pull it back up to cover me and grip it close. Fall must be coming. It's the change of the season that's throwing me off. I close my eyes and listen harder. Some noises are faint, but they're still present. I just need to relax and accept the approaching transition from summer to autumn. Some things can't be helped.

Still, I check the locks at the front door twice after depositing my cup in the sink. Being alone in a cabin in the country isn't the smartest thing for a young woman on her own. My options for disappearing and starting a new life were limited though, and when you want to hide, it's best to be far away and alone.

I move the curtain away from the large window in the front room and look down the gravel driveway, seeing nothing. The grass is tall and needs to be mowed. I sigh and again the throw slips, but it's warmer inside the main part of the house, so I let it drape over the crook in my arm.

My bed is made and I can't wait to sink into it and drift to sleep, but I need to check over my email and messages one last time before I can pass out. The one good thing about my job is that I can do it from anywhere. When I first moved here, I had to stop working on anything associated with my real name. My blog, my columns and articles, anything else tied to my online presence, you name it—done. I was crushed. I had been a renowned book reviewer, beta reader, and part-time writer. The money was great, but I would have loved it all regardless of the pay.

I had to say goodbye to my former life though because the Cassano *familia* could have found me that way. The mafia that saw me as a rat could have easily tracked me down if I'd continued working under my real name, and it wasn't worth it.

So I started over under a pen name, and it's going better than I ever imagined it could. The experience and knowledge that I gained in my former life helped me tremendously. Now I'm firmly established in the industry, and I'm doing even better than I was before.

This is my life now--books and tea in a remote cabin in the woods. I love it, but lately it's felt empty. I could go on like this, feeling as though I'm living a full life, but I'm so alone. I wanted nothing more than to be by myself when I was running and hiding. But now I find myself questioning if I'll ever have anyone real in my life, and anything substantial.

I've thought about getting a dog—a big one, to help make me feel secure. A dog's love is unconditional. I want that love desperately. I need it from someone, or something. But a dog would need walks and interaction, plus dogs have to be taken to the vet. Those are all opportunities for people to see me. I don't want that. I want to stay hidden. I *need* to stay hidden. But I do need companionship. I've been craving it more and more as I've settled into this new life.

At least I have my business. I have my blogging, my books, and my friends, even if they're all online. I almost didn't start over. I almost gave up and poured my heart into a book of my own. But my life is no romance. And writing it down would make it real. Once I'd gotten over the fear, I didn't want to relive it. So I did my best to move on.

I was hesitant to start from scratch, but I pushed myself to do it anyway.

Within two months my new blog had taken off, and I'd revitalized my income. I log on and see twelve new messages in my email. The first few are easy enough to reply to, requiring nothing more than copying and pasting from a template of other answers I've already given. The next email takes some time to write out though. I'm responding to a new author who messaged me looking for advice on her series. I'll have to get back to her in the morning. I don't have the energy right now. But I take this business seriously, and it shows. And it pays. Just before I close the laptop, I hear a *ping*.

It's a message from a new book friend. She joined my book club a few weeks ago. Right now it's just a small Facebook group, but it's my baby. Although she's not very active in the group, she's messaged me a number of times. I get so many messages a day. Some are from other bloggers and columnists who are just starting out and looking for advice. Others are from authors wanting to send me advanced reading copies and beta reads. I can read two books a day, so I'm always happy to help where I can. But Val's messages are different. They're more personal.

What did you think of the book?

I scan the message twice as my fingers hover above the keys. I read and receive so many books that most of the time I have to sift through my emails before replying in order to make sure I'm keeping everything straight, but not this time. I know exactly which book Val's referring to.

Smut, also known as erotic romance to some, is a genre with which I'm intimately familiar. I prefer the term smut though, because it fills me with life. Like I'm naughty for reading it. The book she picked out though is exceptionally taboo. Arousal heats my core. The idea of being taken by a strange man has certainly been a dark desire of my own. I clench my thighs and bite down on my lip. I won't admit how I touched myself to some scenes.

I decide to respond with a professional answer.

I thought the author did a fabulous job of depicting the scenes with vivid imagery and capturing the heroine's emotions and character arc. Overall a well-written book.

She's quick with a reply. *So you enjoyed it?*

I did, I message back.

Is it so wrong that I'd want it to come true? Her reply makes me stop and consider her words.

I don't think there's anything wrong with the fantasy. But I'm sure real life would be much different.

You don't think you'd enjoy it in real life? Her question forces a small laugh from my lips. Although it's wonderful to get lost in them, these books aren't real. I know I'd enjoy some things. I've often fantasized about them. But this conversation is veering a little more into the territory of my personal preferences and is less about the book. It's also late, and I need to go to sleep while the melatonin is still active or I'll never get to bed. So I settle for a quick reply with a little humor that she'd enjoy.

Oh there are scenes I'd enjoy, but I'll stick to role playing for that ;) Gotta go to bed, ttyl!

Night!

A shiver of want travels through me as I exit her message and look at the list of remaining emails. I'll get to them all tomorrow.

I close my laptop, but I feel more awake now than I was when I first sat down. The book Val mentioned is all I can think about as I change into a nightgown. The imagery of a dark, damp cell and chains flood my mind. I can picture being the heroine. I can understand her desire to please her master. I wasn't a huge fan of the ending though. It wasn't the happily ever after I enjoy from romance. It was more realistic. After all, how could you ever fall in love with your captor, but still be sane? Would it even be possible to have both the sweet fantasy and the dark reality?

As I crawl into bed and lie on my back, I let my fingertips gently brush along my clit as I think about the book. I hear the clinking of the chains and the smack of the whip. I see her back arch as she raises her lower half to him for more. He takes her however he wants, and she's more than happy to let him use her body. My legs part, and I dip my fingers into my slick pussy and run the moisture over my clit. A small moan escapes me as I see the scenes play out in my head.

She's been trained to love the sting of the belt, and the feel of his hand slapping her ass. His bites. His marks. My hand grips my breast and I pinch my nipple between my fingers and pull, imagining it's him. I turn my head as though his lips are touching my neck, as if his teeth are about to pierce my skin. Anything and everything he does to her is a reward. He thrusts into her and takes his pleasure, over and over. Using her body. And she enjoys it. She thrives under his touch. I circle my clit, wanting him to reward her for her obedience. It's all she lives for. She is his, and that's all she desires. She only lives to please him. He doesn't stop until he has his fill and cums deep inside her. That alone is enough to bring her over the edge. And I find my own release with her.

You don't think you'd enjoy it in real life?

I remember Val's question as my breath steadies and I turn on my side, feeling exhausted from cumming.

In real life, that scenario would be a fucking nightmare. Just as I close my eyes, I feel a pinch in my neck. My lips part as I wince and raise my hand to feel what caused the sting, but it falls lifeless to my side. I vaguely make out a dark figure rounding the bed to approach me.

"Sleep, kitten." I hear his voice. But I can't respond as darkness overwhelms me.

CATHERINE

$\mathcal{M}$y shoulders are so sore. I roll onto my back against the cold, hard concrete and wince. After taking a moment to adjust to the discomfort, I push off the floor and into a sitting position. My eyes open and try to adapt to the darkness. I can barely see anything. My heart pounds in my chest, beating faster than it ever has before. I have no idea where I am or how I got here, but this shit isn't good. A cold sweat pricks my skin as I think back to last night. I remember lying down in my bed. I was tired, and then I fell asleep.

I have no clue how I've ended up here, in the middle of what looks like a small basement cellar. It's nearly pitch black. The only light is streaming through three small windows high up on the ceiling of the far wall. Each window is only about the size of a cinder block, and all three are blocked by something, but a small bit of light is still shining through. Terror runs through me and seems to freeze my blood.

I open my mouth to scream, but I'm too scared. *They'll* hear me.

I've been taken. They found me, and they took me. I know exactly who it is. The Cassanos. Fuck! I never want to go back to him, to Lorenzo. I won't let him touch me ever again.

Tears threaten to reveal themselves. But it's useless to cry. Some small part of me always knew it would come to this. You can't escape your death. I didn't really think I'd ever be able to run. I swallow the lump growing in my throat. My eyes fall to the ground. I have no idea why they would keep me alive, since I'm no use to them. I'm certain they'll kill me soon. Or worse.

There are only two options I can think of. One, they left me alive to torture me because I went to the cops. Two, they left me alive to torture me for fun. Knowing Lorenzo, it's number two.

I close my eyes, letting the realization settle in. My body shakes as tremors of fear run through my limbs, but I try to soothe them. I got out before. I'll do it again. I may be a meek little mouse, as that fucker used to call me, but I fight when I have to. And right now, I have to.

My eyes slowly open and adjust to the light.

The air is cold and damp, but my throw is in a pile on the floor next to me. I quickly grab it and wrap it around me as though it can protect me. Fear cripples me as I hear the sound of a chair moving across the floor. My heart stills and a chill prickles my skin. I'm not alone.

As I search the dark, vacant room, I see him. The look of a hunter stares back at me. I don't recognize him. His broad chest and chiseled muscles flex as he leans forward. His eyes are a brilliant light blue and they pierce through me. His cheekbones are sharp and only appear more contoured with the shadows from the dim light. If he had any other expression on his face, I'd think he was the most gorgeous man I've ever met.

As if reading my mind, he smirks at me. The fucking bastard thinks this is funny. My heart tries to climb up my throat as he sits back in his seat and his hand settles on the raging erection in his jeans.

Fuck!

My eyes dart back up to his. That shit's not happening. I'll claw his fucking eyes out. I look for a door and then back to him. I don't see one, but I don't care if I kill him and I'm locked in here and starve to death. I won't let that happen.

We stare at each other in silence. I want to ask him what he wants from me, but I already know. I want to plead for him to let me leave, but I've learned that doesn't work. Instead I wait for his move. He cocks his head after a moment and slowly stands.

As he moves toward me, I resist the urge to scoot away. I can't do that. I can't back myself into a corner.

He crouches in front of me and leans in closer. His eyes hold a hint of danger, but also a spark of desire. I'm just not sure what he wants to do with me exactly, besides the obvious. "I'm supposed to kill you," he says. His deep baritone voice is low and threatening. He tilts his head as I slide slightly backward on my ass out of natural instinct. I take control of my body and tilt my chest away from him, giving myself leverage to kick this motherfucker in the balls if he gets any closer.

His full lips pull into an asymmetric grin. "You can't get away from me just yet." I hate how he's taunting me, like he expected this.

My breathing is ragged, and my heart is beating so fast I swear my chest won't be able to contain it. It feels as though my heart's trying to leap out of my throat. I barely get the words out, but I manage to say, "I don't want to die."

His grin widens into a perfect smile. This man's too handsome to be a predator. There's a darkness about him, but he could fool anyone with just a small amount of charm.

"I don't want you to die either, kitten." His pet name sends a bolt of desire to my clit. Shame washes through me. I shouldn't like it. *This is wrong.* He stands up and towers above me. I tilt my head to keep my eyes on him. "You have a choice," he says.

I wait for him to continue as I stay huddled in a ball beneath him. My blood rushes loudly in my ears and I try to calm my racing heart. He doesn't want me to die. That should relax me; it should make me feel even the faintest bit better. But it doesn't.

"You can die." He speaks to the far wall, not looking at me. I find my eyes searching for a door, looking for a way out. To my right, I finally spot a steel door, with a keypad to its left. "Or," he continues, and I feel his gaze on me as my eyes fly to meet his and my heart thuds painfully in my chest. "You can agree to be *mine.*"

I can't help that the way he says it makes my core heat. A wetness pools between my thighs and I feel ashamed. This isn't a fantasy. This is real life. I feel the blood drain from my face as I become lightheaded. The only reason I'm not dead is because he wants to keep me. But I doubt his intentions are anything but kinky and sick.

I don't want this. Tears leak from the corners of my eyes and I shake my head. "No." My voice is hoarse and barely audible.

This isn't real. This isn't happening. I wait for him to grab me. As soon as he does, I'll strike. But he merely searches my face for something and stands far enough away that I can't do any real damage.

He cocks a brow and his voice softens as he says, "You haven't heard my terms. How sure are you that you don't want to be my pet?"

Terms?

Again the offer makes my pussy clench and my cheeks redden with a violent blush. "No," I blurt out without thinking.

His chest rumbles with a deep chuckle. "Some part of you wants me. There's hope for us after all." He smiles down at me and turns to walk away. My limbs refuse to move and attack him. Instead I stay frozen on the ground. I watch his corded muscles ripple as he walks to the door and enters in a code.

"Where are you going?" I ask before thinking. Apparently the fear of being left alone in this room to rot is greater than my fear of him. I don't want to die here, left to starve because he changed his mind. I may have said no, but I sure as fuck don't want to die here.

He turns and gives me the same sexy smirk. "My kitten needs to eat."

Tension coils in my body. I can't let him leave. I need to get more information. I don't like not knowing anything about this situation and not having any other options.

"Wait. What--" I swallow thickly before continuing. "What are your terms?"

He smirks at me as he opens the door and says, "The first is that you'll listen to me. I'll be back soon."

My chest rises and falls with anxiety and fear as I stare back at him in silence. I pull the throw tighter around my shoulders and watch as he walks through the door and leaves me in the dark room. I'm all alone and barely able to breathe. After a short moment, lights in the ceiling slowly come to life, illuminating the room dimly and gradually getting brighter. I look around my surroundings and see a small toilet in the corner and the metal chair my captor was sitting in, but nothing else. Tears prick my eyes and my blood runs cold. I can't stay here like a prisoner.

I stare at the door waiting for him to come back, letting everything sink in.

I've been taken.

And he wants to keep me.

The only thing I'm certain of is that I need to find a way out of here. Run as fast as I can, and never look back. But I'll have to rely on him to get out of this fucking cell first.

ANTHONY

I've never done anything that's felt this *wrong* before. Nothing's ever come close to giving me this thrill that's surging in my blood. Her reaction was perfect. I knew she'd deny me, but the fight in her is something I didn't expect. I fucking love it.

I had to be in there when she woke up. I didn't want her freaking out, thinking she was going to die. Instead she can be absorbed with thoughts of me and being mine. My dick is fucking leaking in my jeans. I can't help that I want this. I want her. And now I have her. But not her submission though. That much is obvious and expected.

I feel like I'm on the highest high I've ever had in my life. I should feel conflicted. I should have second thoughts about this, or feel remorse. But I don't. *She's mine.*

I pace back and forth in the kitchen as I think about what I'd like to feed her. I'm not sure what to offer her first. I need to make it tempting for her to obey me, but this isn't a reward. I have to stay vigilant. I want to shower her with everything she'd ever want to convince her she'd enjoy being my pet. But that would defeat the entire purpose of all this, and she needs to know what her position is. She needs to earn her rewards just as much as I need to earn her submission.

There are simple truths to this relationship.

I will always give her shelter and food, no matter how disobedient she is. Even if she refuses every order, which I imagine will happen at some point. Hell, I fully expect her to try to kill me at some point, too. Even the best submissives refuse their positions at times. And she's being forced into this, so I wouldn't blame her if she did. There's no reason for me to deliver physical punishment unless I'd like to prep her for pleasure. Which I can't fucking wait to do.

I imagine it'll be her mouth that makes me blister her ass red. My dick jumps in my pants at the thought of watching her ass turn a beautiful shade as my palm smacks against her pale skin.

Equally as important as punishment is reward.

Although I'll always feed her, some kinds of food are definitely a reward. This won't be one of them. But it needs to be good. She didn't eat dinner, so I know she must be hungry. It's far past breakfast, so a light brunch it is.

I looked up her credit card history and I know what she likes to eat. I've taken everything she does into consideration. I know everything about her. I've spent every day for nearly a month studying her habits and learning how best I can meet her needs and reward her. I also needed time to get the rooms together and decide on the best way to go about everything in between taking care of the other hits. I've fantasized about this day since I got the approval from the mob bosses. But I never imagined I'd get this fucking rush of adrenaline.

One thing I hadn't decided was what her first meal should be.

Although she's not too picky, I don't want it to be mediocre. However, I can't spoil her just yet, so I decide on fresh ahi tuna. It's something that will be simple to feed her. I smile as I realize I'm going to feed my kitten tuna. A rough chuckle rumbles through my chest. I'm sure she won't find humor in that, but I sure as fuck do.

I grab the tuna tartare from the fridge. It's fresh. I bought it just for her since it's one of her favorites. I'll give it to her now even though it's certainly on the reward side of food. She needs to know I'll treat her well and give her what she likes so long as she obeys. She'll probably throw it in my face or on the ground, but I'm prepared for that to happen. And then she'll have to settle for something less appealing when I serve her dinner.

If she's a good girl, I'll move her into her room. I don't think she'll react well to being kept and told to obey, but the thought makes my dick press even harder against my zipper. I'm dying for her to disobey me, but there's a very real possibility that it'll take a long time to convince her that she should listen to me. I can't get carried away with my excitement. I have to be patient. I have to give her every reason I can to submit to me willingly.

She will though. I'm certain of it. I know this turns her on as much as it does me. It's what sealed her fate. We both have this fantasy, and I'd be a fucking idiot to let it pass us by. That's why I watched her for so long. I needed to make sure this is really what I wanted. And it is. She's exactly who I want. Everything she does is perfect. She's a natural submissive.

I pull back the plastic wrap holding the delicately pressed chunks together, and place the stack neatly in the center of a ceramic plate. It looks delicious. I grab the accompanying plastic container of sauce and put it on the dish. She'll enjoy this...if she eats it. I thought about using a plastic plate, but I want the dish to be breakable. I want her to think about smashing it and using it against me. Fuck, in all honesty, I hope she tries. That way I can show her how useless her struggle would be. It feeds into my need to train her to be submissive to me. Maybe it's wrong of me to tease her like that and to dare her to disobey me, but I don't give a fuck.

Right now I just need to get her to agree and follow a simple command. To eat.

I have to adjust my erection at the thought of her parting those full lips and letting me slip chunks of tuna into her mouth. I'm so fucking hard for her. All I want to do is pin her down and sink deep into her hot cunt. I know she's turned on by this. If nothing else she wants to fuck me. It's a long way from her craving to be all mine, to wanting to submit to my every wish. But at least her desire is a start. A really good fucking start. I wasn't anticipating that just yet.

I thought she'd be crying by now. I imagined her screaming and begging to be set free. That's not what I want, but that would be a natural response. Maybe that'll come later. I'm hopeful that it won't though. She's too smart for that shit. I think she'll probably pretend to play along and wait for the perfect opportunity, just like she did earlier. She'll go along with everything, waiting to see my hand and then calculate her next move.

I'll be ready though. I can't wait till she lets her claws out and tries to fight me so I can show her just how easy it would be to take her.

I shake my head, hating where my thoughts are going. I'm such a sick fuck.

For as long as I can remember, I've had these dark desires. I want her to fight me, to run from me. I want to feel her body struggle against mine. But I want her to do all of that willingly. I want her eager for me to chase her and pin her down, forcing her legs open and fucking her until she's limp and filled with my cum. I won't give in to that temptation, not until she begs me. Not until I earn it.

I can't get carried away. I need her to *want* this just as much as I do.

As I prepare to head back to her cell, my phone goes off in the dining room. From the sound I can tell it's a text, and I know it's from Vince. I put the plate on the counter and walk to the table to give him the news.

Is the shipment taken care of? he asks in his text.

Usually I'd reply with a simple yes, meaning that the unlucky bastard on my list is dead, but that's not the case this time.

It's been delivered, I respond.

You've kept the shipment?

Yes. I'm quick to answer. My heart beats faster in my chest. He gave me permission, so now I'm keeping her. I don't like that he's questioning me. Maybe he was wondering if I'd really go through with it. I watch my phone and see he's writing a response. Then nothing. Then he starts typing again. I'm not sure if he doesn't know what to say, or if he's just trying to figure out how to word it.

Will the order keep a shelf life? he asks, and I know what he's really asking. Will she live? Am I going to kill her? Or possibly he thinks she'd rather die than be with me.

I stare at my phone and look through the kitchen toward the back room where the door to the basement is. I've got all three of her rooms set up with locks on them. The cell, her suite, and her office. I didn't do all this prep work and make sure she was the one for me only to have her taken away. Or worse, have her choose death. She may have said no to being mine out of a knee-jerk reaction at first, but she's curious, and I know I can change her mind. She doesn't mean it. Before I leave her cell tonight, I'm going to leave her wanting more. I want her to start fantasizing about being mine and what an opportunity this really is for her.

I type in my answer and push send, leaving the phone on the table and walking quickly to get back to her.

I'm keeping her.

CATHERINE

a fter a minute of watching the door, I slowly rise and take a look around the room. It's small and a bit cold. The only escape is the door he went through. The one locked with a keypad.

I can't fucking stay here like a caged rat. My heart stills in my chest. That's what I am to them. My eyes rise with defiance to the door. I did what I thought was right, and the only thing I could do to survive. They can all fuck off. I don't deserve this shit. I'm not a mouse or a rat.

I picture that sexy smirk and hear the man keeping me here call me *kitten*. It sends a shiver down my spine. I'm not his fucking kitten either. Even if I do think that pet name is sexy as hell, and it makes my pussy clench.

I walk to the chair and imagine smashing it against his head when that fucker gets back in here. I don't know the code to unlock the door though. I'd have to be on the other side of the room to get a good view of him punching in the keys. Even then, I doubt I'd be able to make them out; it's too fucking dark. I need to get the fuck out of this room, and I don't know how I'm going to be able to do that unless he physically lets me.

I know pleading with him to let me go would be of no use, but maybe I can beg him to let me out of this room and into another. One without a fucking lock. I need to be smart about this. I grip the back of the chair wanting so desperately to just beat the shit out of him, but I can't. First of all, I'm weak as

644

shit. Second, no matter how much I don't like it, I'm stuck here until he decides to let me out.

My body tenses as the door opens. I watch as he walks into the room with a plate balanced in his hands. Anger heats my blood. This is a game to him. He thinks he can play with me. He stops as the door clicks shut behind him and he stares at me. I try to school my expression to neutral, so I don't reveal how I'm really feeling. But then I see his expression, and he looks *pleased*. He's happy that I'm angry. I release my grip on the chair and take a step back before I give in to the urge to pick it up and throw it at him.

"You look upset, kitten."

My nostrils flare. I decide to settle on the truth. "I am." I keep my hands straight so I don't ball them into fists. It won't do me any good to fight a man like him head on. I need to save my energy for when I'll *have* to fight him off, since I'm sure that's coming. I should also be adopting a more submissive tone considering I've come to terms with the fact that he's the only way I can get out of here. But I'm holding on to my anger. It's better than giving into the hopelessness of the situation.

"With me?" He tsks and shakes his head as he takes slow and deliberate steps toward me. I take another step back as he sets the plate down on the chair. "Don't be angry with me, kitten. I--"

"Stop calling me that!" I scream at him, hating how he's talking to me. Like he's placating a disobedient child.

His shoulders stiffen, and the soft angles of his face harden with anger. "Now now, you shouldn't speak to me that way. You're a smart girl, so you should know better." His tone is soothing, like he's trying to appease me, but it's right on the edge of taunting me with condescension.

"What do you want from me?" I ask with a choked voice. I want to get this part over with. That's really what I need to find out. I want to know what I have to do to get the fuck out of this room.

"I want you to submit to me," he answers simply.

"Fine." I whisper the word. I need to play along in order to get the fuck out of here. I relax my shoulders, trying to channel a softer side of me.

He tilts his head and echoes, "Fine?" A low chuckle rises in his chest, and I have to keep my eyes wide open and my lips slammed shut to avoid showing how much it turns me on. What the fuck is wrong with me? My breathing picks up and I take another step back, not trusting him or my reactions.

"Alright, then...*kitten*." He stares at me, waiting for a response to his pet name for me. I don't give him one. Instead I hold my tongue and push down my pride. "Come over here and get down on your knees."

My heart sinks. I'm not doing that shit. He's out of his fucking mind if he thinks I'm going to suck him off. As much as I want to obey him so I can get the fuck out of here, I'm not going to do that. I'm not a whore. I could bite his dick off though. I feel my eyebrows raise at the thought, and the tiny cellar fills with a deep, rough laugh from the man standing across from me.

"You're adorable, kitten. But that's not going to happen. Not yet." He shakes his head with a small smile on his face.

"What's not going to happen?" I play dumb, like I wasn't that obvious just now.

"You haven't earned my touch yet, and you don't need it right now." He picks up the plate and moves the chair so it's facing me before sitting down. "Now come here and get on your knees so I can feed you."

I hesitate to move. I don't believe him, not for one second. And kneeling before him would put me at an even greater physical disadvantage.

"Come on, I know you're hungry." He sets the plate on his lap and motions with his fingers for me to come to him. "It's almost eleven, and you didn't eat last night. You must be starving."

My eyes narrow on him. I hate that he watched me last night. I knew it. I should have trusted my instincts. I knew someone was out there. "How long did you watch me?"

"I've been watching you ever since I got the hit on you." He's quick with his response, and it chills my blood.

"Are you a member of the mafia?" I ask.

He chuckles and says, "Which one?" The fact that he thinks this is funny really pisses me off.

"Are you a Cassano?" I ask with force.

"No. I'm not."

"So why are you going to kill me then?" My heart sinks. I don't understand. How many fucking people did I piss off?

"I'm not going to kill you," he says with a hard voice. His blue eyes turn dark and I can feel the weight of the conviction in his voice. "It took a lot for me to be able to have you. But I bought you from the Cassanos, and now I'm keeping you." I can't help that my pussy twitches at his words.

"Why?" my voice asks, without my conscious consent.

He leans forward slightly. "I've asked you twice now to come and get down on your knees. You need to learn to listen."

My feet move of their own accord until I'm standing in front of him. My legs tremble as I slowly kneel before him. I swallow thickly. Finally, I sit on my heels and keep my eyes on the door behind him. I have to do what needs to be done. My heart sinks and I just want to cry.

"Look at me, kitten," his deep voice commands me, and I look up at him reluctantly. I feel weak, and I hate it. Everyone assumes I'm weak. Now that I'm on my knees without a fight, it's hard for me to disagree. I look at his gorgeous face with nothing but sadness on mine.

"Don't be sad. You'll enjoy this." He leans forward and places a large hand on my shoulder. I fucking lean into his touch and close my eyes before I can stop myself. "Trust me."

My eyes harden at his words, but before I can spit back that I don't even know him, let alone trust him, he takes his hand away and says, "You'll learn to trust me."

I bite the inside of my cheek and wait for his next move. My eyes are drawn to his fingers as he reaches for a chunk of what I think is tuna. My mouth waters as he dips it into some sort of sauce and brushes it along the side of the cup until none of the sauce is dripping from the chunk of fish. He brings it to my lips and I instinctively lean back and move my hands up in front of my face.

The man's deep voice rings out. "No." My body jumps at his disapproval, and my heart races as I look into his eyes. Half of me still expects him to be violent toward me, even though he hasn't yet. "You know what I want."

He seems to relax some as he registers my fear. "Hands on your knees like they were, and mouth open. You were seated perfectly."

I obey him even though my fear seems to paralyze my body. I'm simply moving to his commands in order to survive. I have to admit him saying I was "seated perfectly" gives me a small thrill. And I fucking hate that. I wish he didn't have this affect on me.

"Open," he commands, and I do as he says. He gently places the chunk of tuna in my mouth and as he does, my stomach grumbles from hunger.

He smiles down at me and dips another piece in the sauce. "I knew you were hungry, kitten." He looks at me again with curiosity, holding the piece over the plate. "Do you like it?"

My heart beats slowly as I search his face. I wonder if he's toying with me. If I admit that I like it, he might take it away and make me starve.

"I'd like you to answer me quickly and honestly, Catherine." His voice holds a note of admonishment, and I feel compelled to apologize.

"I'm sorry, s--" Sir is on the tip of my tongue, but I pause as I realize I don't know what to call him.

"Anthony," he says, answering my unspoken question. "No need to be sorry." His other hand grips my chin to get my attention. "You're learning. I can be reasonable so long as you're making an effort to obey. Is that under-stood?" he asks.

"Yes, Anthony."

"Good." His fingers stroke my jaw briefly. "Did you like that?" he asks.

"Yes...Anthony." It feels odd saying his name again so soon. But I imagine it's what he wants.

He smirks at me, the fucking bastard. "You don't have to say it every time." He holds the fish out and I open my mouth obediently.

It's so fucking good. It's not fair that I am fucking loving this fish. It's sweet, with a hint of spice. I'd eat this every day if I could. My eyes widen. He knew I'd like it. He smirks at me again as if reading my mind.

"Open," he says, holding out another piece.

I do as he says. And again and again. His fingers brush against my lips more and more. He puts a piece up to my mouth, and I take it and swallow before I realize his finger is still in front of my face.

"A bit of sauce, suck." My core heats and stirs as I maintain eye contact and open my mouth. His lips part as he slips his finger slowly into my mouth. I gently suck and massage him with my tongue. His eyes go half-lidded, and his breath comes in pants. And that's when I push my teeth down. Not hard, but enough that they scrape against him as he slowly pulls his finger free from my mouth. I know it didn't hurt him, but he got the message.

Once his finger is finally released, he grabs my jaw forcefully. He shoves his thumb into my mouth, tilting my head slightly. I'm forced to remain still, with my neck bent at an awkward angle. "Be a good girl, kitten. I know you could hurt me if you wanted to." He leans in closer and whispers in my ear.

His hot breath sends shivers down my back. "Just remember, I could hurt you too, *if I wanted.*"

The threat makes me regret my action. My eyes fall, and tears prick the back of them as he releases me. My heart hurts, and anxiety races through me.

"Open." I hear him give his command, but I can't. I feel sick to my stomach. I fall back onto my heels and turn away from him. I can't. I can't do this. I back away slightly as he moves to the floor, setting the plate on the metal chair with a clink. Tears leak from my eyes.

"Hush, kitten," he says as he wraps his arms around me and pulls me against his chest. "I understand, I do." He rubs my back gently and it calms me. I lean into his touch, loving the warmth. It's been so fucking long since I've been held. Once I went into hiding, I was always alone in that house. It's made me weak.

"I don't want to hurt you. I want you to enjoy this, and I don't want you to be sad. But I don't want you to push me either. Not unless you *want* to be punished." I bury my head deeper into his chest, trying to resist how every-thing he's saying is making me want to play. This isn't pretend though. There'll be no stopping this once it's started, and that terrifies me. But as much as I'd like to tell myself it hasn't started, I know it already has. And I'm playing into his hands.

The realization sobers me. I slowly back away and get back into a submissive position, although my eyes aren't on him at all. I stare at the floor and try to gather some kind of composure. I quickly wipe the tears away and chance a look at him as he sits back on the chair. He looks uncertain. It's an expression I haven't seen on him before. It makes me fucking terrified. He's quick to adjust the look on his face.

"Come," he says with a firm resolve. He pats his left leg. "Let's try this again." He waits patiently as I stand and sit awkwardly on his lap. His left arm wraps around my waist and he pulls me closer to him. Even though he's so tall compared to me, his head is nearly level with mine with us seated like this. He rests his left hand in my lap, dangerously close to my pussy. My nightgown has ridden up some and I feel exceptionally vulnerable. I'm stiff on his lap, and I can't relax with his hand where it is.

He waits a moment before saying or doing anything. It's awkward as fuck.

"You need to relax." He dips his finger into the sauce and brings it to my lips. He stares into my eyes rather than giving me the command. I do as he wants and open my mouth. He slips his finger past my lips. His eyes are drawn to my mouth as I gently suck his finger clean. When he pulls his finger away, he gives me a satisfied look.

"Good kitten." He puts another piece of the tuna tartare to my lips and I accept it. Seeing his approval eases something in me. I know so long as he's pleased, I'm safe with him. And so far, pleasing him is simple, but I don't know what other *terms* he has.

On the next bite, I find myself leaning into his fingers. He tsks and pulls the piece away from me. My heart rate speeds up until I realize what I've done to upset him. I swallow and sit back on my heels, exactly the way I was positioned before. His left hand runs along the thin fabric of my nightgown, just above my clit. "Good job, kitten." My pussy spasms around nothing. I close my eyes, hating how my body is betraying me. My nipples are hard, and the light brush of the fabric against them only turns me on even more. Other than his hand edging closer and closer to my pussy, he shows no signs of his own arousal.

"Eat until you're full." He grabs another piece, and we continue like this. Each time he feeds me his fingers brush a little closer to my throbbing clit, until finally his deft fingers are massaging small circles over my clit. I'm soaked for him, and primed for him to fuck me. And I fucking hate it. He's playing me and using my body against me.

He leans into my neck and whispers with his lips barely touching the shell of my ear, "I knew you'd like this. You just need to admit that you want it."

I'm not sure what angers me more--that I've allowed myself to be such easy prey for him, or that he's right. I want him to fuck me, and I fucking hate him for it. But I'm not going to let him reduce me to nothing but a whore.

I push away from him and kick the plate off his lap while I fall to the floor. The dish smashes on the ground as I fall backward.

He rises quickly, somewhat bracing my fall. The anger washing off of him is so strong that I scoot backward on my ass without even realizing at first. My heart races in my chest, and my blood rushes in my ears. Fear consumes me.

Making Anthony angry is something I shouldn't do. I know this as a truth, but I pissed him off anyway. I was going to play along. Why couldn't I just do what I needed to?

I expect him to hit me, or to grab me like he did earlier for my outburst.

Inwardly I'm cursing myself for not just going along with this. But I can't. I'm more than *that*.

I anticipate his aggression. He doesn't get violent. Instead, he turns his back on me.

"I'm disappointed in you, kitten," he says as he carefully picks up several pieces of thick porcelain. He's slow to pick them up, and for a moment I imagine myself grabbing a single piece, the one closest to me. But I don't. I'm frozen with fear. After a moment of him cleaning up the mess I made, he looks me in the eyes as he picks up the last shard.

He turns to the door with an expression of discontent and that's when I realize he's leaving me.

My racing heart tries to leap from my chest. I can't be left here. I need to get out. "Please don't leave me here!" I scream and beg. I didn't want to, but I have to try. I don't want him to leave me here alone. I can't sit here with nothing. No plan, no hope, fucking nothing.

"I'm sorry, kitten," he says as he turns his back on me. "Tonight training will begin. It's best that you put this rebellion behind you. You won't enjoy being punished."

Tonight? How fucking long will I have to wait in this room alone?

"I have a life! Please just let me go!" I feel weak and hate what I've become.

"I know you do, kitten. And I would provide for you in every way you need."

"I want *my* life back!" I don't want to be his version of a pampered pet. I want my job and my friends. I worked hard to create this new life for myself, and I want it back. I don't want it torn from me.

He turns back to me with anger sparking in his eyes. It's enough to make me retreat until my back hits the wall. He strides toward me with a dark aura surrounding him.

"You want an office? You want to go online so you can work? Do you want your books, kitten?" I stare at him, not knowing what to say.

"I told you to answer me when I ask you a question," he says with barely contained anger.

"Yes. Yes, that's what I want." I answer him in a strangled voice I don't recognize.

He smirks at me, and that expression is completely at odds with the aggression choking the air between us. "You would've had all of that, if only you'd behaved." I stare at him with disbelief as he makes his way back to the door.

He's lying. He must be. I can't help but hope.

"Please. Just another chance." I take a hesitant step forward as he punches the code into the keypad.

He turns to face me with sympathy in his eyes. "We'll try again at dinner." Before he leaves me alone again, he turns to face me. "I'm going easy on you right now, but remember this is only because it's your first day and we haven't discussed terms yet." He looks at me expectantly as I wipe the angry tears from my eyes.

"I expect you to answer me," he says with the hint of a threat in his voice. "You will look at me when I'm speaking to you."

My eyes dart around as my breath catches in my throat. I don't even remember what he said. My mouth parts, but words don't come out.

He takes long, quick strides toward me, letting the door fall shut behind him. I cower and find my back up against the wall again. He stops inches away from me like last time, but this time he grips the nape of my neck and pulls me toward him.

"I want you so fucking badly." His low voice sends a chill down my body. "I want to show you how good this is going to be." His fingers tangle in my hair, and he makes a fist at the base of my head, forcing me to expose my neck to him.

He leans forward, pressing his body against mine and his large erection digs into my belly. Being held like this sends a need coursing through my body. Every nerve ending is on alert and ready to spark to life. I clench my thighs as my nipples harden.

He leaves an open-mouthed kiss on my neck. It's so gentle, and so at odds with everything else.

"You'll learn to obey me, kitten, and you'll fucking love it when you do." His hand pushes between my legs and he cups my pussy. His lips brush against my ear as he whispers. "I will give you everything you need. Every-thing you want. But you need to submit to me." His hot breath gently caressing my sensitive skin forces a moan from my lips. He takes my earlobe into his mouth and gently nips it. "You're going to beg me to fuck you, kitten. I'll wait for it. I'll wait for you to beg me."

With that, he leaves me. My body sags against the wall and the chill of the damp cell replaces his warmth. I take in a ragged breath and barely catch sight of him as he leaves me cold and alone. I watch the door close quickly behind him, like he couldn't get out fast enough.

I close my eyes, hating that I'm so turned on by him. I shouldn't be. All of this is wrong in every way. Even worse, I hate that I already crave his touch.

ANTHONY

I hear the door shut with a loud click and lean back, reveling in how perfect she is. She's caught up in her own mind and holding back, but she's exactly how I dreamed she'd be.

It's going to be so fucking good when she finally lets go. I need to break those walls down and I'm doing that as soon as fucking possible. Fuck patience. She needs a push. She's desperate to get out of that room and I can't blame her. Come tonight, if I don't let her out, she'll be sleeping on a hard as fuck floor. I don't want that for her, and I don't want her in that cell. But I don't have a choice. She needs to learn.

The thought brings to mind the memory of her scraping her teeth against my finger. If I'm honest with myself, it was hot as hell. I love how brazen she is, but she knew what she was doing.

She had to be punished. There's a lot of research on the psychology of motivation via punishment and reward. Reward is always better, but when punishment needs to happen it's best if the severity of the punishment is in direct proportion to the offense. Ideally it should also be swift, taking place as soon as possible after the misdeed. If you merely give a slap on the wrist, the behavior is more than likely to occur again, and also more likely to be a worse transgression.

I needed that punishment to be aggressive to keep her from pushing. But I didn't like that I had to do it. It's better now that it's over with. Hopefully things will continue to go as planned, and the next time she pushes it'll be minimal. And that way I can get my hands on her ass and move this along to other forms of play.

My fingers twitch with the need to touch her again. I don't know if she noticed how she rocked her cunt against my hand. I know she was hot and wet from what we did, and she should have been. There's nothing wrong with being turned on by what happened. It's natural.

I just need to break down the social constructs she has built in her head. She has to learn to give in to her needs and desires. She has to learn to trust that I'm gonna give her everything she could ever want. The life she's built; she can have it. But I can add so much more. I can let her give in to her own dark desires and show her a world she's only dreamed of. I'll teach her that. Tonight I'll give her a test, and if she obeys the one command I give her, I'll let her out of that room. That will be huge for us. I only hope she doesn't disappoint me.

She's too headstrong and preoccupied with right and wrong. She knows she wants this, but I don't think a girl like her gives into desires. She's strict in her regimen, and doesn't reward herself much. I'll have to ease her into enjoying this, one reward at a time.

I make my way to the dining room where I left my phone and cringe when I see I've missed messages. Three are from Vince. I put my password in and take a look. The first and most recent text is from Tommy, my brother, but also my partner in the hits.

Cassys have another for us.

Cassys are the Cassanos. Ever since we started taking on outside hits, they've been good customers. Apparently they get pissed off. A lot.

The next three are from Vince. It looks like he sent them within minutes of each other, and the first one arrived almost immediately after my last message to him.

They seem to be under a different impression.
They want a timeline.
We're talking tonight.

Fuck. I don't like any of the shit in those messages. I don't really give a fuck what impression the Cassanos are under. I bought her freedom from them. If they changed their minds, that's on them. I don't have to do shit for them, and neither does Vince.

I finally text back, *I paid for this shipment.*

What the fuck am I supposed to tell them? he asks, and I can practically hear his anger.

The deal's done. I tell him simply.

I know we do a lot of business with them, but I don't like where Vince's head is at. He's the Don and even though technically Tommy and I aren't included in the *familia* shit, we're not fooling anyone. He's the boss, and we're still untouchables. We're still family and *familia* and nothing changes that. It also means I have to listen to the fuck. Usually I agree with him. But on this? No. I don't fucking like the way he's talking.

What do you need from me? I ask after a moment.

I need a timeline.

I stare at the phone. I don't know what to say. I never had one in mind. And I sure as fuck don't plan on making one now.

I don't have one. Your call.

I send the text, knowing full well that whatever deadline he gives me, I'm going to try to and extend it. The phone goes off, but I don't look at it. I'll figure this shit out later. Nothing is going to ruin this for me.

I put the phone down and leave it there, knowing damn well I'm not going to like anything he has to say about this. I need to get started on something to eat tonight and make sure her room is set up.

I don't want to get my hopes up, but I have a good feeling that she's going to pass this test. I fucking hope she does. She desperately needs to cum. My eyes fly to the door to the basement. Fuck! I didn't tell her she wasn't allowed to touch herself without my permission. Fuck me, I didn't tell her anything.

She's a smart girl though, and she's read a lot of dirty books. She should know better.

She had better know better.

CATHERINE

$\mathcal{I}$'m fucking rocking like a crazy person. I could sit in the chair, but it's tainted now. So instead I'm huddled in the corner rocking. It's not because I'm crazy though. It's because there isn't a fucking thing to do, not a damn thing to do in this empty cell.

I've walked around every inch of this room. Even though it's dark, the cell's not too dirty. I should know, since I've searched everywhere for a second door, or crack, or opening. Anything. I bet he watched me; in the books, they always watch. I even expect some kind of punishment for it, but I had to do it. I had to try.

All the flashbacks keep coming forward, and I keep pushing them down. They make me weak. I can't go back to that. He's not one of them.

"Come on, little mouse," *Lorenzo says as he parks his car in front of the restaurant.*

"*I don't want to.*" *I already told him I don't want to, but he's not listening.*

He has his dick out and he's pushing me to go down on him here, but there are people everywhere. At first when we met, I was looking for that thrill. But we kept getting caught by his friends, and now they give me weird looks and make jokes that I don't like.

He moves faster than me, and it takes me by surprise. He fists my hair and yanks my head back. I scream out in pain and try to pry his hand off of me. "Stop, it hurts." Tears prick my eyes. "It hurts!" I scream out.

"Dumb bitch," he says under his breath. "You know what you got yourself into. You fucking want it this way." My heart sinks in my chest. I don't want it, and especially not like this.

"Suck it," he says, releasing me while pushing my head forward. I look back at him with daggers in my eyes.

"Fuck you," I sneer at him, and wipe my eyes. He barks out a laugh.

"Aw, little mouse. You don't want to play?" I feel sick to my stomach. Things never used to be like this. When he's rough with me in bed now, it's different, too.

"I said no." I hate that I have to tell him twice.

"Fine," he says as he tucks himself back into his pants and I feel a small sense of relief.

"Come here, you know I didn't mean it." He leans across the console to give me a kiss and I hesitate, but I lean in anyway. Because I'm a fucking idiot. Because I thought I just needed to make the lines clearer. Like it was my fault.

THAT WAS right before I tried to leave him. I had no one else, and I was afraid to be alone. I was so desperate for his "love" that I stayed with that fucking creep far too long. Things only got worse after that. I remember the night I tried to sneak out and run away. Before I left, I looked down on his sleeping body and thought about slitting his throat. How awful of a person had I become where I thought I should kill him? Not fucking awful at all. That bastard deserved to die. But I couldn't do it. I couldn't lower myself to becoming a murderer, so instead I sneaked out through a window and hoped I could start over. Instead I fell right into a new world of hell.

I HEAR them laugh as Lorenzo backhands me again. This time I fall. I learned to make it look real.

When he was drunk that's the game he played. How many hits until the mouse would fall? He liked his nickname for me even more after I saw what happened. He was daring me, taunting me to be a *rat*. If I stayed on the ground, he'd only kick me a few times. I learned to just stay curled on my side and wait for the beatings to be over, no matter how much he urged me to stand. He only made it worse if I obeyed him. Bruises gave way to broken bones, but by then, I had no way to leave. I was trapped and beaten regularly for his enjoyment. I barely escaped them. And I only managed because they were reckless. Their desires to cause me even more pain is what eventually gave me my out.

They came into the room they kept me in. It'd only been a few days of being trapped there, feeling helpless and weak, trying to recover from the beating he gave me. The three of them came into the room and left the door wide open as they stalked to my bed. I knew what they were going to do. I rock harder, remembering the fear. I fucking bolted. I just kept thinking, *Please don't let them catch me.*

They can never catch me. Never. I had to do everything I could to escape that hell. But I had no one. Not a single soul to run to. My mother was everyone and everything to me. But she'd been dead for nearly a year. I ran to her grave and prayed for a sign. That's when the cops showed up, sirens blaring. I thanked my mom every day.

I thought she'd saved me like she always did.

But they did catch me.

Only they didn't come after me directly like I thought they would. They sent someone else.

I have no clue how long it's been. I don't know what he's doing. Or what this training is going to be like when he gets back. I have absolutely no control in any of it either, and I don't like it. I tug at the hem of my nightgown, wishing it were longer so I could cover myself up more. My knees are drawn up to my chest, and I rest my head on them as I consider my next step.

I don't know what to do. I don't know what my options are. He said he'd give me my life and everything I needed. I want to believe that's true, but what's the catch? I know his intentions aren't pure. And I'm certain his terms aren't negotiable.

I'm eager to hear what he has to say though. I want to know what I've gotten myself into. That way I can figure out how to get the fuck out of here.

My back is killing me, so I keep up my rocking. It feels better than just sitting still for however fucking long it's been. I'd get up and stretch or do yoga, but I don't want to be standing when he walks in. I want to be ready.

Well, as ready as I can be.

I close my eyes and remember his words. An office, my books. How much does he know about me? He's been watching me, obviously. I wonder if there were signs I missed. Red flags I should have seen, but didn't.

The only time I ever felt that things were off was last night. That was the only chance I had. I should have gotten into my car and driven away. I should have listened to my gut.

But I didn't.

I've never felt so fucking helpless. Not when I was with Lorenzo. Not when I was taken by those fucking Cassanos. Not even when I went to the police and they told me I'd have to leave my old life behind forever. Never. Because there was always hope. But now, I only have his word. And I don't trust him.

For all I know, he has a bet going with someone. How long would it take him to get into my pants willingly? And then boom. He'll kill me. Or he'll let someone else in here to have a go at me. How the fuck would I know? I don't know shit. And it's not like he's offering up any information. He's just playing this game with me.

In all the books I've read, there's been some sort of contract, or list. Terms. Like he said before.

That always happens first.

But he's playing with me. Testing me. And as far as I'm concerned, he's winning.

My body betrayed me, and I gave into the weakness. I was practically ready to cum on his lap. If he'd flipped me over and put his mouth on my clit rather than whispering in my ear, shit. I don't know what I would have done. I was so weak. So desperate.

It's pathetic. *I'm* pathetic.

But what real choice do I have? I can fight his game, or I can play along. I can stay here and let him toy with me, or I can use him to get out of here.

Use him.

I like that idea. It almost makes the desire for him to touch me feel justified. That giving in and caving to his touch is alright. I'm merely playing into his hand because it's what I have to do.

As if hearing my thoughts, Anthony opens the door.

My breath stills in my lungs as the loud click echoes off the walls.

I make a promise to myself. I'll do whatever I have to do to get the fuck out of this room. I need to see if I can trust his word at least.

Just as I make that promise to myself, I see what he's pulling behind him. It's a large bench with leather shackles. Fuck! Tears prick my eyes.

I bury my head in my knees and just fucking cry. He's going to chain me to the bench. He's going to fuck me.

A wretched sob heaves through my chest.

I shake my head, and that's when I hear his footsteps. But I don't back away. I have no options. What choice do I have?

ANTHONY

I turn around as soon as I hear her crying.

Fuck. I wanted to shock her, but I didn't think she'd cry.

She had so much fight in her when I left her. I don't know what happened while I was gone. I know that being alone for hours can be torturous when you have nothing. No noise but the sounds you make, nothing to touch but yourself and the walls and floor.

But I didn't think it would affect her like this.

"Kitten," I begin as I crouch down next to her, although I keep my distance. She could be playing me for a fool. Waiting for me to comfort her so she can strike. I'm certain I picked up the large chunks of the plate. There were only three or four of them. But maybe she found a smaller piece and she's planning to stab the shit out of me with it. She doesn't trust me, and I sure as fuck don't trust her.

I didn't watch her in the monitor. I was driving myself crazy watching her do nothing. More than anything seeing her like that pissed me off, because all I wanted to do was to go to her. But she's being punished.

This is a part of her punishment.

"Yes, Anthony," she answers in a strangled voice. She raises her head with tears staining her reddened cheeks. I'm surprised she answered. She wipes the tears from her face and I see she doesn't have anything in her hands. She's not armed, and she's not trying to fight me. She's just genuinely upset.

"Why are you crying?" I ask her.

"Because I give up. I'll let you do whatever you want. I just want this to end." My heart stops in my chest. That's not at all what I expected, and so far she's done everything I thought she would.

I haven't broken her yet. But maybe I've taken away her hope of getting out of here unless she obeys.

"And that makes you sad?" I ask to clarify. "You're upset that you're giving me control?" Truthfully though, she never had any control. Maybe over her own actions, but not at all over the situation. She's a strong woman. I guess that very realization could be troubling her.

She takes in a small gasp and shakes her head. "Of course I'm upset about that. Normal people don't do this."

Although I appreciate her honesty, that fucking attitude is going to be the first thing I correct.

"Watch your mouth, kitten." She looks up at me with nothing in her eyes.

"Yes, Anthony. I'm sorry, sir." She says the words without a hint of sarcasm in her voice. And it's disappointing. I'm surprised by my reaction to it.

"Could I know the terms, please? Before you chain me?" she asks in a flat voice. It's unsettling how much I don't like it.

"No." I watch her as I answer sternly. She merely nods her head slowly, as if she figured I wouldn't tell her anything.

"Okay." Her voice is small and she's finished crying. She sniffles once and nods her head again. "I'm ready."

I was foolish to think that this behavior didn't indicate her inner strength. She's resigning herself to a fate she doesn't want so that she can move forward. That in and of itself is strong. I feel my tense muscles relax now that I understand.

I grip her chin with my thumb and forefinger and make her look me in the eyes.

"You won't regret this, Catherine. I promise you." As I say the words with confidence, I remember Vince and the Cassanos, and I fucking hate myself for thinking of them right now. I won't let them take her. And I won't let her regret this either.

"I'm going to put you on the bench, and I want you to hold onto the straps." She nods her head and then whispers, "Yes, Anthony."

"Once you agree to the terms, and only then, I'll bind your wrists."

She closes her eyes and I can see her pride leave completely as shame overwhelms her. I knew this would happen. But I still don't like it. This isn't the part of this relationship that I looked forward to. But the next part, the part where she learns she can trust me and that it's not the nightmare she perceives it to be? That part will be worth all of this.

"Up, kitten." I stand up and hold a hand out for her. She starts to get up on her own, but then she sees my hand. She looks dejected and depressed. That's exactly what she is. Depressed that she's given in to me. But I'm going change that. I'm going to make her love giving in to me.

I walk her over to the bench and help her on. I fucking love this idea. It's meant for spanking and fucking, and I intend to do both in time. But for now, that's not what we're going do. I lay her down so that her chest is flat against the lowered part and her ass is in the air. Her eyes are focused on the leather binds.

I take one strap out and hold it for her to take. "Go on, kitten. It won't magically wrap around your wrist." Again her eyes meet mine and I see a spark of the smart-mouthed woman from this morning. But it's only a dim flicker of defiance, and she takes the leather without much hesitation. She does the same with the right without my help. She lays her head and body flat with her legs and hand off the side. She waits for my next command with her pussy almost fully bared to me, covered only by a thin layer of fabric.

She's perfect like this, vulnerable and waiting for me. But she's obviously unhappy and only doing it because the other choice isn't really a choice at all. I splay my hand on her back, and although she stiffens, she doesn't move away from my touch. I walk around her slowly, moving my hand in soothing circles until she slowly relaxes her body.

I keep my voice soft and comforting. "The terms are simple. You do your best to obey me. If you don't, you come back here." Her eyes close as I speak. "If you please me, I will reward you. I will give you everything you need. You want your old life, and you can have it." Her eyes fly to mine, but before she can question me I add, "I will simply be a new constant in that life." Her eyes fall to the floor and then close again.

She whispers, "Yes, Anthony. I understand." That was too easy.

"You don't have any questions?" I'm surprised by that.

"What questions should I ask?" My dick finally starts hardening. Her submission is just now starting to arouse me.

"Any questions you have, kitten. I'll answer them all truthfully."

"If I do this, you'll let me out of this room? You said I'd have an office and my old life back?"

"Yes, that's right."

"I'll be able to keep working?" she asks.

"You will," I reply. I walk around to where her head is and place my hand on her chin to make sure she sees my face and knows how serious I am. "It will be heavily monitored though. And any sign that you've disobeyed me by doing anything at all that would obviously upset me will result in you being sent here. And not just for a few hours, kitten."

She nods her head and says, "I understand."

"Anything else?" I ask.

She shakes her head. "No."

"You don't want to know what I'm going to do with you?" I ask. I imagine she's already made up her mind.

"You're going to do what you'd like to me." Her voice is flat, but dampened by sadness.

"Close," I answer. "I'd love to fuck you, kitten. But I've told you I won't do that until you beg." Her head lifts slightly off the bench and her eyes widen with hope. That's the woman I want with me. Her reaction makes me smile.

"You thought I was going to fuck you right now?" I ask her.

"Yes," she answers with a tinge of confusion.

"I told you I wasn't going to until you begged. I mean it," I say.

"Do I have to let you do that in order to get out of here?" she asks.

"No," I answer, and love how much her body relaxes at my answer. I love it because she's showing trust in my words. I'm giving her hope and her strength back. Even if she doesn't realize that.

"Will I ever have to...?" she starts to ask, but trails off. My eyebrows raise and I lay a hand on the small of her back.

"I want to reward you as a dom should reward his submissive." I let my hands travel to her ass. I cup her cheeks and spread them slightly. "I'll let you know if I'd like to be pleasured. But it'll be your choice if you'd like to give me that." I let my thumbs skim along the seam in the center of her panties.

"I do want to reward you, kitten. Do you know what that means?" I ask.

She nods her head, seeming very much at ease with the knowledge I've given her.

"Tell me what you think it means."

It takes her a moment to respond, but when she does, I'm pleased. "It's what you were doing earlier."

I smile at her backside as my fingers slip past her panties. I run them along her slick heat and I'm rewarded with a soft moan.

"You rubbed my clit," she says as she continues her answer.

"Why?" I ask as I gently place her panties back where they belong.

"To reward me," she says.

"What was I rewarding?" I ask her. I'm sure she'll say it's because she was listening to me. Or because she did as she was told. But in actuality it's because she was enjoying it. I rewarded her desire for my control to continue. I'm intentionally conditioning her reactions and her emotions.

"Because I listened to you and obeyed. Because I earned it." She adds the last part forcefully. I smirk behind her. That's how that dirty book went about it. You obey, and you get rewarded. Disobey, and you get punished.

I agree to an extent, but emotions are far more powerful a tool. She'll thrive with my touch. She'll love my control. And it'll only bring her happiness.

"I want to reward you now, kitten. Should I?" I ask her.

Yes. Yes, I fucking should. But right now I want her permission. I want her to control this next step. If she answers yes, I'll have her shackled and cumming harder than she ever has before. If she'd prefer not, that's fine, but I won't shackle her. I'll merely move her to her room, unrewarded in some ways, but feeling safe in others. It's a fair trade. And either way, she's rid of this room so long as she isn't disobedient.

After a quiet moment, I look at her face. She seems lost in contemplation.

"I think so," she finally answers. I chuckle at her response.

"You're being very good, kitten. How would you like me to reward you?"

She bites down on her bottom lip.

"I--" she starts to speak, but stops herself. I know she's ready. I know she's craving a release. Each time I rest a hand gently on her lush ass, she tilts it slightly.

"Tell me, kitten. I want you to know that you can tell me anything. So long as you're respectful, you won't be punished."

"I don't want you to...have sex with me." Hearing those words fall from her lips is disappointing. But I simply tack on the unspoken "yet" to the end. Obviously she won't admit that she wants me just yet. She's angling for control as well. This is her bid to ensure that if she says no, it's not going to happen. And that's a truth. I want to earn it. I want her to yearn for my touch and desire pleasing me more than anything else. And I will. This is just a step, a small hurdle, in that direction.

"I don't intend on fucking you. Not until you *beg* me, remember?" She eyes me warily and I know I should just play my cards so she has more confidence in her decision. I reach inside my pocket and pull out a small vibrator.

"You're doing very well, kitten. I'll be honest, I'm very pleased. But you haven't earned my touch yet." Her brows creases and she almost looks disappointed. "This is all I'll use." She looks between my face and the vibrator.

"You're going to tease me? Until I beg." It pisses me off that she makes that assumption. Although I know she's read that shit in her books.

"No. That would not be a reward. I'm going to put this vibrator against your clit and make you rock yourself on it until you cum. That's all there is to your reward."

She may not notice that her ass raises just slightly, but I sure as fuck do.

"I asked you a question. Do you think you should be rewarded?"

"Yes." She finally gives me the green light in a breathy voice that makes my dick impossibly hard.

"I think so too, kitten." I push the vibrator under her, past her clit and snug between her body and the bench, just to warm it and then walk around to the front of the bench. I take the strap in her left hand and move it into place. She pulls back and nearly falls off the bench. "This is your reward, but you will receive it how I see fit."

Her big brown eyes look up at me with worry. I can't wait to ease her concerns.

"I told you what's going to happen. I won't lie. Once you've cum, I'm going to want you, and I'll ask. But if you say no, or don't beg well enough, I'll release you and show you to your room." She nods her head and places her chest flat on the bench again. Her breathing is coming in pants and I know

667

she's scared. But she's trusting me. In only a day, I've gained enough trust to make her bared to me, completely vulnerable--and she did so willingly.

The realization thrills me.

I strap both her wrists and her ankles, letting my fingers trail along her exposed skin. I gently pull the nightgown up to her waist and then slip her panties slowly down her thighs. They don't go far, but it's enough to expose her. I bend slightly and blow against her glistening sex. She's so fucking wet. I want to lean in and take a languid lick of her sweet cunt. I want to slide my fingers inside and feel her tight walls clench as she cums. But right now, I'm limited. Soon. Soon, she'll beg me for more. She'll desire nothing else. I smile as I pull away and pull out the warmed vibrator and twist it on.

Soon, she'll be begging me.

CATHERINE

$\mathcal{I}$ pull my wrist slightly, but I can hardly move. My arms don't even bend. The leather straps around my wrists have virtually no give. My ankles are strapped as well and I can barely move my legs at all. I'm completely restrained. My heart beats frantically as his hands move down my body. My ass is higher up and I know why. This bench was made for fucking. And I'm strapped to it. Willingly.

As soon as he locked in the first buckle, I felt regret. I don't know him. He's not a good man. That's really all I'm sure of, at least about him. I know one other thing. I have to do this in order to get out of here. And he promised he would let me out. He's made all sorts of pretty promises. My blood heats as his hand lingers on my ass. His other hand moves to the other cheek and he spreads them. I can't help that I'm turned on. I'm so fucking hot for him. It's been over a year now since I've felt a man's hands on me. And I've definitely never felt the hands of a man like Anthony. It's exhilarating.

I'm wet and hot and desperate for his touch. It's sick. I shouldn't want this, but I do.

And he knows it. My cheeks flame with embarrassment. My pussy is fully exposed to him and I'm completely vulnerable. The only sounds I can hear are my own ragged breath and the humming of the vibrator. My lips part and I hold back a moan as he gently pushes it against my pussy lips, just beneath my clit.

"Are you an over or under girl, kitten?" he asks in a sexy-as-fuck voice while putting slightly more pressure against me. I instinctively try to pull away. The intensity is just too much. He moves the vibrator over my clit, and my entire body heats and tingles. The pit of my stomach stirs with a hot, radiating pleasure. My ass bucks up, but the rest of my body remains in place due to the restraints.

"Ah, over it is."

I whimper and turn my head from side to side. I've never felt something like this. It's too intense. My body's pleading to move away as the sensation grows and grows and my legs quiver. "Stay still. You're going to enjoy this," he whispers.

I try to keep my body from wanting to move, but it's useless.

"Move your hips, kitten." I instantly obey him, wanting and needing to move. The motion sends a surge of arousal to my core and soft gasps fall from my lips. I grind harder, loving the intensity of the pulses shooting through me. Close, so close. My neck arches back as I desperately search for my release.

His large hand splays on my lower back and pushes me down harder onto the vibrator. His force is what does it; I cum violently and scream out as the waves of pleasure roll through my body. The first wave is the most intense, then the rest grow dimmer and dimmer. My body feels limp on the table as I take in deep, uneven breaths.

"Have you ever used a vibrator before, kitten?" I shake my head no, and try to answer aloud, but he starts talking before I can respond. "You obviously enjoy the stimulation."

I nod my head and breathe out as I agree. "Yes." I swallow thickly, realizing I'm still pinned down. My eyes open a little more and I look at him to my left as he looks from my bared pussy to my face.

"Do you want to cum again?" he asks.

My breath stalls in my chest. I do want that again. But not from him, not now. I only did that so I can get the fuck out of here.

"You do, but not like this," he says. I break eye contact, hating how obvious I am. But then again, anyone else in my position would be this fucking obvious.

"Time to see your new room." he says, shutting off the vibrator. He reaches down and unstraps the bands. I stay still, feeling uneasy yet relaxed at the same time. I want to be tense and on guard. But I'm too exhausted from all the shit I've been through. He unstraps the last restraint and I try to brace myself on the bench, but his hand comes down on my shoulders, pushing me back down.

It sets off every red flag. My heart beats faster and fear sets in.

"Let me pick you up. Your legs are still trembling." His voice is calming and soothing. I instantly feel myself relax. At the realization, I throw my guard up even higher.

I blink a few times to clear my head. I feel drunk on lust and pleasure. I breathe in deep as his arms tilt my body and he cradles me against his chest. He gently sets my feet down, but holds onto my waist. I want to push him away. I don't need his help. My legs are shaky, but I'm fine. It was just one orgasm, for crying out loud. One intense, earth-shattering orgasm, but still. I can manage on my own.

I'm sure as fuck not going to tell him that though. I just need to be good so I can get out of here and see where he's taking me. His body brushes against mine as he releases me. My eyes nearly close as I feel his massive erection through his jeans. I have to bite the inside of my cheek as my thighs clench and my pussy clamps down around nothing. I trap the moan in my throat.

His hand grips my shoulder and he leans down, placing a kiss on my shoulder before whispering, "You alright?" I can practically feel his smile.

He knows exactly what he's doing. Instead of telling him off, I continue to play the role. That's what I need to do now. "Yes, Anthony."

He lets out a deep chuckle as he reaches into his pocket and pulls out a piece of black silk cloth. He holds it up with both hands and that's when I realize it's a blindfold.

Fuck. I was hoping I'd be able to see where we're going so I can get the layout of this place. I need to come up with a plan to get out of here. I'm sure the next room will be locked as well though, and then what? I'll be fucking stuck there, just like I am now. *He promised though.* I hate that I'm relying on his word. But I am. His word is the only hope I have.

My lips press into a hard line and his response is to smirk at me and raise a brow.

"Come on kitten, behave." His tone is playful and it makes me hate him even more. It's like we're playing cat and mouse, but he's always two steps ahead of me. I swallow my pride and turn around so he can place the cloth over my eyes.

I have no other option but to trust him. And I fucking hate it.

ANTHONY

$\mathcal{M}$y little kitten thinks she's slick. It's fucking adorable. I can practically hear her thoughts. I know all of this is an act, but for a moment, I had her. I had a sweet submissive who trusted me and craved my touch. I want more.

I tighten the sash over her eyes and take a step back. Her arms move out slightly, as though she's off-balance. Without me there to guide her, I'm sure she is. Her mouth parts, but then she closes it and moves her hands to her side.

Good girl. She's trying hard to obey. I know it's only so she can use me. She's not doing it because she *wants* to. Not yet, anyway. But we'll get there. I just need to be patient.

I put my hands on her shoulders so she knows I'm there, and then let them fall to her hips.

"Walk with me and hold my hand." I take her small hand in mine and slowly lead her to the door. Her other hand opens and closes. I know she'd like to reach for the blindfold. But she doesn't. Not yet. It won't do her any good to get it off though. Even if she does manage to get it off and race up the stairs somehow without me on right on her ass, she'd just come to another lock. And the combinations to enter her rooms are all different.

The entire basement is soundproofed. She could scream all she wanted, but she would be locked down here. The doors are programmed to unlock after three days though, if anything were to prevent me from returning to the house.

I punch in the code and lead her through the door. Her right hand twitches, and I know she's fighting the urge to bolt. She's working hard to stay by my side and not take off.

But ultimately she obeys. It's a fucking relief. Also, quite an achievement. A dozen or more scenarios played out in my mind, ranging from her starving herself to her throwing the chair at me. But this is nearly all I could hope for. It's perfect really. She's still resistant, but cooperating. I knew she'd be like this. She's perfect.

She's making it easy while still being a challenge. I like that. No, I fucking love that.

We get to her bedroom and I punch in the code. I see her shoulders sag slightly and the corners of her mouth turn down. She should be smarter than to think I'd place her in a room without a lock. I'm sure she knows better than that.

As soon as the door shuts behind us, I take off the sash. She blinks a few times before letting the astonishment show on her face. I look over her body and realize how unkempt she looks. Her skin's still flushed and gorgeous, save for a few smudges on her face. But her feet are bare and dirty, and her hair's tangled and in need of a wash. Even her nightgown looks rumpled and dirty on the part covering her ass since she sat on the floor most of the day. She was only in the cell for one day, but one was enough for her to get this disheveled. I'm not looking forward to having to send her back there, but I know she's going back. It's only a matter of time.

I made sure her room was spacious and would satisfy her every need and desire. It's a combination of her bedroom and living room. The en-suite is to the left, through a pair of large antique doors, and to the right she has an office that's accessible through another locked door. I hope that it will be hers one day. For now, all contact she makes with the outside world will be monitored. I made sure to take her phone with me when I left. She hasn't received any messages or calls yet, but her social media shit is fucking constant. I have my ways to ensure we'll both be happy as far as that's concerned.

This room that I've prepared for her is nearly the size of her entire cabin. It takes up the majority of my basement. But she needs the space since this is all she'll have from now on. I tried to section it off for her so she'd have a clear separation between the living room and bedroom. It's all the same soft grey in color though, which helps to unite the spaces. Most of the linens are white, giving it a very clean and modern look. The accents are pink though. Very pale pink. I even hung floor-to-ceiling crushed velvet curtains for her. They're only covering small windows that hardly let in any light, but they make the room look larger and more luxurious. I'm hopeful that everything is to her taste. Every piece I selected reminded me of her. I want this to be a dream come true, and the setting is every bit as important as the story.

In reality, her new home is much nicer than her cabin. Everything is new and fresh. I wanted everything to have the same feel as her cabin, just with more luxurious furnishings and decor. A huge bookshelf is in one corner. Some of the books are favorites of hers, but the others are my choices. I even brought her laptop for her so that she can keep working. Of course she'll only have access to it when I'll be present for now, and I installed a tracker and a logger so I'll be able to remotely monitor her, but she should still be thrilled to have it.

I watch her as she walks to each item, putting her hand out, but barely touching the furniture. She seems shocked, but also pleased, and that makes me happy. I'm proud that I can provide for her. I want that. I want her to see how good I can be for her.

She walks slowly to the table in front of the sofa. It's where I set her Kindle. The tablet's in its case, and she pauses as she recognizes it as hers. Her eyes widen, and she looks back at me.

"I told you I'd give you what you need. And I understand your needs," I say. I know all of her needs, and I can't fucking wait to fuck her exactly how she needs it. She looks at me hesitantly, but I don't give her a moment to respond.

"You will obey me." Now's the time for me to start going over the terms since she's seen the alternative. "You will do what I say, when I say. I'll do my best to be reasonable and keep your limits in mind." I smirk and add a touch of humor to lighten the severity of the situation. Her eyes remain clouded with worry. I can tell she's thinking there's a catch beyond what I've told her. "But I will push you, and you will obey. If you don't at least try to obey me, you'll be punished, and this room will be taken from you."

I give her a moment to digest what I've told her.

"You said..." She pauses to clear her throat before continuing. "You said I would have to agree?" I nod.

"On physically pleasing me, yes. I only want your touch if you're eager to give it to me." That's absolutely true. I have no interest in taking my pleasure from her, I want her to give it to me freely.

She nods her head in understanding, appearing a bit more relaxed, but still unsure.

"Kitten, I have desires. And I want you to fulfill them." My hand burns with the need to touch her soft skin. "When I come into the room, I want you to kneel and wait for my command. My needs will be your priority." I want her submission more than anything. I want her to need me, and to look forward to my company. I need her complete trust. I will earn it.

Her breath comes in short pants, and I'm hoping this is turning her on more than anything else.

"Yes, Anthony," she answers in a respectful low tone.

"You can speak freely, so long as you're respectful. But I will punish that smart mouth of yours if you back talk or raise your voice to me. Is that understood?" I keep my voice soft, but firm as I face her. I want to brush her hair off her shoulder and wipe the smudges off her face. She needs to be cleaned and pampered.

She nods her head and says, "Yes. I understand." Her body language tells me everything I need to know. She's scared, and she doesn't trust a word I'm saying. She'll learn though. She just needs time. She needs space as well. I can't rush this fantasy. Deep down, she wants this. I'll still be here when she's ready for it. Until then, I'll have to control my own needs and desires.

"Now," I begin, as I walk to the soft grey sofa and pat the seat next to me as I sit down. She listens and quickly sits with her hands in her lap. Her eyes keep dancing around the room, so I wait for her full attention. It doesn't take long, which pleases me.

"I want to go over your earlier behavior," I say.

Her eyes widen slightly and she inhales deeply. I keep my face impassive, but it makes me happy that she's nervous to discuss it. She should be.

"You know what a good submissive does and how she behaves, don't you? I was under the impression I wouldn't have to teach you that," I say with a frown.

Her eyes lock on mine as she replies. "Yes, Anthony." Her complete attention and obedience is fucking beautiful. And hearing my name on her lips makes my dick jump. I know she has expectations just as much as I do. They'll help us for now, but they can hurt us, too.

"Earlier, you hadn't agreed to be mine. In fact, you said no and chose death at first." Her eyes stay locked on mine, but her mouth stays closed. "Because you weren't aware of my terms, you weren't punished. But now, you're mine. That behavior you displayed will get your ass whipped, kitten."

She nods her head diligently.

"You deliberately teased me." I bring my finger to her mouth and trace her bottom lip. Her mouth parts slightly, but I pull away. "Next time you'll find out what happens when you tempt that side of me." I have to work hard to keep my eyes locked on hers rather than roaming her body and picturing those sweet lips wrapped around my cock. "Do you understand, kitten?"

"Yes, Anthony." A wicked smirk pulls my lips up.

Now that she's agreed, we can really play.

CATHERINE

"You need a bath and then dinner, kitten." Anthony rises, towering above me as I sit paralyzed on the sofa.

"Yes, Anthony." The words fall easily from my lips in a tone I've only ever imagined could come from me. I feel...numb. Almost as though I'm not present in my own body. I don't understand how things have changed so quickly. I've gone from being in a dark, cold cell with nothing, to this room that's more beautiful than anything I could ever imagine.

"Come." Anthony holds his hand out for me and I quickly place my hand in his. I'm relying solely on my instincts and what I've read in my romance novels. My heart flutters as he leads me to a set of double doors carved from wood. I want to touch them, but I don't. Not with him here. I imagine he has cameras everywhere, but as soon as he leaves, I want to touch everything. I need to see what all he brought from my home and what he has for me here. A part of me wants to cry with joy and feel nothing but gratitude. But that part of me is fucking stupid.

And I'm not stupid. This is a gilded cage for his pampered pet. And he intends for me to be that pet, his *kitten*. I can play along. I *will* play along. At some point I'll be able to get out of here. I just need to survive and be whatever it is that he wants me to be until that time comes.

He opens the doors and reveals the most gorgeous bathroom I've ever seen.

The walls are lined with a beautiful pale blue paisley wallpaper. Hanging from the center of the ceiling is a silver and Lucite chandelier positioned directly above a large, oval soaking tub. Running the entire length of the back wall is a huge walk-in shower complete with waterfall shower heads and massage jets arranged symmetrically on the walls. There's a large double vanity to the left, and that makes chills prick over my skin. Is he staying here, too? It never occurred to me that he would. This space is feminine and designed for a woman. I try to ignore the fact that there are two sinks and walk forward to the shower.

My heartbeat picks up. I know what he's going to want. I'm not an idiot.

"Kitten." I hear Anthony's rebuke from behind me and I quickly turn around to face him. I don't know what I did wrong. My knees weaken and my immediate reaction is to lower myself to the ground to show complete submission. I don't want to go back to the cell. I can't. I can't go backward.

Before I can drop to the tiled floor, Anthony reaches out and firmly grips my arm and waist. "Now now, you're alright. I just want you to relax." His hands loosen on my waist and I struggle to look at him. I feel lost and powerless.

"I want you to undress out here. I need to take a look at you." I nod my head at his words. Obviously that's what he wanted. He's already made me cum and seen my naughty bits, so this isn't that far of a stretch. But it feels dirty somehow. I guess in a way it's more intimate. I pull the straps off my shoulders and let the thin nightgown fall into a heap around my feet.

Naturally I want to cover myself, but I don't. I've read enough dark romance to know better. A submissive doesn't hide her body from her dom.

Anthony's quiet. He doesn't move to touch me, and he doesn't say anything at all. I find myself growing more anxious the longer he stays silent. What if he doesn't find me attractive? What if he changes his mind? I close my eyes and try to breathe easy, but I can't.

I'm not skinny, but I wouldn't say I'm overweight either. I've got a pear shape and the cellulite on my ass to go with it. My breasts are small, but perky. I think I could be cute if I wasn't so fucking pale. His eyes don't give anything away. I wish he'd just say something already.

Before I can go into a full panic attack, he reaches out and places his hand on the dip in my waist. He crouches low and puts his face just inches above my pelvis. His fingers trace over a small scar on my hip.

"Where did this come from?" he asks.

I look down at the shiny white scar. It's hardly noticeable. I've had it most of my life and I've never thought twice about it. "When I was younger, I hit something I guess, or fell." I swallow thickly and say, "I don't remember."

He nods his head and walks around my body, looking over every inch. I feel like he's evaluating whether or not he's going to keep me, and I'm terrified he'll find me lacking.

From behind me, I feel his hands gently rest on my hips, and I close my eyes as I feel his hot breath on my shoulder. I gently tilt my neck, expecting him to kiss me there, but he doesn't. In an instant he's gone, and I'm left standing awkwardly as he completes the circle and stands in front of me as though it didn't happen.

For a moment I wonder if he even touched me at all. Maybe I imagined it.

I clear my throat after a moment of silence, but he speaks before I can and says, "You're beautiful. Every inch of you." I look up at him with surprise and wonder. He sounds so sincere. I can't help but believe he really does find me beautiful.

"You're dirty though. Let me clean you." I back away out of instinct as he walks around me toward the shower. My breathing picks up, and I can't hide the fact that I don't want this. I don't want his hands roaming my body for a mix of reasons. He's fucking good at this game, and there's a small piece of me that I know would cave at his touch. I don't trust him. I don't want him to take care of me.

"Would you rather I give you space, kitten?" he asks.

I can't hide my shock. I can hardly believe that he would leave me alone in this room. That's a lot of trust for him to extend to me. I could easily break the glass and use a piece as a weapon. Either on myself or him. As if reading my mind, he cocks a brow.

"You aren't going to make me regret that, are you? You've been so good today. I'd hate for you to upset me just before bedtime." There's a dark threat in his voice, and I'm quick to shake my head and alleviate any worries he has.

"I didn't think you would. You're smarter than that," he says.

"Yes, Anthony." My response earns me a warm smile, and I hate that it eases the apprehension in me, but it does.

"Dinner will be ready in an hour; you'll need to be done by then."

"I'm not very hungry." I speak just above a murmur and stare at the beautiful marble floor. The silence he gives me in return compels me to look at him. He gives me a tight smile.

"I understand not having an appetite, but you need to eat, kitten." He takes a step back and looks into my eyes. I try to break eye contact, but I can't. The intensity of his gaze has me pinned.

"Tomorrow will be different; you know that, don't you?" he asks with an even voice.

Tomorrow I'm his, and I'll have expectations to meet. I know. I know what this is. Regret overwhelms me. I've read this story so many times. Girl gets taken and held against her will. But this is no story. It's not something I can edit and critique. What's happening right now isn't the same as words on a page that can be changed on a whim.

"It's going to be good, kitten." His calm tone eases the stress threatening to consume me. He grips my chin in between his thumb and forefinger. He leans down with his lips close to mine, but he doesn't let them touch. My body ignites from the proximity of our bodies--mine naked, and his fully clothed. He holds such power over me, yet his touch is gentle. I almost lean into him, expecting him to kiss me, but he doesn't. He whispers, "You're going to love this kitten; I promise you."

I close my eyes, waiting for him to kiss me, but instead he drops his hand and turns to leave me. "Sleep well, kitten," he says as he opens the double doors and leaves me alone.

I watch the doors shut as his body leaves my view. The loud click fills the bathroom and I finally wrap my arms around my body. I feel stunned. Confused. And scared. More than anything, I feel lost.

I turn the water on and let the steam fill the room before I finally get into the shower. The heat feels like absolute heaven on my sore shoulders. I stand under the stream, letting the water hit me as I absorb everything. It takes a long while for me to reach for the soap and and wash the grime of the cell away. When my fingers travel lower, the anger comes along with bitter disappointment. I let him touch me.

I scrub my body harder and turn up the heat. The reality of the situation makes my breathing become ragged.

I close my eyes as the tears leak out and lean my body against the cool tiled wall. I slowly slide down until I'm on my ass and holding my knees to my chest.

I don't know how I'll ever get out of here. But I will.

Part of me thinks I should be grateful. The fucking psycho who took me is at least giving me space and letting me stay in a beautiful prison. It could be worse. But it's still a prison. And I don't deserve this. *It's better than death.* I can't deny that. I'm safe for now. Or at least I've been given the impression of safety.

I'll obey him to save myself from punishment, but I can't forget what's really going on here.

I can't let him break me. I can't let him win.

The first chance I'm given, I'm running and never looking back.

It takes me an hour before I finally go back to the bedroom.

I stop in my tracks when I see a tray on the end of the bed. I walk closer to it with disbelief. Sitting on the tray is a sage green teacup with the corresponding saucer on top to keep the heat in. And next to it are two melatonin pills.

I reach down and slowly move the saucer; the steam spills out beautifully from the freshly steeped chamomile tea.

He was watching. I already knew that though. I knew he would be watching me.

I've read countless books where the heroine is taken and forced to submit. I pick the teacup up and put it to my lips. I close my eyes as I take a sip and sit down on the bed. I look around the bedroom, the one he designed with me in mind, and think back to all those dark romances.

I've already read this story, but this is different. The way this story ends is entirely up to me and my choices from here on out.

ANTHONY

I *pull the covers closer around me. I do it every night as though they'll
protect me, but they won't. No one can protect me. This is something that
has to happen. I ruined her life. When she had me, everything changed. She's hurting
because of me. Dad's never nice to her anymore. He always makes her cry now. When
he hits her, she hits me. It's only fair, she says. I deserve it. I should never have been
born.*

*I hear the door creak open and shut behind her. I know it's coming. The belt comes
down hard and I cry out as little as possible. I hear her, but I ignore it. I feel the pain,
but I pretend I'm numb. I think about Tommy. As long as she stays here, he's safe. He
didn't do anything. It's not his fault. It's my fault. I try to be good and stay quiet, but
the belt whips through the air and smacks across my face. I can't help that I screamed.*

*I can't help it. I hear them coming. No! I shake my head as she shoves the belt
under the covers. My heart beats faster. I tried to be good. I tried. Please forgive me.*

MY EYES slowly open and and my body seems frozen. It takes a moment for
my heart to calm. I'm used to this. Everything will be fine. It's nothing that
matters anymore. My racing heart is the only indication that I've had that
fucking nightmare again. I clear my throat and get my shit together. I do my
best to feel nothing, and for the most part that's true.

I don't feel a god damned thing reliving that memory.

I LOOK over to my alarm and move the switch before the clock has a chance to display 6:00 AM and go off. I can't remember the last time the alarm actually had a chance to go off. It doesn't matter though, as long as I'm up to start the day.

I check my phone again. Vince still hasn't written me back.

I look at the last message he sent me. It reads, *1 month*. I have one month with her until the Cassanos want proof that she's dead.

One month, my ass. I'm not giving her up in a month. No fucking way. I've only just gotten my hands on her.

I calm myself by thinking about how she's safe here. Having her in her room soothes the beast inside of me. My kitten is where she belongs, and she's adjusting well.

She cried for nearly an hour last night. I hated watching her break down like that. It's only natural though. And now that it's out of her system, she's taken to her surroundings well. She checked everywhere for an escape though. I chuckle as I make my way to the monitors in the closet.

Her alarm is going to go off at 7 a.m., and she's still curled up in bed. I imagine she's going to want to fight me on this one. She's used to getting up at 8 a.m. I'd be happy to let her have the extra hour, if she asks. I may prime her to ask for permission so she can see that I'm willing to adjust for her. But I'm not sure she'll bring it up and risk going back to the cell. She might be afraid that even just asking me will displease me. Her fear is a big part of what's holding us back. I just need to give her time and let that dissipate.

I watch her sleeping peacefully and something inside of me seems to shift into place. I know everything is going to work out perfectly. Every ounce of worry leaves me.

I walk with purpose to the bathroom and go about my daily ritual. I look at my reflection in the mirror and run my hand over the stubble on my jaw. I need to get myself together before I go to her. And she should be doing the same for me. She isn't though.

I cluck my tongue before pulling out the razor and shaving cream.

I'm happy about that. This will be a perfect training opportunity. I asked her if she needed me to explain what being a submissive means, and she said no. She was wrong. Obviously my little kitten missed some vital information in her books. She should always be presentable for me. I can't wait to show her what happens when she doesn't meet my expectations. My kitten's in for a treat.

As I rinse the razor in a hot stream of water, my phone pings. I close my eyes with frustration.

I've told them I'm taking some time off, but Tommy insists I'm needed. I'd do anything for my brother, but sometimes he gets on my fucking nerves.

I text him back that I'll meet him later tonight. I just want to enjoy this, but instead I feel tense. It's because I know they're going to take her from me.

They can't.

He said I could have this.

He gave me his word.

I don't give a fuck about the business that we get from the Cassanos, or what their expectations were. I bought her, so she's mine to do whatever I fucking want with her.

And right now, I want to get information from her, whip her ass for not being ready and then have her writhing beneath me.

My shoulders loosen up and I let out an easy breath as my dick springs to life. Maybe if I just keep all the blood in my cock I won't get so fucking worked up over Vince and his lack of a god damned backbone.

I splash some water on my face and pat it dry. I'm only in pajama pants that are hanging low on my hips, and my erection is obvious. That's good though. I want her to know how much I want her.

I look back in the mirror and breathe easy.

It's only me and her right now.

Time to play with my kitten.

CATHERINE

I wake up with a shriek ripped from my throat as a hard hand smacks against my ass.

I bolt upright from the bed and grab the covers, pulling them close to my body as I stare wide-eyed at Anthony. My heart beats rapidly with fear, but then is replaced by something else entirely. The brief dread that I feel fucking vanishes.

Holy fuck, he looks like he came straight off the cover of my favorite smutty novels. That chiseled "V" at his hips and his hard and lean muscular body are exactly what I've longed to wake up to. Except that he just spanked me, and he's looking at me like I kicked his puppy.

I have no fucking clue what I did to piss him off. I slowly move into a submissive position, watching him cautiously. But his eyes aren't on me. They're on my ass and probably admiring the bright red mark he left.

"Nice of you to wake up." He finally gives me a clue as to what I did wrong. His tone is playful and it eases a small part of me, but I can't forget. This is an illusion and a game to him. I can't relax; I need to keep my guard up. I pull at the hem of the nightgown I'm wearing. It's the longest one I found in the dresser, but it still shows far too much of my ass.

My eyes home in on the clock on the nightstand, but I can't see the time. I vaguely remember smacking that annoying fucker when the alarm woke me up earlier. My heart sinks, and my stomach drops with fear. Day one, and already I've fucked this up. I didn't fucking know, although I should have.

"What do you have to say for yourself?" he asks with a heated stare.

I'm fucking exhausted because a psycho took me from my home and said psycho happens to get up earlier than I do. Add that to the list of things that make you a prick.

I clear my throat as softly as possible and decide to apologize. I can't risk getting in even more trouble right now. I can't go back to the cell. I remember how nice he was last night, I just need to appeal to that side of him. "I'm sorry, Anthony. I didn't realize."

"You're supposed to be presentable for me." His voice is stern.

I keep my eyes on his as my breathing picks up. He's right, I should've known that. It's not like I thought I could sleep in and lounge around all day.

"I wasn't sure when you'd be here," I say as softly as my voice allows.

"You should *always* be ready." He walks to the nightstand and picks up the clock, holding it out for me to see. "But this should give you a pretty good fucking clue as to when I'll be here."

A yawn creeps up on me and I really do try to hold it in. But I can't stop myself, and I literally let out a huge yawn as he's reprimanding me. I cover my mouth with my hand and shake my head. "I'm sorry, I didn't--"

"You didn't what?" he asks with a hard edge. His eyes narrow as he sets the clock down with more grace and care than is needed. I can tell he's trying to hold in his anger. A darkness I haven't seen yet gathers around him. Fuck, this isn't good.

"I'm sorry, Anthony. I didn't mean to upset you." Fear heats my blood as I scoot backward on the bed. "I didn't mean to yawn. It just slipped out, and I didn't know about the time."

"You seem to have relaxed a little too much, kitten. Did you forget who you are?" he asks. His words send chills down my spine and strike fear into my heart.

I don't know how to respond; my mouth opens, but words don't come out. I don't know what he wants me to say. He puts his knee on the bed and reaches out, grabbing my ankle and dragging me across the bed. The nightgown travels up my body and I desperately try to keep it down. But I don't struggle against his hold, and I don't fight him. I let him drag me over to him.

"Mine. That's who you are. You. Are. *Mine.*" His anger wanes as I look back at him. He commands me in a calmer tone. "Say it."

I hold his gaze and answer quickly. "Yours. I'm yours." His chest rises and falls with his steadying breath. My pussy clenches as I see how my words have tamed him somewhat. I love the power I have over him, but I'm not a fool, and this isn't right. It's wrong. What I feel for him, this entire situation--it's all wrong.

He's still trying to calm himself down and I know I need to say something to make him less angry with me. "I will be pres--present--" I try to tell him I'll be ready for him at all times. But I stumble over the words. Although he hasn't hit me, I'm scared to death he will. Or worse, that he'll throw me back into the cell and leave me there.

"Shh." His hand cups my chin and he looks me in the eyes. "You will be presentable for me by 8 a.m. every morning. Unless that's too early for you?" He cocks his head at me, daring me to disagree.

I swallow the lump in my throat and nod my head. "Yes, Anthony." He looks back at me like he's waiting for more. But I don't know what he wants me to say.

After a moment he asks, "Have you disobeyed me?"

I shake my head no. My breathing becomes erratic as I wonder if I've defied him unintentionally. "I didn't mean to. Not on purpose."

"I know you haven't. But you also haven't been a very good pet, have you?"

"I'm sorry. I'll be better." I don't want to go back to the cell. I can't go back there. My heart begins to thump painfully in my chest as I imagine being imprisoned there again. I'll be better for him. I know I can be better.

"You need to try harder, or this will never work." I search his eyes for sympathy or understanding, but I see nothing. He doesn't wait for me to speak as he continues.

"Right now, for instance. You're hesitating to answer me. You aren't speaking to me. You aren't ready." I draw in a short breath at the no-nonsense list of shit I've done to displease him already. The worst part is that I really should know better. I've read dozens or more books about submissives and dominants. I know all about power exchanges--fuck, I've fantasized about it. And yet here I am. Failing at it. Failing at being a submissive pet like I've dreamt about.

"I don't like that," he says quietly. Fear grips my heart as I register his words. I can do this. I can be better. I need to be better so he keeps me. At least until I can get the fuck out of here. "I'm going to punish you for it."

I start to shake my head; my body feels paralyzed. It was just one mistake. I can fix it. "Please don't send me back--"

"No, kitten," he says as he strokes my cheek and looks me square in the eyes. I instantly close my eyes and hold my breath. "Not a punishment for disobeying me." He gently pulls me by the hands into a seated position and pets my hair. "The kind of punishment that will push your limits and end with both of us being satisfied." His anger completely vanishes as he gives me a small smirk and says, "You know the type of punishment I'm talking about."

Everything in my body relaxes as I nod back and reply, "Yes." I know what he means, and the thought makes my blood race. I have to break his gaze as a blush comes over me and my core heats. What the fuck is wrong with me?

A low chuckle rises in his chest.

"Now that you're here, kitten, it's time to really start playing." I look anywhere but his eyes and end up staring right at the erection in his pants. Oh, fuck, another wave of arousal hits me. I close my eyes and try to ignore it. This is just pretend. This is something I need to get through until I can escape.

I feel the bed dip, and I know he's sitting next to me. I slowly open my eyes as he speaks. "Time to be a good pet and take your punishment, kitten." I want to ask him why he's doing this. I want to ask him to just let me go. But a darker side of me wants to be punished. I want to feel the pain turn to pleasure, just like I've read about before. I want those scenes to come to life. I crawl on my knees and move to drape my body over his lap with my hips atop his thighs. I know that I have this coming. I have to be better next time. It'll be easy. I've read so many god damned books so I should fucking ace this.

I think about them as he slips my gown up to my waist. I'm not wearing any underwear because he simply didn't provide me with any. My heart sputters in my chest as his hand caresses one of my ass cheeks and then the other. My body is stiff and I keep waiting for the smack every time I feel his hand lift up, but he just continues to massage my ass, drawing out my punishment. I turn my head to the side and just breathe. My shoulders ease lower and I close my eyes, enjoying his touch.

He positions me across his lap and places one of his legs over mine. My eyes open, and I know it's coming. A hand gentles on my ass and then lifts before landing hard with a loud *smack*!

"Fuck!" I yell out, and resist trying to move away. My eyes scrunch as another hard, stinging smack lands on my right cheek and then again on my left. I ball my hands into fists and close my eyes tightly as the stinging makes my eyes water. My throat closes, and I can't help that I flinch at the next smack. Tears leak from my eyes. Fuck, it hurts. Fucking hell. I cover my face with my hands as another hard smack lands on my ass and forces a scream from me.

I prepare for another blow, but it doesn't come. He rubs my tender ass and whispers, "You're close, kitten. So close." My ass feels so fucking hot and so damn sore that even the faintest soothing touch stings. He lifts his hand and brings it down over the crack of my ass. His fingertips barely touch my pussy. I try to arch my back as a warmth stirs in my belly. I shake my head as he continues my spanking. Soon the stinging pain turns into a numbing sensation, and the numbness is replaced by something else. Something hot and delightful that makes my core clench.

I groan into the sheets as his hand slaps my tender skin repeatedly. He pauses to rub my ass, and I find myself moving against him.

"Stay still, kitten," he says as a warning. His fingers dip between the folds of my pussy.

"Yes, Anthony." The words fall from my lips with lust. He raises his hand, and another hard spank greets my ass. "Uhh!" I scream out as my body bows. I've never felt this before, this heated need for more. I writhe under him, but then remember his command.

Still.

I force myself to remain motionless as more blows rain down on my ass. Right, left, center. Over and over again. Each time he hits the center, his fingers sink lower.

The pain morphs into something entirely different and I feel myself rise higher and higher. My head thrashes as I try to resist, but my body betrays me. I'm fucking soaking wet for him. After a few more hard swats, he stops and leans down, planting a kiss on my left ass cheek.

"What do you say, kitten?" he asks as his hands gently caress my ass.

I have no fucking clue what he's talking about. My heart beats faster with the desire of wanting to answer him correctly. And then it hits me.

"Thank you for my punishment," I say just above a murmur.

His fingers travel down my ass and over my puckered hole. My lungs stop as his fingertips hover there. They prod slightly, but only for a moment. Then they travel lower and dig into my heat. The feeling is so unexpected, and so shockingly needed.

I grind on his hand as his fingers pump in and out of me. I moan into the sheets shamelessly. He pulls them out, only to move the moisture to my clit and circle it with no mercy. My back stiffens and my body tingles as every part of me is on edge. And then he pinches my hardened nub and I shatter. I fall off the edge and break, with waves of pleasure controlling every inch of my body. It's a paralyzing release that leaves me breathless.

It's quiet for a long moment as I lie limp across his lap. Finally he breaks the silence. "Good job, kitten. You did really well. I'm proud of you." For some reason his praise makes my heart swell. I quickly look away and try to ignore the warmth I feel in my chest. Not to mention his fucking erection digging into my stomach.

He reaches over me to grab something off the nightstand, but I don't see what it is. I hear a cap snap open and I hiss as a cool dab of cream lands on one ass cheek and then the other. He chuckles, and it's the sexiest fucking sound I've ever heard. He gently rubs the cream into my skin and I practically purr with affection. *Aftercare.* A small smile plays at my lips, but then I remember everything. Shame replaces every good feeling. I swallow as spikes seem to grow in my throat. *What the fuck just happened?*

He reaches over to the nightstand for something else, and this time I look. My brow furrows as I catch a glimpse of something that I'm almost positive is a syringe.

He stabs the needle into my ass, making me wince before I can do a damn thing about it. After a second he pulls it out and rubs the tender spot. "There kitten, now you've had your shots."

I look at him from the corner of my eye as he lifts me off his lap to sit next to him. Fuck, my ass hurts! I'm too scared to ask what the shot was, but I can't take my eyes off of it. I need to know what he's putting into my body. I swallow thickly and bite out the words.

"Anthony, what was that?"

"A shot of Depo-Provera," he answers confidently.

Birth control.

He sits me upright, making me cringe from the stinging sensation and moves off the bed. I keep my head lowered and try not to show how fucking worried I am.

"I'll be back in one hour. Be ready for me this time." He cups my chin in his hand. "I've been going easy on you, so don't make me regret that."

His lips hover an inch away from mine, but he doesn't lean in. My breathing picks up and I wait for him to kiss me. But he doesn't.

He drops his hand and walks quickly to the door.

"One hour. Don't disappoint me, kitten."

CATHERINE

$\mathcal{I}$ breathe in deep and look at my reflection as I layer on one more coat of mascara. The cabinet is filled with high-end beauty products that are all brand new. It also contains my makeup bag, which he obviously stole from my house.

I've been watching the clock like a hawk.

My hair's tied back in a loose braid, and my makeup is clean and natural-looking, just enough to cover the imperfections.

The closet is stuffed with all sorts of clothing. From cocktail dresses, to slutty role-playing costumes, to everyday pieces that I actually love. He also brought along a duffel bag packed with a few items that I wear all the time.

The variety of clothing, makeup, and accessories is strangely familiar. Some things I recognize as mine, but the new additions are all nicer, more luxurious versions of what I already own.

The one thing he didn't grab were the owl earrings my mother left me.

They were hers, and when she found out she only had three months left to live, she gave them to me.

They're gorgeous. I'd admired them since I was a little girl. The earrings are yellow gold with ruby flowers in the centers of the owls, but I've never worn them. I was always too afraid I'd lose them. And now they're gone.

I tilt my head back and exhale, waving my hands around my face to cool my eyes and keep me from crying. It's almost time, and I can't ruin my makeup and piss him off.

I don't know why I was so lackadaisical when he came in this morning. Maybe it's because I slept so damn well. It took forever to actually get to sleep, but when I did, I slept wonderfully. I guess allowing myself to cry some helped. I'm not sure why I wasn't more alert this morning. Maybe it's because he was so lenient last night, but whatever the reason, I can't let it happen again.

I calm myself down and put the mascara back. Everything's neat and put away. It makes me feel at ease. I just need to make the bed and then I can wait for him.

I always make my bed in the morning. I think staying at home all day has made me a tidier person than I ever was before. So long as I'm capable of making the bed, I'm able to do anything. I snort a humorless laugh as I move the sheets into place and reach for the duvet. It's so pretty and soft. It's off-white, with thin silver threading making a paisley design throughout.

I bend at the waist to lay my head down on the bed and love how I sink in to the mattress and smell the comforting scent of fresh laundry. As I inhale deeply, I hear the doorknob turn and the door slowly open. I quickly climb the bed and kneel at the end of it. I don't know if this is where he wants me. My heart races. I don't know any of his preferences. He never told me. He may want my hair a certain way, my makeup to be heavier, or my clothes to be different. I have no fucking clue. I need to ask him. He hasn't given me anything. He's not playing fair.

As soon as I find out what kind of mood he's in, I'm asking. So long as it's a good mood.

I hear him walk by the sofa and toward the bed, but I don't look up. I keep my head bowed and wait. I'm on my knees, sitting back on my heels with my hands slightly in front of me, palms up.

I've read a lot of books and there are so many damn positions. I don't know which one he means by kneel. For Christ's sake, in movies they kneel on one foot, but I'm sure he doesn't mean that though.

I watch as he picks up my hand and places it gently on my thigh and does the same with the other. His fingers tilt my chin up so I have to look at him.

"No need to bow, kitten." He pets my hair as he talks. It's soothing and rhythmic. "I want your eyes on me always. You never have to look away."

"Yes, Anthony." I feel like I'm playing a role. It gives me a small thrill, but I have to remember this is an act. All of this is an act.

"Did you find everything you need?" he asks.

I look up at him through my lashes. He's so fucking handsome. It still amazes me that he felt the need to take a woman when he could have anyone he wanted. That a man like him would stoop this low. I realize I haven't answered his question and bite my lip. I want to tell him I want more of my things, but I can't. I'm too scared to do anything to upset him. Because of that, I merely nod my head in assent.

"So I packed everything that you need, then?" he asks with slight disbelief in his tone. The way he says it makes me feel like I'd be a liar now to tell him that I want more of my things. My skin heats and I feel nauseated. I feel trapped in a corner, like no matter what I do, it'll be wrong.

"Kitten," he says as he leans my body against his chest and runs soothing strokes along my back.

"You can tell me anything. I promise I won't get mad," he says.

"I want to go home." The words fall out easily. As though they've been perched there, waiting for me to release them.

"I know you do, but you can't." He keeps petting my back and I hate him for it. I want to move out of his embrace, but at the same time I don't. I need the comfort.

"What else did you want to ask?" he says. I'm quiet for a moment and he adds, "If you want certain things, you'll need to ask for them."

"I have other things I want," I say softly into his chest. I wait with bated breath for his reaction.

"We'll go together. Later tonight." His answer surprises me so much I go completely still. I'm afraid if I move, or if I even breathe, he'll change his mind.

"I want you to be happy here. You know that, don't you?" he asks.

"Yes, Anthony." I respond with the only answer that seems fit, but really, I don't know that to be true. He wants me here to serve him. To play his fucked up game. He doesn't want me here to be happy. He's not doing me any god damned favors.

He finally releases me and I maintain my position.

He looks me over, assessing me before taking me by my hand.

"It's time for breakfast, kitten." He leads me off the bed and to the door.

We're leaving the room. Hope rises in my chest. I wait for the sash, but he doesn't pull it out. Maybe he'll let his guard down today, and I'll have a chance to run.

He looks back at me as he enters in the code. I bite my bottom lip and look away. Damn it. He grunts a laugh and it pisses me off. At the click he opens the door and reaches out to prop it open with his foot. I consider grabbing the door, swinging it open and running. My heart beats fast and adrenaline rushes through my blood at the thought. But I don't do it. I watch as he wheels in a steel cart and the door slowly closes. My eyes fall to the ground and I feel like a fucking coward.

"Now now, kitten, stop that." I look up at my captor, at my dom, with sad eyes.

"I just want to go home." I say the words again and I'm sure I sound pathetic.

"You are home," he says absolutely. It crushes something inside me and I have to work hard not to cry. I stand there while he wheels the cart over to the sofa and sets up covered dishes on the coffee table. I look between him and the locked door.

It could be so much worse. He was supposed to kill me. I close my eyes and steady my breathing as I consider how many other ways this could have gone. I just need to behave. He can't keep me here forever.

"Come, kitten." My feet move toward him before I'm even fully conscious of his command.

I start to sit on the sofa, but he holds his hand up and I freeze.

"On your knees," he says.

I only hesitate a fraction of a second before gracefully sitting on my heels. I put my hands on my thighs where he placed them earlier. I can do this. I know I can. And I can win his trust and I can get the fuck out of here. I just need to role-play. I can do it. I know I can.

"Let's play a game, kitten." He starts talking and I give him my full attention, but I don't want to play a game. I want to go home. I want to read my books, talk to my clients, and engage with my group of readers on social media. Every hour I'm away from them kills the interaction rates. It's fucking horrible for business. I breathe in deeply. My books and my work are my life. And he's murdering both of them right now.

"Between every bite we'll ask each other a question." He lifts a silver dome off of a plate and a delicious scent fills my lungs. I inhale deeply, loving the smell of peppers and sausage and eggs. I eye the dish. Omelets. My mouth waters. "Does that sound like fun to you?" he asks.

No, I think, but of course I answer, "Yes."

"Does it really?" he asks, immediately countering my simple answer.

"Fun? No, it doesn't. But it sounds like something to do," I answer honestly out of instinct. I don't have time to be nervous about it. He barks a laugh at my answer and lays a gentle hand on my hair.

"Thank you, kitten." He leans down and plants a kiss in my hair and strokes me gently. It's soothing, and I hate how comforting it is.

I look his body over as he moves to cut a piece of the omelet. I still don't understand why a man like him would do this. I want to ask him. But I'm not going there. I think I'll stick to, *What's the weather like outside, since I can't fucking see it?*

"I'll go first, kitten," he says as he stabs a piece of the egg and puts the fork in front of my mouth. I obediently open and wait for his question. "I know what happened with the Cassanos. But I want you to tell me what you saw." I chew the food slowly as my blood chills. I don't want to talk about it. I also don't know if this is a test. Maybe he really does work for them. Maybe this is all a ploy of some sort. Anxiety creeps up on me. As if reading my mind, he reassures me.

"It's not a trick. I'm just curious how it happened." He sets the fork down as I swallow.

"Would it help if I tell you what I know?" he asks. I nod my head, still unable to speak. Everything that happened fucking destroyed me. I may have been a sweet, shy, book-loving nerd before, but at least I was strong and confident. Going through that shit robbed me of that. I don't want to go back to that fucked up place.

"You saw three of their soldiers kill Judge Hawthort. He was killed by Michael Davis, and Joseph and Brandon Becker. And later you were able to identify them all as well as account for their missing kilos of dope," he says.

I shake my head no and say, "He was alive. I'm fairly sure he was alive." I didn't testify that I saw him dead, and I'm confident that he was alive at the time that I witnessed everything. His body was never found though. It's a very real possibility that he's dead simply because I saw them. Talking about this triggers the memory. I see the hammers in their hands and hear the sound of

Brandon smashing his against the judge's knee. He was alive. I hear his screams echo in my head. The bricks and the bags are there. My body turns to ice.

He holds another bite to my lips; my appetite is gone, but I take it. "What else did you see?" he asks.

"Nothing. I never saw anything else," I say.

"They were charged with more," he points out.

"Nothing that I testified to," I answer quickly.

"But you testified to attempted rape and kidnapping?" he asks.

I look away and nod.

"I have another question for you and then I'll lighten it up, kitten." My eyes fall. I don't want another question. This game fucking blows. "I want you to be honest."

I wait nervously for his question.

"Did they touch you?" I know what he's getting at.

I shake my head no. "They tried," I answer, looking to the floor. "That's when I left." Not a single one of them did. Not even Lorenzo. He was having too much fun beating me for sport.

"What about your boyfriend?" he asks. I fucking hate that I ever called him that. Lorenzo helped me escape the pain of losing my mother. He made me feel free and wild. And then he destroyed me. I shake my head no, and I don't realize until Anthony says something, but my hand moves to my cheek.

"He hit you?" I lock my eyes on Anthony's. His voice is calm. He's been calm the entire time. But his eyes spark with a darkness I never want to see directed at me. I give one curt nod in response. I'm ashamed that I let Lorenzo hurt me. I'm ashamed that it all ever happened.

He scoops a piece of omelet onto the fork and holds it out for me.

I take it simply to fill my mouth so I don't have to talk.

"Your turn, kitten. Ask me anything."

CATHERINE

I can ask him anything at all. Anything I want. "Why me?" I ask simply. I want to know what I did that put a target on my back.

"Well. I told you I was supposed to kill you," he says. The reminder makes my stomach churn. "You were on my list, and like everyone on my list, I did a little digging. In your case, I liked what I found." He spears a small piece of pepper and puts it to my lips.

"Have you...done this before?" I ask before accepting the bite. I fucking hope the answer is no. If it's yes, I know what my next question will be, but I'm afraid of the answer. *Did you kill them when you were done with them?*

"I've played before, but it was only play. You're the first real submissive I've had. And the first complete 24/7 power exchange."

I don't know why, but I hate that there were others before me.

"What happened to them?" I ask before receiving another bite.

"We weren't a good fit," he answers without looking at me. It's the first time he's done that, and I don't like it.

"What did you do to them?" I ask before I can think twice.

He cocks a brow at me. "You mean, did I kill them?" he asks.

My throat closes as I answer in a choked voice, "Yes."

"No, kitten. I didn't kill them." He doesn't answer my unspoken question. *If we don't fit, will he kill me?* He holds another piece out for me to take. But I shake my head. I'm not hungry. The thought of eating another bite makes me sick to my stomach. Of course he will. I'm already supposed to be dead. If we don't fit, or once he's done with me, I'll be dead.

Tears prick my eyes, but I push them back. I need to be good. I need to be fucking perfect until I can get out of here. And the first chance I get, I need to run as fast as I can. I can never stop running. Never.

His strong arms wrap around me as he picks me up and pulls me into his lap to lean against his chest. "I chose you for a reason, kitten." He gently strokes my back and I concentrate on how good it feels to distract myself from the pain. He kisses my hair and then pets me as I lay my head flat against his hard, hot body. I hear his heart beating as he speaks. "You fit me, and this is exactly what I wanted. *You* are exactly what I want."

For now. I focus on the plan. Survive until I'm given an opportunity. I'll be as perfect as I can be. I'll make him want to keep me. I pull back and he readjusts me so I'm sitting in his lap.

I don't know what to say to move past this, but I really just want to move forward and forget that this breakdown ever happened.

"Do you like your new home?" he asks. I'm grateful to discuss a more casual topic, but I can't forget that the fact he's even asking me that question is fucked up. I didn't need a new home. I loved my cabin, and I want to go back.

I glance around the room again. It's as perfect as a gilded cage can be. "Yes, it's beautiful."

"Do you have everything that you need?" he asks.

"There are a few things I'd like to get," I say quietly.

"Yes, you told me that. Other than a few trinkets, is there anything important that I've forgotten?" I feel like he already knows the answer to his question. Like this is a test.

What's the one thing I need here? One thing he hasn't given me is my laptop. I'm afraid to ask for it. It'd be stupid to ask. There's no way he'd let me go online.

He reaches past me to the cart and my mouth drops open.

"I told you earlier, you only need to ask," he says.

I stare at my laptop in his hands. My fucking life is on there. I reach out to take it, expecting him to snatch it away, but he doesn't. Instead he kisses my hair and gently rubs my back. I hug it to my chest and wait for the other shoe to drop.

"Go ahead. I know you have work to do." I swallow the lump in my throat and slowly open my MacBook Pro. It's ten years old. I got it in college. It's really past time to get a new one, but I fucking love my baby.

I type in my password, and the same screen pops up that's greeted me every morning for the last year. It's a meme that says, "You can't read all day, if you don't start in the morning!" I can't help my smile. I instinctively look to check the internet connection. I have a few books loaded on here that I need to put on my Kindle, but what I really need to do is catch up with my FB group and my blogs, plus the editor for my column. I also need to check my email, my website for beta readers, my Goodreads account, and the reading groups online. I take a deep breath and click on my web browser and then hold my breath and stiffen as the screen pops up. I quickly hit exit and look back to Anthony self-consciously.

"Go ahead, kitten. I want to watch you work." I release a breath I didn't know I was holding and look back at Anthony with disbelief.

"I told you I'd give you your life back. I'm a man of my word." I search his eyes for anything but sincerity, but that's all I see. I bite my lip and look back to the computer.

I have work to do, and this is going to take me fucking forever. I shift in his lap. This isn't going to work, but I don't want to push my luck.

"You typically write on your bed, don't you?" he asks.

A chill runs through me at the reminder that he watched me before taking me. "I do."

"Go ahead. I'll sit here. I have a book I'd like to read." It takes a moment for his words to sink in, but when they do, I take my chances and get my ass up and move to the bed with my laptop. I keep my eyes on him as I put the pillow against the headboard for support, and another on my lap for the computer. I've always typed this way. I imagine I always will. It's a bad habit to break.

I watch as Anthony rises and walks to the bookshelf, choosing a paperback and lying down on the sofa. He crosses his ankles and it's the sexiest sight I've ever seen.

It's fucking unreal that he's letting me get online.

Something's up though. And I don't fucking like it. Everything is a test. Every last fucking thing. My eyes stay on him as I type in my password. My email is slow to open, but it does. I click on my emails one at a time and type my responses, but I keep looking back to Anthony. He simply turns a page, appearing fully engrossed in his reading.

I feel so fucking uneasy. He's not at all what I expected, and the thought that I'd be able to do this is just...insane. He's fucking insane. Not just mentally unstable, but certifiably insane if he thinks I'm not going to message some-one--anyone--that I've been taken. I don't give a fuck that he's been nice, or that he's hot, or that this is literally a fucking dark dream come true for me. There's no way I'm not going to try to get the hell out of here.

I click on a new tab and bring up Facebook. Cheryl's my personal assistant and my go-to gal for everything. My cursor hovers over the box to message her, but she's already sent me five messages. The third one was her freaking out that I didn't respond at all yesterday, but the fourth and fifth are her fixing my shit and wishing me well because she refuses to believe that I'm dead and I better fucking message her back or she'll find me and kill me. Yeah, that's Cheryl.

I type in a lame excuse and don't mention shit. Yet. I want to. Every fucking voice inside of me is screaming to do something and tell someone. But I'd be stupid to think I'd get away with it, right? I watch Anthony for a minute as I copy and paste an email to send to another reader.

What would he do to me if I did? Kill me. The answer is obvious, but he hasn't hurt me yet. My ass smarts at the thought. It still fucking hurts, although the cream he rubbed in did wonders for the worst of the pain. I don't know where I am. I'm not sure that there's any way they'd find me.

Hey, Cheryl. Some psycho took me, I'm not sure where. Could you figure out a way for someone to rescue me?

Yeah...that's not going to fucking work. My heart races and my fingers itch to type something, *anything* to help me get the fuck out of here.

I will be good. I will not email the police and post all over social media that I've been kidnapped. 'Cause that would be fucking obvious. But I could sure as fuck sneak in some clues.

I type in, *Busy with Comfort Food*, hoping she'll catch on. It's a classic book where the heroine is kidnapped. I hope she understands and catches the subtlety. Maybe she can help me. She can relay information for me, and I can figure out where the fuck I am.

She instantly replies, *Whatcha eating?*

Jesus, Cheryl. I barely keep myself from rolling my eyes. As I consider what to type next, Anthony's phone pings in his pocket. He takes it out and looks at it and then right at me. My heart stops. But he merely gives me a tight smile and goes back to his book.

I can't help but think that message was about me. That I'd been caught. My skin prickles with goosebumps and my hands shake. What would he do if he caught me? What good would it do for people to know I'd been taken if they had no way to find me? It takes me a moment, but I'm finally able to type back, *Omelets, brb.*

No more of that shit. I go back to checking all of my notifications. I post a few memes, along with a fun pic of a hot man with a question for the readers to answer about Linda's new book release. I download four betas to my Kindle as I message three authors that I'm a day behind. The hours tick by as I make small dents in my work.

I only look up when I see Anthony rise and stretch. I hold my breath and wait for him as he strides toward me.

"I'll be back, kitten." He leans down and looks over my computer for only a second and then gives me a smile. I feel that sexual tension between us, the need to lean forward and kiss him.

But instead his brows furrow and he looks back at the screen, reading over the posts in my group. After a moment he breaks the silence. "I wonder what your group would suggest, kitten," he says, taking a seat next to me. His arm wraps around my waist. Like this is normal, like we're a couple.

"Ask them this." It's a command.

I click the box and prepare to type in a question. My heart beats chaotically in my chest as he tells me what to write. "What would you do if you woke up in a basement and a man gave you two choices: die, or be his?" I type in his words and hover over the submit button. It's fucking insane that he's having me ask them. But it's also a common thing I do. I pose a question by picking a scenario from a common trope to engage them. I already know what most will answer.

I hit enter, and it doesn't take long for them to start commenting. They love these questions, and frankly, so do I. But not this one. Because this is real.

"Well, your friends have some good ideas as to what you should be doing." I consider pointing out the comment from a reader about gouging his eyes out, but I don't.

I read down the list of responses. Nearly forty comments already. Most say the same thing.

Be his!

I choose the second option!

Well, if he's hot--that's a no brainer!

All their responses seem so natural online. They're meant for humor, and to be cheeky replies. A week ago, I would have said the same. But it's not *real*. You wouldn't really do that. It's not that easy. I want to yell at Anthony. I'm pissed that he would do that shit to me, that he would make me feel like I'm the one holding back.

"Given that the choice is to die or to be his, it's clearly a given." I read the words flatly. It's one of the comments, but also the truth. I keep my voice even and my eyes on the screen.

I can feel Anthony's eyes on me, and I regret opening my mouth at all. I can't look at him, so I stare at the screen. The comments continue coming in.

Agree to be his...duh! lol

Well I wouldn't make it easy for him...

Agree! It could be hot as hell ;)

I close the laptop and try to swallow the lump growing in my throat. I can't read them. I hate the ease at which the replies come in. Normally I love them. I love my group of readers and authors. But right now I can't stand how easy they make giving in sound. Anthony pulls the laptop from me and cradles me in his lap.

"I just wanted you to see why it was easy to pick you." His voice is gentle and it vibrates up his chest. I lean deeper into him. "You're primed to enjoy this because deep down you know how good this can be."

I shake my head against his broad shoulders. Those are fantasies.

He grips my chin in his hand and leans into me. Our lips are closer than they have ever been before. "Real life and fantasy can blur, kitten. This can be whatever you want it to be."

My heart aches in my chest. *Be his.* How easy it seems to give in.

And I do. A piece of my armor cracks enough that I lean into his embrace and brush my lips against his. He doesn't kiss back, not at first. And it kills something deep down inside of me. Before I can pull away, his hands grip my hips and he pushes me down onto the bed and kisses me with passion. His erection rubs against my clit and he rocks against me as our tongues meet and our kiss turns into something more. I feel my walls falling down around me. It would be so easy to give in to him. To live something I've only ever thought would be a dream.

Just as the word touches my tongue, *please*, he pulls back and stands, leaving me panting and lost in lust. I slowly push myself into a sitting position as he climbs off the bed and gives me a heated glare. I know he wants me. I would have begged him though.

I close my eyes and turn back to my computer. A moment of silence passes. I fucking would have begged him. I was going to do it. What the ever loving fuck is wrong with me?

"Time's up, kitten," he says, reaching for the laptop.

"I need to work." I speak without thinking. His eyes narrow and I reword my plea. "I'm really far behind. Please, Anthony." I sound so pathetic and weak. I hate it. *I'm so fucking weak.*

"You can download the books and write your articles without going online," he answers, and he's partly right, but he's fucking wrong, too. I have to be available. That's why I'm so successful. I respond immediately. If they need something done, I get it done that fucking second. Yesterday took a toll on my work already. I'm going to have to bust ass to get it back up. And his internet is so god damned slow that everything is taking longer than it should.

"You don't understand, I have to be available," I say.

"You want to be able to go online without being monitored?" he asks.

I nod my head even as I realize how ridiculous my request is. But he said he'd give me my life back. And this is my life. It's my passion.

"Alright, kitten," he says as though it's perfectly normal. As though there's no harm whatsoever in allowing me to do this without him here. I remember the ping from his earlier text. But that had to have been a coincidence.

Hope rises in my chest. Maybe I can get the fuck out of here after all. I don't need him fucking with my emotions and manipulating me into fucking begging him like he just did. He hands me back the computer and I take it as gently as possible to hide my intentions. I'm going to escape. I just need to figure out how.

ANTHONY

I have shit to do, but I'm waiting. I know she's going to push.
Especially after leaving her all hot and panting for my touch like I did. I walk about five steps away from her door and lean against the wall. If I've learned anything about my sweet little pet, it's that she acts on impulse. And right now, she's not too happy with me. But she needs to learn that she's not always going to get what she wants. I readjust my erection and think back to how she writhed under me. She fucking wanted me. But she didn't beg. And I had to get the fuck off of her before I broke my word.

I log on to my phone that's now on silent and go through the alerts. There's a logger on her computer and I set up a script to monitor what she's doing. Even shit that she types, but doesn't send. Titles of books or authors that could trigger clues. Words and phrases or certain sites that she'd think of going on. There's also a feed. I can watch everything she's doing as she's doing it. And I can veto it, too. I go through the list of triggers again. Three triggers- -*Comfort Food*, "help me, please", and "taken." The last two triggers seem harmless enough in context, but that first one? I know what my kitten was up to. I thought about going over and busting her ass. But I'm gonna wait until she makes a clear offense. Something she can't deny is wrong.

I lean my head against the wall realizing what that means. I don't want her back in the cell. But she's going back. I'd bet my life on it. And that fucking sucks. I was hoping we'd make more progress; I was sure we would, but I was wrong.

Ping. Another notification pops up and I'm quick to hit--blackout. My kitten is about to freak the fuck out. I hear her cuss and move around in the room. Her screen just went black, and she sure as fuck knows why. I pocket my phone and punch in the key code to her room. I check my other pocket for the sash and it's there. Good. I'm gonna need it. I've got all sorts of shit I use for work out here in the hall. She doesn't need to see that and think it's for her.

I open the door and examine her room. She's nowhere in sight, and the room is silent.

I close the door behind me quietly. "Kitten," I call out for her, but she doesn't respond. Even I have to agree the calm manner I'm calling out with is creepy as fuck. But it's better that I'm calm. She's already on edge, and I can't push her away with my anger. She's scared, and I don't need her to turn violent. She would. I'm sure she would.

"Kitten, you will answer me." I take a few steps past the living room area and into her bedroom. "Do you want to make this even harder on yourself?" I ask. There's only a hint of anger in my words. I don't want her scared of me. I want her scared of displeasing me. There's a very big difference.

"I'm sorry, Anthony." I hear her words as I open her closet doors. They came from behind me. I look at the bed, and then at the space underneath. Oh, how...pitiful. I walk over and stand where she should be able to see me, if she has a view from wherever she is under there. At least I feel a little relief knowing she responded to me at all. That's a good sign.

"Kitten, you need to come out," I say.

"Please," she begs with a sob. She sounds remorseful and truly upset. And she should be.

"Please what, kitten?" I ask.

"Please don't kill me," she whimpers. I close my eyes and pinch the bridge of my nose as I exhale with frustration.

"I'm not going to hurt you, kitten." My words come out soft to help her relax somewhat. "I can promise you I won't. You already know your punishment." I hear her sniffle amidst the small sounds of movement. "I knew I'd have to wait to leave. At least I can say I'm only mildly disappointed that you disobeyed me so quickly. It's best we get this out of your system now." A moment passes, and she doesn't appear. I'll give her one more chance.

"Come out now." I make my voice harder and then regret that I did. She cries louder, but I still don't hear her moving to come out.

"If I have to come get you, you're really gonna regret it." The thought of dragging her out makes my cock jump in my pants. Fuck, I would fucking love it. I can't wait until we're at that point. Once that pussy is all mine, I want her to hide from me so I can punish her. I want to punish that ass with my dick, rather than my hand. Soon. I remind myself that I just need to be patient. If I did it now, it would ruin everything.

As I open my eyes, I see her sliding out. Her small body drags on the floor as she squeezes between the floor and the frame. Poor Catherine. She looks so despondent.

I stand with my arms folded across my chest and watch as she slowly stands up. She hangs her head low and she's angling her body in a way that makes it obvious that she expects me to hit her. She should know that I won't. But she's still going to be punished. It will help her. I remind myself that this needs to happen. She'll learn. I only want the pain to be pleasurable. And this punishment will contain zero pleasure.

"I had to try." She looks at the ground as she speaks, and I fucking hate it.

"You didn't. You didn't *have* to." It makes me angry that she thinks she needed to disobey me. She needs to get over that shit. Hopefully a day and a half in the cell will be enough. "You *chose* to."

I pull out the blindfold and she submits to me, turning around so I can tie it and lead her to the cell.

We're quiet the entire way to the cell. The only sounds are the echoes of our footsteps and her uneven breathing. I pet her back with every step and at times she seems like she's ready to lean into me, but she doesn't. She's rejected my touch, my comfort, my trust. I sigh heavily as I take off the sash and prepare to leave her, but then I see mascara running down her cheeks as she crumples onto the floor and scoots away from me.

I need to wait until she's calm. She'll learn to accept her punishments. When she's fully aware of what she'll receive in return, that knowledge will keep her from failing to obey me.

I lean down and stroke her cheek. "It's alright, kitten." She doesn't respond, but she doesn't move away from me either.

"I'll have to go get your things without you. You need to tell me everything you want." I don't tell her that her things will always be there for her. I plan on keeping up with her mortgage and bills. Every contact that she gets will go through me, and to her, and then back to the sender. I don't need any red flags to go to the WPP. Fuck that.

The reminder of life outside of these walls pisses me off.

None of that will be necessary if I have to kill her at the end of the month. I press my lips into a straight line. That's not going to happen. I've only just started to have my time with her. Vince will give her to me. I bring in so much fucking money with these hits. He'll give me this. I just need to deal with the Cassanos.

"I--" She hesitantly looks at me and then back down, grabbing onto her fingers nervously. "I have a pair of earrings in my armoire." She speaks so quietly I can hardly hear her. "I need them. Please." She looks up at me with a pleading expression. "They're owls," she says as her voice cracks and she breaks down at my feet. She bends over with her hands on the floor as a wretched sob heaves through her chest. She needs me right now. This is more than just being sorry about getting caught. It's more than being ashamed that she broke the rules, or fearing that I'm going to hurt her.

I sit on the floor next to her and pull her shaking shoulders into my embrace.

"I'll make sure to get them. Anything else?" I speak softly into her hair and breathe in her sweet scent. Her small body is so warm against me. She's leaning into me like I'm her savior, regardless of the fact that I'm about to leave her in a cell with nothing.

After a few minutes of me gently petting her back and her hair, she pulls away slightly. She still doesn't look me in the eyes. "I can't remember." She wipes her eyes and sighs. "Nothing I can think of."

I'm going all the way to her house for one pair of earrings. It's nearly two hours away. Obviously they mean something to her though. I give her a curt nod that she doesn't see, because she's not looking at me.

I take her chin in my hand and force her eyes on me. "You'll be here until tomorrow night. That's your punishment."

She noticeably swallows, but nods her head and manages to push out, "Yes, Anthony." Good girl. She's taken this well at least.

I have to leave her. I don't want to, but I do. "I have to go, kitten," I tell her gently. I hate that I'm leaving her in here, but she knew the consequences. It's important for her training that I stick to my word.

She leans against my leg as I pet her hair. I know she doesn't want me to leave, but I have to.

I pat her head to let her know I'm going, and she responds by looking up at me with sad brown eyes, glossed over with tears.

"I promise I won't do it again," she says, but her plea is weak. She's resigned to her fate.

"You earned your punishment, kitten. I'll be back to give you dinner," I say.

With that I turn and leave her. She barely grips my leg, but releases me without me having to scold her.

It fucking hurts my chest as I press the keys to leave.

I wish she hadn't done that shit.

But if I was her, I would have done it, too.

ANTHONY

$\mathcal{R}$igs, Vince's giant ass lab, is lying pathetically on the floor begging. He's a good-looking dog. I look to Vince and say, "See, told you the kids would ruin him. He's a biscuit-begging mutt now."

Vince shakes his head and my brother laughs, taking another drink of his beer. All the women are in the living room with the kids. Usually Rigs goes where the kids go, but we're still in the dining room, and so is the food. Smart dog.

"He was so fucking good before the kids. You could drop a steak a foot from his face and he wouldn't move," Vince jokes, and we all have a laugh even though he's shaking his head.

"God, the kids. Cockblocking and dog ruining," Tommy says with his hands over his eyes. He's worn the fuck out with the little ones. But he still says it with a smile.

"Gotta love 'em though," Vince answers.

"I need another beer," Tommy says with a touch of humor.

"Grab me one, too?" I ask him. He gives me a nod and heads out. Vince gets up from his seat to pour more Jack in his glass.

As soon as no one's looking, I give the dog the last meatball from my plate. He swallows it down so fucking fast there's no way he even tasted it. I chuckle at him and watch him lift his head up higher so he can see what's left up here. Greedy ass dog.

Vince takes the head seat again and leans back with his glass at his lips. When he looks at me this time, there's tension surrounding us. I know what it's about, too. I've been waiting for it.

"We gotta talk, Anthony," he says.

Tommy makes his way back with the beers and passes me one. I don't want him in here for this though. I don't want him to know about Catherine. She's my secret. She's *mine*. I wish even Vince didn't know. It kills me that he does. Even worse is that I know he doesn't understand.

"Hey, bro, could you give us a minute?" I ask Tommy as I pop the cap off my beer. He looks between me and Vince with a touch of confusion, but nods his head with a bit of a frown.

"Everything good?" he asks. He's always worrying about me. He always has.

Vince and I both nod as I answer, "Yeah, I just need a minute."

"Suit yourselves," he says, grabbing a bun off the table. He whistles at Rigs and the dog bounds off after him, wagging his tail.

"You need to take care of her," Vince says the second Tommy's out of earshot.

"See the thing is, I *am* taking care of her, Vince. We had a deal." I put my beer down and lock eyes with him. "I paid, and she's mine."

"They seem to think otherwise." He says the words as though them backing out is acceptable.

"That's their fault. They made an assumption. They were wrong."

"They give us almost thirty percent of the income from the hits, Anthony. *Your* income. You really wanna piss them off?" he asks.

"I couldn't give two fucks about them, to be honest." I say it with a hint of menace in my voice. I take another drink, trying to calm myself down.

Vince looks at me with hesitation. "What's gotten into you? You aren't usually like this."

"Like what? Stubborn? Opinionated?" I ask. I know I'm pushing my boundaries. But I don't care. I'm always on the outside with them. I have been for most of my life. I never ask for anything. This is the first and only request I've ever made.

"Look, I know you have your issues and all." He talks in a hushed tone, and

I fucking hate it. I hate how the entire family feels sympathy for me because of that shit with my mother. They talk about it behind my back. I know they do. But they fucking fear me, too. I'd rather have the fear than the sympathy any fucking day.

"My issues?" I ask, putting the beer down on the table and staring back at Vince like he's going to have to spell it out.

I look back at him, and suddenly he's not the Don. He's one of the boys huddled around the broken, bloodied dumb fuck we were supposed to teach a lesson.

They all stare back at me. I can feel their eyes on me as I breathe heavily and try to calm myself. My shaking fists are dripping with his blood. He had it coming to him. They all know I'm fucked up. He should've known better than to push me.

"You alright, Anthony?" Tommy lays an unsteady hand on my shoulder. I look up at him and past him to see the other guys. They look nervous as fuck. Like they could be next. I'm not a savage. I can contain this. I do contain it. Every fucking day.

"Good job, Anthony." Vince says as he looks between the dead fuck and me. "Pops is gonna be proud." He says the words, but there's more to it than that. I don't know if it's jealousy, or if he hates that he fears me.

That day I decided not to give a fuck about any of them. All of them except for Tommy. Tommy's all I have.

That was the day they started giving me a little more space than normal. I had to push my humor onto them to loosen them up. But it wasn't quite the same. Not with us doing jobs together. Thank fuck for Uncle Dante. He gave me the hits and the other shit I could do on my own. It was a release for me, but more than that, it saved me from being the social pariah. I always knew they felt that way about me. But having Vince say the words...fuck, it hurts to know it's true.

"You know what I mean, Anthony." He straightens his back and meets my gaze head on. I have to hand it to him, he deserves to be boss. But I can fucking smell his fear from here.

"I bought her, and now she's mine. That's what happened. End of story," I say flatly.

"It's not the end. You also agreed to one month, and that's what they were told," he says.

"I didn't--" I start to answer, but he cuts me off.

"You did." He says the words with finality. I never should've said it was his call. It pisses me off. I shouldn't have trusted him. It wasn't his decision to make.

"I have work to do, and I need to get home to check on her before bed."

"Check on her?" he grunts a humorless laugh and it takes everything in me not to plant a fist on his jaw. I can hear Aunt Linda in the kitchen and the kids playing not twenty feet from us. I clench my fists at my side, but hold back. I finish the beer and grab my keys off the table.

Checking on her is my job. This isn't about getting laid, it's not about fucking her or using her, or demeaning her. That's not what I want. This is more than that. It's deeper than Vince could possibly know. It's about having someone *need* me. And she does, whether Vince likes it or not.

"I mean it, Anthony," he says to my back.

I don't answer him. I still have time with her. It may be best that I don't get too attached though. I close my eyes as I open the door and step out into the night.

The cold air whips against my skin. She's in a cell for trying to get away from me, for fuck's sake. I shake my head and feel torn. I thought this would be perfect, but it's not.

I'm just damaged goods. That's all I am.

Perfection doesn't exist. Neither do fantasies.

CATHERINE

I wake to the faint hum of the lights being turned on in the cell. I'm so fucking cold. The only thing he gave me besides the chair was my chenille throw. At least it was freshly washed. Not like that matters now though, since I've got it bunched up underneath me as a makeshift mattress. It fucking sucks.

The lock clicks and the doorknob turns. I quickly get into position. I'm mindful of keeping my hands exactly how he likes them.

My heart flutters in my chest. Last night he didn't stay. He left me with dinner and watched me eat it in silence. An air of disappointment and distrust surrounded him. I don't understand why he's angrier with me now than he was when he put me in here. I feel like I'm failing, and I don't know what I'm missing. I wish I could go back in time. If I could, I would.

He walks in front of me and stops. I look up at him, hopeful that today he's in a better mood.

"Good morning, kitten," he says simply.

"Good morning, Anthony," I respond.

He puts a bowl down on the floor. It's oatmeal with strawberries and cream. It's my favorite. I had a shit-ton of it at my house and I find myself wondering if he went back there. I want to know if he was able to find the earrings, but I don't ask. I stay in my position and look at the bowl and then back at him. He didn't feed me dinner last night like he did before, and I didn't think much of it. But this morning reminds me of the first time we met, of him feeding me.

He shakes his head no and walks to the chair to sit down. "You don't get my touch in here, kitten. That's part of your punishment."

My heart sinks as I pick up the bowl and watch him cross his arms. I feel fucking sick. He's so fucking angry with me, and I don't know that I'll ever be able to take it back. I had to try though, didn't I? *No, I chose to.*

"I got your earrings. You won't get them until you're back in your room." His voice has a hard edge.

"Thank you." My voice cracks, and I have to take a deep breath to steady myself.

"What do they mean to you, kitten?" The use of my pet name brightens my spirit and my chest fills with hope. It's not lost on me that if he decides not to forgive me, he could kill me. He *will* kill me. It's not just that though. I hurt him. I disappointed him. That shouldn't affect me like this, but it does.

I jump at the opportunity to answer. And at the chance to do something and to talk to someone after spending hours alone and barely sleeping in this room. "They were my mother's." I wipe the sleep from my eyes and clear my throat of the knot growing there.

"I'm sorry for your loss." His words are short and simple, but I can hear the faint compassion in his voice.

"Cancer," I answer as I stir the oatmeal. I'm hungry, but it's not nearly as appetizing as it was before. I don't talk much about her. I don't like remembering.

"I know," he says, not moving from his position. A small, sad smile forms on my face. Of course he knows.

"Do you want to play the game, kitten?" he asks.

"Yes," I immediately answer, and I don't even care that I sound desperate. I fucking hate that game, but I want him to stay.

"How does a girl like you wind up with a man like Lorenzo?" I hate his question. I don't want to talk about him or think about him. I have to work hard not to show how upset it makes me.

"I just needed something different. He distracted me, I guess." He did. I nod my head thinking about how I went from crying all day and struggling to pack up my mother's things, to getting drunk and doing things I never thought I would.

"So you went for the *bad boy*." He says the words like he's disgusted by them, which is fucking ironic.

"It works in the books," I barely get the words out. It's what I really wanted. I wanted to find love. Even if he didn't love me back at first, I was hopeful that I'd eventually find my own happily ever after. I thought I'd found a hard man who'd melt for me in time. Instead I found an abusive fuckface. 'Cause let's be real, that's what life gives you when you go out looking for Mr. Wrong.

"Your turn, kitten. One question." He leans forward in his seat like he's ready to leave, and I hate it.

I ask the one thing that's been on my mind for hours. One thought that sickens me. I wish he'd just hit me and make that my punishment. I'd let him beat me if it meant this would be over with.

"I'm surprised you haven't hit me," I say. He makes no move to answer me, and there's no change in the expression on his face. He's silent for a moment.

"I don't want to hit you," he finally answers. And I believe him.

"Why?" I just don't understand. Lorenzo thrived by showing me how strong he was. He fucking loved dominating me physically. I keep expecting the dams to break and for Anthony to let loose on me. I expect to be physically punished for my infractions. I'd thought he was restraining himself before, but now that I look back on it, I don't think he was.

"I'll never hit you. My father used to hit my mother, and it made her do bad things. I don't want that for you or anyone else."

"I'm so sorry." My heart twists with agony. That's a horrible thing to grow up with. I can't even imagine. My own father passed away when I was younger in a car crash. I hardly remember him. I can't imagine growing up in a house with abuse. My eyes search his, but he gives nothing away. "Bad things?" I ask tentatively.

"She beat me instead since she couldn't hit my father back." My mouth falls open with a gasp as he continues. "I was young, but I remember." His voice is flat and devoid of emotion. My heart is fucking destroyed by his words.

"I'm so sorry." I shake my head, as though I can deny the truth.

"She's dead now." My throat closes and dries. His life just gets sadder and sadder. I want to scoot closer to him, but it's obvious he doesn't want that. He doesn't want sympathy. I don't even think he'd accept compassion.

"Did your father...?" I don't finish, but I don't have to. He nods his head once with his eyes locked on mine.

"He killed her when he saw what she's done; snapped her neck in front of me. He thought he was doing the right thing."

My mouth hangs open in shock.

"I don't even know if he ever hit her or if he didn't love her. I know next to nothing about what their relationship was like, apart from what my mother told me. We never talked about it. She beat me and he killed her for it. That's all I know." He gives me a sad smirk. "There's a lot of, 'let's not talk about it' that happens in the familia."

"I'm so sorry." I repeat my words; I don't know what else to say. I feel pathetic that I have nothing to offer him. Tears threaten to fall. I feel nothing but empathy for him and the pain he must've felt. Both our mothers are dead, but mine never hurt me. I never once questioned if mine loved me.

"Don't be. My brother's always been there. And in a lot of ways so has my father." His hard expressions soften somewhat. "I have to go, kitten," he says.

"No, please," I say. The bowl falls from my lap to the ground as I crawl closer to him.

"Are you telling me no? Are you the one giving orders now?" My shoulders hunch in as I lower myself to the ground. Tears slip down my cheeks. Some for me, but most are for him. I want to hold him and soothe the broken part of him I know exists. But I also need to be touched. I can't stay here like this.

"Please, Anthony. I want to earn your touch." I say the words with the desperation I feel.

His eyes widen with surprise and the darkness that's plagued him since last night seems to lift slightly.

"What are you thinking, kitten?" he asks.

"Whatever you want. I'm yours." I've never said truer words.

"Lie on your back and spread your legs for me." He gives his command and I obey. I refuse to think of this as anything but meeting my own needs. I need to feel something other than this emptiness.

"Good kitten," he says and rises from his chair. "I'll come back tonight once your punishment is over."

With that, he leaves me.

Alone and pathetically bared to a man who won't touch me, I curl up on my side and cry. I don't know how long, but it doesn't matter. It's not long enough to fill the emptiness inside of me.

CATHERINE

*I*t's been over a week. He's barely touched me or said anything to me. It's as though my punishment still hangs over my head. All I have is this room and my laptop. *My old life.* I'm surprised he gave it back to me.

I feel empty though. It's like I've hurt him. It's like he doesn't want me. I don't understand it. *He* doesn't trust me.

A few nights ago he came for me. Only one night has he touched me like he did before. He said I was being good and I deserved a reward. He laid me across his lap and instead of making my ass red with his hand, he pumped his fingers in and out of my needy pussy. He knows that I've been craving his touch, but I haven't begged him to fuck me yet. I just haven't been able to get the words out.

"I want my mouth on you." I remember him saying that as I came on his hand. I can't deny that I wanted it, too.

He throws me on my back and I part my legs for him. His shoulders dive between my legs, but he bites my thigh. I scream out as his fingers stroke my G-spot. It feels so good. My body heats with need. I wait for his lips to touch my clit. But they don't. He sucks my inner thigh, so tantalizingly close but not quite there, and I wish that touch was where I need it most.

I beg him, "Please, Anthony. Please!" He pulls away from me and fingers me until

I cum again from the ruthless pace of his touch.

I'm breathless and limp. I lie there until my body's no longer useless.

I press my fingers against my hot cheeks. Everywhere still feels hot, but my cheeks and chest are burning. Each time he touches me, it's more and more intense. I've never been so...sated in my life. It's more than foreplay. It's like he's taking me higher than I could have taken myself. And what's better is that he wants to push me there.

It's a game to him though. I can't forget. It's not like he's doing a good deed. He wants me to break for him. He wants me to beg. And I did. The memory reheats my body. He said he wanted to put his mouth on me, and I begged him to, but he didn't.

"I said yes." The words tumble from my mouth without a filter.

He looks up at me with a neutral expression. "I heard you."

His admission makes me feel self-conscious. Why have me beg for him if he wasn't going to do it? I don't understand why, but it hurts. I pull the duvet up and around my body and scoot up into a seated position. I can see him putting his shirt back on, but I don't really watch him. I just want him to leave.

"You hesitated." Anthony sits on the bed next to me, making it dip. I look up at him through my lashes but I keep my mouth shut. An apology is trying to climb out, but I won't. I'm not going to apologize for not begging quicker. I fight to keep my face from showing my anger. He cups my chin and leans down to kiss me and I lean into him. I can't help that I want his affection. I won't deny that it fills a deep need I'm only now realizing how much I craved. His lips break from mine and I miss them instantly. I know he's leaving, and I'll be alone until tomorrow.

He gives me a soft smile and rubs his nose against mine. It makes me close my eyes. When I open them he's already across the room. Before he leaves he says, "Next time you'll answer more quickly, kitten."

The words come out before I'm even aware I'm saying them. "Yes, Anthony."

THAT WAS THREE DAYS AGO. And he hasn't touched me or hinted at anything else since. Most of the time I think he regrets this. I think he really doesn't want me anymore. I'm not the pet he wanted. But then I think maybe I'm just missing something. Maybe he's waiting for me. If that's the case, I'm ready to beg. I hate this empty feeling that I'm not wanted or that I'm not good enough.

I look at the clock and it's almost three. He's come in everyday to check on me around now. My fingers tap on the keys, but I'm not typing anything. I'm just waiting for him. My work's done anyway. It'll pile up quickly, but it can wait.

Finally, I hear the sounds I'm used to. He's coming. I set the laptop to the side and climb to the foot of the bed. I kneel there for him and wait.

I hear the door open and I watch as he walks into my room. He gives me a small smile and it fills my chest with warmth.

"Kitten," he greets me as he walks toward me.

"Anthony," I say his name with a breath of reverence. He cups my chin and I lean into his embrace.

"How are you today?" he asks.

"Well." I look up at him through my lashes and almost don't say the words, but I need to. I need to let him know that I do want this. I'm sick without his presence. "I missed you."

His eyes light with a flash of something I don't recognize. "I missed you as well."

I just need him to touch me and tell me that I've been good. I've done everything he's told me to. I don't understand why he's treating me so differently now. I'm doing everything I can to prove I won't betray his trust again.

"Will you stay with me?" I ask him.

"I have to work tonight, kitten." I love the use of my pet name. "I only came in to check on you."

"Please, don't leave me here." I grip onto him and he gives me a look of reproach, but I don't let go.

"This is your room." He looks around the gorgeous suite. "I made it just for you."

I don't want this room if it comes with this feeling of nothingness. I need more. I say the words that have been eating me alive.

"I want to prove to you that I'm yours." I feel so needy, so pathetic. I just don't want him to turn me down and throw me away. I don't give a fuck about anything other than being his. I need his touch. I need the taste of the fantasy he gave me before I betrayed him. I've had a lot of time to think, and I want to try. I may be forced to be here, but I want to give in to the temptation. I'm scared to do it, but I have nothing to lose. I can't deny that a growing part of me finds all of this incredibly sexy.

He says nothing and a feeling of complete despair washes over me. "Please." I cling to him, needing something. I can't keep going like this. I'm trying so hard to be his, but I feel like I mean nothing to him. I'll beg him; I'm ready.

He strokes my hair and says, "We'll see when I get back."

"Can I give you something now, please?" I would do anything to hear him tell me I'm a good girl.

"Please, Anthony. I want to please you," I say.

A moment passes as he searches my face for something. And then my eyes fall to the button on his jeans. I watch as his deft fingers easily undo them.

"On your knees, kitten." His voice holds a hint of danger to it as he issues the command. I love it. It reminds me of our first morning together. Well, technically the second. Before I disobeyed him. Before he changed.

I climb off the bed and move to my knees for him.

He strokes himself once in front of me. I lick my lips and wait patiently. If he wants me to suck him off, I will. I want to. I'll make him want me. I know he will. My pussy clenches and heats with excitement as I watch him stroking himself, his eyes focused on my mouth. This turns him on as much as it does me. The intensity of my desire rises. I have a power over him that he can't deny and it's simply intoxicating. I'll make him need my touch.

"Open, kitten," He starts to put the head of his dick on my tongue, but then he pulls away. "No teeth this time," he says with a dark look in his eyes. I nod my head and feel a wash of shame. I'd never do that. Never.

Maybe the old me would have considered it, but the new me...Mentally I shake my head. I had an old life before my mother passed away, and a new life after I went into witness protection, but deep down I'm the same person I've always been. It's just taken my time here with Anthony to really open my eyes to that fact. My training with him has awakened all my hidden and taboo desires. All the things I always thought could never be more than unrealized fantasies. But we can make our fantasies come true together. I just need to submit to him fully.

I feel a small sense of shame that he feels like he'd have to tell me that. I've changed. I've accepted that I'm his, but he isn't acting like I have. I open wider and wait for him. I want him to know I'm willing. I want him to see me as his so I can really live this dark fantasy.

He fills my mouth with the head of his cock, but then pulls back. "Only the tip kitten. No more than that."

I look up at him and nod with my mouth still open. I'll take anything he's willing to give me.

I moan around the head of his cock and swirl my tongue. His large hand strokes his cock and I wish I could do it for him. My fingers dig into my thighs as I gently rock back and forth doing everything I can to get him off. The tip of my tongue dips into the slit of his dick and I fucking love that he hisses and throws his head back.

I'm so wet for him, so needy. But this is all for him. I want to take him all in. I want to shove him so far down my throat that I choke on him. But I obey him. It takes all of my willpower, but I do it. I suck his head so hard it hollows my cheeks. He takes it out with a pop and smacks it against my cheek.

"Again, just like that," he says with a ragged breath.

I look into his eyes as I do it again and I see the moment he reaches his climax. He keeps my gaze and parts his lips with an admiration I've never seen before. Hot jets of his cum stream into my mouth and I'm quick to swallow it and gently suck him until he's done.

"Swallow it all," he says with a rough groan that makes my pussy clench. I do.

He pets my hair as I wipe the corners of my mouth. I lick his slit until he takes it away from me. I bite my lip, staying exactly in the position he left me in. I'll prove to him that I've learned to listen and that I can obey.

"I'll be back tonight, kitten," he says as he buttons his pants. "Beg for me tonight, and you can have whatever you want."

ANTHONY

"*D*o you know what I don't want to be doing right now, Tommy?" I ask my brother.

"Taking this guy out with me?" my thickheaded brother answers. He used to be the muscle for the *familia*. Now he does hits with me. He just happens to fucking suck at some aspects. Give him a long-distance kill, and he's fine. Up close though, and he's sloppy as fuck.

I tap my pointer to my nose.

We're in a car parked across from Barcode. It's a dive bar on the strip and we've been waiting in the dark for a good two hours now. I keep looking at the monitors in the app on my phone. My kitten's been lying in bed reading and stretching or doing some yoga shit on the floor. I want to get back to her. I want to hear her beg for me. Even more, I want to hear those soft moans from her lips as she cums on my dick.

Instead I'm doing this stupid shit 'cause Tommy didn't want to do it on his own.

"Hey, I don't wanna be out here either. I've got more important shit going on, but we need to take this guy and not just kill him."

I can't blame him for being hesitant to take over and do this without me. I grunt a response and then think about his wife and my sweet little niece as I

725

say, "Yeah you do. You gotta be happy to not be hearing all that screaming for once."

He smiles back at me. I don't fucking get it. He's overjoyed about that little bundle of high-pitched lungs. She is a cutie, but damn, if only they could come out already talking and walking.

"You know she's adorable." He smiles back at me, finally taking his eyes away from the bar across the street.

"She's real cute, Tommy." I can admit that. She's adorable when she's sleeping. "You did good. I'm proud of you."

"I meant what I said, it's gonna happen for you. You don't have to be so fucking jealous all the time," he says.

I hold in a deep laugh. Jealous isn't quite the right word. I made up my mind a long time ago. That world isn't for me. I'm not meant to be a husband or a father. I don't have that ability. I know I'm capable of love, because I truly love my *familia*. But I'm fucked in the head. I know I am. They know I am.

There's no reason for me to ever think about taking that path in life. Even with my sweet Catherine.

My thoughts are interrupted when I notice the movement from across the street. I lean forward in my seat as the fucker on our list exits the bar, nearly stumbling as he lights a cigarette. Tommy starts talking, but I simply nod my head and keep my eyes on the dumb fuck who skimmed off the top of our shipment. He fucking knew better. He's been on the inside for a while now. He's almost a made member. Maybe he got tired of waiting. Maybe he just wanted the money. I don't know, and I don't care. I just need two pieces of information from him and then we can get this shit over with.

Who'd he sell it to, and where's the money?

Louie leans against the wall, taking a few puffs of his cigarette. I'm sure he thinks he got away with it. He looks like he doesn't have a care in the world.

I take a look down the street and it's busy as fuck. There's a narrow alley in between the two shit buildings. I'm sure we could take him for a walk. I've gotten away with that shit before, and I know I could keep his ass from screaming too loud.

"Let's do this shit," I say.

Tommy looks at me anxiously. "Out in the open?" he asks.

"Yeah, quick and easy. Let me show you how it's done," I reply.

I step out into the street and walk quickly, keeping my head turned to the right. The only camera is on the side of the street where we parked. But it's angled so they shouldn't get shit. Better safe than sorry though. I already messaged Tony about it. I'm sure the owners won't have any problems erasing the feed tonight. Not when the orders are coming from the Valettis, and their business has been going steady on the loan we gave them.

That's one good thing about the *familia*. We want this town running like a well-oiled machine. And it does.

"Louie." I let a grin slip into place as he kicks off the wall and walks toward us like we're his pals. Like he didn't steal from us.

"Anthony, Tommy, what's up guys?" His words are slightly slurred and it pisses me off. I find when they're drunk they're more likely to piss themselves. More than that, they scream louder, sooner. Tonight that can't happen. "You here for a drink?" he asks.

"Nah," Tommy says and he starts to say something else, but I cut him off. I want him to watch this time, so he can see how it's done and be able to do this shit himself next time.

"Louie, we gotta talk." I say the words firmly and hold his eyes. The fucker holds his breath and I know he's scared shitless. I need him scared, but more than scared, I want him willing to talk and wanting to make me happy. I want him to think I need him.

I lean forward and lower my voice so it seems like I'm letting him in on intel. "There's someone," I start talking then look to my left as a group of young women dressed in sequined, glittery dresses that ride up their asses pass behind us. The street's not packed, but it's busy enough to want to get out of the open so we can have some privacy. I make it a point to look at the entrance to the alley and nod my head. "Let's go down there for a sec."

He starts to put his cigarette down with a look of dread on his face. But I don't want that. I don't want him thinking anything's wrong.

"No need, I don't mind the smoke," I tell him as I start walking ahead of him. "You first, Tommy." I need my brother to catch on to the fact that you don't intimidate targets in public. Not till you have them where you want them. Tommy walks ahead of me with a nod. My brother's smart, even if he does do dumb shit sometimes. He's good at reading people. My back's to Louie. It's a sign that he's not a threat to me. The two of us walk quickly while Louie stays behind for a moment. I keep walking. I know I don't have to tell him twice.

It only takes a minute for Louie to follow us down the alley. It's a few feet wide and blocked off at the back entrance by a dumpster and a chain-link fence. That's not good for the clean-up crew. They're going to have a hell of a time getting the body out without anyone seeing, but that shit's not for me to worry about. Tommy stops about halfway down the alley and leans against the wall. I put my hands in my pockets and face the entrance, waiting for Louie to catch up. He's walking slow, but he sure as fuck isn't stumbling around anymore. Having the feeling you're about to get caught by the mafia for stealing from them is a surefire way to sober the fuck up.

"What's going on?" He tries to keep his voice from wavering, but he's shit at it. To be fair though, I've tortured a lot of men. And almost all of them are scared at first, even the ones that didn't have shit to tell because they were genuinely innocent. Poor fucks. But this prick is dripping with sweat and his shifty eyes are looking all around us for some hidden door that will lead him to safety. There's no safety here though. Just me, my knife, and Tommy's gun.

I want Tommy to stay out of this one. There's no need for him to get involved beyond keeping this fucker here.

"Listen, Louie. There are some things I need to know before I kill you." His eyes go wide and he takes a step back. He's closest to the entrance, so he's thinking of running.

Tommy's already got his gun on him and we all hear the click of him cocking it back. Louie's eyes lock on the barrel and he nearly tips back as his legs go weak.

He shakes his head and I know he's getting ready to deny it. His hands are raised in the air. "Hey. I wanna make this easy on us all, Louie," I say as I reach into my pocket for a rag as I slowly walk toward him. He takes a step back and I shake my head. His breathing comes in short breaths as he starts spewing off, "Whatever you heard, it wasn't me. I didn't do it." The desperation is clear in his voice.

I wrap the cloth around my fist a few times. It's thick; thick enough so he won't be able to bite down on my hand. The thought reminds me of my kitten. My sexy-as-fuck little minx, scraping her teeth down my finger. I close my eyes and will the images away. It only fuels my need to get this shit over with. I walk around him and let him retreat until his back is against the wall. We're still almost halfway down the narrow alley. It'd be hard as fuck to see or hear anything from us, as long as he doesn't scream. I look at my left fist, wrapped tightly with the rag and back at Louie.

"You've got one chance. Who'd you sell it to, and where's the money?" I ask him clearly, but I already know I'm going to have to ask again.

He's shaking his head, thinking he can talk his way out of this.

I'm quick to shove my fist in his mouth. He only gets a partial scream out before the rag mutes his frantic screams. He struggles against me, his hands wrapping around my wrist, trying to rip my fist from his mouth. I push my fist harder into his mouth, stretching his jaw. I need to be careful not to break it though. I need this fucker to talk. He's a pretty decent-sized guy and he's doing a good job of throwing my body off of him, but I pull out my knife and hold it to his throat, my forearm bracing his shoulders against the wall. That makes his entire body still. Tommy comes up to my right and holds the gun to Louie's head. Louie looks between the two of us and starts fucking crying. It's pathetic.

"It's just two questions, Louie, then we get to move on from this. You had a chance. You should've taken it." I gave him a warning, and he chose to ignore it. Now he has to accept the consequences.

I nod at Tommy. "Get his hand."

Tommy grabs Louie's right arm, still holding the gun to his head. Louie's quick to pull his arm away, but I dig my knife into his neck, slicing his skin to make a point of what will happen if he keeps this shit up.

He tries to speak into the rag, but it's too late for that. I'll give him a chance in a minute, once the screaming is over with. Louie's got his fist balled, which is a bad move on his part. It would've only been one finger, but with them all bunched together, I slice into his middle finger and thumb as I cut off his pointer. Tommy struggles to keep the fucker's wrist up as I cut his finger off and the dumb fuck screams into the rag.

I let the finger fall and the blood drip down onto the ground as I wipe my knife off on his jacket and push it up to his throat again. I choose a new spot, one an inch up from the first cut. "Stop your screaming," I growl out as I push my fist deeper into his mouth. He whimpers in response, tears flowing down his cheeks as he cradles his arm in his hands.

I talk while I wait for him to calm down. "We have you on tape taking the product, so there's no backing out of this one. You know it. There's only one way out. You just tell me who you sold it to and where the money is, and it's all over."

He cries out something muffled by my hand, but I keep it there until he's calm.

I hold his eyes and wait.

When I take my hand away, his body sags and he closes his eyes. "The Cullums, they bought it."

"Did they know it was ours?" Tommy asks.

Louie shakes his head no.

"Where's the money, Louie?" I bet the fucker's already spent it, but Tony couldn't find it anywhere in his bank accounts.

"I gave it to my brother." Hearing his confession makes my heart sink. I know his brother has a problem with alcohol. They both do. His brother's also a gambler though. And that's not a good combination. I nod my head and wait for him to look me in the eyes.

"You stole from us to get your brother out of debt?" I ask him and I see a flash of hope in his eyes. Like maybe that'll save him. But it won't. As he raises his head to speak, I stab the knife through his neck until it comes out the other side and quickly push it up toward his face, splitting his throat open. It's a silent kill, efficient and quick.

Once his eyes glaze over and his hands fall to his side, I let him drop to the ground. I shake my head as Tommy dials up the crew to come clean this shit up.

He should've known better. No one fucks with us for a reason.

"Damn, Anthony. I need to practice with a knife." I turn around to look at my brother. He's looking at me the same way everyone always has. Like he fears me, because I do this shit without thinking twice and without feeling remorse. It's simple. He had it coming. It had to happen. Catherine used to look at me like that too; only sometimes though in the beginning. Not anymore. She would if she knew I did this shit. If she really knew who I was. When people break the rules, they die. That's just what happens. Just like my mother. I've come to terms with it long ago. I don't get why everyone else gets so shaken up over it.

I don't feel any different than I did when we walked back here. A little bit of a high on adrenaline, but I just want to get the fuck out.

Tommy says, "I don't think I could do that shit."

"Sure you could, anyone's capable of it." My words remind me of my kitten. Her patiently waiting for me, and telling me all the things I want to hear. I don't think she would ever hurt a fly. That's just not the kind of person she is. But if she wanted to kill me, she could. I still expect it at some point. If I was her, I'd try to kill me. The thought makes my blood run cold. At some point she's probably going to try to kill me.

"You alright?" Tommy asks. "It's alright, Anthony. He had it coming to him."

He had it coming to him. I bet that's what she's going to think when she gets the courage to try. I want to believe in her, but ever since that night with Vince, all I keep thinking is that I'm fucked up. That I was wrong. That this is destined to fail.

I school my expression and look at Tommy as I say, "Let's get out of here."

It's late, but I need her right now. Even if my little kitten wants to sink her claws into me. Even if it's all lies. Even if it's completely fucked up. I *want* her.

731

ANTHONY

*a*s soon as I put the keys on the table, I make a beeline for the door. I need to get to her. She could be lying to me; she could be gearing up for a fight. I don't fucking know. But right now I want her, and she's ready to beg for me. I'm giving in. Whether it's my dark needs and *issues* or something else causing this impulsive behavior, I don't give a fuck.

I go straight down to the basement. My steps are loud as fuck. I enter the code and swing open the door just in time to see her falling to her knees and breathing heavily. Her hair's a mess, like she was sleeping when she heard me coming. I look past her at the bed and I know that's exactly what happened.

"You want me, kitten?" I walk to her with hard steps. "You still want to prove to me that you're mine?" I ask her.

"Yes, Anthony," she responds with a deep need in her eyes. I run my hand down my face, knowing this is stupid as fuck. But I'm going to do it. I'm tired of questioning this shit, and I'm tired of waiting.

I lean down and grab her by her waist, carrying her in my arms.

She snuggles into me and stares at my face as I take her up to my room. I want her there. If she's really mine, she'll be mine everywhere. She doesn't look around; she doesn't try to squirm away. She grips onto my shirt and kisses the dip in my neck.

I lay her gently on the bed, but she's quick to pop up on her knees and wait for me.

"You want my dick, kitten?" I ask her.

"Please. Please, Anthony," she begs me as she pulls the nightgown over her head and lies naked on my bed. She's desperate for something from me. Anything. This is what I wanted, but right now, I fucking hate myself for it.

Her lust-filled eyes look back at me as she whispers, "I want to prove to you I'm yours." Fuck, she sounds so sincere.

I nod my head slightly and kick my pants off. If that's what she wants, then she's going to get it. She's going to earn it.

"Fuck yourself on my dick," I command.

I climb on the bed and stay on my knees stroking my cock. Precum's already leaking out and I use it to lube up the head.

She's quick to get on all fours and look back at me over her shoulder. She's too fucking sexy for her own good. She lowers her breasts to the bed and lays her head to the side, keeping her eyes on my dick as she backs her ass up.

I put a hand on her hip to steady her and let her take me in. My breath comes in short pants but I make sure they're low so she can't hear how much I need this. Her ass looks so fucking good. I give it a loud smack. She jumps, and I slip out of her.

"Uh-uh, kitten. You're going to take it. This is your cock right now. Lean back and take it." Her mouth stays parted as she reaches between her legs for my dick. Her small hand strokes the head and I almost cum right there.

Smack! I hit her ass to keep from cumming as she slips the tip inside of her welcoming heat and moves back, stretching her walls slowly around my dick. I watch my cock slowly disappear. So fucking slowly. It's almost too much to take. I ball my hands tightly into fists and fight the urge to just let go. I want to collapse on top of her and bury my head into her neck. I want to bite down on her and fuck her ruthlessly and let my savage beast out. But I need control. I thrive with control. And this is for her, not for me.

She rocks on her knees to get more of me inside her tight little pussy. Fuck, it feels like heaven. I place my hand on the small of her back, but I don't take control. This is for her own needs, not for my pleasure. There's a difference.

I grip her hips, but she's still in control. She slides easily on and off my dick. Her sweet sounds fill the air. That's when it really hits me, she really has given herself to me. I've broken her down to this. She *wants* this. She wants me. She's doing this to please me. What more could she possibly give me? My heart clenches in my chest, and I can't fucking stand it.

Not now. I can't think about this shit right now.

She moans as she slides back deeper and my dick fills her cunt. I can't help the groan that slips past my lips. She feels so fucking good. She rocks forward and I watch as her cream coats my dick. It's the sexiest fucking sight I've ever seen. I want to push deep into her and pound her pussy so fucking hard her body collapses. But not yet.

She fucks herself on my cock, searching for her release, but she's so far from getting that highest high that I can give her. I tilt my hips and thrust back as she impales herself onto my dick. I'm rewarded with a sweet strangled cry of pleasure. "Yes!" she screams out. The sound of her panting and smacking her wet pussy against me is everything I ever dreamed of.

"Please, Anthony!" she cries out as she fucks herself faster and harder. "Please," she begs me.

"Please what?" I ask her. I just want to hear her tell me how much she needs me.

"Please, Anthony," she begs again.

"You want me to make you cum?" I ask her.

"Yes!" she answers.

"You want to cum all over my cock to please me, is that it?" I smack her ass again and again.

"Yes!" she cries out, and it's the last straw. I give in and lose what little self-control I have left.

"Coat my dick with your cum," I growl into her ear as I push her shoulders down and hammer into her. My other hand moves to her slick clit and I strum it until she screaming into the sheets.

Her pussy latches onto my dick and starts milking it with her release. I pump into her harder and faster, and with each thrust her cunt holds onto me tighter, trying to suck me in deep. I nip her earlobe. I bite, kiss and suck all over her neck. Her pussy pulses around me and her body trembles beneath me. She cries out my name, and it's what takes me over the edge. I cum deep inside her. I groan in the crook of her neck, loving that I gave her more than she could give herself.

I slowly release her and her body falls forward and I slip out of her, our combined cum leaking from her pussy.

She lays on the bed panting and curling on her side as I leave her to get a shirt from the hamper to wipe up with. She hums softly in appreciation as I clean her off. She looks so weak and tired as she slips her nightgown back on. I love the sight of my cum leaking out of her tight little pussy, but I need to clean her up before bed. And she's obviously fucking exhausted.

I watch her as I climb in next to her. I expect her to plead with me to stay. I expect her to ask me for something. But she doesn't. She scoots her body against mine and rests her cheek on my shoulder. She cuddles with me. She holds me.

I feel my guard lower from her comforting touch. I should put her back in her room, but I need this as much as she does. I don't think I've ever felt someone hold me with such need and adoration. She rubs her body against mine and I relax into the mattress.

I kiss her hair and pet her back as she nestles into my chest.

"Sleep, kitten," I whisper into her ear.

She looks up at me through her lashes with a small smile. "Good night, Anthony." And she plants a kiss on my lips. I can still feel it as she lies back down and gets comfortable in my arms.

I watch her for hours before I can finally sleep. It never once occurs to me that in the morning she won't be there.

Because I know she will.

ANTHONY

$\mathcal{M}$y eyes slowly open and I move to turn onto my side, but a warm and comforting weight rests against my side. *Kitten.* A slow, lazy smile graces my lips. It feels good to wake up next to someone. I never have before. I'm not angry that I let her sleep here last night. But it's a one-time thing.

I stare at her while she sleeps. Her chest rises and falls in a steady rhythm. Her chestnut hair is fanned out on the pillow. I gently brush the hair off her face and fucking love how at peace she is. *With me.*

This is going better than I ever imagined it would. My hand gently eases on her hip as my eyes roam over the dip in her waist. She begged me to fuck her. She wants me. She truly wants me.

I lie back down on my back and sigh. She's seen my darkness, and she craves my touch.

Only because she has no choice. Only because I've conditioned her.

All traces of her warmth and tenderness leave me. And then she stirs beside me. I close my eyes and wait to see what she's going to do. I've no idea what kind of trouble my kitten will get into if I let her roam the house without supervision.

But I'm curious. The idea that locks aren't needed makes me feel powerful, as though I've perfected the relationship I desired. But there's only one way to find out if it's possible.

I feel her body press against mine as her cheek nudges gently against my chest.

She's trying to wake me, but I don't move.

It's been a long time since I've pretended to be sleeping, but I'm still good at it.

Maybe she has no intention of leaving my side. Maybe she's scared of being punished if she does.

I've never said I would. There are no rules against it. But she's made up in her head what this is supposed to be like. She's decided on her own that it would upset me if she wandered around the house without me. That's smart of her, but I want her to push. I want her to learn I can give her freedom if only she'd ask for it.

I wait as she rests on her side and lies still next to me. I know she doesn't want to disappoint me. That's a good thing, but it's also holding us back.

She runs her fingers along my jaw gently, and I have to stifle a soft groan of tenderness so she won't realize I'm awake. I crave her touch as much as she craves mine. But she'll never know that. I can never show her that weakness.

After a moment, she slowly and easily slips off the bed. My little kitten's curiosity got the best of her. Good.

Excitement races through my blood as I hear her walk through the room. I peek through my lashes as she opens the closet.

She can see all the monitors, but she seems unaffected. She knows I watch her. She closes them after a moment of watching the screens flash to different angles in her rooms. She walks slowly and quietly across the room. Her fingers trace over the notebook on my dresser. She slowly opens it and I don't like that.

It's my list. There are names in there she shouldn't know. Her brows raise and she quickly shuts it, taking a step back as though it bit her.

Good girl. She turns on her heel and walks quietly to the door, looking back at me once.

As soon as she's out the door, it's my cue to get up and follow my sweet submissive who's being a bit naughty.

For all I know she could be trying to leave. But I doubt she would. I'm fairly certain she just wants to snoop. I can't blame her. I listen from my bedroom and hear her walk to the next room. The door opens, and she gasps and quickly shuts it.

It's the armory. If she wanted, she could grab a gun in there. But none are loaded and the ammunition is locked away separately, so I'm not worried. But she doesn't. I hear her feet patter faster away from the room and move on to the next door. It's just a guest room, so there's nothing in there, but I can't hear her any longer and I imagine she walked in.

So I decide it's time to put my kitten to the test. My dick hardens at the thought of chasing her. YES! I need this. I want to prepare her first and give her a fair chance to run. I'll catch her though. I'll always catch her; she can never escape me.

I walk silently to the door and peek in. She's fiddling with a wooden puzzle on the desk.

I walk up behind her and quickly press my front to her back, wrap my arm around her waist and cover her mouth with my hand. She screams out of fear but I gently kiss the crook of her neck and she instantly relaxes.

"My kitten is being naughty," I say as I move my hand from her mouth to her throat and the other lifts her nightgown up for me to splay my hand on her bare lower belly. My fingers tease along her clit.

"Did you find anything you shouldn't have?" I ask.

She nods her head obediently. I smile behind her back.

I could ask her what she found, but I already know and I know she'd tell me the truth.

"Did you find anything interesting?" I ask her instead. She presses her body against mine and her ass rubs against my dick.

"Yes," she says. My dick is so fucking hard for her.

She turns her head slightly to see me and I reward her with a rough kiss.

"I have to punish you, kitten. You should know better than to run off without me," I say sternly.

That knocks the confidence out of her, but she nods her head and stays still in my arms. Once she realizes what this is, she'll fucking love it. So sweet and obedient. She's so fucking perfect.

"This is as much for you as it is for me." She closes her eyes and tries to hide her smile. "It would make me very happy though, if you fought me back." She arches her back and moans softly as I whisper the words into her ear. My fingers slip past her clit and I cup her pussy. She's so fucking wet. "Do you want to fight me, kitten?" I ask.

"Yes," she whispers into the hot air between us as I push my palm against her clit.

"You have five seconds," I say as I pull away and take a step back. She turns to face me, breathing heavily with lust-filled eyes. "Run, kitten," I say.

At my words, she takes off.

It's the longest five seconds of my life. One. She runs out the door, slamming it into the wall. Two. I walk slowly to the hall behind her. Three. Her small feet bounce off each step as quickly as possible. Four. She holds onto the railing and swings around making her way toward the kitchen. Five.

My long strides and taking the stairs three at a time has me on the first floor before she's through the dining room. She doesn't turn around to look at me. Instead she keeps running, pumping her arms and nearly crashing into the table.

She makes a sharp right to go through the hall and I'm on her tail before she can do a damn thing. Her hand grips the doorknob, but she doesn't have time to open it. I grab her waist and pin her to the ground. Her legs thrash against my body and I lay my weight on top of her. She tries to push me off, but I'm bigger. I'm stronger. She doesn't stand a chance against me. My kitten's fighting me though. I fucking love it. Her hands smack against my face and push against my chest.

I growl as I take both her wrists in my hands and pin them above her head, moving them to together so I'm able to hold them with one hand. She continues to struggle against me as I rip her nightgown open with my free hand and pin her down with my hips. I stare down and marvel at her gorgeous body laid out under me. I take one perky breast in my hand and squeeze. Her tiny pink nipples harden and I take it as an invitation to suck them in my mouth one at a time and nibble them as she writhes under me. I pull back and let one out with a pop, leaving a red mark. Fucking beautiful.

Her eyes are shooting daggers at me as she plays along, but they're filled with lust. Her breathing is heavy and labored. I can feel her passion, and that's everything I want. I push my forearm against her chin, pushing her head back so I can lean down and kiss her, knowing she won't be able to bite me.

Her lips are hard at first, but they mold to mine. I'm quick to pull back and keep this fantasy alive.

Her back arches as she tries to buck me off. But I have her right where I want her. My free hand pries between her legs and I push my fingers into her heat. She's so fucking wet.

"You're so fucking dirty. You want this," I say.

I lean down and take her earlobe in my teeth before nipping at her skin, leaving tiny pink marks all over her neck.

"Please!" she cries out.

"Your cunt is *begging* me to fuck you," I whisper in her ear.

"Is that what you wanted, kitten? You wanted me to punish you like this?" I ask as I push a third finger in and pump them in and out as she begs me. "Please, Anthony. Please fuck me. Punish me, please."

She stops struggling and moans as I curve my fingers and stroke against her G-spot. My dick is so fucking hard for her.

My blood heats as I line my dick up. Yes! I've waited so long to sink deep into her hot cunt and take her like this.

I don't ease in slowly, and I'm not gentle as I thrust all the way in and keep myself buried deep inside her. Her walls tighten around me as I rip through her, taking her exactly how I've wanted since I first laid eyes on her.

"Fuck!" She screams and cums as her walls stretch and spasm around my cock. Her arousal leaks out between us and onto my thighs. I easily move in and out of her tight pussy, pumping my hips against hers and watching my cock slide in and out.

"Anthony." She moans my name as her body trembles. I pull almost all the way out and then piston my hips over and over, pounding her hips into the floor. Her arms pull against me, but her wrists are still pinned.

I groan as I rut between her legs, watching her tits bounce slightly with each hard thrust of my hips. I push all the way in and grind my pelvis against her clit until her mouth is open with a silent scream and her pussy pops around my dick.

I want her cumming harder than she ever has before, so I don't let up. I grind harder and let her scream and struggle against me with more force than before. Her legs stick out straight and her head falls back hard against the floor as wave after wave of pleasure and heat consume her body. Her eyes glaze over and it's only then that I pull back.

I let go of her wrists so I can spread her legs wider and sink in deeper. My hands grip her thighs as I pound into her.

"Anthony," she moans softly. Her hands travel down her body and then to mine. She moans into the air and her soft eyes stare at me. I reward her by keeping up my relentless pace and pushing the pad of my thumb against her clit.

"Good girl, watch me fuck your pretty little pussy." Her mouth opens as her body stiffens again. Her back bows and she cums a third time. Her nails dig into my back and she urges me to get closer to her body.

I won't deny her. I lay my forearm above her head and let my lips fall onto hers.

She pulls back to breathe and whisper my name. "Anthony, Anthony."

Her fingers grip my hair, holding my lips close to hers.

Over and over she says my name against my lips and then presses them to mine in a sweet kiss.

I cum violently inside her, harder than I ever have before as her lips part and she kisses me with more passion than I've ever felt.

I stay buried inside her, lying down beside her while we both catch our breath.

* * *

IT'S ALMOST BEEN A MONTH; less than two weeks left. I can't let them take her. She's everything I've ever wanted.

I won't let them take her from me. I pull her body closer to me and kiss her shoulder. I won't let her go. They'll have to kill me first.

CATHERINE

$\mathcal{I}$'m still sore from yesterday and last night. Plus this morning. Ever since he had me in the hall, he fucks me nonstop. That's the only difference now. Every morning's still the same otherwise. I get ready and wait for him. I greet him on my knees. And I still stay in my room.

"Your pussy's open for business now." His dirty words echo in my head.

Maybe it's wrong to be so turned on by him, but I don't care. I am. Just thinking about him has my nipples hardening and my back arching off the chair. I clench my sore pussy and instantly hate that he's not here to sate me. I *need* him.

My computer pings and it's only then that I realize my hand has slipped into my blouse and I'm pinching my nipple between my fingers.

I'm ready for him.

I look down at the message and smile.

My kitten is needy today.

I don't know which camera he's watching so I wave to the screen and nod my head. A blush travels up my chest and into my cheeks.

Get back to work, kitten. I'll take care of you tonight.

I no longer feel trapped. It's like he's given me my life, but filled a hole I was only vaguely aware was empty. All my needs are met. He's seen to that. I

742

have my work, my friends, and a sex life that somehow manages to be hotter than anything I've ever read about. And it's all thanks to him. It hurts to think I may have lived my life without this. Without *him*.

* * *

I'M busy editing this piece for my column, and so immersed in getting this paragraph flowing better that I don't hear the lock or the doorknob turn. I don't even hear the door open.

The only thing I can hear is the language of the text over and over that I keep reading in my head. The wording is just clunky and passive, but I don't know how to reorder them. I bite down on my lip and copy and paste a few times, reordering the sentences. My fingers click against the keys.

"Kitten." His voice holds a threat and my body stills. My heart slows but even with the fear of displeasing him clouding my emotions, my pussy aches with need.

I push the chair away and fall onto my knees. I crawl around, keeping my body lowered. Once I see his shoes I stop and sit back on my heels with my hands where they should be. I don't look up though. My heart beats chaotically. I've never not been ready for him. Not since that first day. Every time I hear the click of the lock, I immediately kneel and wait for him. It's been what, maybe weeks at this point? I've been his good kitten and he's kept his word. But this time, I failed.

"I didn't hear you enter." My neck strains as I resist the urge to look at the clock. He usually comes to me around the same time every day. But I got lost in work today.

His hand comes down and rests in my hair. I close my eyes and wait for his response. "Please forgive me, Anthony." The words slip out and I don't try to catch them. My heart swells with agony in my chest. I don't want him upset with me.

"What were you doing, kitten?" he asks as he pets my hair. I open my eyes and finally look up at him. His stubble is a little longer than usual and his hair is as well. It has a tousled look that's fucking sexy.

"Work," I reply easily, and then realize he may want more. "My column is due tonight, but the editor is overbooked. So I'm trying to get it done myself."

He hums, "I see." He looks past me and to the laptop sitting on the desk. I love this little office he made for me. It's so cute with all the book nerd touches, and the large window gives me more sunlight than I'd ever get in the bedroom.

"I think maybe a short break would be nice. We could go get you more flowers." I look up at him with surprise.

"Would you like that, kitten?" he asks.

"Yes, Anthony." I nearly crawl up his body with the need to press my lips to his. But I'm an obedient pet. I keep my hands planted firmly on my thighs and wait for his direction.

"Do you think you're ready to go out?" he asks.

I nod my head. I'm never been outside of these locked rooms. The only exception was that one night. The night I gave myself to him completely. I crave a different environment. A voice deep inside me tells me I can run; I just need one chance. But it's such a small voice, I barely hear it.

"Come, kitten. I think you need a break." My brow furrows with confusion at first and then I realize he meant I need a break from work. He holds his hand out for me and I take it instantly.

He chuckles as he reads the writing on my tank top. It's a racerback that hangs just past my ass and is almost as long as my yellow shorts. The top reads, *Book lovers never go to bed alone.*

I give him a small smile and walk with him as he presses the keys to unlock the door. I know not to look even though he doesn't try to hide the code from me.

It's cold and dark and empty down here. Only a florescent light is above us. It looks so dungeonlike compared to my room. I stay behind him as we walk up the stairs and he presses in keys to another lock. He doesn't give me the chance to look, but I don't mind. I just make a note of it. I'm not sure why though.

My eyes wince as he opens the door and leads me into an open-concept first floor. I take a look around in wonder as if seeing Anthony for the first time in a new light. I don't remember this room when I was out before.

There's a large slate fireplace with a flat-screen television above it. Everything is modern with dark accents and clean lines. It's orderly and nearly barren of any character at all. For some reason it makes me sad. His bedroom was like this, too.

"There's a farm stand down the street," he says as he leads me through the hall without giving me a moment to look around. There are stairs to the right, next to the front door and a hallway that looks like a dead end. *That's where he took me.* A smile spreads on my face as I remember.

He opens the door and keeps my hand in his. I'm surprised to see that his home isn't in the middle of nowhere. It's just a normal house, in a homey cul-de-sac. There are two kids riding bikes to our right, and a third playing with chalk on the sidewalk. Anthony walks to the left and leads me past the houses to a busier street. The sounds of kids playing and a car passing me by seem odd, but comforting. Out in the cabin, I never had this. I like it. It's different.

It doesn't fit with how I pictured Anthony would live though.

"You look surprised, kitten," he says without looking at me. He knew I'd be surprised. He does this often. He says things or asks questions when he already knows what my response will be. He thinks I haven't caught on, but I have. He needs it though. And I'm happy to give it to him.

"I am," I answer honestly.

"Monsters don't live in the dark; they hide in plain sight." His response makes my heart twist in my hollow chest.

"You're not a monster." I spit out the words and look away. I can feel his eyes on me as we stand at the stop sign and a car drives through the intersection. He tugs my hand and we walk to the front of the development and to the right. I can see the stand ahead. It's a shabby-looking shack that's probably been there before the development was built.

"I don't understand." I can't help that the words fly out of my mouth.

"What's that?" Cars fly by us but the breeze still feels fresh against my skin.

"Why do you think you're a monster?" I ask him. Ever since he told me about his mother, I've thought he was broken, but never a monster. He's just missing a piece of his heart. I ache to fill that hole for him.

"Many people have died because of me, kitten. That makes me a monster in a normal person's eyes." I know he's including his mother in that statement. And I hate that.

I stay quiet as we walk closer to the empty stand. There's an old man sitting behind a wooden counter in the shack. Baskets of produce are on the ground, but the flowers are on the counter.

"What are you thinking?" he asks as he lifts a bouquet of purple and pink flowers to my nose. I inhale deeply and close my eyes.

I shake my head at his question and take the flowers from him with a smile. I whisper close to him so the old man doesn't hear, "I don't think you're a monster." My fingers play with the tiny soft petals, but I'm careful not to break them.

He looks down at me while he digs in his pocket for his wallet. "You did at one point, kitten; you were right about me then."

ANTHONY

$\mathcal{I}$'m so fucking tired. I haven't slept in I don't know how many hours. I drag my hand over my face. Fuck, that hit was brutal. It was a former Cassano who double-crossed Marcus. The Don, Marcus Cassano, wanted him to suffer, but I wasn't prepared for that shit. It was a struggle to get him to say a damn word and when he did, it left me frozen with panic.

"Cassanos are coming for you." His dark eyes stare back at me as blood drips from his mouth. The bruises are already starting to show as he wobbles in the chair he's chained down to. Even with all the pain we've inflicted, he laughs at me as I stare back with anger.

He looked right at me and I knew why. Tommy smashed his fist into the dumb fucker's face. Too hard and too fast though. That's the only info we got from him.

Tommy kept asking me what I thought he meant. I couldn't even look him in the eyes as I lied to him, and told him I had no idea. They want her back. They want her dead. My time's up.

I push the door open to the house and then kick it shut. That didn't go as planned. My eyes fly to the backroom, to where the stairs are to the basement. If I'd die, she'd be in there alone for three days until the door would unlock and let her out. I need to change that shit. She wouldn't be okay for that long.

She'd be hurting and hungry. I decide on twenty-four hours, tops. And then all her doors are opening.

I head to my bedroom and go right to the monitors so I can change that shit now. It's done within two minutes and I find myself staring at her sleeping form on the bed. She's got a book in her hands still. I squint at the screen, but I don't recognize which one it is. That stack of books on her nightstand has been there for a week. I don't remember what books I got her though. It's rare that she's got a paperback. She's usually on her Kindle whenever I check on her. I'm glad she found something that I picked out for her. Well, she fell asleep, so maybe she didn't like it all that much. A lazy smile kicks my lips up.

She should be waking up soon and getting ready for me. Waiting for me. I don't give a fuck that I'm worn out. I'm not making her wait. Not today. Not ever again if I can help it.

I need to program something for her to let her know what the hell happened if those doors ever open because I never made it home. Or maybe leave a note each time I go. I don't know what she'd do. Or what she'd think. I drag my hand down my face. I can't deal with this shit right now. I'm tired as all hell.

I drag my ass to the shower. I want to make this fast. I have one thing on my mind, and I need it as soon as fucking possible.

All I care about right now is feeling Catherine cum on my dick. It's all I want. I need to feel her body against mine and hear those sweet moans as I push her closer and closer to her release.

I'm in and out of the shower and punching in the code before I know it. She's sound asleep. Doesn't wake up at all. She doesn't hurry to get on her knees and in position like she's supposed to. I walk over to the desk in her room and see on the clock that it's already past 9 a.m. The alarm's supposed to go off at 8 a.m., if she set it. Which she didn't.

She finally had the courage to ask me to change the wake up time from 7 to 8. It's one of the first things she asked me to change. And I was more than happy to do it. I think if she never set an alarm though, my kitten would sleep in all morning. She used to on the weekends when I watched her. But then she'd feel like shit when she woke up to all the work that piled up. I love how she told me that. I love how she's starting to open up to me and really be her true self. It's perfect. *She's* perfect.

I sigh heavily with my eyes closed. I don't fucking want to punish her. I don't want to do this shit right now.

I study her beautiful body on the bed. She's still in her shirtdress from last night. I wonder if she ever even got out of bed after I left her. I bet I just wore her out and she wanted to relax.

I make my way over to the bed and see a pad of paper on the other side of her that was hidden from the cameras. I take a quick look at her scribbles before tossing it onto the nightstand. It looks like my kitten is keeping a diary. I make a mental note to read that later.

"Kitten," I say loud enough that should wake, but not so loud that it should startle her. She rolls her head a bit, but she doesn't wake up like I want her to.

I kick off my pajama pants and crawl into bed with her. I fucking need her right now. I lay my body next to hers and pull her in close, loving her warmth and how she molds her body to mine in her sleep. I gently kiss her neck, hoping that will rouse her. I get a small satisfied moan and a rock of her hips, but nothing else.

"Catherine." My lips barely touch the shell of her ear as I speak just above a murmur. "Wake up for me, kitten."

Her eyes slowly open and seem to settle on my face. A faint smile crosses her face before her eyes shut and she settles her head into the crook of my arm. It makes my heart swell. It only takes a minute for her brain to catch up and her eyes pop open and her body stiffens slightly.

I instantly take her lips with mine, wanting to ease her worry. Her lips are hard at first, caught by surprise, but soon they mold to mine and she leans into my touch. Her small hands press against my chest as my tongue slips into her hot mouth. My hands travel along her body. The feel of the fabric pisses me off. I need to feel her. I grip her dress in both hands, pushing her onto her back and ripping the dress open.

She gasps and clenches her thighs as the buttons pop off and her gorgeous skin is exposed to me. Nothing separates us and that's just how I want it.

I kiss the underside of her breast, taking the other in my hand to feel her soft, supple skin. My tongue swirls along her nipple, leaving a wet trail in my path and then I blow lightly until it's a hardened peak. I do the same to the other side and then pinch and pull them slightly. Her back bows and she moans in complete rapture. The sight of her and the sounds of her pleasure make my raging erection leak.

My fingers dip into her heat and thank fuck, she's already soaking wet. I could play for hours, but not right now. I need to be inside her.

"Spread your legs for me, kitten." She immediately obeys and I don't waste a second as I thrust into her all the way to the hilt. Her eyes open wide and her mouth parts with a silent scream as I pound into her tight cunt.

My fingers dig into her hips as I keep up my ruthless pace. She screams out her pleasure and claws at the sheets before fisting them and biting down on her lip. I usually start up nice and slow, but I need her. I need this. It's so fucking sexy to watch her take this punishing fuck I'm giving her. Her breasts bounce with each thrust and her lips slowly part in ecstasy as she gets closer to her release. I don't let up. I need more of those noises coming from her lips. I need her eyes to squeeze shut with the intensity of her pleasure.

I'm hitting her cervix every time, but I still don't feel deep enough. I want more. I turn her onto her hip and straddle her leg, bringing the other up to rest on my shoulder. I fuck her hot pussy and there's nothing stopping me from pounding into her farther and deeper than I ever have before. She thrashes on the bed and tries to move away, but I push down on her hip, forcing her into the mattress and making her take every brutal thrust. Her pussy spasms around me and I lose it. I stay deep inside her until her pussy's filled.

It was a quick fuck, but I needed to feel her. I needed to be deep inside her.

She falls to the bed limp, breathing heavily with her eyes closed. Her body rolls slowly onto her side and those sweet lips part as she winces and brings her knees up. For a second I'm worried I hurt her, but then she gives me a sated look with a soft smile.

I still have to ask. I push the hair out of her face and cup her jaw. "You alright, kitten?"

She nods her head slightly in my hand, "Yes, Anthony." She responds like she should, but then adds, "I am." A blush makes her flushed cheeks even redder. "Better than alright."

"I was worried I hurt you." I want to make sure I didn't. I search her eyes for the truth to make sure she's not just giving me the answer that she thinks I want to hear. And they shine back with sincerity.

"I like it when you fuck me like that," she says with a shy smile. I always knew it turned her on, but hearing it makes it different.

I'm fucking exhausted, but I can't sleep here. I need my own bed. I want her companionship though. I don't want to go to sleep alone.

I wrap my arms around her and carry her to my room. Cum drips onto my hip and leg, but I don't care. I kiss her hair as she snuggles into me. I'm so fucking grateful I have her. I don't know what I'd do without her.

ANTHONY

Catherine pulls away from me slightly as we make our way up the
walkway. "Are you sure?" she asks. No. I'm not sure. I'm taking her
to dinner at my aunt's house, but Vince has no clue. He just needs to see her.
He needs to know what she means to me so he can understand. I know she'll
be good for me.

"No one has any idea about how we got together, and what we do behind
closed doors. That's our business. Just be yourself, and everything will be
fine," I tell her with so much confidence in my voice that even I start to
believe it. I take a deep breath and open the door. If they've accepted me, they
should sure as fuck accept her.

When I open the door, I can hardly fucking breathe. I've never done this
before. I've never asked for acceptance. Maybe because I never wanted it.
Maybe because I never thought I could have it. But now I need it.

The guys look over at me and do a double take. Tommy looks shocked at
first, and it guts me. He's quick to replace the shock with a wide smile. He's
the first to get up and greet us as we make our way to the dining room.

"You brought a friend?" he asks with his eyebrows raised. I look past him
at Vince and answer as Tommy pats my back. "Yeah," I say as I bring her close
to me. "Meet my girl, Catherine."

My sweet kitten blushes a beautiful shade of red and holds her hand out for Tommy. He chuckles but accepts it, which is a good thing. He doesn't need to have his paws all over her.

I expect a lot of things when I walk in, but I don't expect the cheers from the women and Aunt Linda rushing over to greet Catherine.

It's obvious that she didn't expect that either. She holds onto my hand for dear fucking life. The sounds of the kids playing and the men laughing fills the room. But all I can see is Vince, staring at me like I've betrayed him. And maybe I have, but I had to do this. He needs to know she's not going anywhere.

Vince just needs to understand. What happened wasn't her fault. That fucking prick hit her. She had to leave. He can't expect that she wouldn't have done otherwise. She's strong for what she did.

I'm not going to let him take her. He'll listen and he'll understand. My confidence sways, but I ignore it. *She's mine.*

I STAND from my chair in the dining room. Vince is alone in the kitchen. The women are in the den and the men are all in here. Now's my chance to talk to him. I push the chair back, pick up my dishes, and go to him. I need him to hear me out. The tension's been thick between us all night. I just need him to understand. Now that he's seen her, he has to know what she means to me.

"I don't want a rat here. Around my *familia*. In my *home*." He speaks to me in a hushed tone as I set my glass in the sink. It takes all my strength not to break it, not to smash him over the head with it.

"She didn't have a choice, Vince." He just needs to listen to me.

"You're defending her?" I hate that he questions me at all. Someone has to defend her. She's not a rat. She doesn't deserve to be killed, and I won't do it.

"He beat her. When she saw that shit, he made her life hell. She had no choice!"

"He kept her? Are you fucking serious? What'd he keep her as, Anthony? A fucking pet?" He sneers the last word and it's the last fucking straw.

"How fucking dare you!" That fucking prick! He has no right!

"How can you do that to her when you were supposed to kill your own wife? Catherine's not good enough to spare?" I ask, raising my voice.

"I love Elle. She's my *wife!*" he screams at me. I don't hold back any longer,

I can't. I let loose and swing as hard as I can, landing a punch on Vince's jaw. He staggers back a few feet, cupping his chin and looking up at me with daggers, but he doesn't make a move to counter. He stands there waiting as he rubs his jaw. He gave me a pass this time. But I won't get another.

He takes two steps and spits in the sink. "If you can tell me right now that you love her, I'll back off. You going to marry her, Anthony?" He's asking like it's a dare. Like he knows me. It fucking tears me up inside that he's right. He doesn't know her. He doesn't know *us*.

"She's as close to a wife as I'll ever have." I didn't even know how true the words were until I spoke them.

"Until you kill her." Vince says the words just as Catherine walks into the doorway. Her mouth parts and her eyes widen as she looks between us.

"Fuck you," I say with disdain at Vince and quickly go to her. I take Catherine by the hand and brush past my brother as he walks into the doorway.

"Whoa," he says with shock. "You guys alright?"

"We're leaving," I answer with my back to him and drag her out of the house with everyone staring at us.

As the door slams shut behind us, I look at my girl, but I know she's not okay.

My heart hammers with a fear I've never felt before. Although I'm gripping onto her like my life depends on it, she's already gone. I've lost her.

CATHERINE

I sure as fuck wasn't expecting this to be so...comfortable and normal. I'm usually a bit awkward with people—and I still am today, don't get me wrong—but I don't feel the nervous energy I thought I would. I'm able to relax somewhat and just be my usual awkward self. At least around the women.

"So, do you want to be a writer?" Elle asks me. She's Vince's wife. Her voice is soft like you'd think it would be after taking one look at her since she's sweet and petite. Vince isn't. He looks scary as fuck. All the men are intimidating. I'm super fucking happy to be in a room with just the girls.

Being around the men is different. I felt like a sheep brought to the slaughter. I couldn't stop trying to determine which position in the mafia each man had. I couldn't even breathe for the first few minutes. So many fucking flashbacks made me feel like I was drowning. But this is nothing like what I experienced with the Cassanos.

Lorenzo would start talking about things with the other members of his *familia* anywhere, and then look at me like I shouldn't have been there. Like it was my fault. It happened a few times, and then they started doing it on purpose and blocking me from leaving. They liked scaring me and taunting me by calling me the meek mouse. I never felt safe, and they said that was a good thing. Lorenzo said it was good to be afraid. And I was. They made damn sure to keep me afraid.

I stayed with Lorenzo far too long because of that fear and then...well, by the time I had the courage to leave, that's when I actually saw shit. Shit that changed my life forever. I shake my head and try to forget. I don't want to go there in that headspace. Not now.

It's not like that here though with the Valettis. Everything is lighthearted. It took me a while to even want to eat, but when I did it seemed to help. I just kept something at my mouth the entire night hoping no one would talk to me. It's odd how I still felt included in conversations even though I only really ever smiled and nodded. It felt nice though. It's been a long time since I've even talked to anyone. I've been too afraid. Back when I was in hiding, I had the ridiculous idea that the very first person I talked to would somehow know the Cassanos and they would tell them where I was.

But that doesn't matter anymore. I have Anthony now. I've never felt more safe in my entire life than I do tonight. It's the first time I've felt like I could fit in, like I could have a family again. And I want it. I haven't wanted for anything in so long. But I want this.

The kids are all in bed now and the men are in the dining room. Anthony left me alone with the wives. I start to answer Elle's question, but hear a crash of toys from the living room. His aunt, Linda I think, is straightening every-thing up. I feel weird sitting here not helping. Even though it's not my mess.

"Should we--" I start to ask.

"No," Becca answers before I can finish. She's a bit older than me and she's a no-nonsense kind of person. "Trust me," she places a hand on my forearm, "she will not let you help."

"Okay." I draw out the word and the girls all laugh. It forces a smile from me. I can't help it. I feel included. It's been a long time since I've felt that. My mom was everyone to me. She was my best friend. When she died, I had no one else. It feels good to feel like I belong here. Even though I don't.

"So do you want to write? Or do you just do the columns and blog thing?" Elle asks again and I know she's genuinely interested. She's been asking me questions ever since Anthony told them that I work in romance literature. I literally laughed when he said it like that. *Romance literature*. I love *smut*. That's my genre. Smutty smut smut. I shut the fuck up real quick when he gave me that look though. I'm still a little worried about that look. It could be a good thing though.

"I think I'd like to," I start to answer, but I hear Anthony yell something. We all look to the doorway to the kitchen. But none of the women stand up. Elle grabs my wrist as I start to walk toward him, but I shake her off.

"Don't," I hear her whisper, but I ignore her. The women stand up, but they don't stop me. I know they're right and I should stay away. But something deep down is telling me Anthony needs me. I need to be there for him.

I walk into the kitchen in a daze and see Vince and Anthony yelling at each other. Their hair is a mess and they're both breathing hard. Vince has the start of a bruise showing on his face. Anthony doesn't see me as he says, "She's as close to a wife as I'll ever have." It soothes my soul to hear those words coming from him. But then my heart shatters as I realize what's happening.

"Until you kill her." Vince's words ring out clearly, and I hear them repeated in my head. Over and over. *Kill her.* Anthony finally sees me and I expect to see something in his eyes that proves to me that Vince didn't mean that. That there's no truth there. But it is true. I can barely breathe. I feel him take my hand in his and squeeze, but I don't return the gesture.

People move around us as he leads me away. It's as though I'm watching this scene play out from a distance.

"We're leaving." I barely register Anthony's words as he leads me away. What just happened? *Until you kill her.* No. I shake my head. No, it's not true. But he said it with such conviction. And didn't I always think he would? Didn't I know this would happen? *I should have run.* A small voice whispers inside of me. *Weak, you're so fucking weak.*

"You said they didn't know." I barely speak the words as Anthony leads me to the car. I have to keep blinking to focus. I feel lost and confused. That didn't just happen. It couldn't have. Everything was perfect. It was perfect. *It was fake.*

"Vince was the only one." *Was.* But now they all know.

I remember the look in Vince's eyes and everything changes. My world tilts on its side and my vision blurs with my tears. Vince isn't a forgiving man. He wants me dead, just like the Cassanos. I don't belong here. I watch Anthony as we drive away and the same cold, impassive look he had when I first *met* him is on his face.

In this moment I don't know why Anthony brought me here, but I do know two things for certain. The first is that Anthony lied to me. And the only other thing I know is that the Valettis want me dead.

ANTHONY

"*Y*ou're going to kill me?" she whispers as I shut the front door behind me. She walks aimlessly in the hall.

"No," I tell her again. She said it in the car and I shut that shit down. But she won't look at me. She doesn't believe me.

"I don't understand. Why?" She still doesn't look at me, and I hate it. What we had was pure. But now it's tainted with doubt.

"I've told you repeatedly I won't hurt you." She finally looks at me, but I can tell she doesn't believe me.

"Come here, kitten," I hold out my arms for her. She just needs my touch. I'll keep her safe. Vince can go fuck himself. They all can. I'll run away with her if I have to.

She looks at me, but takes a step back.

"I said come here." I take a step forward and she turns her back on me to run. She's defying me. She's running from me. It only takes three strides until my arms are wrapped around her small body and she's shrieking for me to let her go.

It hurts. It fucking kills me.

I walk to the basement with her struggling in my arms. She flails and kicks. She yells and cusses as I take her down the stairs. I almost drop her as I enter in the code. She's fighting me. She hates me. I know she does. My heart hurts, but I ignore it. I hold on to the anger. I hate that she thinks I'm lying to her. I've done nothing but tell her the truth. I will take care of her. She needs to calm down and listen. She has to listen to me.

I open the door to her cell and she looks up at me with anger and then betrayal in her large brown eyes. She needs to learn she can never question me. She'll learn.

She shakes her head and backs away from me as I stand in the doorway. Her body language and the look in her eyes make my heart squeeze with pain.

"You *will* obey me." I say the words with force, but they're choked. She looks back with defiance in her eyes. I don't recognize her, and she doesn't recognize me.

What we had is gone and I wish I could take it back. I hate Vince. I hate myself.

* * *

I WATCH in the monitor as she huddles into a ball on the concrete floor. Hard sobs rock through her small body, making her look weak and fragile. I know she's not at all weak. But she's become reliant on my approval and I know this hurts her.

I've seen this before. I've only had two subs before who thought they'd enjoy a complete power exchange.

They think they want to be told what to do. And they think they'll be able to listen, and be rewarded and pampered. But there always comes a time when the desire to obey is challenged too far. The desire can be lost over some concept of degradation or pride, or an issued command can simply be too far outside their comfort zone. Submissives have to learn to trust that everything their dom does is for their benefit. Doubt and lack of trust are the real issues.

Susan and Cassie were sweet girls. But when it came time to push them, it ended up like this. It would have never worked with them anyway. They cried and then left me. The only difference here is that Catherine can't leave me. Instead she'll hate me.

She doesn't trust me. I pace my room, not knowing what to do. I can't leave her in there to think about leaving me. Her cries ring out from the monitors and I walk quickly to turn them off. I can't take it.

It's my fault. It's all my fault. I don't think about anything other than what I want. And right now I want to comfort her. I want her in my bed. I need her in my arms. I take the stairs two at a time until I'm at her door. No more locks. She'll learn to trust me. I'll do anything I can to prove it to her. She just needs to stay with me.

Stay with me.

I walk into the room with purpose, but she doesn't lift her head. I scoop up her body into my arms and hold her to my chest. I rock her gently and pet her back and her hair. Just holding her calms the beast pacing within me. She needs me, and I need her. That's all that matters. Doesn't she know that? She's all I need. I kiss her hair, but she doesn't look up. I walk us slowly to my room, but I don't even know if she notices.

I try to kiss her, but she shoves me away. I hold her closer to me, but she tells me, "No." She won't let me in. I watch her deny me over and over as she sheds her pain in my arms.

I want to make love to her and show her what she means to me. But I feel like I've already lost her. My need to control her was wrong. I shouldn't have punished her. It's my fault. I hold her close to me as she cries herself to sleep.

"I'm sorry," I whisper into her ear as her shoulders gently shake. "Please forgive me." She doesn't respond and I don't know if it's because she never will, or if she's fallen asleep.

I hold onto her as tight as I can and watch her. That security I've had since I first laid eyes on her is gone. I look down and I know I've lost her.

I shake my head and swallow the lump in my throat. I don't know if I can make this right. I don't see how it's possible to move forward. I've broken her trust. I need her to forgive me, but I know she won't.

CATHERINE

J can hear his steady heartbeat and feel his warm body against my
back. We fit together perfectly, and that very thought frightens me
to the core. My heart hurts as I try to ignore it. But this isn't right. I'm not
okay. I'm falling in love with a man who's taken me against my will. These
feelings can't be real. I need to leave. I have to get the fuck out of here before I
lose what little sanity of I have left. Before he kills me.

I slowly move away from him and hate myself. I watch him sleeping peacefully and I have to cover my mouth to keep the sob from coming up and
waking him. If I don't leave now, I may never have another chance. And I
know I have to leave.

I walk as quickly and quietly as I can. I remember him leaving the keys in
the dining room. I know it's a risk trying to leave. He could come down here.
He could take me back upstairs by force, or he could lock me away in the cell,
and part of me hopes he does. I'm sick for having these thoughts, and I know
it. But I use the knowledge that his *familia* won't keep me safe to motivate me.
I summon my strength and force my limbs to move and go to the door. I take
one last look around, gripping the frame and try to keep down the sickness
threatening to come up.

I can't even take anything with me, because it's all locked in a room I don't have a code for. If that's not a fucking sign that this was never real, I don't know what is.

Rain beats against my skin and thin clothes as I run to the car. My heart pangs sporadically and I don't know if it's from the pain or the fear.

What hurts the most is knowing I would have stayed. I never would have questioned him. What we had was fucked up. But it was my fucked up fairy-tale come true. I loved him. I know I still do.

Tears cloud my vision and I brush them away, shoving the keys into the ignition. I look over my shoulder and hate the pain growing in my chest. I'm leaving him. I don't want to, but a small part of me is saying if I don't leave him now, I never will. Is it so wrong? I can't answer the question. "Forgive me," I whisper as I put the car in reverse and turn the wheel.

I don't care if it's wrong, I fucking loved him. Even knowing he was going to kill me, I still love him and all his broken pieces.

I wipe the bastard tears from my eyes and sniffle as I speed away. I've left him. He's the only man I've ever truly loved, and I've left him. The car swerves and I fight the steering wheel in the rain to stay on the road. I try to steady my breath as a pain radiates in my chest.

In two turns, I'm out of the development and onto the busy road. It's late. It's nearly deserted, with just three cars parked at the front of the entrance.

I had to go, didn't I? I'm not safe with him. I shake my head in denial. He'd keep me safe, but he'd have to fight the world to keep me. I feel so torn and so confused. I hit the brakes and turn off the side of the road. I let the tears consume me.

I know I need to keep going. I need to run as fast as I can. He's going to find me if I stay here. The thought brings me more comfort than anything else. Maybe I'm sick. Maybe the feelings I have aren't healthy. But I hold on to them so I can calm myself. As I look in my rear-view mirror I spot the three cars from earlier driving toward me. None of the cars have their headlights on.

Something triggers inside of me and I quickly put the car into drive and hit the gas. As I speed up, so do they.

My heart beats in my chest with a fear I haven't felt in so long. They've found me. I swallow thickly and search the cars for a face. I don't know if it's the Valettis or the Cassanos, but as I make a sharp right and see them follow me, I know it's one or the other. I wish I could turn around and drive back to him. To Anthony. I wish he were here. I wish he could save me.

He would save me.

Out of instinct, I yell for Anthony. Tears fall down my face. No! I hit the gas harder and the back end of the car swerves. I try to straighten the wheel as my hands grip the leather and I pull to the right, but the car spins out, and in a blur my body smashes to the side. My head smacks against the wheel and my body falls limp. My hand touches my forehead and I look down at my fingers only to see blood. My vision spins and my breath feels hollow, but I have to run. I unbuckle the seatbelt and prepare to run. I have to run. I have to fight.

As my hand grips the handle, the door opens and I look up to see a sick smile from the last person I ever want to see.

"My little mouse came back to me." I hear his words, followed by the smash of his fist against the side of my temple. I'm vaguely aware that he's gripping my hair and pulling me out of the car, but I can't move my legs. Slowly, darkness overwhelms me, and I lose the battle to stay awake.

ANTHONY

I push the curtain back and watch her drive away. I see her look over her shoulder with one last glance at the house, and it kills me not to run out and get her. I couldn't move as I felt her stir next to me and leave me. I knew that's what she was doing, and it took all of me to lie still and let her go free.

I knew she'd leave me. I was a fool to think I could have her. I was wrong to think she'd be safe with me.

She needs to leave me. I can't protect her. I need to let her go. She doesn't love me, and Vince will never let me keep her if she doesn't love me back.

They'll never understand.

If I could tell her anything right now, I'd tell her to run. Run far away from me.

It hurts. The pain in my chest hurts so fucking much as I watch the car disappear.

She left me. I really thought it was love in her eyes.

Mom. I thought she loved me too.

When Dad killed her in front of me to get rid of the fear and the night-mares, she cried out how much she loved me. I thought that was love, too.

Maybe I'm wrong and I just don't know what love is.

If love is what's causing this pain, I don't want it. But I still want her. Fuck me, I do. I want to lie to myself and think that we can be together in this fucked up way and that the world will leave us alone. But I can't put her in danger. I've been selfish and stupid, and I fucking hate that I ever took her the way I did. At the same time, she's all I want. If I could go back upstairs and keep her lying in bed with me, I would. If I had to lock her up and never let her out again, I would. That's only more reason that I need to stay here and let her go. She deserves so much more than a man like me.

I sit outside in the rain, letting it soak through my clothes, just thinking about how I should have let her go right from the start. I should have let her go free. I thought I made her happy though. I thought she wanted the same things I wanted. But I was wrong.

I hear a car swerve in the distance and my heart starts pounding in my chest. I run inside for the keys to my pickup truck and haul ass as fast as I can. It can't be her. I pray she's okay. It takes too fucking long to get there. I'll save her. She needs me. I'll protect her. I slow the car as I see skid marks, but there's nothing there. It looks like a car crashed, but then drove off.

I stay at the scene for a long time, thinking it wasn't her. It wasn't my kitten.

She's left me and now she's safe. She's better off without me. I wish I had a way to track her to know for sure. Again, another reason she needs to run from me.

The pain won't go away.

I can't get rid of this hurt in my chest. I just know something's wrong.

I close my eyes and shake my head. It's all in my head. I'm only hurting because she left me. I'm looking for reasons to search her out. It's my own sickness.

I need to let her go. I settle on that truth as I drive back home. But I can't sleep. When the sun filters through the curtains and my phone pings a few hours later, I reach for it like it was meant to go off.

I expect it to be my kitten. I don't know how, but I do. All night I've waited up, hoping she'd come back to me.

I stare at the phone and I fucking hate myself. I click it off and move as quick as I can.

Cassys want a meet.

I know why. And I'm ready to end this. They're all fucking dead.

ANTHONY

$\mathcal{I}$ can't stop pacing. It's not a fucking coincidence that the night she left we got a call for this meetup. We're supposed to meet at the garage in an hour. It's not right. Something's horribly wrong. She's not okay. I can feel it. My girl's not okay.

"Vince, it can't just be us two," I say. I know this is a setup. It's not just going to be Marcus there wanting to clarify the situation. There's more to this, and I know it deep down in my gut. He texted Vince to come meet with him, and later asked to bring me along. But I know this is a trap. I fucking know it.

"We can't trust them," I tell him again.

"What the fuck, Anthony?" Tommy asks me for the fourth fucking time.

I just shake my head. "It's not good. It's not going to be good."

Vince has been watching me like a fucking hawk. I haven't told him yet.

We're all here and I haven't said shit, but I can't shake this feeling. I need to tell them.

"Let me go in first," I finally speak up and look back at Vince.

He doesn't answer.

"You're freaking me out, Anthony," Tommy says, grabbing my arm.

"You couldn't fucking listen!" Vince yells out, and it gets the attention of everyone. The air is thick with tension.

"You know I wasn't going to." I can't reach his eyes. I know I fucked up, but I need him right now. I can't let them hurt her. Not her. She didn't do anything wrong. She can't pay for my sins.

"What the fuck is going on?" Tommy asks with a pain that breaks through his words. He's worried. He's worried for me and it's all my fault.

"They have her; I know it." I say just above a whisper.

"Catherine?" Tommy asks, confused. It breaks my heart to know I've betrayed him. I betrayed all of them.

"Why? Why would they do that?" Tommy asks.

"War. It's the start of war." I answer him with pain in my chest.

"What'd you do?" Tommy demands to know as he shakes my shoulders, and I have to look him in the eyes, but I still can't tell him.

"Catherine's a rat. She's supposed to be dead." Vince answers over my shoulder and Tommy's grip loosens until his arms fall to his side. He looks at me like it can't be true. But it is.

"She had no choice." I try to defend her. They have to believe her; they have to believe me. She needs me. *She's mine.*

"This is over Catherine?" Tommy asks with doubt.

"She's mine," I say with finality. A look of hurt flashes in my brother's eyes. He doesn't understand. They'll never understand.

"You fucking bought her as a slave--" I understand Vince's anger, but I don't need it right now. I need him on my side. I need my *familia* to help me get her back. I need her. I need her right fucking now.

"I don't care if you don't understand. None of you ever understand me. That doesn't make me any less family. If I say she's mine, then she's fucking mine," I growl out.

"If she's yours, then how did they get her?" Vince steps up to me like he knows. Like he already knows that she left me. But that makes no difference to me. I let her go because I love her, and I'll save her because I love her. Even if she doesn't love me back.

"She left me."

Tommy grips his hair like he can't believe this shit. I hear the men walking around us, waiting on their orders, even though they already made up their minds. No one fucks with us. They mess with one of us, they fuck with all of us. The only thing that would hold them back is if Vince told them not to.

"You didn't let her go?" Vince asks with disbelief.

"I watched her leave me. She needed to." I swallow the lump in my throat as I add, "But I know they have her. I know they found her." He looks at me with doubt and then nods slightly.

Vince looks past me and addresses the *familia*. "It doesn't matter what started it. Get your guns ready, boys, and call for the rest of 'em." I nod my head. Thank fuck. Thank fuck I have a real chance to save her, if they didn't already kill her.

"Anthony," Vince says to get my attention. I look up at him. "We're going in first." I put my hand on his shoulder before he has a chance to move away. I lean in and give him a quick hug. He's shocked, and it takes him a moment, but he pats me on the back in return.

I don't let him go. "I have to save her, Vince." I pull back to look him in the eyes. "She can't die. I can't let her die." His brow furrows with confusion and I know I'm not getting through to him. He doesn't have to understand. He just has to give me his word.

"Don't be stupid--" he starts to answer me, but I cut him off.

"If it's between the two of us, save her. I can't let her die," I say.

That's the moment his look changes.

He gives me a small nod, and only then do I release him.

* * *

THERE SHE IS. Just like I fucking knew she'd be. Fuck! She couldn't run fast enough, could she? It's my fault. She's on her knees with that fucker's hand gripping her shoulder, pushing her down. She looks up at me with the saddest expression and cries out, "I'm so sorry." The man behind her whips his hand across her face and she lands on her side. My hands fist at my side and my blood boils.

Not her. He's not going to get away with it. He cocks the gun in his hand and aims it at her head. His eyes are on me though.

"Was this little bitch worth it, Anthony? Was she worth war?" I hear the words but I can't take my eyes off of her. Lorenzo is still standing behind her. And behind him are a dozen or so of his men. I know I've walked into a sentencing. Her sentencing.

"Knock it off, Lorenzo." Marcus finally speaks. He puts his hands out as if to welcome us.

"What's this?" Vince asks from behind me as he walks up to my side. It's just the two of us, for now. "It was just supposed to be us, Marcus."

Marcus gives him a twisted smirk and shrugs his shoulder as he says, "Thought I might need a few more men to make my message clear."

Vince looks at Catherine and motions to her. "Is this really necessary?" He's keeping his voice even. If you didn't know him, you'd think he was completely unaffected. But I know him, and he's fucking pissed.

"It's the fucking rat your boy didn't fucking kill like he was supposed to."

"You know that's not what the deal was," Vince says as though he's on my side, but I know he's not. All this is my fault. I brought this onto my *familia*. I put us all in danger for her. Simply because I wanted her. I wanted to break something so beautiful. And I did. And now I have to take my punishment. I hope I fucking die today. I'll never forgive myself if I see her die though. I've watched death all around me my entire life, and it's never affected me. Not since my mother. But I can't today. Not her. Not my Catherine.

I walk toward the men and a few take a step back, but Marcus and Lorenzo hold their ground. "I bought her fair and square." I say the words like I'm not ready to rip them apart. Like this isn't war. Like this is just a business meeting over terms.

I hear the rest of my *familia* walk in behind us. A few guns cock. The clicks fill the air. Marcus' eyes turn hard. He tried to set us up, but the dumb fuck wasn't ready for an even match. The doors behind the Cassanos open and more of our crew walk in, guns loaded and ready. We have on our vests; I'm sure the Cassanos do as well, but this is nowhere near an even match. They're fucking dead.

"You really wanna do this, Vince?" Marcus sneers at my boss behind me. My eyes are locked on Lorenzo's. My hand's on my gun.

"You brought this on yourself. You wanted to put on a show," Vince says as he reaches for his gun, but keeps it pointed at the ground.

"What'd you think was gonna happen?" he asks. Silence fills the air and the men line up on both sides. We're in the middle. Vince is by my side, and my kitten on the floor just a few feet away from me. Everyone's armed but her. My eyes dart to hers and I can see she's already accepted it. She's gonna be the first to die.

I can't let it happen. I can't.

A few men start moving around. They're lining up. Some of the Cassanos start looking behind them, but most are going to be gunning for us. It doesn't matter either way, they're all going to die. The only thing they can do is try to take out a few of us first. I can't let that happen. I have to do something. She can't die, and our men can't go down because of my mistakes.

"Give her back, and we'll go away." I say the words and hate the weakness in my voice. I also hate that Vince is looking at me like I've lost my damn mind. He's ready for a fight. No one takes us on like this and makes fools of us. I know he won't stand for it. But I have to try. I'd beg them for her. I'd trade places with her if I could.

"It's not happening, Anthony. Not after you betrayed us." Marcus' voice rings out with clarity. He's firm in his decision.

"Take me instead then. Take me and it's over." Vince still hasn't said anything. I hear Tommy yell out from behind me. But Vince holds up his hand and silences him.

"Your gun," Marcus says loud enough for everyone to hear. I don't hesitate to lower myself, place my gun on the ground, and kick it away.

As I stand up, the fucking prick in front of me, Lorenzo, shrugs his shoulders and raises his gun at me. Every man in the room raises their weapon but me. I'll make the trade. I'll do it for her.

Catherine looks up with wide eyes and shakes her head. As the reality presses down on her, she does the stupidest fucking thing I can think of. She jolts upright and grabs the gun. She yanks it out of Lorenzo's hand. It falls to the floor with a loud clack and goes off. The room fills with the sounds of bullets.

"Fucking bitch," Lorenzo yells out and reaches for the gun. A bullet flies past me, but my eyes are on his gun. He's going to get it first. I see it happening in slow motion. I run to her and cover her small body as the sounds of bullets firing and men yelling ring out and ricochet off the wall.

She screams and cries. She tries to push away from me to fight. But I can't move, or she'll be in danger. She'll die. I have to protect her. I can't let her die. *Not her.* If I do anything good with my life, it'll be keeping her safe and alive. I need to get her through this. Even if I die, at least she'll know what I felt for her.

My body flinches with impact of a bullet, this one at close range. I feel a radiating pain throughout my shoulder as the bullet comes out the other side. The vest can only cover so much. I duck my head and tell her to stay down. I hear her crying and the thud of bodies hitting the floor. I lift my head for only a moment to look into her eyes and she looks wretched with guilt. I push my lips to hers to try to take the pain away. And as another bullet rips into my back, I do everything I can not to let her know.

I just want one more moment with her. One real moment where she can see the real me and what we really had.

The pain expands inside of me. I've been shot before, and more than once, but fuck it hurts. My body loses its strength and I fall onto her body, unable to brace myself any longer. I hear a few more shots and then silence. I don't look. I can't move. I can't risk her. It hurts. Fuck, it hurts. I cough and blood spills from my mouth. Men yell, "Take those three." Fists are smashing against flesh. I recognize the voices. We won. It's over.

"Anthony!" Vince calls out.

"Anthony," she cries out. Her grip on me is strong. She's okay. She's safe.

Vince pulls my body off of her and I lie flat on the ground. A pounding ache in my chest makes it hard to breathe.

"Anthony," she says as she holds on to me as she frantically searches my chest for the wounds. She's okay. She's on her knees, hovering over my body. Tommy comes up behind her.

"Take her away!" Vince yells.

I use the last of my strength and grip onto his shirt, pulling him close to me.

"Promise me she'll be safe, Vince." I hold his stare and make him promise me. "Promise me."

"I swear on my life, Anthony. But I don't need to tell you shit." He's bull-shitting me. I know he is. Blood fills my mouth and it's hard to breathe. I should've died a long time ago. It's alright with me, as long as she's safe.

"You're gonna be fine. You'll make it through this," he says. I shake my head and let my head fall back.

"I love her, Vince. I don't deserve her, but I love her." I have to tell him. He has to believe me and take care of her when I'm gone.

"You can tell her yourself." Vince looks down at me as my vision starts to spin and darkness fades. "I promise I'll keep her safe for you."

The last words I hear come from her mouth as she pushes Tommy away and runs for me. "Anthony," she cries out. But I can't answer her. My world fades and I dream of her touch. Of her love.

CATHERINE

"*N*o!" I scream while shaking my head in denial. They try to pry me away from Anthony. My hands grip onto his shoulders and my tears fall onto his chest. I feel numb everywhere, but my heart is aching.

Blood's soaks into Anthony's shirt and pools around his back as he lies still on the ground. "Help him!" I frantically scream out. They need to do something. He can't die. No! He can't leave me like this. He can't die because of me. *Please, God, save him.* I pray as I watch Vince rip off his shirt. Anthony doesn't move. His limp body sways as Vince looks over the bullet wound in his back.

I vaguely hear the grunting of men as they haul off dead and limp bodies. I hear the smash of a fist pounding into tender flesh and threats being made. They took prisoners, but most of the men are surrounding their own man, the only Valetti to fall. My Anthony.

"Get her out of here," Vince yells back. He looks directly past my shoulder at Tommy who's holding me back.

"I can't leave him," I say. I search for understanding in Tommy's eyes, but he's not looking at me. He looks like he's carrying the pain that Anthony must be feeling. His eyes are full of anguish. He grips me closer to him as I try to push away and go back to Anthony. I can't let him die. He can't die.

"Right now you need to," Vince says as he looks at me, but it's not said with hate or anything other than sympathy.

"The cops are going to come and you can't be here. You shouldn't be anywhere around them." He motions to our left, where the Cassanos are all lined up execution style. My heart twists. I don't care about them. I don't care about any of this.

"I can't leave him," I cry out to Vince as Tommy drags me back.

"I won't tell you again." Vince looks me dead in the eyes. "If you never want to see him again, go ahead and stay. Have him try to explain it to the cops."

"You can't stay. Just listen to Vince. He'll take care of Anthony," Tommy whispers into my ear. I know he's hurting, too. I turn around in his arms and close my eyes tight, willing Anthony to be alright.

From my left, I hear a grunt of a laugh and someone spit. My eyes open and I see that prick. The bastard who started all of this. His hands are tied behind his back and he's on his knees. He's lined up like the others. Two of them are getting the shit beat out of them. But not Lorenzo. He looks at me with one black eye and gives me a bloody smile, and I've never wanted to hurt him more. I've never felt such a strong need for vengeance. It's his fault. All of this is his fault.

I don't think about it, and I don't consider the consequences. I just reach for Tommy's gun tucked in his waistband.

I hear his scream as I pull out of his grasp for just enough time to pull the trigger. I fire once, and it hits the fucker in his shoulder. I take a single step and scream with all the rage and pain I'm feeling. He falls backward with a cuss ringing in my ears. My second shot hits him square in the chest. Tommy's arms wrap around mine. Several men yell. I don't care. I stare at the man who made my life hell. The man who laughed at my pain. And I watch the life leave his eyes.

A strong hand rips the gun from my hand and I look up to see Vince scowling at me. He looks between me and Lorenzo. I can't look him in the eyes. I swallow the lump in my throat and stop fighting against Tommy. His hold on me loosens, and I instinctively try to go to Anthony. But Vince is blocking me, and Tommy's still gripping my wrist.

"Your ex?" Vince asks.

I nod my head as tears fall down my cheeks. I look back at him. That piece of shit should have died long ago.

"You snitched 'cause of him?" he asks me. I fucking hate that he brings it up. I want to cower, but I don't. I nod my head in response. Vince looks me in the eyes and gives me a small smile as he says, "He fucking had it coming." He pats my shoulder and leans into my ear as he reassures me, "You did good."

He pulls away from me and I feel the faintest bit of relief. But it's not okay. Nothing can change what's happened. Lorenzo being gone won't bring Anthony back. He can't die on me.

"But don't do that shit again," Vince says to me, handing Tommy back his gun. "Get your shit together, Tommy."

"Let's go," Tommy says, pulling me away from the scene.

I hear someone ask Vince a question. I don't know what the question was, but I hear Vince's response clear as day.

"All of them. They're fucking done." Bullets ring out in an instant. I look over my shoulder to see the Cassanos falling to the ground, blood splattered on the ground in front of them. I should feel a sense of shock. But I feel nothing. I turn back around and let Tommy take me away before I give in to the urge to run back to Anthony.

I walk, but not by my own free will. I keep looking back, but they're surrounding Anthony. I can't see him. It hurts. It hurts too much. I feel like I'm dying. I get in the car, but I don't know how. All I can see is the look in Anthony's eyes as the bullets hit his back. I cover my face with my hands and let all the pain out as I sob.

"Catherine?" Tommy asks me after a long time. I look up and see that we're driving, but I don't know where we're going. He pulls over and holds me against him as I cry. His hand rubs gently on my back and for a moment I pretend it's Anthony. I pretend it's okay. "I know Anthony has problems. It's not his fault." He chokes on his words and refuses to look me in the eyes, "I'm sorry." I don't know how to respond, so I say nothing.

"Did he hurt you?" I hear the pain in Tommy's question and I look up at him with confusion. Did *Anthony* hurt me? It takes me a long time to gather the strength to answer. "No. Never." My heart twists with a pain I've never felt before.

"I didn't know he was keeping you against your will. I'm sorry," he whispers. "I'll take you anywhere you want, Catherine. You'll be safe. I'll make sure of it. He'll never find you if you don't want him to."

I shake my head frantically. "You don't understand. It's not like that. I want to go to Anthony," I insist. I hold onto Tommy's arm with an unrelenting grasp. My heart stammers in my chest and anxiety races through my blood. They can't send me away. I need to know he's okay.

"Do you love him?" Tommy asks.

"I do; I don't care if it's wrong." It's the truth, and I pray Tommy knows that. But he doesn't respond.

"He can't die for me; tell me he'll be okay." He has to be okay.

"I wish you'd ask me for something I can give you, Catherine, but I can't give you that."

CATHERINE

The faint humming of the machines and the steady beeping of the monitors are the only sounds in the room, but I need to keep hearing them. They tell me he's alive. They removed the breathing tube from his throat today. It's been three days and they keep telling me he's going to wake up soon since now he can breathe on his own. They're just waiting on him now.

I'm waiting on him, too.

Tommy comes back into the room and hands me a styrofoam cup with a lid on it and the string from the teabag draped over the side. I give him a small smile and say thank you. I haven't slept at all. I didn't realize I haven't had to drink my tea or take my pills to sleep until I found myself curled up in the hospital chair, wide-awake and watching Anthony.

My voice is hoarse as I thank him.

"You can go if you want," Vince says from across the room as Tommy sags in the seat next to him. He keeps telling me that, and I give him the same response I did last time.

"I want to stay." He nods his head and looks down at his phone then back up at Tommy. They start talking in hushed tones. I don't mind. I don't listen. I just keep my eyes on Anthony's chest as it slowly rises and falls.

I put my cup down and scoot my chair closer to Anthony's bed. The clink of the metal is the only sound in the room. I take his hand in mine and rub my thumb along the palm of his hand and wait. I need him to hold me back. I just need a sign that he'll be alright.

I look up and my heart stops beating as Anthony clears his throat and his head turns to the side. He's waking up. My eyes widen and I do what I've been trained to do. I get onto my knees in the chair and kneel as best as I can. I watch my dom, my master, my love, and my life as I wait for him to wake and acknowledge me.

I see Vincent and Tommy rise from their seats from my periphery. I don't look at them though. I don't care what they think. I need Anthony to see me waiting for him like this. I need him to know I was waiting for him, that I would always be here for him.

His eyes slowly open and he looks down at me with confusion as he takes in a heavy breath and winces. My heart hurts for him. I know he's in pain.

"Kitten," he barely manages to get out.

"Anthony," I say as I look up at him and move my hands to his bed, crawling to get close to him.

"Can I get in with you?" I ask him. I know he's in pain, but I need to feel him. I need to be next to him and be by his side.

"Please," I beg him. "I need to feel you." He gives me a nod and watches as I quickly move to him. I never want to leave his side again.

I climb onto the small bed and hold him close to me. Tommy and Vince stand and talk to Anthony, but I don't listen. I can't do anything but hold him.

Once they're quiet I finally speak.

"I'm so sorry, Anthony," I say as I bury my head into his chest.

"Nothing to be sorry about." He kisses my hair and rubs my back. He's consoling me when he's the one who's so badly hurt. I pull away and brush the tears from my eyes while I shake my head.

"I never should've left you." I push down the sob threatening to choke me.

I look over to the left and see Vince and Tommy watching us. Both look confused and are obviously judging us, but I don't care. I need him to know how much I want him, how much I need him. I can't go back to a life without him. Never.

"I'll go to the cell. I deserve to be punished." I speak clearly and I know the other men heard, but I don't care if they know. It's none of their fucking business, and what they think of me is none of my business. I've never felt more safe and complete as I do with Anthony. I'm not letting that go.

"No, you need to go. Now," Anthony says dully as he stares at the back wall.

"You're throwing me away?" I ask him as my heart shatters in my chest. I shake my head in complete denial. I feel so broken. Every part of me hurts all the way to my soul.

"Please, Anthony," I beg him. "Please don't throw me away."

He closes his eyes and refuses to look at me. "You don't understand, Catherine. You're free now. No one will come for you. You can live your life in peace."

"We'll make sure you're safe and settled in." Vince interrupts us and motions for Tommy to follow him. He holds the door open and they both look back at us. "Whatever you two decide, we'll make sure you're safe, Catherine." He locks eyes with Anthony for a moment before leaving and closing the door behind him.

"But I don't want to go." My shoulders shake and my voice cracks. I try to scoot closer to him and he lets me. Thank God he lets me. "Please, Anthony. I can't live without you."

"You can." His hand cups my chin and his thumb strokes against my jaw. I lean into his warmth and kiss his palm.

"You'll find a man who can love you." It breaks my heart that he's willing to let me go. That he's shoving me away. "I don't deserve you." He says the words with finality.

"Just the fact that you're saying that means you do." I breathe out the words, my hands clutching his. I need him to take me back.

"I'll do anything." I will. I'll do anything he wants for him to take me back.

"Then leave me," he says.

"I won't." I almost yell the words, but somehow, saying it in a calm voice and locking my eyes on his, it comes out with force.

His eyes heat with anger and a dark lust that I've missed. "Are you disobeying me, kitten?" he asks. His chest rises and falls with a sharp intake of air.

"Yes. I am." I stare back at him defiantly, hoping it's enough. That his need to punish me is enough that he'll keep me. Even if he doesn't realize it, I know he loves me. And I love him.

I close my eyes and gather up the courage to spill my truth to him. "I love you, Anthony." I wipe the tears away angrily. "You'd better not throw me out. I'd rather die."

"You wouldn't," he says as though he knows it to be true.

"I would. I can't live without you." The pain in my chest is unbearable. I know I won't be okay without him. Never.

"I did that to you," he says with regret.

"You did what I wanted, Anthony. You always did what I wanted." I take his hand in mine and press his palm to my cheek. "I need you now more than I ever did. I'll beg until you cave. I swear I will."

He looks at me for a long time and I remain still, waiting for his verdict. My heart pumps slowly in my chest as though it's prepared to stop beating if he denies me.

"Come here, kitten." I crawl up to him, loving my pet name. I nestle into his side, careful not to hurt him. "You've been very disrespectful," he says, staring into my eyes. "And you disobeyed me. You left me, and then disobeyed me again. You put yourself in danger." His admonishment makes my shoulders droop in shame. What's worse is that it's all true.

"I'm sorry, Anthony."

"Don't be," he says, taking my chin in his hand and tracing my lower lip with his thumb. "If you come back to me now," he says, "I'll never let you go."

My heart swells in my chest and I push my lips to his. My tear-stained cheeks heat as he kisses me back with the passion I know he has for me. I break our kiss and finally breathe.

"Never let me go, Anthony." I look into his tortured eyes and I hurt so much for him. For everything he's been through, but also because I know leaving the way I did hurt him, and I fucking hate that. "I love you." I'll say it every day until he believes me, although I'm not sure he ever will.

His forehead scrunches and he takes in a deep breath. He swallows thickly and looks out of the hospital window. Finally, he looks back to me and says the words I want to hear every day for the rest of my life. "I love you, too. But that's not even close enough to describing what I feel for you. I want you to remember that. Always."

ANTHONY

MONTHS LATER

I've been looking for Catherine everywhere and I'm trying to push away the feeling that something's wrong. I keep waiting for her to leave me again, no matter how many times she says she loves me. She says I just need time to accept it, and maybe that's true. I don't care what holds us together, so long as she never leaves me.

I almost pass by the pile of two-by-fours and cans of paint, but then I catch sight of her out of the corner of my eye. She's curled up in a ball on the reading nook I built for her. Each wall is a shelf for her books and there's a giant window with a bench that I plan on padding for her. She's curled up on the wood, napping.

"I gave you a fitting pet name, kitten," I say as I pet her hair. She blinks a few times and yawns. She's been tired from the move and from all the changes, but the one thing that stays the same is the look of devotion I get from her every waking moment. The move's been good for her. She said she needed to be close to family. My *familia. Our familia.*

I have to admit it's been good for her. For me, too. Which is surprising. Even Vince seems to be as happy as a pig in shit. And Catherine and Elle are thick as thieves when it comes to planning these fucking get-togethers she forces me to attend. Apparently having a girl that gets along well with everyone looks good for me and makes me more approachable. I'm still on my own when it comes to work, but that's the way I want it.

I'm about to whip her ass though and she should know it. "You were supposed to be upstairs twenty minutes ago," I tell her with a hard voice. She knows it's play though. There's a time for that side of me to come out, and right now, it's time. She wanted to play, and so did I. She should've been there to greet me on her knees.

Her eyes go wide and she's quick to pick up her phone. She checks it and shakes her head as she taps the screen and looks at her alarms. She winces and holds the phone up for me to see. She never turned the alarm on.

"I really hate to have to do this," I say even though I fucking don't hate it at all. She looks up with a bit of apprehension, but her eyes are full of lust and her legs subconsciously fall open. She knows she's going to be cumming soon. She's a spoiled pet. But I fucking love it.

I sit next to her on the bench and she quickly sits up and waits.

Since moving I've punished her ass at least a dozen times. Not for disobeying me, since she knows better than that. She deliberately disobeyed me once before we moved. She sought out Vince after I told her not to. I told her to leave it alone and let us break off from the *familia*. I thought it was best, but she defied me. My hand twitches remembering how I spanked her. I got her on edge and left her there, alone and crying. She took her punishment and waited for me to go back to her. It couldn't have been more than fifteen minutes. I'm not a man who makes love to a woman, but if I ever have, it was with her that night. And then of course I gave her what she wanted.

"What's my punishment, Anthony?" she asks as she looks up at me with big doe eyes. She's an awful actress. There's nothing but excitement on her face.

"I set the bench up in the dungeon." I can't help but smile at her name for the basement. She bought a whip and a riding crop, stuck them in the corner on top of a bed and called it the dungeon. My little kitten is fucking adorable.

Her eyes glaze over with longing and she speaks in a breathy voice. "Yes, Anthony." She loves that bench. I had to reinforce it because I almost broke it the last time I fucked her on it.

My brow furrows as she waits for me to lead her to the basement so she can take her punishment.

"Do you still want to play, kitten?" I ask her. After everything we've been through, I keep thinking one day she won't want this. One day she'll decide she doesn't want this anymore.

"Always," she answers. "I'll always be your kitten, and you can be my bad boy." She tells me like it's a fact.

"Boy? No, kitten. I'm a bad man." It's the truth, and I wish she'd just accept it, but I don't think she ever will.

Her eyes go soft and fill with sadness.

"You aren't a bad man." She shakes her head and it breaks my heart. I wish I'd never burdened her with my shit. None of that matters; it's in the past where it belongs. And my sweet love is my future. It's all for her.

"Bad boy?" I ask her. She's gotta be fucking kidding me.

"It's a genre of romance," she explains.

Jesus Christ.

"Call me whatever you want, kitten, when we're home. But please don't call me your romantic bad boy in front of another human being ever." That has her eyes filling with laughter and a silent giggle shaking her shoulders. That's my girl.

I finger the ring in my pocket nervously. I just got it back from the jeweler. I had it custom designed for her to match her owl earrings. It took a little convincing, but now that she doesn't fear losing them, she never wears anything else. I thought rubies in her engagement ring would be a nice touch. It's the entire reason I wanted to play today. I need her to do this for me. We need this.

"You know you love it," she teases me. As she says the words I slip the ring on her finger. She pulls back with a gasp and stares down at the diamond. She covers her mouth with her other hand.

"Marry me, Catherine." I tell her simply. I want everyone everywhere to instantly know she's mine. Always.

She nods her head as tears slip down her cheeks. She rises from her chair and wraps her arms around my neck as she says, "Yes, Anthony."

"I love you, Catherine," I whisper as I lean down for a kiss.

"I love you too, Anthony."

EPILOGUE

CATHERINE

I type away and continue hitting the keys even though I hear him coming. I just have to get this thought out before I forget. I was hit with a wave of inspiration for this scene and I don't want to lose it. I've been writing steadily ever since we moved into the new house. My office has a huge window, just like it did at our old place. Well, this one's even bigger, but the feeling is the same.

He walks up behind me at the back of my desk and rests his hands on my shoulders, but other than that, he doesn't interrupt. It only takes a minute for me to finish my thought and when I do, I'm quick to look up at him and give him a small smile. I reach my hand behind his neck and pull him down to me for a kiss.

"Mmm." He hums against my lips. "What is my naughty girl up to?" I blush at his low tone and rest my head against his chest.

"I wanted to write our story." I feel him stiffen behind me, but I keep going and decide to spill it all. "All of our stories."

"Kitten," Anthony says in an admonishing tone.

"No, no. It's fiction. Under a pen name. No one will ever know." I look up at him searching for approval. I love romance novels, and I just have to write all these love stories I've heard. The whole family is filled with fairytales, albeit dirty smutty fairytales, that have to be told. I've never felt compelled so much in my life to write them down. Ours will be last, because in my completely unbiased opinion, it's the best.

He smirks at me and places a hand on the nape of my neck, massaging slightly. "Can I read them?"

"If you want to." I wouldn't be shocked if he did. He reads over my work from time to time. I used to think he was making sure that I wasn't trying to put clues or hints out there for someone to come rescue me from him. *As if.* But then he started doing things in bed that were incredibly familiar from my blogs and columns.

"Well, I definitely want to read ours. I wanna know what my kitten was thinking when I brought her home." He smiles warmly at me with love in his eyes before leaning down to give me a sweet kiss. My chest warms with his affection.

"I have a question I need to know... for the story." I don't know what he'll answer. But I really do want to know. "Why didn't you have me call you master?" I ask him.

It takes him a moment to answer. "I knew from the second I saw you that I would be just as much a slave to you as you would ever be to me. If not more." Tears prick my eyes. I fucking love his answer. "Doesn't matter what you call me, babe," he says as he tips my chin up so I have to look at him, "You'll always be my kitten."

"You'll always be my *bad boy*." That earns me a chuckle as I lean into his chest savoring how happy we both are.

It might not be ideal or perfect, but I'm more than satisfied with my happily ever after.

ABOUT WILLOW

Thank you so much for reading my romances. I'm just a stay at home mom
and avid reader turned author and I couldn't be happier.
I hope you love my books as much as I do!

More by Willow Winters
www.willowwinterswrites.com

CPSIA information can be obtained
at www.ICGtesting.com
Printed in the USA
BVHW030931040520
579154BV00001B/53